THE REDWING SAGA

BOOK THREE

THE
BLOOD
IS THE
LIFE

SHARON K. GILBERT

THE BLOOD IS THE LIFE
BOOK THREE OF THE REDWING SAGA
BY SHARON K. GILBERT
WWW.THEREDWINGSAGA.COM

First Print Edition December 25, 2017
Kindle Edition December 25, 2017

ISBN-10: 0-9980967-3-3
ISBN-13: 978-0-9980967-3-5

AVENUE FICTION
514 ROSE AVENUE, CRANE, MO 65633

Published by Rose Avenue Fiction, LLC
514 Rose Avenue, Crane, MO 65633

TABLE OF CONTENTS

FROM THE AUTHOR

When I originally conceived of this series of books, I wanted to teach spiritual warfare through the Jack the Ripper murders. I never imagined more than three books back then, but as I grew to love Sinclair, Aubrey, and the duchess—as their backstories and planned futures grew far too dense and rich for a mere trilogy—it became clear to me that I'd need to create many, many books. Therefore, I plan to release three per year in the form of 'mini-trilogies'. Each of these will centre around a major theme. The first mini-trilogy (each title containing the word 'Blood') has served to introduce the primary plot and players, and it's launched Charles, Elizabeth, and Paul on their journey. The next (each title containing 'Realms') will delve more deeply into the histories of the human and inhuman members on both sides of the spiritual battle.

Eventually, the entire series of mini-trilogies will run through 1948, and as we near the turn of the 20th century, it will become clear to the reader just why Charles Sinclair is so very special.

I'll not spend much time in this section, for it's my hope that you're itching to jump into the action of the tale, but allow me to gently remind you that spelling in these books uses British convention. Hence, my American readers may initially stumble at words like 'marvellous', 'mould', 'storey', 'judgement', 'travelling', or 'jewellery'. If ever you doubt the spelling I've employed, I suggest checking the *Oxford English Dictionary*. It is a wealth of information.

I've spent weeks editing this final version, but it's impossible to 'fix' everything, so I beg your indulgence should you find something I've missed. If you've written to me about the books, allow me to say thank you—*very, very much*. Your encouragement helps during those arduous days of typing and editing.

Sharon K. Gilbert
15th December, 2017

This book is for my wonderful husband, Derek,
who daily acts as my knight.

I love you with all my heart.

"For the life of the flesh is in the blood, and I have given it to you upon the altar to make an atonement for your souls..."
– Leviticus 17:11

PROLOGUE

6:53 pm – 8th November, 1888

Joseph Barnett had been sitting on the edge of Billingsgate Dock for nearly an hour, pondering the sorry state of his miserable life. Over his right shoulder, he could see two uniformed sentries, taking a leisurely break from their duties as night guardians for the Custom House. Inside the building's imposing, limestone and marble façade, the famous 'long room' stretched from end to end; its enormous, unsupported canopy of architectural braggadocio soaring majestically overhead; whilst within the beast's cavernous belly, an intricate labyrinth of secret vaults shielded dusty oubliettes stacked to the ceiling with seized treasures, each inmate held within awaiting liberation upon receipt of unpaid port fees and taxes.

In the upper storey regions, nearly two thousand clerks and government overseers buzzed like an efficient hive of worker bees each day, their uniform cubicles now fallen silent and empty in the evening's dank chill. Higher still, claustrophobic attics provided cramped housing for chars, cooks, and bachelor clerks. Along the sloped, grey slate roof, a forest of brick chimneys belched smoke and grease from dozens of hearths, where mutton roasted and stew simmered.

In all, the building seemed more community than mere edifice, and the night watchmen saw themselves as gatekeepers of a miniature city. The pay was meagre, but the job brought one prime benefit: keys to unlock cloisters filled with casks of wine, barrels of whisky, and wheels of cheese; as well as sea cans bursting with chocolate, spices, tea, exotic silks, and even sparkling gemstones. So long as they kept their pilfering small and confined to lesser items, the governor of the house turned a blind eye. After all, his hands were soiled as well.

Tonight's excursion had taken the guards into a holding area filled with casks of *Boutelleau* cognac. Though considered a premium wine, they reasoned that one small cask amongst many dozens would never be missed. Standing now beside the western doors, the underpaid watchmen whispered together as they shared tin cups of purloined cheer and coarse amusements—most at Joe Barnett's expense, for they cast their inebriated eyes upon him often, sometimes pointing in his direction.

The Custom House perched upon the Thames shoreline like a grand goddess of the waters. Architect David Laing's impressive design ran for nearly five hundred feet along the river and featured two wings that branched from a protruding central base, decorated with six ionic columns and terra cotta *bas-relief* figures, representing the world of commerce. Atop this magnificent edifice, rested a massive, nine-foot tall clock dial, supported by marble statues of the chief gods of economy, 'Plenty' and 'Industry'. The gods' frozen faces looked down upon the lonely figure of Joe Barnett as if contemplating his isolation. The unemployed fish porter cared nothing for fine architecture or pagan imagery, content only that he'd found a solitary place in which to think.

Joseph shivered in the cold night air, his bumpy, florid nose wrinkling at the pungent reek of Indian spices, rotting fish, dead flowers, and horse muck. A light rain cut through the thick mist, spattering upon the rough cobbles that lined Lower Thames Street, and the clip-clopping of horseshoes echoed against the pea soup fog like a familiar drumbeat, percussing a dissonant refrain of endless toil and agony.

"Got some for me?" a thin woman asked, startling Barnett, as she emerged out of the grey haze like a pale ghost.

"Cor blimey, Ida! You'll give a man an 'eart attack, you will, appearin' like tha'!" he exclaimed.

The woman stared, motionless in the night air, as if she were nothing more than a renegade statue, escaped from the Custom House façade; her pale eyes mere orbs of painted ceramic. Then she blinked, thawed from her frozen state as though touched by an unseen, warming hand.

"Sorry if I gave you a fright, Joe. I wonder if you've got a bit o' gin to share; that's all."

"Bit o' gin ta share?" he repeated, showing her an empty bottle. A lifelong speech tic caused Barnett to repeat the last few words he heard in conversation before forming his own reply, but his friends had grown accustomed to it. "Sorry, Ida. I done drunk it all away."

Ross sat down beside him, the thin folds of her cotton skirt billowing across emaciated legs like a pale blue shroud, making her seem more ragdoll than human being. "That's all right. Mary's not with you tonight?"

Joe shook his head. "Not wif me tonight? No, no she ain't. Mary's go' no need o' me, I reckon. Took up wif another o' them trashy women friends. I don' understands it, Ida. Mary used ta love it when I come 'round. Now, she go' no time fer the likes o' Joey Barnett."

"Don't give up on her, Joe," Ross urged him gently. "Mary's worth it. Really, she is." Ida grew silent for a moment, her eyes on the grey waves below them.

A watchfire burnt in an iron barrel near the southwest corner of Custom House Quay. The stoop-shouldered guard had finished his wine and now warmed gloveless hands against the damp, the bright flames painting his round features in flickering shades of yellow and orange.

"Have you seen any more of those strange animals about?" Ross asked as the sentry glanced her way.

"Strange animals about?" Joseph repeated. "No' you as well! Like I done told Mary, there ain't no wolves in London. Not ones what walks abou' on two legs, anyhows. Now, iffin ya wants ta talks 'bout them wha' preys upon the poor o' this city, then tha's another thing. Like them men buildin' this 'ere bridge," he said, pointing to the skeletal frame of Tower Bridge, begun two years earlier. "Bunch o' la-dee-da layabouts, iffin ya arsk me! Fancy boots an' fancier clothes. Lily white skin an' all. No' a callused 'and amongst 'em. It's enough ta make a real man wanna drown 'imself in a barrel o' gin, it is. Where you been, girl? I ain' seen you in nigh on a month."

"I spent several weeks in hospital," she sighed. "But I'm better now, and I got work. I'm back with Mrs. Hansen, up on Columbia."

"Up on Columbia?" he repeated, absentmindedly. "Say it ain't true, girl! I thought you was done workin' on yer back."

"Don't scold me, Joe. Whorin' at the Empress means clean sheets, a few coppers in my pocket, and regular meals. And it's a sight lot better than working the streets."

"Better 'n workin' the streets? You don' look like a girl what's sleepin' sweet, Ida. Is them bruises on yer face? An' them ain't silks on yer limbs, my dear. Don' Meg Hansen pay you enough, so's you can buy a new frock now an' then?"

Ross smoothed the creases of the blue muslin, and Barnett could see that she shivered. "I don't like to wear those pretty clothes when I take a walk, Joe. B'sides, I've got other plans tonight."

She grew silent again, her thoughts far away. Finally, as the chimes of St. Margaret's Church tolled the hour of seven, she took a deep sigh, changing the subject as if trying to distract her own mind. "I heard Liz Albrook say that Mary might be meeting her and a couple o' friends at Ten Bells pub later. Why don't you go see if she'll talk to you, Joe? I got a real bad feelin' about tonight, and I'd hate for Mary to be alone."

"Mary ta be alone? A bad feelin'? What sort o' feelin', Ida? You get another one o' yer visions or summat?"

"I don't know," she whispered, her voice nearly lost in the night wind's howl. "Joe, would you do me a kindness? Nothing that'll cost you much. Just a bit of time."

"A bi' o' time? What's tha', Ida?"

She opened the drawstring of her crocheted handbag and removed a slim white envelope. "Post this for me, will you? I've already put a stamp on it. All it'll cost you is the time it takes to walk to a pillar box. There's one at Mitre Square."

"Mi're Square? Cain't you do it?" he asked. "No' tha' I minds, ya know, Ida. I don'. Jus' tha' I migh' forget. My memory's no' the best—no' since tha' accident in the fish market down at Shadwell las' year."

She grew pensive, and he noticed that her eyes followed the path of a rusting trawler as it steamed past, bound for the dock beneath London Bridge. "Don't you wish you could board one of those boats, Joe, and sail away to another country? Put all the bad choices behind you and start all over?"

"Star' all over?" he repeated as he scratched his pockmarked nose. "You shore is funny tonigh', Ida. Nah, I ain' never wanted ta visit nowheres else. London's all a man needs. Tha' an' a warm woman ta come 'ome to on a winter's evenin'. Why don' you lemme buy you a drink over at the Ten, eh? It's gettin' migh'y cold out 'ere, an' I ain' so sure it's safe."

She shook her head, causing several of the restrained, strawberry locks to tumble from their pins. The fallen strands whipped about her face in the rising east wind. "It's not all that cold," she lied. "If you'll just post that letter for me, Joe, it'd be a blessing. And tell Mary how much I appreciate all she did for me. Tell her I tried to get away. I really did."

"Ge' away? Whatcha mean, girl? Ge' away from wha'?"

"Get away from *him*," Ross answered as the trawler sounded its horn. Overhead, the shadow of a large bird skittered across the iron grey waves of the river, and a seagull's cry split the air in chorus with the fishing boat's call. "It's not safe out here anymore," she said mournfully, looking towards the inky vault overhead. "Something's coming, Joe. Something hideously dark. Darker than any night."

Barnett tucked the envelope into the right pocket of his moth-eaten coat. "Darker 'n any nigh'? No' safe no more? You're startin' ta sound like them women down at Shadwell! Them wha' crosses themselves like some ghost'll get 'em iffin they don'. It's just gulls, girl. Naught bu' one o' them seagull's nibblin' on a dead fish or summat." He placed a brotherly arm around her slender shoulders to offer warmth and fellowship. "I don' like ta leave ya, Ida," he said gently. "Come wi' me, won' cha? We'll share a buttered tater an' a pint o' bitter. My treat."

"No, thanks, Joe. That's kind of you, but I'd like to stay," she insisted. "Just post that letter for me. It's important."

High in the sky, the lengthening shadow lingered upon the murky waters, its form impossibly still, as if the night bird hovered just over their heads. Ross glanced up, and a shiver ran through her bones. "It's getting late. You'd best go now, Joe. Find Mary and see if she won't make up with you this time. She needs a man with her, Joe. She needs protecting."

Barnett pushed himself up by steadying his right hand against the stained brickwork that lined the dockside. "She needs protectin'," he repeated, the persistent tic sticking stubbornly in his brain. "Don' stay 'ere too long, Ida. Keep close ta them watchmen. Does ya need money fer a ride 'ome? I go' a copper in me pocket. It's yourn, iffin ya wants it."

"That's generous of you, Joe. I've got a little money, so you keep it," she assured him, though she had none. "Go on. I'll keep safe," she promised.

Reluctantly, he turned to go.

As Barnett left the dock, Ross could hear the sharp echo of his thick-soled, black boots upon the limestone setts. The watchmen for the Custom House shared one last laugh, but within ten minutes, they, too, had departed, leaving Ida Renée Ross all alone in the freezing fog. The twenty-seven-year-old could hear the rhythmic waves slapping against the sides of the concrete stairs below her vantage point, as if the hypnotic voice of Old Father Thames, the river god, beckoned her to leap and join him in eternal sleep.

High above her head, on the east side of the massive clock dial, a winged figure perched upon the head of Plenty. He'd been watching the entire time, listening to the conversation, calculating the woman's intent. Now that she sat completely alone, the spirit entity wrapped himself in human form and descended to the street.

"Why do you sit by yourself?" he asked, causing Ross to turn around. He stood tall and regal, dressed in elegant attire, and the silvery moonlight fell upon his perfect features, revealing ice-blue irises and long, raven hair.

"I'm not working tonight, sir," Ross replied. "I hope you're not looking for anyone just now."

"I look only for you, Ida," he answered gently. "May I sit?"

His voice bore a strange accent, yet it sounded familiar to Ross, although she could not fathom why. "Do I know you, sir?"

"In a way," he told her, his voice entrancing and sweet as he sat beside her. "You are quite lonely, aren't you, my dear?"

"Not really," she insisted. "My memory's not the best, sir. Not since my illness. How do I know you? Did we meet at the Empress?"

"No," he answered, placing his warm cloak about her shoulders and touching her frozen hand. "We did not meet there. I've known you for a very long time, Ida. I've been watching you since you were a small child. That letter you asked Mr. Barnett to post; why didn't you place it in the pillar box yourself?"

"How do you know about that?" she asked, finding her mind strangely fragmented.

"I know a great deal about your life, Ida. I know that you left home because your father molested you in the months after your mother died. You were only twelve years old when you arrived in London. A woman named Isabel Crighton took you off the streets, and she sold you to rich men. She taught you to perform degrading acts for them. Taught you to please them, and how to convince each of your maidenhood, selling you night after night as a perpetual virgin. Mrs. Crighton shared very little of her income with you. Isn't that so? And when you could no longer convince the wealthy bankers and businessmen of your innocence, she tossed you back onto the streets, where you slept in overgrown graveyards and church doorways for almost two months before encountering the woman who would become your friend. Irene Winters. Little Irene who shared her food, her lodgings, and helped you to find employment; though not the respectable sort. It was she who introduced you to Margaret Hansen, wasn't it? Hansen convinced you that whoring was your only skill—that it was the only way a solitary woman could survive the unforgiving streets of London."

Ross's head lowered in shame. "Yes, sir, but Irene was right. Whoring is all I know."

He took her chin in his hand, tilting her face upwards. "Untrue. However, your entire life changed direction whilst there, did it not? Just one week after arriving at the Empress Hotel, you met two men who would forever alter your life. One would abuse you mercilessly for the next ten years. The other served as the solitary ray of hope in that nightmarish darkness: the handsome policeman with the beautiful smile and azure eyes."

Her face went white. "How can you know that?"

"I told you; I know everything about you, Ida. I know that you are in love with this ray of hope, though you would never tell him. I also know that he cares about you as well. Charles Sinclair would be most upset if you do this."

"If I do...*what?*" she asked, stunned.

"The river is very cold tonight," he said. "Cold as the grave. Won't you allow me to escort you to safety? The myth of the beautiful, drowned woman is only that: a myth. *L'Inconnue de la Seine* died hopeless and alone, despite her famed beauty. I also tried to stop her, but she refused my help. I hope you will not follow in that poor girl's futile footsteps and pursue a watery grave, my dear Ida. Only poets profit from such an ignominious death."

The dark waves licked hungrily against the dockside stairs, as if the ravenous river god awaited her decision. "Who are you? How do you know so much about me? About my thoughts?"

"I am your true friend," he assured her, standing. "Take my hand, Ida Renée. Allow me to help you."

Ross's heart warned her to resist the beautiful man's tempting smile, but the offer felt so welcome, so right, as if sent from heaven above. She had come to Billingsgate Dock to end her life, but the oppressing gloom and despair that haunted her thoughts suddenly felt lighter. Despite her doubt, she accepted the long, pale hand, and he drew Ida to her feet. Standing now beside him, Ross could see just how magnificently tall the man was, and that his regal bearing seemed strangely familiar—like something from a distant dream.

Ross smiled, her mind no longer fixed upon suicide. "Who are you, sir?" she asked.

"I shall tell you my name soon, Ida, but for now, just think of me as your guardian angel." A crested brougham drawn by a pair of midnight black Friesians stopped in the lane that ran beside the Custom House, and he pointed towards it. "Come with me, Ida. I shall take you to safety and a new life."

Ross allowed the enigmatic stranger to lift her into the interior of the sumptuous coach, and within seconds, the entire rig had disappeared into the dense fog.

As the coach departed, a second spirit creature landed upon the Custom House roof. Two small imps, their contorted limbs covered in rough scales, flanked the taller being. The gargoyles' claws gripped the heads of the marble statues; leathery, bat-like wings folded against their curved spines.

"Do we eat now, my lord?" the taller imp snarled.

"Patience," the Watcher replied. "All in good time."

"Good? Time is not good! Time is a prison!" the second imp bit back; its black spittle dropping as frozen pellets upon the slate roof. "Why must we wait? Do you fear your brother?"

"I fear nothing!" the Watcher snapped, his eyes points of fire. "Nothing and no one. Our ultimate triumph draws ever nearer, but it requires that we free my other brethren."

"All of them? That could take years, Lord Raziel! It is too long to wait. We hunger now, my lord. We crave sustenance!"

"As do I, Shishak," the fallen angel replied, stroking the imp's pointed ears. "The veins of this city's humans pulse with a dark buffet of sweet delights. I do not think it would cause too many ripples if we enjoy a small taste."

"A taste merely whets the appetite," the younger complained. "If we must share this sweet buffet with your brethren, who then will be the first to emerge, my lord? Which merits such an honour?"

The Watcher smiled, his ice-blue eyes twinkling. "The foolish men of Redwing have uncovered the prison belonging to Saraqael, so he will be the first to join my army."

"Did not Sara once aid in your imprisonment, Lord Raziel?" the elder enquired, his chameleon eyes twisting in all directions. "Why must he be freed at all?"

"Because I require all thirteen brethren, you fool! Do you know nothing of the old texts? However, once his usefulness is finished, I shall repay Sara for his treachery. I'll repay all the traitors who bound me within that stone."

The two imps gazed at one another, and the younger's head tilted to one side. "Yours is the greatest power," he declared with a low bow. "Since you speak of traitors, do you think Lord Samael has taken the woman for a reason, my lord?"

"Reason eludes my brother," the Watcher answered with a sardonic smile. "Sama's mind has turned to sentimentality, which makes him weak."

"Then, might he be vulnerable, sir? Might he be easier to slay?"

The Watcher laughed. "Slay the slayer? A delightful thought, Globnick. Perhaps, we should follow him to see just why Samael has taken the woman. Summon your packs—both of you!—for we require many eyes to spy upon one so deviously powerful as Samael the Betrayer."

Leaping with glee, the hideous gargoyles unfurled their wings and sounded their battle cries—squawking and squealing in high-pitched calls audible to few, save their loyal minions.

Below the slate roofline, Eddy Morrain, the younger of the two watchmen, had just left the west entry of the Custom House to relieve himself, when he heard animal cries rise up in the distance. A shiver ran through his rawboned frame, and Morrain felt certain he heard a kind of cruel laughter, ringing like an unwelcome, animal chorus against the city's night sky. Hundreds of black rats rushed past, and a red fox ran across the lanky lad's path, stopping to stare at him with eyes that looked eerily human; its sharp snout open as if to speak.

Suddenly, the voices of a thousand animals of all kinds rose up from every direction. The nocturnal chorale followed the retreating coach, and the Cerberean pack snapped at its turning wheels; the terrifying cacophony causing yellow gaslights in houses along the path to spring to life.

Hastily buttoning the fly of his woolen trousers, the young night watchman wanted only to return to the refuge of the Custom House, but a monstrous, inky shadow suddenly obscured the white face of the waning moon, and the air temperature dropped by ten degrees. Turning about, the youth could see something *enormous* leave the roof, the shadowy figure shaped like a gigantic man; but then it sprouted wings so wide that even the stars winked out momentarily.

As he raced back into the building, Morrain crossed himself, certain that he'd just seen Satan himself.

Not far from the Custom House, Maxwell 'Stinky' Tubbs, one of the city's few remaining nightsoil men, guided his laden cart towards his next stop in the east, just the other side of Bishopsgate. He, too, saw the mammoth nightmare pass overhead, but Tubbs could also see the dense, supernatural pack that pursued the black brougham. This hellish mob rushed towards the coach and pair, eyes red as flame, and it seemed to Tubbs that the animals' shaggy legs never touched the ground. But there was no mistaking what they were: Wolves. Enormous, grey wolves, some on all fours, some running upright like men, calling to one another in hideous, black speech.

Tubbs could hear their dark conversation. Even understand it, for something translated it inside his head:

> *Snarl! Claw! Rend and bite!*
> *Satan rises on this night!*
> *Blood and flesh and cracking bones;*
> *Enter all their happy homes!*
> *Destroy the world of men and then;*
> *Our fallen world will rise again!*
> *Crush the skull and bind the head;*
> *And hail the king amongst the dead!*

Far away, on a lower level hospital ward, beneath the streets of Hackney Wick, a desperate man writhed upon a narrow cot, his pointed ears twitching as he listened to his altered brethren sing the hideous rhyme.

The king amongst the dead, he thought to himself, as the remaining portion of his once human brain strained to recall the boy's face. Five years old, he was. Tall, kind, with eyes of a unique, azure blue. He'd once called the boy his friend—or so the hybrid man believed.

Had the boy been there that day? The day when his father had died?

Now, why is it I keep remembering it? the man worried. *I was there, all right. Standin' alongside the other one. The cruel angel with the pistol smoking in his hands.*

A beautiful woman had rushed out of the mansion at the sound of the gun's report, and she'd bent low to hear the dying man's last words. Then, she'd turned pale with fright and raced back towards the house to find the child.

But the boy was already there, standing upon the green. He'd seen it all. Watched his father shot down like a helpless rabbit upon the manicured lawn of his own home.

Rose House.

That was the name of it. Rose House!

Why does the story make me sad? the man wondered. His transformed mind struggled with the painful memories. Why should blood make him sad? Why should a child's pain—his tears—make him so very sorrowful?

And where had he seen those same eyes since that day? He'd smelled the child only recently—on that other one. The hospital visitor. The old man with the white hair and top hat.

But I'm an old man, too, the patient thought, looking down at his leather-bound wrists and forearms. Their once papery skin used to hang upon the thinning bones like crepe upon a widow's back, but not today. Not now. New, firm muscle and glorious hair rippled along the powerful limbs now!

But the boy. What of the boy? He'd seen those same, distinctive azure eyes here in London once. He felt certain of it. He'd seen them in the east...but where?

The boy was an adult now, and he'd worn a uniform.

That's it! A uniform made of darkest blue with brass buttons, and a tall helmet sat upon his curling black hair, just above those unforgettable eyes of azure blue.

The king! the unbalanced hybrid thought wildly. *My king! The boy king with the beautiful eyes and the perfect blood.*
And he was crying.
Now, why does that make me sad?

Fury overwhelmed the man's altered mind, and a hideous strength surged through his bound limbs. *No, I'll wait,* he reasoned, the human part of his brain regaining control over the animal instinct. *I'll wait a little longer. Wait until HE calls me. The Other One. The nice angel. Perhaps, he'll help the boy again. Allow me to help, too.*

A tear ran down his cheek, and the hybrid creature began to weep great, anguished tears. "Forgive me, sir!" he whispered aloud. "Lord above, forgive me! If there is redemption for one such as myself, I beg you to reveal it!" he whimpered. "I don't want to do these things anymore!"

CHAPTER ONE

8:56 pm – Queen Anne House, Westminster

"That was the most delightful lamb I've had in months. Nay, make that years," James Stuart, 11ᵗʰ Duke of Drummond, gushed, patting his belly as the family left the mansion's dining hall. With Mary Wilsham on his arm, the head of the Stuart clan led everyone into the music room. "Do sit, Mary," he told the plump woman. "Della, why don't you entertain us with a few of those Scottish airs I like so much. A bit o' Bobby Burns settles the stomach as no other music can."

Dressed in a yellow silk skirt and white blouse, trimmed in blue ribbons and ruffles, Lady Adele Marie Stuart skipped lightly to the Bösendorfer grand piano, where she lifted the hinged seat and glanced through a collection of sheet music. "I don't see any of them here, Uncle," she told the duke. "They must still be packed with my things at your house."

"I had Mrs. Chambers send over all your bags, Della," Elizabeth Stuart told her young cousin. "Lester and Carter carried them upstairs whilst we ate."

"Did they?" the girl asked, her eyes bright. "All of them?"

"All of them," the duchess answered as Charles Sinclair helped her to a soft chair. "Your Uncle James has agreed to allow you to remain here with me until after the wedding. I require your expert advice on music, but also in choosing the perfect flowers and jewellery."

Adele threw her arms around the duchess's slender neck, kissing her liberally on both cheeks. "Oh, Cousin Beth, that is so very nice! Thank you! But is it all right with my brother? He is my guardian, you know. When is he returning, Cousin Charles?" she asked the marquess. "Hasn't Paul been at Whitehall a very long time?"

Sinclair drew a second chair close to his fiancée. "Your brother plans to be out most of the evening, Della. Dull government business, I should think. Won't I do? Perhaps, I could help plan out some of those flower arrangements. Do they usually include weeds and lots of scrap metal? Bits of broken glass, perhaps? I've an old emblem from my first policeman's helmet that would make a splendid centrepiece."

Adele giggled as she embraced the marquess. "You are so very silly, Cousin Charles. I think it's best that you don't help with the flowers. Aunt Mary may do it, though. Shall I play some Brahms for you, Cousin? I've memorised almost all of *Wiegenlied* and several others, so I shouldn't need the music."

"That sounds quite lovely, Della. Yes, please."

The girl started to turn, but suddenly stopped. "Cousin Charles, are you and my uncle meeting later?"

Sinclair took the girl's hand, his dark brows arched in curiosity. "That is a very pointed question, little cousin. Why would you ask?"

"I'm just adding up all the clues," the eleven-year-old told him, her blue eyes twinkling. "I have observed long tables, arranged into a single surface inside the library. Paper and pens for writing. Lots of wines and other drinks men seem to enjoy, though I cannot imagine why anyone drinks whisky."

The duke huffed, his waxed moustache twitching. "What sort of Stuart would say such a thing? Della Marie, shame on you! I may just have to strike your name from the clan rolls for that."

The girl offered a knowing smile, her own brows arched in defiance. "You cannot do that, Uncle James. I am a Stuart through and through, and there is no denying it. My eyes are just like my brother's, which are like our mother's. I even look rather like Cousin Charles, too. Don't you agree?"

"Wouldn't that make you a Sinclair?" the marquess teased. "If so, then I'll side with you on the whisky. It's a bit too powerful for me," he whispered, "but then perhaps that's because I'm only part Stuart. Do play for me, though, won't you, little cousin?"

Adele kissed his cheek and then took her position at the gleaming, ivory and ebony keyboard, her slender hands slowly beginning the first measures of the lullaby.

As the music filled the room, Martin Kepelheim entered with Lady Victoria Stuart on his arm. He eased his companion into an overstuffed, chintz-covered chair nearest the piano. "Shall I fetch your cigarette case?" he asked amiably.

"Not just now, Martin," Tory answered. She wore a grey flannel skirt and crisp white blouse, accented with a striped tie and burgundy waistcoat. The spinster's dark hair showed hints of silver at the temples, and fine lines around the deep brown eyes made the duke's sister appear careworn. "Elizabeth, I thought you intended to retire early tonight. You mentioned a headache coming on before we sat down to eat. Has it improved, for if so, your eyes have failed to register the change. You have the look of someone in great pain, my dear."

The duchess had spent most of that day planning the wedding and reception with her aunt and Maisie Churchill, and she now glanced at her family, her heart-shaped face paler than usual. "I do have a slight headache," she admitted, looking guiltily at her fiancé. "Charles, I thought I'd told you about it, when you came home earlier. I'm very sorry, if I didn't. It's nothing. Really, it isn't," she explained rapidly at seeing his surprised reaction. "I'd like to listen to this song first, and then I'll go upstairs and sleep. I promise."

"If you've a headache, then you should go to bed at once," Charles insisted. "Beth, you promised Price that you'd follow his instructions to the letter, which of course, you have not. He required that you rest all day today, and instead you've spent most of it working on the wedding."

"Our wedding will not organise itself," the duchess argued, her hands set demurely against the dark velvet of her skirt.

"Perhaps not, but must you be the one who does the organising? Darling, if such activity causes you physical duress, then let's hire someone."

"There's no need to hire anyone, Charles," Victoria interrupted. "Maisie and I are quite capable of arranging a simple ceremony and reception, though with nearly five hundred guests, it presents a few challenges. Beth does not actually work, you know, but merely offers opinions as bride. That is all. However, you do look quite tired," she told her niece. "There is a paleness about your cheeks that is not flattering. Perhaps, an early bedtime would be wise."

The twenty-year-old duchess sighed and put out her hand. Sinclair helped her to stand, but she nearly fell into his arms. "As I thought," he said, clearly worried. "You're exhausted. Here now.

Lean upon me, and we'll climb the stairs together. Everyone, do excuse us. I'll be back in a few minutes to hear Della play."

As they climbed the winding staircase, the detective spoke more gently. "Darling, I'm very sorry if I seem angry or overbearing. It isn't my intent. I'm just concerned about your welfare."

She took the marble steps slowly, her weight against his arm. "Yes, I know," she assured him, "and I try not to be a bother."

"You are never a bother, and if I make you feel that way, then I've much to answer for."

As they neared the landing for the first floor, she almost collapsed again, and rather than risk a faint, he lifted her into his arms and carried the duchess into the master apartment, crossing through the warm parlour and into the main bedchamber. Once inside, Charles set her upon the soft mattress of the four-poster bed, and then turned down the quilted covers. "Is it the headache, or do you feel dizzy?"

"Both," she confessed. "You're right, I suppose. Perhaps, I have been overdoing. It's been a rather long day."

"Then I'll say goodnight and ring for Alicia," he said, but she stopped him, her hand on his forearm.

"No, please, Charles, don't go. Not yet. Might we have a few moments to talk first? I know you're worried, but I need to tell you something. It's quite important. I tried to speak with Paul about it before he left this evening, but I wasn't able to catch him. Where did he really go?"

"A last minute meeting with someone in government, I imagine. You know the earl—in demand by everyone in high office," Sinclair answered, though he knew Aubrey had actually gone to Egyptian Hall to seek out news of Lorena MacKey.

"Oh," she said, her eyes downcast. "Charles, when you came home this evening, you had a worried look. What did Commissioner Warren say to you that left you so agitated?"

"Only that he's resigning," the detective answered, offering a partial truth. "He wished to sound me out on it before word gets 'round the force. As you might imagine, the Ripper murders have taken their toll, both on Warren and on his family. He has a new grandchild, by the way. A lovely little girl. I got to hold her, Beth, and I kept thinking about our own child—about the future."

She smiled and took his hand. "I think about that nearly all the time now, and I know it's why you're so worried, but don't be, Captain. Really, I'm all right. Merely tired."

He sat beside her. "Of course, you're tired, but not only because of the pregnancy. These past weeks have been filled with excitement as well as terrors, haven't they? Elizabeth, forgive me when I'm overbearing and demanding. It's not my intent to tell you how to live your life, but as the man who's about to marry you, I feel my responsibilities keenly. It's why I asked your grandfather and Victoria to allow me to sleep in here at night. To keep you safe."

"And your presence helps more than I can ever express," she answered. "No, Charles, I don't mind—well, not very much. I confess that I do bristle just a little, when you tell me what to do, but I know your intentions are only to protect us both," she said, touching her abdomen. "However, I am stronger than you think. You may share your concerns with me. It is my job to be your helper, is it not? For instance, there's more to your meeting with Mr. Warren than you're telling."

"Do all the Stuarts read minds?" he asked, smiling.

She leaned against his chest, and he placed an arm around her shoulders. "Only those who love you," she replied. "As I said, I'd hoped to speak with Paul, for I'm very worried about him. I keep dreaming about him, you see. I asked him not to tell you about those dreams, for I cannot recall all of their content, but each time, I've a strong sense that Paul—and you are in danger." She sighed, worry creasing her pale brow. "You expect me to obey your commands, but will you obey just one from me?"

"What is that?" he whispered, kissing her cheek.

"Nothing burdensome. Just promise to be careful."

He laughed softly. "I promise, little one. And our cousin is quite capable of looking after himself. However, I shall convey your concerns when next I see him. Is there anything else about these dreams that distresses you? Anything you're not telling me?"

She nearly confessed the nightmare she'd suffered earlier that week: the dark dream of the tall man and the blood-spattered ballroom, but as the disturbing events made Charles seem cold and uncaring, she decided to keep it to herself for the time being. "Not really. Ring for Alicia, if you wish. I shan't argue, for I am quite tired."

"And the headache?" he asked as he stood and crossed to the fireplace to pull the bellrope.

"Fading, thanks to you."

He returned and kissed her lips. "And your stomach? Is it still unsettled? I noticed you ate none of the lamb, though it's one of your favourites. Only a few vegetables and a bite or two of bread."

"I am sorry about that, but it's the best I could manage. Victoria has also asked about my appetite. She suspects, I think. May I tell her about the baby?"

"Of course," he answered, "but not Paul. Not yet. And say nothing to any of the staff, Beth. If that new maid hears of it, she'll spread it all across Westminster. Everyone will reason it out soon enough, but I'd prefer they do so *after* we're married on the eighteenth."

"You don't like Gertie, do you?"

"I don't trust her. I know the employment service Laurence used to engage our new staff was recommended by your grandfather, but Miss Trumper fails to live up to their usual standards. Frankly, I'm shocked that she passed muster with them. She has much to learn about living in a large house. Ordinarily, I would try to be as compassionate as possible, for I understand Gertie's life has proven challenging thus far, but your welfare and safety depends upon the reliability of all who live here, Elizabeth. I may have to dismiss her, if she continues to abuse her position."

"I understand your concern, Charles, I do, but please, give her another chance," the duchess implored. "Perhaps, she could serve in a different capacity. With the gardeners, or in the kitchen."

"I thought only men worked in the gardens?"

"That is true, but she might be able to tend the indoor plants or help with seedlings in the greenhouse. Charles, I'd hate for Miss Trumper to lose her place, if there is any way we might prevent it. If you and I are to underwrite a charitable hospital in the east, then that same compassion must also extend to our home."

"By allowing a gossip to remain on staff?" he complained. "No, you needn't answer. I promise to consider it, but let's leave off discussing it for now. Is there anything you require before I return downstairs? A glass of water? A few biscuits? They might settle your stomach. Which reminds me, Mary mentioned to me that water crackers can soothe a queasy stomach. I think she, too, suspects."

Elizabeth's smile widened. "I'm sure she does. Mary is an observant woman, after all. She kept bringing me peppermint tea this afternoon and placing cushions at my back. She's such a dear, and I'm delighted to have her in our home. May I tell her as well?"

"If you wish, but remember, say nothing to Paul. I hope you understand about that, Elizabeth. I'm not intentionally keeping secrets from him, but it would crush him just now. He's dealing with enough as it is."

"I promise, but I think you're wrong about him. Paul would understand. I'm certain of it."

"I am not wrong," he insisted. "As another man who loves you, I'm able to comprehend his emotions better than you do, Beth. Now, if food does not please, then, what about a book? Where is your Verne novel?" he persisted, searching the nightstand. "I don't see it, Beth. Have you moved it?"

"No. It should be next to Father's picture, where it always is," she told him, pointing to the mahogany drum table beside the bed.

"It isn't here," he said. "Might it have fallen to the floor, when the maids cleaned this morning?"

"Possibly, but don't worry about it," she said easily. "I've another copy in English, though the French is still my favourite. I hope it isn't lost."

"Shall I ring for Mrs. Meyer? She could assemble the maids and conduct enquiries for you," he suggested.

Beth began to laugh softly. "Superintendent Sinclair, I don't think we need mount a formal investigation. My darling, you are so wonderfully predictable sometimes!"

"Do not force me to place you under arrest, Duchess," he teased. "It may require that I conduct a thorough investigation of your recent whereabouts and activities. Perhaps, even smother you in kisses!" he told her, demonstrating the last statement with much affection.

"Do you treat all your suspects with such familiarity, Captain?" she asked.

"Only the very pretty ones, and she must be a duchess and engaged to me," he assured her. "Beth, why do you call me Captain Nemo? I'm not complaining, mind you, but I've never quite understood it."

She smiled sweetly, her dark eyes fixed upon his face. "You look like a Captain. At least, I've always thought so. Yes, I know the description of the book's character isn't much like you, but he is a solitary, lonely figure. When I first saw you, all those years ago, your eyes made me think of Nemo. They seemed so very sad that it broke my heart."

He drew her into his arms. "I hope your heart is now mended, little one; for mine certainly is. Never does a moment go by without a thought of you inside my head. Not one moment. Not one second. Honestly, Beth, you saved me that day. And each day since, you make me a better man."

"I love you, Captain."

"And I love you, little one. Now, sleep. I shan't be up for some time yet, I shouldn't think. I need to speak with your grandfather and Martin, but it's only about tomorrow's circle meeting. We've decided to compose a list of topics for discussion. Shall I wake you when I come up?"

She nodded just as her lady's maid knocked at the open doorway. "Good evening, Alicia," the marquess said. "Your mistress has a headache. Might Mrs. Meyer have some of Dr. Price's sleeping powder remaining?"

"I believe so, my lord," the slender maid replied. "I'll fetch it right away. And there's a letter arrived for you, sir. Mr. Miles asked me to let you know, if I saw you. It came by way of special messenger."

"Thank you, Alicia. If you find the opportunity, could you see if you might discover the whereabouts of the duchess's Verne novel? It's generally on the night table, but it's disappeared."

"Has it?" the maid asked, clearly puzzled. "Yes, sir. I'll speak with the chamber maids whilst I'm fetching the powder. Shall I bring up cocoa, my lady?"

"No, thank you, Alicia," Beth answered, her eyelids already grown heavy.

"It seems you're wearier than you thought," Sinclair said, kissing her forehead. "Good night, little one. Sweet dreams."

"Goodnight, Captain," she whispered as the marquess shut the door.

"My lady?" the maid began as she arranged the duchess's night clothes at the edge of the bed. "I see that you're weary, but we should get you out of that evening dress. Won't take but a minute, and then you can have a lovely rest."

"What?" she asked, having lain back on the pillow. "Do forgive me, Alicia. It's this headache. Don't tell the marquess I said this, but it is quite awful."

"I'll fetch one of your powders, my lady. Right after I help you with your night dress. It's getting quite cold outside, isn't it? Mr. Miles says it'll snow soon. Wouldn't that be lovely?"

"Yes," Beth answered drowsily.

The maid felt her mistress's forehead. "You're a bit flushed, my lady. I hope you're not coming down with measles." She crossed into the bath and ran cool water onto a linen hand towel, but when Alicia had returned, she found one of the windows open; frigid air gusting into the room, causing the fire to crackle in the hearth.

Despite the chill, the duchess had fallen asleep. The maid shut the window and latched it. "You surely did that quick, my lady," she observed, assuming her mistress had opened the window. "I've not been out of the room more 'n a minute."

Still puzzling through the mystery, Mallory softly closed the door and headed towards the servant staircase to fetch the headache and soporific powders from the housekeeper.

Inside the darkened bedchamber, the window slowly opened on its own, and the night winds blew into the room. The candles upon the mantlepiece guttered as a great Shadow drifted into the chamber. The shapeless visitor sat upon the bed's edge, slowly shifting into that of a man, its wispy fingers reaching out for Elizabeth's hand.

Beth twisted in her sleep as though experiencing a terrifying nightmare. The intruder touched her forehead. An evil, amorphous grin crossed its face. "Dream, Duchess. Dream of darkness and the beautiful night; for soon, you shall be mine. All mine."

Ida Ross stood inside an ancient house, her eyes blindfolded. "May I look now, sir?" she asked her host. "Am I back at the Empress? I hear no voices. Usually, this time o' night, there are lots of men talking and music playing in the parlour."

She felt warm hands upon her face; someone untying the soft folds of cotton. As the cloth left her eyes, the prostitute blinked away strands of red thread from her lashes. She could see very little, for only a few candles burnt in a chased silver candelabrum to the right of a lit fireplace. The glow of the coals and burning wicks painted dancing fingers of amber upon the silk-covered walls.

"Where am I?" Ross repeated.

Still holding the red cloth in his right hand, the man who'd taken her from the docks stepped around Ida so that she might see him. "Forgive the blindfold, my dear," he said. "It is necessary to keep this location secret. To answer your question, you are in my home; or one of them, at least. I do not always reside here, so the contessa keeps house for me, you might say."

Serena di Specchio huffed angrily, her powdered nose in the air. "You think me your servant? Really, Anatole. Your sense of humour escapes me."

The handsome Russian laughed. "Most of what I say escapes you, madam. It is one reason I so enjoy your company. I have brought Miss Ross here to keep her safe and permit her to rest." He turned towards Ross. "Ida, my dear, we've prepared a lovely apartment on the first floor that will meet all your needs. It has a spectacular view of the west garden, which is yours to explore."

Ross seemed perplexed. "I don't understand, sir. Am I to work for you now? On my back, as I did at Mrs. Hansen's?"

Prince Anatole Romanov stroked her emaciated face. "No, dear, you are my guest. No strange men will encumber you here, and the entire staff are at your command. You have but to ask, and your needs will be met. Katrina is your lady's maid, and she will answer any questions you might have regarding our household."

Ross stared, wondering if she'd gone to some level of the afterlife and if her lifeless body now floated along the Thames beneath the Custom House stairs. "Me with a lady's maid, sir? I've never heard of such a thing! Girls like me don't have servants. We serve others."

"Oh, but you do have your own. Now, allow me to introduce you to Andrija Nikolaevich Vasiliev. He has served as my butler and valet for many years. He will show you up to your apartment. Just call him Vasily, if it makes it easier. Like myself, he is from St. Petersburg, but he speaks English quite well."

A thickset man with straight black hair, parted severely down the centre, offered a deep bow. He wore white cotton gloves, an elegant coat of black wool and matching trousers, and his shirt was of bright white with crisp pleats down the front. The striped silk waistcoat, like all the man's livery, looked out of fashion, but as with the prince's attire, appeared quite expensive. His skin was pale, and his piercing eyes were black as soot.

Despite his imposing exterior, the butler spoke in a polished manner, and his alabaster cheeks rounded high as he attempted to offer her a brief smile. "It is my honour to serve you, Miss Ross."

Di Specchio shrugged in irritation. "Do not introduce me!" she complained. "I am merely your caretaker, apparently!"

"Miss Ross, this rather rude woman is the Contessa Serena Sofia di Specchio," Romanov told Ida. "The countess has many other names, but few that she uses in England. She is Italian—or so she claims."

"I could mention your many names, Anatole Petrovich. And perhaps your many faces as well, but I will not," the dark-haired woman replied angrily, extending a pale hand towards the newcomer. "It is my pleasure, Miss Ross. We are very glad you have agreed to join us."

"Join you?" the young woman asked. "I'm not sure what you mean."

"All will become clear very soon," Romanov told her. "For now, you must rest. I've had a food tray sent to your sitting room along with a bottle of red wine. I suggest you sleep until you wake naturally, my dear. We rarely keep to schedules in this house, so we set no alarms. I have other matters that require my presence this night, but I promise to look in on you tomorrow. I've also taken the liberty of providing a wardrobe for you. I hope it pleases. Katrina will assist you with all the many silks, satins, and jewels that a lady wears these days."

"Are you leaving, sir?" Ross asked, finding herself troubled by the possibility. Though she knew practically nothing about this strange man, she felt bonded to him already, and the thought of his departure distressed her.

"For the evening, yes," Romanov told her, "however, I shall return before morning. I hope my home is to your liking, and that you remain with us for a very long time." He kissed her hand and left the drawing room, passing into a dimly lit foyer, where he spoke briefly to the butler before exiting through the front door.

Ross crossed to a set of gothic windows and followed the prince's departing steps—or tried to do so, for though he had left only a moment earlier, she could see no one anywhere upon the shadowed lawn. Two gas lamps illuminated a broad, brick pathway, leading to a circular, gravel park. Near the end of this area, the black coach stood waiting, but its door was already closing.

"He's very quick," Ross said, her hand pressed against the window pane.

Di Specchio laughed. "Anatole is swifter than you could ever imagine, my dear. As if borne on wings! Now, allow me to see you to your apartment. I believe you'll find it is quite perfect. Exactly like you used to dream of when you were a girl."

Turning, the former prostitute stared. "What do you mean by that? How could you know anything about my childhood dreams?"

"Anatole knows everything about you, Miss Ross. Now, follow me. Vasily!" she called, snapping her fingers. "Tell Cook to send up a special glass of my favourite vintage along with the wine. I plan to sit and talk with our guest for a time. And then, I, too, must go out for the night. I've a call to make at a theatre in Piccadilly. There is a magic act that I simply must view."

"Do you mean that I'll be here all alone tonight?" Ida asked, suddenly fearful.

"Not at all, Miss Ross. Here, as you will soon discover, one is never truly alone."

Ida sighed, reluctantly leaving the drawing room to follow Vasily and the countess to the upper reaches of the mysterious castle. Each mounting step took her further from her past, but to what kind of future?

Before long, that question would find an answer, but it would lead the former prostitute into a telescoping maze of ever-deepening, infinitely puzzling questions, beginning with a single revelation: the true identity of Prince Anatole Romanov.

CHAPTER TWO

Queen Anne House – Below stairs

"Evening, everyone," Alicia Mallory said politely as she entered the staff parlour. The pleasant space sat betwixt the kitchen and a small apartment currently in use as an infirmary for the household's measles cases. "I wonder, Mrs. Meyer, might we have more of the sleeping powder that Dr. Price left for the duchess? Also, my lady complains of a headache."

The buxom housekeeper sat in an oak rocking chair near a brick fireplace, a crewel needle in her right hand, a deep blue swatch of cotton velvet across her lap, with a basket of woolen thread alongside. "We've half a bottle of the headache preparation left and two packets of the sleeping powder," she replied, pointing towards the kitchen. Within its warm walls, head cook, Mrs. Hilda Smith oversaw a trio of chattering scullery maids, performing the evening rituals of washing up glassware and china; scrubbing out copper pots; and cleaning the two cookers, four ovens, and every table and counter surface with carbolic soap and lemon oil.

"You know where I keep my medicine chest, Alicia," Meyer instructed the young maid. "In the glass cabinet within my office. The packets are in the top section of the chest, next to the migraine tincture. The key to the chest is here, girl," she added, reaching into the right pocket of her dress.

Alicia crossed to the rocker and took the heavy ring. "Is it this one?" she asked, holding up a small brass key.

"It is," Meyer answered as she knotted a bit of green thread. "Is the duchess having troubles again? Is she feverish? If so, then perhaps I should come up."

"No, ma'am. No fever. The marquess isn't to know about the migraine—per my lady's instructions—but his lordship did express concern regarding her poor sleep of late. He's quite worried."

"Such a lovely man, he is," Meyer observed. "The duchess shouldn't overprotect him from worry, though. However, it speaks to her character that she does, I suppose. Young love, isn't that right?" she mused, clipping the thread. "I believe Dr. Price is staying with his friend, Dr. Whitmore, over in Mayfair this evening, but he's promised to check in on all our patients tomorrow. I'll mention the duchess's headaches and poor sleep when he comes 'round." Then turning to one of the maids, she asked, "Gertie, you're not catching these measles, are you? I noticed you hardly ate at all this evening."

Gertrude Trumper had said little since finishing her afternoon tasks at Haimsbury House. She and Agatha MacGowan sat together in the northeast corner of the parlour, working through a wooden jig-saw puzzle of the Tower of London. Most of the mansion's footmen had decided to spend the evening playing cards with several grooms and gardeners, whilst the remaining male servants patrolled the park or kept watch upon the exterior doors. With four maids and a char still recovering from measles, the healthy female staff had dwindled to only seven, making Trumper feel even more isolated than usual.

"I'm fine, Missus," the Londoner answered. "Just a mite bit weary. No fever nor bumps, ma'am."

"Good," Meyer answered, threading a long line of scarlet into the needle. "Have you ever sewn, Gertrude? Did your teachers at the workhouse instruct you in piece-work?"

"They did, ma'am," the girl replied. "Only not like you're doin'. Nothin' so fancy as tha'. I can mend as needed, though. I can make real small stitches."

"Can you? You know, there's a rather nice overcoat that might fit you, but it has a rip in the lining of one sleeve. It belonged to Constance Morrow, the duchess's former lady's maid, but she forgot to pack it when she left to marry her intended last year. I wrote to Connie, and rather than have me forward the coat, she asked that I pass it to someone in need. Remind me once you're ready to go up, and I'll give it to you. If you can repair the coat properly, it's yours."

Trumper tried to smile, for she supposed that the offer was in-tended as kindness, but as she'd received very little positive feedback in her short life, she had no idea how to respond. "Thank you, Missus," she muttered.

"Not at all," Meyer answered, her eyes on the two maids. "Aggie, did I hear that you spoke informally to Lord Haimsbury on Wednesday morning?"

"Only as replyin' ta his lordship, Missus. I never started it," MacGowan answered.

"I hope not. We must always remember to offer respect to the family, my dear. The Stuarts have a reputation for great kindness, and the marquess still accustoms himself to his lofty position, but that does not give us leave for familiarity. Even when our employers behave informally, it is up to us to respond with deference and respect."

"O' course, ma'am," the Scottish maid answered, noting that Gertrude Trumper's attention had wandered.

The cosy parlour contained two tall windows, both facing east, and the Londoner watched as a man wearing a cloth cap peered into the window on the right.

"Who's tha'?" MacGowan asked.

Rather than reply, Trumper jumped up so quickly that the movement nearly toppled the wooden chair onto its side.

The underbutler, Simon Stephens, nephew to the cook at Branham Hall, stood and straightened his waistcoat. "Return to your seat, Miss Trumper. I shall deal with this."

Stephens crossed through the busy kitchen towards the east entrance. Just as he reached it, the stranger knocked. As the servant opened the heavy door, the evening breeze blew a rusty collection of brittle oak leaves across the flagstones of the freshly mopped floor.

"If you seek employment, sir, we're not currently hiring," Stephens told the disheveled caller, assuming him to be a tramp.

The unkempt man appeared middle-aged with light eyes, thinning brown hair, and a thick nose. He wore no whiskers, and a long, red gash disfigured the left side of his face from temple to jawline. He squinted as he spoke.

"I ain' arskin' fer no jobs, guv. Bu' I wondered if I might speak wiv his lordship. 'e knows me, sir." The stranger handed the underbutler a grease-stained calling card, embossed in gold with the Stuart and Sinclair crests, showing the name 'Supt. Charles R. A.

Sinclair, III' on the first line, '11ᵗʰ Marquess of Haimsbury' on the second and 'Haimsbury House, Westminster' on the third.

"His lordship gave you this?" asked Stephens doubtfully. "When? Where?"

"At the thea're, sir. The Lyceum. Migh' 'is lordship be at 'ome? I called over at t'other 'ouse, bu' were told ta come 'ere."

"Your name?"

"Tawbry, guv. Gus Tawbry."

"Wait here, Mr. Tawbry," Stephens instructed.

Fifteen minutes passed with the uncomfortable visitor doing his best to avoid scathing glances from the scullery maids and other servants who occasionally stared from their places inside the warm parlour. With November almost half over, the nights had turned quite cold, and before the underbutler finally returned, the light rain had changed into a downpour. As the kitchen's clock began to chime the hour of ten, Tawbry could hear male voices speaking from nearby, and to his great relief, he recognised one.

Charles Sinclair crossed through the wide kitchen and reached the open door, extending his right hand in fellowship. "Mr. Tawbry, sir, do come in. Forgive us for keeping you waiting upon our doorstep, particularly in the rain. Mrs. Smith, I wonder if we might offer this gentleman a cup of tea?" he called to the head cook. "Sit, won't you, Mr. Tawbry?"

The Lyceum flyman gulped audibly. "Thank you, my lord. I don' need no tea nor nothin', though 'tis a kindness tha' you offer it, sir. It's jus' tha' you arsked me ta let you know iffin I ever 'eard anythin' more 'bou' the goin's on over a' the thea're, an', well sir, I 'ave. So I come righ' away. It's 'bout tha' singer, sir. Miss Soubret. There's a fella name o' Parker, sir, wha' kep' comp'ny wiv tha' good lady, an' 'e's been braggin' to all an' sundry tha' 'e's come into a good bi' o' coin. Says 'e won the money a' the dog fights, bu' tha's a lie, sir. This feller's a dark one; a righ' scoundrel! When I challenged 'im on it, 'e gimme this," Tawbry explained, pointing to the jagged wound. "Cut me wiv 'is knife! Real long blade. All the girls is righ' scared of 'im, sir. Parker's been showin' tha' blade an' freatenin' 'em wiv talk o' Ripper an' all."

Sinclair listened carefully, his experienced ears accustomed to the truncated, Bow Bells dialect of the poorer people of London's streets, but even he struggled to decipher some portions of the man's rambling confession.

"Mr. Tawbry, do I understand that this Parker person has been flashing a knife around the theatre's female population? That he's threatened them with it?"

"Tha's jus' wha' I been sayin', my lord! Parker's a righ' bad man, sir, an' Mr. Irving's sent 'im packin', bu' it ain' made no diff'rence. Parker's still comin' 'round, insistin' on showin' tha' knife. Bu' there's more, my lord. I seen Parker wiv one o' them creatures, sir."

Charles stared, suddenly concerned for the maids who stood within earshot. "Shall we go outside, Mr. Tawbry? Delicate ladies are present."

Taking an umbrella from Stephens, Sinclair led the visitor towards the formal gardens along the St. James's Park side of Queen Anne House, finding shelter beneath the canopy of a small gazebo. "Forgive me, Mr. Tawbry. Our young maids might find references to these creatures somewhat disquieting. Do you refer to the wolf-men you described to me on Wednesday morning as I was leaving the theatre?"

Tawbry nodded, his hair dripping wet, the cloth cap twisting in his dirty hands. "Tha's right. Them creatures was back, sir. Las' night. I been sober as a judge since tha' nigh'—when poor Pamina were killed—an' I know wha' I seen. My lord, I 'eard them wolfmen talkin'. They's powerful strange! Ears all pointy an' thick 'air all over their faces, and e'en the palms o' their 'ands, ya know!"

"They have hair on the palms of their hands? How is it they spoke so openly in your hearing, Mr. Tawbry? Didn't they see you? Oh, do put your hat on," the marquess advised at seeing the man's condition. "You'll catch your death!"

"Thank you, my lord," the flyman gulped, setting the cap over his plastered hair. "I cain't rightly say if they seen me, sir, bu' I reckon they migh' o' done, fer I 'eard the big one speak yer name, sir. Charles Sinclair. Lord 'aimsbury. Called ya sumfin' strange, sir. Wha' were i' now? King o' sumfing."

"They called me a *king*?" Sinclair asked, glad now that he'd removed the caller from the kitchen. "Try to remember precise words, Mr. Tawbry."

"I fink it were sumfin' like king o' the dead, sir. No. Tha' ain't quite righ'. Wait a minute. I got it, sir! It were *king amongst the dead.* Tha's it! King amongst the dead. Makes no sense ta me, bu' tha's wha' them creatures called you."

The detective took a deep breath, his eyes closed. *I am but king amongst the dead,* he remembered. The Tennyson quote he'd felt sure was the translation of the strange markings upon the card given to him that week by the photographer, Mr. Blackwood. "Is that all?" he asked the flyman.

"Yes, sir. I reckon so."

"I see. Has anyone treated that wound for you?" Sinclair asked, his demeanor grown kinder. "You say this fellow Parker did it? Cut you?"

"Aye, sir, bu' I don' need no tendin'."

"Yes, you do. Come with me. I'll ask my housekeeper to look after you. She's a very skilled nurse. What happened to your spectacles?"

Tawbry's hands unconsciously touched his bulbous nose, where a slightly cleaner stripe of skin connected the thick brows. "They go' broke in the figh', sir."

"Then we shall see that they are replaced. Come with me."

The marquess led the man back through the side garden and into the kitchens once more. After leaving him sitting at the table surrounded by a ring of curious scullery maids, Charles pulled the cook and housekeeper aside to a solitary spot near the bottom of the servants' staircase.

"Mrs. Meyer, I hope you and Mrs. Smith will forgive the interruption to your evening. This gentleman may not possess graceful manners, nor is he of pleasant countenance, but he is in need of medical care. I hope that I do not overstep. My experience in life is as a policeman who orders men about, so if ever I treat either of you unkindly, you must let me know. This man—Mr. Tawbry—has been a wealth of information to me regarding the murder at the Lyceum on Tuesday night. I feel that he has earned our indulgence. Do you mind?"

Meyer actually blushed. "Oh, sir, you mustn't ever think your actions are anything but kind! Had we known this gentleman was one of your—what do you call them, sir? Informants?"

"Yes, that's correct, Mrs. Meyer," the detective answered, smiling. "Of course, most in the east have a far less gentle way of referring to those who offer information to the police. I've heard them called grasses, snitches, rats, rossers, even spawns of Abaddon, if you can believe it."

Smith blinked. "Is that so? I must say, my lord, that your experience in the world makes ours seem quite ordinary!"

"I seriously doubt that, Mrs. Smith. Though I've only been part of this family for a short time, already I've heard tales of your bravery in the face of danger. The duke mentioned a time when you aided our little duchess in the herb garden, saving her from a poisonous adder. And Mrs. Meyer, you served with the duke in two theatres of war, I understand, and comported yourself most admirably; particularly as regards your time in Turkey during the Crimean. But I have interrupted your quiet evening with all this, ladies. Again, forgive me."

"Really, my lord, it is no interruption at all. None at all," Meyer answered as she peered around the corner at the bashful visitor. "You say his name is Tawbry, sir?"

"Yes. Gus Tawbry."

"Mr. Tawbry!" she called to the man. "Do come through, sir. I shall fix you up in my office, if you don't mind." Meyer turned back to the marquess. "We can handle it now, sir. Oh, and I've sent the medicine you requested with Alicia. Is my lady feeling better? Mrs. Smith and Mr. Miles both mentioned that the little duchess is still off her food."

"Her stomach is rather delicate just now," he whispered. "Nerves."

"Ah, yes," the housekeeper replied, though her expression made it clear that she doubted the diagnosis. "I suppose that makes a *kind* of sense, doesn't it, sir? Getting married is a big step, after all."

Hilda Smith agreed. "Aye, gettin' married can set a lady's stomach all aflutter. The duchess has always been right sensitive, ya know. I'll make sure that we offer something light and easily digested at every meal from now on."

Meyer started to follow Tawbry into the office, but then turned, glancing at Sinclair. "Lord Haimsbury, I wonder, might Dr. Price have left any instructions regarding a special diet for my lady? Foods that will help in nourishing her, uh, *delicate* constitution?"

Charles stared at the perceptive woman. *She knows,* he realised. "None that he mentioned to me, but I shall ask when next he stops by. And may I say, Mrs. Meyer, that you and Mrs. Smith are the foundation of this home? We should all be lost without you." He kissed the right cheek of each woman, causing the prim housekeeper to blush profusely, and the plump cook to giggle like a schoolgirl.

Charles climbed quickly back up the stairs, and the women returned to their duties, each stroking her cheek thoughtfully, eyes twinkling.

Standing nearby, just inside the door to the butler's pantry, Gertrude Trumper began to consider what she'd overheard. *She's off her food and faintin'. Reckon I know the real reason 'er 'igh and migh'y is poorly. I wonder which one is the father.*

With this playing in her mind, the Londoner left the doorway and tiptoed through a connecting hallway towards the housekeeping office, where Meyer now tended to the flyman's wounds. Gertrude's objective—the medicine chest—stood open as if daring the maid to theft. The housekeeper's back was to the door, and Trumper entered, treading softly to avoid detection. Cynthia Meyer's attention was upon the hand lens she now used to examine her patient's eyes. Taking advantage of the distraction, the newly hired maid quietly removed the remaining paper packet from the chest's top layer. After stuffing the powder into her uniform pocket, she hastily left the office and followed the narrow staircase up to the third floor living quarters.

Entering the small room she shared with Aggie MacGowan, Gertie made certain no one else lurked in the hallway and then shut the door behind her. After unlocking a dresser drawer, she withdrew an ornate, green bottle and opened its stopper. She then added the packet of sleeping medicine to the vial. Including the liquid already inside, the addition filled it to the three-quarters mark.

"This'll fix 'er," the girl whispered to herself as she stoppered the bottle and stored it once again in the locked drawer. She gazed into a beveled mirror that stood over the simple dressing table she shared with MacGowan.

"You there, sir?" she said aloud. "I done wha' you asked. I got that bottle o' medicine from the old gypsy, an' I added somethin' extra, jus' ta make sure she sleeps through it."

A shadowy figure materialised within the mirror's surface, the indistinct form slowly assuming a pleasing shape: tall, regal, dark-haired. The image smiled.

"When shall I use it?" she asked him.

"I shall tell you soon, my dear," he replied in heavily accented English. His ice-blue eyes were rimmed in black lashes, and to Gertrude, he appeared as beautiful as any god.

"You shore is 'andsome, sir," she told the lying creature. "You ever gonna meet me, sir? You know, in the real world?"

"Soon, Gertrude," the image promised, his eyes smoking to a crimson hue. "Very, very soon. For now, keep the bottle of medicine safe. Allow no one to discover it."

"And when it's done, sir?"

"Then, I shall give you the reward you deserve, my dear. You will join me forever—as a lady of the night."

Once back inside the drawing room, Charles found the duke perusing one of the evening papers. "What did Stephens want?" the Scotsman asked his nephew.

"Do you remember that Paul and I mentioned a flyman from the Lyceum?" Sinclair began.

"Aye," Drummond replied, reaching into his pocket for a pipe. "You spoke to him about a peculiar shadow that Paul had seen onstage, as I recall."

"That's right, sir. His name's Gus Tawbry, and we gave him our cards and asked that he contact us if he ever learnt anything new, which is why he's here now. Tawbry tells me that a fellow calling himself Parker has been flashing a long knife and wads of money, hoping to impress the actresses at the theatre. The unsociable behaviour has cost this Parker his job, but he continues to harass anyone who challenges him, and Tawbry did so to his detriment. Meyer is patching him up now. The poor man will wear a long scar upon his face for the rest of his life, I should think."

"He was cut? Charles, do you think this Parker could be Ripper?" Drummond asked.

"He certainly claims to be—or so he has implied to all at the Lyceum. Where is Martin, by the way? Did he already leave?"

"No, our tailor is on an expedition in search of a bottle of wine, and Victoria's gone up with Della. With Paul out, it's just the three of us for the evening."

Charles took a seat just as Kepelheim returned, holding a dusty bottle of wine in each hand. "Do forgive the wait, Your Grace. It took me longer than I'd thought, for the cellars here have been re-arranged since my last visit, but I believe this vintage will suffice. Did I miss anything interesting? I overheard Mrs. Meyer speaking to some fellow in her office when I walked past. It looked to me as if he'd taken the worst in a rather energetic fracas."

"The man's name is Gus Tawbry," Sinclair answered.

At that moment, Samson the terrier scampered into the room and began sniffing everyone's hands as if inspecting their washing habits. "Hello, boy," the detective said good-naturedly. "Have you decided to spend the evening with the men?"

Martin set the wine bottles onto a carved, rococo-style table that stood behind one of the sofas. "Tawbry? Isn't that the fellow who spoke to you as we were leaving on Wednesday morning, Charles? The rather dirty-faced one who reeked of gin?"

"I think he's left off strong drink for the present, Martin, but yes, the same," the marquess answered, scratching the dog's ears. "He claims a man named Parker has been keeping company with a group of hybrids."

Drummond struck a match to the pipe. "Hybrids? The man used that word?"

"Not exactly. He calls them wolfmen, actually—or wolves that walk like men. This Parker was recently dismissed from Irving's employ, but was flashing money about, regardless, claiming he'd found luck at the pit dog fights. When Gus called him out as a liar, Parker wounded our flyman and broke his spectacles. Gus is being tended by Mrs. Meyer just now, but I wonder if another visit to the Lyceum is in order."

"To see the play again?" the tailor asked with a wink.

"Not if I can avoid it," the detective answered, turning to look at Victoria's dog. The terrier had leapt upon a nearby chair, deciding to take a snooze. Samson circled several times and then lay upon his back near the window. Within minutes, he'd begun to snore, all four paws in the air, twitching as he dreamt.

"Samson likes this house, I think," Sinclair noted. "Is he allowed on the furniture?"

"He's allowed wherever he wishes to go, apparently. Tory's much too permissive. My dogs know better," Drummond grumbled, casting a disapproving glare at the Parson Russell. James placed the pipe into the corner of his mouth, chewing on it as he spoke. "Charles, if you must return to the theatre, wait until Paul or one of us can accompany you. I've begun to worry about you, son."

"I'm fine, sir. Policing Whitechapel has taught me caution," he replied, pointing to the pistol inside his coat.

"Nevertheless, I want you to have company," Drummond insisted. "Consider that an order. I'll not have my great-grandchild's father out and about where Redwing's experiments might bring him harm. Oh, I do hope it's all right that I mentioned it. Martin told me that he knows."

"It's fine, sir," the marquess said, smiling at the animal's curious posture.

"Look here, laddy," Drummond continued, "there are a few things I'd like to discuss with you, when you've the time. One of them has to do with Loudain House."

Kepelheim had set three glasses onto the table, but suddenly recalling a promise, he reached into his pocket. "I nearly forgot, Charles. I've a note for you. Lester gave it to me as I passed him in the foyer earlier. I'm pouring glasses for all of us. A sort of celebration, in honour of our beloved duchess. Whilst in the cellars, I uncovered an entire rack of this lovely wine, if you can imagine it. Château Lafite '65. A very nice year. I'm sure it was Connor who added these to the inventory. Patricia never cared much for Bordeaux, as I recall. Didn't the late duchess prefer white wine, Your Grace?"

"Patricia? Aye, she liked Chablis, but only because Connor preferred the opposite," the duke replied, his voice revealing a low opinion of the late duchess. "Trish was contrary when it came to my son. That reminds me, Martin. Charles has agreed to become my heir. Did I tell you that?"

"Has he? That is absolutely wonderful news! Another cause for celebration! I'm sure Connor would have approved," the tailor answered as he poured a sampling of the wine into a long-stemmed glass. "I wonder if I should allow this to breathe a bit?" he whispered aloud as Charles read through the letter.

The duke laughed. "Don't ask me. Ring for Miles, if you're unsure. I'm content with whisky, but you do as you please. Charles, I'm told that you had some photos taken wearing the Stuart tartan on Wednesday. We'll need to get one o' you wearin' the full Drummond regalia. Better yet, a painting! You're nearly Connor's size, and I'd imagine his kilt would fit you. I think it's packed in a trunk at my house. I'll have Booth send it over."

"Thank you, sir," the marquess answered, looking up. "I'm not sure I have the knees for it, but I'll wear it, if you wish."

"Who's the letter from?" the duke asked as he fiddled with the pipe to make it draw better.

"Edmund Reid. He voices concern regarding tomorrow's meeting time. With the mayor's procession planned for ten, it's likely the streets will become impassable by eight. In fact, most of them are already shut to wheeled traffic twixt here and Leman Street. We may have to reschedule, yet again. Is that the evening *Gazette*?"

"The *Times,* actually. Not much news," James said, tapping the paper next to him. "Most of it's filled with columns about tomorrow morning's doings. You'd think the Lord Mayor's being crowned the new monarch, for all the fuss the press is making! As you say, he's shutting down most of the streets 'twixt here and the city. It'll be a chore for anyone to make it tomorrow morning. Reid may be right, but if we do postpone, then let's move it to Loudain House. I could have Booth and his men open it, if you approve."

"James, you're the leader. I'm pleased to participate whenever, wherever you wish, but let's not delay it too long. Monday?" Sinclair suggested. "We'd planned to overlook Loudain House that day, anyway. A circle meeting would allow the full London membership to help us make decisions regarding how best to utilise the space."

Kepelheim swirled the sample of the wine, examining it for signs of sedimentation. "Monday? Mr. Blackwood will want to see you again early next week, I should think, Charles. Did we tell him Tuesday?"

"Yes," Sinclair answered. "I think so, at least. I've yet to hire that secretary you mentioned, though I promise to interview him once the wedding's done. I suppose Sunday is impossible."

"We're having the Churchills and Cartringhams over for luncheon following morning services," Drummond explained. "My sister has arranged it all. Charles, make sure your cousin attends, won't you? Delia Wychwright will be singing that morning, and I suspect it's primarily to impress him."

The policeman rolled his eyes. "That girl is certainly persistent! Very well, Sunday is out, or the afternoon is, at least. Might we meet that evening, sir? Warren gave me information that we must discuss as a group, and with Beth's recent nightmares, I think it important that we gather as soon as possible."

"Have we ruled out Saturday?" the tailor asked, sniffing the wine's bouquet.

"I don't believe so," the duke answered. "What about Saturday morning at ten?"

"I have to visit Whitechapel that morning, sir, but I could return by noon. Would early afternoon work for everyone?"

"Let's make it one, and we'll serve luncheon, but it will have to be here, since the kitchens at Loudain haven't been used in decades. Martin, write that time and date down in your enormous brain, will you? In the meantime, we can meet as a family tomorrow morning. Pull the bellrope, will you, Martin? I've an errand for our Mr. Miles."

The tailor complied and in a moment the efficient butler answered. "Sir?"

"I'll need one of your footmen to run to the telegraph office, Miles."

"Most of the footmen are enjoying entertainment with the grooms, sir."

"Cards?" Drummond asked, winking. "They work hard. I canno' begrudge them a few hours o' play. Is your underbutler available?"

"He is, sir."

"Good. If you'll bring me a scrap o' paper, I'll write it down. It goes to Sir Thomas Galton at his home in Mayfair. He'll make sure everyone else receives the message."

Within five minutes, James Stuart had composed a short note regarding the altered date and time for the circle meeting, and Miles dispatched Stephens in a coach to carry out the order.

"Tomorrow, we'll go over anything you think important, Charles," the duke told his nephew. "I'll see if Tory might find a means to distract our duchess."

Sinclair felt weary, but adding to the sense of fatigue was the weight of an incomprehensible foreboding. "I promised Elizabeth that we'd share a picnic at the other house on Saturday afternoon. If we could finish by five, I'm sure she'd appreciate it. Will Dr. MacPherson be able make it tomorrow morning?"

"Aye, he lives this side o' the city, so I imagine he can. Why?"

"Spiritual questions that I'd put to him."

Drummond leaned back against the sofa. "If these pertain to Beth's experiences, I could ask her to join us as well."

"No, James. I prefer she did not."

The brown and white terrier's eyes popped opened, and the dog squirmed to a new position on the upholstered chair, his attention captured by a large, black moth at the window. The animal's head cocked to one side, and a stripe of bristly hair rose up along his spotted back.

The three men took no notice, continuing their conversation.

"Why shouldn't Elizabeth be part of the meetings, son?" Drummond asked. "She's at the centre of all our discussions, and her experiences with these entities could bring insights we lack."

"I appreciate that, James, but I prefer those experiences be relayed through myself or the earl for the present. I've no wish to stifle her input, but Beth is very delicate at the moment. I'm sure you understand."

Drummond grinned, his dark eyes twinkling. "Aye, I certainly do understand. Tis a delicacy that makes this old man very happy. Very well. I'll not press the issue. What did Warren have to say this evening? Is he resigning?"

The dog growled softly, its body posture altering once more, so that the chin was low, tail held high, ears back. In response, the moth fluttered against the panes of the south window. The gas lamps of the portico shimmered against its iridescent wings and revealed two marks that looked for all the world like a pair of red eyes.

Martin held the wine glass up to the chandelier's light, swirling the Bordeaux slightly before tasting. "Oh, this is quite delicious!" he exclaimed, pouring himself a full glass. "Charles, you really must have some. Lafite is spectacular, but also medicinal. It settles the stomach following a heavy meal and even aids in sleep."

"I've no trouble sleeping most..." Sinclair started to answer, but the dog's sudden movement caught his attention. The animal pounced against the glass as if trying to strike or bite the persistent moth. "Samson!" the marquess cried out as he rose to remove the dog. "What has you so upset? It's only a moth."

Bending to retrieve the animal, Charles froze, for he could now see precisely what the dog saw: not a moth at all, but an enormous, inky figure with two red eyes within a blank face.

Drummond and Kepelheim perceived nothing, for the two men continued to chat genially as they sampled the wine. Finally, noticing his friend's prolonged silence and frozen position, the tailor spoke. "Charles?"

"Does anyone else see that?" Sinclair asked the others, his eyes wide.

Drummond stared, but perceived nothing amiss. "See what, son?"

Kepelheim set down the wine glass and walked to the window, joining the marquess. "What do *you* see, Charles?" he asked pointedly.

"A creature. It's looking at me," the marquess explained. "It's approximately nine feet tall with an oval sort of face, though there's no nose or mouth. Just red eyes. It's watching me as I speak, Martin. Listening. Wait! It's moving backwards now, away from the window. Good heavens!" he gasped. "It grows even larger: fifteen, sixteen feet in height—and it has wings!"

Kepelheim squinted at the retreating moth, trying to see past the veil that disguised the demonic presence. His attention thus distracted, the tailor nearly missed it when Sinclair started to fall.

"Charles!" the duke shouted, leaping to his feet and reaching his nephew just as Kepelheim clutched at the collapsing peer's shoulder.

"Sit, my friend. Sit! Shall I send for George Price?"

"No, I'm all right," the detective assured the tailor as he leaned back against the chair. His breath came quickly, and a cold sweat covered his brow. "Neither of you saw it?"

"I saw only a peculiar looking moth," Kepelheim told him.

"A moth?" the duke asked. "No, it was more like a bat!"

Charles sighed. "Neither, though it's likely this creature conceals itself beneath multiple layers of lies. I'd take some of that whisky you mentioned, sir," he told Drummond.

The duke rang for Miles, and the butler entered. "My lord?"

"Bring us some of your strongest whisky, Mr. Miles," James told the man.

"Very good, Your Grace."

"I wish Paul were here," Drummond said, moving to a chair beside his nephew. "Did you see anything else? Sense anything?"

Sinclair shook his head. "Nothing I can explain. Is this how Beth feels when she sees visions that elude the eyes of others? I know that creature was there, James. Staring into this room like a hellish spy of some kind. Sir, do you mind if we speak more of this tomorrow? I'd like to go up to Beth soon. I've an unsettled sense, and I would make sure of her safety."

"Of course. You go sleep, son," he said as the butler returned with a decanter of Drummond Reserve. "That was quick!"

"From the library, Your Grace. Some that I'd already decanted for tomorrow's meeting. I fear that it's the last of the '22 Reserve. Would you prefer to save it for tomorrow? I could fetch the Glenlivet."

"Certainly not! I've six casks of the '22 and plenty of other years at the castle, if we run low. Pour our marquess a large glass, will you? Has my sister gone to bed?"

"Lady Victoria and Lady Adele retired to the upstairs library with Mrs. Wilsham, sir. They mentioned an embroidery project."

"And what about Mrs. Marchand? Is she about?"

"Lady Victoria's nurse has gone out, sir. I believe she is walking the north gardens. The rain has stopped, and she said something about stretching her legs. Shall I send a footman to fetch her, sir?"

"The woman's taking a walk this time of night?" Drummond exclaimed. "Yes, Miles! Send a man out to escort the woman indoors at once. No one's to go out after dark from now on unless another is with him, and that includes you. Did my nephew happen to say when he planned to return?"

"The earl did not know when he might be finished, sir," Miles said as he handed the glass of spirits to Sinclair. "However, he did indicate that he hoped to return to the house before dawn."

Charles smiled. "Typical of my cousin. Miles, would you please send Granger to look in on the earl? He told me he planned to visit someplace called Egyptian Hall. It's in Piccadilly. I'd feel better knowing he's home and unharmed."

"At once, my lord," Miles replied, setting the decanter on a table.

The butler left the room, and Kepelheim lifted the stopper on the decanter, sniffing the whisky. "I've always loved the Drummond Reserve. Spicy with notes of vanilla and cinnamon."

The duke took the flask from the tailor and put his nose to the opening. "I'd not thought there was any left here. The Reserve was always Connor's favourite. It's aged in two different types of wine casks for fifteen years each. Strong stuff, this. Careful, Charles."

The marquess gazed at the caramel-coloured liquid in his glass. "Down the hatch," he said, tipping it back and swallowing every drop in one gulp. His eyes began to water, but the detective maintained composure, despite the intense warmth at the back of his throat. "Not bad."

Drummond began to laugh heartily. "Heavens above, laddy! It's clear you're a Stuart, through and through. Now, off to bed, wi' ye. Martin, I'm goin' along to make certain my nephew doesn't roll down the steps, but I'll be back."

The duke took hold of Sinclair's arm and the two of them left the drawing room. Once they'd reached the duchess's apartment, Drummond paused before opening the door into the parlour. "Are you sure you'll be all right, son?"

"I'm fine. Thank you, James. As promised, I'll leave the doors open again, for propriety's sake. Let me know when Paul returns."

"You should sleep," Drummond insisted, "but I'll tell him to stop in to say hello, if that's what you want. Give my granddaughter a kiss from me, will you? Goodnight, Charles."

"Goodnight, sir."

The detective entered the dimly lit bedchamber, finding his beloved sleeping peacefully beneath several quilts, for the entire room felt cold. Despite his warnings to all staff, Sinclair noticed that one of the four windows stood open, so he closed it and turned the brass latch to lock it.

Wiping at his eyes, the marquess considered taking a bath to relax his weary muscles, but the combination of two glasses of wine at dinner and the large whisky had left him somewhat tipsy, so he settled for a quick splash of cool water upon his face. He then brushed his teeth, combed his hair, and returned to the bedchamber.

To his shock, the window stood open once more. Charles had heard no one enter the apartment, but he crossed through the adjoining parlour and even peered into the corridor to make certain that he and Beth were actually alone.

After relatching the window, he removed his coat and waistcoat, draping both across an armchair near the fire. He unbuckled the metal fasteners on the leather shoulder holster and added it to the chair as well. Charles then pushed the long sofa close to the duchess's bed, aligning it so that it paralleled her mattress, drawing it near enough so that he could touch her hand if she reached out in the night.

Sitting upon the chair, he removed his boots and socks, and then unfolded the trio of quilts that Mrs. Meyer had left for his use, placing these and a pillow upon the couch. Remembering the conversation regarding the Verne novel, he dropped to his knees and examined the underside of the duchess's bed, swiping his hands underneath the shadowy space, but found nothing. *What happened to it?* he wondered.

As he stood, intending to lie down on the sofa, he felt a deep chill. Inexplicably, the window had again sprung open, despite the fact that he had very carefully secured its lock.

Elizabeth stirred in her sleep, turning towards the window, and she reached out as if trying to touch something. "Paul," she moaned, her eyes moving rapidly beneath closed lids.

She's dreaming about him, Charles realised. *Why?*

As he reached for the window latch, a large bird or bat flew past. The skies were still overcast, though the rain had stopped. The vault overhead appeared like an impenetrable dome of iron, for it seemed as though all the stars had winked out at once.

"Paul," she whispered again, her voice raspy.

He sat upon the edge of the soft bed. "It's Charles, dear. Paul isn't here."

She reached for his hand, though she still slept, perhaps trapped in a nightmare. He leaned over and kissed her soft cheek.

"Paul?" she called again, and the agony caused by the single word drove its sharp point into his heart as no material dagger might—so keen was the disappointment. *Why does she dream of him?*

"No, darling. It's Charles," he told her, his voice coloured with despair.

Her eyes flew open, and even in the dim moonlight filtering through the windowpanes, he could see the large black pupils, and it seemed to the detective that her gaze fixed upon something other than his face.

"Paul! He's in danger! We have to help him!"

Josette Marchand cared little for England. Though French by heritage, the thirty-six-year-old widow had lived most of her life in Bouillon, a scenic village in the south of Belgium, near the French border. The nurse found Londoners noisy and ill-bred. The Stuart family were kind enough, but Josette missed the pastoral hills and farmlands of her former home. Walking through the scenic beauty of Queen Anne Park, especially after a rain, provided an escape from the clattering chaos of London, and she'd made a habit of strolling here after supper.

"Madam Marchand!" a man's voice called from five hundred yards to the south. She turned to find a slender youth approaching. "Madam, you are wanted inside the house," he said politely. "The duke and marquess ask that you return at once."

It was a footman named Peterson, a handsome young man with copper hair and a constellation of pale freckles across his nose and cheeks. Marchand sighed. "I am needed?" she asked, her voice heavily accented.

The footman walked swiftly towards the nurse, his gloved hands in his pockets against the chill. "His lordship asks that no one be out after dark, madam," the youth continued as he drew near. "Allow me to escort you into the conservatory."

Marchand shook her head, irritated by the interruption. "Why this rule for me, eh? Am I not strong enough to keep myself safe? I wear a coat. Cold does not affect me as it might others. I am not frail duchess, m'sieur!"

Peterson's steps slowed as he reached her position, just to the east of a boxwood knot garden. "Please, madam. I'm only following orders. Allow me to see you safely indoors."

She shrugged. "*C'est dommage.* Such a pity, for the moon, she is lovely. *Mais oui*, I go, if it must be so." She started towards him, but a movement along the north wall of the mansion caused Marchand to stop in her tracks. "What that?" she asked, pointing to the windows of the master apartment. "Is large bat or nightbird?"

"It might be a bat. We often see them 'round here." The sharp-eyed footman turned 'round to look, and the sight forced air from his lungs in a great gasp of shock. "Good heavens! It's a man!"

Sure enough, a humanoid creature was scaling the limestone façade, creeping upwards, inch by inch, using claws of living shadow—but as it approached the duchess's window, it transformed into a vapour and entered her room through the tiniest of cracks, disappearing from sight.

CHAPTER THREE

One hour earlier

Susanna Morgan had been waiting since eight o'clock. Sitting in a small salon just off the main theatre of Egyptian Hall in Piccadilly, the buxom singer waved to the slender young man who served as waiter for the private meeting room. "You there!" she called. "What time is it?"

The youth glanced at his pocket watch. "Three minutes 'til nine, Miss."

Morgan tapped her empty glass. "Another white wine, then, I suppose. When does Maskelyne perform?"

"Ten o'clock, Miss," he told her as he poured her a fourth glass of Chardonnay. "Do you wish to speak with him?"

"Hardly. His so-called magic is mundane, predictable, and really quite boring. Is he still working with that cabinet maker? That awful little twist—oh, what is his name again? Cooke?"

"Yes, Miss. However, we've another magician and a singer as prelude who'll begin at half nine. And there's also an amusing musical number on Jack the Ripper. It's been quite well received."

Morgan yawned. "Ripper is becoming somewhat clichéd, don't you think? I see my friend has finally arrived. He'll have whisky, I imagine. Be sure it's your best. He'll know the difference."

"Yes, Miss." The waiter bowed and departed, his somewhat effeminate face breaking into a broad grin as the newcomer walked past. "Welcome to the Egyptian, sir. May I bring you a drink whilst you wait for the prelude to begin?"

Paul Stuart handed the youth a sovereign. "Your best whisky. To the table in the corner."

"Very good, sir," the young man said, clearly appreciating the earl's apparent wealth, muscular physique, and attractive face.

Paul's raised eyebrow sent the lad packing. The earl strode towards the American, pulling out a chair and then sitting. "A rather strange place to meet, Susanna," he said, removing his leather gloves. "I wasn't aware you enjoyed magic acts. Forgive the late arrival. Couldn't be helped. Have you found our errant physician yet?"

Morgan heaved a sigh, the movement straining the tight laces of her corsetted evening gown. "You crush me! Not even a moment of small talk? A 'my you're looking lovely tonight, Susanna', or 'is that a new perfume'? Is this how you treat me, when you're already an hour late? As though I'm cutting into your family's precious time? Really, Paul, I should just leave," she complained, pouting as she stood to go.

Ignoring the woman's theatrics, Aubrey remained seated, but he took her hand and kissed it nonetheless. "Do sit, Susanna. I might be late, but I would never deliberately ignore your charms. If it soothes your wounded vanity, then allow me to start again. It's been a rather busy day, and I'm short on sleep, as I'm sure you know. But if anyone has cause to complain, it is I. After all, you stood me up on Monday."

"A conflict arose," the American cooed. "You know how that is. It couldn't be helped, much like your family problems, but I promise to make it up to you, if you'll allow me."

"Not tonight, my dear," he said, his blue eyes bright. "Another time, perhaps. What have you to tell me that's so important that it cannot wait until a night when I'm less weary?"

"Now you really have hurt my feelings," she complained. "I've not seen you for more than five minutes in over a month, and when you finally do meet me, it's all business. Still, you're looking rather well for someone who's operating on little sleep. Quite well, in fact. Given the opportunity, I'm certain that I could wake you up," the cat purred, leaning against the table to allow her generous bosom to push forward. The gown's material shimmered like ice, for its pale blue satin was overlaid with hundreds of clear glass beads. Beyond form-fitting, the dress looked as if it had been painted on, making her assets seem rounder and more prominent.

Aubrey responded by smiling ambiguously. He'd known Morgan for nearly five years, and in that time, she had continually failed in all attempts to entice him into bed, but the Chicago-born songstress never wearied of trying.

"I imagine you would find ways to awaken me that are quite creative, Susanna, but as you already know, I'm not interested. It is not that you lack beauty, my dear..."

"Yes, I know. Your heart lies elsewhere, but why, Paul? Why waste your affections and energies on a woman who is now engaged to another? How did all that come about anyway?" she asked, her foot stroking his left calf.

Aubrey shifted position. In his time with the inner circle, the handsome earl had fended off many such feminine assaults, but her question drove into his mind like an icepick. *Why am I still focused on Beth? Is it mere habit, or could it be I hope she will change her mind?*

"It's been in the works for a long time," he lied. "Charles and Elizabeth go back many years. He's just come into his inheritance, and..."

"Yes, yes, that is what the brain-dead reporters are fed, and they swallow it like a rainbow trout going after a tasty minnow, but you can tell *me* the truth," she insisted. "When Clive and I shared your theatre box at the Lyceum last month, you and the duchess seemed quite close, but then perhaps she's been secretly in love with this policeman all along."

"Beth's affections for Charles have been no secret to our family," he said honestly, though the truth still stung. "Susanna, you slipped me a message on Tuesday evening, saying you had information of interest regarding Lorena MacKey. If you have nothing to share other than gossip and innuendo, then I'll be going."

The waiter arrived, and he set down the whisky, intentionally brushing against the earl's hand as he did so. Paul glanced up. "Thank you, young man, but I assure you that I not interested. You are simply not my type."

The youth's countenance fell, but the earl smoothed it over by handing him half a crown as a tip. "Why, thank you, sir!" the lad grinned, a gold incisor glittering inside his otherwise nondescript mouth. "You're most kind. Will you be stayin' for the entertainment, sir?"

Aubrey shook his head, the long chestnut hair gleaming in the gaslight. "I fear that I cannot. I have business elsewhere."

57

The waiter departed, pausing near the doorway to chat with a fellow employee, apparently boasting about his generous tip and the very handsome man who offered it. Paul saw it all and laughed.

The American touched his hand. "It seems that everyone wishes to share your bed, Lord Aubrey."

"Not everyone," he heard himself say, instantly regretting it. "Never mind. I'm more tired than I thought."

"I like the beard," she said, hoping to banish the duchess from his thoughts with a change in topic. "It suits you."

"Does it?" he asked, stroking the coarse hair on his chin. "I'm leaving soon for a protracted assignment, most likely in Egypt. This will help me to blend in a bit more."

"I doubt you'd blend in anywhere. It's darker than I'd have expected. Your hair is such a beautiful shade of golden brown, I'd have thought your beard would be closer to auburn, yet it's nearly black."

"My father's influence, I imagine. He had black hair."

She smiled. "I saw him once—in your company. Ten years ago. I'd only just arrived in England, barely sixteen, and Clive had taken me to the opera. He pointed out you and your handsome father that night. Do you favour your mother?"

"Yes, actually. She had auburn hair. My sister Adele looks much the same. She is my mother made over, in fact."

Morgan's face pinched. "Didn't Clive tell me that your sister is adopted? Don't tell me that she was born on the other side of the blanket!"

Paul's thoughts scattered, scrambling about for a means to cover the careless blunder. *What is it about this woman that makes me say such things?* "I've no idea where that rumour arose, but Della is a Stuart by blood. Clive is mistaken."

She smiled, the sort of practised curl of the lip that implies secret knowledge. "Ah, well, that explains it."

The earl rarely felt ill at ease, but he suddenly longed to be elsewhere—anywhere but here. Looking about for an escape route, he noticed Serena di Specchio enter the salon on the arm of a gentleman who looked almost as if he could be Prince Anatole's twin, though several inches shorter.

"Excuse me," he told Morgan, standing. "I shan't be more than a moment."

Aubrey strode towards the corner, where the contessa was just sitting, her chair held by the stranger. "Good evening, Countess," he told di Specchio. "Have you come for another evening's entertainment?"

The Italian noblewoman showed little surprise at his appearance. "It is Lord Aubrey, is it not? Yes, I find magic acts most enjoyable, don't you? Allow me to introduce my friend, Prince..."

"Razarit Grigor," the earl finished for her, recognition hitting him at last. "It's been a long time."

The Romanian's eyes sparked hotly in response. "I'd thought that might be you when we entered."

Serena gasped, feigning amazement. "You know each other?"

"We do indeed," the earl replied, sitting. "How long has it been, Rasha? Four months? Five?"

"Since the end of June, I think," he said as the waiter arrived. "Vodka for me, young man. Your finest red for the lady, and I believe the earl is fond of whisky. Or perhaps you have altered your desires since last we met, Aubrey. Much has changed since then, I understand."

The earl's mouth upturned at the edges, and he glanced up at the waiter. "Nothing else. I'll finish my drink when I return to my own table."

Grigor laughed. "Perhaps, one glass is all a Scotsman can handle! One woman, one drink. You are wise to curtail your inclinations."

Under other circumstances, Aubrey would never have fallen for such obvious bait, but fatigue had dulled his wits. "Have you any Drummond Reserve in stock?"

"We do, sir. It is quite strong, however."

"I'm accustomed to its strength. A tall glass."

"Very good, sir," the youth replied, leaving the table.

The prince's full lips widened into a sneer. "It's my understanding that a wedding is planned. Congratulations! You finally won the fair duchess's hand."

Paul counted to ten before replying. "My cousin is the victor, actually. The Marquess of Haimsbury. I'm not sure you've ever met."

"I shall seek him out," the prince said, glancing at di Specchio. "Won't I, Serena? Perhaps, you and I shall attend the ceremony, arm in arm, eh? Elizabeth did not choose you," he continued, his gaze returning to Aubrey. "It must gall you. Tell me, how does it feel to be spurned by the duchess? Rather stings, doesn't it?"

Stuart leaned forward, his voice low. "I know what you did to her, Grigor. If you *ever* touch her again, I will kill you."

Razarit threw his head back in mockery. "Is that so? You and your cousin are certainly two of a kind! Oh, didn't he mention it? Charles Sinclair and I have already met, you see. He threatened me as well, but neither of you frightens me."

"Then you're a fool as well as a coward, for only a man with no backbone strikes a woman!"

"Now, now, gentlemen," the countess cautioned, "must we make a scene in so public a place? If hot words must be exchanged, then there are other ways to settle your disagreement."

"Name the place," Aubrey said foolishly.

Grigor remained calm. "Are you so eager to die? I am far more powerful than you can possibly imagine, Lord Aubrey."

"Shall we take this outside and find out?" Stuart suggested. "I haven't fired my weapon all week."

"Do you really think that bullets affect me?" Grigor taunted. "Ask Sir Robert Morehouse if material weaponry is of use when battling my kind."

Di Specchio tried to intercede, fearing Anatole Romanov's reaction were any harm to befall the earl in her presence. "We have no need for such trifles, Rasha. You are better than ten Scottish earls! He isn't worth your time."

The prince stood. "Indeed. Forgive me, Lord Aubrey. I have an appointment elsewhere, but I promise to return to this conversation very soon. And when I do, I shall not be alone."

"Let's finish it now," the Scotsman insisted, his jaw set.

Razarit snapped his fingers, and the room grew still, populated only by human statues. Paul felt his arms turn to lead weights. He was frozen, unable to move.

"Do not tempt fate, my Scottish friend. I could slice your throat right here, right now, and you would be powerless to stop me," the demonic hybrid whispered, bending close to Aubrey's ear.

Unaffected by the parlour trick, di Specchio looked all about for signs of Romanov. "Rasha! Are you mad? If Anatole finds out, *he* will slice *your* throat, and you know it! Even your father's intercession will avail nothing, if Anatole chooses to punish you!"

"Romanov does not frighten me. My father is far more power-ful than that blind traitor! He grows slow and stupid in his dotage!"

"And you risk eternal death, if he learns of your actions," she re-minded him. "Now, release the earl before we all end up in chains."

Grigor's breathing slowed, his intense eyes returning to their normal hue. "You owe the countess your life, Scotsman. Now, fin-ish your whisky and your conversation with the American. I have work elsewhere this night." The hybrid entity's body thinned, like a fading shadow, and in the blink of an eye, both Razarit Grigor and Serena di Specchio had vanished.

The sudden blare of ribald conversation and stage music struck Paul's ears like a clap of thunder, and he fell against the table, his muscles suddenly unlocked as time once more moved forward.

Morgan rushed to his aid, genuine concern in her voice. "Paul! Good gracious! Are you all right?"

"Yes. Yes, I'm fine," he told her, though he felt anything but fine. The earl had never in his life experienced such a supernatural event, and it rattled him to the core. "I should go."

"No, you aren't going anywhere. You sit down, now! Come on, let me help you," she insisted, taking his arm. "Do you need a doctor?"

"No, Susanna, I'm fine, but I will sit with you for a moment," he answered, allowing her to lead him back to the table. She seemed deeply worried, which surprised the earl. "Perhaps, there's more to you than I thought," he said as she handed him the half-empty whisky glass.

"What just happened?" she asked. "One minute I saw you talking to that man and some woman in red, and the next you were collapsing against an empty table. Where did they go?"

"To hell, no doubt. Did you know him?"

"Yes," she whispered, "but don't ask me to say anything about him, Paul. I can't."

"You can. You will. Susanna, if you truly wish me to trust you, then tell me all you know about that man and his *femme fatale* courtesan."

She returned to her chair. "Promise you won't tell Clive?"

"I promise. Now, speak."

Morgan looked all about, her hazel eyes scanning for signs of Redwing. "I don't know much about her. Serena di Specchio, I think. I met her only once, in company with a Russian."

"Anatole Romanov."

She nodded. "Yes. He and the man you want to know about are related, I think. Through a third foreigner named Raziel Grigor. Prince Razarit Grigor is his adopted son. I first met Razarit at Clive's home, perhaps six months back. He seemed exciting at first. Genteel manners with a hard edge to them. More like the men I knew in Chicago. One night, though, Clive was entertaining some of his more influential, government friends, and Razarit arrived late. I remember it, because I'd decided to leave. It was almost two in the morning, but Clive insisted I stay. Sir William was also there that night."

"Trent?"

"Yes," she said, her voice filled with intense regret. "I detest that man, Paul. He's coarse and vulgar and *evil*. He and Razarit hit it off as if they'd been pals from long ago, and before I knew it, all three—Clive, Trent, and this supposed prince—had decided that I was to be their personal plaything for the night." She grew quiet, her eyes downcast. "I don't claim to be pure as the driven or anything. I'm not, but they forced me to do things, that..." her words stuck in her throat, and tears formed on her lashes. Morgan sniffed, embarrassed by the display of emotion. "Sorry. I hadn't intended to do that."

The earl touched her hand gently. "You don't have to finish the story, Susan. I think I can guess what they did to you, and I'm very sorry. Not all men are like that."

She began to weep, and he could see that it was not pretense. "There, there, now," he said, wiping her face with his handkerchief.

"Clive will kill me if he learns I've said anything."

"He'll learn nothing from me. Do you have a place to go, where you might avoid him?"

She shook her head. "No, I've no one and no other home. I lost contact with my father when I left Chicago. I've no money without Clive. He owns my home, and he owns me. He'll send all the resources he can muster to find me, if I ever leave. I know far too many of his secrets."

"Then, we'll have to secure you where he will never think to look. Go to the Carlton Hotel and ask for the manager. His name is

Spencer. Tell him that I sent you, and that you're to have my suite for as long as you want."

"You don't have to do that, Paul," she said. "Really."

"Yes, I do. Really. Go there tonight. Now," he said, handing her ten pounds. "Take a hired coach, but don't register under Morgan or your real name, for that matter."

She blinked. "What do you mean? Morgan is my real name."

"No, it isn't. You were born Cassandra Calabrese. Your father is Antonio Calabrese, and he works with the Chicago branch of Red-wing. I've known it for many months now, and I'd hoped you'd admit it on your own. No, no, you needn't explain," he said kindly. "We'll discuss it tomorrow. Come now, I'll walk you outside and get you a coach. Or you can go with me in a hansom, if you're afraid to travel alone."

"I don't know what to say," she told him. "This makes no sense. You're part of the inner circle! My father told me that you and your family use people for your own ends. That all you want is to put one of your own on the throne of England. I'm the enemy, Paul! Why would you treat me with such kindness?"

"Because you need kindness, and the last thing we want is to assume England's throne," he said, helping her to stand. "Come now. Remember. Spencer at the Carlton. Use any false name you wish, and I'll make sure you're safe."

"Lorena MacKey is staying at the Langham Hotel," she confessed as they walked towards the exit. "Suite 512. She goes by the name Elaine Michaels and has changed her hair colour. Dyed it blonde."

"Thank you, Susanna."

Once they'd reached the lobby, a uniformed usher held open the door, and the two left the Egyptian just as Hamish Granger approached the entry.

"Granger, what on earth are you doing here?" Aubrey asked.

"Lord Haimsbury insisted I fetch you, sir. I believe he requires your presence."

"Is the duchess all right?"

"She is well, sir, and sleeping, I'm told. Lord Haimsbury did not say more."

Paul considered the situation for a moment. "Very well, but first, we take this woman to the Carlton Hotel. It's on Waterloo."

"I'm familiar with it, sir. Ma'am, if you'll step into the coach?" the driver said as they reached the brougham.

Morgan sat next to the earl, and as the pair of bays moved forward, she wiped her eyes with his handkerchief. "I only have about quarter of an hour before we reach the hotel, but I'll use it wisely. I want to tell you what I know about Redwing and their plans. And I think it explains just what's been going on in Whitechapel."

Charles Sinclair stared in shock as the unwelcome phantom seeped through the crack beneath the locked window. Elizabeth's eyes stood open, but her rhythmic breathing and slack limbs made it clear that she still slept. The detective advanced towards the intruder, his right hand on the pistol he'd removed from the shoulder holster.

"Do you bleed?" he whispered to the man shape.

The Thing's wispy hands moved towards the sleeping peeress, but paused near the everpresent Bible that sat atop her nightstand.

"That is a barrier you cannot cross, isn't it?" Sinclair said, stepping closer. "God's Holy Word."

"God's book of lies," the shadow hissed as it tried to find a way around the Bible.

"If you touch her, I will find a way to remove you from this world permanently."

The amorphous Thing turned, slowly transforming into a familiar shape—solidifying into a man whom Charles Sinclair had been pursuing since 1879.

Sir William Trent.

"Good evening, Superintendent," the baronet said, brushing a bit of grime from his gloves. "How very nice to see you again after so long a time. I've anxiously awaited this encounter. Dreamt of it, you might say. Shall we dance?"

Charles did not flinch. "I fear my dance card is already full, but, if you want to speak with me, then you may do so outside. Leave her now, or I shall make sure you never walk this earth again."

Trent smiled, his light grey eyes narrowing. "And how would you do that? The pistol you carry does nothing to my kind. Your feeble attempts to harm me will ever fail, Prince Charles."

"Why do you and your demonic fellowship call me that?"

Trent left the bedside, avoiding any contact with the Bible, and then stepped towards the parlour, passing through the open door and into the darkened interior of the sitting room.

Sinclair followed and shut the connecting door.

"Tell me, Charles, did you enjoy sleeping with her?" he asked. "I have always imagined how satisfying that must be. How very erotic and intense. Sublime indeed. Elizabeth has a perfect body, don't you think?"

It took considerable effort, but Charles fought the urge to strike the intruder, to rip the lying, black tongue from his deceitful mouth. "I think you're weak, if you want to know the truth. It is easy to prey upon women. If you want a real challenge, then, touch that Bible. You cannot, can you? The gospel of Christ is anathema to one like you. It burns."

"I used to collect photographs of Elizabeth," the shadowy figure replied, ignoring the challenge. "How I enjoyed looking at them in the quiet of an evening! Imagining her—picturing myself with her. Hearing her breathe in my ear. Ah, yes, I can see from the expression on your face that you know what I mean, Charles. That lovely whisper of breath as you touch her soft skin..."

The baronet paused, as if waiting. Sinclair said nothing, but instead, shut his eyes tightly, silently praying for strength and wisdom.

"Not even a slight response?" Trent asked. "Not the tiniest spark of moral outrage? You disappoint me, Detective. *She's a pretty thing*," he quoted. "That's what you said the very first time you saw her, isn't it? All those years ago. And so she is. Pretty, I mean. Very pretty. Even as a girl, those dark eyes enticed. She had an innate light which draws one into her orbit like a moth to a flame. Are you happy, little moth? Do your wings feel her heat? Are you mesmerised by her hot flame? Careful, lest you burn," he continued, moving about the room as if he owned it.

Suddenly, it occurred to Sinclair that Trent had been inside this room before, not once, but perhaps many times whilst married to Patricia. *He must have a key! Is it possible that the doors were never rekeyed after her death?*

"Still no reply, little moth?" he asked, sneering. "You have me to thank for your current state of bliss. Had I not left Elizabeth and her foolish mother upon Commercial Street, you'd be living an entirely different life now. In fact, you'd probably be dead."

Charles ignored the comments. The hybrid creature's intent was to unsettle him and muddle his mind, and the detective had no intention of granting the baronet the satisfaction. "You keep avoiding my question, Trent. Why do you and Rasha call me Prince Charles?"

"Because, it is your true title," he answered, returning to the fireplace. "I call you that out of respect."

Sinclair laughed, carefully keeping his voice low to avoid waking Elizabeth. "You call me that because it pleases you, Trent. You respect no one, and you have no permission to enter these rooms or this house; so leave."

"Once, I had free rein to roam this house anytime I wished. And I left items here and there. Perhaps, you'll discover them over time—but will it be *in time*, I wonder? Oh, but you look so very lost, little moth. You grow weary of this exhausting maze, don't you, Detective?"

"What maze is that?" Sinclair asked, still praying.

"The one made of blood! A tortuous course that twists and turns, this way and that. You must despair of ever solving the mystery." Trent's head tilted to one side, and he swiped at his silvering moustache with one finger. "Tell you what. As you are a friend, beginning tonight, I grant you an exit from this taxing catacomb. The ritual nears its end, and your overworked policemen deserve a rest; particularly poor, bumbling Warren. Such a troubled soul. He blames himself for London's current calamities, but it was always meant to be. Warren merely served as a means to an end; that is all."

"You imply that the murders in the east are rituals. Perhaps, you take credit for someone else's actions," Sinclair suggested, choosing to disregard the references to Warren.

"Nonsense! The murders belong to me—well, to me and my friends, that is. The crimes form a single, blood-forged link within a long chain of incantations. One phase of a dark, proscribed necromantic ritual that reaches back more than five thousand years. I shall miss them, you know. I find them absolutely invigorating! The screams of the women are a delight to one's ear; don't you agree?"

Sinclair nearly swung, but he managed to restrain his arm. "What you find delightful is reprehensible to sane men."

"Yes, I'm fully aware of that," the other replied. "Did Elizabeth tell you about her childhood? All those times that she provided entertainment for me and my debauched friends?"

The detective's fist clenched and unclenched, itching to connect with the baronet's face. "What do you want, Trent? Just why are you here?"

"I want so many things, but there is always a cost. Paid in blood, which brings me back to our revels. Tonight, our current ritual ends, and the players must take their bow, but before that great moment— our company shall provide you a theatrical *pièce de résistance* that will leave London breathless! Look to a tiny flat near Dorset, Detective. I shall see you again very soon. Shining like the dawn."

As the little dog clock on the mantel began to strike the hour of eleven, Trent's figure winked out of sight, and Charles heard two things: the sharp barking of Victoria's dog beyond the closed door that led into the hallway, and Elizabeth calling his name.

"Captain! Charles, please, answer me!" she shouted, and he rushed back into the bedchamber to make sure the hybrid fiend hadn't harmed her.

"I'm here, little one. I'm here," he said sweetly, taking her into his arms. "It's all right. You're safe. Hush now. It was a dream. Only a dream. Nothing more." She seemed half asleep, and he caressed her face with one hand whilst holding her with the other. "I'm here, my love. There's nothing to fear."

Samson's persistent scratching finally paid dividends as Alicia Mallory opened the door. The determined animal rushed into the bedroom and leapt upon the bed. The maid followed, but paused inside the open doorway.

"Begging your pardon, sir, I thought you were still downstairs with the duke. I'm very sorry! I was turning down the bed in Lady Victoria's apartment, and I heard the duchess cry out," she blustered, completely embarrassed at finding the engaged couple in so intimate a pose.

"Do come in, Alicia. It's all right," Charles assured the maid. Ordinarily, he would have moved immediately, but not this time. The marquess remained on the bed's edge with the duchess cradled in his arms. "She's had a dreadful nightmare. I think Samson must have sensed it, for he's been scratching at the door. Would you mind tending to her whilst I fetch another quilt? She's shivering."

Mallory curtsied and opened a linen cupboard in the connecting bath. "I'll fetch it, my lord. Sir, if I may, there was a commotion downstairs, 'twixt Mr. Miles and the French nurse. She claims she saw something trying to climb up the side of the house. Might it be a thief, sir? Should we call the police?"

"Sorry, Alicia. I'd nearly fallen asleep when the duchess awoke. I wasn't aware of the commotion, as you call it," he explained, deciding to keep Trent's visit to himself, but certain that whoever—or *whatever*—the nurse had seen must have been the loathsome baronet in an altered form. "There's no need to call A-Division. I'll go outside myself in a moment. Where is the nurse now?"

"In the kitchen, sir. Madam Marchand is most upset. She's been telling as how she wants to return to Paris, but I doubt that Lady Victoria would go, sir."

"Yes, I can see how Marchand might wish to leave a house where it seems as though strange men crawl up the sides, but I'm sure it's nothing. Probably just the shadows of trees upon the irregular stonework." He took Beth's hand and whispered, "I'm going downstairs, but I shan't be long, little one. Go back to sleep now. I'll return shortly, and I'll never be far from you in the night. Just a foot or so away on your couch." She did not reply, and he felt certain the duchess once again slept soundly. "Alicia, do you mind remaining until I return? If she awakens with any fears, send for me at once."

"Of course, sir. The duke might already be out there. He and Mr. Kepelheim mentioned something about having a look at the bushes near the foundation. Shall I keep the dog in here?"

"Yes," he answered, realising that Samson's sight was far keener than any human's, and he might provide protection for Elizabeth. "Perhaps, we should consider adding a second dog to our household. One a bit larger."

Leaving the apartment, the marquess hurried down the stairs towards the foyer, where he joined his uncle and Kepelheim. In a matter of moments, the trio had wound their way through the pathways to the north face of the mansion. As they searched, the tailor pointed to a line of tracks that ran from the edge of the park, past the pond, through the knot gardens, orchard, and the willow trees, finally ending at the north wall, directly beneath the duchess's window.

The tracks began as human, made by a man wearing large boots; but as they rounded the pond, the marks slowly transformed into something far different: the paw prints of a massive wolf.

"When I moved to London ten years ago, it was because my father had ordered me to spy on England's branch of Redwing," Susanna Morgan, born Cassandra Calabrese began. "I was sixteen years old. I'd grown up as the only daughter in a Sicilian family. Four brothers, all older, and all I wanted to do was please my pop. I started singing in my Uncle Salvatore's cabaret when I was thirteen. I'd already been hardened to the realties of how women are treated in places like that, but at that time, I thought it exciting. My father is second in command in Chicago's branch, but it's an uncomfortable position, because the leader owns so much property that he could buy and sell my family a hundred times over, which meant Pop would do whatever he was told."

She paused, her eyes dry but thoughtful, filled with regret. "Anyway, I got here, and Clive sort of took me under his wing." She smiled. "I guess that's a joke, since he's a member of Redwing."

Aubrey watched her, assessing the truthfulness of her tale, based on years of experience interrogating both men and women. "Urquhart probably assumed you had influence with the American wing of that wretched bird. But he came to trust you, apparently."

"Yes," she replied. "I underwent a series of tests. I won't tell you what they were, but I'm sure you can imagine the sort that Redwing employs. Starting last year, I noticed an increase in the number of meetings, some of them at Clive's home. Not the one in Grosvenor Square, but another one in Hackney. It's near the marshes. An old mansion built back in the 17th century. It's a spooky place, but it sits over a natural cavern that connects to a system of underground rivers beneath the city. Clive said he bought it because something was buried there. An old mirror."

Paul sat forward, his eyes intense. "A mirror? Why would someone bury a mirror?"

"Redwing isn't exactly sure just who buried it, but it had been there for thousands of years. I overheard Trent tell Clive that it may have been put there before the flood."

"What flood? Do you mean Noah's flood?"

She nodded. "Yes. As crazy as it sounds, that's what they believe. Trent said he learned about it in '71, when he was living in Austria. I'm not sure if he was telling the truth, though, because William lies so often, his mouth is crooked."

Aubrey smiled. "An apt description. What happened in '71?"

"I'm not sure, but I'm told that's when this plan was first discussed. Redwing's always been run by men who communicate with ghosts and spirits, but that year, the London leader at the time, a man named Sir Arnold Winterfeldt, announced he'd been visited by something he called a Watcher."

"I've heard of these creatures," Aubrey replied. "They are very powerful beings from a realm outside our own. Fallen angels. Did this Watcher give his name?"

"If he did, I never heard it, but Winterfeldt became terrified of the direction the group took afterward. Clive said that he eventually tried to deny this creature access to the meetings—that Winterfeldt even contacted someone from the inner circle for help, but he died quite suddenly in '74, and Sir William took his place."

All of this was new information to the earl. "Do you know the name of the circle member Winterfeldt contacted?"

She shook her head. "No, I don't, but he was Scottish. That much I do know. Clive made great sport of it, saying that Winterfeldt's folly was to go the Scots for help. I'd always assumed it was your family."

"Possibly, but if so, then neither my uncle nor my father mentioned it in any of the meetings I attended. Perhaps, they thought me too young, but no one has mentioned it since. Never mind. I'll speak with the duke about it. So what happened then? Did this Watcher begin to steer Redwing's course?"

"Yes. As I said, a new plan was devised, beginning with the search for this mirror I mentioned. That's why Clive bought the house in Hackney Marsh. Last June, their diggers uncovered a hidden cave, and within a month, they'd found the mirror."

"And?"

"And this Watcher said that one of his brothers was imprisoned inside it—and that Redwing had to free him."

Stuart's mouth lengthened with dismay. "A brother? Another Watcher, you mean?"

She nodded. "Yes. Paul, this first creature—someone named Raziel—he taught the members a ritual that would allow them to release this other Watcher. It required a stone key and collecting organs from thirty-three murdered women."

The earl's face blanched. "The Ripper killings."

"I think so. Clive never admitted his involvement to me, but I'm sure that this ritual is behind the murders. You have to tell your cousin."

"But thirty-three? I'm only aware of half that number, and that includes a few the press know nothing of."

"Not all of them were in London. A group of men commit them—or I think that's how it works. Some of the spirits that advise Redwing participate. This Watcher—Raziel—he's begun to alter a few of the members, and he's teaching them to transform. That's how they evade detection," she explained.

"And once this ritual is complete? What then?"

"Then the mirror's imprisoned Watcher will be released," she whispered.

"A second such creature will roam the streets of London?" Stuart asked, his mind scrambling to make sense of the dark news. "Will the London branch answer to *both*?"

"I'm not sure, but probably. I don't think everyone agrees as to the direction the group's to take from now on, though. I've heard hints to that effect. However, Clive and Trent continue to meet, so if there is division, those two stand together on one side of that divide."

The carriage had turned south onto Regent Street, and Aubrey knew they had little time remaining. "Is that all you know?"

"Almost," she said, her face turned towards the window. "Three days ago, Clive received a telegram from France, which caused him great excitement. He immediately wired Trent."

"Did you see the telegram?"

"Part of it. I saw the words 'mirror found'. Paul, I think it means that another Watcher has been located."

"Another? Susanna, do you mean that Trent intends to unleash a third fallen angel into London?"

She nodded. "Yes, but it gets much worse, Paul. Clive and William found an old scroll that describes this long ritual. It indicates that there are thirteen mirrors in total. And if all thirteen are joined together in the right location and the correct incantations spoken, then Redwing could unlock Time and release *all* the Watchers held within the Abyss."

Paul stared at the woman, scarcely able to comprehend the scope of her claims. The universal *evil* of it all. "The Abyss mentioned in the Bible, you mean? The place where Abaddon reigns?"

"Yes. That is my understanding," she finished as the coach pulled next to the Carlton Hotel. "If anyone from Redwing learns that I've told you this, they will kill me. There is no way they'll let me live, and the death described for traitors is slow and painful. I know it sounds crazy coming from someone like me, but would you pray for me?"

Hamish Granger appeared and opened the door. "Sir, we're here. Shall I accompany you and the lady inside?"

"I'll take her on my own, Granger. Stay with the coach."

The earl helped Morgan down from the interior and held her arm as they entered the expensive hotel. A night manager was speaking to a portly gentleman and his female companion, registering them for an overnight stay. Paul waved as they approached the desk.

"Good evening, Lionel. This is my cousin, Violet Stuart. She'll be staying in my suite for a few weeks whilst she visits London for the wedding. Do give her your best service," he said, handing the agent ten pounds. "Her luggage arrives tomorrow."

The desk agent took the money, offering a knowing smile as he handed the earl a key. "We shall provide your cousin with everything she may require, Lord Aubrey."

The earl escorted Morgan up a curving staircase to the third floor, where he unlocked the door to number 301. "I think you'll find it comfortable," he explained, leading her inside. "There are two bedchambers in addition to this lovely parlour. Also, there's an *en suite* water closet and bath, and a large dressing area in the main chamber. I'll send one of my men to keep an eye on you. He'll be discreet, but I prefer you were not alone."

She set her handbag upon a burnished maple table that stood at the centre of the foyer. "It's beautiful. Do you keep this as a second home?"

"Of a sort," he answered. "I own the hotel."

"You constantly surprise, Lord Aubrey," she said, taking his hand. "You've treated me with far more kindness than I deserve."

He gave her the key. "You asked if I would pray for you, Susanna. Of course, I shall. All of us in the circle will lift you up to God, but you must also seek him out. *Behold, the Lord's arm is not shortened that he cannot save; nor his ear heavy, that he cannot hear*," he quoted. "There's a Bible on the nightstand inside the larger bedroom. You'll find that verse in Isaiah, chapter fifty-nine. It's in the Old Testament. God waits to hear your voice, my dear."

"I promise to read it."

He kissed her sweetly on the cheek. "We don't dare send for your clothes, but I'll have a woman friend of mine gather the items required to get you through until you may safely shop on your own. Will that do?"

She threw her arms around his neck, tears welling up in her eyes. "Thank you, Paul. Thank you so very much!"

For a moment, he considered kissing her—really kissing her properly—but his heart refused to allow it. Somehow, it felt like he'd be betraying Elizabeth. Instead, he kissed the palm of her hand. "You may thank me by forever abandoning Redwing. Their path will lead you to destruction, Cassandra Calabrese."

He left, and she locked the door. *Who am I? Susanna? Cassandra? Or do I sever all ties to my old life?*

"Violet Stuart," she whispered to herself as she gazed into a framed mirror hanging over the parlour fireplace. She could alter her hair colour, just as MacKey had done, and put her feet upon this new path. Violet sounded delicate and pure—it sounded like hope.

Will God hear me? she wondered.

Leaving the looking glass, she sat upon a velvet sofa near the fireplace and closed her eyes. "Our Father, who art in heaven," she began, recalling the words her Catholic mother had taught her many years before. "Do you even hear me, sir? If so, then I have a lot of sins to confess. It may take me all night to name them, maybe even all week, but if you're willing to listen, then I'll try."

CHAPTER FOUR

Just after midnight - 13 Miller's Court

Mary Kelly welcomed the handsome man to her tiny bedsit, grateful for the hot meal he'd brought her.

"Fish and potatoes," he said. "Your favourite. Now, let's shut these blinds, shall we? I'd like a bit of privacy whilst we talk."

The man was well-dressed and tall. He placed the carved rosewood cane with the wolf's head handle against the side of the narrow bed. "Shall we dance?" he asked, his lips curling into an enigmatic smile beneath a silvering moustache.

"You're ever so good ta me, sir," Kelly told him, oblivious that this would be the last meal of her life.

"Think nothing of it," the visitor whispered. "I'm sure you'll find a way to repay me. Eat it all now. Every last morsel."

In less than half an hour's time, the sleeping powder contained within the food had rendered the girl unconscious. Satisfied that his victim would be unable to protest or fight, the hybrid human known to the inner circle as Sir William Trent had transformed. He'd arrived in one of his many guises, a west-end gentleman named Sir Daniel Outerbridge, who'd squired Kelly to France several times, and who lived in a comfortable home near Kensington.

The mysterious baronet opened the weathered door to his trio of hybridised friends, who entered one at a time, each eager for a share of the tasty spoils. One of the three took the form of Kelly. "I'll keep the nosy neighbours from hearing our revels with a little song," the Kelly-shape promised. "Any requests?"

"How about 'A Violet from Mother's Grave'?" one of the other hybrids asked, grinning. "Sing it nice and loud, though. I've such a hunger tonight, that I make no promises about how quiet I might be!"

The demonic Kelly-thing took a deep breath and started to sing very loudly, so that everyone who lived within Miller's Court might hear. *"Scenes of my childhood arise before my gaze...bringing recollections of bygone happy days...when down in the meadow, in childhood I would roam...no one's left to cheer me now within that good old home!"*

The others began to laugh, and their leader banged his cane against the floor. "Hush, you fools! Even with the song as cover, we must be quiet as mice."

"Church mice?" one mocked, causing all to break into riotous laughter.

The baronet grinned, and his eyes shifted colour from light grey to intense amber. "Church mice, indeed. Or better put, wolves in sheep's clothing, who invade and inveigle the pious and paltry pews of the faithful. Now, one of you remove her clothing, so that we might begin our feast. This one's blood fulfills our quota, and at midnight tomorrow, we shall free the first prisoner."

The smallest of the three companions ripped the dress and apron from Kelly with his claws, leaving the pitiful victim clad only in her cotton chemise.

"Throw those into the fire," Trent ordered, and the hybrid opened the iron door of the small stove. Only a few coals burnt there, and the addition of the clothing caused the dwindling flames to flare. "Much better," the baronet said. "I'm sure anyone walking past the window will assume Miss Kelly has just stoked her fire for the night."

He reached into the inner folds of his overcoat and withdrew a long knife with an ivory handle that had been carved with occult symbols. "And now, to begin," he said, placing it beneath the unconscious woman's jawline. "Precise and deep. We must sever the carotid to offer up her blood for this, our final sacrifice—well, final as regards our current phase."

"And then?" one of the others asked, his voice soft, his posture subservient. "What then, Master?"

"Then, phase two of our ritual commences, my dear fellow! We unlock the first prisoner and use any remaining material to advance our experiments. If you think your animal forms beautiful now, just wait until we sprout our wings!" He positioned the point of the sharp blade beneath Kelly's right ear, just over the carotid artery. "May this offering bring us riches, power, and eternal life!" he exclaimed as he pressed down, causing bright blood to spurt like a fountain from the woman's throat. The resulting spray splattered the walls, and began to pool along the floorboards. Trent licked the knife's edge, his yellow eyes glittering. "There is plenty for all, my hellish friends. Enjoy!" he told them as he began cutting slices of muscle and skin and organs. "But I shall keep the heart. I've an idea how best to use it."

The false Kelly continued to sing, 'her' voice raised high and loud. "*Father and Mother, they have passed away...Sister and Brother now lay beneath the clay. And while life doth remain, in memoriam, I'll retain this small violet I pluck'd from Mother's grave...*"

Lorena MacKey hastily threw her belongings into an overnight case. A terse telegram lay upon the table near the fireplace, bearing a single line: GET OUT NOW. STUART ON HIS WAY.

Fearing that the inner circle would exert all their considerable influence to find her, she had coloured her hair to a light blonde and changed her name to Elaine Michaels, but it seemed her location was now known.

As she packed the leather bag, MacKey fought rising panic that threatened to take hold of her heart. What if Paul did find her? Would he kill her? Would Sinclair seek revenge for himself and the duchess? Had she lost a chance at redemption by fleeing the duke's castle?

"I thought you liked it here," a deep voice called from the open doorway.

She turned, fearing it might be Aubrey, but then seeing the visitor's face, MacKey slowly smiled. "How you come and go at will, my lord!"

Anatole Romanov stepped into the room. The prince was dressed formally, his raven hair tied behind his ears with a crimson ribbon. He picked up a lace undergarment, lying beside the open case.

"Expecting to entertain, my dear?"

She snatched at the delicate chemise. "How may I serve you, my lord?"

"By telling me the truth, Lorena. Or should I now call you Elaine? An interesting choice in names," he said, playing with her long hair. "Is it after Elaine d'Astolat from the Lancelot tales? The isolated princess who lived in a tower, and could only watch the world through a mirror—the cursed Lady of Shalott? Poor Lorena! Do you despair of never seeing your Lancelot again? Which man might that be, I wonder? The elder or the younger cousin?"

"I despair for no one," she whispered, her green eyes diverted.

"Another lie," he replied, sitting near the fireplace. Noticing the telegram, he tapped the paper. "Trent is a busy man, yet he takes the time to warn you. Do not risk your eternal life by siding with him, Lorena. His path soon closes."

She snapped the valise shut and sat opposite him, feigning ease despite her fear. "I never know quite what to expect from you, my prince. It is as if you are two people in one body."

"I have not changed since we first met, Lorena, but you have. Your insights into Redwing's true agenda sharpen, and you begin to doubt the wisdom of their goals. Does Trent know you secretly hope to align with his enemies?"

"What do you want from me, my lord?"

"Honesty," he whispered. "Something most difficult for you, I know. For now, I shall settle for your promise to follow my commands. Sir William has overstepped, and I intend to remove him—permanently. How do you feel about that?"

"Is this a test?"

"Perhaps."

She managed a nervous smile. "Then command me, my lord. For that is the ultimate test. If I fail, then I fail."

He stood and took her hand, and his eyes turned soft. "Once you trusted in my plans for you, Lorena Melissa. When did that cease?"

A traitorous tear slid down her cheek, but she maintained defiance. "Command me."

The Watcher sighed. "You must do all in the precise manner which I describe. I have seen numerous futures for you, Lorena, and your next choice will determine your happiness. Do you trust me?"

She paused, recalling her first meeting with the dark angel—how he'd rescued her from a broken home, from danger and penury. How he'd placed her feet upon a better path; even assisted her in her studies. *Do I still trust him? Is he now my enemy?*

"I am not your enemy," he told her, reading her thoughts. "Nor have I altered, Lorena. Allow me to assist you once more, and you may see your Lancelot again, without the aid of mirrors. For now, though, I prefer that the inner circle not speak to you—not yet. I have arranged accommodations at Claridge's, under the name Carla de Longe. You are a famous singer, but you prefer to be left alone. The hotel's staff will comply with your eccentricities. But do away with these altered locks. Your true hair is so much more beautiful. The radiant auburn complements your skin and eyes."

"And then?"

"Then, I shall visit you and reveal the rest of my plan. Look for me tomorrow evening. My coach now awaits you in the hotel drive to convey you to Claridge's. Go quickly, for it is quite likely that the earl will call here yet tonight."

"But what of *your* plans?" she asked boldly.

"That is not for you to know. If you wish to find true happiness, Lorena, then you must trust me. Your tower imprisonment nears its end, my dear." He kissed her hand. "Until tomorrow evening."

She blinked, and he'd vanished.

MacKey sat upon the bed, considering her position, wondering now if she might not be better served to go directly to Aubrey and confess everything.

What game is Romanov playing?

"I play no game," she heard his voice speak from the air all around her. "Trent is doomed. Do not join him."

Fear clutched at her heart, and the physician lifted her bag and rushed out into the hallway. In less than five minutes' time, a black brougham spirited her away to the confines of Claridge's, and Lorena unpacked, wondering just what it was the prince would ask her to do.

Far away from the modern atmosphere of Claridge's Hotel, within the darkened halls of a 17th century castle, Ida Ross shivered upon a lonely bed. She'd been awakened by a noise outside her chamber door, and now she could hear persistent scratching at the wood, as if a dog tried to get in. Ida pulled the velvet blankets up close to her chin, biting her lips from fear.

"*Little whore, little whore, let me in,*" a gravelly voice called from the other side. "*Or else I'll huff, and I'll puff, and I'll blow this door in!*"

"Go away!" she shouted. "Please, please, go away!"

"*Little whore, little whore, let me in,*" it called again, and Ross heard what sounded like sniffing, and she could see a dense shadow pass back and forth beneath the door, as if something knelt upon the hallway's carpet and tried to peer through the narrow space, just above the threshold.

There was a momentary silence, and then without warning, a heavy thud echoed throughout the upper storey, as the unwelcome visitor threw its considerable weight against the heavy door, trying to shatter it. "*Let me in! Or I'll huff, and I'll puff, and I'll blow this door in!*" it shouted. "*And then I'll eat you up, little whore!*"

"Go away, please! Oh, please, leave me in peace!"

The shadow's form lengthened across the threshold, and Ida's eyes widened in panic. A huge, hairy paw had forced its way underneath the door, the claws clattering and scraping upon the oak floor. She pressed against the headboard of the bed, weeping from terror. The hideous paw probed and pushed, and the woman feared it might actually breech the door, but suddenly she could see the blinding rays of a brilliant, white light flooding the area, and a sharp, high-pitched howl split the air.

Moments passed, and Ross sat still as a statue; listening, fearful of making even one sound.

She jumped from shock as a hand knocked. "Ida?" a genteel voice called. "Are you all right?"

"Go away!" she shouted again, certain that it was the intruder, merely using a different tactic.

Though she'd locked the door from the inside with a key, it opened of its own accord, and Ida's host, Prince Anatole Petrovich Romanov, entered, wearing a tall hat and sweeping, black opera cape. He carried an ebony cane, as if he'd just returned from an elegant evening out.

"Please, forgive the intrusion, dear Ida. I worried that you might become frightened in this old house. I'm very glad I returned, for one of my other guests had somehow managed to break free of his confines and was roaming about the upper floors. I have ordered Vasily to return him to his room and lock it securely once more. He will not trouble you again, I assure you."

Ross broke down weeping, her pale face in her hands. Anatole removed the cloak and lay it across a brocade sofa that sat before the warm fire. He crossed to her bed and touched the girl's hand. "You are trembling! I am so very sorry that he frightened you, Ida. Had I known that Mr. Stanley had escaped his restraints, I would never have gone out for the evening."

"Mr. Stanley? I don't understand, sir. That wasn't a man! He could talk, yes, but I saw an animal's paw beneath that door! It tried to get in!"

"Yes, yes, I know how confusing it must be, but you'll understand all about our household soon. My home provides shelter and medical treatment to a select few whose lives have been altered by certain devious individuals within our city. I had thought this guest confined firmly inside his apartment, but I shall not make that mistake again," he said, his thoughts turning to the only other person who had a key: Serena di Specchio. "If someone intentionally unlocked it, then I shall see to it that he or *she* pays for such neglect. Mr. Stanley still struggles with his recovery, which is why he remains confined at night. Regardless, he deserves our compassion and sympathy."

"But he wanted to eat me!"

"That was his altered personality speaking, my dear, but that part of him already begins to die. It is only the moon that stirs up these dark compulsions. It's my hope that by next month, he will no longer require chains or locks. Tomorrow, when he awakens, I shall introduce you. He is quite docile when in his normal state. A most tender man who wishes only to be of service to mankind. Mr. Stanley once served with the Metropolitan Police, in fact."

"I just want to go!" she sobbed. "Oh, sir, you should have let me die!"

He drew Ross into his arms, the ordinarily serene prince appearing somewhat perplexed. "How could I allow you to end your life, when there is so much for which you must live? I cannot foresee all aspects of your future, but certain events are known to me, and I assure you that happiness awaits."

"Not for me, sir. Never for me," she argued, her speech interrupted by heavy sobs.

He stroked her hair, his ice-blue eyes blinking. "Why is it women weep? Is it always fear, or are there other emotions that cause these tears?" She clutched at his body, and he held her like he might a child. "Forgive me," he whispered. "I am a poor companion for such moments as this. Perhaps, I should fetch someone else. A human, perhaps."

"No, please, don't leave me! I'll be good. I will, and I'll not complain. I could make you happy, sir. If you wish to stay—there is room aplenty in the bed. If you wish to... To sleep with me, I mean."

The Russian shook his head. "That is not why I've brought you here, Ida. You are my guest, not my mistress."

She seemed confused. "Sir, I've no other use in this world. I only know of one way to please a man."

"Then, I shall be happy to teach you other ways. Ways that are dignified and uplifting. Now, try to sleep. Do you require something to aid in this? A soporific powder? Wine?"

"I don't want to be alone," she whispered. "Can you not stay with me, sir?"

He touched her face with such sweetness that it caused Ida's heart to skip two beats. "I shall remain with you until you fall asleep, but I am sincere when I say that I have no plans to use you as other men have done. In this house, you are a lady, and I insist all here treat you as such."

Finally, she lay back against the silk sheets, her eyes round as she gazed at his ethereal beauty. His features might have been carved upon a Greek statue, not with lifeless, marble eyes, but iridescent orbs of icy blue, rimmed in the blackest of lashes. He had untied the scarlet hair ribbon after leaving MacKey, so that the raven waves fell across the broad silk jacket with such softness that Ida longed to touch the locks, for even these held power to fascinate. His skin was pale as alabaster, but his full lips shimmered with radiant life.

"You referred to yourself as if you are not human, sir. Are you an angel?" she asked.

The lips widened into a soft smile, and his ebony lashes fluttered as he blinked. "Of a kind," he replied. "I promise to tell you more about my life another time. For now, as it's your first night here, it is important that you rest. Think not on the trials you've borne before, dear Ida, but only of the future. Like you, I wear the burden of past choices upon my back, and there was a time when its weight nearly crushed me, but it grows ever lighter. Yours will, as well."

"I don't understand, sir, but I'll try to sleep, if you wish it. You're far too kind to me, my lord. You could have any woman in

England—probably any woman in the world. Why do you show *me* such compassion?"

He drew the blankets across her body and sat beside her. "I'm not sure," he admitted. "Love, as you comprehend it, is something that is still somewhat foreign to me. I've walked this world for longer than any bard may find the words to express, but the bondage of the human heart has only recently found its way into my life. It was nearly eighteen years ago, when I first beheld her. I perceived the tears in her innocent eyes, and suddenly all the selfish aspirations that once defined me fell into nothingness. However, though I might speak of my admiration, I would never act upon that desire. If I did, then the weight of all my past choices would return a thousandfold and render me lifeless, and I would lose her forever. Besides, she loves another."

"I am sorry, sir."

A single tear slid down his alabaster cheek, and Romanov rose to his feet. "Close your eyes, Ida. I shall keep watch by the fire, and I shan't leave until you are safely nestled within the land of dreams. No one will harm you this night. Not whilst I stand guard."

CHAPTER FIVE

Friday morning, 9ᵗʰ November, 1888

Few slept well at Queen Anne House that night. Dawn had long since broken over the Thames by the time Sinclair rose. He quickly shaved and dressed, trying not to waken the duchess, who'd suffered from troubling dreams that lasted until dawn. He entered the earl's bedchamber through the open door, but found the bed empty and already made; the room tidied.

Leaving the master apartment, the detective hurried down the stairs to the foyer, where he could hear the duke speaking to a man, whose voice did not sound familiar.

"Charles," Drummond called. "Son, we're in here."

Sinclair entered the morning room to find a handsome gentleman in a charcoal cutaway and slate blue waistcoat. He stood about six feet in height and wore a thick crop of silver hair, cut short and neat. His equally silver beard was closely trimmed into a goatee that looked as if it had once been sandy brown in colour.

"Good morning. Sorry I'm late getting up, Uncle James. I hope I haven't kept you waiting," the marquess said, extending his right hand to the stranger. "I'm Charles Sinclair."

The visitor smiled broadly, revealing unusually deep dimples, just below fleshy cheekbones, and his grey eyes twinkled, making him appear younger than his sixty-two years. "Good morning, my lord. Edward MacPherson. It's a very great honour to meet you at last."

"Mac's the pastor at Drummond House Chapel," the duke explained. "He'll be marrying you and Elizabeth come the eighteenth, and he sits on the circle, so you'd best get used to his weathered mug. Let's all sit, shall we? We've much to discuss."

"Haven't I seen you before, Dr. MacPherson? In Whitechapel?"

"Your reputation as possessing a keen memory for faces is true, it seems; much like your good father, may he rest in peace. Yes, I occasionally attend to the spiritual needs of patients at the Eastern Dispensary and also at the London and French hospitals. I meet weekly with what you might call a 'religious confederation' of fellow clergymen to discuss the conditions there. That borough hosts many dark spirits, I fear. The duke's been telling me that you and the duchess have suffered spiritual attacks in recent weeks."

"We have, sir. In fact, there was another last night," he said, sitting. "I'm sure my uncle has mentioned it already. Elizabeth has been suffering from distressing nightmares, and she worries that Paul might be in danger. Where is my cousin, by the way?"

"He went out very early, eight or so," the duke replied. "When he finally returned, he took Kepelheim and the two left for Mayfair. That was, oh, half an hour ago, I think. Paul never explained his earlier destination, but he and Kepelheim have gone to collect some of Galton's records about the '79 murders at Victoria Park. He said you'd understand, but he also said he's discovered some very important information for the circle."

"But Paul is all right? Unharmed?"

"Yes. He seemed fine to me," his uncle answered. "But you needn't worry about our earl. Paul's more than capable of taking care of himself, Charles. Believe me. Before you ask, I gave him your message last night, when he returned around eleven. I explained that Beth was very worried and that is why we sent Granger to collect him, but as you were both asleep, he decided not to wake you."

"I thought I heard him tiptoe into the other bedchamber, but it was long after midnight. I assume you and he talked for awhile before he came up."

"I needed help finishing up that decanter of whisky, didn't I? Your cousin was happy to assist," the duke said, his eyes merry.

Charles began to laugh. "At least, the whisky served its purpose! Actually, even if Paul had come into the room, I doubt that I'd have been coherent enough to discuss anything. Once I finally found my way into dreamland, I remained there a good long time—until Beth's nightmares started again."

"She's all right?"

"Yes, sir. Sleeping soundly at present." He turned back to MacPherson. "I'm very glad you're here this morning, Doctor."

"Just call me Mac, Lord Haimsbury. Everyone does."

"Thank you. I hope you'll call me Charles. This lofty title still feels rather like a coat that's three sizes too big."

"You'll soon grow into that coat," MacPherson assured him. "You said something earlier about a spiritual visitation last night. What did you mean by that?"

"The duchess has been suffering from recurrent nightmares, which I believe are spiritually derived. Last night brought more of these troubling dreams, but we also had a visitation from something not entirely human."

"Not entirely human? A curious way to describe this visitor. What do you think it was?" the clergyman asked as the butler entered, pushing a tea cart.

"Would you mind shutting those doors, Miles?" the duke asked. "I'd not want my granddaughter or Lady Della stumbling into our conversation. Go on, Charles."

"You're right, sir. Perhaps, it would be best if we reserve this sort of talk for our meeting," Sinclair suggested. "Miles, would it be inconvenient if we adjourned to the library? I assume the room is still arranged for the circle meeting."

"Yes, sir, but it is no inconvenience at all. If you wish, I can serve breakfast in there."

"Yes, thank you, that would be most helpful, Miles. Uncle James, let's continue this discussion in private. But first, I may walk the grounds again to see if our visitor left any tracks we missed last night," the marquess said as Victoria's dog ran past the open doorway, his lead taut. Lester quickly followed, a woolen overcoat flapping open as he tried to button it with one hand. Sinclair began to laugh, and he called to the dog. "Samson, do be careful with our first footman, will you? Shall I lend a hand?" he asked the servant.

The disheveled footman pulled gently on the leather cord, dismayed but ever stoic, replying drily, "Thank you, my lord, but I believe the animal is more than capable of exerting his preferences unaided."

Charles laughed again as he reached for the dog's leash. "My offer is for you, Lester, not the dog. Here now; allow me. I'll take him for a walk. No need to fetch my coat. I've spent many a chilly morning investigating crime. I'm not dismayed by the cold. Perhaps, you could be of service to Mr. Miles. We're convening a small meeting in the library. Come on, boy," he said to the animal. "Let's see what your superior nose might sniff out around the grounds. Uncle, I shan't be long!"

The air was thin and cold, and the skies showed very little blue amongst the thick nimbus clouds. Most of Westminster's chimneys belched billows of acidic grey smoke, and the detective wondered if he'd made a mistake by not donning an overcoat. The dog seemed to have a definite direction in mind, heading quickly 'round the water-lily fountain, through a statuary park, and straight towards the small pond near the south wall that overlooked St. James's Park. With his long legs, Sinclair had no trouble keeping up with the terrier, and he tucked his left hand into his pocket to warm his bare fingers, his experienced eyes scanning the area for footmarks upon the frosty grass. To his surprise, he found dozens of tracks—apparently left by a very large animal—perhaps a mastiff or wolfhound.

Samson stopped to relieve himself in several spots, all of them close to the strange paw prints within the hoary grass, marking them as proof of an enemy invasion. A stocky man in dark, cotton twill coveralls, topped by a single-breasted woolen overcoat stepped towards Sinclair. He carried a broken shotgun, crooked against the inside of his left elbow.

"Mornin', my lord," Frame said. "Mighty early ta be out fer a stroll. I reckon Samson's a might anxious 'bout them tracks."

"Good morning to you, Frame," the marquess said cheerfully. "Yes, he's been furiously marking this curious set of prints. Was there a large animal running through here last night? A neighbour's dog, perhaps?"

The gardener shook his head. "I don't think so, sir. Them prints is too big fer any dogs known ta me. Seems most peculiar, specially after tha' nurse thought she seen a great bat or summat crawlin' up the side o' the house. Me and Mr. Powers have our men scourin' the park ta make sure everythin's as it should be, sir."

"And is it?" the marquess asked as Samson pulled free of the leash. "Oh, fiddle! Victoria's going to be cross if he gets away. Are all the gates shut?"

Frame pointed down the long, gravel lane, to the south. "Aye, sir, though it's hard ta see in this 'ere fog. Young Mr. Childers is down at the main entrance now, keepin' watch from inside the gatehouse. We usually open the gates at nine, but Lord Aubrey ordered 'em all kept shut. Is everythin' all right, my lord?"

"Yes, I think so," Sinclair replied. "We've guests arriving this morning; though, not many. The duke had hoped to host a large meeting of the inner circle, but the city's new mayor had other plans. Most of the streets that lead here are closed to wheeled traffic not part of the mayoral procession."

"We been told as much by the earl. His lordship was walkin' the grounds this mornin' as well, sir. Round 'bout seven o'clock. He spoke ta Powers 'bout them tracks. I don' reckon it's dogs, sir. Iffin you asks me, sir, I think it's them wolves."

"Wolves?" Haimsbury asked as he followed the dog's path. "Do you refer to normal wolves or something less so?"

Frame smiled and pointed to the shotgun. "Let's just say that we's all prayin' it's the normal kind, sir. Don' reckon buckshot'd take down one o' them other types o' wolves. Looks like her lady-ship's dog found summat, sir. He's gone ta ground."

Not far from the rowan trees, Samson had begun to dig a deep hole. "I'm not sure the duchess would approve of your labours, Samson," Sinclair said. "Those pink asters are some of her favour-ite flowers."

The gardener knelt beside the dog, carefully examining the sur-rounding area. "There's lots o' them tracks, 'ere, too, my lord. All 'bout these beds. I reckon Samson don' like 'ow they smell. Well, look at tha'!" he exclaimed. "The dog's found summat."

Samson turned about and sat before the marquess, looking up at Sinclair proudly. The terrier's spotted muzzle was stained with rich brown earth, and he presented a package, held firmly betwixt his teeth.

"Can you get it from him, Frame?"

"Come on, boy. Show ol' Frame what cha got," the gardener said smoothly as he gently tapped the dog's nose.

Obediently, Samson dropped the parcel, which was tied with thick twine. Picking it up, Frame brushed away the damp earth. "If-fin tha' don' beat all! It's go' yer name on it, sir. Writ in red ink."

"Hand it to me, Frame," Charles said, a dark foreboding creep-ing into the pit of his stomach. The package was approximately four inches by three and wrapped in brown butcher's paper. "Would you mind taking the dog?"

The gardener complied, and Charles returned to the house, the muddy package clutched within his hand. In a few minutes, he arrived inside the library. "Shut that door will you, Uncle? I want none of the staff to see this."

The duke secured the door and joined his nephew at the table. "What on earth is it?"

"What 'in earth' might be a better question," Sinclair answered. "Our intrepid terrier uncovered it. See here? Marked in red ink? It is my name," he told the two men.

MacPherson put on a pair of tortoise shell spectacles and reached for the box. "May I?" he asked. The marquess nodded, and the clergyman took the strange package, holding it up to the chandelier's light. "It's also marked with a date. See? Here, on the underside, again written in red."

"Beth's been receiving taunting messages from a fiend who calls himself 'Saucy Jack', and each is written in red ink," Charles noted angrily. "I imagine this is another of his hideous pranks."

"Nine November," the duke read aloud. "That's today."

Charles grew quiet for a moment, his thoughts running back to the strange conversation with Sir Charles Warren the previous evening. "The ninth day of the ninth month."

"No, son. The eleventh," the duke corrected.

"Yes, November is the eleventh month of the Gregorian year, but doesn't the name imply it is the ninth month?"

MacPherson agreed. "I see what you mean. In the old Julian calendar, November, from the Latin *novem*, was the ninth, just as December is the tenth. Why, Charles?"

"One might then say that today's date is 'nine, nine'—or rather ninety-nine, sir. Thirty-three times three. Of course, the eleventh month also works, as eleven times nine also equals ninety-nine."

"Is that significant?" asked MacPherson.

"Yes, I think it is. Last evening, I spoke at great length with Sir Charles Warren regarding his discovery of a stone marker in Syria. He believes this stone once held an imprisoned fallen angel."

"*Once* held?" MacPherson asked, worry creasing his forehead and mouth. "Why do you say once? Does Warren know this as fact, or does he guess?"

"He deduces it, based on an inscription written upon the stone, but also from incidents that followed its removal from Syria and subsequent installation in London."

"Syria," the cleric whispered. "Was this stone found on Mount Hermon by any chance?"

The marquess nodded. "Yes, but how did you know?"

"I shall explain later, but do continue, Charles."

"Very well, but I would hear what information you hold, Dr. MacPherson. Warren told me that the marker was delivered to London in 1870, and the following year, on the thirty-first of March, its crate was opened by a curator, who died for his trouble; found slain beside that open crate. Warren gave me a long and intricate explanation as to the numerology behind *why* he believes that stone had to be opened on that particular date. He's convinced that the entity once imprisoned within it, derived maximum occult power by emerging on the third of March, 1879. Sir Charles insists that thirty-three holds high significance with the fallen realm, as does the number three. Ninety-nine combines both numbers. 1879 is a prime number, but more to the point, this creature emerged only nine days before Elizabeth's third birthday. The very day she first began having nightmares."

The duke stared at the box, slowly nodding, as comprehension took hold. "Aye. She had that first dream that very night, and they continued for weeks afterward. Connor told Robert Stuart and me about it. I assume it was Paul told you."

"Yes, but I feel as if I have a lot of catch-up work to do regarding the spirits that swirl around my fiancée's life. Warren feels certain that this stone served as a prison, and that its former inmate now roams the streets of England. Now, we find a package left in Beth's garden, overwritten with a date that might be construed as 'nine, nine'. But regardless of how we interpret it, the result is ninety-nine. Is it possible that the date written upon this package is part of a coded ritual to summon such an entity?"

Edward MacPherson removed his spectacles, staring at the detective with wide eyes. "The duke was right about you, Lord Haimsbury. You have learnt a great deal since returning to your family. Our circle needs men such as you."

The marquess shook his head. "I have no special talents."

"Oh, but you do!" James insisted. "However, now's not the time to debate that point. Open it, son. Let's see why it was buried here last night, and why your name is written upon it."

The detective found a letter knife in a small desk near the door and used it to cut the twine. The butcher's paper unfolded like a flower, revealing hideous contents that shocked all three men: crimson flesh that looked as if it had been purchased from a pork seller lay inside.

"No wonder the dog found this of interest," Drummond observed. "Is it animal or human?"

During his years as a detective, Charles had learnt a great deal about anatomy, and he immediately recognised the familiar shape. "It is a human kidney," he declared.

"Wasn't a kidney removed from one of the Ripper's victims?" MacPherson asked as all three men huddled over the gruesome gift.

"How did you know that?" Charles asked. "We didn't release that information to the press."

"Reid," the duke replied. "His circle loyalty is fierce. Is this sent by Ripper then?"

Charles sighed. "I cannot say, but if so, it isn't Elizabeth Stride's. Only a portion of her kidney remains unaccounted for. Also, this is too fresh to be hers, though it does bear signs of glycerin preservation. It might be from one of the Victoria Park victims. They both had organs removed." He took one of the sheets of writing paper, intended for use during the circle meeting, and used it to lift the excised organ from its packaging. Beneath it, they discovered a message, written in what appeared to be blood with a man's finger. Sinclair bit his lower lip, for the implication was clear. "It's an address in Spitalfields. James, I fear I must find a way to reach Whitechapel this morning, despite the congestion of the streets."

"13 Miller's Court," MacPherson read aloud. "You know this place?"

"I do. It's a dangerous rookery behind Dorset Street, not more than a block from where we found Elizabeth's mother nearly a decade ago. Please, James, apologise to Beth for me; and when my cousin returns, tell him that I'll be at this address. If what I fear has indeed occurred, then I may be away for a very long time."

CHAPTER SIX

Early that morning - Miller's Court

Dorset Street in Spitalfields ran east-west from Crispin to Commercial, connecting White's Row on the south to Union on the north. Towards the east, the lofty spire of Christ Church rose gracefully into the brisk morning air, its bells declaring the Lord Mayor's procession day. To the west, the poor children of the Ragged School gathered in a muddy gravel yard, each wide-eyed pupil counted twice by Headmistress Hazel Parmenter before the excited group commenced the long walk towards Leadenhall Street, where each impish set of eyes would strain to catch a fleeting glimpse of the city's new mayor, attired in colourful regalia. He'd be riding in a grand coach amidst a circus of mounted and mechanical followers, that included the ancient guardians of Guildhall: hand-carved effigies of England's giants of legend, Gog and Magog.

It was half ten in the morning, when Thomas "Indian Harry" Bowyer arrived to collect twenty-nine shillings of overdue rent from the young woman who let the tiny room at no. 13, which sat just inside the narrow enclosure known as Miller's Court. The entry to the claustrophobic yard of crumbling brick and misery stood next to 27 Dorset, site of a chandler's shop run by slum landlord John McCarthy. Annie Chapman, who'd fallen victim to the Ripper's knife on the eighth of September, had once lived at 35 Dorset. Spitalfields had a reputation for playing host to debauchery and crime, but those who lived in the east considered Miller's Court and Dorset Street the black heart of an ever-lengthening, evil shadow.

'Indian Harry' Bowyer (so-called for his army career in the far east) served as McCarthy's right arm in this low-rent, high-crime section of Tower Hamlets Borough. Two small children ran past the bearded man's legs as he reached the door to the tiny bedsit.

"Oi! Watch it, there!" Bowyer shouted, as the boy bumped against his side in an attempt at pickpocketing. "I'll clout your 'ead next time, ya little toerag!"

The outraged man continued to mutter complaints about unruly gangs and indifferent schoolteachers as he knocked on Kelly's door. He'd been here almost daily for many weeks, but each time the pretty blonde had convinced the stocky army pensioner to delay just one more day, claiming that she hoped to receive a windfall from a distant relative. Today, Bowyer would accept no excuses, for landlord John McCarthy, owner of Miller's Court, had warned his employee that failure this time meant the overdue amount would be taken out of his pay.

"Mary!" the rent collector shouted angrily.

A woman named Liz Prater, another denizen of the shabby court, walked past in company with a visitor named Sarah Lewis. "I doubt she's awake," Prater told Bowyer. "She were up 'alf the night singin' and entertainin' some toff. I seen 'im go in wiv 'er. Drunk an' actin' like she were the Queen o' Sheba 'erself!"

"Queen or no, she's payin' what she owes," Bowyer declared as he pounded on the door, but not a sound emerged from within the quiet room.

Prater shrugged, glancing knowingly at her companion. "Like I tolds ya, 'arry; Mary's dead ta the world."

The two women continued on their way, and the rent collector pounded again, calling louder this time. "Mary! I know you're in there! Open up, or I send for Bobby Blue!"

Receiving no reply, Bowyer walked around the corner of the building, where he noticed a break in one of the window panes. He pushed through the opening, against the closed blinds, so that he might see into the dimly lit room.

The horrific vision within the small chamber chilled his blood, and Bowyer nearly fell backwards, his heart skipping beats as it tried to calm his addled brain. Stumbling in shock, the rent collector headed back towards no. 27 and rushed into the chandler's shop, shouting at John McCarthy. "She's dead! Mary's dead, an' it's 'im again! Lord above, it's 'im!"

McCarthy dropped his pen, spilling India blue ink across the desk. The two men sprinted back to no. 13, and soon the entire Dorset Street congregation whispered the tragic news: Jack the Ripper had once again crept into their midst and sliced away a woman's life; but this time, his insatiable madness had reached horrors beyond anything imaginable. This time, he'd practically devoured his victim, cutting into her like one might slice open a roast pig before serving it up for supper. It was like something out of a German fairytale, some said. Like a ravenous wolf devouring an old woman or an innocent child in a cloak of red.

As Bowyer and McCarthy shouted for constables, a trio of flies lit upon the windowsill inside the flat; their iridescent wings flicking, compound eyes reflecting the bloodstained scene like a hundred rainbow mirrors in a carnival sideshow. The largest of the three left the window and landed upon the dead woman's face, its head tilting as it pondered the congealed blood.

If flies could smile, this one would have been described as grinning like a Jack-O-Lantern. Satisfied with its handiwork, the shapeshifter flew back to the window and signalled to his friends. The trio buzzed out through the broken pane to await the arrival of their ultimate prey.

Charles Sinclair.

Elizabeth Stuart awoke at half past eleven, disappointed to find Charles had left the house. Breakfast had long since been finished, but the cook prepared a bowl of oatmeal and toast along with a pot of peppermint tea, beaming with satisfaction when she learnt that the duchess had eaten nearly all of it.

At one, Beth met with George Price, who pronounced her much improved, though still somewhat pale and undernourished. The kind-hearted physician also examined the cadre of measles patients and admonished the housekeeper to keep all five in bed for another two days, when he'd return for a follow-up examination.

Having been given permission to walk outside, the duchess wrapped herself warmly and strolled towards the stables, intent on visiting Snowdrop, who had yet to foal. As she neared the main doors, a sudden gust of cold wind nearly blew her off her feet, and Elizabeth put up her hands in defence.

"I cannot stay long," a man's voice whispered as a warm hand touched her shoulder.

Elizabeth stopped, her boots causing no sound at all. She looked up at the overcast sky, and even the clouds had ceased to move.

"Forgive me for appearing to you without warning, Duchess. It is rare that you leave the confines of the house of late, so I took the opportunity when I sensed you had come outside."

"Prince Anatole," she said, her breathing rapid. "What is this? How are you here, and what has happened to the clouds? What do you mean you *sensed* it?"

"So many questions combined into one," he said as he took her gloved hand. "Sit, please. The bench is not cold."

Though the air temperature stood near freezing, the stone bench felt warm beneath her coat. "How? The seat is warm, almost like it glows with heat. "

"A minor manipulation of matter," he answered. "As to the clouds, I have paused time for you. I may not hold you here for long, though. Elizaveta—may I call you that?"

She nodded.

"Good. Elizaveta, I know that you do not trust me entirely, but I wish only for your happiness. I fear that a time of great trouble lies ahead for you. A time of testing. May I show you?"

"Show me?" she asked. Romanov answered by touching his hand to her forehead, and a series of images filled her mind.

She found herself looking down upon a scene covered in white. Slowly, Elizabeth realised that the white was actually snow, and she could feel the cold snowflakes as they fell upon her face and hands. She wore no overcoat, and her unbound hair blew in the breeze. Below her vantage point, chaos reigned. She could hear frantic calls, shouts, and the clanging of bells. Horses neighed as if panicked, and the clatter of wagon wheels on cobblestone rose up in the darkness. Despite the stars overhead, a strange, orange light flickered upon the snow-white ground.

Then she saw him. Charles Sinclair, and he appeared injured. He lay upon the snow, his sea-blue eyes open and staring. His limbs still; face pale as death. Delicate snowflakes collected upon his dark lashes, but he did not react. A stain of red slowly seeped into the virgin white ground, surrounding his frozen body in deadly stripes of crimson.

Terrified, Elizabeth began to weep, her breathing quick and sharp, and she squeezed Romanov's hand. "Why have you shown me this?" she begged him. "Why? Tell me this is but a vain image! A lie! Charles cannot die—he cannot! Please, Anatole, I implore you! Tell me that this will never happen!"

"I fear that it will, my darling Elizaveta. Trent intends to hurt you, and his actions will affect many, including your beloved Captain. Will you trust me? I seek to alter these images, but if I cannot, I shall do my utmost to save him. Promise me this only: that you will stay away from Trent. His crimes have reached the point of no return, and he must face judgement."

She started to reply, but the bench cooled, grower ever colder, and the icy winds began to howl as the clouds moved once more.

Snow, she remembered, standing alone near the stable entrance. *Red snow.*

All turned to darkness, and the next time the duchess opened her eyes, it would be almost four o'clock.

CHAPTER SEVEN

Detective Inspector Arthur France loved his wife. "Brenda, you are a treasure," he told her as she poured him a third cup of tea. "Not too much now," he said. "I expect Sergeant Williams will be serving that gut-wrenching syrup he calls coffee this afternoon, and I wouldn't want to have too much in my belly when it hits. Is that the morning copy of *The Star*?"

"It is, but there's not much in it besides reports about His Worship's big doings."

Brenda France stood five-foot-six with auburn hair and hazel eyes rimmed in long copper-coloured lashes. A sea of pale freckles spattered the ivory skin of her face, making her seem much younger than twenty-nine. "Must you go back to Leman Street already?" she complained to her husband of eight years. "You worked most of last night, Artie. Can't one of the other inspectors mind the shop this afternoon?"

"It isn't to Leman Street I go, Brenda, m'lass, but to Charrington Mission. H-Division has been charged by the Home Secretary to provide policing at the lord mayor's banquet. I'm to be there at one."

She sat down just as their youngest, a boy of two years, toddled into the room carrying a stuffed bear. "Come here, Charley, my lad!" the inspector said, lifting the toddler onto his lap. "You're gonna be as tall as your namesake, you are."

"I wonder if Mr. Sinclair will attend the banquet as well," Brenda said, breaking off a bit of rye bread for her son. "You're right. Our Charles will be tall, just like his godfather. Must be quite a shock, learning you're a marquess. You reckon he's changed much, cause of it?"

"Not a whit. The superintendent's the same as always. A kind and thoughtful man," France replied. "Where's Deidra?" he asked, referring to their six-year-old daughter.

"She's making her bed," Brenda answered proudly. "We'll have no slackers here. And speakin' o' which, I suppose you'll need ta be leavin' soon."

As if on cue, their front doorbell rang, and Brenda rose to answer. "I hope this isn't another o' them travellers come by to ask about sharpenin' our knives." Arthur fed the remains of a mutton sandwich to the boy, one ear halfway listening to his wife's conversation with the visitor. He recognised the man's voice: Constable Antram from Leman Street. "Sorry, son," he told young Charles France, setting the boy onto the floor and standing. "I'm to leave at once, I take it," he said as Brenda returned.

"I'm afraid so. The constable says there's been some sort of crime over on Dorset, but he won't say more than that. I've a very bad feeling, Arthur. Do be careful."

He wiped his hands on a linen towel, and then took her into his arms, kissing her cheek. "I'll be fine. Promise you'll keep both the doors locked. I'll ask Constable Brightman to make regular stops to check on you and the children."

He left, taking a hansom rather than walking, but due to the processional's street closures—and the overflow traffic being redirected through Aldgate—the ten-minute journey took the young inspector nearly an hour. By the time he reached Leman Street, the entire station house had erupted into chaos. Edmund Reid met him at the door, and next to the booking desk, stood Charles Sinclair.

"Sorry to interrupt your luncheon, France," Reid said, glancing at his watch. "I'm afraid our assignment at the mission is now altered."

"So I understand, sir. Good day, Superintendent. I'm surprised to find you here."

The marquess handed an empty coffee cup to the desk sergeant. "About two hours ago, a man named John McCarthy reported a murder to a young constable who'd been patrolling Commercial Street. When the constable investigated, he discovered a woman's body that appears to be the work of Ripper. Arthur, this is to remain as quiet an investigation as possible. Even though most of the city's press is covering the procession and related events, we have very little time before their legions descend. Reid has sent two men to the crime scene to secure it, but I wanted to wait for you before going there myself."

Reid finished signing a series of reports and handed them to the desk sergeant. "There you are, Williams. Send those to Whitehall right away. They're actually for our superintendent here, but I'm sure Mr. Sinclair prefers to survey our monthly rolls at a later date. We'll leave as soon as we can get a hansom." He turned to Charles. "I'd prefer we didn't take your carriage, though it is convenient. Cabs are scarce this morning, but I shouldn't want your fancy coach left near such a place. Miller's Court is the most crime-ridden section of the east."

"It's probably best we cancelled our full meeting this morning, else we'd all have been there when this happened, Edmund. Has anyone from the city police arrived?"

"Major Smith's men, you mean? No, and I doubt they will," Reid replied.

Sinclair had been reading through a series of Whitehall mandates, recently delivered to all three station houses in H-Division. "Do I understand these orders right? Has the commissioner decreed that bloodhounds have to scour the scene before any police officers may enter?"

"That is my reading of it," Edmund answered angrily. "Look, here, are you certain Warren has resigned? We've received no word to that effect."

"He has, Ed," Sinclair whispered. "But with the mayor's doings today, it's likely that most divisions won't learn of the change until Monday. Warren told me last night that Matthews had already accepted his resignation. It became official as of ten this morning."

"Then, it's possible that the order regarding the bloodhounds is now void," the inspector answered. "Look, I don't want the people living at Miller's Court to muddle up the crime scene, so I'm ready to go, if you approve it. You're the seniormost detective on site. As far as I'm concerned, Superintendent, you're in charge."

"Then, I approve," the marquess said. "Has anyone wired Abberline?"

"Fred's still with His Worship," Reid answered. "I've sent word to Superintendent Arnold to meet us at Miller's Court."

A hansom pulled up to the entrance to the station house, and Reid, France, and Sinclair squeezed into its cramped interior. Behind this, a second and then a third hansom arrived, followed by a pair of Metropolitan Police maria wagons, each drawn by a team of sturdy horses. "Did you contact Thomas Sunders?" Sinclair asked Reid as they drove north towards Commercial Street.

"He's at K-Division today, finishing his study of the Victoria Park victims. I wired and asked him to join us. Knowing Fred, he'll want Dr. Bond to examine the woman as well. Good heavens, Charles, is this nightmare ever going to end?"

"I pray it does," Sinclair replied.

"Is the duchess aware of this new murder?" Reid asked his friend.

"No, and that is yet another of my prayers today. That she will never have to hear about this woman's death."

The sidewalks that lined Commercial were packed with handcarts and temporary stalls from which the costermonger class sold their wares: flowers, fresh fish, assorted bric-a-brac, new and second-hand clothing, household goods, vegetables, knives, meats and game birds, pies, oysters, and nearly every other item a buyer might find useful in his daily life. The stink of horse manure, a constant in any modern city, mixed with that of decaying produce, human sweat, caged songbirds, flowers, and chimney smoke; their strange admixture accented by another, less common ingredient, the unsettling scent of fear.

Charles Sinclair felt a chill run along his spine as their hired conveyance took them past Christ Church. As he gazed upon the crowded sidewalk to his right, he could almost see the scene unfold, playing through his memory like a ghost from the past. The headless body of the torn woman, the blind flower girl, a terrified witness who'd discovered the pitiful victim, and beside the dead woman's remains, an unconscious child named Elizabeth Stuart.

Beth had been petrified with shock, unable to remember her own name, recalling only a single memory; that she had a cousin named Paul, and that he would rescue her. Thinking of it now, Charles puzzled through the events of that pivotal night and the day that followed. Again and again, Elizabeth had asked for Paul. "He often goes to Paris," she'd told Charles many times. "He's handsome and wonderful."

Handsome and wonderful. Have I stolen her from him? Charles wondered with a sigh. *Did meeting me alter Beth's entire life as it has mine?*

"You're lost in thought," Reid said as they turned west onto Dorset. "Is it the duchess?"

"It is both duchesses. Beth and her mother," Sinclair answered. "You weren't here in '79, but France and I both responded to that call. Do you remember it, Arthur?"

France sat betwixt his superior officers, and he took a deep breath before answering. "I still dream about it sometimes, sir. That sweet little girl and how she stood up to her stepfather. Cor, blimey! There never was such an evil man!"

"Trent is far more insidious in his crimes that you can imagine, Arthur. The savagery inflicted upon Duchess Patricia was beyond the scope of any sane man's mind. Honestly, nothing Ripper has done thus far exceeds it for ferocity and horror, though the slaying at the Lyceum came close."

"Let's pray we've seen the worst of that demon's crimes, then," Reid said as they neared their destination. "We'll not get any of these vehicles into Miller's Court. It's accessible only through a narrow opening next to McCarthy's shop. We might get a handcart back there, though, to carry out the victim's remains. France, we should probably tell you how it is our marquess knew to come to Leman Street today. I did not send for him. This morning, the superintendent found a package addressed to him, buried in the south gardens at Queen Anne House."

"Buried there?" France asked, stunned. "Ripper left you a package? Why would he do that, sir?"

"His reasons are yet to be determined. My aunt's dog found it, but there's more to the story. If you can spare the time, I'd appreciate your input on this mystery, Arthur. Perhaps, you might drop by Westminster later this evening."

"Certainly, sir. May I bring my family? I'd prefer not to leave them on their own—given all that's happened this past month."

"Yes, of course. I'm sure the duchess would love to meet your wife and children, and I've not seen my godson in more than three months. First, we'll see what awaits us here and then make our plans."

They left the hansom and passed on foot through the entry to the courtyard. Just on the other side of a narrow passage, the policemen were met by a stocky man, wearing a green apron. He wiped his hands and extended the right. "Name's McCarthy, sir. My man Bowyer's the one who come ta see ya. We been waitin' for word on them bloodhounds, but as local folks was ready ta break the windows, I figured we oughta get in first, so I busted down the door with a pickaxe."

Reid's face reddened with anger. "You did what?" he exploded. "And why would you imagine we'd approve of that, Mr. McCarthy? You can expect to spend a very long time in my interview room when we've finished here. A guilty man might find such interference to his benefit!"

To those within his purview, John McCarthy was the local powerbroker, for he leased rooms to nearly everyone now standing upon the sidewalks of Dorset and along the narrow lane within the courtyard. However, his proud voice fell to a whisper as he replied, not wishing to appear obsequious or deferential to the police, whom many listening not only distrusted but actually despised.

"If you'll excuse me, I only wished ta help. If I done anythin' wrong, then I am sorry, Inspector Reid. I just wanted ta make sure nothin' got thieved."

"And how are we to know you've not disturbed the scene or thieved anything yourself?" France asked as they followed the chandler to number 13, where a dense crowd gawped and pickpockets ran wild.

"You boys, clear off now!" Arthur shouted at the urchins. Turning to his sergeants and their constables, the young inspector began to issue orders. "Applebaum, look to those rascals. See to it they return to their Fagin's headquarters, emptyhanded. Prescott, take your men and walk this entire area. Search for anything amiss. Lance, start interviewing everyone hereabouts." He turned to Sinclair. "Is that all right, sir?"

The detective superintendent nodded. "Yes, of course. Well done, Inspector." He then faced the throng of onlookers. "Some of you may know me, but if not, my name is Superintendent Sinclair. I'll be leading this investigation. I know that this is a great shock to you all, but the inspectors and I require time and solitude to conduct our investigation. We wish to uncover all evidence available, therefore, if anyone here has information to offer the police, let us know, and we'll speak to you soon. For the present, I ask that you return to your homes, please. Allow us to do what we must to find this woman's killer."

"We already know who dunnit!" a bent woman shouted from one of the tenement houses beyond the community dustbin. "It were one o' them Jews; that's who killed poor Mary! Wore tha' leather apron an' all!"

Charles motioned to one of France's sergeants. "Applebaum, see to that woman. If she has anything substantive to offer, then take it down, but I want this area cleared." He turned back to the chandler. "Mr. McCarthy, you say that this door was locked when you arrived?"

"It were, sir. There's a window on the other side, near to the dustbin, that's got a broken pane. That's how my man were able to look inside, bu' we had ta break the door in ta get into the room. We ain't touched nothin' nor gone in."

"Have you no key, Mr. McCarthy? Surely, as landlord, you possess keys to all your properties. Could you not use it?"

McCarthy's rough cheeks tinged with pink. "I lost it, sir. Mary 'ad the only copy."

"Good heavens, man, you could have made another from hers, could you not? Never mind, we'll discuss it at length later—at Leman Street."

"Ain't we ta wait fer them bloodhounds, Superintendent?" a young constable enquired. "Commissioner's orders."

"The commissioner's orders are null and void as of this moment, Constable. Neither he nor the dogs will be forthcoming. If you take exception with my orders, you may write to Scotland Yard and complain."

"I do not, sir," the youth answered, gulping.

"A wise decision," Sinclair said as he stepped through the open doorway. The pickaxe had splintered through six layers of peeling paint, and the marquess moved cautiously, avoiding the dull rainbow of debris as he passed into the chilly room. Despite the cold, several flies had discovered the gore in number 13, and one flew past his ear as Charles crossed the floor. "We'll need some kind of temporary walkway; otherwise, we'll be leaving our own bloody footmarks all over. I prefer to inspect those left by our killer. Inspector

Reid, no one is to come in yet. France, see if you might find a scrap of lumber or old carpet."

Superintendent Thomas Arnold had just arrived, and the portly, uniformed policeman peered into the room from outside the doorway. "Charles?"

"Hello, Tom," the marquess answered. "I hope I'm not intruding into your domain."

"Not at all. Scotland Yard is always welcome in Whitechapel, but I thought we were to wait for Warren and the bloodhounds. His standing order is that no investigation commences before his arrival."

"You'll be waiting a long time, if you do that, Superintendent," Sinclair answered, his eyes memorising every detail in the cramped space. "Warren's resignation was accepted by the Home Secretary last evening. I expect James Monro is already decorating his new office over at Whitehall. For now, I am senior investigator. Is that clear?"

"It is," Arnold answered, relieved to hear it. "My men are yours to command, Lord Haimsbury."

Charles now stood beside the bed, where the remains of Mary Kelly lay. "It's nearly identical to the Lyceum," he told Reid, who watched from the doorway. "Like there, the killer or killers have displayed some of the excised tissue and organs around the victim's body. Do we have a name for this poor woman?"

"It's Mary Jane Kelly, sir," McCarthy said, a cotton handkerchief to his face. "She was behind in her rent."

"You will never collect it now," Sinclair answered soberly. "Superintendent Arnold, ask your men to start making a list of everyone who was resident last night—anywhere within earshot. I want to know this poor woman's every action from yesterday: where she went, whom she saw, what she did. Also I'll need the name of all her visitors during the previous fortnight. If she has relatives or close friends in the crowd, ask them to wait in Mr. McCarthy's shop."

"Right away, sir," the police superintendent replied before turning and issuing commands to his uniformed men.

Edmund Reid remained outside. "Can you tell if the kidney left at your home is from this woman?"

Charles wished the earl had come with them, for Paul's knowledge of medicine and anatomy would prove most useful now. "No, not yet. This is monstrous! She's been carved like a game hen, Edmund. One thigh is nothing but bone, and her internal organs have all been removed, as if she'd been hollowed out for stuffing. The viscera lie scattered all about the body. We'll want Sunders or another surgeon here as soon as possible. Also, we'll require a trusted photographer. For the present, who has a pencil and paper?"

Nearly every policeman's hand went up, and Charles motioned towards Antram. "Constable, how accurately can you depict a scene? With a drawing, I mean."

Reid answered. "He's very good, Charles. Do you want him inside?"

"Yes."

A lean young man in a neatly pressed uniform with brass buttons joined Reid at the threshold. "Superintendent?"

"Come in, Antram, but step carefully. Try not to leave too many footmarks," he told the policeman. "I want everything diagrammed as to its precise location in the room. Begin by drawing the body as it lies upon the cot, and then add details as we discover them."

The lad sketched out a rectangle, which he labeled with the address, date, and victim's name. He also added Sinclair's name as chief investigator. "Ready, sir."

Charles moved closer to the bed, careful to avoid altering any evidence. "Do you take stenography?"

"I do, sir."

"Good, write as I speak. Make drawings as you can. The victim is lying prone, eyes open. These are blue in colour. Her upper torso is flat against the mattress, shoulders even, the head turned towards her left. She is dressed only in a chemise. There is no obvious sign of other clothing. Her legs are splayed, positioned approximately two feet apart, knees flexed, angled in opposing directions outward. The neck tissue has been thoroughly excised down to the bone. The abdominal wall is cut through, commencing at the breastbone and extending to the pubis. The gastric cavity has been excavated; all organs removed." Charles donned leather gloves and gazed into the vacant eyes. "She must have been lovely in life. We should see if we can find someone with a photograph of her. What is this?" he asked as he lifted Kelly's head several inches to look at the pillow. "Sketch this if you can, Constable. The killer's left bits of her beneath the head, obscured by the hair. I see what might be an intact uterus and one breast. Why do this? Is it meant as a message? I count two kidneys, also, beneath the hair; both intact," he added, looking up at Reid. "This rules out the one sent to me as being relevant to this case."

"The Victoria murders, perhaps," Reid suggested. "It may not be human, Charles. Sunders will be able to tell us when he examines it later today."

"Yes, all right," Sinclair answered, sighing. "The room is painted in blood, though not equally so. There is a large flap of skin and associated tissue, possibly from the abdomen, lying upon a near-by table. Mark the location on your diagram, Constable. The other breast has been positioned beside the right foot. Is that a liver? There betwixt her feet?" he asked as a most welcome face appeared at the door.

"I got here as soon as Granger's driving could get us through the maddening traffic," Aubrey told his cousin. "Good heavens! Did one man do all this?"

"We don't know yet," Sinclair replied. "Come in, Paul, but mind where you walk. The floor's covered in blood and tissue. See there, by her feet? Is that a liver?"

"Part of one," the earl answered. "This is monstrous. James told me how it is you came to learn about the murder. Are both kidneys present?"

"So it seems. We'll have to examine the one sent to me later. I left it in Reid's dead room. What do you make of the scene?"

The earl stood still, examining the room carefully, then turned as he made sense of the various clues. "Her throat was slashed first. You can see the arc of arterial blood along this wall, just to the left of the bed. See the large pool, here, near her foot? That's probably from the initial cut, which means she was deliberately posed. Moved by the killer or killers and displayed as we see her now. Charles, help me to turn her, if you don't mind."

Using their gloved hands, the two men gently moved Kelly's body towards her left side. "Yes, you can see more blood beneath her. I doubt that she was conscious when she was killed."

"Why do you say that?" Reid asked as Antram continued with his drawing.

"No defensive wounds on her hands and arms, though the carving makes it tricky to determine for certain. There is a small wound on her right thumb, but not where one would expect if she were trying to defend herself against an attacker. Poor woman. What's her name?"

"Mary Kelly, or so I'm told," Sinclair answered. "She looks no more than mid-twenties, I'd say. I'm told she was quite pretty in life. Tall. Fair complexion. Large blue eyes. Lovely blonde hair."

All colour suddenly drained from Sinclair's face, and the detective rushed out of the cramped room, emerging into the courtyard. The crisp November air clouded with vapour as he took deep breaths, his back bent whilst he grasped his knees.

"Steady on, Cousin," Aubrey said as he joined Charles outside. "Perhaps, this is too much for you just now, with all that's happened. I'm told you had very little sleep, and that you had a bit of a spell last night."

"The note, Paul. Saucy Jack's second note. He referenced a former crime from long before. How did it go again? That 'she of the pretty blonde hair had pleased him once and would again'? Good heavens, he'd already selected Kelly as his next victim, when he wrote that! Don't you see it? This poor girl bears a striking resemblance to Patricia Stuart!"

"No, surely not," the earl argued. Then as he considered it further, his own face paled. "Nothing more is to be said of this. Not here," he warned his cousin and Reid. "And certainly nowhere within Beth's hearing. Charles, why don't you go home? I can stay, if you wish and help Reid."

"No, I'll remain," he said, regaining composure. Thomas Sunders arrived in company with Dr. Thomas Bond from A-Division.

"Hello, Superintendent. Lord Aubrey," the amiable Scottish surgeon said as he approached the two cousins. "I'm sure you both know Dr. Bond. He's with Mr. Dunlap's division."

"Yes, hello, Bond," Sinclair said, his breathing slowing. "This one is particularly vicious. I think you can go in now, if you wish. I've had a constable named Antram making sketches of the scene. He has a strong stomach. I think he'll make an admirable assistant."

"That is always a blessing," Sunders replied. "You're a bit green, if I may say so, Lord Haimsbury. Is it that bad?"

"It is that bad," the earl answered for his cousin. "The room's quite narrow, Sunders. Be careful as you walk. We'd not want to obscure any footmarks left by the killer." Aubrey stood still, but then his head turned towards the open doorway. "Footmarks. Footmarks! Charles, when you entered, were there any tracks upon the floor?"

Sinclair shook his head. "None. Only blood and tissue. No prints of any kind," he whispered, pulling his cousin towards the chandler's shop, away from the crowd. "How can that be? How can such a crime be committed, so much blood expelled without even one stray mark within that blood? But more to the point, how did the killer escape a locked room?"

"It was locked?"

"It was. The chandler had to break it open to admit the police."

Aubrey swatted at a fly. "I hate mysteries like this. Look, Charles, let's go back to my coach to speak of this. Granger's keeping watch on it. It's parked behind your marias."

The two men left the area, and as they passed through the narrow opening that led past McCarthy's shop, they noticed a slender man in formal dress—completely out of place in such a neighbourhood. "Did that man come with you?" Sinclair asked the earl.

"No, I came alone," Aubrey answered, glancing at the well-dressed gentleman. "He seems familiar, though. Most likely a westender looking for a cheap thrill. With the procession today, most of the banks declared a holiday. The sad truth is that some of our class enjoy touring the east, so it's possible this fellow heard of the crime and hopes to sate his unsavoury appetite for titillation."

Charles shook his head. "Or he is a unprincipled reporter, thinking to wear the guise of a slum tourist. Hello, Michael. That's a rather splendid suit. Did you steal it?"

"I find your insinuation insulting, Superintendent. My attire is my own."

"Is it now?" Sinclair asked, crossing to the lurker. "Just how did you hear about this crime? Did your Whitehall advocate whisper into your ear? Do not think yourself immune to police justice this time, Mr. O'Brien."

The reporter turned to leave, but Aubrey grasped his collar and spun him about on his heel. "Oh, no, old chum. You and I have unfinished business."

The earl used both hands to pat along the reporter's pockets, and the slightly built man objected. "Now, now, Lord Aubrey! I'm really not that sort of fellow!"

Paul held up a long knife, which he'd discovered in O'Brien's left jacket pocket. "I've seen gamekeepers use knives like this to skin rabbits and foxes. A strange item to keep in such a fine suit. What employment do you have for such a weapon?"

The reporter reached out, trying to retrieve the knife.

"Oh, no," the earl warned him. "This joins other evidence at Leman Street."

Sinclair called to one of the constables keeping watch on the waiting marias. "You there! We've a suspect who requires a comfortable ride back to Leman Street. Here you are, Mr. O'Brien. It's a banner day for you, it seems. You'll get to enjoy our hospitable accommodations once more. This time, however, it's likely you'll be remanded for arraignment. I'll have our sergeant send someone to pack a bag, if you like. How many socks does one need whilst awaiting the rope, I wonder?"

"Now, now, Superintendent," O'Brien began, his voice low but calm. "You proceed from a complete misapprehension! I merely came here to obtain eyewitness testimony for *The Star*'s next edition. I'd been overnighting with a friend following an evening's entertainment at the Cambridge, and I happened to be walking past when the commotion arose."

"You may tell us all about it once we've made you comfortable," Sinclair argued. "Constable, see to it that this hack is booked into one of our lower-level cells. He has a nasty skin condition which requires he spend many hours in dark, dank rooms. If we have any spare rats, I'm sure he'd appreciate the company."

The young policeman helped the reporter to mount the steep wooden steps that led into the maria's interior, and in a moment, the wagon departed for Leman Street.

Reid appeared at the two cousins' elbows. "Did I see you arrest someone, Charles?"

"Our old friend, Michael O'Brien. Abberline will be quite pleased, I imagine. The reporter claimed his presence mere serendipity, but I suspect someone tipped him off. You know, Paul, I think I will go back to Westminster, but you needn't stay. Reid can take charge. Do you mind, Edmund?"

"Not at all. I've sent for Abberline. I'm certain he'll make haste, and Sunders is a thorough man. With him to guide Bond's eye for observation, we're assured of accurate assessments of the woman's wounds. France's men have begun a survey of everyone living near-by and assemble the woman's history. I heard a neighbour mention that Kelly has a common-law husband named Joseph Barnett. I've asked France to find out all he can on the man."

Sinclair smiled. "You're thorough as always. I want you to speak with Henry Irving at the Lyceum regarding a man he recently dismissed named Parker. The man's been sporting a long knife and bragging about being Ripper. It's probably nothing, but I'd like to eliminate him as a suspect. Oh, and Edmund, as you'll be tied up the remainder of the day, would you ask France to attend the circle meeting with you tomorrow rather than drop by tonight? We hope to begin at one, barring anything unforeseen."

Inspector Reid followed his friends to the Branham coach, parked behind the remaining maria. "Yes, I'll tell him, and I'll be sure to send your other coach back to Westminster, once I return to Leman Street. Shall I assign someone to question O'Brien?"

"No, let him stew a bit. He'll keep until you and Fred have fin-ished here. I doubt that I can return today, Ed," Sinclair answered. "I've a nagging thrumming at the back of my mind that needs tend-ing. I suspect the answer lies with Mr. Baxter at Branham Hall, so I might take the earl's train to Kent this afternoon. See you tomorrow."

The cousins left the area and entered the Branham coach, sitting opposite one another. Granger called to the horses, and the matched pair headed away from the narrow lane. Knots of curious citizen-ry had gathered near Christ Church, most still discussing the lord mayor's parade and the planned meat tea to be served later that day at Charrington Mission. A few had learnt about the horrific murder near Dorset, and rumours that a slightly built toff had been arrested spread like wildfire amongst the gossipers. By four that afternoon, most in Spitalfields believed Jack had indeed been caught, a mis-taken impression which brought temporary peace to many, but also aided the police in their efforts.

Paul sighed as the coach passed the church. "That place always brings back troubling memories. I can still see Beth's little face when I arrived in your station house, Charles. All those years ago. You said you hoped to speak to Baxter. What about?"

"It's because of that little face that I go, Paul. I want to learn more about Beth's childhood terrors, and I believe our butler can offer insight. And I want to bring back Bella. I'd feel better if we had something with keener vision than mine inside her bedroom at night."

"You're bringing Beth's Labrador back with you? Why? What happened during my absence?" he asked.

"William Trent paid a call on us last night. Didn't the duke tell you?"

"No. He never mentioned Trent. James said you had an incident, and that Marchand saw someone climbing into the house, but little beyond that. This morning, I left early to speak with Morgan—long story, but she's flown the coop. I should have known she'd refuse my help."

"I don't understand."

"I spoke with her last night at the Egyptian about MacKey. In fact, Lorena had also fled by the time I reached the Langham. That's where Susanna insisted our doctor had holed up. Now, I wonder if any of it was true. Morgan convinced me that she wanted to leave Redwing, and I foolishly put her up at a hotel I own. When I returned this morning to look in, she'd gone. The man I left to keep watch on her, said she'd departed sometime during the night."

"I'm sorry, Paul. Not just for you, but for her. Redwing uses women most cruelly. Your decision to offer help is laudable."

"Foolish, is more like it," the earl muttered.

"Not at all. Look, as I'll be away, would you keep watch on Beth tonight? Sleep on the sofa, if you don't mind; inside her bedchamber. It makes her feel safest."

"Are you sure?" the earl asked.

"Quite sure," Sinclair told his cousin. "I trust you with her, Paul. Once we get to Queen Anne, I'll pack a bag and leave at once. Is your train in Victoria?"

"One of them is. Are you sure you wouldn't like company? I don't think it's safe for you to travel alone, Charles. James can watch Elizabeth."

"No, I prefer you stay with her. If Trent calls again, I want you there. Keep your weapon and a Bible with you at all times."

"And if he calls upon you at Branham?"

"Then I'll have the staff there as guardians," the marquess answered, smiling. "The most capable Mr. Baxter and his well-trained team. There is no finer army this side of Scotland."

CHAPTER EIGHT

As Charles entered the foyer, Della ran to meet him, her small feet flying beneath a taffeta skirt. "Beth had a small spell, Cousin Charles. She's sleeping now. Dr. Price came by and says she's fine. She's just—what was his word now?—oh, yes, overwrought."

"What kind of spell?" he asked as they climbed the staircase.

"A bit of a faint. We mustn't waken her, though. As I said, she is sleeping."

"I shan't. Promise," he told his cousin, as Victoria met them both at the top of the stair.

"Hush," she warned him in a whisper. "Make no sound, Charles. Beth's finally asleep. Where have you been?"

"Investigating, Aunt. Only investigating. However, I must spend the night away. I'm here only to pack a bag. Paul will explain."

The girl bobbed behind him as Charles reached the apartment door. "Are you coming back tomorrow?" she asked in a whisper. "Uncle James says lots of members of the circle are coming. I thought I'd bake them a raisin cake."

"Save a slice for me," he told her, kissing her forehead. "Now, let me pack quickly before Elizabeth awakens, all right?"

She left with their aunt, and Charles entered the apartment, using the second door that led directly into the bedroom where Paul now slept each night. Finding a large, leather valise, he selected enough clothing to cover a two-day visit—just in case—and snapped the clasp shut. He then sat at the parlour desk to compose a letter to Elizabeth. He longed to tell her goodbye in person, but believing her rest more important, the marquess wrote a short note, sealed it in an envelope with red wax, and then left it with Miles before departing for Victoria Station.

Two hours later, Charles arrived at Branham village station, where he was met by a crested coach, sent by Mr. Baxter. The long drive through the countryside allowed him the leisure of watching the passing autumnal scenery whilst composing his thoughts.

"Things have changed for you since you took this journey in October," a voice spoke within the coach.

Sinclair was the brougham's sole occupant, therefore the sudden appearance of another *should* have shocked him; however, with recent experience to draw upon, he found himself merely curious.

"I'd have been disappointed if you'd failed to show," he told the unwanted passenger. "I prefer that you follow me rather than antagonise my fiancée."

The entity's full lips widened into what was intended as a smile but came across more like a sneer. "Am I keeping you busy?" Prince Rasha Grigor asked.

"How so? With rude conversations or with something else? I do have other things to occupy my time besides conversing with the likes of you."

"Why do you visit Branham?" the creature probed. "Is there something there I have missed?"

Charles intentionally withdrew a notebook from his pocket and began scribbling a series of instructions to his inspectors. He offered no reply.

"I shan't go away, if that's what you intend. What did I miss?"

"Why ask me? If you're so all-knowing, you've no need of my opinion."

The creature's upper lip curved into a lopsided grin. "I saw you last month. Inside her childhood rooms. And later, within the maze."

Charles continued to write. It was a method he often employed when dealing with annoying visitors to his office at Scotland Yard.

"I very seriously doubt it, Rasha. In fact, I suspect that you lay claim to works not your own. I rather think your fellow demons will take umbrage at such theft."

"Demons! I am no mere demon, Superintendent! Those pitiful wraiths have no power. They serve me, just as your driver serves you. Bowing and scraping."

"My driver does no such thing," the marquess answered, his head still down. "But as you're here, make yourself useful, won't you? Explain how it is that demons defer to you, a failed human experiment."

The hybrid's head tilted to one side. "I could crush you with mere thought, if it suited me."

"Then do it, or else leave my coach."

"Why should I leave, when the conversation is so very pleasant?" he asked, his left hand reaching for a cigar. "Oh, do forgive my manners. Would you care for one?"

"Even if I smoked, I'd say no. Just what is it that you expect to gain from this conversation, Grigor? Surely not my friendship. I loathe you, as does Elizabeth."

He lit the tobacco with the snap of his fingers, causing the end to spark. Puffing thoughtfully, the altered human tapped ash onto the floor of the carriage. "Elizabeth has no idea what she wants, but she'll soon learn the hard truth of her predicament. Much is about to change."

"Is this Romanian wisdom or just fanciful imagination? Shall I see if a doctor from Bedlam is available to offer an opinion? I hear the jackets there are comparable to none. Such lovely, long arms."

The creature took a deep draw from the cigar, his icy eyes rolling back thoughtfully. "Very droll. A woman you know spent time at Bedlam recently, Superintendent, and she wore those pretty jackets to keep from tearing out her own hair. Knowing how much you care about her, I saw to it that she was moved to kinder, more gentle accommodations. As your friend, I thought it wise to act in your stead. She'd been misdiagnosed with a fatal disease. Ida Ross is her name."

Sinclair's right hand cramped as he struggled to continue to write, but the slight pause was enough to reward his opponent's efforts. Clearing his throat, the marquess answered the adversary. "You took her out of Bedlam?"

"Indeed. She found succor and healing at the second hospital. Such a fine staff of alienists. It's quite modern."

"And what hospital might that have been?"

"One you'll soon come to know quite well. Did you appreciate my little joke?"

Charles looked up at last. "Do you see me laughing?"

Rasha smiled. "I see you weeping. Inwardly, at least. You're such an obedient little puppy, Charles. You really are! I dangle a clue, and you sniff it out, just like that dog of your aunt's. Saucy Jack, indeed! But it has turned out well, has it not? That first letter sent Beth flying to you, and thence to this very hall," he said as the coach neared the turn for Branham.

"Hubris will gain you an eternal berth in hell, Rasha. Taking credit for the Lord's gift is blasphemy. It was His design that Beth came to me. He merely used you and your kind to achieve his perfect end."

"Blaspheming requires belief, Detective. I believe only in myself; therefore, no blasphemy has occurred." He tapped on the window with a signet ring, its bright enamel forming the shape of a white dove bearing a red spot on its upraised wing. "Blonde hair, blue eyes. Kelly's height and measurements are perfect matches, also. Perhaps, I should send that information to Elizabeth. She'll appreciate a man who actually tells her the truth."

The pencil broke in half as Sinclair's anger finally overwhelmed his reason. "You speak of truth, when your mouth knows nothing of the term! If you *ever* approach her, I will..."

"You will what? Kill me? How quaint," the hybrid laughed. "Of course, I do not work solely in England. It is true that my exploits currently lie in London, but Paris is a beautiful den of iniquity! A peer might find himself lost in its depraved streets and garrets. Even an honest policeman might yield to temptation; find himself trapped, if not careful."

Charles stared, for the creature's taunts struck close to home. Whilst in Paris in early '79, Bob Morehouse had insisted his junior officer attend a raucous party in the countryside, just outside of the city. Sinclair had awoken the following morning with no idea what had actually occurred, but afterward, he'd begun receiving blackmail letters. Written threats that Amelia soon discovered. The implied infidelity within those pages had destroyed what little affection remained of their marriage. He'd felt certain that nothing had happened with the actress, that the implications contained within the letters had been fabricated; but Charles had no way of proving it as fact, for he had only vague memories of that wretched night.

"Don't worry, my friend," Grigor laughed, the smoke from the fat cigar curling about his face. "I would never reveal your dark secrets to anyone. Neither the truth of Paris, nor the truth of your son's death. I prefer to save those revelations for a more important day. Perhaps, your wedding."

His breathing quickened, and Charles prayed again, begging the Lord to prevent him from making a terrible mistake. In answer, a sense of calm filtered through his spirit, as though a cool hand touched his face. *Beth loves me. She loves me and believes in me. We are together for a reason—and it is not to please Redwing.*

"My wedding day?" he asked, regaining composure. "How very thoughtful of you, Rasha. I'm sure you long to attend as groom, but Beth chose me, not you. And how is it that your so-called father allows you free rein? You're giving the nether realm a bad name, Grigor. Failure becomes a habit with you."

"Clever human!" the prince laughed. "Too clever by half."

"Doesn't that describe you?" Charles volleyed back. "A weakling half-human hybrid with angelic aspirations? Part divine, yet part profane, as your comrades might call the human condition. I see no advantage to striding the line betwixt worlds. You stand neither in Jehovah's camp nor in that of—who is it that you serve again? Lucifer?"

"I serve no one!" he shouted angrily, his icy eyes flashing into orbs of bright crimson.

"I see," the detective replied with feigned ease, though his heart beat wildly. "Then, by implication, you serve yourself. How does that work? Are you king of the heap, or are you the heap itself? Perhaps, it is both."

Rasha's hand flew to strike, but froze a mere fraction of an inch from Sinclair's face. Then, just as quickly as he'd appeared, the unwanted passenger vanished from sight.

Exhaling slowly in an effort to calm his heart, Charles focused on thoughts of Elizabeth, internally praying for her safety and for God's protection upon her and their unborn child. As he lifted his head, yet another uninvited passenger sat opposite him.

Prince Anatole Romanov.

"Good afternoon, Lord Haimsbury," he spoke in crisply accented English. "Forgive the impertinence, but I thought it prudent to curtail Razarit's temper tantrum. He can be such a noisome child at times."

"Strangely enough, I grow accustomed to these unannounced visitations, but I confess to only mild surprise at finding you capable of such feats, Romanov. This explains much about your effect upon Elizabeth," the marquess replied, wondering now if he'd actually fallen asleep in the coach and all of this were but a dream.

The Russian smiled. "I am no dream," he told Sinclair. "Nor am I a nightmare, though both types of slumberous adventures have the innate capacity to host visitations from beyond. Midsummer is not the only time for such delights, though Shakespeare's play seems to imply it. How does it go now? 'The lunatic, the lover, and the poet are of imagination all compact: one sees more devils than vast hell can hold.'" The prince quoted. "If only that were true. Hell holds an incalculable number of devils and expands itself ever larger to accommodate all that the human world now breeds."

"You would know," the marquess said as the coach passed the gravel turn that led to Henry's Copse.

"Has the duchess ever tell you about the cottage she once visited down that lane?" Romanov asked, pointing towards the road. "It was in a stand of trees, three miles south of the brewery. King Henry the Second is said to have planted the copse himself, but that is only legend. Much has altered since."

"No, she never mentioned it. Why?"

"There is an old Germanic tale of a brother and sister who chanced upon a cottage in such a grove. I believe the most recent version of it is called *Hänsel and Gretel*, but the tale's origin reaches back much further than the Brothers Grimm."

Sinclair sighed. "What has this to do with Beth?"

"This mysterious cottage was constructed of tasty building materials that enticed the children—or so the Grimm's version attests—but in truth, it was nothing of the sort. The house did not tempt children, but was only *visible* to children, or rather to one very special child."

The marquess leaned forward, comprehending. "Are you saying that Elizabeth saw something in that old stand of trees that others did not?"

The prince nodded. "Indeed, so. A house and occupant that appeared only for her eyes. Ask her about it."

"I'm asking you, since you began this. What did she see?"

"Not what, Superintendent. Whom. Whom did she see? It is an important difference. She was but four, and her father had allowed her to disappear from his view. A woodland creature attracted her eye, leading the child into the meadow near the brewery; thence, across a narrow bridge and through a veil of shadow. Beyond it, within the copse, Elizabeth perceived the cottage. Oh, I see that my time is nearly up," he said suddenly, his hand upon the door.

"And my patience is nearly gone! Just what did she see?"

"You must ask Baxter. My time is at an end."

"Why are you here then? To torment me, or to drive me insane?"

"Neither, though, I can see why you might think it is both. I have enjoyed our talk."

Sinclair grasped the angel's hand. "What did she see?"

The prince's face remained serene. "I know that you think me your enemy, Charles, but I wish only for your fondest dreams to come true. It has ever been my goal."

"So you say, but you offer no proof. Rather, it seems to me that all of your kind have but one goal: to terrify my family, but most of all Elizabeth."

"It is a sad consequence of an old plan; one which has now fallen out of favour," the prince replied. "I did not anticipate revealing myself to you so soon, but as Razarit intended to harm you, I had no choice. Or rather, I chose to intervene. A subtle point, but a salient one, as free will goes."

"No word games now?"

"I've no need of them," the prince answered. "You had already guessed that I am far more than human, but you do not yet understand exactly who and *what* I am, so I shall allow you and your circle to continue positing theories. For now, I am permitted to answer one question for you."

Charles wished he were dreaming. "Permission? Such a word is charged with its own questions. From whom did you receive permission? From a more powerful entity? I assume that you, like the creature claiming to be your nephew, are only part human; otherwise, how could you pop in and out of existence so readily? What kind of hybrid are you? Wolf or other?"

"I do love your mind, Charles Robert," Romanov said, his smooth hands on the chased silver grip of the ebony cane. Both the handle and stick bore a series of symbols, which looked completely alien to the detective's eyes. Charles tried to commit a few of them to memory with an idea towards discussing them with Kepelheim.

"You admire my cane? Although your memory is keen and your capabilities are quite extraordinary regarding ciphers, you would fail to decrypt these symbols. They are older than Time. This symbol near the handle, for example, is my name."

"Which name might that be?" Sinclair asked. "Anatole or some other demonic epithet?"

"No, my friend, I am no lowly hybrid. My brethren and I awoke in the earliest days of creation. I shall tell you my full story one day, but for now, ask your question, for our time grows short."

"Whom did Beth see?"

"William Trent in one of his many guises."

"Guises? What do you mean? It is a related question," he argued. "Not an entirely new one."

"So it is," Romanov agreed. "He is much older than you suspect, and he is part human, part demon. Inhabited, you might say."

"Why does he wish to harm Elizabeth? What is his plan for her, and why appear to her when she was only a girl? Her father still lived at that time. Had Trent already begun luring Patricia into his web?"

Romanov laughed, his icy eyes twinkling. "So many questions! Even as a boy, you found ways to break the rules, Charles. I have truly missed our conversations."

"What conversations?"

"No, no. That is an unrelated question, therefore, I cannot answer it. As to Trent, he is a hybrid of human and spirit. He has gained certain capabilities because of this demonic presence, however the familiar spirit within him lacks finesse and true access to the higher planes and powers. If we make comparison according to Darwin's ridiculous theories, then Trent is a bit of slime emerging out of a thick soup of nucleic acids."

"A soup of what? Nucleic acids? What sort of acid is that?"

"Oh, do forgive me. Your science has not yet advanced that far, but you comprehend nonetheless. Sir William Trent is not even his true name. He's had dozens through the centuries. His plans for the duchess began long ago, before she was born, but revealing these to you, at this point in time, defies the limits of the current visit. Although I doubt you'll believe it, I care very deeply for you both. You and the duchess. Now, I must leave you, but before I go, allow me to offer something additional. As you suspect, Trent is involved with the east-end crimes, but he is not their sole perpetrator. He shares these rituals with three others."

Charles started to respond, but the visitor had vanished. Closing his eyes, the detective began to pray softly. "Lord God Almighty, thank you for protecting me. Please, sir, help me to understand why these things are happening to me and to my family. Strengthen my resolve and calm my fears, I beg you. I have no experience that I may draw upon, and I feel utterly out of my depth! I want only to protect Elizabeth and our child," he prayed, his eyes shut. A great sense of dread overwhelmed him, and a shudder ran through his soul. "Our child. What will they do to him?" he moaned, tears spilling down his cheeks.

As this dark foreboding threatened to rob Charles of all hope, he felt a strong hand upon his shoulder. At first, he tensed, assuming Rasha or Anatole had returned, but then a sense of unspeakable, unimaginable calm spread throughout his entire being. He lifted his head and beheld the same man he'd seen near the maze at Branham in October.

The gardener, who'd told him that he mustn't continue to sleep.

"It's you!" Sinclair exclaimed. "But who are you?"

"A friend," he said. "Even before you called, I was dispatched to find you, Charles. One who knows you better than anyone else asks me to remind you of the nail-scarred hands and to tell you this: Trust only in me, Charles. Remember that nothing reaches you that I have not allowed. You are safely cradled within my hand. Though winds may buffet, though the enemy attacks again and again, I am with you always, even when you cannot see me. You abide beneath the shadow of my wings. My truth is your shield and buckler. Fear not the terror by night, nor the arrow that flies by day. The enemy hopes to confuse and frighten you, but their time grows short. These creatures will never truly harm you, for you are mine. Trust only in me." The man's face shone with an inner light beyond any artifice, and his radiant smile caused the marquess to weep. "Do you understand, Charles?"

"I think so," Sinclair answered, wiping at his eyes. "Am I dreaming?"

"You are more awake than any other man upon the earth. Your path will soon lead you into dark byways littered with traps and terrors, but you must continue to follow it. The Lord God Almighty has purposed this pathway for his honour and glory. He exalts you for a reason, which will become clear to you only at the end—at the moment of your passing."

The carriage turned, and one of the wheels hit a deep rut in the road, jarring Charles from his meditation. Realising that his eyes were still shut, he lifted his head, seeing no one, but outside, the wide Branham gates came into view, and the detective wiped tears from his face. Perhaps, he'd seen a vision, but it was from the Creator of the Universe, the Redeemer of all who call upon His name.

"Thank you, my Lord, for allowing me to hear your words; for sending your messenger," he said as the coach passed through the massive stone lions. "You are the Lion of Judah, my King, and I place my faith only in you. And I abide within the shelter of your nail-scarred hands."

CHAPTER NINE

Ida Ross had never been in such a place as this. After a long and fit-
ful night, she awoke at noon. As promised, a young woman named
Katrina Gasparov brought her a breakfast tray and then helped her to
bathe and dress. She arranged Ida's copper-coloured hair into a styl-
ish collection of loose curls at the crown of her head, and then assisted with an assortment of beautiful silk undergarments topped by
a very expensive, blue and cream sleeveless dress and matching day
jacket, trimmed with a high collar that made Ida feel like a queen.

It was mid-afternoon by the time Ross joined the others for tea
in the castle's drawing room. Contessa di Specchio offered a broad
smile as the former prostitute entered the beautifully appointed salon. "Miss Ross, we'd begun to worry that you had, perhaps, decided
to slumber the day through! A sleeping beauty, one might say. Oh,
that dress is quite becoming, and the fit is perfect. The empire style
works well with your slender frame. Anatole's taste is excellent, is it
not? Come, my dear, allow me to introduce you to our other guests."

Ross now noticed that the men in the parlour had all stood as she
entered; a gentlemanly act completely foreign to her, and the small
gesture had a profound effect. She felt important, like a true lady.

"Thank you," she replied nervously. "I'm sorry to be so late in
getting up. I'm not used to the sounds of the house, I guess, and I
had a wakeful night."

"Strange surroundings may prove trying to a sensitive soul,"
a somewhat bent man said as he stepped towards her. "Do not
permit them to disarm you, Miss Ross. We all want you to feel at
home here."

"This is Count Riga," the contessa explained. "He has been with us the longest. The count hails from the Carpathians, but his English has improved much, since his arrival. Has it not, my dear Riga?"

The man's back was hunched, the spine curved slightly to his left side, and he walked with a strange, limping gait, but his manners and smart attire were impeccable. "It suffices," he said simply. His eyes were a peculiar shade of yellowish grey and held a deep sadness, which touched Ross's heart.

"It's a great pleasure to meet you, my lord," she said, reaching out to shake his extended hand. Instead, he lifted her palm to his lips and kissed the soft skin.

"Delighted," he told her brightly.

Ida's cheeks pinked from embarrassment. "I hope you'll forgive me, Count Riga. I'm not much when it comes to gentility. I'm afraid I've spent my whole life serving others—men, I mean."

The count's eyes grew even more sad. "So I understand, my dear, but that life is behind you now. Prince Anatole provides second chances for all who reside within these walls. If I told you the truth of my troubled past, it would shock you indeed, yet here I am: a respected member of a respectable, though somewhat unusual household. Were we a literary work, we might be called a *pastiche*."

The countess laughed. "Ah, yes! Your new word for the day, I should imagine, Count. Ida, Count Riga is our philanthropist. Is that it?"

"Philologist," he corrected. "Philology is a love of words and language. As English is not my native tongue, I endeavour to master its usage through the study of a book I discovered only recently."

Di Specchio tapped Riga on the hand. "Yes, yes, philology. My dear, our friend regales us with a new word from this new book every day. What is it called again, Count?"

"*A New English Dictionary on Historical Principles*," he replied in his heavily accented speech. "It is a series of volumes, based upon materials collected by the British Philological Society. I confess that I find their work quite fascinating, though most of the others here think me rather mundane, if not thoroughly tiresome for doing so."

"Nonsense, Riga! We find your study of these things most stimulating. We all look forward to being enlightened each day by your research. Miss Ross, the count's word yesterday was 'megalomania'. Of course, he referred to this Ripper fiend, and aptly so. Now, my dear, allow me to introduce everyone else."

She drew Ida farther into the enormous room. The muralled ceiling soared overhead by forty feet, and every inch within its wide, coffered beams was covered in intricate brushwork that detailed gold-accented imagery that seemed Biblical to her untrained eyes. The walls were covered in red silk, bearing a subtle pattern featuring the Romanov crest, and many of the furnishings had once adorned the prince's grand palace in St. Petersburg. The chairs and settees were sumptuous and deep-cushioned with carved arms of rich mahogany and varnished in gold-infused lacquer. The windows were heavily draped in damask prints sewn with gold and red threads, and beyond their sparkling panes, Ida could see that the east gardens ended at a pair of enormous iron gates, now shut fast.

"The grounds here are quite beautiful," Riga said. "Beyond those gates, lies the village of Walham Green. And to the east, farther on, is a lovely old cemetery. I like to walk there in the evening. My deformity causes people to mock, you see, and I find comfort in the company of silent sleepers."

"Do be careful, Count," another of the company said. "You may give our newest member the wrong impression."

The contessa laughed. "Miss Ross, this is our Mr. Blinkmire," she said as the man bowed deeply. He was exceedingly tall with a large head and tiny eyes, like that of a pig. As he reached out, Ross noticed six fingers on the hand, but she shook it nonetheless.

"Charmed," the giant said politely. "I understand that the prince rescued you from a socially unacceptable occupation, Miss Ross, but you've no need for concern. Not one of us is without our sins. Mine is one of an ill-designed birth and unwilling subjugation to additional intrusion into my nature. I do not intentionally obfuscate, but there is a long explanation to it, which is better left for the evening hours, I should think. Perhaps, if you wish, I shall provide it tonight. Despite all, I endeavour to rise above it, with the prince's medicinals as my therapeutic aid. As I say, Miss Ross, you are amongst friends and fellow sufferers."

"Thank you, Mr. Blinkmire," she said, though despite his kind words, Ross felt entirely alone.

"And here we have Miss Kilmeade, an Irish lady with her own secrets, though she hasn't revealed them to me," di Specchio explained, referring to a woman with blazing red hair and eyes of a strange, purplish hue. Her skin was garishly white, and her lips plump.

"Do no' let me appearance put ya off, Miss Ross," the woman said cheerfully in a thick Irish brogue. "It's no' catchin'. Jus', I was born with a sensitivity, ya might say. Ta the Lord's own light. Prince Anatole's been workin' with me, though, an' it's a wee bit better. I can e'en go outside for nigh on ten minutes now. Me hair was once white as a lamb, if ya can believe it. Bu' look at it now. And me eyes used ta be bright red like a rat's, bu' they's slowly turnin' a loverly shade o' violet. I'm told tha' afore too much longer they'll be blue as a bluebell, an' I'll be cured. Wha'ever it is that's brought ya here, the prince can mend it."

"Even a broken heart?" Ross asked, suddenly wishing she'd not said it.

"Aye. E'en that."

"That is everyone in our present company," the contessa finished. "That is except for Mr. Stanley, of course, whom I understand you encountered in his *other form* last night."

Blinkmire's piggy eyes squinted rapidly in succession. "Oh dear! Miss Ross, that is most unfortunate!" he worried. "Mr. Stanley is ever so nice when not in *that* form. He will be mortified when he learns how he behaved!"

Di Specchio seemed not to care, shrugging. "Yes, I imagine he will. Miss Ross, won't you join us for tea?"

Ida sat down beside Blinkmire, opposite Kilmeade and Count Riga. The contessa took her own chair, near the fire. "Anatole has asked us not to wait on him. He plans to be away most of the day and possibly part of the evening. I fear there's been a most upsetting crime in the east, which draws him from us. I, too, shall spend part of the evening elsewhere, so I shan't be here for supper. I dine with an old friend," she added mysteriously.

"The countess has many, influential and very interesting friends, Miss Ross," Riga observed as a liveried footman entered and began to pour tea from a beautifully adorned *samovar* of gold and ivory enamel. "You will notice that the tea served here is somewhat different from what you English normally drink," the count explained. "It is sweet and strong, in the Russian style. We add orange peel and even lemon with hints of cinnamon and clove. It is deliciously spicy.

You will find yourself unable to drink the bland English version once you've had this, Miss Ross."

Ross took the ornate, gold-edged teacup from the footman. "Do I add anything? Milk or sugar?"

"Try it first, but wait until it has cooled a little," Blinkmire suggested. "I have a somewhat peculiar, nervous constitution that allows me to drink even the hottest of liquids, but your lips look quite delicate to me. Oh!" he exclaimed. "I do hope that is not forward of me! I meant no offence."

"I took none," she answered with a smile.

"That is kind of you. Sergei?" Blinkmire asked the footman. "Are those carriage wheels I hear?"

The servant turned to look out the heavily curtained windows, and a black coach with gold embellishments upon the doors had just entered the long drive. "As always, your superior hearing outmatches my own, sir. It is Prince Rasha's coach, if I'm not mistaken. I'm sure His Highness was unaware of the prince's intent to call, else my lord would be here to greet him."

Di Specchio rose, casting a sharp look at the perceptive footman. "I shall deal with Grigor," she told Sergei. "If you will excuse me, everyone."

She left the drawing room and closed the pocket doors to prevent anyone else overhearing. Exiting the house, she emerged onto the large portico and waited for the coach to stop. She waved to the driver.

"No, no! There is no need for you to jump down, my good man! I must speak to your master, for he will not be leaving the coach." She opened the carriage door herself and entered, sitting opposite the hybrid prince.

"What are you doing here? You know that Anatole has barred you from this house," she chided him.

"I had Sinclair just where I wanted him, and then that meddling Russian chose to interfere! I shall see him dead for that!"

"What do you mean? Rasha, have you acted unwisely?"

"At least, I have acted. My father spends nearly all his time in France of late. Someone must Careful, my dear," the countess advised. "Time is on your side, but you will never achieve your goals, if you risk your life by baiting Anatole. Remember his office! Only our rituals will weaken his power. Trust in me. Have I ever failed you? Did I not protect you in Milan?"

"I require no protection. Not from anyone, but especially not a woman!"

Her dark eyes smoked with anger. "Season your replies with honey rather than vinegar, Razarit Grigor. You have so much to learn. I have lived a very long life, but not without its dangers. Milan nearly proved your downfall, and you know it to be so. Learn from us. Trent and I have succeeded where others failed, because we have acquired patience and cunning. Let us offer you what wisdom we have gained from centuries of life."

"Trent be damned! What power does another hybrid have that I lack? He is less than I!"

"True. Very true," she said soothingly, "but he has influence in Redwing's round table—for the present. We use him, my dear. The baronet is an instrument that helps to bring your bride to your side. Consider him your court jester, if you wish. Allow his plans to amuse, but remember that he is merely a hireling whom you may dismiss when that usefulness ends."

"And this collection of cattle that my uncle finds so endearing? These misfits? What of them?"

"They will burn when this house burns, as befits failed experiments, but you must tame your temper. Sinclair is close to discovering our truths. Lie low, if you are able to manage it."

"I can manage the lying part," he said with a wink, "but if that means I may not visit my beloved, then I cannot agree."

"Leave the duchess and her cousins to us! Trent and I have lived much longer than you, Razarit. If you dare touch her now, Anatole will kill you."

The prince laughed. "Let him try!"

"He will do it," she warned him. "You are too weak yet to stop him. Go now, and do not come here again, or else your visit will be reported. His servants and his guests are fiercely loyal."

"Unlike you," he said, running a gloved hand across her pale cheek. "It is a trait I admire."

Serena di Specchio would have blushed, had she been fully mortal, but such biological responses had forever been altered, centuries earlier. "As I admire you, my prince. Now, go. I will see you tonight."

She closed the door, and the driver snapped his whip.

Di Specchio turned back towards the house, fear gripping her heart. She played a very dangerous game. Were Anatole to unmask her subterfuge, she would find herself without a friend in the infernal realm—for traitors inevitably betray one another. She hoped Trent's perceived power proved true, but even if it did not, she had her hidden ace: the one with the greatest, oldest power, equal to that of Romanov. Prince Raziel; recently escaped from his stone prison, now free to challenge Anatole's leadership.

Rasha had charms, but Raziel the Ancient, one of the Seven, had power great enough to break the world.

Cornelius Baxter dipped an almond-flavoured biscuit into the bone china teacup, a broad smile colouring his ample cheeks. "My lord, this is a delightful surprise," he said to Sinclair. "Lord Aubrey wired, of course, and forewarned us that you were on your way. Mrs. Alcorn has seen to it that the master apartment is ready, and we've laid in all your favourite foods. Mrs. Stephens has been baking for the past two hours, and there's roast pork with apples for supper."

Charles had been relaxing in the Branham kitchen for a quarter of an hour, and he realised he'd not felt this carefree for many days. "That's very kind of you, Mrs. Stephens," he told the plump cook. "You will spoil me, if you're not careful, and Mr. Kepelheim will have to let out all my new suits."

Myra Stephens clamped the lid onto a pot of stewed chicken, and then took a chair next to Esther Alcorn, the hall's housekeeper. "It's a pleasure, my lord. We didn't get ta see much of ya when you an' Lord Aubrey came back with the little duchess. I reckon you've had a real interestin' month. Do ya like bein' a marquess, sir?"

"I grow more accustomed to it each day, I suppose, Mrs. Stephens, but I still feel like a man with a thirty-four inch waist trying to fill out a pair of forty-two inch trousers."

The cook laughed, as did the others, and Baxter took two more biscuits from a plate near his elbow. "An apt description, my lord, but it always seemed to me that your bearing is that of a peer. There was something quite familiar about your eyes and other facial features, if I may be so bold. The child grown into the man, you might say. I had the honour to meet you several times when you were a boy, and it is a very great pleasure to see you come into your true inheritance at last."

"Honestly, Mr. Baxter, I find it difficult to shake off the modest garb of a policeman, but each day takes me a step closer to complete acceptance. Our little duchess has helped a great deal in that regard, and she is most patient with me."

"Our lady is patient with all of us, sir. As Mrs. Smith mentioned, we had very little time to catch up with you and your cousins when last you visited. Much to our dismay."

"Forgive us for that, Baxter. When we came down from Glasgow, I'd thought our purpose was to spend a week or two doing nothing but relaxing, for we were all of us quite exhausted. However, it immediately became clear that the duchess's many friends throughout the county had other ideas. I've never been to so many dances! It's a good thing my aunt and uncle forced me to learn basic steps, else I'd have embarrassed myself and my fiancée many times. Her tender feet could never bear my untalented prancing about, otherwise. But those many dances kept us away from Branham nearly every night."

Alcorn agreed. "Aye, sir, tis true tha' you and our dear little duchess trod many a ballroom floor, but I'm sure she enjoyed showin' ye off ta all her friends. When word came down to us of your engagement, Mr. Baxter said that the postman would soon bring invitations ta a rash o' balls and the like—but many were hand-delivered, ya know. Alicia started cleanin' all the duchess's gowns right away, so as ta be ready. Bu', if I may, sir, wha' is it brings ya down to us now? And without Duchess Elizabeth?"

"I have need of your counsel," he told her plainly. "Not personal, though that is always welcome, but investigative. We've had another murder in London, and as I examined the scene, my mind kept going back to 1879."

Baxter nodded, looking at the women. "Yes, we'd thought you might eventually wish to speak to us of that, sir. Sir William Trent. Am I right?"

"You are, as always, exactly right, Mr. Baxter. When we visited in October, Mr. Kepelheim and I explored the east wing. Do you remember?"

"How could I forget, my lord? It was here, in this very kitchen, at this very table, where you asked me about that wing, and I shared my experience with you regarding the ghost."

Charles had finished his tea, and Mrs. Smith poured him another cup. "Two sugars and a splash o' milk. Isn't that right, my lord?" she asked. He nodded, and the cook stirred the mixture and handed him the refilled cup. "Those choccy biccies'll be done in half a tick. If I remember right, you've a sweet tooth, sir."

"And so I do! I can smell their delightful aroma even now, Mrs. Smith. I've missed your chocolate biscuits. Mr. Kepelheim will be crushed when I tell him you made them. Yes, Baxter, the ghost. You told Martin and me that you encountered a spirit you thought must be Duke Henry, the little duchess's great-grandfather. Is that right?"

"It is, sir," the butler replied as the cook rose to remove the baked biscuits from the hot oven. "I'll have two when they've cooled, Mrs. Smith. No, make that four," he corrected. "Yes, sir, Duke Henry was a very different sort of person from his son. Duke George was distant and somewhat cool in his emotions, whilst his father was fiery and unpredictable. Richard Henry George Robert Linnhe, 8th Duke of Branham knew no strangers, but as he aged, he became rather reclusive—or so I've been told. The eighth duke was killed the very year I was born, sir. 1827. His son inherited the Branham title when he was, I believe, eighteen. Is that right, Mrs. Alcorn?"

"Seventeen, if memory serves," the housekeeper corrected as she stood to leave the kitchen. "I can make certain of it, if you wish. I gathered up all my old diaries, my lord, in anticipation of your interviews."

Charles laughed. "Am I that obvious? Do you think yourself subject to police interrogation, Mrs. Alcorn?"

The buxom Scotswoman laughed, leaving the table for a few moments. "I do hope I'm not a suspect!" she called from the interior of her office. In minutes, she returned, wearing a pair of reading spectacles and carrying a stack of diaries in her hands. "I'm guilty of nothing more than the odd sweet before bedtime, Superintendent," she added, winking. "Mr. Baxter is a few years my senior, but I also remember Duke George as a youth. I'd entered service as a char, you see, following in my mother's footsteps, who had followed her mother. Both worked their way up from chars to housekeepers, remaining in service until their final days. We moved down from Scotland when I was seven, taking over a sheep farm, not far from the Baxter cottage; just this side of the brewery. It's not far from Parker's Clearing, where that wonderful balloon of Mr. Reid's waited for you and the duchess."

"A day that will live forever in my memory, Mrs. Alcorn," the detective answered with a bright smile.

"And in mine, as well, sir," Baxter said, his brown eyes turning soulful. "Our band of soldiers certainly came up to the mark that day. But as we were saying, the east wing contains many a ghostly presence. Is it because of Sir William that you bring it up, my lord? Do you think him involved with these mad murders in London?"

"I think him behind much of the evil in England," Sinclair replied simply. "Which is why I'd like to see inside his apartment. The one he used whilst married to Patricia. Kepelheim and I weren't able to open the door, so we'd planned to return later, but then everything went rather mad, didn't it? I wonder if I might ask for the key, Mrs. Alcorn? I'd like to examine the contents of those rooms; as a policeman."

Baxter finished his tea and wiped his mouth, gazing fondly at the cooling biscuits. "May I suggest, sir, that it is unwise to journey into that dark domain on your own? Perhaps, it would be best to have accompaniment by one familiar with the surroundings. And one who, unfortunately, knew Sir William whilst he lived here."

"I'd hoped you would suggest that, Baxter!" the detective said happily.

Alcorn stood and returned once more to her office. When she reappeared, she carried a large ring of keys in one hand and a Bible in the other. "Well, let's get started then, gentlemen. If his lordship is to return to London tomorrow morning, then there's a great deal to accomplish in the interval."

Charles bowed. "You are a woman after my own heart, Mrs. Alcorn. Were I not already engaged to be married, I should give serious consideration to courting you. And when we return, we will have Mrs. Smith's chocolate biscuits to nourish our constitutions whilst we make sense of anything we find there."

6:13 pm – Queen Anne House

Elizabeth read through the short letter for the third time, setting it against her lap with a heavy sigh.

"It's no good trying to wish it away, my dear," her aunt noted, handing a pinch of brown bread to her dog. "Not everything in life goes as we like. Our response to disappointments is what defines us."

"Nothing is going as I would like," Elizabeth said. "I'm allowed to sleep away half the day, and now Charles leaves for the night without bothering to explain why he's gone to Branham, saying only that there is information there he lacks. Whatever does he mean by that, Paul?"

The earl had been reading through the press coverage of the lord mayor's procession, glad that every reporter but one had yet to discover the horrors that lay inside Miller's Court. It was Sir Thomas Galton who'd alerted Aubrey to a single column near the back page of *The Star*. A letter to the editor from a man named Dr. Hermann Adler, Deputy Chief Rabbi, who addressed a rising conviction that was currently running rampant throughout the Jewish population of Spitalfields: That the Ripper was, in fact, a *dybbuk*, a type of malevolent spirit thought to have been brought into London as a possessive entity during the massive influx of Jewish immigrants fleeing the Russian pogroms in 1881. Rabbi Adler hoped his letter would calm the fears of Jewish readers through scientific argument, but he also wished to address the mistaken belief that Ripper was, in fact, a man of Jewish heritage.

The earl had never thought the demon who now savaged the women of the east connected to the Jews, but with mention of this dybbuk demon, he began to wonder if a *spiritual* explanation might not draw near to the truth of the matter.

He set down the newspaper and focused his attention on his cousin. "Charles merely wishes to confer with Baxter regarding some of the conversations the two of them had with Kepelheim, Beth. There is nothing dark or mysterious about it. I'm sure he'd planned to speak with our enigmatic Mr. Baxter whilst we were there recently, but the dance floors of Kent County had other plans."

"Do you imply that I encouraged those frivolous plans?" she asked angrily.

"I do no such thing," he assured her, folding the newspaper and hiding it beneath a small pillow. "Tory, your dog will grow fat if you keep feeding him."

"Samson is to be praised for his quick wit," she insisted, breaking a biscuit in half and allowing the terrier to nibble.

"What quick wit is that?" the duchess asked, oblivious to the animal's earlier discovery of a human kidney, buried overnight in the gardens.

Aubrey glared at their aunt. "Tory refers to Samson's persistent barking whenever an intruder nears the house. One apparently tried to enter our backdoor last night. Madam Marchand saw him, in fact, trying to scale the walls. No doubt a reporter hoping to enter and garner an exclusive story from your fiancé, but Marchand was quite overcome by it, poor thing. It seems to have overtaxed her flinty constitution, for I've not seen her all day."

Victoria Stuart huffed in irritation. "That is because that peculiar event has more than overtaxed her, my dear, it has sent Josette packing! My ordinarily taciturn nurse has taken the early train to Dover and left me on my own."

Paul began to laugh, surprising both women. "Then you're the better for it, Aunt! You have no need of a nurse, and though I do not begrudge you a companion, I'm sure you can find one more agreeable than she. Shall I advertise for you?"

"You'll do no such thing. To be frank, I am content to be on my own. Besides, Josette returns to my home, if you must know. I've asked her to report to Dr. Calvet that I am fully mended." Victoria turned to her niece. "Elizabeth, you are far too brusque with your poor cousin. He does not imply that dances are frivolous, nor did he blame the flurry of social invitations on you. Really, you must not take such comments so personally."

The duchess said nothing, choosing instead to re-read Charles's letter:

My Darling,

Forgive the sudden departure. As I write, you sleep soundly, and I've no wish to disturb that much-needed rest; hence, this inadequate letter.

I need to speak to Baxter—in person. Were there an alternative, I would never leave your side, little one. I hope to return Saturday afternoon for our picnic. I shall write this evening to let you know I've arrived safely.

Until I return to your smile, I am less than whole, for you complete me, Elizabeth.

Your Faithful Captain,
Charles

Beth glanced up from the letter, tears brightening her eyes. "What did you say?" she asked Victoria.

"Do pay attention, Elizabeth," the duke's sister admonished, brushing crumbs from her skirts. "All of the strange activities of recent days have left you out of sorts, which is why Paul and I have arranged a distraction."

"Have we?" the earl asked, his mind now returned to sifting through the scene at Miller's Court.

"Of course, we have! A small gathering of friends. I sent word to Maisie Churchill to come by this evening following supper, along with a few others. You suggested it to me earlier, Paul, and I thought it a splendid idea. We shall have light refreshments and play games. Charades, I think was on your cousin's list," she said, looking at Elizabeth. "Maisie's nephew is also coming. Winston is about Della's age and might teach us youthful games unknown to my generation."

"Must we have company tonight?" the duchess asked, massaging her temples with both hands. "Truly, I don't wish to be difficult, Tory. It's just that I'm very worried about Charles."

"Hence the notion of a distraction, Princess. The games will take your mind off those worries," Aubrey replied, moving so that he might sit next to her on the sofa. "In the meantime, why don't you let me take you for a walk 'round the park? The stars begin to emerge, and the rains have subsided. It's actually a lovely evening. The walk will aid in your appetite as well. You hardly eat at all these days."

"That's a very good idea," Victoria added. "My brother won't return with Adele until seven, so a short walk will increase your vigour, my dear. Remember what Dr. Price said, that you should enjoy the outdoors whenever possible."

"I suppose you're right," she answered, thinking of the tiny life growing inside her. *Don't tell Paul*, Sinclair had warned her. *But how can I not? He has been my dearest friend for all my life. He deserves to know.* "If you'll give me a moment or two to change my shoes, I'll take you up on the offer."

He helped her to stand, and then the earl walked Elizabeth to the staircase. "I'm not to allow you to climb or descend on your own," he reminded her. "Charles made me promise. You might grow dizzy."

"I'm not an invalid," she complained. "I'm quite capable, if I take them slowly."

He took her hand. "No, darling, I will not allow you to defy your doctor's orders. Come now, lean upon your old cousin."

Once inside the apartment, she changed into a pair of sturdy boots and added a short, woolen overcoat. The earl again helped her to climb down the winding stairs and then accompanied the duchess out the conservatory doors and into Queen Anne Park.

"You seem more delicate to me, Beth," he said as they walked together along the gravel path, arm in arm. "Is there something I should know? Price keeps visiting you. Darling, are you ill?"

"Of course not," she assured him, wishing she could tell Paul the truth. "What did you and Charles do today? I overheard one of the maids mention that you were in Whitechapel. Was it to do with the murders there?"

"In a way," he replied, trying to find a way to soften the blow. "Another woman was found dead. She might be Ripper, but the evidence is still being collected."

She stopped, her eyes boring into his. "That's why Charles left for Branham, isn't it? It's to do with Ripper, but what can he possibly learn at the hall that he cannot find in London?"

"I'm no policeman, so I'm afraid I cannot answer that to your satisfaction, darling. You'll have to ask your fiancé when he returns."

They had reached a lovely, old knot garden that featured a miniature maze consisting of boxwood interspersed with lavender, barberry, and a variety of colourful herbs. Surrounding this intricate island of formality, stood staggered rows of graceful willows, and beneath these sat three curved ragstone benches. He led her to the central bench and the two cousins sat, holding hands.

"You miss Charles terribly when he's away from you, don't you?" he asked. "I know it tears at him as well, darling. Being parted from you, I mean. He loves you very much."

Without warning, the duchess began to weep, her gloved hands covering her face. Certain he'd said something wrong, the earl drew her into his arms, holding Beth close to comfort her, much as he'd done so many times before. "I'm sorry. I'm so very sorry, Beth. I've made you cry."

"You've nothing to apologise for," she said. "Nothing at all. Paul, it is I should apologise to you! I've been so unfair to you during the past few weeks. In early October, I promised to accept your marriage proposal at Christmas, and I've broken that vow. What sort of woman am I to intentionally hurt such a noble heart as yours? All my life, you have been there for me—consoling me, protecting me, making me laugh in times of great distress; making me feel safe when I'm most fearful. I would never have made it through those years living with Trent without you, Paul. Never! Oh, I am so very sorry for all I've done to you. You must hate me!"

"Of course, I don't hate you. Beth, what's caused this rush of self-recrimination and doubt? Is it the dreams you've been having this past week? This new crime in Whitechapel? Charles's departure? What, darling? Tell me the source of your woes, and I shall slay that dragon, if it lies within my power. I'd do anything for you."

She wiped at her eyes, and he handed her a handkerchief. "You would never understand," she told him. "I'm sorry. Yes, it's probably just the nightmares. Paul, promise me you'll not leave me. Not ever!"

"How could I? Such an act does not lie within my power," he admitted. "I've belonged to you since the day you were born. I shall remain bound to you for all eternity, Princess. Don't you know that?" His words caused her to weep all the more, and he noticed that she shivered. "Perhaps, this walk wasn't a good idea, after all. Are you sure you're not ill? Did Price look in on you this afternoon?"

"He did, and he's pronounced me overwrought," she told him honestly.

"Beth, I have two ears to listen, should you require them. And I can keep secrets, if needed."

She shook her head. *You promised Charles that you would say nothing to Paul*, she reminded herself. "It's only a case of nerves. Walk me indoors, will you? It's grown quite cold."

He helped her to stand, and the two loving cousins walked arm in arm into the conservatory.

Gertrude Trumper watched the pair from one of the oval windows that dotted the perimeter of the fourth storey, which served as attic space and contained the various junctions for the mansion's electrics. She'd gone there to fetch a small mirror, left stored in the main attic cupboards many years before. As the maid left the window, she gazed into the dusty reflection, hoping to find the familiar eyes she'd come to expect, even admire.

He wasn't there.

Sighing, Trumper placed the mirror into her apron pocket. Perhaps, the beautiful man would appear in another silvery surface and explain why he'd instructed her to obtain this rosewood-handled looking glass. Explain why *she'd* been chosen to fulfill his dark commands.

But the reward was worth it. Soon, Gertie believed, he would make her his paramour, and the possessions she now cleaned and polished and pressed, would be as nothing compared to her own.

All would fall down to worship *her*, when Gertrude Trumper became the beloved bride of the *prince to come*.

Esther Alcorn stared at the large circle of brass and iron keys. "I felt certain it was on this ring, my lord," she told the marquess. "I'm sorry ta make ya stand there whilst I plunder through these. It's an old ring, ya know, sir. It belonged to Mrs. Larson before she died and was left ta me when I took over. My that would be almost twelve years ago now! Hold on a minute. It's this one, my lord. I'm sure of it." She inserted a long iron key into the oil-rubbed bronze lock. Whispering a short prayer, Alcorn tried to make it turn. "Well if that doesn't beat all. I'm sure it's the correct key, but it won't budge," she said in dismay.

"Allow me," the marquess offered.

She stepped to one side, and Sinclair placed his hand on the key. To his surprise, it felt oddly warm. "Strange," he muttered, half to himself. "It makes my hand tingle. There it goes," he added as the key clicked from vertical to horizontal.

"Well done, sir," the housekeeper praised as Charles pushed the door open. "Clearly, the key and door recognise you as rightful lord of the manor."

Sinclair shrugged. "Perhaps, but that title is still a week away. It's quite dark inside."

A strong whiff of ancient dust and mould rushed to greet them, and amongst the odours that one often met when unlocking a long-forgotten space, arose another that smelled far different; yet all too familiar to the detective.

The stench of death.

Baxter gently touched the marquess's forearm. "Allow me to lead, my lord, if you don't mind. Mrs. Alcorn, I suggest you follow behind Lord Haimsbury, so that we might protect you should any-thing other than...*ghosts* lurk within."

Esther nearly argued, but instead obeyed, taking the third posi-tion behind the men. "If there are ghosts inside, then we'll need this," she told them, showing the small Bible to the marquess. "Psalm 91 is one of my favourites, sir. I've marked it. If you wish, I can read aloud whilst you men explore."

Charles kissed the intrepid woman's brow. "As always you provide what we men lack, Mrs. Alcorn: a woman's instincts. Yes, please, do read it aloud, softly; and I think Mr. Baxter is correct. If anything resides herein with material capabilities, I'd prefer you remain safely behind us."

"And what about you, my lord?" she asked, opening the Bible to the marked page.

Sinclair drew his grey woolen suitcoat to one side, revealing the everpresent shoulder holster with its gleaming Webley Bulldog companion. "If someone living breathes herein, then he'll soon re-gret it, Mrs. Alcorn. I'm a crack shot. I never miss. Baxter, is there a lighting switch?"

The butler entered first, his heavy footsteps causing the oak floorboards to creak. Suddenly, a mouse darted past, quickly skirting the wide boards of the trimwork along the far wall; its dun colour blending into the murky shadows of the room.

"I shall have to put down traps," the butler sighed. "This wing is not wired with electrics, sir. It was shuttered long ago, but re-opened when Duchess Patricia married the baronet. He insisted on using this apartment, despite its rundown condition. Sir William refused to allow anyone to enter, save those from his own private staff. He had a somewhat ill-mannered young woman who cleaned for him, and I believe that she provided other, uh, *entertainments*. Ah, here we are, sir. I think this small table will offer aid."

The butler opened the centre drawer, withdrew three candles along with a box of matches, and then placed one into the nearest wall sconce. He lit the wick, and instantly the room grew more friendly.

"Much better," Sinclair observed, searching the table for more candles. "Ah, here are several brass chambersticks. Do you need one, Baxter? Alcorn, here is yours," he said, handing her the small lighting source after striking its wick with a match.

"Thank you, sir. It makes it easier to read," she said.

"Thank you, my lord," Baxter replied after he'd placed candles into two other wall sconces and lit each.

The yellow glow of their lamps flickered against the peeling wallpaper, revealing a highway of ancient cobwebs and two rather new constructions, each hosting a fat, black spider. The larger of the two webs held numerous moth parts, an array of dead flies bound up in silk, and a rather energetic wasp, struggling to free itself from the sticky trap.

"Much like the man who once occupied these rooms, the spiders draw helpless prey into their dark realm," Baxter said, using a handkerchief to sweep the largest cobwebs out of the marquess's path. "Step carefully, sir. It seems numerous rodents have left their marks."

"I police in Whitechapel, Mr. Baxter, where numerous dogs and horses leave their marks every day. I'm accustomed to minding my feet. How many rooms are there in this apartment?"

"Six, sir. It was once used as the master by Duke Henry George, who was the little duchess's three times great-grandfather. He was injured quite badly in a fall from his horse during a hunt. The duke remained confined to a bath chair until his death. I believe that he was only forty-seven when he died. Is that right, Mrs. Alcorn? Your head for history is superior to mine."

"Yes, that's correct, Mr. Baxter. Duke Henry George was a fine looking man, my lord," she told the marquess. "There's a portrait of him in the great gallery, astride his favourite horse. I've often thought he looked rather like Duke James, your uncle, my lord. Duke Henry George spent most of his youth in Scotland, in fact, as his mother was the only child of the Earl of Keel. Castle Keel stands in ruins now, but the farmland is still rich and productive. In fact, it provides barley to the Drummond distillery. Keel's not too far from Lord Aubrey's castle, sir. A day's ride east of Inverness, if memory serves. And the earls of Keel were also Stuarts."

"It seems that Scotland is everpresent in our bloodlines, is it not, Mrs. Alcorn?" Sinclair observed; knowing full well that the grand lady of the Branham staff hailed from Glasgow.

"Aye, sir, it is," the housekeeper answered proudly. "My family worked for the Drummonds for six generations, but my father moved here to help young Duke George with his sheep. My old dad was a master herdsman, sir. I'll go back to speaking the psalm now," she whispered, continuing to read softly. "'He shall deliver thee from the snare of the fowler, and from the noisome pestilence. He shall cover thee with his feathers, and under his wings shalt thou trust: his truth shall be thy shield and buckler.'"

Charles turned about, his eyes wide. "Say that last again, will, you, Mrs. Alcorn?"

"The last verse, you mean, sir?" she asked.

"Yes, please."

She complied, holding a candle in her left hand, the book in her right: "'He shall cover thee with his feathers, and under his wings shalt thou trust: his truth shall be thy shield and buckler.'"

"May I?" Sinclair asked, reaching for the Bible. "I know I've read this psalm before, but I'd not realised these very words are contained within. 'Thou shalt not be afraid for the terror by night; nor for the arrow that flieth by day,'" he read out to his companions. "This may sound quite mad, but I heard these very words not an hour ago, whilst sitting inside the Branham coach."

"You *heard* them, sir?" Baxter asked. "Didn't you ride alone?"

"Yes," he answered cryptically, "yet another person quoted this passage to me—by way of offering comfort."

"Is this a riddle, sir? I do no' understand," Alcorn said.

"I'm beginning to," the detective replied. "Of late, living riddles appear all around me and offer conversation. Shadow and light. Evil and good."

"Do you imply that you've seen such spirits, sir?" the butler gasped. "As in my tale of Duke Henry's ghost?"

"I not only imply it, Mr. Baxter, I declare it. Redwing's spiritual members appear when I least expect them; but I am learning not to fear. Those very words—the promises within this psalm—were spoken to me by one of the gentler spirits in answer to prayer."

"Ah, I think I understand, my lord. It is always comforting to hear the Lord's promises, is it not, sir?" Baxter observed as he opened a door that connected with a hallway.

"More than you might imagine," the marquess replied. "Thank you, Mrs. Alcorn. I shall add the 91st Psalm to my nightly reading list. Where does this corridor lead, Baxter?"

"It branches off towards three bedchambers, my lord. Sir William rarely allowed anyone in here, but I entered once, whilst the baronet was away. I'd grown concerned for the little duchess—then called the Marchioness Anjou, of course. I'd feared that she might be inside. Her nurse had reported her missing, you see, and we'd convened a search party. I drew the straw for this wing."

"How often did the duchess enter this area as a girl, Baxter? She's told me some terrifying tales about her adventures inside this house, and some defy belief. However, I would never doubt her word. Not ever."

"Nor should you, sir. The little duchess is brave beyond measure, and that fortitude has taken her into some very dark and treacherous paths, as you have learnt firsthand. But that day, I found her sitting outside the main apartment door, and she appeared quite dazed. The little marchioness said she'd talked with a monster man, and that he'd threatened her."

"A monster man? Wait a moment, Baxter. Did she call him that, or did she say his name was Monstero?"

Baxter blinked, his thick brows pinched together. "I cannot say, sir. The latter may be correct. Was there such a man?"

"The duchess once told me about a gigantic creature whom Trent referred to as Monstero, and this horrid person often visited. Beth said he looked rather like a... *What a fool I am!*" he exclaimed without warning, slapping his forehead so hard that the report rang throughout the enclosed apartment.

"Careful, sir! You'll do yerself a mischief!" Alcorn exclaimed, holding the candle to his face to examine it. "That'll leave a mark for a day or two."

"Then it will remind me to pay more attention to what my fiancée has to say, Mrs. Alcorn. Beth told me that she saw a horrid, shadowy creature on the south lawn of Queen Anne House on Tuesday morning of this week—the same day we attended a rather awful play—but she described this creature as *looking like a spider*. The very same words she used to describe this Monstero person to me last month."

Baxter's eyes widened as he began to understand. "Might this strange creature that my lady saw on Tuesday be the same as the Monstero person who visited Trent ten years ago?"

"Yes! It might very well be, Mr. Baxter. I wonder what sort of demon appears as a spider to a human's eyes?" he asked, passing through the corridor into the first bedchamber. "You needn't answer that, my friend. It is more rhetorical than anything else. Although, Dr. MacPherson may provide a more substantive answer." The marquess crossed to one of three windows. "Baxter, what direction do I now face? North?"

"North of a kind, sir. This wing does not proceed in a direct line from the central portion of the hall. It branches from the original east wing at an acute angle so that it points towards the northeast."

"Wait a moment, Baxter. Did you say that this wing branches from another? There are *two* east wings?"

"In a manner of speaking, sir, yes. The original east wing is used daily by staff and contains three apartments along with a small guest library on the first floor. When looking at the hall from the south, one would see only that magnificent edifice stretching eastward from the centre, however this strange arm was constructed as a sort of 'secret wing', sir. It juts outward from the centre at an angle of forty-five degrees and bisects the original east wing from that of the north."

Charles turned 'round. "It isn't original to the house? When was this wing built then?"

"During Duke Henry's time, sir. Duke Richard Henry, I mean; the one whose persistent ghost haunts these halls. Originally, there was a dower residence connected to this side of the house, extending northwards from the original east wing, but Duke Richard Henry, whom we generally just call Duke Henry, had it torn down and replaced with this hideous structure. Were you to overfly the mansion in Inspector Reid's excellent balloon, you'd find that the basic shape of Branham Hall is somewhat unusual. The original house is rectangular and quite large, with an enclosed courtyard in the centre. The original east and west wings, along with the dower house, were added twenty-five years later by the first duke. The north wing and conservatory were constructed one hundred or so years afterwards by the fourth duke."

"And this curious wing was built by the eighth duke; correct?"

"Correct, sir. That same duke also constructed the wooden maze, which we call the very peculiar stairs that you and Mr. Kepelheim traversed to get here during your first visit, and which we so mercifully were able to avoid this time 'round. Per Duke James's orders, I had the bars removed to this wing on Saturday last; thus we were able to enter by way of a much less stressful route today."

Charles gazed through the mullioned windows, noticing now that they overlooked a small circle, made entirely of stone. "What is that?"

Baxter joined the detective at the window. "Ah, yes, well, that is the stone ring, sir. There is an old legend regarding the ring that links it to a labyrinth beneath the current maze."

"You know about that?" Sinclair asked. "Powers, the Chief Gardener, mentioned that to me last month. How is this ring connected?"

"I cannot say, sir, but if you'll notice the two bluish stones, there on the end, farthest from our view? They predate the hall. In fact, it's said they were here long before Christ walked the earth. These two form a narrow doorway that encloses the rising of the sun, each summer on the solstice. It is a pagan structure, to be sure, and the duchess has no love for it, sir. It was she who told me that the ring connects to the tunnel maze. I'm not certain that my lady understands the entire layout of the underground system, but I recall her mentioning last year that she would like both the ring and the blue stones torn down."

"I agree with her, as it is clearly a pagan site. We'll see that it is razed once the weather warms again. I wonder, might that be why this wing was erected at such a strange angle? See there, Baxter. The blue stones appear to align with the direction of this very wing. Might this wing also track with the rising of the midsummer sun?"

Both the butler and housekeeper peered out the window at the stones. Alcorn gasped. "Never did I consider that before, sir! My goodness! It gives me the shudders to think that this entire wing may have been built for a dark purpose!"

"Well said, Mrs. Alcorn," Baxter replied.

"Trent must have known all about these structures," Sinclair added as he turned from the disturbing view. "This house has many dark secrets. I'd see this entire hideous wing razed along with that ring."

Sinclair turned to examine the rest of the room. A large bed occupied a long wall, its posts carved with hideous imagery that seemed unholy to the marquess's eyes. "Is it the light, or do these carvings look demonic?"

Alcorn bent closer and gasped. "They look like writhing creatures," she whispered. "Lord above save us from such hellish strange things! I've never seen this room before, my lord, and I'm glad of it. I wonder if tha' awful man brought this bed with him."

"I'd say he probably did," the detective answered.

An oak desk sat opposite the bed beneath the centre window, and Charles opened the only drawer. Inside, he found a shallow box, which he removed and set upon the bed. The rosewood container was hinged with a keyed hasp of brass, which bore the scratch marks of repeated use. "I don't suppose we know where the key might be for this?"

The butler took the casket and examined it in the candle's faint light. "It isn't the sturdiest construction," he said, shaking it. "I hear nothing breakable inside, sir. May I?"

Charles smiled. "Allow me, Mr. Baxter." The marquess took the mysterious box in both hands and threw it to the floorboards. The hasp sprang open. Sinclair picked it up once more and set it upon the bed.

"Photographs," he said as he sifted through many dozens of images. "All are of Beth as a girl; perhaps five, six? Does either of you recall these?"

The housekeeper took one of the photos, which showed Beth on a small pony. She wore dark trousers and boots, and her eyes squinted as though looking directly into the sun. "I remember that day. My lady was not yet four when this one was taken, sir. That's

Crispin, her first pony. And that's Lord Kesson, proudly holdin' the reins. What a lovely man he was."

Charles smiled, thoughtfully. "I wish I could have met Beth's father. Elizabeth inherited the Stuart eyes and hair." He turned one over, looking for signs of a hallmark. "Dryden Photographic Portraiture, London," he read aloud. "It's dated April, 1872. It looks as if all these are of Beth, in fact. Taken at various moments in her childhood. Trent mentioned that he had such a collection of photographs. I've no doubt that he left them here for me to find."

"You spoke to him, sir? Does this means he's in prison?" Alcorn asked, hopefully.

"Sadly, he is not," Sinclair answered. He paused for a moment. "Mr. Baxter, do you recall the night we returned here from Scotland? The twenty-fourth of October."

"Certainly, my lord. Twas an exciting day for all of us at the hall, when your company arrived back safely. Why do you ask, sir?"

"That first night was spent relaxing before the fire in the main drawing room. The very same room where Lord Aubrey lay near death, actually, but that night was filled with life and laughter, rather than worry and fear. As we enjoyed Mrs. Stephens's refreshments, Elizabeth shared hundreds of photographs with us, from various moments of her life—most of them taken by her father. I saw none with this hallmark upon them. None." Charles paused, shutting his eyes as though weighing his thoughts. "Baxter, I know that you and Alcorn loved the late duchess, but I'm afraid I have some very troubling news for you. It pertains to an unposted letter I discovered in Connor Stuart's bedroom whilst at the castle. It was written to Patricia, and its contents revealed that she was less than faithful to my cousin."

Baxter took a deep breath. "Shall I, Mrs. Alcorn?"

The housekeeper shut the Bible. "Perhaps, this would be a good time to return to the kitchen and tuck into those biscuits, Mr. Baxter."

"Yes, I believe you are right, Mrs. Alcorn. Shall we, sir?"

"Certainly. I've seen enough for now, but I want to come back here when the duchess and I return at Christmas."

Alcorn followed alongside the butler. "Mr. Baxter, as the marquess will no doubt have more questions, perhaps, you might see if there's a cask of *Danflou* in the cellars—with your permission, my lord," she said, looking to Sinclair.

"Why ask me? The cellar and its contents belong to my fian-cée," he said as the trio left the apartment.

Baxter blew out the sconce candles and then locked the primary door before handing the key to Alcorn. "I'll bring up those vermin traps tomorrow," he muttered to himself, his mind on the mice. "My lord, all the wines and other spirits will become yours in just over a week's time. As my lady's husband, you will have control of the entire Branham estate."

"Not true, Baxter. The laws have changed regarding husband's rights," he said as they headed towards the double doors that sepa-rated the strangely angled wing from the main portion of the man-sion. "*The Married Women's Act of 1882* changed all that. No longer does a woman lose her legal identity when she marries. A wife now retains control of her property, though some husbands willfully ne-glect that law."

"So I understand, sir, but the little duchess spoke to Alcorn and myself before departing for London last Sunday. She insists that all on staff consider you the new lord of the manor. As such, the cellars are in your control."

"Really?" he asked, his dark brows rising high. "Then, I think we should make sure the *Danflou* has not soured, don't you, Mr. Baxter? And whilst we wait for the decanting process to accomplish its good work, we'll finish examining Trent's box of secrets."

CHAPTER TEN
9:26 pm - Queen Anne House

"Shall we play telephone?" Delia Wychwright asked as she nibbled on a watercress sandwich.

The Cartringham ladies, accompanied by Lord Cartringham and Delia's parents, Baron and Baroness Wychwright, had arrived at half past eight. As promised by Victoria Stuart, Maisie Churchill, a widow of ten years, had brought along her great-nephew Winston, whose parents were out of the country visiting Lady Randolph Spencer-Churchill's father, American financier Leonard Jerome, in New York.

"What is telephone?" young Winston asked. "Is it like Dr. Bell's device?"

Delia Wychwright set down the remains of the small sandwich and daintily wiped her hands on a lace-trimmed, linen serviette. "I'm not sure," she admitted, for Delia cared little for inventions and science, "but it's rather fun, if not entirely scandalous! Everyone's playing it in the city; or so, I'm told. My friend Tamsin Callgerton taught me how to play it last weekend whilst we were at her cousin's home in Kent. Lord Aubrey, you and your family were in Kent at that same time, I'm told. Pity we couldn't have gotten together."

Lady Cartringham cast her cousin a sharp look. "Just what is this game, Cordelia Jane?" she asked, using the girl's full name as a reminder to behave more like a lady.

Ignoring the subtle remonstrance, the determined ingénue leaned towards the younger members of their company. "It's also called Lover's Line, you know, which is probably why my cousin is rather annoyed at my suggesting it," she whispered, causing Adele to burst into laughter.

"Lover's Line!" the younger girl exclaimed, looking at her brother. "Oh, I know all about that game, and I'd already arranged for us to play it. I told Paul about it—or at least, I think I did. Did I tell you, brother mine?"

The earl sat beside Elizabeth on a very small settee, which allowed no room for Delia Wychwright, who had done her best to move ever closer to his side. "Did you?" he asked. "If so, then I'm far too old and ignorant to have remembered it. And aren't you all a bit young to be playing a game called 'Lover's Line', Della?"

Wychwright objected. "Not at all, Lord Aubrey! It is never too early for a young maiden to learn the ways of romance and all its lovely mysteries. Juliet wed her Romeo at thirteen."

Winston shrugged at this. "I'm not sure that exemplar supports your argument, Lady Cordelia. Juliet's marriage ended rather badly. Aren't there any other games we could play, Lord Aubrey? A board game like *Hare and Hounds? Fox and Geese? Mansion of Happiness?* Why not a game of chess? I'm quite good at that, you know. This telephone game sounds quite dull to me."

The twelve-year-old's Great Aunt Maisie had been going through last minute details for the upcoming wedding with Victoria Stuart, and she looked up over her gold spectacles. "I imagine you will find such a game *very* interesting one day, Winny. However, if you don't wish to play with the girls, then perhaps you could help us decide where to place our guests at table. We've five hundred to seat and many of the men are currently at loggerheads in Parliament. It's a bit of a game in itself."

Master Spencer-Churchill shook his head, the light-coloured locks shining in the chandelier's glow. "That doesn't sound fun at all, Auntie," he objected. "I should prefer the company of girls to making long lists of boring old party details."

Aubrey laughed. "The company of girls will have great allure for you one day, Winston. If you're interested in learning about politics, perhaps you could accompany me to Egypt or even Bolivia, when you're older."

The young nobleman stood. "I should very much like to explore Africa with you, Lord Aubrey. My mother says there are people living there who haven't the foggiest idea where England is. I'd like to tell them."

"Then you shall," the earl promised. "Della, as you're an expert, tell us how to play this game. To start, why is it called by two names?"

Delia Wychwright interrupted. "I suppose its name depends on who refers to the game, Paul," she said, instantly wishing she'd not used his Christian name, for her cousin Margaret shot her an angry glance. "Do forgive me. I meant Lord Aubrey, of course."

Stuart squeezed Elizabeth's hand, and she leaned her head against his shoulder. "Darling, shall we play this game?" he asked her.

Beth smiled brightly. Despite her fears for Sinclair, the unabashed exuberance of youth inside the mansion brought colour to her pale cheeks and lightened her heart. "I think we must," she told him. "How do we play, Della? What are the rules?"

The earl's daughter—raised as his sister—picked up a sheet of linen paper and began to sketch a simple diagram. "It's like this," she explained. "On each end of a line is a tin can. I'd hoped we'd play, and I asked Mrs. Smith to wash out two of sufficient size for our use. Oh, and dear Mr. Frame filed down the edges to make sure there is nothing sharp, and he's punched a hole in each with his awl. Very clever, our Mr. Frame. He was also quite obliging, as he even volunteered to attach the string for me."

"Quite obliging," the earl agreed, winking at the duchess.

Della showed the diagram to her brother. "It's very simple, actually. A cotton string connects the two cans, and each person holds one end of the device to his ear or mouth. One person talks whilst the other listens."

"Very scientific," the duchess observed. "And then what? Is that the entire game?"

"Oh no!" Cordelia Wychwright interrupted once more, brazenly sitting upon the arm of the settee to be close to Aubrey. "Then the fun begins. The speaker writes down a phrase. It could be the title of a book, line from a poem, whatever he likes, and then hands it to the judge. The listener must leave the room, taking the other end of the Lover's Line, or telephone, with her—or him, of course," she added, smiling coquettishly at Aubrey. "The speaker must convey the phrase to the listener to achieve a score, starting in a whisper and speaking more loudly with each attempt. After four tries, a judge calls time, and the listener is brought back into the room by the conductor. She or he—the listener, I mean—is then asked to tell everyone what he or she heard. If the answer is correct, points are awarded. Ten for the whisper, five for the next loudest try, then two and half, and only one point, if heard on the fourth attempt. The judge has the final say, if arbitration is required. At the end of the game, the tallies for the couples are made. The overall winner gets a prize."

"What prize is that?" the earl asked, dreading the response.

Adele laughed. "It's a kiss, silly! That's why it's called Lover's Line, dearest brother! The winner may ask for a kiss from anyone he or she wishes. Of course, the person doing the kissing is usually the one on the other end of the line. It's quite fun. We played it at Violet Aiken's home last June."

"Did you, indeed? I really should spend more time at home," the earl said. "Very well, then. Let's play. Do we draw lots to choose up our teams?"

"No, you pick a number 'twixt one and one hundred. You write it down, and whoever comes closest to your number is your partner."

"No nought?" he asked, teasingly.

Lady Adele glared at her brother. "No. There is no nought. It is not a true number, but a placeholder. Ask Cousin Charles. Do you plan to play by the rules or not, brother mine?"

"I do. Forgive me, sister mine. Give us a scrap of paper and a pencil. The duchess and I shall choose our numbers."

"But you mustn't peek," Cordelia warned him. "You must play by the rules, if you're to win your kiss, Lord Aubrey. And be sure to write your name on the paper, so we may know who our partner's to be."

Victoria Stuart bit her lower lip to keep from laughing, and even Samson the dog seemed to have trouble ignoring Wychwright's overt flirtations. He'd started circling the audacious guest, growling now and then, pawing at her skirts and standing on his hind legs in an effort to gain her attention.

"Samson, come!" Victoria called, causing the animal to rush back to her side. "James, are you playing?" she asked her brother.

Drummond sat near Martin Kepelheim, and the two men had been commenting on the lord mayor's procession, intentionally avoiding all talk about the latest Ripper murder. "I think I'm a bit too old for parlour games, Tory. Perhaps you should play."

"I prefer making boring old lists of party guests," she teased, glancing at Winston.

Beth and Paul scribbled their numbers, as did most everyone else in the room. Even Sir Thomas Galton and Malcolm Risling joined in the play. Both circle members sat near the duke's chair, their numbers in hand.

Adele folded her choice and then glanced up. "Has everyone finished? You should all have a number written on your paper that lies 'twixt one and a hundred. No noughts," she added, her blue eyes fixed on her brother's face.

Wychwright raised her hand. "Who will act as judge?"

The duke volunteered. "Martin and I shall serve as empanelled judges. Will that serve your needs, Lady Adele?"

"It serves quite well," the youngest Stuart answered, bobbing up from her chair and collecting everyone's paper. "Here, Uncle James. You read them out."

The duke passed the papers to Kepelheim. "My fellow judge has younger eyes than mine. He'll have the honour."

The tailor took the basket of numbered slips. "Oh, my, such a responsibility! Lord Haimsbury will be very sorry that he's missed all the fun. Very well. I shan't delay longer. The first name is our young Harrow student. Master Winston has chosen the number twenty-one. A fine choice, I think. Here, Your Grace," he told the duke, handing him a clean sheet of cream paper and a pencil. "You keep the list as I read it out."

"A fine job for me," Drummond jibed. "Winny, you're twenty-one. Next."

"Delia has given us forty-nine. Seven squared. Another fine number," Martin continued. "Let's see now, who is next? Lady Cartringham has written the number nought. Very droll, my dear," he told the countess. "I wonder, does this mean you won't be allowed to play?"

"I do hope so," the countess admitted with a smile.

"We'll see how our judge decides," Martin replied, grinning. "Lord Aubrey has given us the number fifty-two," he continued. "Quite close to Lady Cordelia's, isn't it?"

Wychwright could scarcely contain her enthusiasm, and she reached absentmindedly for a chocolate *petit fours* filled with thin layers of raspberry jam.

"Adele Marie is next," Kepelheim continued. "Our lovely Scottish lady has chosen twenty-six. Quite close to Master Winston. Well done, my dear. Sir Thomas has given us forty-seven. Lady Cordelia, you may be showing our handsome baronet how to play the game," Kepelheim told her, much to Wychwright's dismay. "Now, Lord Malcolm is our next contender, and Pembury's dear son has chosen thirty-nine. Baron Wychwright gives us a very reasonable number. Ten. Sensible and to the point. His dear wife, Baroness Wychwright gives us ninety-four. Rather a large disparity there, it seems, but perhaps it is to be expected from two such enlightened individuals."

The duke laughed. "Baron, does your good lady also dispute your opinions with regard to Parliament?"

"Only the bad ones," Wychwright answered amiably, taking a sip of whisky. "Good this, Duke. Might there be any more about?"

"We'll get the youngsters started with their game, and then you and I shall nip off to my granddaughter's cellars and see if we might find some."

"You must take this seriously, Uncle James," Adele chided. "You are the head judge, and you must set the example. There's only Beth left, and then, you must tell us our assignments."

The tailor opened the final slip of paper, offering the duchess a knowing smile. "It seems that we have saved the best until last. Our beautiful hostess has chosen the number... Well, this is quite extraordinary! The duchess has written fifty-two. The very same number as the earl. Blood will always tell, I suppose."

Aubrey sighed in relief, looking at Elizabeth. "I suppose it will," he said, smiling. "All right, then, Della. Who goes first?"

Cordelia Wychwright fought back tears as she reached for the last of the chocolate ganache *petit fours* cakes. "Are we playing elimination?" she asked suddenly. "If a partnership fails to score any points, then each member must be reassigned."

Adele looked at their guest, her light blue eyes round. "I don't recall that rule."

"It is new," Delia replied quickly, for she'd only just invented it. "I suppose the earl and duchess should get us started. Where is the telephone?"

Della had hidden the device in a willow sewing basket, set behind the drawing room door, and she now retrieved it. She handed one end to her brother. "Will you speak or listen?" she asked.

"I'll do whichever Beth wishes."

"I shall listen," the duchess told the assembled players. "Does the earl write down the message?"

"Yes, but only after you leave the room," Della explained seriously. "The telephone has plenty of line. I think Mr. Frame said we have three hundred feet, so you should be able to go across to the morning room, or even the library. Be careful when walking with it, Cousin Beth. Keep the string wrapped about the little dowel as you go; else it will knot."

"Rather like a kite string," Beth said, kissing Della as she took the string and second tin can. "All right, I'm on my way. Paul, do speak clearly. We wouldn't want to lose now, would we?" she asked him, offering a conspiratorial smile.

"Absolutely not!" the earl replied honestly. He took a bit of paper from his sister and quickly wrote down four words: *I love you, Princess*; and then without allowing anyone else to see it, he handed the short message to the duke. "Where am I to stand?" he asked Adele.

"You must remain in here," she declared. "That way, we are certain you do not cheat."

"Would I do such a thing?" he asked, his dimples deepening within the dark beard as he smiled. The string grew ever more taut as the duchess moved farther and farther along the foyer, towards the rear of the great mansion. Eventually, it grew quite tight, and Adele glanced into the foyer to make sure the duchess was nowhere in sight.

"I think we're all ready," she told him. "I'll act as conductor. Brother mine, you must speak softly at first, and you may get louder each time you speak, but you have only four chances to make Cousin Beth hear you. I'll stand in the foyer and let her know that you're about to speak."

"Sounds simple enough," he said.

Adele shouted in the direction of the library doors. "Cousin Beth, are you ready?"

The duchess called in return, her voice sounding very far away. "Ready!"

"Go!" Della exclaimed.

Paul wished now that he'd used a less intimate phrase, but there was no altering it, so he whispered, "I love you, Princess."

Della called to Beth. "Did you hear it?"

"I'm afraid not!" the duchess called in return.

Paul sighed, knowing Delia Wychwright would inevitably overhear. Why should that bother him? He had no interest in the impetuous ingénue, but neither did he wish to hurt her. "I love you, Princess," he said again, a trifle louder.

"Cousin Beth, did you hear it this time?"

"I may have," the duchess answered. "I'm not sure. Might I hear it once more?"

Inside the library, Elizabeth held the tin can to her right ear. The second attempt had brought a mysterious buzzing through the line, and she thought she could discern Paul's distinctive voice telling her that he loved her. Surely, he'd not use such personal words in mixed company.

She wondered which would bother her more—hearing him speak the words before their guests, or realising she'd been wrong, and that he'd not said them at all.

"Cousin Beth, it's the third try now!" Della called.

The line buzzed again, and Elizabeth heard the words more clearly. "I love you, Princess," the earl told her. She felt tears slide down her face, and she was about to let Adele know that she'd heard the words, but before she could speak, the line buzzed once more; this time the voice much louder. *"Does he love you, Princess? Then, why do you lie to him? Poor faithful Aubrey! Like a lapdog without his mistress!"*

Beth dropped the can, and it hit the uncarpeted portion of the mahogany floorboards, denting the side. From the hallway, Adele noticed the line fall, so she dashed back to the drawing room and told her brother, "I think she's moved. Don't speak yet."

The eleven-year-old followed the line through the long corridor and found that it dipped beneath the closed library doors. Opening one door, Adele found the room dark. Not even the fire was lit; a strange thing, for it had been burning brightly only an hour earlier.

The duchess lay upon the hardwood, her eyes shut. Della bent down and touched her face. "Cousin Beth? Did you faint again?"

Elizabeth did not respond. Her skin felt like ice. "Paul! Uncle James! Hurry!"

The earl reached the room first and knelt beside her, wishing he'd never admitted his feelings. "Beth, are you all right?" he asked, touching her hand. "What happened to the fire and all the lights?" he asked as he lifted her to a sitting position. "Beth, open your eyes."

Her eyelashes fluttered, and the lids slowly parted. "What happened?" she asked. "Did I faint again?"

"Yes," he told her. "Can you stand?"

She nodded, and the earl eased the duchess onto her feet.

Delia Wychwright had reached the open doorway. "Did she guess it?" the interloper asked, seemingly unmoved by her hostess's condition.

Elizabeth managed a slight smile, determined not to reveal her fears. "I think so," she said, leaning into the earl's strong embrace. "I love you, too, Lord Aubrey."

He held her close, relieved that she seemed unharmed. "It's an old phrase, I know, darling, but one I shall never stop saying," he whispered. "Come now. You and I shall resign from competition and allow the younger generation to continue whilst you rest."

Cordelia watched carefully, noting with dismay that the earl's affections for the duchess showed no hint of diminishing. If anything, they seemed to have intensified. "If only Lord Haimsbury were here," she said aloud. "I expect that he'd be very good at this game."

"Do forgive me, everyone," Elizabeth said as Paul helped her to the settee. "I should have eaten more at supper. Paul, would you ring and ask Miles to bring me a pot of tea?"

"I'll do it," Adele offered, returning to the foyer to find a footman.

The duke knelt beside her, taking her hands in his. "Maybe this gathering wasn't such a good idea, Princess. Why don't you let your old grandpa take you upstairs? Your fiancé would insist you retire, if you're too weary to keep on your feet."

"A cup of tea will revive me, Grandfather. I'd like to stay."

The duke kissed her cheek. He assumed that the child she now carried might be causing the physical weakness, but he also recognised worry in his granddaughter's eyes. "Charles will be fine, Beth. He's probably enjoying a long talk with our Mr. Baxter. You know how much those two enjoy each other's company. I imagine you're right about supper. You scarcely ate a bite. If you don't find any of the finger sandwiches appetising, I could see if Mrs. Smith might make you a cup of cocoa. You used to love that as a girl."

She brightened at the suggestion. "Yes, I think that might be better than tea."

Delia had decided to use a different tack with regards to catching the handsome earl's eye, so she turned to Galton in an effort to evoke jealousy. "Shall we go next, Sir Thomas?"

The earl's first lieutenant for circle matters bowed, extending his hand. "I'd be honoured, Lady Cordelia. Shall I speak, or do you prefer to do so?"

"I think I shall also take the line into the library and see what secret message you might wish to convey to me, dear Sir Thomas. Remember now, that it is called Lover's Line for a reason."

Galton actually blushed. "I shall endeavour to comply," he said haltingly.

Baron Wychwright huffed in irritation, turning a page in his newspaper. "Delia, do show a bit of common sense. Not everyone here knows what a jester you are. Forgive my daughter, Sir Thomas. She assumes everyone understands her perverse sense of humour."

The baroness said nothing, for she'd instructed her daughter to pursue the earl aggressively—no matter what it might take. A marriage with the influential Stuart clan could only enhance their family's position in society, particularly now that the earl's cousin was marrying the duchess. As Lady Aubrey, Cordelia would usher their family into high-peerage circles, a mere stepping stone away from the queen, herself!

"I hope I've not embarrassed you, Sir Thomas. Twas not my intent," Cordelia whispered, feigning shyness. "I can be rather too forward at times. A fault of my generation, I suppose."

Galton bowed gallantly. "I find it refreshing," he told her, as he scribbled a message across a bit of paper and handed it to the tailor. "I shall do my best to help us win."

The baron's daughter giggled and then left the room, taking her end of the 'telephone' into the library. Acting once more as conductor, Adele made sure the doors closed. "I think we're ready, Sir Thomas."

Galton took a deep breath and then whispered softly, "Women may fall, when there's no strength in men," he quoted, glancing at the earl, who instantly recognised the line, for they often quoted it at circle meetings.

Aubrey smiled. "Act II, scene iii."

"As we all know," Galton replied. "Too much, you think?"

Risling laughed, and the duke also joined in the merriment, winking at Kepelheim. "Do forgive us, Baron," Drummond said to Wychwright. "'Tis a line that's meaningful to our family."

"Act II, scene iii of what?" the plump baroness asked, reaching for a plum-filled *petit fours* just as a footman entered bearing two silver servers, one of tea and another of cocoa.

"*Romeo and Juliet*," Aubrey answered. "Thank you, Lester. Which is cocoa?"

"The smaller one, sir. Cook thought the others might appreciate tea as well. Shall I pour?"

Beth nodded. "Please."

"I'll do it, Lester," Aubrey insisted. "You pour for the others. Baroness, do not mistake our intent," he continued as he added the warm chocolate to a red and yellow teacup. "We gentlemen do not imagine ourselves in any way superior to the fairer sex. Rather we consider ourselves your lifelong servants," he finished, his eyes fixed upon the duchess. "Lifelong."

He intended to return the silver pot to the tray, but as Beth took the cup, Paul appeared to lose his balance and fell against Beth's arm, spilling the pot's contents across the settee and causing her to drop the cup, sending cocoa flying into her lap and onto the thick carpet.

As a consequence, the entire room stood at once, becoming a whirl of commotion, causing the terrier to bark furiously. Strangely, its attentions were focused not on the scene near the settee, but rather on the open doorway. As the humans in the room huddled near the duchess, Samson raced into the foyer, chasing an unseen adversary to the front door, barking and biting at the air.

"Oh, Beth, I am sorry!" Aubrey exclaimed, righting himself and using a serviette to clean chocolate from her skirt. "I've ruined your beautiful dress."

The footman calmly intervened, taking the pot from the earl's hand and offering a small towel, which he'd brought on the tray. Kepelheim removed several soaked newspapers left in the vicinity, whilst Victoria and Maisie lifted Elizabeth to her feet. "You should change at once," the elder Stuart told her niece. "Alicia will want to soak your dress in cold water right away. Chocolate leaves such stains."

Samson returned at this point, apparently satisfied that he'd accomplished his task and scampered over to the carpet, greedily licking up the sweet drink.

"That isn't yours!" Victoria scolded the dog. "You'll need another bath. First mud, now cocoa! Paul, do stop cleaning and take Beth upstairs, won't you?"

"Yes, of course. You're right. I am sorry, Beth. Really. It's all my fault. I'll replace your gown with a new one."

"It's fine, Paul," she said, her eyes on the dog to keep from stepping on him. "I could change and then return, if you think that's all right."

"I think Charles would want you to rest, dear. Come with me," he said, putting an arm 'round her shoulders. "It seems you and I are far too weary for company. A night's rest will soon set us both to rights."

"Very well," she sighed. "Goodnight, everyone. I hope you'll continue to play. Victoria, it might be best to move everyone to the yellow drawing room. I apologise for causing such a mess."

"Nonsense," the earl objected. "'Twas I who fell; not you, Princess. Goodnight, all. Thomas, I'll see you tomorrow morning. Easy now," he whispered sweetly to Beth. "Shall I carry you?"

"No, I can walk," the duchess insisted. "Did you see him?" she asked, glancing back towards the front door.

"See whom?"

"The man, who... Oh, never mind. No one."

"You're already half asleep. Here now. Arms 'round my neck," he told her, lifting her into his arms. "You're far too weary to climb."

Delia Wychwright emerged into the foyer just in time to see the couple disappear into the recesses of the west wing corridor. *I wonder how much Lord Haimsbury knows about his cousins' behaviour,* she thought to herself. *Perhaps, someone should tell him.*

High overhead, perched upon the slate-roofed cupola of Haimsbury stables, a being materialised into a realm the fallen often referred to as 'sen-sen'. No sooner had he appeared than a second emerged through the aether, his form fiery; and he struck the first creature with a bolt of flame, nearly causing him to fall.

"Fool!" the second one shouted. "How often must I warn you, Rasha? Your abilities may grant you powers in the human world, but they have addled what few wits you once had!"

The hybrid prince steadied himself by grasping the copper weathervane. "It was only a small joke," he argued, rubbing his jaw. "The earl is overconfident and proud. I thought to humble him a little."

"Liar!" Anatole Romanov exclaimed angrily, his eyes twin flames. "The only reason you live is because I was able to intervene. Had the duchess consumed that beverage, her child would be at risk."

"Really? I know nothing of that, Uncle. I thought only to help her sleep. Her dreams keep her awake at night. Is not rest important to the nourishment of the child?"

Samael grew large, overshadowing the hybrid as a man overshadows an ant. "The duchess and her child are *not* to be touched! Never! This is your final warning, Rasha. You may have avoided punishment in Milan, but my patience is at an end. Neither di Specchio's pleas nor Raziel's wings can shelter you from my arrows, Razarit. They bear bitter poison, and no alteration to your human cells is enough to save you from their bite! I allow you to live for one reason only: because you are useful. For now. If you *ever* enter that house again, I shall strip your hybrid flesh from your bones and dip your skinless carcass in boiling oil!"

An imp who served Anatole appeared near the cupola—his wings tucked, head bowed in subservience. "You called, Lord Samael?" he asked.

"Yes, Bí-za-za, I did. Escort this fool of a hybrid back to his home in the human realm. And when you have accomplished that task, return to me. I've another assignment for you." He then addressed Razarit. "Think yourself a prince, do you? I keep watch upon you. Never forget that. I know all about your works with that young maid."

"What works are those?"

"Silence! Remember, that you live only at my pleasure. The Trumper girl is vulnerable and weak, but she is still a daughter of Eve."

"Which means she has free will," the human dared to argue. "Tempting her is permitted; as you know quite well. Your pretense at honour shows cracks, Uncle."

"Do not call me that! Raziel may claim you as son, but he does so only to appeal to your pride. Nothing more. Once your usefulness to my brother's plan is done, he will toss you into the destroying winds like so much chaff."

Razarit paused, considering this revelation. "No. You are wrong."

"Time will prove me right. Now go!"

The imp touched Rasha, and the two popped out of sight. Samael slowly grew smaller, until at last his form resumed that of Anatole Romanov. Deciding that the duchess remained in danger, he emerged into the human realm, concealing himself in the guise of a barn owl and flew to a tree near her bedchamber window.

He remained there for many hours, watching.

Inside the house, Paul Stuart helped his cousin into the bedchamber and set her upon the sofa, which had been returned to the fireplace. "Tory's right about that dress, Beth. I'll ring for Alicia, so she can place it in cold water."

"Stay with me, won't you?" she begged, stepping into the connected bath. "You needn't ring for Alicia yet. I can manage, as it buttons in the front. It won't take me more than a minute to change. I'd like to talk, if you don't mind."

"If it allows me respite from Lady Cordelia's persistent flirtation, then I'm more than happy to hide up here for the next week! But you are all right, I hope?"

Don't tell Paul about the child. She could almost hear her fiancé's warning, echoing in her mind like a persistent refrain.

"Yes, I'm well enough."

"Beth, are you sure you're not ill?" he called to her.

She unfastened the pearl buttons of her silk waistcoat and draped it across the porcelain tub. The bath had one small window, circular and placed high, and she could see the moon, shining beyond the branches of a graceful elm tree, and upon one of the slender twigs sat a large owl. The dark eyes looked like jet beads against the snow-white feathers.

Snow, she thought, the visions Anatole had shown her playing in her mind. The owl's head tilted to one side, and the terrifying images faded, as if removed from her consciousness and stored inside a mental photograph album—waiting to be opened.

Paul's voice continued; the earl completely unaware of the night creature's actions. "I've seen you faint half a dozen times this past week, Beth, and you hardly eat anything at all lately." He stood and moved to the closed door, placing his hand on the polished wood. "Beth, it isn't my intent to order you about, but Tory said you had a dizzy spell in the stables today, and that afterward you slept for several hours. Perhaps, I should send for Price. He's at Reggie's home still, I think. In fact, it might be wise to have them both come by. I'm sure Charles would want you seen by a physician. He's just as worried as I am. I can see it in his eyes each time you have a spell."

Elizabeth had removed the high-collared blouse and velvet skirt, along with her undergarments, and laid all upon the tub. She gazed at herself in the cheval mirror, picturing the unborn child she carried and wondering how the truth would affect her relationship with the earl.

Charles, I have to tell him the truth. I owe it to him.

"Beth?" Aubrey called again. "Speak to me, darling. Tell me you're all right."

"I'm fine," she answered. "I'm nearly finished."

Five minutes more passed, and she joined him in the bedchamber, wearing a satin night dress, topped by a blue velvet dressing gown trimmed in ivory lace. "Sorry to take so long," she said as she sat beside him.

"You said you wanted to talk," he whispered, taking her hand. "What about?"

"About last month—whilst we were in Scotland," she began. "Do you remember the night you told me that Della is your daughter?"

"What has this to do with your fainting spells?" he asked, puzzled by the apparent shift in topic. "You're intentionally ignoring my question."

"No, actually, I'm not. I'm trying to explain something important. Do you remember that night?" she asked again.

"How could I forget?" he answered, kissing her hand. "I'd feared that you would hate me when you learnt the truth, but instead you said that it made you love me all the more."

"Yes, and I love Della all the more, too," she reminded him.

"Why do you bring it up, Princess? Surely, you've not changed your mind."

"Of course not, but I'd intended to tell you a secret of my own that night. Do you remember?"

His dark brows rose in surprise. "I'd forgotten, actually. Charles had become ill, and we were interrupted."

"Yes. He was terribly ill and spent three days in a state of dreams, half-conscious with fever and chills. You and my grandfather started having a series of private meetings after that, and then the wolf attacked, and..."

"And Charles proposed. Yes, darling, I remember all that. Why do you bring it up?"

She took a deep breath to steady her nerves. "Because I really must tell you my secret. Charles and my grandfather, both, have urged me to keep it to myself until after the wedding, but you deserve to know. Paul, you have been my closest, dearest friend for all my life. How can I not tell you?"

"Darling, if Charles has asked you to keep it secret, then you must do as he asks."

She shook her head. "No. In this one case, I must disobey him. He will be cross, but I owe you this." She began to weep, and he put his arm around her. "Oh, Paul, you are going to hate me!"

"Never. Not for one second of time could I hate you."

"Oh, but you will; I know you will, but you must promise not to hate Charles."

He pulled back, looking at her in confusion. "Hate Charles? Why would I do that? What has he to do with your secret?"

She began to tremble, her voice high and nervous. "The night at the cottage. That small farm near Dr. Lemuel's house. Charles and I stayed there after the doctor was shot."

"Yes, I'm aware of that."

"Charles and I were alone in that cottage, and someone had put poison into the tea. Do you remember?"

"Yes, Beth, of course, I remember," he told her. "We feared for you both. Charles was delirious, and you were unresponsive.

Both your eyes showed signs of some dark drug. Dear, where is this all going?"

She swallowed hard, her lower lip trembling. "Charles thinks we may have suffered from more than poison that night. Grandfather told me that Laurence and his men discovered wolf tracks as well as human footprints all 'round the cottage grounds and beneath the windows. As if someone performed a ritual of some kind whilst we were there."

He sighed. "I know all this, Beth. We've discussed it many times in our meetings," he replied, his deep voice tinged with irritation.

"Then, you surely must know that the combination of enchantment and poison had altered our ability to make... Well, to make free will choices."

His face paled to ash. "Free will choices? Beth, what are you saying?"

She bit her lower lip, her breath catching in her throat. "I'm saying...that I am pregnant."

All colour in the earl's face drained away, followed by a sudden flush of anger that infused the pale skin with angry patches of crimson. He jumped to his feet, both hands clenched. "How dare he force himself on you! He is thirteen years your senior and knows better. Charles claims to love you, yet he would do this to you? Force you? I shall kill him! With my bare hands, I will wring every last breath from his traitorous lungs!"

"No, Paul, please! He did no such thing!" she implored, reaching for his hands, but he eluded her, stepping backwards as if trying to remove himself bodily from the shock.

"How can you expect me to think anything else?" the earl shouted. "Beth, he took advantage of you. Charles is much more experienced, and you—my darling, you are an innocent. No amount of enchantment or poison can explain such selfish, such appalling behaviour!"

He turned away from her, for he felt completely lost. His Elizabeth had forever altered—forever *been* altered. Charles Sinclair had stolen a gift that should have been his! Now, Elizabeth would never be—*could* never be the same.

"You hate me," she wept, and the anguish in her voice broke his heart.

"No, no, of course, I do not," he assured her, falling to his knees and taking her small hands in his own. "But how can I not be angry, Beth? How can you expect me to simply pass it off as nothing? Charles did take advantage of you! He must have done!"

"He did not," she said simply, tears sliding down her cheeks. "Charles told my grandfather all that happened the very next day, and he wanted to confess it all to you, but I insisted that I be the one to tell you. Then, he fell into a fever, and time passed. Each day brought new challenges. Charles told the duke that he feared I might have conceived, Paul, but he would have stepped aside had I chosen you as husband. Charles knew it might mean abandoning his own child, yet he would have made that sacrifice, because he loves us both. If you think him blameworthy, then you could not be more wrong. Do you really think either of us would betray you that way? Both of us love you! I love you."

He began to weep, his head in her lap like a penitent child. "I don't know how to feel," he admitted. "Honestly, I grow numb with the anguish of it. Beth, I want to hate him, but in truth I do love Charles. He is the brother I lacked as a child, but that love only sharpens the edge of this cruel blade. It is a pain—a betrayal beyond all description!"

"And what of my betrayal? Do you also hate me?" she whispered.

"I could never hate you, Elizabeth. I love you more than I love life. If you asked me to fall upon that blade—drive it into my heart, I would do it."

She stroked his chestnut hair, wiping the tears from his face. "And if I asked for your forgiveness? For Charles?"

"Dying is easier," he admitted.

She took his hand and placed it upon her abdomen. "If George and Reggie are correct, then a tiny life now rests within my body. You often speak of how you took me as a baby in your arms and became my guardian. I ask you now to become guardian to this dear life. A boy. A girl. I cannot say, but he or she needs you. Would you ignore that need in favour of vengeance?"

"Of course, I would not, but you've had time to adjust to this. Allow me the same, won't you?" he begged her. "Perhaps, by morning, I might find the repose you so need of me."

She pulled him back onto the sofa, and he folded her into his arms. "I shall always need you as my knight, Lord Aubrey. It is selfish of me, I know, but it is true nonetheless. I cannot stop loving you, no matter how my life may alter. Your very name is etched upon my soul."

"And yours on mine," he admitted. "I understand now why Charles has been so worried about you, and I shall join him in worrying, I suppose. Beth, I still love my cousin, but it seems to me that he did take advantage of you," he told her. "No, no. You needn't plead his case any further. Inside my head, I believe your testimony, but my heart is the problem, you see. It aches with anguish and regret."

"Regret?" she asked. "Why?"

"Because it should have been I who rode to your rescue that night," he confessed.

"And if you'd fallen prey to the same poison and enchantment?"

"Then, this would be my child within you," he whispered, and the agony in his voice broke her heart. "Forgive me. That was unfair, and I should never have said it. Pray for me, Beth. I want to understand. I do. It is just...difficult."

She kissed his cheek, but without thinking—almost instinctively—he pulled her into his arms and took her lips. They'd not kissed this way in many weeks; not since she'd accepted Sinclair's proposal, and his desperation drew her into a depth of feeling that frightened Elizabeth. She did love the earl, only not in the same way she loved Sinclair. Stuart's faithfulness and steadfast love formed the bedrock upon which her entire life was built.

But Charles—her handsome Captain—*he* was her future. Beth felt connected to him as to no other human on earth. Charles kept her anchored to reality. Without his tether, she would forever be lost.

Aubrey released her, shock and regret painting his lean features. "Forgive me. Oh, please, forgive me, Beth. I had no right to do that. None at all."

She encircled his waist, her head against his chest. "If you can forgive me, my darling knight, then it is easily forgotten."

He helped her to bed, and then rang for the lady's maid. "I've a few things to do, but I shan't be long. An hour, no more. I can send up another pot of cocoa, if you wish. To settle your stomach."

She smiled, still holding his hand. "That would be lovely. Thank you, Paul."

The earl bowed and then left the apartment, his cheeks burning from embarrassment and guilt. He had to find a way to forgive both his cousins, but for the moment, that ability seemed very far away.

CHAPTER ELEVEN
11:41pm

Mansell Street in Whitechapel sat only four blocks west of the Leman Street police station, forming the western edge of a large square with Great Alie Street to the north, Great Prescot to the south, and Leman to the east. Within this enclosure, stood a smaller square formed by Tenter Streets North, South, East, and West. The neighbourhood was a mixture of decaying tenement houses, goods yards, rundown churches, public works buildings, a police mews, and two public houses. The Widows Home stood at the southeast corner of Great Prescot, not far from Garrick Theatre, with the Jewish Men's Refuge on a corner nearby.

Mansell also hosted a congregation of abandoned warehouses, four of which had once belonged to Dryden Imports, now defunct and bankrupted into receivership; their slowly deteriorating buildings listed with the tax assessor's office for a quick sale. Being empty and isolated, these provided the perfect meeting place for the London branch of Redwing.

"Rasha is late," Sir William Trent complained, glancing at his pocket watch. "You did remind him?"

"Of course, I did," di Specchio answered as she took a seat at the large, circular table. "Is the altar arranged?"

"It is complete and prepared for our guest's enjoyment," Sir Clive Urquhart answered, handing a black silk cloak to a heavy-set doorman. "Prince Anatole is coming? He has sent word, yes?"

"Tolya will not be joining us tonight; and possibly never will again," the countess replied. "I suspect that he is afraid to face the elohim whom he imprisoned."

"And who wouldn't be?" laughed a red-haired man in formal dress as he took the chair beside the contessa.

"My dear Sir Christopher," she cooed. "I'd feared our new mayor's party might ensnare you tonight. Is our overtaxed estate agent to attend, or does he still linger in hospital?"

"We'll see no more of Lewis Merriweather," the man replied, smiling. "Honoria, do sit by me."

Slowly, the table began to fill with men and women who wielded great power in England: Sir Christopher Holding, owner of a major ironworks company that supplied metal to the shipping industry; Mrs. Honoria Chandler, the widow of David Chandler, founder of Brighton Stone and Pebble, a quarry that provided construction materials to the city of London; Lord Peter Andrews, a lifetime peer and politician who'd led the 1877 negotiations in Cyprus; Alvin Meyerbridge, munitions manufacturer, specialising in production of rapid-fire armaments; Dr. Laurence Malford-Jones, a chemist who pioneered methods for birth control and altering the human species; Gerald St. Ives, 5th Earl of Wisling, owner of three steel foundries; Sir Robert Cartwright, a slightly built baronet, who rarely spoke in the meetings, but who had the trust and companionship of two very important royals; and Dr. Alexander Collins of the Castor Institute, site of numerous experiments in hybridisation.

"Is Prince Raziel coming?" Collins asked Trent.

"We'll discuss that in a moment," the baronet replied, mysteriously. "And our estate agent will not attend at all. He now sells properties in much hotter climes."

Di Specchio laughed. "Then, he is dead, I take it. Good! We should drink to his eternal death!"

As the members each took his or her chair, a servant filled cups with a red liquid that bore a striking similarity to *Sangiovese* wine.

"Lewis was a bumbling fool. May he roast on Lucifer's spit!" Wisling told his companions. "Perhaps, we should look to his magnificent building as our new headquarters. These old warehouses provide secrecy, but they are damp and dusty. What do you think, Serena?"

"I think Redwing belongs in the heart of the city, and what better street than Wormwood?" she answered, sipping the dark liquid.

"How apt, my dear!" Clive agreed, as he took the last chair. "I'm pleased to see our round table full this evening. I'd feared that our illustrious, new Lord Mayor might entice many of you into his political web for the night, but here, at this table, is where true power lies. England's government agents are mere window dressing. Is that not so? Mundane fools with no eyes to see the hidden hand, lurking behind them in the dark, pulling the strings and making the monarchs dance."

"The shadowy Professors animating a hellish Punch and Judy show!" Wisling jibed.

Trent stood. "Well said, Lord Wisling. Are all our cups filled? We shall toast, and then to business."

"It's true, then. You have found it? The obsidian mirror?" Collins enquired.

"It is why we assemble this evening, Doctor. We completed the excavation a few months ago, and tonight we perform the rite," Sir William replied. "To the annihilation of the inner circle and the enthronement of our infernal king!"

"To the King amongst the Dead!" they all shouted in unison as each tipped back the goblet and drank.

Trent set down his empty cup and reached into his left coat pocket, withdrawing a small round object that resembled a black rock. "Here is the key, purchased with pain. There stands the glass, which will open again," he quoted. "Sir Robert, would you do the honours?"

"One moment," Serena objected. "Perhaps, we should wait for Lord Raziel. These are his incantations, after all. If we err, our lives may be at risk."

"Are you afraid, *mon ami*?" Sir Clive asked.

"Of course, not. I merely wish to avoid... Disappointment."

Trent gazed intently at the countess, as if taking her measure. "Only those with reason to fear will be disappointed, Serena. Let us unveil the glass!"

Sir Robert left his chair and walked to a tall rectangular shape, concealed beneath black velvet draping. The mysterious device dominated the northeast corner of the basement area, where the round table now met. "Yes or no?" he asked the others. "The incantation must be spoken at midnight precisely. If not tonight, we must wait until the next, correct lunar phase."

"Yes! Uncover it," several of the members shouted in unison. "Let us see it!"

Di Specchio finished her drink and joined Sir Robert at the mirror's side to demonstrate her fidelity with their cause. "Allow me.

After all, mirrors are my business. However, we must give credit to our builder, Sir Clive Urquhart, without whom we would never have located this revered glass."

Sir Clive stood and bowed, swiping at his waxed moustaches with one hand. "It is but a small contribution."

The contessa pulled at the velvet covering, and every member gasped. Beneath the drape stood a perfect sheet of obsidian— black volcanic glass. Its gleaming surface had been polished and etched with a thousand sigils, containing a spell used to imprison the Watcher bound within.

"That which is bound, let it be loosed. That which is hidden, let it be found. That which is silent, let it *roar*!" Trent cried out, as he held the black rock aloft.

The round table commenced a hideous chant, and the orb began to glow; with each spoken word, a sigil on the obsidian surface brightened, then disappeared as if wiped clean. When all the etched figures had faded, the orb grew dark, and every torch and lamp in the room snuffed out at once.

A low hum slowly reached their ears, its unearthly sound composed of a thousand dissonant pitches, as if an entire chorus of demons sang in black and hideous speech. The ears of all within the circle began to bleed. A massive wind rushed into the hall, and the obsidian surface shattered into a million shards of glass; each piece flying in a whirlwind throughout the room, narrowly missing the humans surrounding the table.

A great Shadow appeared within the glittering whirlwind, and the entire building began to shake. Something *very powerful* was coming through.

CHAPTER TWELVE
3:03 am – Branham Hall

Bella the Labrador had begun to pant, her large black paw pushing against Sinclair's right side. Turning in the bed, the marquess opened his eyes.

"Forgive me for interrupting your sleep, my lord," a man's voice whispered in the darkness. "It's just that we've a situation, you might say. Outside, on the grounds. Shall I fetch your clothing, sir?"

Sitting up, the policeman wiped sleep from his dark lashes. "Baxter, what do you mean by a situation?"

The butler switched on a small electric lamp and started collecting the detective's trousers, socks, waistcoat, and shirt. He laid each, in orderly fashion, upon the foot of the wide bed whilst replying. "Let us just say, sir, that Clark and Powers have ordered their men to carry shotguns as they search the buildings. I'm afraid that one of my lady's horses is dead."

This news jolted Sinclair into wakefulness. "Which one?" he asked as he reached for the trousers.

"Ambrose Aurelius, my lord. A four-year-old Andalusian worth nearly five thousand pounds. Or at least, he was."

"Black with a white blaze on his head? Quite tall?"

"Yes, sir. I believe Lord Aubrey rode him during your pleasure ride last month. Ambrose is—*was*—unusually large for such a breed. Just over seventeen hands. The duchess purchased him last year to form a new line with Paladin's descendants. Mr. Clark found him inside his stall about half an hour ago. I do apologise for waking you, sir, but I assumed you'd wish to know."

"Yes, of course. Send no word to London about this, though. I'll tell the duchess myself," he said, hastily donning the clothing and pulling on boots. After making sure his pistol was fully loaded,

Sinclair followed the butler out of the apartment, down the main staircase, and into the cold night air.

Voices rose up from every direction as grooms, footmen, and gardeners searched the estate grounds and nearby woods. The waning moon stood high in the cloudy sky: its silvery light shining brightly upon the dying blossoms and vegetation of the gardens. As the detective walked, he could hear the sharp calls of a peacock and several foxes near the edge of Henry's Wood. The daytime temperature had cooled considerably, and he noticed that he could see his breath.

It took nearly fifteen minutes to reach the stables, where a knot of armed men stood near the entrance to the largest of the six barns. Each tipped his hat, one stepped forward. It was Chief Groom, Edwin Clark, who'd been injured during the Branham Battle in early October.

"Sorry to wake you, my lord," he said as Sinclair approached. "I reckon Mr. Baxter's told you about Ambrose. He's in here, sir. I've touched nothin' aside from makin' sure the horse was dead, o' course. Nothin' we could do, I'm afraid."

The detective followed Clark into a stall near the end, where three lanterns hung from ceiling hooks, illuminating the crime scene. The dead animal lay on his left side, the head towards the door; a slender stream of blood stained his powerful neck. Before entering, Charles surveyed the scene, assessing each item present and where it now stood or hung.

The stall was approximately ten feet by twelve; the packed earth floor covered in sawdust and straw. A four-foot long trough stood parallel to the east wall, and it was half filled—the water within looked clear. A black leather halter, decorated with the initials A. A. in silver, hung from one of the doorposts, and a dark green, woolen blanket embroidered with the name 'Ambrose' lay draped over the animal's withers.

"Clark, did you place this blanket here?" Charles asked.

"He had it on already, my lord. If you look closer, you'll see it's buttoned at his throat, so that it draped 'round his chest. Ambrose had been off his feed the past two nights. We wanted ta make sure he kept warm."

"Had a vet visited?"

"We'd called one, sir, as we'd wondered if it might be connected to the sheep what's died, but Mr. Soames—he's the hall's game warden, but also trained in animal medicine—well, sir, he thought the horse might have strangles, for there's a swelling on his head, just beneath the left ear, but that's an unusual spot for strangles. We'd hoped to get Mr. Stillwell's opinion once he returns from holiday."

"Stillwell? Is he the hall's vet?" Sinclair asked as he knelt beside the horse.

"Yes, sir. He studied in France. A bright man, sir. He lives over in Margate, and as I say, he's been on holiday, visitin' his mother up in Yorkshire. We wired him, and he promised to come down once his mum recovered. She's been right poorly. I don't reckon it'd make no difference now, though. Don't think this is strangles at all, sir. Looks more like somethin' bit 'im or even attacked him ta me. There's blood on his neck, but it don't come from his ear. There's a mark, but as the animal's coat is dark, it's hard ta see in this light. I'll fetch a lantern."

After removing one of the hanging lamps, Clark bent down to cast light across the horse's head. "See here, sir? Ain't this a wound o' some sort?"

Charles used a handkerchief to wipe the drying blood from the area. "Move the lamp to your right, please, Clark. Yes, there. I see two wounds. Both quite deep. Is there a major artery near a horse's ear, as is in humans?" He thought of the exsanguinated women from Victoria Park. Was it possible that the same bloodthirsty killer who'd drained the life from those victims also preyed on animals?

"That'd be a question for Soames, sir. I could send Stephens ta fetch him from the game warden's cottage, but it's a ways off; over by the brewery, near ta Fairy's Copse."

"Fairy's Copse? I've not heard the duchess mention that."

The man's breath hung in the air as he spoke, creases around his eyes revealing lack of sleep and worry. "It's not somethin' my lady's likely to speak about, sir. She got lost there as a girl. We used ta call it Henry's Copse, but after the duchess saw the fairy there, it sort o' changed name."

"I see," Sinclair answered, recalling Prince Anatole's strange tale of a cottage seen only by children. He started to ask about this fairy, but a sudden rapid series of gunshots sliced through the cold, night air, drawing all their attention. Charles took to his feet, rushing out of the stable and into the moonlit paddock. From beyond the fence line, he spied movement in an area populated by a stand of tall elms, ringed by mulberry trees. Foxes cried in the distance, harmonising with the insistent yelping of the dogs, set to the staccato drumbeat of more gunfire and men's boots upon gravel and turf.

"Over here!" he called to Clark and his men. Cornelius Baxter had stood guard near the stable entrance, and he, too, dashed towards the commotion, a loaded derringer in his livery pocket.

As he ran, Charles suddenly worried about Elizabeth, as if the fears were meant to distract him from the current task. He forced the duchess's face from his mind, concentrating solely upon finding and apprehending the intruder. He could hear his own, quick breaths as he ran past one of the large storage sheds used by the gardeners. His long muscles pumped like pistons, propelling arms and legs and expending oxygen faster than his lungs could provide.

Most of the men had reached the mulberries, but as the detective neared their position, he slammed bodily into something unseen and was knocked to the ground; the sharp blow nearly rendering him unconscious. The entire left side of his head felt as if a blacksmith's hammer had struck it, but Charles ignored the intense pain and regained his feet. Sudden movement to the right caught his attention, and he spun on his heels to find himself staring at an enormous shadow, shaped like a man, standing no more than six feet away.

The being's face held no definition, yet its eyes burnt like live coals. Fear threatened to overwhelm him, but Sinclair took a deep, painful breath and burst forward, rushing towards the supernatural creature. The apparition turned and fled; its unnatural speed quickly outpacing the human pursuer.

Despite his injury, the detective forced his legs to pump faster, whilst the great Shadow led him on a dangerous and winding chase beneath overhanging limbs and through razor sharp brambles with the ease of a gazelle. Bella and Briar, the two dogs who lived inside the hall, raced alongside the marquess, Briar taking the lead, for the animals also perceived the supernatural figure.

As he ran, Sinclair began to recognise the path as the one he and Elizabeth had taken in early October; the road which led to the old abbey and its subterranean altar, where Trent murdered Duchess Patricia in 1879. Not six weeks past, Charles and Elizabeth had ridden Paladin through these same trees, pursued by Trent's hybrid army, and now he ran alone, pursuing a hellish shade in a race that began with the death of another of Beth's prize horses, Ambrose Aurelius.

The low hanging branches, barren of leaves and fruit, reached for his eyes as he plowed through them, but miraculously, none brought him any harm—as if unseen hands restrained even the woodlands. Many minutes passed, and it seemed to Charles that he'd been running for more than a mile, perhaps even two, and he feared that his body might fail him, for it had been many a year since he'd chased down criminals as a police constable. Despite the intense pain in his lungs, he refused to slow; instead, he forced his long legs to move faster as he ran past the original hall with its crumbling stone towers and bat-filled chambers.

Then he saw the impossible.

The Shadow stopped without warning and turned. Its contours became fluid, like ripples upon water, and the arms elongated, morphing and stretching into massive wings. It rose high into the air, hovering there above the trees, taunting its pursuer. It emitted an ear-piercing wail, and then flew towards Sinclair's position—pursuing him now.

The enormous night bird was making straight for the human's head, its mouth yawning into a black cavern.

Just before the creature's red eyes reached him, just before the enormous claws tore his tender flesh, a blinding flash of light illuminated the path and surrounding trees.

Startled, Sinclair immediately stopped, but the abrupt change in momentum caused his boots to slide upon the gravel path, and he toppled forward—but before his body crashed into the hard-packed earth and stones, a pair of strong hands caught the marquess in a desperate embrace.

It was Cornelius Baxter, his fleshy brow white as chalk and beaded with sweat; cheeks pink with the rush of blood and the night's brisk chill. "There now, sir," the butler said gently as he helped the detective to his feet. "Take a moment. Slow, deep breaths."

Sinclair's eyelids squeezed together, and he gasped repeatedly, the vaporous exhales clouding the night air. Every muscle in his body screamed in agony, and his head and eyes stung, but he managed to maintain composure.

"Just a...leisurely stroll...for you, I take it, Mr. Baxter?" the marquess panted, wincing as the calf muscles of his left leg tensed into a tight ball of pain. "I, uh...I fear you're the better man. I'm only glad...none of my constables...was here to see me...try to run beyond my limit."

"No one could have run that far, my lord. I certainly didn't. Clark and I were in one of the dog carts. When we saw that foul creature knock you to the ground, Clark broke all speed to put Little Girl into her traces. It's no wonder you're out of breath, sir. I know of no man who could have done as you have. You've run over ten miles!"

"Ten? Whatever do you mean? It cannot be more than two," Sinclair argued, his brain gobbling up oxygen, that now slowly filtered through his bloodstream.

"No, sir, it was ten or more," the butler insisted. "No mistaking it. That's the old abbey up ahead, which is the eleven-mile marker from the hall, and since you started half a mile from the house, I make it nearly ten-and-a-half. Quite remarkable! Come with me, my lord. Let's get you back to the hall and see to your head. It's bleeding."

"Yes, all right, but did you see it? The creature, I mean. Did you see what it did? How it flew?" the marquess asked as they turned about towards the waiting dog cart.

"We did, sir. But let us speak more of it inside. You look close to fainting. You took quite a blow."

"Yes, all right," Charles managed. His vision began to dim—telescoping inward as consciousness faded. "Wings. It had wings," he finished, collapsing into the butler's arms.

"Yes, sir. We know," the butler replied. He and Clark lifted the marquess into the dog cart, carefully laying him against the straw bales. Climbing into the back, the massively built butler gently placed a horse blanket around Sinclair's shoulders. "It's starting all over again, Ed," he told Clark. "God help us, those monstrous shadows have returned."

As the cart rumbled along the pathway towards the hall, the enormous winged bat landed upon the parapet of the mansion near a second spirit being, this one clad in human flesh. His skin was pale, eyes a radiant crystal blue, and his hair flowed like a river of ebony upon broad shoulders.

"Welcome back to the night, Saraqael," he told the bat-like creature. "I regret that I was unable to attend your ceremony, but business in France detained me."

"Raziel!" the creature exclaimed. "Can it be you? I saw you chained within the stone. Samael and his followers placed you inside and covered it over with spells and runes to conceal its hiding place. I don't understand. How are you free? You were doomed to remain there for all time."

"What you say is true, yet here I am," Raziel Grigor replied. "The *how*, as you might guess, is due to the actions of a foolish human. The *when*? In the year 1871, according to their reckoning. It is now 1888, late fall; one and a half cycles past the blood moon. Soon, the day and night will share equally—bringing with it great power, and we shall use that power to free the third of our number. Designer of patterns, discerner of wheels."

The enormous bat blinked, its black tongue licking hungrily at the horse blood remaining on its upper lip. "Do you mean Araqiel?"

"Indeed. We require his skills to locate the remaining prisons. For now, my brother, you must master your rage against the Sinclair family. We require his blood to achieve our ultimate goal. That is why Samael punished you—do not anger him again, lest you suffer a worse fate than imprisonment. Remember his office."

The ancient vampire tore a section of iron railing that formed the edge of the roof and dashed it towards the ground. "Samael the Betrayer! Samael the Torturer! Samael the Prison Guard! Yes, I remember his office quite well. I shall find my own poison and bring him to the lowest pit of the deepest night for what he did to me—and to you!" he shouted. "Surely, you must hate him as much as I."

"Five thousands years have taught me to appreciate what he did," Raziel insisted calmly. "Do not mistake me. I loathe Sama, and eventually, I shall repay him, but he did save me from the fires."

"Was it you who freed me, then?"

"Indeed. The humans think themselves clever; yet they are easily led. I know that you hunger, my brother, but you must curtail these urges—for the present. Surely, you recall the fragile nature of human understanding? It was your impetuous actions which saw you chained inside that prison, Sara. I'm told that you struck at the very heart of the bloodline—one which harkens back to *my* time. And all for spite."

"Revenge," he whispered bitterly. "Why must we rule through humans? They are fit only for food."

"I agree," Raziel said patiently. "Their blood is sweet, but their minds have potential. If we are to rule this realm, then we must cajole, not consume. Teach, not terrify."

The creature's rage slowly dissipated, and his form shifted from monstrous to something more human-like. His wings became arms; claws became fingers; the flat nostrils, a refined nose; beady eyes rounded into a man's pupils, surrounded by ice-blue irises; and fur lengthened into spirals of thick hair as black as night.

The monstrous had become exceedingly beautiful.

"A significant improvement," Raziel observed drily. "I'd forgotten how much you resembled Samael when in this form. That similarity may aid in our plans. However, you will require clothing, Sara. It is still customary for one to dress when visiting the fashionable parlours of London."

"Is it?" the new arrival quipped. Saraqael snapped his fingers, causing expensive thread to wrap around each perfect muscle, weaving a tapestry of gold and silk. In less than the time it takes for a fledgling's feather to fall from a nest, the imposter had clothed himself in luxury. "Have I your approval now?" he asked, his raspy voice softened into a curious accent.

"The ladies of London will swoon, dear brother," Raziel replied with a sideways smile. "Of course, my own reputation in such circles is quite impressive. Women are readily fooled by a handsome face and genteel manners, but do not bleed them dry. The harlots of the city can be tricked into believing our need to consume their blood is but another style of sexual play. A taste here, another there can provide nourishment, but you must leave no evidence that leads to us. Instead, find ways to blame the humans. If they go to prison, so much the better."

"Tasting only?" the other asked with a sigh. "It will require many women to provide the quantities I require, Raziel. I have slept for nearly thirty years inside that ancient mirror! My hunger is great!"

"Yes, yes, I recall that savage hunger when first awakening, but you and I are but the forerunners of an assault. Consider yourself a spy within the human realm. Spies do not draw attention to themselves. Killing the horse was a mistake."

"But a delicious one," Sara parried back, smiling.

"Temper your urges, my brother. You remind me too much of my son. He is rash and indiscreet."

"Son? Have you taken human women again?" he asked greedily.

"Not as before," Raziel answered, the light wind blowing through his locks. "I take them to my bed, of course, but I am careful. Herbs and plants keep the seed from growing, and a knife proves useful when these remedies fail. I speak of a son born of magic. I have perfected the rituals that alter the innate structure. Rasha is my first experiment."

"A successful one?"

"I cannot yet say. If a failure, then I shall begin afresh."

"Then you will fail again, for no magic can transform a human into one of our kind," Saraqael argued. "They are inferior stock."

"Perhaps, but that stock can be reshaped into useful creatures. A similar process has proven successful in hybridising men into all manner of animals. You might consider satisfying your thirst on them, Sara; rather than on horses. Or roam the fields in search of sheep. If a few are found slain, the shepherds will lay the blame on predators such as dogs or wolves."

"Or bats?" he asked, winking.

"Perhaps," Raziel answered. "You must keep to the shadows. Allow Sinclair to recover, for we require him whole and able to rule. Now, let us fly. The moon rises, and I have much to tell you."

The two humanoid shadows thinned, and within seconds, only the wind remained. A white-faced barn owl flew past the parapet, its round eyes scanning the roofline.

The ancient vampire, Saraqael, is free, the owl thought as it turned upon the air currents, towards London. *He will seek human flesh and blood. He will kill indiscriminately. And no matter what Raziel may advise, Sara will eventually seek vengeance, for he is dangerous and decidedly evil.*

Samael the powerful *elohim*, Angel of Death, Poison of God, sailed easily through the cold night air, traversing invisible doorways that connected the hidden realm to the human one, returning at last to the manicured park of a west London mansion, where he kept watch upon the duchess until long after the sun had risen.

CHAPTER THIRTEEN

11:31 am – Saturday, 10th November, 1888

"Charles, over here!"

The embattled marquess stepped off the Aubrey train and walked towards a tall man wearing a long, burnished leather overcoat but no hat. Two black Labradors flanked the returning policeman, who held a braided dog leash in each hand.

"I'd not expected anyone to meet me, though I'm always pleased to see you," Sinclair greeted his cousin. "I've brought two of the best companions a man might have. I hope Beth approves."

"Of course, she will. Elizabeth loves both of these dogs. Well, hello there, Bella," Aubrey said as the animal sniffed his gloves. "Yes, I've been petting another dog. I'm sure you remember Samson." He rubbed the male's ears affectionately. "Tory's dog may have to fight Briar when it comes to any rats wandering the grounds. He's the best hunter on the Branham estate. I imagine Powers will be at a great loss, though he has three other dogs for company. Briar's own sons, in fact. Charles, are those bruises on your face? Did you get into a spat with Beth's cook?"

"Actually, Mrs. Stephens and I get along quite well, thank you. No, my battle scars result from a scuffle in the middle of the night. I'll explain it at the meeting," Sinclair replied, wincing, for his entire body ached along with his head. "You know, Paul, I don't recall ever seeing you sporting outerwear. Are you expecting snow?"

"Actually, no, but I thought the coat prudent," he replied mysteriously. "You might say it's part of my customary attire when anticipating danger. One of James's men reported a break-in at our rail shed, and I've spent the past hour there, inspecting the damage. Hello, Sparks," he said to the pleasant-faced porter carrying Sinclair's overnight bag. "How fares your good lady?"

"Mrs. Sparks keeps busy, my lord," the amiable servant replied with a broken-toothed grin. "We've just had our third grandchild, in fact. My son's named him James Stuart Sparks, after the duke, o' course, as His Grace has been gen'rous enough to let us lodge on Drummond property more 'n ten year now. I don' see a coach, sirs. Where might it be parked?"

"Two streets over," the earl replied, taking the bag into his right hand. "Allow me, Sparks. You go back to the train and tell our intrepid engineer to put her into the rail shed for a few days, but number three rather than one. We're repairing the locks on that shed. I don't think anyone in the family will be travelling again until after the wedding, so you can both take a few days off and spend them with your families," Aubrey added, handing the silver-haired grandfather three, five-pound notes. "A fiver for each of those precious grandchildren. Invite us to young Master James's christening, won't you? I'm sure the duke will want to see his namesake's special day."

The man bowed and placed the notes carefully into a tooled leather wallet. "You're a great gentleman, my lord. Mrs. Sparks reckons it'll be sometime after Christmas. Maybe even first o' next year, but we'll send you an invitation, my lord—soon as the date's been set. Pleasure seein' you again, Lord Haimsbury," he said, tipping his hat. "Best o' wishes to you and the little duchess, sir, as you begin your wedded life together. I hope it's as joyful as mine's been with my dear Emma."

"Thank you, Sparks," Sinclair answered, pressing twenty pounds into the porter's hand. "Consider this an early Christmas gift. Buy your wife something nice."

The man gasped. "You are both too kind, sirs! But I shall put it all to good use. I promise!" He then turned about and headed back towards the Aubrey train.

"We're parked on Gillingham," Paul said as Sinclair accompanied him past a long line of travellers, several of them with small children, bound for points north. Several of the youths smiled at the two dogs, and one lad tugged at his mother's coat sleeve, begging to pet them.

"Only if this gentleman approves, Mickey," she told him.

Charles overheard the exchange and stopped to smile at the boy. "Mickey, is it? How old are you, young man?"

"Seven and a half, sir. Are these your dogs?"

"They are my fiancée's dogs, but soon we'll share them, as we're about to get married. Do you like dogs, Master Mickey?"

"Oh, yes, sir! Very much, but I can't have one, cause o' the cost. Might I touch them, sir?"

Charles nodded. Bella's tail wagged happily as the boy tentatively reached for her head. "Careful now," the detective cautioned. "When meeting a new animal, one must always proceed slowly. Show her the back of your hand first. Let her sniff it, to show that you mean her no harm."

The boy complied, his eyes wide. "Now what, sir?"

"Slowly overturn your hand and touch the top of her head. Avoid a dog's mouth until she knows you are safe."

"Safe, sir? I wouldn't hurt a dog."

"I'm sure you wouldn't, Master Mickey, but some would. Some men find no issue with injuring or abusing an animal." He thought of the dead horse, and of the sheep; eleven in all, according to Baxter. "She likes you. See her tail wag? Now, try it with Briar. He's Bella's husband."

The boy used the same procedure to acquaint himself with the male, grinning with delight.

"You are a natural with animals, young sir. Tell me, where are you and your mother headed?"

"Nowhere, sir," he told the marquess. "We're waitin' for my pa. He's been up north with the railroad."

"That's enough, Mickey. We mustn't delay these gentlemen any longer," the mother said, gently pulling him backwards, closer to her skirts. "Forgive my son's impertinence, my lord. You're him, aren't you? Lord Haimsbury, I mean. I recognise you from the newspapers, sir."

"Yes, I'm Haimsbury," Sinclair answered, removing two gold sovereigns from his pocket and handing both to the boy. "For you, Master Mickey. Perhaps, they might help with finding a dog—if your parents approve, of course. It was very nice to meet you. And if ever you and your family are close to Haimsbury House, I hope you will stop and say hello."

The boy's fist closed 'round the coins. "Blimey, sir! Thank you!"

"Take care of him," the marquess admonished the woman. "He's a lovely boy."

"Thank you, my lord. You're kind to say so."

187

The two cousins left the platform and continued on their way. Aubrey reached for Briar's lead. "Let me help, Cousin. You're limping," he said as they headed towards the main exit. "Are you sure you're all right?"

"Yes, I'm fine, Paul. Just weary. We had a long night."

"I see," the earl remarked, deciding to let it drop for the moment. "You packed light," he added, jostling the overnight bag.

The detective laughed. "Unlike you, I don't carry an arsenal with me. Is Beth feeling well today?"

"She slept late and was just finishing breakfast when I left an hour ago, but yes, she's fine, though somewhat tired. The circle meeting commences as soon as you and I return. Tory's promised to keep Elizabeth occupied whilst we meet."

"Good. I admire her enthusiasm and bravery, but it often leads to trouble. I prefer she not overhear our conversation."

Hamish Granger met the cousins at the coach and took the leather bag, placing it into the boot. "Welcome back, my lord," he said. "I trust all is well in Kent."

"As well as one might expect," Sinclair answered cryptically. "Granger, I'd like you to attend part of our meeting this afternoon, if you can spare the time. And Miles, as well."

"Lord Aubrey had already suggested it, sir, so we've arranged to join you after luncheon, if that suits."

The marquess smiled. "As usual, I'm dragging far behind the earl. Yes, that suits quite well. Thank you."

Once the cousins had settled into the rich leather seats, Stuart grew serious. "Charles, I decided to meet you, because I needed to speak to you in private. Before we join the others."

Sinclair felt weary from lack of sleep, and every muscle and joint ached as if his entire body wore a massive bruise, but he discerned deep strain in Paul's voice that surprised him. "What's wrong?"

The earl took a deep breath to steel his resolve. "I know."

Sinclair's dark brows rose together in confusion. "I don't understand. What is it that you know?"

"I know the truth," Stuart said.

"I'm still not following, Cousin. What truth do you mean?"

"I know that Beth is pregnant."

Sinclair's mouth dropped open, and he grew quiet, his azure eyes still. The earl, too, sat silently, anticipating his friend's response. "Who told you?"

"Beth did, but don't scold her, Charles. I think it's been burning a painful hole in her heart, and though it was a relief for her to get it all out, she now feels as if she's betrayed you, because she disobeyed your admonition to say nothing."

"That admonition wasn't intended to exclude you, Paul, but to spare you. James is the one who asked me to keep silent."

"Yes, he's admitted that to me."

"And how do you feel about it?" Charles asked, leaning forward slightly.

"I'm adjusting."

"Paul, I wanted to tell you at once, but Beth insisted she do it," his cousin explained.

"Yes, I know all that. She told me everything, and I'm embarrassed to say that I reacted quite badly."

Charles sighed. "If it's any consolation, I'd have reacted quite badly were our positions reversed, but neither Beth nor I chose to betray your trust. Please, do not for one second imagine that we did! The night in the cottage forever altered us all, but it was Redwing's intent that it do so. I beg you not to think any differently of Beth."

"But she is different, Charles, and there is no going back," the earl insisted. "Hear me out, please. I hadn't realised it until last night, but I've foolishly been clinging to a vain hope that Beth might change her mind and agree to become my wife. Yes, I know that I gave her up to you in Scotland, but surely you understand how difficult, how impossible such a concession is! I've loved her far longer than you have, Charles; known her longer, and her image and name are engraved upon my very soul!"

The detective touched his cousin's hand to offer strength. "Paul, I understand. I do. It's why James advised me to keep Beth's pregnancy a secret until after the wedding—not because we feared telling you, but because we feared *hurting* you. You are my dearest friend in all the world. As much as the prospect of a child thrills me, it means that your heart is endangered because of it. I would never willingly have done that to you, nor would Elizabeth. I hope you know that."

Aubrey grew silent, his eyes on the passing scenery. "Mentally, I do," he admitted, "but I fear that my heart lags far behind my head. I spent all last night praying about it whilst Beth slept—or nearly slept. She had some disturbing dreams, I think, for she seemed restless, calling out the word *snow* over and over. I found her window open once, which may explain it. I'd heard Samson scratching at the door and left the room to bring him inside, and when I returned it had blown open. We had flurries overnight, and the room had grown quite cold because of it."

"Her window was open? Did Samson act disturbed by it?"

Aubrey seemed confused. "By what? The wind? It was only that, Charles. Nothing more. No, the dog had been ill, and he wanted comforting, I think. I put him into bed with Beth, and both she and Samson grew quiet after that. If there's blame to be assigned for her dreams, then look to me. My anger and disappointment almost overwhelmed me, and it caused her great sadness."

"I can imagine it would. Elizabeth loves you dearly."

"So she does," he whispered. "Far more than I deserve. Hoping to make sense of what she'd confessed, I read through several psalms, seeking the Lord's comfort, and as dawn broke through the windows, an indescribable peace filled my heart. I've never experienced anything like it before in all my life," he continued, tears filling his clear, blue eyes. "To my surprise, all the anger, all the guilt had vanished. Do not think me cured of my jealousies. I am human, after all, but God has accomplished in one night what men could not achieve in ten lifetimes."

Charles thought of the visitor who'd brought the same kind of peace to him aboard the coach the previous day. "The Lord's messengers are beyond our capacity to comprehend or describe. I'm very glad our Saviour brought you this peace, Cousin."

"As am I, and I promise you this, my dearest friend: I shall do all within my power to protect you *both* from this moment on. I only pray that you can forgive my selfishness. It is to my shame that I admit it."

"I could forgive you anything, Paul. Anything. Our friendship is formed from an insoluble, inscrutable bond. I'm only sorry that I didn't tell you what happened right away."

The earl smiled at last. "Then, let's make a pact. No secrets from now on. Not amongst the three of us. Tis a mystery indeed, but for God's reasons, you, Beth, and I form a strange sort of triangle, and our love for one another makes each of us stronger. Victoria called you and me 'twin arrows in God's quiver', but it is Beth's love for us that provides the delicate fletching that enables us to fly truer and farther."

"Well put," Sinclair said, also smiling. "No more secrets. Beth and I would be lost without your friendship."

"And I without yours, but let's speak no more about it," the earl insisted as the coach turned off Grosvenor and onto Queen Anne Walk. They passed through the great gates, and in less than five minutes, the two cousins entered the magnificent foyer.

"Welcome home, my lord," John Miles said as he took the marquess's overcoat and hat. "I see you've brought reinforcements. Shall I take the dogs for you?"

"I'll keep them for now. I want to surprise the duchess first. Where is she?"

"In the dining hall, sir. She and the other ladies are working with floral decorations, I believe."

"Sounds quite dull. Paul, tell Uncle James that I shan't be long," the detective said as he and the animals headed towards the north-west end of the mansion's main floor. Along the way, he passed three maids who dusted portraits, vases, and mirrors within the smaller of two galleries. One such maid was Agatha MacGowan.

"Hello there, Aggie. Meet Bella and Briar. Ordinarily, they keep order at Branham Hall, but I've brought them here as a surprise for the duchess. I understand she's in the dining hall."

"She is, my lord," the Scottish servant said with a slight curtsy. "Such lovely dogs, there are, too. Bella reminds me of a bird dog we had at the castle some years back. I suppose you heard about last night, sir."

He tugged on Bella's lead, for the animal seemed to know her mistress was nearby and strained to be released. "Patience, Bella! Last night?"

"I'm sure it was the cocoa what done it, sir. Lady Victoria's dog got right sick. He's better this mornin'; though sleepy."

"The earl mentioned that the dog was ill, but what's all this about cocoa?"

"That's what Lady Victoria thinks, my lord. The cocoa, I mean. Samson licked it up after the duchess spilt it. Alicia told us at breakfast this mornin', tha' my lady were all aflutter last evenin'."

"Whatever do you mean?"

"Only tha' with all the company 'ere las' night, I reckon she were a wee bi' off kilter. Might she be gettin' these measles, sir?"

"I don't know, but I doubt it. Thank you, Agatha. If you'll excuse me," he said, hastening towards the dining hall. As he entered the grand chamber, he found Della, Mary Wilsham, Victoria, and Elizabeth seated around the mahogany table, now protected by a cloth of waxed linen. Each was fastening dried blossoms, berries, and ivy cuttings to straw and wire forms. Samson lay quietly near his mistress's side, his manner subdued, but he perked up and began to bark when the Labradors appeared.

"Do be quiet, Samson!" Tory commanded the animal. "You remember Bella and Briar. Hello, Nephew. It's time you got back."

"And so it is, Aunt. I've never seen such a beautiful collection of blossoms all in one place," he said. "And the flowers are lovely, too."

"Charles!" Elizabeth exclaimed as she jumped to her feet and threw her arms 'round his waist, her head against his chest. "Oh, my darling Captain, you're home—and safe. Promise you won't leave like that again!"

"I promise, little one," he whispered, kissing the top of her head. "I've missed you far too much even to consider it,"

The dogs tugged at the leads, and Beth bent to greet them. "And you've brought my dogs! What a wonderful surprise. Is this the reason you left so suddenly for Branham?"

"Partly," he said honestly.

"Hello, Bella! Hello, Briar!" she said, scratching each animal's ears and head. Both offered a flurry of kisses, and Elizabeth laughed and laughed, sitting at last on the flagstone floor to receive their affection. "Now, now, you mustn't undo my hair," she warned them, referring to the fashionable, fishbone braid Alicia had arranged in her dark curls. "It is intended as practise for the wedding, so you mustn't pull at it. Thank you so much, Charles," she said, glancing up at the marquess. "I've missed these dogs so very much."

Sinclair reached down and helped her to stand. "You're welcome, darling. Hearing you laugh like that is worth the price of a thousand dogs. I'm sorry if I worried you. Do sit, now, and tell me all about Samson. I'm told he's been ill."

"Serves him right for lapping up Beth's cocoa," Tory replied. "He's a glutton and paying the price for his appetite. Charles, whatever happened to your face?"

"It was the telephone game," Adele interjected before Sinclair could reply. "It caused Beth to faint again."

"What's this?" he asked, worry creasing his brow. "Paul didn't mention another faint. Shall we send for Price?"

"No. Really, I'm fine, besides George saw me only yesterday and said I'm much improved," she insisted. "Ask Tory, if you don't believe me."

"Is that true, Aunt?"

"Mostly true," she told him. "George did come 'round yesterday, but he told Elizabeth she's overwrought and that she should rest more often. Your disappearance did little to aid in that, Charles."

"I don't think it was a faint, anyway," Elizabeth continued. "Not really. The lights failed in the library, and it caused me to stumble, but I'm quite all right. Mrs. Meyer took my temperature, and she pronounced me fit, which is more than I can say for you. Victoria's right about your face. It's all scratched and bruised. Whatever happened? Have you been fighting? Is this why you suddenly left for Branham? Please, don't tell me something there connects to crimes in London!"

"No, darling. Nothing. Nothing at all," he assured her. "My face bears the marks of my own clumsiness in the dark. I'd forgotten where I was and tumbled down that short flight of stairs off the master suite. Ask Baxter, if you doubt me. As to why I travelled to Branham, I merely wished to consult with our knowledgeable butler on a personal matter. His experience proved quite insightful, so it was time well spent. Look, darling, I have to attend this circle meeting, but I promise that you and I shall catch up later this afternoon. Ask Mrs. Smith to prepare us a picnic basket, and we'll share it at Haimsbury House. Then, after we eat, you can help me choose colours for the master apartment. Five o'clock?"

She nodded, and he could see tears forming at the corners of her eyes. "Yes. Oh, yes! I've looked forward to that picnic for many days, Charles. I'll speak with Mrs. Smith right away, and I'll be ready—whenever you are."

He kissed her again before leaving the dogs to keep watch on the ladies. Following quickly behind him, Adele Stuart passed through the broad doors and then shut them firmly so that she stood in the anteroom with Sinclair, out of sight of the others.

"Might I have a moment, Cousin Charles?"

"Of course, little cousin. What is it?"

"Let's move away from the door, if that's all right," she said, taking his hand and leading him into the main corridor. "I just wanted to apologise for playing that game last night. I think it upset Cousin Beth, despite what she claims. I realise that I'm not yet fully grown, but I do see things, you know, and I draw conclusions from what I see. Beth isn't herself lately, and I wonder if she needs to see a doctor. A different one, I mean, as Dr. Price keeps saying she's all right. He must be wrong, for she keeps fainting. I'm very worried—as are you. I can see it on your face each time you look at her."

Charles had half a dozen, disparate thoughts fighting one another inside his mind as he tried to decide how best to respond. He had no wish to rush—even though the circle members sat waiting for him—nor did he want to patronise the girl.

"In here," he said at last, leading Adele into the music room. "Sit," he told her as he shut the door. "Della, I consider you very grown up, and as such, I'm about to tell you something that only a few of us know. You must promise to keep it to yourself. If you wish to share it, you speak to me first. Is that clear?"

Her blue eyes widened. "She is ill, then. I knew it. I just knew it!"

Charles sat beside her on the settee. "No. Beth is not ill. Della, has anyone talked to you about the... Well, about the special relationship 'twixt husbands and wives? The kind that leads to the birth of children?"

To his surprise, she began to laugh. "Oh, yes! I know all about that. Mrs. Kildare, our cook at Briarcliff, told me everything when I turned eleven in June. She said it was high time I heard the truth, and that my brother would never think to tell me. Why?"

"Your cook told you? Does your brother know that she spoke to you about it?"

Again she laughed. "I very much doubt it. My brother still thinks of me as a child. Paul doesn't realise that I'm almost grown up. In Scotland, girls can marry at twelve years old, and I shall be twelve next year."

Sinclair blinked. "Scots can marry at twelve? Della, please, promise me that you will never do anything like that! Wait until you're eighty, at least."

"I promise," she laughed. "But why do you ask me about that?"

"It has to do with Beth's—condition. You see, she's not ill. She's going to have a baby."

Adele's face lengthened into an oval as her mouth opened with shock. "A baby!" she exclaimed.

"Quiet, please!" he warned her. "Remember, this is still a secret to nearly everyone here. Paul knows, and so do James, Tory, and Mr. Kepelheim, but we've told no one else."

"A baby," she whispered, breaking into a wide grin. "Oh, this is simply wonderful! But wait, does this mean that you and Cousin Beth have been married all along?"

He paused before replying, wondering how best to explain. "We've not had a formal wedding, no. It's rather convoluted, but she and I were given a strange drug in Scotland that caused us to behave in ways quite unlike our usual selves, but perhaps to God, we are married now. To be honest, I'm not sure. Della, I hope this doesn't make you think any less of me. I respect the duchess and would never willingly take advantage of her."

The girl considered this for a moment. "No, you wouldn't. It's quite strange, you know. I don't think less of you, Cousin Charles. On the contrary, I respect you even more, if that makes any sense. May I talk with Cousin Beth about it?"

"Yes, of course, you may, but you must keep the secret."

"Is this why she fell down the stairs last week?"

"Possibly. Probably, in fact. Her balance is rather unpredictable, and she finds eating a challenge. Might you keep an eye on her for me?"

"I shall be your little spy, if you wish it, Superintendent Sinclair," she whispered. "I think that I would make a splendid detective, which is why I wonder about the dog," she continued, her chestnut brows furrowing into an eleven over her nose. "I mean, if someone drugged you in Scotland, mightn't it happen again? I've read that story, you know. The one printed in *The Strand* magazine from Dr. Doyle. *A Study in Scarlet*. I think our mystery might aptly be called 'A Study in Chocolate', for it's quite possible that Samson got sick, because someone tampered with Beth's drink. Shouldn't we investigate the cocoa? Ask who made it and all?"

He smiled proudly. "Apparently, spying and investigative skills are inherited through the blood. Very well, then, Detective Constable Stuart, give me your report, and then I shall assign your next task."

"Constable? May I not be a detective sergeant?"

"First, let me hear your report, and then I'll decide if your skills merit promotion."

"All right, then," she said seriously. "When Beth took the telephone line into the library, the electrics were switched on and the fireplace lit. I know this, because I watched her go in, you see. However, when I saw the line had slackened, I entered the library and found it dark. All dark. There was not even one single ember glowing, which makes no sense at all, unless someone snuffed it all out with a great brass snuffer of some kind! She was cold, too. Her skin, I mean. Cold to the touch."

"And your brother then helped Beth into the drawing room?"

"Yes. Paul was most upset, but he showed a brave face—as he often does. My brother is far more sensitive than he pretends," she noted.

"You're quite perceptive."

She nodded. "You are much the same. You want everyone to think you are terribly fierce, but I see through your façade, Cousin Charles," she told him. "That is not part of my report, Superintendent. Once Beth returned to the drawing room, she seemed to improve very quickly. Someone—I think it was the new footman, Mr. Peterson—returned to the library to relight the fire, but he found everything in its previous condition: the electric lamps lit and the fire burning brightly. Quite odd, don't you think?"

"Quite."

"And then, my brother suggested that Elizabeth have some cocoa to help her sleep. She's been rather restless of late."

"Yes, so she's told me," he said, finding the girl's mature observations quite remarkable. "Go on, Constable."

"Well, the cocoa arrived, and as Cousin Beth was about to take a sip, my brother suddenly lost his balance and fell into her lap! He'd been pouring the drink into her cup when it happened, and he dropped the pot onto the sofa, and this caused Elizabeth to spill the cup all across the carpeting."

His face darkened. "Paul lost his balance? An accident?"

"No! It looked to me as though someone or something bumped into him. My brother is quite graceful and athletic, yet his balance failed him. As I told you, Superintendent, it was as if someone shoved up against him and caused it all. Rather like dominoes, but no one stood nearby. Isn't that strange?"

"And the dog then lapped up the spill?"

"Most of it, yes. Paul took Elizabeth upstairs as soon as it happened, for cocoa had stained her dress something awful, but before he came back down, Samson had begun to vomit. Perhaps, half an hour or so had passed. No more than that, though."

"Quite observant," Sinclair said as he stood. "And deserving of a promotion to Detective Sergeant, I should think. I'll have your ICI warrant card issued along with my own."

"Don't you mean CID?" she asked as they walked to the door.

"ICI, actually. Your brother and I have decided to start our own detective agency. It's called Inner Circle Intelligence. ICI."

"ICI," she whispered to herself. "I do like that. It's somewhat like Sherlock Holmes, you know. He's a consulting detective. Cousin Charles, all jesting aside, will women be allowed to serve in the ICI?"

"We have women on the inner circle, so I think the answer is yes," he told her. "But only those with the ability to observe and keep secrets."

She winked. "Then, I shall be your very first female inspector."

He bent low and kissed her cheek. "You make me very proud, little cousin."

Adele kissed his cheek as well, putting her arms around his neck. "I do love you, Cousin Charles. And I'm very glad about the baby. Will it be a boy?"

He thought of Albert, remembering that he would have to confess the truth of his death to Elizabeth later that day. "Perhaps," he answered. "We'll know only after it's born."

"Might that be in June?"

"July, perhaps. I'm not certain how doctors calculate these things. Why?"

"My birthday is in June."

"Is it? So is mine. The tenth."

"Mine is the twelfth! We're almost birthday twins."

"So we are. But we missed Paul's birthday, I'm told. Why don't we have a party after the wedding to celebrate all our missed birthdays?"

"A very good and logical idea," she said, adding another wink. "Now, you must go to your meeting, and I have flowers to add to my arrangement. Do you like pink roses or yellow?"

"Yellow," he said, the thought of China Pink roses reminding him of Prince Anatole's multiple baskets. "Though red ones are nice, too. Are these flowers for the chapel?"

"No, but they are for the wedding reception. We're making them to decorate the tables and doorways at Uncle James's house. Oh, but also here, of course. There's to be a family party afterwards. Will Cousin Beth feel like celebrating?"

"I'm sure she will, little cousin. I mean, Detective Sergeant."

"I think I like little cousin, actually," she admitted. "For now, at least, but when I'm on duty perhaps the title is better. See you later!"

She skipped off towards the dining hall, and Charles watched her leave, a smile widening his face. Sighing happily, he followed the corridor away from the music room and entered the library just as the mantel clock struck the hour of one.

1:33 am Castor Institute

"Sister, where is your new nurse? I'd like her to meet me in the lower ward. What is her name again?"

Charge Nurse Cynthia MacArthur had been on her feet for over sixteen hours, having stayed over to replace the day supervisor, who'd come down with measles. "It's Bridget, sir. Bridget O'Sullivan, but I thought we were to employ only males in that section, Dr. Kepler. Have the orders changed?"

"We require a female trainee, as we plan to add a women's section to that level, Sister. I thought we'd discussed this with you last week. The special room our patron has asked us to construct is nearly complete and will require a fulltime nursing staff to monitor our patient and keep her secure whilst she enjoys her stay with us."

"Forgive me, sir. I'd misunderstood. I thought you intended for Nurse O'Sullivan to tend to the male patients. This new ward, though, sir. How many female patients will reside there? Shall I hire more nurses?" she asked, her stomach growling.

"No, I believe our current complement will suffice. There's to be one patient only—for the present. We hope to add to that number with time, but we begin with just the one."

"Very good, sir. If I may, Doctor, I noticed that Mr. Thirteen has been moved. Shall we expect a replacement for him?"

Kepler's beady eyes blinked. "Moved? I gave no orders to move Thirteen to different quarters. If he is not in his room, then, I fear that we must assume the worst! When did you last see him?" the alienist bellowed, hastening his steps towards the door to the lower levels.

"Seven o'clock, sir. When I was asked to replace Sister Campion. She's taken to bed with measles. Her employment record indicated that she had them as a girl, yet her illness was diagnosed by Dr. Collins, himself. It seems our Miss Campion either had a similar illness as a child, or else was misinformed."

"I care nothing about this measles tale, Sister!" he said, his voice rising in pitch. "Damn this key! It isn't fitting. Has someone changed the lock?" he shouted, his hand shaking as he tried to turn the stubborn key.

"Dr. Collins ordered all the locks changed following the incident with Miss Amberson. Her drinking, sir. Shall I?" The nurse inserted a new key and easily turned it. The door swung open, and the two hurried down the hallway towards a set of broad stairs. Four flights later, they emerged through a second, locked door into the sub-basement.

Two male interns waved from their office, the larger of the pair emerging, still chewing on a steak and kidney pie. "We'd not expected ta see you down 'ere, Doc," he said to the physician. "Are you alterin' yer schedule, sir?"

"Where is Thirteen?" the diminutive alienist demanded. "Sister tells me that he was not in his room when she made her rounds this morning."

"He's still with Dr. Collins, I reckon, sir. On that outin'."

"Outing? Mr. Carstairs, we do not take these men on outings! They have aberrations which make them highly unsuitable for such frivolous pastimes. I seriously doubt that my colleague would have done such a foolish thing!" he shouted as he led the way towards cell thirteen. "Gone!" Kepler wailed as he opened the narrow door. "Sound the alarm and get men on the grounds at once! Sister, when did you last check on this wing?"

The charge nurse remained calm, for her twenty-six years of experience with doctors had taught her to retain composure in all situations. "If you look at the chart outside this room, you will see my comment, sir." She donned a pair of reading spectacles and lifted a leather-bound notebook that hung from a hook to the right of the metal door. "It was at 7:07 am, precisely, Dr. Kepler, when I noticed him gone. You will see that I mention that the linen on Mr. Thirteen's bed had been changed, and that the room appeared to have been scrubbed clean with carbolic. The last time I tended to that gentleman, previous to this morning's visit, was at 7:39 yesterday evening. At that time, the patient seemed quite agitated. Therefore, I administered a sedative, per Dr. Collins's standing orders. You can see my signature just to the right of the dosage and time of injection: '7:41 am, six millilitres of three-percent sulphurous morphine'. It is the same dosage we've been using with Mr. Thirteen for the past eight weeks, sir."

"Well, it is clearly not strong enough!" he shouted, sweat beading across his brow. The second-in-command for Castor Institute swiped at his face with a peacock blue handkerchief. "Don't just stand there, Sister! Set the entire building to finding this man! He is dangerous, but more to the point, his mind is unreliable and unbalanced. Should anyone discover what we do here, then, we shall all find ourselves answering some very uncomfortable questions from the police. Do you understand? Find him!"

"Calm yourself, Dr. Kepler. Remember your blood pressure." She turned to the attendants. "Now, Mr. Carstairs, you and Mr. Brine begin down here. I'll have the attendants and porters upstairs begin a thorough search of the upper floors. I'm sure Mr. Thirteen is somewhere on the grounds. After all, we have guards at every gate, and our walls are higher than anyone might scale. So, let us keep our minds sharp and use the brains God gave us."

Kepler shot the woman a scathing glance. "God gave us nothing! Anyone with a modicum of scientific knowledge surely knows that!"

The woman cleared her throat, her strawberry blonde brows riding high upon her face. "As you say, sir. Shall I send word to the French Hospital? Perhaps, he went there again."

"Yes, yes, do so, but find the man before the police do!"

Theodore Kepler felt the ever increasing weight of fear pressing upon his narrow shoulders, and his legs threatened to give way as he climbed the stairs towards the ground floor. Alexander Collins would fly into a rage when he learnt that Thirteen had escaped their confines again; but worse, Sir William Trent would surely learn of the error. Of all Redwing's members, Kepler feared Trent the most.

Perhaps, I should speak to Prince Raziel directly and report Collins's errors in judgement, he thought to himself as he climbed. *It might be time to replace loyalty to Trent with loyalty to the true source of power. The one who brings the greatest reward with him.*

Picturing a future where Collins and Trent lay writhing in torment—where *he* was put in charge of the entire hospital—Theodore Kepler's step quickened, and he actually began to whistle.

CHAPTER FOURTEEN

"I hope his nibs enjoyed his gilded ride yesterday," Galton said as Miles entered the library along with two footmen, bearing pots of coffee and trays of food. "The diverted wheel traffic cluttered up every byway twixt here and Cheapside."

Risling laughed as his friend and comrade joined the table. "Despite his protests to the contrary, the new lord mayor seemed quite pleased with the pageantry. Whitehead pretends to be a man of simple tastes, yet he has no problem with pomp and ceremony."

"It's a long tradition," Galton noted as he accepted a cup of coffee from a footman. "At least he toned down the usual circus atmosphere, Gog and Magog notwithstanding."

"I'm surprised Mr. Whitehead allowed those figures to remain in the procession," Edward MacPherson complained. "If anything smacks of circus, those huge beasts do! I write to the Archbishop every year regarding those pagan monstrosities, but does he listen? Of course, not!" The cleric reached for the sugar. "Oh, thank you, Mr. Lester. Very kind of you," he added when the cordial footman passed him the hand-painted bowl.

"Whitehead couldn't very well leave them out," Sinclair told the gathering as he shut the door. "Good afternoon, all. Forgive the delay, but it couldn't be helped. I had a fiancée to kiss and two dogs to deliver. Hello, James. I trust we're all present and accounted for now."

"Good to have you back, son. From the bruises on your face, it seems you have a tale to tell."

"It can wait," the marquess answered as he took a chair.

"Then, let's begin, shall we?" Duke James said, rising to address the assembled circle members. "Mrs. Smith has prepared a selection of sandwiches and the like, and we'll dig in as soon as we've offered a prayer. But first, let me say a few words of welcome. As some of you already know, we've had to reschedule this meeting several times for one reason or another. It's gratifying, then, that you've made the effort to join us today. This is Charles's first full, circle meeting, for in Scotland, we were able to assemble only a few of our members. Therefore, please, introduce yourselves and tell my nephew how it is you came to be a part of our work."

The marquess and his cousin sat to the duke's right and left, respectively, and the man beside Aubrey stood first. "As you already know, Lord Haimsbury, I'm Malcolm Risling. My father is Lord Pemsbury, and he sends his best wishes. He and my mother look forward to meeting you at the wedding on the eighteenth. My elder brother would be here as well, but he's with the army in Afghanistan presently. My family have served on the circle for six generations."

"It's good to see you again, Risling," Sinclair said. "I shall be pleased to meet your parents. I've followed your father's career in the House of Lords. His advocacy for the police endears him to many of us at the Yard."

"He'll be pleased to hear it, sir."

The next man stood. "Sir Percy Smythe-Daniels, Lord Haimsbury. It's a very great honour to meet you. As with most of us, my family have served for many generations. Malcolm didn't tell you, but he also served in the army and is an expert in several fields of endeavour, including advanced weaponry, which I'm told you'd already learnt in Scotland." Everyone laughed. "I believe our Malcolm hopes to convince you to build an armoury on the Haimsbury estate grounds."

"An idea already proposed by my cousin," Charles said, causing everyone to smile and nod. "Of course, Lord Aubrey keeps a small armoury in his bedchamber from all accounts, so I may call upon that in time of need—for now, at least. And your speciality, Sir Percy?"

"Languages, sir. I've always had an ear for it, which has allowed me to learn sixteen spoken languages, and I can read six that are considered dead. Also, I work with Mr. Kepelheim on ciphers as required."

The next members stood, each in turn introducing themselves:

- Algernon Winters, son of a prominent banker, whose ability to recognise patterns in world markets and political news allowed the circle to finance and launch specific operations abroad.

- Dr. Allan Callerson, a chemist who'd been researching coal tar applications.

- Sir Ralph Epperson, an engineering and scientific genius who'd perfected a combustion engine six years before Daimler, but also designed the electric plants used by Queen Anne House and Branham Hall.

- Dr. Andrew Carrington, a medical doctor and chemist who'd studied tropical diseases in South America on behalf of the circle and had only just returned to England the previous week.

- Dr. Simon Allerton, the duke's leading chemical expert, but also a surgeon, who'd arrived that morning from Germany.

- Sir Anthony Meadows, a skilled archaeologist and anatomist who'd toured the American southwest with Lord Aubrey, and helped to return the skeletal remains of two giants, now stored in a circle warehouse.

- Dr. Deidra Kimberley, a chemist and medical doctor who specialised in diseases of the blood.

- Mavis Carrington, an American heiress representing her father, Matthew Carrington of the New York branch. Accompanying Miss Carrington was her cousin, Peter Carrington, a specialist in ciphers and numbers.

- Sir Dennis Richeson, government attaché to the Argentine and an expert in finance.

- Robert Ludlum, an architect currently designing an underground facility for the duke, who'd brought plans for renovating Loudain House.

- René du Land, an adventurer who'd explored west Africa in search of ancient texts, but also spoke six languages.

- Sir Thomas Canton, an old school chum to Lord Aubrey and a circle historian.

And finally, Mrs. Louisa Gilmore, the Dowager Lady Bramstile, widow of the late Lord Bramstile. As she stood to introduce herself, the entire room grew quiet and respectful.

"Lord Haimsbury, it is a very great pleasure to be here with you on this day. It was precisely six years ago that my husband, Ronald Gilmore, died at the hands of Redwing, slain by a masked man in

Romania. As we had no children, I have asked the duke to allow me to attend on my late husband's behalf. Victoria and I have been friends for nearly thirty years, but it's my understanding that she has forgone attendance so that she might keep our duchess company. We often refer to Elizabeth as our 'dear one', but to me, she is much more than that."

The sixty-seven-year-old widow wiped at her eyes, and the cheeks of the men shimmered with similar tears. "You most likely do not remember me, Charles, but I met you briefly in '79 at the memorial service here in London. Our Beth had specified that you were to sit with her at that service, and I can still see it as if it occurred only yesterday. Our darling child, newly named Duchess of Branham, dressed in black crepe, held your hand as she wept. You bent low and whispered to her, promising that she would be all right; that she was safe. I sat behind you, you see. I could hear your words, and could see her posture alter as you encouraged her. I knew then that you loved her just as we do, but I had no idea who you truly were.

"It wasn't until this past spring that the duke told me of his suspicions, and that he had tasked Martin with finding the evidence of your inheritance, but I should have seen it. Charles, you are the gentle-hearted boy grown into manhood. I see not only your dear mother in your face, but also your good father—and the late Lord Aubrey as well. It's remarkable how much you resemble him. You descend from a mighty heritage, Charles, and I believe that it's always been God's plan that you return to us this year. Don't ask me to explain why, for it is more feeling than evidentiary fact. As a policeman, you would probably find such feelings irrational and inadmissible."

She wiped her eyes once more, her thin frame shuddering as deep emotion took hold. "I hope you brave men will forgive me. I grow sentimental in my older years. Seeing you here, in company with your cousin, brings me such joy, Charles! As you continue to learn about your childhood and the many trials you experienced as a boy, it will all make more sense, but let me end by returning to 1879. When I watched you with Elizabeth, somehow, I knew that your connexion to her would become very important one day. It seemed too deep, too profound to be mere accident. It was as if a great ribbon of light formed betwixt you. And that same beautiful light shines within your eyes now. It is the light of Christ. May he continue to guide you both as you enter into this marriage. May he strengthen you for the inevitable battle ahead."

The dowager countess returned to her chair, and all of the members wiped their eyes. Charles rose and walked to her place, where he took her hand as he bowed. "Countess, it is a very great honour to meet you again, and I do recall being introduced to you in '79. I remarked on how lovely your blue eyes are, like a delicate pair of robin's eggs. They still strike me as such."

She smiled and touched his face. "Yes, you did say that. I'd forgotten. I don't know if your uncle has told you, but the Bramstile earldom passed to the late Lord Aubrey, as he was the closest relative when my husband died. He and Ronald were second cousins, you see. When Robert Stuart died two and half years ago, the title fell to your cousin, but I suppose it rightly belongs to you, as you are closer to my husband's side of the family. Ronald was your first cousin through the MacAllens. The Bramstile earldom is much younger than the Aubrey title, though, and far less important than your marquessate. Oh, Charles, I'm rambling now! Do forgive me."

He kissed her cheek. "I could forgive you anything, Countess. But as we are related by marriage, would it be presumptuous of me to ask if I might call you Aunt Louisa?"

She began to weep openly. "Oh, I'd like that very much!"

"Thank you, then, Aunt," he whispered sweetly. "As to the rest of you, I already know Reid and France. Glad you came along, Arthur. And Kepelheim has become a dear friend, of course, as my improved wardrobe will attest."

All laughed, and the tailor's plump cheeks rounded with pride. "It is an honour to design them for you, but my creations pale in comparison with your rugged charm."

Charles laughed as he clapped the tailor on the shoulder. "One of these days, I must hear the truth of your history, Martin. I suspect you are far more than a fast and efficient needle, your cipher and deductive abilities notwithstanding."

"One day, we'll tell you all about our intrepid tailor, son," the duke promised. "Over a cognac or some Drummond whisky. Louisa, did you wish to leave?"

The dowager countess nodded. "Yes, James. As I told you whilst we awaited your nephews, I think the best use of my presence is to keep Elizabeth company. I'd originally planned to listen to all the reports, but I'm sure you prefer that Beth remain outside these doors."

"I doubt that she'll try to enter, Louisa," the duke countered. "Beth has a strong aversion to circle meetings. Though she is curious about our discussions, she fears what may happen if she actually sits inside the room with us. I'll explain it to Charles at a later date."

"May I not have one hint, James?" the marquess asked. "As her guardian, any strong aversion within her nature is important to me."

The duke sighed. "It's a long tale, son, but allow me to give you that hint. Do you recall the seizure she suffered whilst at your home in '79?"

"How could I forget? I'd asked her to tell me about the person she called 'the man in the park', and she had a dreadful reaction! Her entire body shook, and I thought she might collapse entirely."

Paul reached over and touched his cousin's hand. "I know how terrifying that was for you, Charles. Can you imagine, then, what it was like for us, when we asked Elizabeth to answer a few questions about Connor's death? We wanted the fellowship within our circle to hear her replies and try to make sense of it all, but when I asked if she remembered seeing any other humans upon the moor, she had a similar reaction—only far worse than you described. A mere seizure would have been a blessing that day! Poor Beth collapsed to the floor, her entire body stiffening into an arc, and she literally elevated to the height of the table! It was as if unseen hands had lifted her, and she screamed the entire time. No, we will not bring her in here again. Not ever."

Sinclair grew thoughtful, and he glanced at the sober faces surrounding him, finally nodding in agreement. "Yes, I can see how her attendance might prove harmful, but this makes me appreciate her remarkable strength all the more. Beth has suffered contacts from another realm since childhood, yet she's kept her sanity and sense of humour, despite all."

The dowager countess smiled. "Little Beth possesses a quiet strength beyond that of many men, and I am very glad that you appreciate it, Charles. Not all men would. So, as we prefer she remain occupied, I shall join her and Victoria."

"I'd like it if you would stay, Aunt Louisa," Charles implored. "However, if you choose to leave us, please, wait until after I've made my announcement."

The duke cast a curious glance towards the detective. "Do you prefer to make it now or after the prayer?"

"I'll do it afterwards, sir."

"Very good, then," the duke continued. "As I'll soon be passing leadership to Charles, I'd like to pray this one last time, if I may. Let us bow our heads, ladies and gentlemen." He paused for a moment, and then the duke's rich, Scottish baritone rose up as he held his nephews' hands. "Lord of all that is good and honest, just and true, we come to you with humble hearts this day. Tis an honour to sit with this assembly of your united warriors this afternoon. I would that such a gathering were not necessary, my Lord, but it is. Redwing's crows flock about London and about my granddaughter like ravenous birds of prey, and so we seek your guidance in how we might prevent their plans from achieving fruition.

"To be honest, my King, when I consider all that happened whilst in Scotland last month, it fills my human heart with dismay and fear. I imagine it affects Charles in much the same way, yet he seldom shows it. You've given him a unique ability to remain calm, when the world all about him races towards insanity. Perhaps, that's one reason you chose to allow Redwing to take him from us at so young an age. The past thirteen years as a policeman have honed his mind into a razor sharp blade that will cut our enemies to the quick! Paul and he have become great friends, but I know that already, Redwing plots how best to sever that alliance, for they fear the united strength of these two cousins. I ask that you show them the path you've designed for them to follow, and that you light that path, my Lord. Arm them for the battle and grant them the courage to stand against the foe until their final breath is taken.

"I ask also that you be with our little duchess, my Lord, and help her to remain healthy and strong. Calm her fears and lighten her heart. Banish all the nightmares and replace them with sweet dreams filled with joy, for she brings joy to all our hearts. As this wedding approaches, keep all within our households and within this circle safe from the enemy's wiles, for this event is the culmination of centuries of planning on both sides.

"Teach us to honour you in all that we do, to see with your perfect vision and discern with your perfect insight. Keep our heads clear, our minds sharp, and our hands ready to wield whatever weapons you command us to employ. May we serve you faithfully until our dying breath. In the name of your only begotten Son I ask—even the name of Christ Jesus. Amen."

As the assembly wiped their faces, Dr. MacPherson stood. "I was honoured to spend yesterday morning with this fine young man, my friends. Charles Sinclair is indeed a remarkable servant, who loves the Lord with all his heart. As the duke has said, the enemy thought to destroy him in his early years, but that altered path not only taught Charles to discern the human heart, but also to see things most of us cannot."

"What do you mean by that, Mac?" Risling asked.

"I'll allow Charles to explain further, but suffice to say that Sinclair's eyes are attuned to matters beyond the ken of most. I shall be honoured to pronounce him husband to our beloved duchess on the eighteenth."

Sinclair stood. "Thank you, Dr. MacPherson—I mean, Mac. I cannot begin to tell you just how pleased I'll be to hear that pronouncement on the eighteenth! The prospect of calling Elizabeth my wife brings me greater joy than mere words could ever express. Which brings me to my announcement. I know this will likely surprise many of you, but those who know what happened in Scotland last month may not be at all surprised. Let me quickly explain for those who are unaware of those events. On the eighth of October, shortly after our arrival at Drummond Castle, the duchess was given an unknown drug or combination of drugs by the late Dr. Lemuel, a man who betrayed this circle and whose background still requires our attention."

Risling's hand went up. "When I give my report, I have something to offer along that line of enquiry."

Charles cleared his throat, for he felt nervous suddenly. "Thank you, Malcolm. I look forward to hearing it. As I said, Lemuel had given the duchess something to render her unable to struggle, and then he abducted her. Because the earl had been shot on our rail journey from London to Branham, the man whom I may now call uncle sent me into the night upon his fastest horse to rescue Elizabeth. When I finally caught up to Lemuel's carriage, a shooter on the heath killed the man, so I rushed to take Beth to safety. I had no experience with those roads at night, and I became quite lost. Beth was unconscious; therefore, could not aid me in my ignorance. We came upon a farm, and I sought shelter for the night. The couple put us up in their son's empty cottage. Whilst there, I kept watch on Beth's welfare."

He stopped for a moment and took a long sip of water. "What I didn't know as I sat beside that fire, was that the farmer's wife had put something into our tea. Beth drank half a cup before falling asleep again, and I consumed an entire jar of it. That night, she and I shared the same dream."

Charles took another long drink, and the duke tapped his forearm. "You needn't get into this, son. We all know you're not to blame. What's done is done."

"But I feel as if I'm to blame!" Sinclair objected. "I should have been more aware. More careful, but I wasn't. As you say, what's done is done. The dream the duchess and I shared, my friends, was rather... Well, it was quite intimate. She and I realised later, when we compared our experiences, that it was not a dream at all, but rather a real event."

"Charles told me all about it as soon as he recovered enough to remember," Drummond explained. "My nephew is a man of honour and compassion, and he worried then what Redwing might have intended."

"It's clear what they intended," the marquess added, taking a deep breath to strengthen his resolve. "What I'm trying to tell you all is this: Elizabeth has seen two doctors, and both are convinced that she is with child."

Most of the company knew nothing of this news, and their expressions ranged from surprise to great joy. Kepelheim spoke for all as he rose to his feet.

"My dear friends, this is the best of news! Yes, I've been privy to the diagnosis for a day or two, but I think it likely that this has been the ultimate goal of Redwing all along: to unite our marquess's blood with that of Elizabeth. Charles, your uncle and I had a lengthy discussion about this last evening, and we agree that Redwing's members have committed a very grave error in judgement. They have underestimated you, my friend. Our sovereign king, Christ Jesus, has designed you for this moment in time, Charles. I know it as surely as I know my own name! He *allowed* your abduction, and he's been with you on each step of your perilous journey since that day, forming you and shaping you as his servant.

"Victoria has called you and Paul twin arrows in God's quiver, and it is imagery that I can never forget, for it is a perfect description of your office. Both of you love our duchess, and both of you are required as her protectors. Both. And I believe we are only seeing a tiny sliver of God's plans for your lives—you three. It occurs to me now that in one way, the three of you are the central triangle within our circle. A triple bond, which adds strength to our formation. May we band of brothers and sisters tighten about you as a protective hedge during the coming trials. And once this child is born, may we surround him or her with all our energies, all our might!"

The entire table broke into applause and shouts of 'hear! hear!'. The earl took to his feet, tears staining his bearded cheeks. "I can add little to what Martin has said in honour of my cousin, but I would make a confession, if you'll indulge me." He paused, his clear blue eyes on Sinclair.

"I've come to love and respect this man. Charles Sinclair, whom I first met ten years ago. I think of 1879 as the year every-thing changed. Not just for Beth, but for Charles, for me, for all of us. Redwing tipped their hand, you might say, though we were blind to it at the time. What Charles has told you about Scotland may sound like fairy tale, but it is hard fact, and it nearly sent me reeling into our enemy's clutches when I learnt about it! Despite her fiancé's admonition not to tell me about the baby, the duchess did just that. Last night. Elizabeth told me, because she loves me, just as much as she ever has. I'm not proud of my reaction, for in truth, my entire being was overwhelmed with outrage, even hatred. I actually told Elizabeth that I wanted to choke the life out of my cousin."

These last words rode upon waves of intense regret, and the earl lowered his head in shame, his broad shoulders spasming. Many of the members prayed silently as Aubrey took a moment, his head against his chest. Charles reached out and touched his cousin's hand to offer strength.

Paul raised his eyes at last, wiping tears. "Of course, I didn't really intend to do it, but I *felt* it. Deeply, intensely, and it revealed a darkness to my heart that shocks me. Charles, I pray that you can forgive me!" he exclaimed as he gripped the marquess's hand. "I beg you to understand my anguish, for I love Beth with all my heart!"

Sinclair took to his feet, and the two men embraced before the entire company. Not an eye remained dry around the long table, not one heart unmoved; even the two footmen began to weep. James Stuart stood and threw both arms 'round his nephews, and soon all the company drew near, their hands joined, many of them praying softly as the cousins wept.

Louisa Gilmore, who walked with a cane, made her way to the pair, and the gathering parted as she approached. Like a wise mother-figure, the dowager countess took the hands of both men and began to pray aloud. "Father in heaven, may your Spirit fill this room and bring strength to these two, remarkable young men. May you touch both heart and mind, to cleanse them of any doubts or resentment, and may you then replace those darker emotions with your clear resolve and fellowship.

"It's easy to see the love these two men hold for one another, but the enemy would turn that love to hatred, for as our tailor wisely observed, they form a bond with our dear duchess that requires them both as her protectors. At the heart of all this, lies the future and safety of an unborn child. I ask especially for your protection upon that small life. Help it to grow and thrive. Provide your guardian spirits to minister to this child's mother and father, for this is the child the enemy has long sought. And may you equip both Charles and Paul to shelter that child, as they now shelter the duchess.

"Guide our small fellowship, my King! Guide us and instill within us a firm resolve, so that we do not fear whatever lies ahead. May each of us within this ring remain true to you, but also true to these two men. Twin arrows in your quiver describes these remarkable cousins so very well. May they never waiver as they take flight! May they fly straight and true without fear, trusting in your perfect aim. It is in Christ's name I ask all this, Father. Even, he who taught us to pray. Our Father, who art in heaven, hallowed be thy name..." she continued, and all joined her, finishing the Lord's wonderful prayer of supplication and praise with one voice.

As the company spoke the final words, Charles, who still embraced the earl, opened his eyes. "My life is yours," he whispered.

"And mine yours," Aubrey echoed back. "Today and forever."

The duke wiped his dark eyes. "There's no man richer in this world!" he told his nephews. "Not one. Now," he continued as the assembly returned to their chairs. "Louisa, if you still wish to leave us, this would be a good time, but I agree with Charles. I'd like for you to remain. You ladies of the circle provide insights that we foolish men lack. Will you stay?"

Charles escorted the dowager countess to her seat. "I hope you'll stay with us, Aunt Louisa."

She smiled, touching his face. "Yes, of course I'll stay. We women shall serve the roles of Mary and Martha, though I shan't try to cook."

Everyone laughed softly, and the marquess returned to his position on the duke's right. "So, whose report begins us?"

The duke tapped his water glass. "Reports require nourishment. Mr. Miles and his men have brought us a substantial luncheon. Everyone should fill their plates whilst we discuss matters, but first I'd like to hear how you earned those bruises, laddy," he told Charles. "Did Baxter give you a boxing lesson?"

"He could have, sir, but these marks owe their root to a far less pleasant pastime. One of Beth's horses was killed last night. Ambrose Aurelius. Drained of blood by a spirit that led me on an exhausting chase through Henry's Woods."

"You say the horse was killed?" Paul asked. "How?"

"I'm not sure, but it reminded me of the Victoria Park murders. The only obvious injuries are two puncture wounds upon the throat. The sheep who died at Branham recently may also have been slain by the same dark hand, or another like it. It is a creature of immense power, capable of flight. A new type of hybrid, perhaps, beyond that of the wolves with which we're familiar."

The earl stared, trying to sort through the information. "Then, it's beginning again. Spirits and shadows. Here and at Branham. But why now? Charles, you say you pursued it? Judging from your face, I assume it attacked you."

"It did, but there is more to the story. The creature intended only to gain my attention, or so I believe. It may have been the same entity that appeared inside my coach on the road to the hall."

"Son, what do you mean by that?" the duke asked.

"I had three, very interesting conversations during that journey. One with Prince Razarit Grigor, the second with Prince Anatole Romanov, and the third with a being whose name I do not know, though he brought me comfort beyond all capacity to explain. I think this third was sent by God."

All grew silent, and MacPherson raised a hand. "The first two names are outside my knowledge, but how is it they rode with you in the coach?"

"They appeared to me, Mac, as uninvited guests. I'd already had one encounter with Razarit, and I'd begun to suspect Romanov is more than human, but now I know for certain. The former is evil and arrogant and believes Beth will become his soon. The latter's loyalties remain unclear, for he acted on my behalf, preventing Razarit from harming me."

"Then, how is your face bruised?" the earl asked.

"It happened last night, after we discovered the dead horse. Truthfully, I'm still trying to puzzle through it all, but their abilities imply that both Grigor and Romanov are spirits or hybrids of a type unknown to us. Further, they may be but a vanguard of what is to come."

MacPherson stood. "Forgive me for pressing the issue, Charles, but I'd make one further observation. If you pursued this creature, then it is because this spirit *wanted* you to see it. You say that it struck you?"

Sinclair nodded. "Yes, Mac, as if daring me to chase after it."

"Sounds rather infantile to me," Drummond observed. "Like a child's prank."

"Our experience indicates that these spirits have personalities, the same as humans," MacPherson explained. "Some exhibit more maturity than others. And scripture reveals an order to their ranks, a hierarchy similar to our peerage system."

Reid stood. "I am sorry to interrupt, but if I may, Charles?"

Sinclair nodded. "Yes, Ed, of course. There was a time when all I had to concern me were police matters, but my duties widen. Please, speak."

"Thank you," Edmund answered. "Charles, I've not yet sent this report to your office at Whitehall, and you'll understand why momentarily. I've brought typed copies, but for circle eyes only. With that in mind, allow me to introduce Inspector Arthur France. Charles asked me to bring him along, my friends." Reid turned to look at the young inspector. "Arthur, you'll want to meet with a few of us privately to learn more about our core command and history, but I think you already understand a little of our mission."

France stood. "I'm catching on a bit, sir, and I'm honoured to be here, Your Grace, my lords and ladies. I'll most likely have a cartload of questions, but Mr. Reid has told me the basics whilst on our drive from Whitechapel this morning. It helps explain many of the strange things going on in the east just now, but it also helps me to understand some of the hushed conversations 'twixt the superintendent and Reid of late."

Many of the members smiled at this, including Sinclair. "I imagine it does, Arthur. I'm very glad you're here. Ed, what is it you've learnt? I take it this pertains to Mary Kelly."

"It's in the written report," he said, handing copies to both Charles and the duke. "Sunders has performed an initial examination along with Bagster Philips and Bond. As you can imagine, Abberline sees the hand of a man behind these murders, but there are signatures we in the circle recognise as spiritual. Charles, you mentioned the lack of footmarks in the blood. We made a thorough inspection of the room and could find nothing left by our killer—or killers. Witnesses claim that Kelly sang for many hours during the night, continuing until close to dawn. A neighbour reported seeing a man leaving the area, but she may have only seen McCarthy or Indian Harry. We're trying to prompt the woman's memory, but she admits to having enjoyed several pints of gin before bedtime; therefore, we cannot be sure of her faculties. Kelly's heart is indeed missing, by the way. I've collected photographs, delivered to me this morning by Lord Aubrey's friend. The entire east end was riotous when France and I left. We require more men to handle the brawlers, sir. Lusk's support widens, and he may have gained political ground as well. I strongly advise against anyone driving within four blocks of the Leman Street station house. Our forces are overstretched, and the rioting worsens by the hour."

"I'll speak with Monro about seconding men from other divisions," Sinclair offered.

"Thank you, sir. The sooner they can arrive, the safer it will be for all who live and work in Whitechapel."

Galton raised his hand. "And O'Brien? It's my understanding that he once again enjoys your hospitality, Edmund."

Reid smiled. "So, he does, and I hope our marquess will agree to spend an hour there with me later on. O'Brien claims to have information of interest. I'm not sure just what he fears, but he is quite nervous."

"I'd hoped to spend time with Beth today, Ed, but if you think O'Brien might talk, then I'll drop by later this evening. Is there anything else that involves the circle?"

"Only that we've also arrested Kelly's common-law husband, Joe Barnett. He's unable, or unwilling, to account for his whereabouts Thursday night," Reid explained. "I am curious, though, sir. I've heard tell of a new endeavour involving an investigative body called the ICI. Are the rumours true?"

"They are, Edmund, and I'd planned to speak with you about it, but I'd like to postpone that conversation until after the wedding. Is that all right with you, Uncle James?" Charles asked the duke.

"Fine with me, son. For those who don't already know, the ICI is to be our circle's private intelligence organisation. The queen and her privy council have approved, granting us the royal warrant. We'll be serving as the Crown's eyes and ears in foreign lands as well as here in England, but we shall remain private and independent. I've provided information in your packets. Once we're through the wedding, and Charles has found a little free time, we'll host the first meeting at ICI headquarters, Loudain House."

Dr. Kimberley flipped through the pages of the duke's packet. "I've never been inside, of course, but the house looks suitably large. Will we be using it as office space?"

"Eventually, yes," Charles answered, still standing. "Forgive me for monopolising so much of our time, but before we begin other reports, I'd like to read something to you all. As some of you may know, I paid a call on Bob Morehouse's widow this week, and she gave me a letter, which Bob asked his solicitor to send me. Apparently, with my travels over the past month, the envelope failed to find me, so it was returned to Lady Morehouse. Martha received a similar letter from Bob, though the copy sent to her did not include this confession."

Reid's hand went up. "Fred Abberline said Morehouse sent something to him as well. I wonder if it's a similar sort of confession."

"Bob and Fred were quite close," Sinclair replied, "so it's possible. However, this revelation is about me. I doubt Abberline's version contains the same. In addition to the letter, Bob included documents he'd purloined from the Yard. Reports he'd written regarding Duchess Patricia's murder. And there was one other inclusion, wrapped in newspaper."

Charles handed a folded newsprint sheet to Aubrey. The earl unwrapped the package. "It's a stickpin," he said.

The duke reached out. "Let me see it, son." Taking the slender pin, Drummond examined it carefully, and then donned his spectacles to peer at a fine line of engraving. "We shall pass this 'round, but it's probably familiar to Paul. We've both seen this many times."

The earl took the stickpin once more, his young eyes sharp and aware. "Why would Morehouse have this?"

Charles took it once more, turning it in his hands. "Whose is it?"

"It was worn nearly every day by Sir William Trent," Aubrey said darkly. "At least, every time I saw him, it was on his cravat. He wore it as a symbol of pride."

"Yes, but what we never saw then was the engraving on the reverse, son," Drummond noted, reaching out for the pin and showing it to both nephews. "See here? How brazen can a man get? *Nox Lupus*. Night Wolf."

"He certainly isn't trying to hide his true colours," Kepelheim remarked. "Charles, what does Morehouse's letter say? Do you mind reading it aloud?"

"Not at all. It says the following," Sinclair began.

'Dear Charles,

This letter serves as my final confession, dear friend, and you receive it, because I am dead. By now, I suspect that you may already know some of my misdeeds, but because they concern you in particular—and from what I have learnt, also a lady known to you—my soul will not rest until I make a clean breast of it.

When you first came to my attention as a new recruit all those years ago, I was ordered to provide you full instruction and opportunity for advancement. Those orders originated from a position very high in government. Therefore, I assumed, that your origins must be, let us say, from the other side of the blanket. My high-level confident also tasked me with finding out all I could about your background. You would not have been the first man born from an illicit union, and I thought little of it at the time.

Later, additional orders arrived from this same person—and no, I shan't tell you his name, but he is someone known to you. These orders included taking you to Paris and introducing you to his contacts there. It shames me to think of how I left you to their influence that night at the party. Shames me to the core, but, Charles, you did nothing wrong. Nothing. You were a gentleman and a Christian, despite their attempts to lure you into debauched situations. I know the woman who blackmailed you—know who she really is. However, I cannot reveal that either. Not in a letter. I pray that you discover it on your own. I suggest you have Aubrey's team investigate that party. It will lead to her, and to many other, dark truths.

However, it was that singular night in March, 1879, when my curiosity was at last roused from complacent slumber. You remember that night well, I know, but you were not privy to all that happened. Recall that we received word that Duchess Patricia's body had been discovered on Commercial sometime just after midnight. I was called out to Leman Street a little after one, and you shortly afterward. You and I searched the scene and then conveyed the victim's remains to the station house—for the child found beside her was already there, so we had learnt. What you did not know, Charles, is that I discovered evidence at the scene, which I concealed.

Prior to that long night's work, I'd been called upon by an envoy who represented a royal personage from Romania. Prince Alexei Grigor. Both Downing Street and our Foreign Office vouched for this gentleman, and he was working with our own Special Branch. The envoy informed me that a lunatic—a close friend to this Romanian prince—had escaped from an asylum, and that he had been seen in our borough. This escapee was foreign, and of high birth—*very high* birth, Charles—and it was imperative that any scandal be avoided. I would add that such a scandal would have involved the royal family, as this escapee often attended public events in company with Her Majesty. At the time, I thought myself acting rationally.

As you and I searched the ground near the body, I discovered a figural stickpin, which I then pocketed, saying nothing to you. I never logged it as evidence; never revealed its existence to any other policeman. The pin bore the image of a white bird, that I understand you now would recognise as representing a dark group called Redwing.

I'd instantly recognised the image, my dear friend, because as a youth—twenty or so years of age—I'd fallen in love with a woman who served this evil cabal. An ageless witch who lured me into detestable activities. I shudder to think what rites I once performed with her and her wretched friends, but when I finally broke free of her bonds, I thought myself emancipated at last!

Not true. Not true. I fear all my follies are discovered, and tonight one comes to claim my life, if not my soul. He signs his name as 'A', and I fear this man more than any, Charles. He may be someone already in your intimate circles. If so, you must keep him away from our little duchess! He seeks to use her—but also *you*—to satisfy both his lust for power and his lust for flesh.

No longer will I keep their hideous secrets. I pray that you and the inner circle will find a way to use the enclosed evidence, though I hand it to you ten years too late.

I realise now that I was duped, and I pray our Saviour has forgiven me for these sins and so many others.

My final piece of information is this: My investigation into your true identity as a Sinclair hints at some strange component within your blood—something connected to an ancient lineage that reaches much further back than the circle is aware. There is a Russian prince who may be able to tell you more, though I cannot vouch for his allegiance. He once aided me in France, and though you may not remember it, this same prince came to your rescue when you were a child.

His name is Anatole Romanov.

Forgive me, Charles. I go to Our Saviour now, praying that *His blood* may yet wash away all my unholy sins.

Robert.'

"It ends there," the detective concluded. "He implies that Romanov is an ally, but if this 'A' person isn't Anatole, then who might it be?"

"Despite what Morehouse claims about the Russian's help in the past, I'd still place my money on Romanov," the earl replied. "He is overly attentive with Beth."

The jewelled stickpin had made its way 'round the table and returned to the duke's possession. "Does this letter serve as evidence implicating Trent in Patricia's murder? Is it enough to see that man hang at last?"

Sinclair shook his head. "I doubt it, Uncle. Trent's lawyers would deny that the pin is his, but merely another that looks like it; or that it was stolen; or that Patricia had it with her when she died. After all, it can be assumed she had access to his jewellery. It *is* enough, however, to remand him for questioning, and I look forward to doing so, providing we can find him."

"William Trent hovers about these Ripper murders like a carrion crow," Aubrey remarked, glancing at the pin. "Just who is Trent, anyway? How did he become a hybrid? Rituals? Science? Can he even be killed, I wonder?"

"I don't think him purely spirit," MacPherson said. "Our experiences reveal him as hybrid of man and demon, and it's clear that he brags of it. *Nox lupus*, indeed. An enhanced human with transformational powers."

"Powers gained through blood rituals?" Charles asked. "He mentioned to me that the Ripper murders are but one part of a ritual that is nearly complete."

"What do you mean, Charles?" the earl asked. "When did you speak with Trent?"

"I've already told James and Martin about this, Paul, but night before last, Trent appeared to me inside Beth's apartment. He entered by way of a crack beneath the east window."

"A crack?" MacPherson asked, his elbows against the table, his eyes wide. "Was it in the form of smoke or mist?"

"Yes, how did you know, sir?"

"It's a favourite method employed by these spirits. I'd no idea Trent had such powers! But if these murders are meant to enhance his capabilities, then perhaps they're working."

Paul shook his head. "You could be right regarding Trent's personal abilities, but the murders and the bloodletting provide far more than personal gain. An informant tells me that they power a ritualistic machine that will lead Redwing to the location of a hidden mirror."

"A mirror?" Kepelheim asked, his face darkening. "Oh dear. This is bad. Very bad."

Charles had been making notes, and he glanced up. "What do you mean by that, Martin?"

"The riddle, Charles. Don't you recall it? Yes, I know it's been a very busy week with much to occupy your thoughts, but Saucy Jack's riddle implies a mirror. Let me see if I can remember it..."

Sinclair closed his eyes, his eidetic memory turning through pages in his mind. "*Find the glass, the shining one, numbered 'mongst its brothers near, keyless doorway to the dawn, crying child awakens fear. Dying dreams of princes be, to subtle asp and owls arise, Keepers howl and Watchers beam, as Wormwood's poison seeks its prize,*" he quoted. "The glass is a mirror. A shining mirror?"

Paul smiled. "Your memory is like mine, Charles. And Beth's. She can recall nearly every conversation heard or item seen. Blood will tell."

"And blood provides power in ways human knowledge cannot fathom," the marquess answered. "I may have a nearly perfect memory for some things, but my insight into Redwing's supernatural advisors is sorely lacking. Why blood? How can it power their rituals?"

"It's likely that blood provides energy for their transformations," Deidra Kimberley observed. "Our human bodies require food, air, and water. Perhaps, these hybrids require blood for the same reason. Doesn't the Bible say that very thing?"

"The blood is the life," MacPherson quoted. "Charles, when you encountered the creature at Branham and earlier inside your coach. what did it say to you?"

"He threatened me, but that's no surprise. However, I got the distinct impression that Razarit has no permission to harm me; that even he has commanders. My experiences thus far have taught me this much, though: when these creatures speak to me, I notice that worldly motion stops, as if time itself holds its breath."

The minister nodded. "It's said that is how we perceive such visitations. As though the entities must pull us outside of our reality in order to commune with us. The duchess has often entertained these visitors, but despite her remarkable mind, her recollections are often clouded. Either she is incapable of retaining such a troubling memory or is deliberately manipulated to forget."

"Trust me, my limited experience with these creatures confirms what I've known for a long time: that Beth's mind is incredibly strong," Charles said with pride. "Few individuals, man or woman, would remain sane after all she's endured. She is a brilliant person. Simply brilliant."

"Yes, our dear one generally recalls details others would forget," Kepelheim said as he reached for a sliced beef sandwich. "You say that Romanov appeared as your benefactor? Is he our ally, then?"

"I cannot yet say," Charles answered. "Perhaps, he plays both sides, but it's clear that he exerts power of some sort over this other—the one who calls himself Razarit or Rasha."

"This is the second time Rasha has appeared to you, Charles," Kepelheim observed as he poured a glass of lemonade. "I wonder why."

"Probably because he's jealous," the earl answered. "I can appreciate his anger. No, dear friends, I do not return to my former state. I merely call attention to it. But I, also, have seen Rasha Grigor. He appeared to me at Egyptian Hall two nights past in company with Serena di Specchio. I'd intended to speak to you about it, Charles, but with Mary Kelly's murder, time got away from us."

"What did he say to you?" the marquess asked his cousin. "Did he threaten you?"

"In a manner of speaking," Aubrey replied stoically. "Nothing I couldn't have handled, so sending Hamish Granger to fetch me was unnecessary."

"I'll leave that to our Chief of the Mews to confirm," Haimsbury answered with a slight smile. "The informant you mentioned earlier. I presume you mean Susanna Morgan?"

"Yes, but as I told you at the station this morning, both she and MacKey have disappeared."

"Charles, why do you pursue Lorena MacKey?" asked Martin Kepelheim. "Hasn't she done enough damage to you and Elizabeth?"

"MacKey could provide access to Trent's mind," the detective answered. "When she and I spoke in Scotland, her mask dropped, only for a moment, but in that moment I saw regret in her eyes. I believe we can turn her to our cause."

"I doubt that," Aubrey answered, pouring a cup of tea. "If her mask slipped, then it was deliberate. She's a witch, Charles. Pure and simple."

Sinclair sighed. "Must we assume her unredeemable? You place your faith in Morgan's defection. Why wouldn't Lorena hold the same hope for independence?"

"She demonstrated no such hope in my presence," Aubrey said. "Perhaps, she found you more charming, Cousin," he then added with a mischievous grin.

"Paul, I think your charms ever true, if Delia Wychwright is any indication!" the duke teased "That girl has certainly set her cap on you. Shall I speak with her father and ask him to rein her in?"

"No, sir, I'm capable of doing so, if it comes to it. However, Lady Cordelia was casting her eyes upon Sir Thomas towards evening's end. Perhaps, I've slipped the hook."

"Or perhaps you're already netted and being prepared for supper," Galton answered.

The doors opened, admitting Granger and John Miles. The two servants bowed and took the last empty chairs, near the end of the table.

Charles rose to his feet. "Welcome, gentlemen. Thank you both for joining us today. I'm sure that you have plenty to keep you busy, but I'd ask your help with several matters. Mr. Miles, can you tell us if anyone working here presently or in the past might be considered suspect? It occurs to me that the first letter from Saucy Jack bore no stamp, and the postman assured the duchess that he did not put it into the post bag. Do you remember?"

"Of course, my lord," Miles answered. "Do you suspect someone within the household?"

"It is one possibility," Sinclair replied. "I'd be remiss if I ignored it. Another possibility is that the house was never rekeyed after Patricia's death."

Drummond glanced at Paul. "I don't remember having it done. With the funeral and so much to worry about at the time, it may have slipped past us. Paul, did you rekey the locks?"

"No, sir, and I cannot believe it never occurred to me! Miles, are the current keys the same as in '79?"

"They are, my lord. No one ordered them changed. Do you think Sir William used his old key to enter?"

"He requires no key," Charles answered, "but a human would. If Trent's key is involved, then he has given it to someone fully flesh. I'd like a list of everyone who's worked here, say, in the past ten years. And the names of anyone else with access to house keys."

"Yes, sir," Miles replied. "I'll work with Mrs. Meyer to provide that information to you. Ordinarily, only she and myself have keys, but I do not dismiss the possibility of someone stealing a latch key and having a copy made, or, as you say, obtaining one from Sir William."

Aubrey shook his head. "I should have had all the locks changed when Beth told me about that letter! Charles, you once told me that I left nothing to chance, but I neglected to perform that simple act. I'll contact a trusted locksmith today."

Galton raised a hand. "I've a man who can do it, Lord Aubrey. Alvin Chambers. If you've no further need of me, I'll fetch him and begin the process at once. We'll have all the exterior locks changed by end of day."

"Good," Sinclair answered. "Sir Thomas, is there anything else you wish to ask or report before you leave?"

"Only that my man at the Empress Hotel has been forced to vacate his rooms. He did manage to obtain some information that may prove valuable, but he couldn't be here in person today. Elberton's mother is dying, and he asked leave to go to her bedside."

"Of course," the marquess replied. "Is that why he left the Empress?"

"No, sir, but it was a blessing he had, otherwise, he might not have learnt of her illness. He left because he was recognised by another customer. Dr. Alexander Collins."

Kepelheim wrote the name into his notebook. "Isn't Collins with the Castor Institute?"

"Is he?" Aubrey asked. "That place keeps coming up, Charles. You and I should pay a call on this Collins. And we should return to the French Hospital and revisit this woman doctor who treated Moira Murdoch."

Reid sighed. "Dr. Kennedy has left the French, Charles. I went there to enquire about Murdoch's death, but our physician had fled, leaving no word as to her whereabouts."

"Why is it women doctors grow so shy around us, Cousin?" Aubrey asked.

"Because you offer them opportunity to do so, gentlemen," Deidra Kimberley noted. "When next you must question a female in the sciences, I suggest you call upon me. My knowledge of medicine and current research allows me to compose pertinent questions, but more to the point: men are easily led by feminine tricks. I have no such limitations."

Charles laughed softly. "Strange, I just had a similar conversation with Paul's sister."

"Does my sister also call me 'easily led'?" the earl jibed.

"Not really, but Adele thinks we lack a female perspective. She hopes to be the ICI's first woman inspector."

"Well, if anyone would qualify, it would be Della!" the duke interjected. "Shall we discuss the ICI, then? I assume that's why you asked both Miles and Granger to attend, Charles."

"Yes, it is, but before we get into that, I'd like their input regarding Sir William. This stickpin is evidentiary regarding Trent's ability to transform into a wolf. Of course, I'd have a difficult time offering it as evidence at the Old Bailey, but in this circle, I am confident of your belief."

"Does this mean that I get to act as judge?" the duke quipped.

"It does, sir. As do we all. Martin, do you recall our excursion into the east wing last month?"

The tailor wiped his mouth, for he'd been enjoying a slice of apple tart. "Oh, yes. Yes, of course. How could one forget such a ghastly journey up and then down those peculiar stairs? Surely, you didn't traverse them again, Charles!"

"No, thankfully, I didn't have to. Our good Mr. Baxter had removed the seal on the entrance to that strange wing, and we entered via the main section. Much preferable, I can tell you. Branham Hall's history is rife with spiritual oddities. For instance, I was unaware that there are two east wings."

John Miles stood. "If I may, sir? I worked as first foot under Mr. Prescott at the hall for a year. He served as underbutler there before moving to Glasgow to join the duke's household."

"Ah, yes, I remember Prescott quite well," Drummond remarked, smiling. "A good man. He sailed to New York, Charles.

Fifteen years ago. He works with the Albany branch of the circle now, though his public position, you might say, is as Beth's butler."

"Beth's butler? I don't understand," Sinclair answered.

"Elizabeth's portfolio of properties includes an 18th century home in upstate New York called *Beau Rêve*."

"My French is rather limited," the marquess admitted. "Beautiful dream?"

"Aye, that's right. It came into the Branham holdings when Duke George Linnhe married Countess Carlotta d'Oradour. Her father died with no male heir, so Carlotta inherited all. Those properties were subsumed by the Branham estate. The house sits on a cliff overlooking the Hudson River. It's quite lovely. Beth went there as a little girl, but she was far too young to remember it. Prescott now keeps the house ready, should Beth ever visit, and the Albany branch meets there each month."

"I've much to learn about my fiancée's life, it seems," Sinclair said, standing. A series of peculiar sounds had arisen from the hallway, as if someone scratched upon the library doors. "Excuse me, I suspect I know who that is." He walked to the doors and opened them, finding Bella sitting on the other side. "Hello, girl. Have you a message, or do you require a stroll in your mistress's garden?"

The dog's thick black tail wagged, and Charles could hear the patter of quick footsteps from the north end of the hallway. He followed the Labrador into the foyer to find Adele running towards him. "Cousin Charles!" she gasped, nearly out of breath. "I'm to tell you that Elizabeth and Aunt Victoria have gone to the stables. Something's very wrong with Snowdrop!"

"The mare that's about to foal?"

"Yes! She's breathing heavily and lying on her side. Mr. Powers thought her about to deliver, but the baby seems stuck, and poor Snowdrop's eyes are all pale!"

Duke James and the earl joined the pair. "Has Powers sent for a vet?" Aubrey asked.

"He has. Mr. Marsden, I think his name was. Oh, poor Snowy looks so sick!"

"I'm sure she's just having a little trouble delivering, Della. She'll be fine," he assured his sister. "Charles, I can go, if you want to remain in the meeting."

Edmund Reid appeared at Sinclair's elbow. "It sounds as though our meeting might need to adjourn. Charles, if it's all right with you, France and I shall return to Leman Street and begin questioning O'Brien and Barnett."

"I'd also like this Parker brought in, Ed. The one who's been threatening the women at the Lyceum."

"We'll see to it right away. Will you be joining us?"

Paul interrupted. "Charles, you should go with them. I'll tell Beth. She'll understand. If the mare's labour becomes difficult, this could last for many hours."

"Very well," Sinclair said as he checked his pocket watch. "It's nearly two now. Tell Beth I'll try to be back by six."

"I will, and don't worry. I'll remain by her side at all times."

Miles had already fetched the marquess's overcoat and hat. "Your gloves are inside your right pocket, sir. Mr. Granger has gone to bring the coach, and there are blankets and umbrellas inside."

Sinclair donned the coat, turning one last time to speak to Aubrey. "Let her know how much I want to share that picnic, will you? If we must postpone, I'll make it up to her. I promise." The earl nodded, and Sinclair left the mansion. Though he knew the choice to be logical, it left his heart heavy.

Reid and France followed close behind, and soon, the trio departed the pleasant avenues of Westminster for the riotous roads of the east.

CHAPTER FIFTEEN

Joe Barnett had never felt so alone. He'd spent most of the day sharing a cell with a pit setter named Billy Soames, who'd been arrested for trickery, animal abuse, and hosting illegal ring matches. Soames had a nasty look about him, and he'd made vile threats against Barnett, vowing to break his neck should the fish porter so much as glance his way.

It was nearly four o'clock when a constable arrived to conduct Joe into an interview room, and though he feared the police, he dreaded the dog setter's actions even more.

"Good afternoon, Mr. Barnett," Reid began as he entered the tight quarters of the room. "We've removed your manacles so that you might sign your confession."

"Sign a confession?" Barnett repeated, his mental tic persistently causing him to repeat words before answering. "Confess to what, sir?"

"To murder," a tall man in a fine suit replied. He'd entered in company with Reid. Joe Barnett had never seen the man before, but assumed he was CID.

"Ta murder?! I ain't done no murder, sir. Iffin you means Mary, I ain't done it. I don' know who done it, sir, bu' it weren't me!"

"Then why do Miss Kelly's neighbours all imply that you did, Mr. Barnett?" the well-dressed man pressed.

"Joe, this is Superintendent Sinclair. He's in charge of this investigation. If you are innocent, we shall do our best to help you, but if you lie, we shall see you hang."

"See me 'ang?" Barnett repeated, audibly gulping so that his Adam's apple slid up and down beneath a knotted kerchief. "Sir, I canno' tell nuffin bu' trufe. I go' no reason ta lie."

229

"Joe," the tall man began, sitting opposite the porter, "numerous witnesses place you outside Mary's lodgings that evening. Thursday the eighth. You had words with her, didn't you? You and she argued, and you stormed out of there vowing to see justice done. Isn't that so?"

"Tha' so?" he repeated, nervously, his head bent low. "I canno' say, sir."

Sinclair took stock of the man, his experienced eyes running over Barnett's face, his posture, the placement of his hands—any and all 'tics' and 'tells', including the persistent repetition of questions asked. "How old are you, Mr. Barnett?"

"'ow old am I? I ain' sure, sir. Firty, I reckon. Mayhap firty-five."

"Thirty-five?" the marquess repeated, making sense of the dialect. "You're about my age. I shouldn't want to spend the rest of my life in prison, much less be hanged for something I didn't do. When you spoke to Mary, was she alone?"

"Were she alone?" he echoed, nervously scratching at his nose with grease-stained hands. "No, sir. Tha' womern were wif 'er. Liz Albrook from number two. Lor' Almighty! Them womern cleaves ta Mary like she's a priest, sometimes! Confessin' their sins an' beggin' fer some sorta 'elp—'elp wha' Mary can't give."

"Not now, she can't," Reid observed. "Not thanks to you. Why did you kill her, Joe?"

"Why'd I kill 'er?" he parroted blankly. "I never done it! Never! I loved Mary, sirs. Loved 'er and wanted 'er ta come back ta me. Ida's the one wha' told me ta go. I seen 'er down by the Custom 'ouse, an' she said Mary needed protectin'."

"Protecting from whom?"

Barnett's entire face had gone pale. "The letter," he said, his brain so distracted that he failed to repeat the last words spoken by Reid. "Tha' letter wha' she gimme. Tha's 'ow I know yer name, sir. Migh' your full name be Charles Sinclair, Superintendent?"

The detective nodded. "Yes, why?"

Barnett reached into the pocket of the ragged coat he'd won from a Chinese seafarer in a card game three months earlier. When his hand reappeared, it held a stained envelope—once white in colour, now marked in greyish fingerprints and drips of cooking fat. "She gimme this fer you, sir. Down by the docks tha' nigh'. Ida did."

"Ida?" Charles asked, not making any connexions, for the name was common enough.

"Ida Ross, sir."

"Ross?" Sinclair asked, unable to hide his shock. "Why would Miss Ross give you a letter for me?"

"A letter fer you? I go' no idea, sir, bu' 'ere it is." Barnett passed the letter to the superintendent, who left the room to read it.

When he'd finished, Sinclair tapped on the window to get Reid's attention. Edmund left a constable in charge of the prisoner and joined his superior in the detectives' lounge. "What is it?"

"Ida," Charles responded, his face pale. "I think she's dead."

"Dead? What do you mean? I thought Ida Ross had been consigned to an asylum for her illness. Sunders admitted her himself."

"It seems she was released. By William Trent and another person, whom Ida does not name. Edmund, have any bodies washed ashore?"

"You think her drowned?"

"Yes. Look, I want to speak with Paul about this, for the letter is more than a suicide's last confession. It contains information regarding Redwing."

Reid's face opened in surprise. "Yes, of course. Are you returning to Westminster?"

"Yes. I'll wire Paul to let him know. But first I've an errand to run, and if we've time I'd like to stop by the docks. If that dear woman is dead, then it's a pity beyond reckoning, but her valiant final words may help us in ways even she could not imagine. However, if there is any chance that she lives, I want to find her."

Sinclair handed the letter to Reid. "I offer you this only because you're a member of the circle. It contains aspects which are quite personal, but I want you to read it. I'll wire Paul whilst you read."

Edmund entered his office and shut the door to assure privacy.

8th November, 1888

Supt. Sinclair:

Forgive my cowardice for not telling you in person, but I cannot go on, and I have no right to come to your home.

When I finish this letter, I'll go to the docks and end it all. It is the only way to be free of him.

You've asked me over and over to tell you his name, and I kept it back because I was afraid. With me dead, he cannot hurt me anymore, so I'll tell you all I know. His name is Sir William Trent, and I met him two days before I met you.

When I started working at Mrs. Hansen's, I thought I'd found a better life. I'd just been there a few days, when she brought a customer who seemed nice at first. He bought me chocolates and a new dress, and he treated me well enough— never demanded anything unusual or hurtful, if you know what I mean. The same day that I met you, he came to see me and told me that a little girl was staying with the policeman across the road. He said the little girl was very important, and that she was in danger from a wolf. This wolf would find her, and she had to stay with the policeman to be safe.

Not more than two hours later, I saw you running out of your house, without a coat or hat, and you said you were looking for a little girl. I'd seen her run out of the house after the local publican, so I knew who you meant. What you didn't know is that I'd also talked with her—before she left your home, sir. I called at your door, but no one answered for several minutes. I was about to walk away, when the girl answered. She was so sweet, sir. Sweet and kind, and she asked what it was I needed. I told her what Sir William had asked me to say, and it frightened her—I could tell, for her face went all pale. Then, I left, but I kept an eye on the door. A moment later, Mr. MacArthur walked past, and the girl flew out your door after him. I was about to return inside the Empress and fetch my coat, when my friend Irene came out to smoke. She didn't know about Sir William's words to me, so I said nothing. Then you rushed out your door and asked if we'd seen the child. I nearly told you all, sir, but with Irene there, I didn't dare, as Sir William had made me promise.

Over the years since that day, I sometimes heard about the girl, and I learnt who she was. You were kind enough to befriend me, but I feared telling you about Sir William. He often beat me, sir, as you noticed, but he did far worse than that. I got to know his friends, too, and I heard them talk about you and their plans for the little duchess. Evil plans to use her. They talked about a child and how this baby would fulfill those plans.

I knew their threats were real. I'd seen those wolves, sir. When Trent and his friends gathered for parties at Mrs. Hansen's, they'd sometimes 'turn'. Can you see why I was afraid to tell you? I know their names—all of them. I've written them all down and left the list in a safe place.

Do you remember where you took me once, a few years ago? You introduced me to a kind gentleman with physical problems. He has the list.

It's funny, but by writing this letter, I feel free now. I'm not worried about dying, sir. The river will be a lovely place to sleep.

It's been so long since I last slept soundly. Tonight, I will finally find rest.

I've never told you, but I do love you, sir. It feels good to finally say it. I love you with all my heart. Thank you.
     Ida

Reid's head lifted, and he wiped his eyes. Sinclair knocked on the office door, entering when Reid waved.

"Poor Ida," the inspector said, pointing to the letter. "I pray she isn't in that river, Charles. I'd hate to see her end her days like that. But this mention of a list. Do you know what she means by this 'kind gentleman'?"

"I do, Edmund. And he's a man known to you as well. We'll stop by the London on the way to Billingsgate. Have Barnett returned to his cell for the present, but don't release him. I don't think him guilty of Kelly's death, but he may know more than he's telling. As to O'Brien, his interview will have to wait until tomorrow."

The west gardens of *Istseleniye* House provided solace and serenity to all, and Ida Ross touched each delicate blossom and leaf as she wandered through its fading flowers. Never before had the former prostitute had the luxury to enjoy a garden, much less visit one attached to a home in which she lived, and the idea of remaining here forever began take root inside her heart. As if summoned by her thoughts, Anatole Romanov appeared beneath an overhanging juniper branch, attired in Russian costume, his unbound hair draping across his shoulders like a raven waterfall.

"I'm pleased to find you outdoors," he said as he approached. "I do hope my arrival did not alarm you, Ida. Won't you join me for tea?"

Though she'd not noticed it there before, a table had been set with gilt-edged bone china, crustless sandwiches, cakes, fruit, and a silver samovar, as if he'd expected her. Romanov held the chair as she eased into it, careful not to wrinkle the folds of her new silk gown.

"You treat me much too well, sir," she told him as the prince sat opposite.

"I treat you as you deserve. Did you sleep more soundly last night?"

She nodded. "I did, my lord. Much better, thank you. I met Mr. Stanley at breakfast this morning. He is quite nice; in his normal state, that is."

Anatole smiled. "Believe me, when I say, Ida, that he regrets his behaviour. Tell me, was the contessa also at breakfast?"

"No, sir, she was not. In fact, I haven't seen her since last evening. Has she left us?"

Romanov began to laugh as he poured her a cup of tea. "I seriously doubt that I would be so lucky as that! I see from your expression that you find the comment surprising. My history with di Specchio is *slozhno*, what you English call complicated. Like the workings of a watch—the complications—our partnership relies upon one gear moving effortlessly in cooperation with the next. The contessa begins to rust, I think. Her usefulness and even her loyalties are in doubt. I'm told she had a visitor yesterday. Did you see him? A tall man, who somewhat resembles me?"

"I did, sir. I thought he might be your son, or some other kin. He never came into the house, though. Just sat inside his coach. Is he your son?"

"In a manner of speaking, Rasha is my nephew. One of my brothers has adopted him."

"Have you many brothers?" she asked innocently.

His light eyes twinkled. "Far too many to count, but I once knew every name amongst that host. Raziel is the one to whom I refer. He hopes to find immortality through paternity. I prefer other ways to eternal reward."

She placed a monogrammed serviette against her lap, a light breeze playing in her strawberry locks. "I'm surprised to find it so pleasant here, sir. Usually this time of the year, the air is cold, and it even snows, but here—in your garden—it feels almost like spring."

"This house and its gardens lie beyond the reach of seasons."

"Does it?" she asked, puzzling through the curious response. "I find it hard to follow you sometimes, sir. It isn't because I'm not interested, but my education ended when my mother died. I hope you'll forgive my ignorance."

He reached for her hand, stroking it gently. "I speak nonsense at times. Pay me no heed. Are you happy thus far—here, I mean? In my home?"

"Oh, yes, sir. Very happy. Katrina is quite nice, and she's teaching me how to dress properly. Is she also Russian?"

"She is, yes," he answered. "I first met Katrina long ago, and she has taught several young ladies the rules of dress and society. But you say that Rasha did not enter the house? Why did he come? Did he speak with anyone?"

"I cannot say why he visited, sir. The countess slipped out the front and spoke with him in the prince's carriage. That is right, isn't it? Razarit is a prince?"

"He is. Razarit's original name at birth was Nicolae, but he changed it six years ago to Razarit, in honour of his adoptive father. Rasha, as he often calls himself, is Romanian and descends from a long line of Carpathian princes. He thinks himself wise and sophisticated, but I find him abrasive and cruel. He has little understanding of how his actions affect the lives of others. I have barred him from my home, but he is persistent, and may find a way to reach you. Therefore, you must tell me if he visits again. You are under my protection, Ida. I will not suffer anyone to harm you. Not anyone. Not even my brother's so-called child."

She blushed. "I don't know why you treat me with such kindness, sir. You've already admitted to me that you are in love with another. What makes me special?"

"It is...complicated," he said, adding milk to his tea. "Have you ever had a dream that came true, Ida?"

"Once or twice, sir."

"Then you will understand what I'm about to say. I do not sleep, you see, not as you understand sleep. What you call dreams come differently to me. They display inside my waking mind as meandering rivers of possibilities; some brighter, more colourful than others. These are more likely to come true, whilst the less colourful ones are less so. I have foreseen you in many of these bright rivers, and in each, you play an important role in the life of the woman who is so dear to me."

"Who is she, sir?"

"I cannot tell you that. Not yet. Soon, however, you will meet her. Tell me, Ida, do you worship? Are you a believer?" he asked as he offered her a plate of iced desserts. "The orange-cranberry sponge cake is quite nice. The others are lemon-blueberry and apple-pecan. I have a sweet tooth, as they say. A small vice."

She selected the sponge cake and placed it on her plate. "Thank you, sir. I'm not much of a believer, no. God never seemed to notice me. I wish he had, but I suppose I'm not important enough. Or perhaps he gave up on me. My sins are mighty grievous."

"They are not," he insisted. "We hold no formal services here, but as tomorrow is Sunday, I could see if the others would be interested in beginning something. Mr. Blinkmire has a keen interest in theology. Perhaps he could assist."

"Do you worship, sir?" she asked innocently.

"Once, I worshipped every minute of every day," he said, his eyes taking on a distant look, as if gazing backward into an ancient past. "How I long to return to that, but it is not to be. Perhaps, that is why I call this home *Istseleniye*. It is Russian for 'healing'. I would find such healing for myself, but as it evades me—for the present—I endeavour to bring it to those who've been wounded by my kind."

"Istseleniye," she repeated. "It is a beautiful word, sir. If I may be so bold, my lord, you always seem so very sad. Is it because of the woman? The one you love?"

"Partly," he admitted. "Sugar?"

"Just one."

He added a single cube to her teacup, took a sip of his own, and then wiped his mouth with the linen. "Ida, you mentioned your grievous sins. Mine would make yours seem like the purest wool, my dear. Once, I thought myself justified in my actions, but some years ago, I saw my *true* self in the eyes of a child. I will not tell you the boy's name, but his father was slain by one of my own brothers. It was as if I looked into a mirror—and what I saw there tore at my heart. Since that day, I've tried to change. You wonder if God understands, but I tell you his compassion is limitless; beyond all imagination! Despite my former, rebellious choices, God always had a plan. That boy has grown into manhood, and actions I took in ages past, now prove useful to him and to those he loves. God truly does work all things together for good, despite the actions of fools."

Vasily approached and bowed deeply. "My lord prince, word has come from your brother. Last night's meeting appears to have been successful."

"Yes, I'm aware of that. Sara has emerged. He will make our task much more difficult."

"So I have learnt, my lord, but the ceremony not only opened the gate, it revealed the location of another."

"Where?" Romanov asked, standing.

"It is where you theorised, sir. In France, near his ancestral home."

"Forgive me, Ida, I must attend to a matter, which cannot wait. Vasily will see that all your needs are met. I have enjoyed our little talk. I believe Mr. Blinkmire walks each afternoon in the east garden, near to the cemetery. He might appreciate your company, if you would offer it. Until this evening," he said, bowing and kissing her hand.

In a moment, he'd vanished from the garden in company with the butler, both speaking rapidly in Russian as they walked. Ida sighed as she considered the cemetery with its dead and dying flowers placed near many of the tombs. "Perhaps, that is where I belong," she said to herself. "Do you listen?" she asked the sky, thinking of God and whether he hated her for the choices she'd made.

Only the wind answered, so she remained in her chair, sipping tea, and pondering the idea of rivers.

CHAPTER SIXTEEN

The London Hospital, often simply called 'the London', began in the mid-18th century as an idea put forth by seven men at the Feathers Tavern in Cheapside, who saw the need for an infirmary in the growing city's east end. The London was originally intended as a medical service for merchant seamen and warehouse workers, but before long the facilities expanded to include a broader class of poor, requiring construction of a larger building. In 1752, Mount Field in Whitechapel was chosen as an ideal site by a committee headed by the Earl of Macclesfield, and in 1757, construction began. During the intervening years, Mount Field had altered from a countryside meadow to a crowded inner city block, but the five-storey, brick building still overlooked small but well-kept flower and vegetable gardens, used by patients and staff alike.

On any given day, the hospital housed over six hundred patients within three hundred rooms and wards, but one special resident made his home on the ground floor in a small chamber overlooking a rose garden. As he knocked upon the resident's door, Charles Sinclair recalled the many times he had visited here since first meeting the gentleman in 1886. A mumbled voice replied softly through the dense wood, and the detective entered the room.

"Superintendent!" the patient exclaimed happily, his speech encumbered by the peculiar formation of his mouth and teeth. "Oh, this is a fine surprise. Do come in, old friend. Yes, come in!"

Sinclair and Reid bowed gracefully, and the superintendent reached out to shake the resident's misshapen hand. "Mr. Merrick, it is always a great joy to see you, my very dear friend. I'm remiss for not visiting sooner. You remember Inspector Reid, don't you, Joseph?"

"Yes, yes, of course! Of course! But you mustn't apologise for not calling, Charles. The newspapers report daily just how busy you've kept since we last visited in September. Your life has taken many wonderful turns, has it not? From St. Clair to Sinclair, from a policeman to a peer."

"And from desperately lonely to engaged to be married," the marquess continued. "May we sit?"

"Yes, of course," he answered, his breathing strained. Merrick sat upon his small bed, which bore half a dozen plump pillows: gifts from hospital staff and friends, many of them embroidered with pastoral scenes. "Shall I ask the sister to arrange for tea?"

"No, I'm afraid we cannot stay," Charles told him. "Another time, perhaps. We've come to speak with you about a mutual friend."

Merrick suffered from a disfiguring disease that caused his skin to harden into bumps and knots all over his body. His spine and limbs were twisted, and his head overgrown by the ravages of the illness. He had spent most of his twenty-six years confined to side show cages and tents, gawped at by those who came to stare and throw refuse at 'the Elephant Man'. Though his stony exterior made it arduous to speak, those who knew him well had come to understand the refined words and gentlemanly expressions. His eyes grew soft now as he sat upon the bed's edge, leaning upon the carved handle of his walking stick to keep his balance. "You mean Ida, don't you, Charles?"

"Yes, Joseph. Did Ida Ross visit you recently?"

"She did. Only last week, in fact. I'd not seen Miss Ross in many weeks, but that is not unusual for her, as you know. She seemed in a terrible state. Thin, pale, and excited to the point of exhaustion. I suggested that she allow one of the nurses to examine her, but she insisted she was quite well."

"Ida has always been proud," Reid said.

"So she has," Merrick replied. "Ida told me that she intended to speak with you, Charles. I take it that she has, else you'd not be here."

Charles removed the letter from his pocket. "Ida left this for me. She'd given it to a man named Barnett. There's a stamp on it, so I assume he was meant to post it, but the man's wits are dulled by drink, and clearly he forgot. In the letter, Ida mentions a list which she left with you."

"Yes, I have it. There behind you, Inspector Reid, you will find a silver box inlaid with ivory. It is a music box given to me by a dear friend. I secured the list within."

Edmund located the box and handed it to Sinclair. "May I?" the marquess asked before opening it.

"Oh, yes. Do."

The detective turned the delicately wrought latch and the lid opened, revealing the interior workings and tines of the unwound mechanism. "I see no list."

Merrick smiled—or did so to the extent to which his malformed face could manage. "The lid contains a hidden compartment. If you push up against it, a spring will reveal it."

Charles did so, and a rolled scrap of paper fell out of the secret chamber. He handed the box back to Reid and then unrolled the note. "Have you read it?" he asked Merrick.

"I have, but I do not know why these names are joined together. Ida would not say. She only wanted to secure the list, for your eyes only."

"Joseph, I want to put a constable on your room from now on. I'll speak with Mr. Treves about it. Would that meet with your approval?"

"Why, Charles? Am I under suspicion of some crime?"

Sinclair smiled. "Hardly, old friend. Rather, I worry that a crime might find you. The men on this list are very powerful, and if any suspects you have read it, he might decide to pay a call on you, and that is not a risk I'm willing to take."

"I see," Merrick answered thoughtfully. "I have no fear, if you are on my side. Very well. Post your man, and I shall keep watch also. The hospital has a telegraph room, so I shall ask an orderly to send a wire, should anyone come 'round snooping. How is that?"

Standing, Sinclair shook Joseph's hand. "Quite sensible. Joseph, I'm getting married in a week, and I'd like you to come."

He shook his head. "Charles, I find large crowds difficult, but I shall say a prayer for you and the duchess. It gladdens my heart that you and she have found each other at last. Perhaps, you would bring her by sometime?"

"We'll make a point of visiting often," he promised. "Edmund will have one of his men come right away, so expect a constable to be outside your door from now on."

"If you select one that plays chess, it would be most gratifying."

"I'll see what I can do," Reid replied. "Goodbye, Mr. Merrick."

"Goodbye, Inspector. It was a great pleasure to see you again. Charles, remember your promise to bring the duchess to visit me. Her photograph is most pleasing, but I suspect she is even more lovely in person."

"Elizabeth is beautiful beyond the capacity of any camera to reproduce," Sinclair answered. "We'll come by next week. The twentieth or so."

The two detectives left and returned to the Branham coach. "Where to now, sir?" Granger asked as the men entered.

"We'll leave Reid at Leman Street, but I'm going back to Queen Anne, Granger." The driver left, and in a moment, the carriage moved forwards. "We'll deal with O'Brien tomorrow, Ed. This list must get to the circle right away. Be sure to send a reliable man to Merrick's room, will you? The names on this list are extremely powerful, and their reach long."

"You said nothing to Merrick about Ida's possible death," Reid noted.

"I'll not distress Joseph without cause. Until her body is discovered, I refuse to believe her dead."

"We're not going to the Custom House then?"

"No, not today. I'd appreciate it, though, if you would send France to enquire about Barnett's claims. Perhaps, a watchman saw him there in Ida's company."

"Consider it done."

Charles read through the list again. Thirteen names in all, led by Sir William Trent and followed by Sir Clive Urquhart, Lewis Merriweather, and many others, including Razarit Grigor. The Romanian did indeed sit on the exclusive 'round table' of Redwing.

Charles briefly wondered if it might be safer to take Beth far away from London, but he knew Redwing's reach stretched 'round the globe. No matter where they might travel, the ravenous birds would follow.

Snowdrop's breathing had grown shallow and quick, but there'd been no sign of the foal's movement into the birth canal. In fact, Mr. Marsden believed the foal was dead.

"Your Grace, I'm very sorry to tell you this, but the kindest thing would be to put the mare out of her misery. There's no internal movement at all, which is surprising at this stage. She's showing waxing in the bag, and her pelvic muscles are beautifully relaxed, yet it's as if she's reluctant or unable to do more. I have to assume it's the latter."

Beth had stood beside the open gate to the stall for almost two hours, and she'd begun to grow weary. "Excuse me, Mr. Marsden, but I must sit." Finding a wooden chair, she took it, and a stable boy brought her a cup of clear water. "Thank you, Master Keith. You're as considerate as your father." She looked at the veterinarian. "Might she feel crowded?"

"Crowded? In what way, Your Grace?"

"When I was a girl at Branham, we had a broodmare who refused to deliver whenever watched. It was as if she worried that her foal would be in danger, even from those whom she knew well. If we left Snowdrop in peace for a few hours, then might she feel safe?"

"It's an old wives tale that horses have such thoughts, my lady. Medical care and intervention in an expedient manner is best."

"I know that you are considered an expert, Mr. Marsden, but Snowdrop is my horse, and I'll not have her put down unnecessarily. If she's to die, then may we not allow her a little time to try foaling without us first?"

"It will cause her a great deal of discomfort if the foal is dead, my lady."

"But we do not know for certain that it is dead, do we?" she countered patiently. "Mr. Powers, let's clear the stall and leave Snowdrop in peace until morning. Send someone to check on her hourly, but no one is to remain where she might see. Is that clear?"

Powers nodded. "Clear as a bell, my lady."

Marsden disliked the suggestion. "If you did not intend to take my advice, Your Grace, why did you send for me?"

"Your expertise is appreciated, Mr. Marsden, but I am not without experience, and neither is my Chief Groom. Our concern was that Snowdrop appeared ill—not that she is having difficulty with foaling."

"She is not ill," he declared as he put on his hat.

The earl entered the stable area, a telegram in his left hand. "Charles is on his way back from Whitechapel. How is Snowdrop?"

"Dying," the vet replied matter-of-factly.

"Not another one!" Aubrey exclaimed. "Is it the same as with Ambrose?"

Beth stared at him, shock painting her face. "What are you talking about? Ambrose is fine. You rode him only a fortnight ago, in fact."

Paul wished he'd said nothing. "No, dear. I'm afraid Ambrose died last night. I'd assumed Charles had already told you."

"Charles knew about it and said nothing to me?" she bit back angrily. "Why would he do that?"

"To spare you, I imagine," the earl answered. "Marsden, is there any sign of injury to Snowdrop's neck? Ambrose Aurelius had two puncture wounds below his ear."

"Wounds? No, none that I perceived. What does Clark think? Shall I go to Branham and perform a necropsy, Your Grace?"

Beth had begun to weep. "Oh, I don't know. Paul, take me back to the house, please. I just want to sit down for a moment." Bella and Briar drew near, concerned to see their mistress weeping. The female licked Beth's hand as if trying to comfort her.

"Sorry, darling. Yes, I'll take you back inside." He turned to the vet. "Mr. Marsden, we'd appreciate it if you'd pay a call to Branham tomorrow. Stop by here first, though. If Snowdrop is still in distress, then we will take your advice—whatever it might be."

Elizabeth leaned upon him, clinging to his side as she wept. The earl held her close as they walked, and Della met them at the door. "Has Snowdrop had her baby?" she asked her brother.

"Not yet," he answered. "Beth, would you like Della to play for us? It's two more hours until supper. I'll read the news, and you can have a little lie-in whilst Adele entertains us."

"Is Cousin Charles coming back?" the youngster asked as they headed towards the music room. "Uncle James had to leave, by the way. Something about a meeting at the palace."

"Another? Our uncle sees more of the queen than the prime minister these days," Aubrey said with a grin. "Yes, Charles is on his way back. He'll join us for supper."

"Good. I have a report about the cocoa," she told him. "Shall I play my new piece? I've been learning one for Christmas."

"That would be lovely," her brother replied. Beth continued to cry softly, and in a few moments, he'd laid her upon a long, velvet sofa within the music room. Adele searched through a tall stack of music she'd brought with her from Scotland. "I've a wonderful book of Christmas songs that my piano teacher gave to me last year. My favourite is *Away in a Manger*; but there's also *March of the Kings*, *Sing We Now of Christmas*, *How a Rose E'er Blooming*—that's Uncle James's favourite—and *O, Tannenbaum*. Do you prefer one over another?"

"Play them all, dear," the earl said softly. "I think the duchess is already falling asleep."

Elizabeth had turned her face towards the back of the sofa, preferring no one see how upset she'd become. It felt as if the entire world's weight crushed her now, and all she wanted was to see Charles's face and hear his voice.

"I'll play softly, then," the girl said as she set the music upon the piano.

Paul left momentarily to find that afternoon's collection of newspapers, returning quickly and carrying six editions beneath his arm. He listened to the music whilst reading various reports of crimes in the west, financial news, Parliamentary decisions and debates, and several articles on Ripper. Two included quotes attributed to Reid and Abberline, but the earl doubted that either man had given reporters the time of day, much less any comments.

As he read, something Della had said tickled at his brain, and he glanced up. "Della," he called in a whisper.

She paused, turning to face him. "Yes, brother mine? Am I playing too loudly?"

"No, not at all. It's just I was wondering what you meant earlier about the cocoa. You said you had a report for Charles."

"Oh, yes," she told him as she continued to play. "I spoke with Mrs. Meyer. She'd seen it all."

"Seen what?"

"The maid. The new one. She's from London, I think."

"Gertrude Trumper?"

"Yes, that's the one," she said, leaving the piano and joining her brother on the settee. "It's quite a curious story. The maid offered to take the chocolate upstairs. Mrs. Meyer had watched from her office. She'd been going through the ledgers, and Mrs. Smith was teaching one of the scullery maids how to make cocoa. This maid—Trumper, I mean—sat nearby at the kitchen table. When the cocoa was finished, the scullery maid poured it into a silver pot and started to place it onto the tray for the footman. That's when it all happened."

"When what happened?" he asked, looking at Beth to make sure she still slept. The duchess lay quietly, her breathing regular.

"That's when Miss Trumper added the cinnamon."

Paul blinked. "How is that important?"

"Because she poured it from a bottle kept in her apron pocket. Why would a chamber maid keep cinnamon in her pocket? You must admit that it's a mystery, brother mine. A very deep mystery. Might it be that it wasn't cinnamon at all? That the maid was mistaken? Something certainly made Samson ill, and I doubt it was anything as common as cinnamon."

Paul's entire body went cold. *Had Trumper intentionally tried to poison Elizabeth? Surely not! But what if Beth had drunk the cocoa?*

"I'm sure Miss Trumper did nothing deliberate," he assured Adele. "You're quite a thorough investigator, sister mine. I'm very proud of you."

"Shall I be the ICI's first female inspector then? Cousin Charles promised me a warrant card."

"I'll make sure you are the first ever, darling. Do continue playing now. It is helping our cousin to sleep."

Adele returned to the bench, and her talented fingers caressed the keys, filling the room with sweet music. However, in Aubrey's heart, a great sense of dread had taken hold. He'd have to speak with Charles right away.

Gertrude Trumper might be a Redwing spy.

CHAPTER SEVENTEEN

Sunday 1:24 pm – Drummond House

"Lady Delia, that song was perfect," Sir Thomas Galton told the blushing seventeen-year-old. "I'd no idea you had such a lovely voice."

Cordelia Wychwright sat opposite the handsome baronet, a demitasse spoon in her right hand, a cup of Darjeeling in her left. She stirred three cubes of sugar into the tea as she replied. "You're very kind to say so, Sir Thomas. My music teacher, Mr. Primrose, thought me good enough for the stage, but of course, my parents would never agree to such a public display. And by 'the stage', of course, I mean opera. Music halls are so very common, don't you think?"

"I cannot imagine your beauty upon any stage other than Covent Garden," Galton replied. "Do forgive me, I see that Haimsbury and Aubrey have arrived with the duchess. I must offer my hellos."

He set down his cup and bowed slightly, kissing her hand before departing. Wychwright glanced at her mother, who sat across the large drawing room along with Victoria Stuart and Lady Cartringham. The baroness nodded towards Aubrey, silently reminding her daughter that her prey was not Sir Thomas Galton but Paul Stuart. The subtle prompt caused butterflies to rise up in the girl's stomach, and she reached for the cake plate in an effort to banish them.

"Well, if it isn't Delia Wychwright," a pleasant voice spoke at her elbow.

The girl's chin jerked up. "Good heavens!" she gasped, using a serviette to wipe cake crumbs from her small mouth. "Michael Emerson. When did you get here? I'd no idea you were in London!"

Dr. Emerson laughed. He stood six feet tall with short, prematurely grey hair, laughing blue eyes, and a smooth face. He removed his gloves and placed them in the left pocket of his cutaway. "An honour to see you once more," he said, taking her hand and offering a friendly kiss. "May I join you?"

She gulped audibly, for her mother's visual remonstrance cut through the air like an angry shout. "Uh, yes, of course," she answered politely. "Only, Lord Aubrey might also be joining us. Were you in church this morning? I didn't see you there."

"Yes, I was. Towards the back. Your song was quite lovely," he answered, sitting beside her. "Aubrey's joining you? Excellent. The earl probably doesn't remember me. I challenged him at one of Oxford's chess matches, failing miserably. He's far too skilled for me, I fear. I suppose, like most of us country folks, you and your parents are in London for the wedding. Quite exciting, isn't it?"

Her eyes were fixed on Aubrey, and Cordelia replied automatically, as trained to do. "Yes, I suppose it is."

Emerson took note of her apparent coolness, assuming she preferred to be left alone. "Well, as I said, it's a delight to see you again," he continued, standing. "If you'll pardon me, I should say hello to our host." Emerson bowed slightly, and then left to find Duke James, who was engaged in an animated discussion with Reginald Whitmore near the turning to the gallery.

The physician noticed Emerson and called out, "Michael! Over here, lad!" Once Emerson drew near, Whitmore made the introductions. "Duke, this is Michael Emerson, the finest physician ever to leave Edinburgh. Michael, this is His Grace, Duke James."

"A pleasure, sir," the young man answered, shaking Drummond's hand. "Thank you for inviting me today. I assume I'm here to meet my new patient."

"If by that, you mean my granddaughter, she's just arrived. I say, Charles!" Drummond called. "If you can tear yourself from your fiancée's side, there's someone you should meet."

Sinclair stood just inside the gallery, some ten feet away, speaking to Beth and Kepelheim. "Excuse me, darling," he told the duchess. "I believe this may be the new doctor Reggie mentioned to me. Paul will keep you company whilst I sound him out. Do you mind?"

"No, I suppose not," she answered. Elizabeth had been somber during the church service, her mind still on Ambrose and Snowdrop. The mare had given birth to a white and grey colt overnight, but as of eight that morning had failed to rally. Marsden felt certain she would die before the day was out, and Beth hadn't wished to leave her.

Stuart put an arm 'round her shoulders. "Come with me, Princess. I require a chaperone when speaking with Lady Cordelia. Stay close and keep watch upon me, will you?" His teasing brought a smile to her face, and the two left. Charles joined the duke, Whitmore, and Emerson.

"Is it my imagination, or is the duchess somewhat out of sorts this morning?" Reggie asked.

"She's lost a stallion and possibly a mare as well. You know how much Beth loves her horses."

"So she does. I'm very sorry to hear it. Elizabeth takes such losses to heart. It's the sort of thing a good physician must keep watch on, you know, which is why I'd like to introduce the man I mentioned to you last week. Lord Haimsbury, this is Dr. Michael Emerson." Whitmore turned towards the younger practitioner. "Michael, I've told Lord Haimsbury all about your eminent qualifications, and he and the duchess have decided to give you a try. Tread carefully, now. Remember, Sinclair is with the CID."

Emerson extended his hand, and Sinclair noticed he wore a gold band on the right, ring finger. His palms were smooth, his grip firm, eyes filled with intelligence and mirth. He had the look of someone trustworthy. *I just pray he is.* "A pleasure to make your acquaintance, Dr. Emerson. I understand you're Lord Braxton's son."

"Guilty and proud of it," he replied with a bright smile. "Our family seat lies close to your own, Lord Haimsbury. I believe Rose House overlooks the Eden, correct?"

"So I'm told. My childhood memories still lie in a mist, but they slowly return."

"That's right. You were thought long dead, were you not? Extraordinary! I remember it now. My father spoke of it many times when I was a lad. I think you and I are close to the same age. I was seven, when your father died. Tragic, the way it all played out. His murder, I mean."

"Murder?" Drummond asked. "All my sources indicate it was a duel."

"That's true, sir, but locals believe it was unfairly fought. There was even a coroner's inquest to determine if trickery were involved. Only one witness was called, though—a footman."

"Then you know more than I," James answered. "Charles, I'm going to visit with my granddaughter. Emerson, I'd speak more to you of this, when you've the time."

"Of course, sir. I look forward to it," the man answered. He turned to Charles. "I do hope I didn't overstep. I'd forgotten your mother was also the duke's sister."

"I'd love to hear about my family," Charles said. "There's so little known about my disappearance. Anything you might add can only help."

"In truth, I only know a little, but my father could tell you more. He'd hoped to come down for the wedding, but poor health precludes travel at present. Congratulations, by the way. I've known Elizabeth for many years, though the last time we spoke, she was only twelve. She's grown into a remarkable woman."

"I look forward to meeting your father, Dr. Emerson. I'd no idea the Braxton estate was so near Rose House. Before you leave today, I'd appreciate a word in private."

"Would now work? If you're amenable that is, Lord Haimsbury." Emerson smiled, and his already handsome features brightened, giving him an almost childlike appearance. He bore a faded scar above his left brow and signs of an old infection dotted the area below his right ear. When not speaking, Charles noticed the man's head tilted slightly to the left.

"Yes, thank you. Reggie, do you wish to join us?"

"I think I'll tuck into those little cakes," Whitmore answered, winking. "Be sure to mention Kelly," he whispered to Emerson before walking away.

"Kelly?" Charles asked as he led Emerson into a small drawing room beyond the gallery. "In here, Doctor. Booth, could you let my uncle know where we are?" he called to the butler. Once inside, the marquess shut the door and turned the key.

"I prefer no one stumble in whilst you and I speak. Which Kelly does Whitmore mean?" he asked as they took matching leather club chairs on either side of a tall fireplace.

"Marie Jeanette," Emerson answered. "I understand she is your latest victim. I may know her."

"We list her as Mary Jane, though they might be the same person. Is your connexion professional or personal?"

It took a second for the implication to resonate in the physician's mind, but once done, he shook his head vigorously. "Oh, no, not personal! Not at all. I treated her. I spent two years at the Castor Asylum. Miss Kelly suffered migraines, brought on from poor diet and despondency. I assume my patient is the same woman as your victim. Moderately tall, fair hair, blue eyes. Quite pretty, in fact. Well kept. Clean, I mean. Many of the local patients, particularly those from Limehouse and Spitalfields, seldom bathe. Even if water were abundant, most would avoid washing. Marie often arrived in company with a well-dressed gentleman. His name escapes me, but I could consult my records, if it assists your investigation."

"It might," Sinclair said. "Miss Kelly died quite horribly. I prefer not to offer details, for there's much we're keeping out of the press, though Fred Best from *The Star* has already penned a scathing report." He paused, weighing whether or not the man could be trusted. *Both Price and Whitmore recommend him. Please, Lord, don't let me make a mistake!*

Emerson waited patiently, his breathing easy. Finally, he leaned forward in the chair. "You're concerned about the duchess, and you wonder if I'm trustworthy. Sir, I understand. I do. My late wife meant the world to me," he said, glancing down at the gold band. Twisting it, he explained. "She passed away from typhus three years ago. Shortly after the loss of our only child. Both are with our Saviour now. I wear the ring on my right hand as a reminder that they stand at the right hand of the Father, nearest our Lord. Tis a comfort on dark, lonely nights."

"I'm very sorry for your loss," Sinclair answered. "I lost my son in '78. Smallpox. My late wife and I were separated when she died, but I believe I understand the depth of your loss. Were I to lose Elizabeth, all life would stop for me. My heart would simply cease to beat."

"Then you have found your perfect mate," he said thoughtfully. "Lynette was mine. Reggie said you're concerned about the duchess's health. He's reviewed his findings with me, and though I've not yet had an opportunity to speak with George Price, his reputation amongst London physicians is incomparable. Both men have diagnosed pregnancy. I assume that is why you wished to speak in private."

251

"Yes, and I'm very glad Reggie explained it to you. The circumstances of conception are difficult to explain, but..."

"You are with the inner circle," Emerson interjected, causing Sinclair to stare, mouth open. "You're surprised. Yes, I know all about that august group's noble cause. My father served as an agent when a young man, and he's consulted with Dr. MacPherson several times since. Both men research ancient languages and texts. I assume the circumstances you mention relate to Redwing in some way."

"Is it possible that our Lord has brought you to us? Honestly, I have worried endlessly about Beth's condition, not because of any possible scandal. Neither she nor care a whit for that, but because of how it all came about—and now, her health issues. Doctor..."

"Michael. Just call me Michael, sir."

"Then you must call me Charles."

"An honour," Emerson replied. "By health issues, do you refer to these early symptoms Whitmore mentioned?"

He nodded. "To a degree, yes, but also the extremity of them. She rarely has a moment when her stomach isn't roiling, and she finds eating quite challenging. Tea and dry toast form the bulk of her diet, but even those can send her reeling. My late wife's pregnancy had few such troubles. Does Elizabeth's extreme nausea and dizziness indicate a problem?"

"You seem to me a man who appreciates candor, Charles, so I'll be blunt. Yes, the symptoms you describe can be caused by complications, but there are a few women whose delicate constitutions react violently to pregnancy. We're only now studying the physiological changes during the months of infant growth and maturation, and I fear that very few physicians have enough experience to be considered experts. It is one reason I served at Castor. The large female patient population included many with pregnancies in various stages, and I kept copious notes, asking many questions throughout. I've several theories regarding the duchess, but I need to examine her before offering them."

"Then, we should arrange for you to do so as soon as possible," Sinclair replied. "Would tomorrow be opportune?"

"This afternoon is better, if you haven't other duties," the doctor answered. "I have two visits to make outside London tomorrow, but if that is your only option, I could reschedule them. I shall make myself available to you as a priority."

Charles stood, shaking the man's hand. "I feel as if a great burden is lifting off my shoulders. It's been a whirlwind week, and I pray the one before us brings a season of rest. Knowing that Elizabeth is well would offer that repose to us both. This afternoon at five?"

"Certainly. At her home, or do you prefer your own?"

"Hers. Queen Anne House, just north of St. James's park and west of the palace."

"I know exactly where it is," Emerson said, adding the appointment notation to a small leather book. Charles led him to the door, opened it, and the two men returned to the main drawing room, where a small crowd had gathered, including Edmund Reid. The duke motioned to his nephew.

"Charles, it looks as if you'll be leaving us," Drummond explained, pointing to the inspector. "Beth wants to say goodbye, though. She's in the music room."

Without pausing, he found his way there, entering and shutting the door. The duchess stood alone at the piano, her right hand playing a haunting melody.

"I hope this sad tune isn't an indication of your mood," he said as he drew near. "I'd no idea Reid would come to fetch me, Beth. Really, I am so very sorry. After missing our picnic last evening, you must now doubt the wisdom of becoming a policeman's wife." He expected her to argue or play coy, but instead she threw her arms around him and began to weep. "It's Snowdrop and Ambrose, isn't it?" he said gently. "I'll tell Reid that I cannot leave."

She shook her head, though her face still pressed against his chest. "It isn't that. It's memories, I suppose. When I saw Edmund enter, I knew he'd come to fetch you. He insisted to me that there is no new case, but only the continuation of another. I cannot explain why, but I suddenly felt overcome with emotion, so I retreated here and asked Grandfather to tell you. Do you think me a coward?"

"You? Darling, you are the bravest of us all. What memories tug at your heart?"

"Memories of you. Of the man I first met in '79. Your extreme kindness and unabashed love. Charles, it frightens me sometimes—the way I feel about you; the way I desperately need you. If the enemy ever took you from me, I don't know what I'd do. It would kill me, I think."

He kissed her forehead, upturning her heart-shaped face in his hands so that her eyes looked into his. "My precious little one," he whispered, "you are the brightest star in all the heavens. I would scale any mountain, slay any dragon, swim any ocean, were to ask it. Our connexion is beyond that of poets to describe. One week from now, you and I shall stand in this house as husband and wife. Nothing will prevent that. Nothing. That's what you fear, isn't it?"

"Yes," she whispered, her eyes lowering. "Rasha has said he will take me from you. Trent vowed to prevent us from marrying. Oh, Charles, please, promise me that you'll stop them!"

"I will, darling. I will stop them. I promise," he said, sitting at the piano bench and taking her onto his lap. "Next Sunday, you and I begin the rest of our lives, and this child serves as a beautiful reminder of our bond. I've spoken with Michael Emerson, and he'd like to meet with you at five this afternoon. Is that all right?"

"Yes, I suppose so, but will you be back by then?"

"If not, I'm sure Emerson can proceed without my input. Both Whitmore and Price vouch for him, and having met with him briefly, he seems a man of great faith. Your opinion matters most of all, so put him to the test."

"I will. Charles, before you go, I want to make a confession."

She had worn her hair down, and several stray locks obscured her face as her eyes lowered. Sweeping the curls behind her left ear, he traced the curve of her face. "What confession, dearest?"

"The dream. I told Paul about it, but I've been afraid to tell you."

"Afraid? Why?"

She took a deep breath, the last of it catching in her throat in a stuttering manner. Tears formed on her lashes, and it seemed as if a great tempest brewed. "Because it made you seem uncaring, but I do not think of you that way! Not at all!"

"What happened in this dream?"

"It takes place inside a ballroom, and every time, the orchestra transforms into animals as the music changes key. You stand alongside the dance floor, staring at me, with a young girl beside you. I think she is my younger self, though I cannot be certain. My dance partner is Paul, but then another man forces him to leave, and this man is taller with long, dark hair. He insists I dance with him again and again, and as the musicians transform, I stumble and fall. The floor is bathed in blood, and the animal musicians rush into the costumed crowd and rend the dancers with their teeth and claws. Not noticing any of this, Paul leaves with another woman—a redhead. Finally, you notice my predicament and come to my rescue, abandoning the child. There's more, but it is difficult to remember, and I think there is a black mirror..."

"A mirror?" he asked, Morgan's claims and the words of Saucy Jack's riddle entering his thoughts. "Can you describe it?"

"Not well, for it's a part of the dream that eludes me. I think it has writing upon its surface, and the frame is very old. But it is an unusual mirror. More than that, I cannot remember. I'm sorry, Charles. Is it important—this mirror?"

"Perhaps. Beth, I think that both you and I need time away from all of this. All of Redwing's plots. If you're well enough, why don't we take a short trip after the wedding?"

"Really?" she asked, her eyes brightening. "Where?"

"I doubt we can stay long, but think of a city you'd like to visit for, oh, a week or so. It's not a real wedding trip, but it's better than none. After the baby is born next year, we'll take a long voyage to a faraway land. Anywhere you like."

She threw her arms 'round his neck, kissing his cheek. "You are so very good to me! Might we go to Tory's château? It's private, beautifully wooded, and lies close enough to Paris that we could attend the opera; though, all I really want is time alone with you. I don't care if we do anything else, because being with you is the most wonderful, most special thing in all the world!"

A hand knocked on the door, and Charles helped her to stand. "That's Reid, I imagine. I'll try to be home in time for supper. Don't worry. Enjoy the party. Paul will need your aid in dealing with Cordelia Wychwright, you know."

She laughed, and he was happy to see it. "I'll do my best, but it is a challenge. Adele will be disappointed that you'll miss her recitation. She's been practising Tennyson poems all week."

"Ask her to reprise them for me later. Darling, I miss you madly when we're apart. When Paul and I get the ICI established, it will allow me to work from home. Would you like that?"

"Oh, yes, Charles. Yes!" she replied, tapping her abdomen. "Both of us would like it very much."

They opened the door, and Edmund apologised. "Sorry to take him from you, Your Grace. I'll do my best to keep it short."

"I understand, Inspector Reid. Next time, though, bring your wife along. Mrs. Reid can remain with me, and we shall commiserate one another."

"I'll do that," he promised. "Charles?"

Sinclair waved to Paul, who excused himself from his conversation with Baroness Wychwright, relief painted on his lean face. "I hope this is an escape plan," he whispered as he joined his cousin in the foyer. "Another moment in that woman's clutches, and I might book passage to Australia."

Elizabeth clucked her tongue. "Shame on you. The baroness only wants to make a good marriage for her daughter. Do you mean to say you wouldn't wish the same for Adele?"

"I beg the court's indulgence," he said, laughing. "Charles, am I to go or remain?"

"Go, if Beth can spare you. It seems Michael O'Brien wishes to confess. Are you up to assisting, Lord Aubrey?"

"Always, Lord Haimsbury. Beth, will you be all right without me?"

"I shall endure," she answered, winking at Sinclair. "I'll make use of the time by listing all your best points to the Wychwrights." She turned to go, casting both a triumphant smile before joining the main group in the drawing room.

"Perhaps, we should send Beth to interrogate O'Brien," the earl suggested as they walked out the front door.

Charles laughed. "O'Brien deserves such a fate! Those dark eyes cut to the quick, when she's angry. So, what is it our reporter wishes to confess, Ed?" he asked as the three of them entered a Branham coach.

"He claims that he'll reveal all of Redwing's plans in exchange for safety. With news of his arrest, he fears his compatriots will hang him out to dry as Ripper, and he hopes to avoid such a fate."

"As would anyone. Good, we'll see how useful his information is, and if it proves true, then we'll find a location where he might live out his life in security. Newgate, perhaps."

The carriage moved eastward along Great George Street, neither the driver nor its occupants aware of the great bat following above, its humanoid eyes blinking greedily.

CHAPTER EIGHTEEN
7:15 Sunday evening – Queen Anne House

Gertrude Trumper sat on death row, or so she believed. She'd been called to Cynthia Meyer's office at half six. Now, nearly an hour later, the girl still sat upon a wooden chair, waiting for his lordship to return from Whitechapel, when the ax would certainly fall. Aggie MacGowan kept her company, hoping to encourage her friend, but Trumper found no solace in the Scottish maid's presence. "Go 'way, Aggie. There's naught ta be done fer me."

"I'm sure his lordship will be fair, Gertie," MacGowan insisted as voices rose up in the stairwell beyond the office. "He's a kind man."

Before the Londoner could reply, the housekeeper entered with Lord Haimsbury. "His lordship wishes to speak with you, Gertie. Answer his questions honestly, and all will be well. Lie, and it will go against you, girl." The housekeeper departed, leaving the door ajar.

The marquess seemed as tall as any mountain to Trumper at this moment. She'd always thought him handsome, even generous, but now his face bore a stern expression that sent shivers down her spine.

Sinclair's visit to Leman Street had proven pointless, for Michael O'Brien refused to speak once Aubrey entered the room, claiming his earlier promise to confess had been misunderstood by Reid. Three hours of intense interrogation had made no difference, and the superintendent reluctantly left, ordering that the reporter be placed alone into a cell and kept on twenty-four hour watch, with no visitors.

During their journey, the earl had shared Della's story of the cocoa, and Sinclair had decided to get to the bottom of the mystery himself. As he entered the room, Trumper stared—and her expression reminded him of the recalcitrant reporter; a fact that did little to soften his manner.

"Do you know why you're here?" he asked brusquely.

She shook her head. "No, my lord."

"Do you like your work?"

Trumper licked her lips, nervously. "Aye, milord. I reckon so."

"Then, why is it that your behaviour indicates the opposite?"

"I'm not sure what ya mean, sir. I work real 'ard, an' do as I'm told ta do."

"I find that answer inadequate, Miss Trumper. Since the first day, you have proven obstinate and unreliable."

"Wha', sir?"

"You disobey orders, Gertrude. When told not to do something, you invariably do it, and when asked to perform a task, you find ways to avoid compliance. Were these the only complaints against you, I'd recommend a reprimand only, however, your actions go beyond that of a poor employee; they may be illegal. Tell me why I shouldn't dismiss you now."

She'd hoped to have a moment to explain, to say how none of it was her fault—for in her twisted mind, it wasn't. "I cannot say, my lord. I reckon you know all 'bout them jewels."

Charles made certain his face showed no sign of surprise. He'd planned to ask about the cocoa. Beth had not mentioned missing jewellery. "Tell me about them," he replied.

"Nothin' big, sir, though it were still thievin', I reckon. A bauble or two. I been sellin' 'em off to a fella I knows near Cheapside. He peddles salted pork from a wagon there, an' 'e buys up the odd trinkets now 'n then. I'll pay the duchess back, sir. I still 'ave most o' the coin I got fer 'em."

"What is it you stole, Gertie? Precisely."

She gulped, her eyes cast downward, fingers twisting. "An emerald ring. A pair o' blue and gold earbobs. A flower pin wif writin' on. Four velvet hair ribbons, decorated wif little pearls. That's all, sir."

"And what else did you take?" he asked, thinking now of the Verne novel. "Did you remove a book from the duchess's nightstand?"

She looked up, and tears tracked her thin face. "Migh' o' done, my lord. Bu' only as wantin' to read it."

"Read it? A book in French?"

She blinked. Gertie had stolen the book as ordered by the man in the mirror, but she'd not looked inside—she had no idea it was printed in anything other than English. "No, sir. I'm sorry, sir."

"Gertrude, why would you take a book you cannot read?"

"I dunno, sir."

"You don't know? Girl, say something in your own defence! Selling stolen goods could send you to prison. Must I arrest you?" he shouted.

Her face began to twitch, just above the left eye. "He made me do it."

"Who?"

"You wouldn't believe me, sir."

"I might," he said, softening his tone. "Miss Trumper, if a man put you up to this, you must tell me. I shan't blame you, if you've been coerced."

Her shoulders jerked back and forth, and her left hand began to tremble. "He ain' showed hisself since last Friday. I reckon I done sumfin wrong."

Charles drew his chair closer. "Who, Miss Trumper? Tell me his name."

"You'll say I'm mad, cause 'e lives here, sir. Inside the mirrors."

Sinclair stared, dread invading all his bones. "Did you just say this man lives *the mirrors*? Have you any idea how mad that sounds? Such a claim could send you to an asylum."

She burst into tears, her hands to her face. "Please, sir! Don' send me ta Bedlam! Mayhap I am mad, like as them teachers at the workhouse said, bu' I didn' wanna bring the duchess no 'arm, my lord. I don' e'en know what were in tha' bottle!"

"Finally, we get to the truth," he declared. "You admit to adding something to the duchess's cocoa? What did you use? Where did you find it?"

"Some of it were wha' tha' doctor left. Fer sleepin'. The rest, I don' know, sir, 'cause I bough' it off a gypsy. The man in the mirror, 'e tol' me ta go there an' arsk fer sumfin' called—I canno' remember, sir. It were a new word ta me."

"Think carefully, Miss Trumper. Remember that I am far more than your employer. I am also a police detective. Bedlam might be preferable to ten years' incarceration at Holloway."

She began to shake all over. Cynthia Meyer watched through a small window that communicated with the hallway outside the office, and she was joined by the butler.

"Is he dismissing her?" Miles asked.

"I cannot say. The duchess has said Lord Haimsbury's to be in charge of how this is handled, but the poor girl looks terrified. Perhaps, I should go in."

"Allow his lordship to deal with this, Mrs. Meyer. Speaking to a policeman might be just what the girl needs."

Inside the office, Sinclair continued, his voice stern and commanding. "The concoction inside that bottle could have made the duchess very ill, Gertrude. Is that what you intended? Did you wish to harm her? Why? She has only been kind to you."

"I dunno," the girl muttered, her shoulders rounding.

"What was in that bottle?"

"I don' know!" she shouted, her chin jerking up, eyes wide. "And I don't care! I hate her! She thinks she's 'igh and mighty, and every man loves her and wants her fer 'is own, but she's a liar and a cheat! She cheats on you, sir. She's been sportin' abou' wif the earl, an' 'e's prob'ly the baby's real fawver! Arsk 'im, iffin ya don' believe me! She don' love you, sir. She ain' never loved you!"

He started to interrupt, but the girl's spine arched backward, and she began to shout in a foreign language; her eyes rolled into her head, showing only the whites. Threats spewed from her mouth like dark water, and blood ran from both her eyes. Trumper's entire body rose up into the air, all on its own, leaving a great gap betwixt the floor and her feet. She literally hung suspended in mid-air; arms and legs stretched out impossible angles, as if unseen hands pulled the poor girl in four directions at once.

Trumper began to scream. Meyer and Miles rushed into the office. The girl's face contorted into animalistic shapes, the irises returning to the front; only now, the pupils had elongated into slits like that of a snake, the eye colour shifted from grey to yellow.

"She will die!" Trumper cried. Her voice was no longer her own, but that of many; most of them male. It sounded almost like the scratching of a bow upon out-of-tune strings, and the dissonance sent shivers down the detective's spine. "She will die," the hideous voice continued, laughing. "And her brat of a child will die with her!"

Charles reached out to take the maid's arm, but she struck him so hard that both he and the chair slammed into the corner, knocking over a small bookcase and spilling half a dozen reference books and ledgers onto the floor. John Miles tried to help the marquess, but Trumper's floating body flew towards him, biting at his ear as her left hand wrenched the butler's shoulder, dislocating it.

As the servant fell to the floor, the possessed girl rose higher towards the ceiling, the butler's blood staining her chin. A deep-throated laughter gurgled from her throat, but the voice was not human. It was a low-pitched, growling, mixed with the irritating voice of Prince Razarit Grigor. "*Find the glass, the shining one,*" the demonic presence inside the maid sang out, "*numbered 'mongst its brothers near.* Have you deciphered our riddle yet, Superintendent? You search for a key in vain. We require no such convention to enter this home! All mirrors are our doors, and soon we shall use one to steal your bride and claim her as our very own! As for this foolish human, her usefulness is at an end."

Charles stumbled to his feet, taking the girl by the hand. "Gertie! Listen to me, you don't have to allow this creature to control you! God hears, and he loves. He died for you!"

A shudder ran through her body, and she looked down at him, her eyes returning to normal. "God doesn't care," she whispered.

"He does," Charles answered. "Tell this creature that you no longer wish to follow his cruel path. Tell him, Gertie!"

"God has no time for me."

"He does. His word says that God resisteth the proud but giveth grace to the humble, Gertie," Sinclair quoted. "I know that in your heart, you are a humble young woman. Submit yourself unto God; resist the devil, and he will flee from you!"

A tear tracked down her cheek. "But I've sinned," she said. "I've hated and thieved and lied."

"As have we all. We are of us sinners. Christ alone is perfect, but His perfect blood can wash you clean. Don't you want that?"

"Yes," she whispered.

"Then ask Christ to cleanse your heart. God so loved the world that he gave his son for us. All you need do is ask him to accept you," he told her; his voice filled with anguish, tears running from his eyes.

Slowly, her body lowered to the floor. As her feet touched the boards, Sinclair pulled her into his arms. "God loves you, Gertie."

She collapsed against him, whimpering like a child. "God, help me, please. Forgive me! Take me to heaven. I don't want ta hurt no one no more." Gertrude Trumper smiled as she looked up at her employer, her eyes filled with tears. "Thank you, sir. No one's ever shown me such love afore. Tell the duchess I'm real sorry. Can you forgive me?"

"Yes," he whispered. "I forgive you, just as God forgives you."

Her body relaxed completely, and her eyes closed. The waiflike smile remained, but Gertrude Trumper was dead.

CHAPTER NINETEEN

14ᵗʰ November, Wednesday afternoon – 4 Whitehall Place

As Charles Sinclair sat at his desk, he reflected on the events since of the past few days. The shock of Trumper's death had thrown the household into deep mourning. At Beth's insistence, Gertie was buried in the family cemetery beyond the deer park at Queen Anne, overlooking a regal stand of graceful willow trees that grew alongside King's Creek. Sinclair read several psalms at the funeral, and Edward MacPherson conducted the service. Aggie MacGowan planted a white rose bush beside the grave, and she promised to visit her fallen friend every week.

Snowdrop succumbed to her illness, and necropsies performed by Marsden revealed a severe infection of the liver in both Ambrose Aurelius and the mare, caused by the introduction of foreign material—most likely bacteria. The presumed route of infection was determined to be puncture wounds found upon the horses' necks, just over the carotid arteries. The newborn colt was named Drummond's Delight and appeared to be thriving, nursed by an experienced broodmare called Branham's Heart.

Sinclair finished his photography session with Blackwood that Tuesday afternoon, including a series of ten poses at Queen Anne House with Elizabeth.

Michael Emerson met with the duchess twice in follow-up visits and received approval as her new physician. He confirmed the diagnosis given by Whitmore and Price: the duchess was indeed pregnant, and he estimated a delivery date near the middle of July, based on objective signs present during his examinations. Emerson felt her severe symptoms raised no immediate alarms, believing them nothing more than delicacy and nervous prostration caused by the trials the family had suffered of late.

After days in isolation, Michael O'Brien had finally confessed, and his information proved enlightening. The reporter corroborated the names on Ida Ross's list, but also revealed the locations of Redwing's meeting places throughout the city. Aubrey placed Malcolm Risling in charge of inspecting each site and removing any evidence discovered.

Sinclair personally investigated the claim made by Trumper before her death: that a mirrored entity had gained control of her and ordered her to poison the duchess. As a precaution, he'd asked Miles—now recovered—to assign footmen to search the house for any unusual mirrors, and they discovered the rosewood-handled looking glass Trumper had removed from the attics along with three other mirrors, apparently stolen from Haimsbury House. Gertrude had also written a rambling diary in a variety of hands and languages. These were given to Kepelheim and MacPherson for deciphering.

Lord Aubrey searched through stand after stand of pork sellers in Cheapside, finally locating a middle-aged Welshman named Pinky Jones, who'd recognised Trumper's description as a girl he'd known at Stepney Workhouse. Not surprisingly, he denied buying the stolen jewellery.

Aubrey also found the gypsy, working in a carnival sideshow, operating two miles east of Hackney Wick. The palm reader called herself Magda Kováks, and she told the earl that a girl claiming to represent an unnamed peeress had purchased half a bottle of valerian root and penny royal elixir so that she might induce miscarriage. Kováks had a long and colourful history with the Metropolitan Police, having been arrested dozens of times. When told that the mixture caused an unwitting animal to become quite ill, the gypsy claimed that she'd no idea what the actual ingredients in the bottle were, as she'd purchased it from a fellow traveller near the Marshes for half a penny.

"Blame him!" she'd exclaimed. "If you can find him. The man is *szellem*; a ghost!"

Finally, as Wednesday afternoon arrived, Elizabeth's health had improved dramatically. Her cheeks held their former blush of pink, her eyes were clear and joyful, and her hands steady. Though he'd seldom left her side since Sunday evening, Charles at last felt he could spend an hour at Whitehall, tying up loose ends at the Yard.

"Much has changed in six weeks' time, hasn't it, old friend?"

Sinclair smiled at his fellow superintendent, George Haskell. "Has it only been six weeks? Feels like six months at times."

"I hope that isn't an indicator of doubt, Charles. I've seen your good lady's portrait in the press. She's absolutely beautiful. Surely, you're not having second thoughts."

"Not even one. Honestly, George, I'm happier than I'd ever thought possible."

The portly superintendent crossed the room, perching upon Sinclair's desk. "Not even a twinge of worry? Marriage is a big step, after all."

"Not even a hint of a twinge. We've had a busy time of it, that's all, but we manage. What do you think of our new commissioner?"

"It's hard to say," Haskell answered, removing a pipe from his pocket. "Monro seems a decent enough chap. He served as a magistrate in India before coming back here in '84. He certainly stepped up to the mark as Assistant Commissioner for Crime, I thought. Didn't you?"

"I suppose he's all right. I've always got along well with Monro. Special Branch might not agree with the Home Secretary's choice, but it's no longer my concern. I'm resigning."

"What?" Haskell gasped. "You're doing no such thing. You bleed blue, Charles. Your peerage notwithstanding, of course. Why, I can't imagine the Yard without you in it. Why would you even consider resigning?"

"My cousin and I are starting a private investigation service. I'm tired of being given a task with no funds to implement it."

"Must be nice to have wealth," Haskell observed, lighting the pipe. "If you ever need advice on how to spend it, call on me. If I can't give you an answer, I'm sure my wife can. Or my two daughters."

"Shall I let Helen know that you said that?" Charles quipped with a wink. "Actually, I think I'll pay Monro a call this afternoon and let him know my plans in person. He's a good man, and I'd not want to leave on a sour note."

"He'll likely try to stop you," his friend countered as he returned to his own desk.

A constable knocked on the door frame, a calling card in his right hand. "Superintendent Sinclair, sir?"

"Yes, Wells. What is it?"

"You've a visitor. A right fancy man."

Sinclair laughed. "Is he long-haired and well spoken?"

"He is, sir."

"Then it's probably my cousin, Lord Aubrey. Send him up."

"No, sir. I know Lord Aubrey, sir. This is a foreign fellow. Says he's a prince."

Sinclair felt a chill run down his back. *Which prince?* "Send him up. George, do you mind?"

"Not at all. I'm not really the princely type, anyway," Haskell, answered. He clapped the pipe against his teeth, grinned, and left the office, passing by Anatole Romanov in the corridor.

"Good day, Lord Haimsbury" the prince said as he entered. "I ask your forgiveness for calling without warning, but you are always so very busy."

Charles met the prince at the door and motioned towards a pair of club chairs, flanking a blue-tiled fireplace. "Shall we sit?"

"Thank you, yes."

"As you say, Your Highness, I'm a busy man these days. How may I help you? Have you come to offer more of your riddles?"

Romanov removed his gloves, smiling. "No. I come to speak plainly."

"That will be refreshing."

"Yes, I imagine so. Charles, I am hosting a ball at Kensington Palace this Saturday evening. It is in honour of your upcoming wedding. You and the duchess are the special guests. I sent an invitation to your home, but have not yet received a reply."

"A ball?" he asked, thinking of Beth's nightmare. "That's kind of you, but as it's the night before our wedding..."

"Yes, I know this, but it would mean a great deal to me. The Duke of Edinburgh also hosts the ball, along with myself and the Russian Embassy. You must come, Charles."

"I'll agree to come if you answer a few questions for me. No tricks, no riddles."

"What would you ask of me?"

"Who are you?"

Romanov's smooth cheeks rose high upon his serene face. "That is a complicated question. I am more than human, as you already know. Am I your enemy? No. I am your friend."

"Prove it."

"Very well. There is a man whom you should locate. He is called Mr. Thirteen, but that is not his name. It is a designation used by those who have kept him prisoner these many years."

"Why would I want to find this gentleman?"

"Because you need him to recover your lost memories."

"How so?"

"Find him, and you find your answers."

"More riddles!" Charles shouted, rising to his feet. "Get out, if that is all you offer."

The prince remained calm and seated. "I also know you found a letter from a woman whom you admire. The names on her list will begin to die, so if you wish to learn anything from them, you must act quickly."

Sinclair paused, his anger dissipating momentarily. "Why would they die?"

"Because they have been exposed. The list's existence is known, Charles. It throws their current plans into a temporary state of chaos, but the round table will rebuild."

"With Trent at its head?"

He smiled, his right hand twisting the head of his cane. "No."

"No?"

"I shall not explain further, but allow me to offer this. You have a fitting with your tailor this afternoon, no?"

"How do you know that?"

"I know many things, and no, I do not spy upon you through mirrors as do some of my kind. My knowledge derives from other methods. Not only do I see what Redwing does, I hear their little whispers."

"You've not yet answered my original question."

"Haven't I?"

"Whose side are you on?"

"The one that will win," he said, standing. "Keep watch for packages. One never knows what they might contain."

He offered his host a deep bow. "Until Saturday, then."

The prince left the office and vanished, leaving no hint that he had even been there at all.

Elizabeth Stuart read through the young woman's résumé, finding herself impressed. "Miss Jenkins, you served as private secretary for the Countess Morell, may I ask why you left? You do not say."

The woman was twenty-six, gracefully tall, auburn-haired, and pleasant with a serious, freckled face. She wore good shoes, an expensive dress that reflected fashion from three seasons past, and she had a tendency to tap her foot.

"She—well, it's difficult to say, Your Grace. That is... If you must know, the countess dismissed me, due to my condition."

Beth looked surprised. "Your condition? Are you ill?"

"No, no, I am quite healthy, my lady. But I was unmarried and—well, I still am, but you see, I was with child. I'd been engaged, you understand, to a wonderful young man from our parish named Thomas Willoughby. Tommy and I planned to wed last April, but he got cold feet, I suppose, especially when it became clear that we'd already begun our family. The countess was very kind to me, and she—well, I must admit it, her ladyship helped me to find a family to adopt my little boy. I've only now fully recovered my strength, but the countess hired another woman to take my place during my confinement. You may speak to her regarding it. I did not wish to keep any truths from you, Your Grace, it is just that the story is a difficult one, and I'd hoped..."

"You'd hoped you might avoid telling it. I see, and I understand. Where is your son at present? You say he was adopted? Does he live in London? Do you see him from time to time?"

"No, Your Grace, I do not. He lives with a family in Ireland. Friends to the Countess. I'm never to contact him, because his new parents must now be his only parents."

She began to weep, and Elizabeth offered her a handkerchief. "Dry your eyes, Miss Jenkins. When would you be able to start?"

"Do you mean you'd still consider me, my lady?"

"I would, and I do—in fact, if my fiancé approves, then you may begin as soon as you're available."

"Oh yes. I recall seeing your wedding announcement in the newspapers. Will you remain here, then, or do you plan to return to Kent?"

"Both and neither, I suppose. I'm sorry to be so vague, but we are only now finalising our plans. When we return from our short wedding trip, we shall reside in Lord Haimsbury's London house, which is not far from here—a short walk across the park behind Queen Anne, in fact. Which means, I shall be able to visit my old home and see all my friends here whenever I wish."

She looked puzzled. "Friends? You have friends living here with you, Your Grace?"

"Most would simply call them my staff, but many have known me since I was a little girl. To me they are more like friends, and some are like family. Now, your home could be either here or at Haimsbury House, but it would work best for me, if you could be available during regular hours. Ten to four, I should think. I do not desire someone who is always on call. I merely need an assistant to keep track of each day's demands, write a few letters, and maintain communication with my solicitors, estate stewards, and so forth. Does that seem attainable?"

"Oh, yes! It is very attainable, Your Grace."

"Good. The salary is two hundred pounds a year to start, but once we've an idea of how efficient you are, you will be considered for a pay rise. You'll have one week off each August, one at Christmas, and another in the spring for Easter week. All with pay, of course."

Her eyes grew round. "Those are very generous terms, Your Grace."

"I'm glad you think so. I had a secretary in Paris last year, who thought them positively meagre. Oh, and if my Aunt Victoria tries to second you for her own projects, you must tell me. Tory should be willing to pay for your time, if she chooses to employ it."

"Thank you so much, Your Grace. Oh, is that the marquess there?" she asked as Paul Stuart's tall form and Kepelheim's short one passed by the windows.

"Actually that is my cousin, Lord Aubrey, and the other gentleman is his tailor and our friend, Mr. Martin Kepelheim. They've arrived to finalise fittings for the wedding clothes. May I contact you at this hotel, Miss Jenkins?"

The young woman nodded and stood, realising she was being dismissed. "Yes, of course. Thank you, Your Grace."

"Thank you for meeting with me today, Miss Jenkins. I shall contact you tomorrow morning either way, but unless Lord Haimsbury has an objection, you are hired."

She beamed, and Beth could see the woman's entire demeanor alter.

"We let ourselves in. The foyer is devoid of servants," Aubrey said, peering into the drawing room. "Are we early? Where are all your staff?"

"Miles is at the other house, and Stephens conducts a meeting in the kitchens, I think. I'm not sure why Lester isn't available. He was here a moment ago," Beth answered. "Miss Jenkins, this is my cousin Paul Stuart, Earl of Aubrey, and this is our most esteemed and talented Mr. Kepelheim. Gentlemen, Miss Jenkins may soon be joining our household as my secretary. And no, I do not believe you early. Charles is late."

The tailor removed his hat as did Paul, and both men bowed. Jenkins found it all too much, and she blushed beautifully in return. "You are very kind. Lord Aubrey, it is an honour to meet you."

Paul smiled, his blue eyes twinkling. "Miss Jenkins, you will find that so long as you take good care of our duchess, you will never cease to have friends here. Beth, I'll take our tailor upstairs, so he may chalk my hems. Wait—did you say Charles is late?"

She nodded her head as the secretary left. "He is. I expected him an hour ago, and since I promised not to chase him all over Whitechapel, I am cooling my heels here."

The earl kissed her cheek. "It's clear that your old fighting spirit has returned, Princess. Shall I send a footman to forewarn your fiancé?"

"Oh, no. Allow me the pleasure of reminding the marquess just how accurate his timepiece is."

Paul and the tailor left the room, both laughing, and even Beth found cause to smile. In only a few days, she would become Mrs. Charles Sinclair, and nothing she might imagine could ever make her happier. She left the drawing room, intending to find that afternoon's post, but she overheard Jenkins speaking to someone at the front door. As Lester had not yet returned, Beth decided to discover who it might be. The secretary stood in the open door, and the duchess could see the young woman's coat and hat, still in her left hand, but she could not see the other person.

Rather than ring for a footman, Beth ignored protocol and answered the door, opening both sides, so she could observe the entire front portico. A man and woman stood near one of the chairs. He was tall and thin and wore a waxed handlebar moustache upon his long upper lip. His dress was formal: cutaway coat, striped cravat, and lavender gloves. She was medium height with greying hair done up in an elaborate coif topped by a yellow rose hat, bearing three enormous heron feathers. Her turquoise and yellow dress echoed the latest fashion, but her pale face and tight lips gave her an aged look.

"Good day," Beth said to the strangers. "Miss Jenkins, are these friends of yours?" she asked. It seemed a perfectly reasonable question under the circumstances.

As was often her way whenever at home, Elizabeth had dressed simply in a royal blue skirt and white silk blouse; topped by a yellow and blue, striped waistcoat. Her hair was down but neatly pulled back behind her ears and secured by a yellow ribbon, edged in white lace.

The man spoke in reply. "My good woman, we are family to the marquess," he announced. "We wish to speak with Lord Haimsbury. Would you announce us?"

Beth nearly spoke to clarify her identity, but realising who this couple must be, decided to allow them to continue in their error. She cast a conspiratorial glance to the new secretary. "Thank you, Miss Jenkins. You may expect word tomorrow." The girl nodded and turned to offer a departing smile before she walked down the long gravel drive to hire a cab back to her hotel.

"This way," Beth said, leading the couple into the smallest of the three drawing rooms, painted in rich reds and gold, and trimmed in creamy white. "Lord Haimsbury is delayed, I'm afraid. Would you mind waiting here until he arrives? May I offer you tea?"

"Tea for my wife, but I'll have coffee," the man said curtly. handing Beth his hat along with the woman's fur-trimmed cloak. Without a word, the duchess took the items and returned to the foyer, where she handed them to Lester, who had now appeared, a small canvas bag filled with chips of ice in his left hand.

"I am sorry…" he began, but Beth signalled for him to remain silent.

"Could you serve our guests tea and coffee? When Lord Haimsbury arrives, bring him to me in the library," she whispered, and then left to read through the afternoon post.

All this took place at quarter past four, and another quarter hour ticked by before Sinclair returned from Whitehall. "Afternoon, Lester. Have Lord Aubrey and Mr. Kepelheim arrived yet?"

"I cannot say, sir," the first footman replied, the ice bag still in his hand. "I'm to tell you that my lady awaits in the library, sir."

"Thank you, Lester. Headache?"

"Yes, sir."

"Sorry to hear it. You must take the afternoon and rest."

Entering the library, Sinclair found the duchess busy at her writing desk.

"Sorry I'm late," he said happily. "I've had a rather strange day. You wouldn't believe who paid me a visit at Whitehall."

Elizabeth rose and took his hand. "You needn't worry about being late. Paul's making use of your time. He and Mr. Kepelheim are working upstairs now. I don't suppose your visitor brought his wife?"

"What? No, why?"

"Because the man now sitting in our drawing room brought his."

"Who might that be?" he asked, as she led him back into the long foyer, towards the front drawing room.

The male visitor's rose up in annoyance, filling the entire floor. Simultaneously, in the downstairs kitchen, the drawing room bell clanged over and over again. "Good heavens!" the man shouted. "Is there no butler in this house? Shabby way to run a London home!"

Beth shrugged, and Charles, having recognised the voice, opened the door. Elizabeth entered first, but before she could speak the man began to rant.

"My dear girl, your household is a shambles! Does the duchess approve of this sort of poor management? Not only does a mere girl greet us, but we're left to ring for assistance without reply. This is intolerable! I shall speak to your employer, young woman. Where is Lord Haimsbury—oh, there you are," he said, his manner altering completely as Sinclair followed Beth into the room. "Charles, my dear, dear son. It is so good to see you again."

The woman in the hat kissed Sinclair fondly. "Charles, we have so missed your visits! When we saw in the *Gazette* that you now reside here, well I said to Frederick that we simply must pay a call on our dear son-in-law."

Beth had correctly surmised the identities of the two in her parlour, and she remained quiet, standing demurely to one side, as if awaiting orders. Charles didn't know whether to laugh or begin shouting, but following his fiancée's lead, he offered Margaret Winstone a perfunctory peck on the cheek and his former father-in-law, Frederick Winstone, a firm, albeit less than enthusiastic handshake.

"I believe we ordered tea, young woman," Frederick said to Beth.

She stood her ground, making no effort to respond or tend to his demands.

"Are you deaf, girl? Will you leave your lord's relatives seeking a simple cup of tea?"

Just then, Stephens the underbutler and two young footmen entered, carrying trays laden with tea, coffee, fruit, finger sandwiches, and beautifully iced cakes on chased silver trays.

Beth said nothing to the servants, but before Stephens left, he turned to her and bowed. "Will there be anything else, Your Grace?"

She shook her head. "No thank you, Stephens. Oh, and please tell Lester that he must take all the time he requires for that headache. I know how they plague him. Has Mr. Miles returned?"

"Not yet, my lady. He promised to be back before six, though."

Stephens shut the doors, and Beth turned to smile sweetly at her guests. Frederick Winstone appeared to be in the middle of an apoplectic fit, and Margaret had turned into a pale, stone statue, her extraordinary feathered hat now skewed to one side.

Charles kissed Beth on the cheek, taking her hand. "Allow me to introduce my fiancée, Elizabeth Stuart, soon to be Sinclair, Duchess of Branham. Beth, these are Amelia's parents, Fred and Meg Winstone," he said, deliberately shortening their Christian names, something he knew both found intolerable.

"I am delighted to meet you both. Mr. Winstone, are you unwell?"

The man cleared his throat and took a moment to find his voice, but he nodded. "Uh, yes, well. Forgive me, Your Grace, we clearly entered your beautiful home under a misunderstanding—ours certainly."

Beth patted the older man's hand kindly, and Charles adored her for it. "No harm done, my dear Fred. None at all. Please, do sit, won't you? You find our household in a rush of preparation, as you might imagine. And with another murder in the east, my fiancé keeps irregular hours."

Winstone showed surprise. "Charles, surely you are not continuing with police work! You are a titled lord, my boy! Does your time and station even permit remaining in your position with the Yard?"

Charles was thoroughly enjoying this unexpected visit. "You'd be surprised at the number of titled men working at Scotland Yard, Fred."

"Perhaps, yes, but surely only in the highest tiers. Sir Charles Warren is still commissioner; I presume?"

"No, Warren's resigned," Charles replied. "Monro's taken over."

"Poor Sir Charles!" Beth added. "He took a great deal of political pounding, but politics is a cannibalistic enterprise, is it not? Where elder brothers consume those viewed as less fit, and younger siblings roust out the old? Charles, you mustn't delay too long, darling. Paul and Mr. Kepelheim await upstairs."

Sinclair kissed her on the cheek. "So they do. Forgive me, Fred, Meg. Perhaps we might catch up another time. My tailor's here to perform one last fitting, and my cousin, who will serve as best man, requires my attendance."

Margaret's light grey eyes lit up. "Oh, Charles, would that be Lord Aubrey?"

"The very same."

"He is quite a dashing young man!" she gushed. "Is it true that he and Cordelia Wychwright have become quite close?"

"They are friends," Sinclair answered, wondering just who might be spreading such rumours. "Nothing more than that."

"Oh," Meg whispered. "I suppose I misunderstood Baroness Wychwright, then. She and I serve on the Mission School committee together. Do you think we might meet your cousin, Charles?"

Beth answered for him. "I'm sure he'd be pleased to say hello. In fact, the earl should be down shortly, and I'm certain he'll want to meet you both and hear all about your Mission School meeting. For now, if you'll excuse me for just a moment? I must speak to my fiancé before he goes upstairs. I shan't be long."

She walked out with Charles, and once they reached the staircase, he began to laugh for the first time in many days. "Oh, Beth! That was marvellous! Simply marvellous! Thank you so much, darling. Now, I can truly say I've seen the proud made humble. You played your part to perfection. Have I told you today how very much I love you?"

She pulled him down and kissed his cheek. "Not since morning, but I am always, always glad to hear it, Captain. Did you speak with Commissioner Monro?"

"I did, and he's promised to consider my resignation, but he plans to confer with the Home Secretary first. It's likely Matthews will try to keep me on, but he may consider himself well rid of me."

"I doubt that."

He touched her waist. "And you're still feeling all right?"

"Much better. Dr. Emerson's dietary suggestions have allowed me to eat at last. And now that everyone knows my condition, Mrs. Meyer and Mrs. Smith conspire to make sure I eat."

"It sounds as though you're in good hands. Meyer and Smith make a formidable duo, and I like Emerson very much. We've a great deal in common, it seems. You being the most important— both of you."

She blushed, suddenly imagining herself as mother of his child. "We both love you," she said. "I pray that all the anguish of the past week is over. Perhaps, with your resignation, our household will settle into a lovely sort of boredom."

He pulled her close, kissing her hair as he held her. "Boredom sounds wonderful."

"I hope you still say that six months hence," she whispered. "Now, go see to your wedding clothes, soon-to-be husband!"

His eyes lit up. "Call me that again—only without the soon-to-be part."

She rose up on tiptoe to whisper into his ear as he bent down. "I do love you, and I shall call you husband soon—for all the days of my life."

His entire face broke into a smile. "That is all I needed to hear; I am now energised for the task ahead." And with that, Charles dashed up the curving staircase, two steps at a time, singing all the way.

Beth turned around and headed back towards the drawing room to speak with the Winstones, but to her surprise, she noticed a white package with a large red bow sitting near the main entry.

For days now, wedding gifts had been arriving, so she assumed this to be yet another delivery from one of the many social contacts or friends on Aunt Victoria's guest list; or from the hundreds of others who had not yet received an invitation but hoped to be added at the last minute.

The drawing room doors remained shut, so she walked past and knelt down to see what sender's name might be on the label. There was none; only her name, written in red ink: Elizabeth Stuart Sinclair. The colour chilled her blood, but surely this was no message from the man calling himself 'Saucy Jack' for he never included her last name, and certainly not one she'd not yet claimed.

The box, though wrapped in expensive paper, looked odd to Elizabeth. It had not been sealed, and the top was wrapped separately. It showed no evidence of having been opened by anyone else, nor did it bear a postmark. There was no return address.

She nearly rang for a footman to fetch Sinclair, but Beth hated alarming him for what was probably just a silver platter or monogrammed teacup, so she retrieved the box from the floor and placed it on the foyer table. As she touched it, a small voice sounded a warning near the back of her mind. When was this delivered? No one had rung the bell, else Lester would have answered it. How then did it arrive? Perhaps, Miss Jenkins set it inside before she left, or the delivery person had knocked whilst she and Charles spoke with the Winstones.

The Winstones! She had nearly forgotten them, so to put an end to the mystery, Elizabeth lifted the lid and found the surprise inside.

Beth had never screamed so loudly in her entire life.

The terrified wail pierced the air, and in seconds, every member of staff, Paul, Charles, Kepelheim, and even the Winstones rushed into the massive, four-storey foyer to find the duchess lying on the Roman tiles in a dead faint.

Wearing only his wedding trousers and a silk shirt, Charles knelt at her side, patting her face, which was ice cold. Aubrey had finished his tailoring session and had dressed to leave for Whitehall. He stood beside the table, overlooking the mysterious box. His lean face had gone ashen. Kepelheim stepped forward and looked inside the box.

"Good heavens!" the tailor exclaimed. "She saw this? Who would send this to her? This is madness!"

Charles looked up at Paul. "What is it?" he demanded. "Another of those horrible notes?"

The earl shook his head solemnly. "No, Charles. It is a human heart."

CHAPTER TWENTY

It was early evening by the time Michael Emerson finished his visit with Elizabeth, and the young physician left the duchess to sleep whilst he washed up and took a much-earned tea break. Charles had been sitting in the library ever since Emerson's arrival, and now that the house had calmed down—and his former in-laws finally left—his head had begun to clear enough to think.

Right after the hideous heart had been discovered, Aubrey sent messages to their Uncle James, Galton, Reid, and France—the last at Charles's insistence. He wanted a full meeting of as many inner circle members as possible. The earl then left, promising to return within a few hours, not saying where he planned to go.

Emerson entered and closed the door.

"Is she all right?" Sinclair asked, bracing himself for the worst.

"Are all your days like this? Sorry, you await my news. Sit down, please," the doctor said. "We are safely alone, I take it?"

Charles nodded.

"Good. May I lock the door?"

Again the marquess nodded. "Michael, if you have bad news, please, just say it quickly."

Emerson took a seat. "Forgive me for keeping you waiting. It is only I do not wish to be disturbed or overheard. Firstly, let me put your mind at ease. The duchess's health has not been harmed by the ordeal. And neither has that of the child."

Charles began to weep softly, wiping at his eyes. "You're certain that the shock of that—that hideous gift did not cause anything to go awry?"

"The duchess is somewhat delicate physically, but her heart and will are mighty. Her reaction to that package is understandable.

Even in the best of times, a woman—or even a man—might faint at such a sight, but as Elizabeth's pregnancy progresses, she will display strong and perhaps unexpected, even inexplicable emotions. Her body is undergoing great changes, as I'm sure you can imagine. Also, she will be far more vulnerable to events such as occurred here today, so it would be best to protect her from such, which I'm sure you already endeavour to do."

"We do our best, however, Elizabeth is sometimes headstrong," Charles told him.

Emerson smiled. "Yes, I've seen evidence of that already. Your household appears to suffer violent episodes from time to time. Are these related to Redwing?"

Sinclair considered his answer carefully. Emerson appeared to be a genuine believer and trustworthy, but dare he tell him everything? "Possibly," he answered cryptically. "Forgive me for not being completely candid with you, Michael. As Beth's doctor, you deserve full knowledge of anything that might threaten her health—and that of our baby," he added, imagining himself as a father again. "This child will change everything."

"Yes, it very likely will, but I would speak to you of another, although related issue. Your Aunt Victoria accosted me outside Elizabeth's apartment, before I could come down to see you, and asked if the duchess were in danger of miscarriage. She mentioned that Beth's mother had trouble with child-bearing."

Charles looked puzzled. "Emerson, that makes no sense. Beth was the only child that Patricia carried."

"Not so. At least, according to the admirable Lady Victoria, it is not so. It seems that Patricia miscarried three times before Elizabeth was born. All three before six months, and all three sons."

"What?" he asked. "All three? All…sons? But, surely not because they were males. Can that be the cause? Is there some medical reason why a mother might succeed only in carrying daughters?"

Sitting back, the doctor thought for a moment. "None that I know of, but that does not preclude it. I asked if Patricia's mother had difficulties, or if perhaps her grandmother had trouble carrying to term, and Lady Victoria referred me to Dr. Price. I shall call upon him tomorrow, but for now, I admit to being puzzled. I tell you this because I know how much you love the duchess. I can see it on your face anytime you say her name or see her enter a room."

"Thank you, Michael. May I see her?"

"Yes, of course, and I shall set my mind to unravelling this mystery regarding the miscarriages." Emerson moved towards the door, his medical bag in his left hand. "I've given Elizabeth a very small dose of a sleeping powder. It will not hurt the child, so don't worry. Let her sleep until she awakens naturally, and that may be as late as tomorrow afternoon. She has a life inside her demanding resources and energies, making her a little more fragile than usual. I'm staying at my father's house in Mayfair. Call on me anytime."

Charles watched him go, but Emerson's tale of miscarried babies echoed in his mind like an unwelcome ghost. Climbing the stairs towards the master apartment, he began to imagine their family in a few years—one child, perhaps even two—but he knew each would be vulnerable to Redwing. Every new life brought fresh danger, but he must not think about that yet.

He found Alicia sitting by her lady's side, and the young woman curtsied and left, allowing Charles to take her place. Elizabeth lay beneath the velvet duvet, wearing a cream lace and royal blue satin night gown, her small hands resting upon the covers.

"Beth," he called, taking her hand. It felt warm, not icy like before. *She lives. She breathes.* "Beth, darling, can you hear me?"

Her eyelids fluttered, and she slowly opened her eyes. "Captain?" she said, her mouth dry from the sleeping draught. "What—why am I in bed?"

"You're in need of rest. That's all, little one." He laid his head on her shoulder, and she raised a hand to stroke his hair.

"Did I faint again?" she whispered hoarsely.

"You don't remember?"

She shook her head. "No, I'm sorry. My mind's rather muddled. I think Dr. Emerson gave me something to help me sleep. I was dreaming. About you—and another. He looked so much like you."

"Who, dear?" he asked.

"Albert," she said, the single word tearing his mind with the speed of a bullet.

"What did you say?" he asked, sitting up.

"Albert. Your son. I saw him, though it was only a dream."

How can she know about him? "What do you mean?"

She tried to push upward, but the effects of the sleeping draught weakened her arms, and she fell back against the pillow. "Could you help me? I'd like to talk about him. Do you mind?"

"You should sleep."

"No, I want to hear about him, Charles. Please, don't be cross with me."

"I could never be anything but in love with you," he assured her. "Do you prefer to sit in bed, or would you like a chair?"

"Bed is fine. I'm very sleepy, but it's on my mind. He's on my mind."

Sighing, he decided now might be the best opportunity to confess his failings, so the detective assisted her in sitting against the headboard. "Let me add another pillow to support your back. Water?"

"No, I'm content. You look as if you need something stronger. Charles, if you prefer not to talk about him, I understand."

"It is difficult, but I'd always intended to tell you. In fact, it's why I wanted to have that picnic with you, though something always came up to make us postpone." He grew silent for a moment. "How did you learn about him?"

"You mustn't scold her, but it was Mary who let it slip. She'd brought me the scrapbooks Amelia kept when you were married. Sunday afternoon, when you and Paul were in Whitechapel. I'd asked if she had any photographs of you in uniform, and she brought out those books. We had a delightful time poring over those pages, and I removed several for framing. You made a very handsome constable, by the way," she said, offering him a smile. He took her hand, squeezing it. "One photograph showed you with a baby, and I asked about it. Mary had no idea that you'd never told me about Albert, but when she mentioned his name, I immediately remembered that it was the name you called over and over whilst in your fever in Scotland. I'd thought then that it might be a child."

"You never said anything," he whispered. "Why?"

"Because you did not. I'd assumed there must be a reason why you kept silent on it. I waited to see if you would tell me. Charles, how did he die?"

Charles grew quiet, his pale face revealing the deep pain the memories evoked. He said nothing for many moments, and Beth allowed him the silence, for she suspected that her question—and her condition—had uncovered deeply hidden grief within his heart.

His eyes turned away from hers, as Sinclair fought emotions and memories he'd kept in check for ten years.

"His name was Albert Frederick," he began. "Amelia never liked living in Whitechapel. She liked very few things related to my life, but as her husband it was my duty to provide for her happiness. I failed in that nearly every day we were married. I often wondered why she married me. She was a lovely young woman back then, and I remember how she would laugh in those early days. That soon changed."

He halted, lost in a spiral of old wounds, old regrets. Then regaining composure, he continued. "That perceived bliss was short-lived, if indeed it ever really existed. After only a few months, we settled into a complacency that dragged at my heart. I truly wanted to make her happy, but Amelia seemed so desperately miserable, that I began to wonder if she might not be better off without me. I actually spoke with a solicitor about divorce."

This completely surprised the duchess. "After only a few months? Was it so awful?"

"It was I who was awful, Beth. Amelia repeatedly told me how I'd disappointed her, and she hated my career choice. I was a policeman when we met, but she pushed me towards the practise of law. She said my university degree was being wasted, and that I should apply to one of the inns. My aunt and uncle encouraged me to divorce, saying Amelia didn't love me. However, it all became moot, two days before my birthday in '77, when she told me she was pregnant."

"You hadn't planned for a child?"

"No. I hadn't, at least. Truthfully, it was a great shock, and I admit to doubting if the child was even mine, for we generally slept apart after the first month. Amelia had headaches most of the time. However, once he was born, it was obvious. Albert looked exactly like me. Amelia begged me to let us move in with her parents, but I refused—out of selfishness to be honest. I'm not proud of my behaviour then, Beth, for at that time, my mind was fixed only on policing and learning that craft. I was one of a very few men who'd been named to form the new Criminal Investigations Department for Scotland Yard, and I wanted to live up to the faith Morehouse had placed in me. The promotion also bumped my rank from Police Sergeant to Detective Inspector, for of those selected to found the

CID, I was only one of two men with a university degree. Also, I'd already solved three murders by then. I was assigned to H-Division in early '78, and we relocated from Lambeth to Whitechapel. My citizenry lived within the borough, and that is where I believed my family should also live."

"That makes sense," she said. "Didn't Amelia agree?"

"She agreed with practically nothing. If I said black, she would argue that it was white. Up for me was down for her. But it wasn't only a desire to remain in Whitechapel that drove me. The truth is that I had no wish to find myself beholden to her parents—her father in particular. It's strange to say it, with all that I now know about my life, my true heritage, but Frederick Winstone always seemed to enjoy putting me in my place. You've met him. He was a very diffi- cult man to please. His daughter inherited that flinty character, and I suppose I simply decided that failure would be my fate, regardless of what I did. Therefore, I did not try."

She listened quietly, her hand in his, and his grip tightened as the dark past rushed to intersect with the present.

"I adored that boy, Elizabeth. From the moment I first held him, I knew Albert was mine. Amelia reacted strangely to him, though. She seemed cold, almost hateful towards him. So much, that I was forced to engage a wet nurse to care for him, but Amelia assumed her to be my mistress."

"Your mistress! Why would she think that? Charles, you are so faithful, so true!"

"Am I?" he asked. "No, the girl wasn't my mistress. Don't think that, darling. Still, Amelia was convinced of my infidelity, and she dismissed the nurse. But Albert began to grow despondent and weak. After consulting with a doctor, I hired Mary Wilsham to keep house and switched Albert to a mixture of cow's milk, cream, and honey, taken from a glass bottle. Though I wasn't fond of the idea and wondered if the mixture offered adequate nutrition, it did allow me to feed him, which I did as often as possible. Over the course of '78, he steadily grew and even began to thrive. Amelia's icy exterior slowly thawed, and she began talking about having a second child."

"When was Albert born?" she asked.

"December of '77, on the twentieth, but he never saw his first birthday. When we moved to Whitechapel, all that I could find was a tiny flat above a jeweller's shop, but after two months, the house on

Columbia Road became available. It was much larger and in a safer part of the east. I thought Amelia would be pleased. It was relatively new and had a back garden. It's the house you stayed in for a few hours—do you remember it?"

"I remember it very well, Captain. Those few hours forever altered the course of my life."

He smiled for a moment, grateful for her patience. "Somehow that small house came to life when you entered it, Beth. It was always a cold place—cold in many ways. Its sole source of warmth is in three fireplaces. We had gas lamps but no boiler for central heating. This wasn't unusual for Whitechapel rents, and I'd been saving to purchase a small place of our own. A new development was going up near Kingston with modern amenities, and my plan was to give Amelia this gift as a surprise for Christmas. It occurs to me now, that this was only a few months before William murdered your mother. That winter was cruel, was it not?"

He paused again, closing his eyes, and she could see the cost of this retelling, written in pain across his handsome face. "In early November, some of the residents of Whitechapel began to fall ill. Within a week, dozens had died, and by the end of the month, hundreds. Eventually, the source for the epidemic was traced to a seaman returning from China, who'd carried the disease, which rapidly spread to dock workers, hauliers, prostitutes, and thence to costermongers, local merchants, and eventually to policemen and their... To their families."

Charles paused again, and tears formed like drops of heavy dew upon his black lashes. He took a deep breath and continued, his hands shaking.

"At first, it looked like seasonal cases of chickenpox or even measles, but its true, terrifying name was soon discerned. Smallpox. Doctors at the Eastern Dispensary and the London came to us and asked that our constables be dispatched to every home, warning of the disease and ascertaining if anyone there had shown symptoms. Morehouse asked me to lead this initiative, and we found many hundreds infected, and dozens already dead or dying. Some merely developed the rash and cough, but others—oh, others," he whispered, his voice cracking, "they, they..." He wiped at his face, struggling to maintain composure. "Their skin turned black and sometimes...

Sometimes it sloughed off. Beth, it was devilish; unthinkably horrible! I'm so glad you weren't in London to see it, or even hear of it."

He paused again, great tears sliding down both cheeks. She squeezed his hand, patiently listening.

"Early in the outbreak, Amelia asked me whether she might go to her mother's home, and I—well, I selfishly insisted she remain with me, that I preferred she and Albert stay in our own home. I foolishly thought them safe there, you see? Mary tried to convince me to send both my wife and son to another part of London, but my pride kept them within my reach; though, I foolishly believed myself protecting them.

"It was several weeks into the outbreak, and more and more corpses began to choke our streets. The hospital and police morgues could no longer house all the bodies, and a shuttered warehouse near Leman Street became a makeshift crematorium. It was hideous work, but dozens of desperate, able-bodied men lined up to receive a shilling a day to stuff the dead into hastily built ovens that burnt 'round the clock. The stench over the east was overpowering. It is a smell you never, *never* forget." His hand trembled as it tightened around hers. "Our doctors feared that the bodies carried disease, you see, so all who died of the illness, regardless of social position, were so dispatched. That also included—children."

His shoulders began to shake as grief took hold of his entire body. Beth held him close, saying nothing, merely being his sounding board, his helper, but it broke her heart to hear the deep pain and regret in his manly voice; to see such sorrow etched upon his noble brow.

"For some reason, I never became ill, not for a day, not a moment—dear God in heaven! I have so many times wished that I had died instead!"

His head dropped to his chest in shame and regret, and grief spilled down his face like bitter rain. Sinclair wept for many minutes. Beth held him close, saying nothing, allowing him to grieve. Finally, after gathering up his courage and straightening his shoulders, the marquess continued as he wiped away tears.

"Amelia panicked when the disease began to spread towards the north. Without my knowledge, she and her mother took Albert to a city doctor who claimed to have a cure, and this man—whom we later learnt was a charlatan—injected my son with some unknown chemical agent. Within hours, Albert's small body grew hot, his eyes unable to focus. He wasn't even a year old, Beth. We'd planned to celebrate at Christmas, and I had my surprise: the new house, but it... It never happened. She took him to her mother's doctor that very hour, and within a day, Albert was dead. I never saw him again. Not to hold him, not even to say goodbye. Amelia never forgave me, and she never let me forget that it was *my* fault that our son died. And she was right. It was my fault—all of it!"

He broke down completely, his head in her lap, great tears of agony raining down his face and onto the quilts. "Beth, I never saw him grow up; never got to—oh, Beth! Please, please, I could not bear losing another child! Nor can I ever lose you, so promise me, *promise* you will take care, please!" He clutched her to his chest, holding her tightly, desperately as he sobbed. "He was a beautiful boy, Beth, and I as much as murdered him!"

"Charles, that's simply not true. You made the best choices you could. Diseases come upon the wind, and no matter what we do, sometimes our loved ones die."

"Do you hate me?"

Her heart-shaped face widened into a soft smile, and Beth stroked his cheek. "How could I hate you, Captain? It is beyond my capacity. Forever out of reach. I love you all the more for your great heart, and I promise to do all my doctors ask of me. If you want, we can name this child Albert," she suggested. "Providing it is a son, of course."

He shook his head. "That is kind of you, but no. Albert was named for Amelia's cousin—a rather loathsome creature. Actually, I thought we might name him Connor."

"Or Charles, perhaps?" she suggested.

"We'll talk of it once he's born, all right?" He stroked her cheek, his eyes shining. "I love you so much, and I love this child—*our* child, our son or daughter. Beth, you are the love of my life—do you know that? I know you are independent, but allow me to take all the risks from now on. Let me stand 'twixt you and danger. Trust in me to care for you, and I shall do all within my power to protect both you and this child," he vowed. "And though it may take my life, I'll make sure no harm touches either of you. Not whilst I have breath in my body."

Mr. Thirteen peered through the crack in the boards that covered the window. Outside, upon the banks of the Lea, a Romany youth dipped a handmade fishing pole into the muddy water, hoping to catch a carp for that night's supper. The terrified former patient watched the lad, his belly stretched and taut from hunger. The escapee had been holed up in a ramshackle boathouse since fleeing the institute, living on what few fish he could catch with his hands, or the odd rat, when his efforts proved futile.

The boy couldn't be more than twelve, and his costume looked completely foreign to the man. The waning moon would rise again tonight, her own shape grown hungry. Thirteen's ears twitched, and his sensitive hearing perceived footfalls upon the sandy marshland. Fearing capture, the terrified man hid beneath a damaged boat, his entire body trembling.

"I know you are there," a refined voice called. Despite his keen ears, Thirteen hadn't heard the door open, nor had he heard footsteps inside the shack.

"Come out, won't you, Mr. Thirteen? You've no reason to fear me."

"Go away!" the altered human shouted. "I might hurt you!"

"You cannot harm me. My powers are far greater than yours, my friend," the voice continued as a gloved hand lifted the heavy boat with ease. "There now. See? I am not from the institute. Do you remember me, David?"

David? "Who is David?" he asked, his teeth chattering.

"That is your name. Can't you remember it? Fear not. I shall help you recall everything, in time."

The hand reached out, and to his surprise Thirteen accepted it. As he touched the stranger, all terror fled from his bones, and a sense of warmth surged through his frame.

"Am I dead, sir?"

"No, David. You are finally alive again. Come with me, and I shall help you to heal."

CHAPTER TWENTY-ONE

After the arrival of the package, Drummond called an inner circle meeting for seven that evening. In attendance were the primary members: the duke, Kepelheim, Sir Thomas Galton, Edmund Reid, Victoria, and Paul Stuart.

"Let us begin with prayer," the duke said, bowing his head. "Lord, we stumble and fall, but you are always there to pick us up, to take our hands, and for that we give you thanks. Help us to see what dangers lie ahead, and to rush towards them without fear, knowing you are by our side. Be with our Elizabeth and keep her body and spirit strong. Be also with Charles and Paul as they show their love for her and for one another, in service to your wonderful Son, Christ Jesus. Keep us united, though the enemy seeks to divide us. And may we ever keep our minds focused upon the task you have appointed for this day, looking neither to the right nor to the left, but ever forward, though the way may bring danger and even death. All this we ask in our Saviour's blessed name. Amen." The duke glanced at the earl. "Is Charles joining us?"

Aubrey seemed distracted, even irritated. "Yes, I imagine so. He and Beth were talking when I started to knock, and I didn't wish to disturb them. I'm sure he'll find us when they've finished."

"I see," Drummond said, deciding not to pursue it further. "Galton, you mentioned that you wanted to speak first."

Galton stood. "Thank you, Your Grace. That heart took us all by surprise, but this may help us put an end to such surprises and see where Redwing's plans are taking us." The baronet spread out the map Reid had given him at The Brown Bear the previous month. "See here, sir, there are marks upon each Ripper site. Note the shape."

"Redwing's symbol," the earl observed as he leaned over the map. "This one—the one on Miller's Court. This was the most recent Ripper event, but Edmund when came you upon this map?"

"In early October, following the Eddowes murder. Honestly, we had no idea then what it meant, but note the names upon the back: Ankerman and Swanson. This map was found by Swanson in the pocket of a dead man, and then passed to Ankerman who gave it to Reid, and thence to me. Though I've searched the entire city, neither Ankerman nor Swanson can be found. It's as if they've vanished off the earth."

James Stuart wore a grim expression. "Both were spies for Redwing."

Nearly all gasped. "But they have our codes, our signs! They know all our operations!" Galton cried out in shock, for William Ankerman had nearly married Galton's younger sister. He'd been both friend and confident for over fifteen years.

Only Paul showed no surprise at the duke's news. "My uncle's correct. Both men were traitors, and both are now dead. The duke asked me to follow them back in late August. They met separately and together with known Redwing operatives, many of them high up in the organisation. Both men helped in the transportation of scientific materials from a laboratory in Chicago to a warehouse in Hackney. Ankerman's chemical expertise made him an attractive addition to Redwing, but Swanson had a secret, which he kept hidden even from us."

Galton could not believe his ears. "Secret? Paul, you and I have known Swanson since Eton! What secret could have avoided detection for so long?"

"He is—*he was*—altered."

Reid thought for a moment. "Was?"

James touched his nephew's hand. "Paul mustn't be blamed. I gave the order for their execution, and he merely followed that order. We've already seen the effect these chemicals have upon human subjects. The hybridisation experiments grow more and more sinister and bold. Yet, there is an aspect to Redwing's dark deeds that even you gentlemen are unaware of, and it may be related to their plans for Elizabeth's child, but I pray not. Lord in heaven, I pray not."

"What plans are those?" called a voice from the doorway. Charles Sinclair had entered without making a sound, and he now stood before them, his eyes red from exhaustion and weeping, but his face set.

"How is she?" Paul asked.

"Sleeping. What plans?" he asked once more.

"We're not yet sure," the earl answered, holding out a chair for his cousin. "Sit, Charles. You look exhausted."

"I am," he answered, wiping at his eyes. "Forgive me, I'd not realised you'd already begun, sir."

"You had other duties, son," the duke answered.

"My friends, may I speak with my cousin in private?" the earl asked.

"Victoria, gentleman, let's continue this discussion elsewhere." The others agreed, and soon the two cousins stood alone inside the large room.

The earl walked to the fireplace, his eyes upon the yellow flames. Charles sat into one of the armchairs, wondering why Aubrey asked to speak to him in private. He'd learnt enough about the man over the years to recognise when his mind was troubled. "What is it you're keeping back, Paul? I beg you to trust me. You are dear to me, Cousin."

The earl turned, wiping at his face. "Yes, as are you to me. And to her—for many years now. I suppose it's only now hitting me. The baby, I mean. I spoke with Emerson briefly before he left, and he confirmed that Beth's carrying your child." He paused momentarily, sighing. "She's loved you for a very long time, Charles. Longer than you know. It was that day I first saw it. The day you dropped by my home in '84. You'd brought me the last documents from H-Division's files on Patricia's murder. Though you knew it not, my uncle had already asked Kepelheim to discover all he could about you. I realise now that James must have recognised Beth's feelings before anyone else. She'd just returned from Scotland, you see, and as Beth always confides in her grandfather—well, I expect she told him."

Charles remembered the visit as clearly as if it had occurred only that week. "Told him what?"

"That she loved you," the earl replied. "I think about that day often. That pivotal day in '84. It was early summer, and she'd just turned sixteen. How she had blossomed! The pale girl had matured into a radiant young woman. I'd watched Elizabeth grow up from infancy, and I tell you that her mother's death was not her first shock. As you know, when Connor died, Beth was witness. It was the wolf that slew him. That same wolf that chased you on the moors; the one we all saw the night it threatened Beth and Adele—the one we hoped we'd killed at Drummond."

"If she saw it kill her father, why does she never mention it? How could Beth forget something that traumatic?"

"Beth's forgotten many things over the years, Charles, and we've yet to discover why. James and Kepelheim believe her mind has been manipulated by someone in Redwing—possibly one of their spirit members. Surely, you can relate to this. Many of your own memories remain in shadow."

Sinclair nodded. "Paul, do you have any memory issues?"

"No. None. Only you and Beth, which may be further proof that it's always been the plan for the two of you to marry. But would you try to recover yours, even if the events were so traumatic, that they might scar your mind forever?"

"I'm not sure. Is that why you discourage Beth from recalling her lost memories?"

Aubrey sighed. "I've seen what remembering does to her. Trust me, Cousin, it is more than she can bear. It's part of what Whitmore meant last week, when he asked if Beth's 'old trouble' had returned. That day, at Drummond, the wolf tore Connor Stuart apart, and she watched it all. He died saving her."

Sinclair thought of his great love upstairs, how she had stood up to William as a child at Leman Street, and then protected Adele at Drummond. She could be fearless, but an unborn child now depended upon his mother's continued calm and safety—and upon his father's ability to protect that mother.

"Paul, you and I both saw the damage done to Patricia. Something tore her apart, and though I didn't see Connor Stuart's body, your description sounds like the murderer might be the same entity. Could that wolf be Trent in another form?"

"We believe so. When I saw Trish in your dead room back in '79, I immediately noticed the similarity. Of course, I could say nothing to you about my suspicions—not then—but it's why my father suggested we move our conversation to Uncle James's porch rather than risk Elizabeth's overhearing."

"That's right, he did. I'd mentioned her fear of an animal; that she'd experienced a seizure when recalling it."

"My father and I had seen Beth suffer similar episodes, when recalling this animal. Once at Drummond Castle—a tale you now know—but also at Briarcliff. Beth sometimes calls it the 'beast'. I'm sure it is a hybrid of some kind."

"I wonder how many crimes can be laid at the hands of such altered men."

"No one knows," Aubrey replied. "But Trent seeks greater and greater powers through something Redwing calls blood magic."

"And the Ripper killings aid in that search. Have you heard anything more from Susanna Morgan?"

"No, and I begin to grow concerned," Stuart told his cousin. "With both MacKey and Morgan on the loose, anything might be in the wind, but this heart, Charles. Is it the one from Kelly?"

"Only Sunders can tell us that. I've dispatched the box to Leman Street for examination. Strange, I received a visit from Romanov this afternoon at the Yard. He warned me of packages. Might he have sent it?"

Aubrey shrugged. "Who can say? St. Paul spoke of seeing through a 'glass darkly', but I feel as if our eyes are bound, causing us to stumble. Never before has Redwing launched this many assaults in so short a period."

"It's because of the child," Sinclair answered, closing his eyes. He thought of the cavernous rock temple beneath the abbey. "Paul, you've not yet seen the place where William murdered Patricia, but it was a quarried and elaborately carved, unholy temple. It lies directly beneath the abbey's sanctuary in mockery of Christ's blood sacrifice for us, for in that unholy ground, Trent and his fellow believers performed unspeakable rites. Beth witnessed them. Bestiality, sodomy, and even blood sacrifice were committed there. She watched it all, but being only a child, she was too terrified to understand or even speak of it."

The earl fell into a chair, his head dropping against the high back. "We always think of Beth as fragile, and in some ways she is, but to witness such acts as a little girl—I marvel that she has kept her sanity, Charles. During one of my undercover investigations, I witnessed those acts, and they are beyond description. These foul men actually invite demonic possession, for that is the ultimate agent of change for them. In return, the men gain supernatural abilities and powers."

Charles pressed the latch on his watch case, reading the engraving there: *'To my Captain, whom I shall ever love—your Beth'*. "Scotland. Beth's father. When she spoke of it on the train to Branham, I thought your reaction cruel, but now I see more clearly, perhaps."

The earl nodded. "I prefer she not remember it, Charles. During the wolf attack that killed Connor, Elizabeth was injured. She only remembers it as falling down a cliff, but the wolf tried to kill her. If that animal was Trent, then perhaps he cannot fully control himself whilst in that form, for I saw the monster rend her small leg as she ran to help her fallen father. Connor saw it, too, and despite his own injuries, he threw himself twixt Beth and the animal. That's how he died. Saving her. He sacrificed his life to keep her from further harm."

"You saw this happen?" Sinclair asked.

"James and I both saw it. Connor had followed Elizabeth out onto the moors. It was late at night—a blood moon high overhead. We'd been playing cards, talking about Redwing, and we all thought Beth asleep upstairs, but Connor suddenly had a strange premonition. He survived his injuries for almost a day before succumbing, and he told us that he'd heard a voice in his head, warning that Beth was in danger. He left us and went upstairs, but she wasn't in her room. The voice told him to look out the window, and he saw her walking outside in her night dress—just like Adele did whilst we were there. Terrified for his daughter, Connor ran out to bring her back inside. Beth had been known to sleepwalk even at Branham, but more often in Scotland. James and I heard the front door open, and Connor cried out Beth's name. As we left the castle, we heard the howls of the wolf, and we ran as quickly as we could. By the time we reached him, Connor's body was being shaken in the wolf's massive jaws, and Beth was screaming; her face and hands covered in blood. James shot the monster many times, whilst I went to Elizabeth. She nearly died that night."

"That's when you gave her your blood. She told me about it, but she thought it an accidental fall."

"I'm glad that's all she recalls, Charles. She was under treatment for the injury for many weeks, but it was her mind that we feared for most. Dr. Lemuel, whom we thought we could trust, administered sedatives to keep her calm, but it was as if she could not awaken from a horrible nightmare. She would thrash about and scream for hours on end, and she kept repeating that the Shadow Man had her."

Sinclair sat forward, his mind focused. "The Shadow Man? This creature has pursued her since '71. Paul, if Warren is right, then this Shadow is actually a powerful being that was once imprisoned inside the Mt. Hermon stone."

Paul sighed. "I wish I'd believed her from the start, but we thought her just imaginative. Had I known that Trent awaited them at Branham, I'd never have allowed Trish to take her. I cannot tell you how many times I've longed to undo that choice. If the wolf was Trent in altered form, then he killed Connor so he might marry Patricia and have access to Elizabeth. Trish never believed in the Shadow Man, Charles. She had little love for the circle and all we tried to do to help her. She did love Christ, and I've no doubt she's with him now, but she wanted nothing to do with her ancestry, nor did she wish to speak of it. Did I tell you that Patricia nearly married my elder brother?"

Charles's brows shot up. "Ian? No. Why didn't she?"

Paul gazed out the window. "My brother was a wonderful man—or so everyone has told me. As I explained to you in Glasgow, Ian died the year I was born, but I'd never heard it told as resulting from a duel. In some ways, it helps me to understand Patricia. She and my brother were madly in love, so much so that they'd made plans to wed in Scotland. We don't require bans or even a church wedding. Hand-fasting can be done by nearly anyone."

"I'm aware of it," Sinclair told his cousin. "Greta Green earns many an English pound from that practise."

"Trish wasn't yet sixteen, and her father refused to consent to a marriage with my brother. Uncle James and Duke George led the circle jointly back then, and both believed Trish should marry Connor. She was stubborn and decided to defy them both. She assumed that, once married to Ian, nothing could be done about it. She'd arranged to meet him in Carlisle. Then, they'd cross the border into Scotland together, but he never arrived. When Trish learnt of his death, she immediately hired a coach to Briarcliff and confessed the plan to my mother, who told me shortly before she died in '78. I'd always thought my brother's death a tragic accident. Now I know better. A tall man with a sword of fire murdered Ian. Perhaps it was Trent, perhaps not. The description is more akin to Beth's Shadow Man."

Charles let his head fall against the chair. He began to understand the long history of enmity betwixt the circle and Redwing, and it was an enmity that would continue, he feared. "Paul, I think she still sees him. Since returning here, Elizabeth's had visions and troubling dreams of shadowy, animalistic creatures. "

The earl turned to face his cousin. "Charles, you and I must make certain your son or daughter *never* sees that Shadow. I fear that Redwing will do all within their power to lure that son into a trap."

"What did James mean by plans for our child?"

"It is the ultimate goal," Aubrey answered. "The child of the bloodlines that would provide an extension for the Man of Sin. Hellish leader of their infernal order. To do so, may mean altering that son's human form or cellular construction through blood magic."

Sinclair showed no surprise, for he'd already considered such a possibility. "Paul, do you think Redwing would kill any child that isn't a son?"

"I'd say yes," he told his cousin. "But let's trust in the Lord, shall we?"

Sinclair nodded, his eyes filled with worry. "I shall, but once the ICI is up and running, I intend to work from home."

"That will help Beth more than you can imagine, Cousin," the earl told him. "It's why I began this story with talk of '84. Beth and I had argued about the Shadow Man that day. I'd ordered her to remain at Aubrey House, but she refused, saying she had no wish to continue speaking to me, as I never believed her. As we both know, Beth is headstrong, and my insistence that this Shadow was but a dream angered her considerably. I'd just started after her, when you arrived."

Charles nodded, smiling as the memory took hold. "Yes, I remember. Your butler told me you were in the library, and I said I could find it on my own. Beth bumped into me as I entered."

"Yes, she did, and she stopped in her tracks at seeing you. Charles, I watched her face change from anger to bright hope—and something else was upon those sweet features: Love. Beth had never looked at me with such eyes, Charles, and I knew then that she loved you. I'm ashamed to say this, but it was I who suggested our uncle send Elizabeth to Paris, and it's why I didn't tell her about your wife's death. She would have come back to support you in your grief; I knew it. I have stood in the way of her love for you from the beginning, and it's time I step aside."

Charles felt no malice towards the earl; rather, he understood completely. "Elizabeth has both of us to love her now, Cousin, and I shall do all within my power to make her happy and keep her safe; I promise you."

"Well, Nephews?" Victoria Stuart called out—startling both men, for they'd not heard her enter. "May we now meet, or do you wish to delay us further?"

Standing, the two cousins laughed. "We have completed our discussion, Tory," Charles replied. "Forgive us for causing any delay."

The earl kissed his aunt's cheek. "Has Reid deciphered the map at last?"

"He believes he found several enticing hints. Charles, you're still limping. Perhaps, Emerson should have examined you."

"My muscles complain, but Mrs. Meyer's liniment works wonders," he said, taking her arm. "I've some work to finish once supper's done, and then I intend to sleep until noon."

Bella entered, her thick tail wagging, and the three humans followed the dog into the library, where the circle continued until Miles called them to supper.

CHAPTER TWENTY-TWO

That same evening - Castor Institute

Bridget O'Sullivan glanced at her reflection in the mirror. The twenty-three-year-old nurse had passed the institute's rigorous qualifying examination the previous day, and this would be her first night in the lower level.

"Miss O'Sullivan," a man's voice called from the hallway beyond the dressing room. "I am waiting."

Using the mirror, O'Sullivan made certain her hair was neatly arranged, her pinafore tied securely, and the pink-ribboned cap sat straight upon her head. She then shut the door and walked towards Dr. Kepler.

"We must keep to our schedule, Miss O'Sullivan," the alienist warned.

"Yes, sir," she answered, hurrying to catch up with the strict physician. "Shall I be working with Sister MacArthur today?"

"No. I prefer to begin your training personally. It's important that you fully appreciate what it is we do here, and Sister MacArthur—whilst a consummate health professional—does not always agree with my methods. I hope I'll encounter no such difficulties with you, my dear."

"No, sir. I promise to follow your orders to the letter, sir."

"Very good. Note that we must keep this door locked at all times. You will receive your own keys once you complete your orientation week. After we pass through, we must always lock the door behind us. You will notice there is an electrified bell, here, near the door frame. Press the button, should you find yourself without your key, or if you have need otherwise."

"Yes, sir." She watched as the physician turned the key in the brass lock. He returned it to his pocket, and they began to walk down a long, tiled corridor. The entire ward was illuminated by electric lighting, and the floor and wall tiles shone like white mirrors.

"The room on the right contains one of our newest patients. This ward is for a special type of ailment, but I believe you strong enough of mind to see them as pitiable rather than monstrous."

She wondered what he could mean by this strange statement, but wanting to make a favourable impression, O'Sullivan nodded. "My own sister sometimes suffers from epilepsy, sir, and I would never think her monstrous."

He nodded, pleased with her reply. "That is one reason I recommended you for this duty, Miss O'Sullivan. Now, be very quiet as we enter. You will notice the lighting is subdued inside the rooms. We find that men with this affliction suffer from light sensitivity."

He led her into the shadowy cell. She could make out the shape of a large bed, much longer and wider than the ones on the other wards. It had rails along the sides like a crib, but there was no bedside table.

"May I ask, sir, where the medical supplies are kept? I see no table or closet," she whispered.

"We endeavour to remove all items that might prove—let us say *useful* to these gentlemen."

There was no window, but a dim bulb burned in one corner, near the ceiling, casting ominous shadows across the gleaming tiles. "Hello, Mr. Ascot. How do you feel this evening?" Kepler asked.

A large man lay upon the bed. He wore no clothing, but a thin sheet covered him, from the waist to his feet. As her eyes accommodated to the low light, Bridget noticed the man had a large cranium and jaw, and that his ears appeared unnaturally pointed. His eyes were closed, but his face and even earlobes were covered in coarse hair.

Kepler looked at his new student. "You observe his deformations? They are normal for this malady of the mind. These men reach a point where their ancestral, evolutionary forms begin to emerge. They can be quite violent at times, particularly if moonlight touches their skin or enters the eyes. That is why we keep them below ground, for here there are no windows that permit the mischievous moon to enter."

"Can he hear us?"

"That is a good question, Miss O'Sullivan. Yes, he can, though he looks to be asleep, does he not? He is, in fact, in a strange state of twilight rest. Our medications maintain this state. It is the safest condition for him, and for us."

"How does he eat, then, sir? And—well, there are bodily functions which must surely require a waking state."

"Astute observations, my dear. We once thought so, too. However, these men are capable of enduring many weeks without food, water, or other bodily functions, as you appropriately call it. In some ways, it seems to me that a return to a more natural, ancestral state is a boon. His nutritional requirements are minimal, yet his strength when awake is that of ten men. We hope to learn more through microscopic study of the blood, but so far the answer eludes us."

"What is that?" she asked, pointing to a strange shadow on his chest. "A birth mark?"

"No, it is our way of keeping track of them. These men have a strong tendency towards natural states, which is why he wears no sleeping shirt or dressing gown. We've tried many times to enforce this, but they always tear them off, leaving the clothing in shreds as they howl and scream. It is my belief that the clothing burns those so afflicted."

"How terrible!" she said, genuinely pitying the man. "So, he would remove any identification as well?"

"Quite so. Therefore, we tattoo each whilst under anaesthetic. If the symbols make no sense to you, do not despair. It is our own system. We keep a roster of each man's name and the symbol. You will find the roster in the porter's office. All records must remain in the ward. You must never, I repeat never remove any item from this ward. To do so, would mean immediate dismissal."

Bridget recognised the need for security and patient privacy. "Of course, sir. I'll follow all the rules."

"I know you will. Now, we shall leave Mr. Ascot to his twilight sleep and continue to each room and patient until we finish. I want you to note each man's characteristics and when you begin your own visits with them, you must record any new alterations. Is that clear?"

"Yes, sir. Quite clear."

"Very good. You'll do well here, Bridget. Dr. Collins was wise to see your potential. Now, our next patient is a Mr. Brightman…"

Bridget followed, her mind still fixed upon the hideous man sleeping in room number one. His ears and size were enough to frighten, but what disturbed her most was the blood—just a small, caked stain at the corner of his mouth.

The creature known at Castor Asylum as Mr. Thirteen gazed at himself in the long, cheval mirror. "Is that me?" he asked Vasily.

"It is, indeed, you, sir. Prince Anatole awaits downstairs. He hopes to introduce you to the others."

"The others? Are they also patients?" he asked, resisting the urge to scratch at the clothing.

"They are guests. If you will follow me, sir?"

The Russian butler led the hybrid creature down a magnificent staircase and into a grand parlour, where a man with a curved spine played a stringed musical instrument, held betwixt his knees. A giant man with six fingers on one hand sat nearby, talking with two women. A third man, stout and round-shouldered, glanced at Thirteen as he entered the room. Instinctively, his nose twitched, and he bared his teeth.

"None of that, Mr. Stanley," Romanov commanded as he strode towards the doorway. "Do come in, Mr. Thirteen. You find us enjoying Count Riga's cello. Allow me to introduce you to our company. May I use your true name, rather than that impersonal designation?"

Thirteen trembled. He could smell the perfume of the women, their soap, hear the crisp rustle of their skirts as they moved. Something within his mind spoke of blood and mayhem. "I don't deserve a man's name," he told his host.

"Nonsense! Of course, you do. Our Mr. Stanley was once known as Mr. Seven. He escaped his fetters several months ago. His captors were also yours, but neither of you will ever see those cruel corridors again."

Thirteen's teeth clenched. "I hate those men."

Former CID detective Elbert Stanley crossed the room and shook the newcomer's hand. "As do I," he said. "Each day, the memories grow a little more dim. You'll soon begin to mend, my friend. Cast off the impersonal designation those hateful scientists gave you and reclaim your true name!"

Thirteen's face contorted as he struggled to recall it. Tears filled his eyes, and he lowered his head in shame. "I have no name."

"But you do, my dear friend. You do! Prince Anatole will uncover it, though it is likely he already knows it. His Highness is most informed."

Turning to Romanov, the pitiful hybrid's eyes grew round as he wiped at them. "Do you know my name, sir?"

"I do. It is David Anderson. You once worked in a great house as a trusted and much beloved footman. Do you remember any of that?"

"No, my lord."

Ida Ross crossed the room and touched Anderson's hairy hand. "Welcome to Istseleniye House, Mr. Anderson. I'm Ida Ross. This other lady is Miss Brona Kilmeade. Count Riga is our cellist, and that is Mr. Blinkmire near the fireplace. We are all of us outcasts of one sort or another. Despite our many and varied sins, the prince makes room for one and all."

Anderson slowly moved forward into the room, bowing slightly to Kilmeade. "A pleasure, Miss. Where is this place, my lord?" he asked the prince.

Romanov took a glass of punch from a tray and handed it to Anderson. "This house has been in my family for over two hundred years. It lies beyond the reach of those who pursue you. In time, they will forget all about you, David, and you may then choose a new path for yourself."

"They did things to me," he whispered, looking down at his hands. "I used to be old."

"As was Mr. Stanley, but the youthful aspects of your altered selves will not depart once the treatments are complete. As I say, a new life lies ahead."

"Treatments?" he asked, nervously. "You're not going to inject me like those doctors did? Hurt me?"

"Not at all," the prince assured him. "The doctors you knew sought to change your humanity. Our therapy will return it to you."

"The medicine is but a powder, dissolved in water," Stanley explained. "Once every hour at first, then thrice a day; becoming less frequent over time. I take mine but once a day now. My last turning occurred only recently—a slight relapse due to a failed dosage, but the prince was very kind to me, despite my actions." He glanced at Ross, who nodded in understanding. "The cravings can make you mad, but Luna's rays no longer hurt me or cause me to fear. Isn't that remarkable?"

"Does it always work?"

"It always works," Romanov assured him. "Mr. Stanley's failed dosage, as he puts it, was caused by the deliberate interference of someone who no longer resides here. Now, let us enjoy Count Riga's music, shall we? Ida, I would speak with you for a moment."

She left the room along with the prince, and the two of them withdrew to a small parlour on the opposite side of the great house.

"Sir?"

"Mr. Sinclair has found your letter, and it has worried him terribly. He now looks for your body in the river, but prays it is not there—that you are alive and unharmed."

"That is kind of him. Did he obtain the list?" she asked, her hands twisting nervously.

"He did. Your help to him is immeasurable. Does this make you happy?"

"I suppose it does," she replied softly. "I wish I could see him once more, to let him know I am alive."

"Not yet," Romanov told her, cupping her chin gently. "But soon. Now, would you play hostess to our household? I've a call to make on an old friend. She, too, requires rescue."

He kissed her cheek, and his lips felt like velvet. Ida watched the prince leave the house, and in seconds, the black coach disappeared from view.

CHAPTER TWENTY-THREE

Thursday evening – Queen Anne House

Charles entered the library and found the earl in deep discussion with Michael Emerson. "No one told me you'd arrived, Michael. I was just upstairs with Elizabeth."

"And is she better?" the physician asked.

"Much. I assume you're here to examine her again."

"Not unless she requires it. I promised to report back after I spoke with Price. I met with George this morning."

"Did he offer insight regarding Beth's mother and these purported miscarriages that Tory mentioned?"

"May I speak freely?"

"Charles, should I leave the two of you to speak in private?" Aubrey asked as Miles and a footman entered with refreshments. The earl held the door whilst the footman carried in the second of the two large trays, nabbing a small sandwich from a plate and nibbling on it. "Oh, this is made from that scrumptious pork roast Mrs. Smith served at supper tonight. Michael, you must try one."

"I'm not really hungry, but a cup of tea would be welcome."

Charles added a sandwich and two small cakes to a plate whilst the efficient butler poured wine. "Just half a glass. Thank you, Miles. We can take care of ourselves, gentlemen. Thank you both. Has our uncle left?"

"He departed an hour ago, sir, in company with Lady Adele and Lady Victoria."

"Tory and Della aren't staying here tonight?" he asked the earl.

"Tory has last minute plans to make with James, and Della wanted to help. Both promised to return before eleven."

"Did Granger go along?"

"He did, my lord," the butler interjected. "As did Powers. Both are well armed, of course—per your orders, sir."

"That's a relief," Sinclair answered. "Miles, would you make certain we're not disturbed? Unless, of course, the duchess needs us."

"Certainly, Lord Haimsbury," the butler said. Both he and the footman left.

Charles locked the door to assure privacy.

"You've spoken to Price?" he asked the doctor once they all sat around a circular table near the fireplace.

Emerson nodded. "Yes, I had an enlightening conversation with that noble gentleman. He is a wealth of medical knowledge, and I hope to learn much from his experience. I asked him about the late duchess, if she had indeed lost children prior to Elizabeth's birth. Price told me that it was so, and that each loss puzzled him."

Aubrey sat opposite his cousin. "Tory told me that she'd spoken to you about those miscarriages, Michael. I'd wondered if that might be what you planned to discuss with my cousin."

"You knew about them?" Sinclair asked, dumbfounded. "And you said nothing to me?"

Wiping crumbs of the sandwich from his mouth, Aubrey poured a shot of whiskey into a small glass. "Forgive me, Charles, it never occurred to me to mention it. Tory told me about it last summer, and I asked Price about it myself soon after. He used that same phrase: that the miscarriages puzzled him."

"How is it the miscarriages puzzled him, Michael?" Sinclair asked, clearly worried. "Medically, you mean?"

"Yes, medically, but also personally, I think. Here is what he told me, and if you have occasion to speak with Price directly, I suggest you do so. As a detective, it's possible you would find clues, where I miss them, but here is how I understand it. Lord Aubrey, feel free to speak, if my sequence of events is incorrect, or if you have additional information I lack."

Paul nodded. "I shall."

Emerson continued. "Patricia Linnhe married Connor Stuart, the duke's son, in December of '61."

"December the tenth," the earl added. "Beth was born in April of '68."

"Yes," Emerson said. "Price tells me that the duchess became pregnant within a few months of her marriage, and that, at first, she carried the child with no sign of difficulty. She took care with her diet, refrained from strenuous activities, and avoided distressing situations. In short, she did everything right. Regardless, in the sixth month, in the fall of '62, the duchess miscarried a son. You can imagine, I'm sure, how this grieved both parents, for Price tells me that Connor Stuart was a tender-hearted, good man, much like yourselves, gentlemen. The second pregnancy was announced the following summer, in late August. To assure success, the late earl—Connor Stuart held the courtesy title of Earl of Kesson, I'm told..."

"Yes, that's correct," Paul interjected.

Emerson nodded. "Yes, well, Lord Kesson hired a live-in nurse, a woman of superior reputation and extensive medical experience, who kept watch over Patricia's diet, activities, and even over the her visitors. This may sound extreme, but it is not uncommon in such situations. As I said, this was in late August or thereabouts that the happy news was shared with the staff, and at that time the duchess anticipated delivery in March the following year—in '64. She miscarried on the very day of her wedding anniversary in '63."

"Another son," Charles said, his imagination picturing the beautiful Patricia Linnhe Stuart and her Scottish laird mourning yet another dead child.

"Quite so. Now, Price is not sure of this, for he did not directly examine the duchess, but his fellow surgeon, a man named Wilkes, who was keeping watch over Price's patients whilst he and Mrs. Price attended a family wedding in France, told him what occurred. It was late summer of '66, and the nurse still lived and worked at Branham, and Wilkes had stopped by to see if the duchess or anyone on the estate required his services. The nurse, a woman named Moira Stopes, refused to grant him entry to her lady's bedroom."

"What? That's nonsense!" Aubrey shouted.

"Yes, it is, but this nurse had gained considerable authority in her time at Branham, and there are certain personalities that refuse to relinquish power, even when commonsense requires it. Wilkes tried several times over the following weeks to see the duchess, and each time, he was refused entry. The staff begged him to send word to Dr. Price, for they were convinced the nurse had assumed an unnatural influence. The earl, you see, was serving in Constantinople at the time, and since he'd hired her, only he could dismiss her. The staff thought if Price wrote to the earl, saying that the woman posed a danger to the duchess, then Lord Kesson would return home and intervene."

Charles smiled, thinking of the staff at Elizabeth's country estate. "Michael, when you meet Mr. Baxter and Mrs. Alcorn, you will appreciate that story all the more."

"I look forward to it," Emerson answered. "A few weeks passed, and Price returned and heard his colleague's tale. Immediately, both physicians called upon the duchess. Now, this is what most disturbs me, Charles. The nurse had decamped, leaving no word to explain her absence or inappropriate behaviour. The duchess, however, was found in a deplorable state—her health endangered, her mind a shambles, and showing signs of a very recent miscarriage."

Charles was shocked. "Connor had no ability to restrain this devilish woman?"

"He knew nothing of it. It was only Price's subsequent letter to the late earl that broke the news. Connor Stuart had returned to his posting four months earlier, and when he'd left, the duchess had been well and healthy. Had he been told of his wife's condition, I feel certain he would have booked passage on the first steamer back to England. But there is more. Price interviewed everyone in the house, trying to determine if anyone had known of the duchess's third pregnancy. The lady's maid had been denied entry for many weeks, and she could give no reply, but she had suspected. Mrs. Chambers, who served as housekeeper at that time, said she was sure the duchess had been pregnant, for she'd asked for foods she had previously requested during earlier pregnancies. Many women have such cravings, and in most cases, it is best to satisfy these whims. However, this observant housekeeper had noticed one other thing. It was a strange herb that the nurse sometimes mixed into the duchess's tea."

Charles thought of the belladonna—the Devil's cherries—that both he and Beth had ingested in a hideous tea mixture, and he now wondered if Patricia had been watched by Redwing. *Of course, she had*, he thought to himself, wondering why he had never thought past Elizabeth's early years to those before her arrival. "What herb?"

"Pennyroyal."

"Pennyroyal!" the earl exclaimed. "Isn't that one of the ingredients in the elixir Trumper added to Beth's cocoa?"

Emerson's eyes rounded. "Tell me Elizabeth did not drink it! In strong quantities, Pennyroyal is an abortifacient! It can bring on miscarriage."

"She drank none of it, praise the Lord," Charles said. "Poor Patricia. The nurse had intentionally killed the unborn child. She remained at Branham until her work was accomplished. Redwing wanted a daughter, and all sons were expendable."

"Yes, that is my conclusion, as well," Emerson said. "Lord Aubrey..."

"Call me Paul," the earl said softly. "If you're to take care of our little duchess, Emerson, then we must dispense with formality. I vaguely remember you from Oxford, but I knew your younger brother quite well. Dickie and I have a longstanding fencing match that goes back to Eton."

"Yes, he told me about that. Richard claims he's bested you ten times out of twelve."

The earl leaned back against the chair. "Six of twelve, actually," he corrected. "We left the count at a draw—for now."

"Ah, well, I shall soon hear his side of it again. I plan to Christmas with my father and brothers in Carlisle this year," he explained, standing. "It grows late, and I should head home. It's been a pleasure visiting with you both. Charles, you look as though you could use a long sleep. Avail yourself of the duchess's soporific if you wish. Alicia has the envelope. It is half a teaspoonful per eight ounces of water, though for you I'd suggest tripling that dose."

"Thank you, Michael," Sinclair said as he shook the man's hand. "I hope you received our wedding invitation."

"I did, thank you. I look forward to attending as you begin your lives together. Call if you have need of me. I shall stop in again tomorrow afternoon as soon as my other calls are complete, but if there is any change that alarms you, send for me at once. I've begun reassigning most of my patients to colleagues in order to make myself available to you and the duchess as needed."

In a few moments, Emerson had gone, and Charles returned to the fireside, where his cousin poured two glasses of brandy. "This is one of our uncle's favourites. Trust me, you'll require no sleep aid after two glasses of this."

Sinclair took a small sip of the amber liquid, his eyes widening as the alcohol warmed the back of his throat. "This is even stronger than Drummond whiskey," he noted. "Have you a few minutes before we retire? I'd like to talk to you about Beth. She asks over and over if it's going to snow. Do you know why?"

"Most likely, she's had some dream that disturbs her. I used to discount Elizabeth's dreams, but I'm learning they sometimes reveal a future event, or elucidate one from the past."

"Yes, I've found myself dreaming of things that come true," Sinclair said, stretching his long arms. "I've encountered spirit beings in Queen Anne Park twice now—and I continue to host uninvited guests; some clearly evil, others with loyalties yet unfathomable."

Aubrey grew thoughtful, his eyes on the brandy as it swirled in the glass. "Beth used to see this Shadow Man in the park. She ran into the stables once when she was seven or so, claiming the Shadow was by the apple trees, but when I followed her there, he was nowhere to be found. She was quite upset."

"Paul, you told me earlier that Beth's seen this creature here, many times. When did it begin?"

The earl sipped the drink thoughtfully. "When she was four, I think. Spiritual beings have haunted Branham and Queen Anne for a century or more. When she'd had a little wine, Trish would sometimes speak of the ghosts that surrounded her, but she usually put it down to fatigue or the influence of circle members. She resented all of us, especially me towards the last."

"I'm sorry, Paul. Beth told me that you and Patricia had an argument after she married Trent."

"We had several, but the last was a major fracas. If Elizabeth has a temper that measures a ten, then Trish's measured a hundred. She screamed and shouted, and I dodged a windstorm of porcelain, and in the end, Trish ordered me to leave. She actually threatened to have Trent shoot me if I did not."

"Would she have followed through on that threat?"

"I've no idea. Trish's behaviour had altered beyond all recognition. I'd merely asked to take Beth with me for a short holiday. I told Trish it would allow her to spend time with her new husband. She shouted that neither I nor the circle would ever have a part in Beth's life again. She said she would kill Beth before letting me take her."

Charles's eyes widened. "Surely not! No mother would say such a thing! Trish must have been under a spell."

"Yes, I think she was. I told you earlier that Beth had been seeing this 'man in the park' since her fourth year of age. I say this, because 1872 was the summer my father brought me to London to stay with Thomas Galton, my Eton friend and fellow warrior. He and I were both Oxford-bound, so I'd asked if we might spend the month of August together. My father was unwilling to say yes at first, for my mother had been ill. She was never very strong after giving birth to me, and she'd deteriorated that summer after falling down the stairs. I'd assumed the plans with Galton off, but then Father suddenly changed his mind one morning, announcing that he and I would leave that afternoon for London."

"Had your mother improved?" Sinclair asked.

"No, but by that afternoon, a nurse had been hired to keep watch on Mother, and my father and I were on a southbound train. He said little to me during the journey, and I could tell that he was worried. I assumed it had to do with my imminent departure for Oxford, so I tried to reassure him that I could handle myself. This failed to cheer him, and I decided to read instead. We arrived in London quite late, but rather than proceed to Aubrey House, we came here. To Queen Anne."

"Why?" Sinclair asked.

"My exact question. To my knowledge, the house wasn't occupied, for I'd thought Patricia at Branham that month. She loved to spend summers at the seaside at Hampton. To my surprise, Baxter answered the door."

"Miles didn't work here at that time?"

"No, our Mr. Miles has been here only since the duchess's death. He worked at Drummond until then. When Trish died, James sent a dozen of his most efficient and trusted servants here to keep watch on the house and on Beth, whenever she was here. That evening, it was our prosaic Mr. Baxter who answered the bell, and he did not seem the least bit surprised to see us."

"Interesting," the marquess noted, finishing the last of his brandy and pouring a second glass. "Is Baxter prescient?"

"He might be, but I learnt later that he'd written to my father. Wired him, and the telegram arrived with the morning post at Briarcliff."

"Why did Baxter write?"

"He was worried," Paul explained. "James was in Austria at the time, conducting business for the Foreign Office, else Baxter would have summoned our uncle. Charles, Elizabeth was only four years old, and she was all alone in that house. No adults other than the staff were with her. Patricia had brought her to London and abandoned her here."

Sinclair stood and began to pace back and forth as a rising tide of anger took hold. "How could Patricia do that? Did she have no sense of motherly feeling?"

Aubrey sighed. "At the time, I was as angry as you, and my gentle father said words that one might only hear from stevedores! He was positively outraged! Trish had left orders that no one report her presence in London. She arrived with Beth and then departed the following morning, telling Baxter she'd be gone for a week. We had no idea where to find her."

"How can that woman have been so callous?"

"I begin to wonder now just what influence Trent had on her back then, and when it commenced. The letter Connor penned—the one you discovered at Drummond Castle—certainly indicates a history of infidelity. Trish had probably gone to meet Trent."

"What year was this again?" asked Charles.

"1872. It had been a relatively quiet year politically, but there'd also been a series of crimes in Westminster and Lambeth that kept the Metropolitan Police puzzled. Look in your archives for 'The Songbird Killings'. Six music hall performers—five female, one male—found from March through September with their throats slashed, their left eyes removed."

"I remember reading about that case when I first joined the force. They were still unsolved at the time."

"Yes, well, one of the victims was discovered in Haimsbury Park. Did you know that?"

"No!" Charles exclaimed in shock. "She was found on my family's grounds? Why did no one say anything about that?"

"Most people are unaware of it. Even the press never learnt that information. My father had his men hush it up. The Queen Anne gardeners discovered the body, you see. They kept up the Haimsbury gardens as well, since the estate was being overseen by Uncle James at the time, and they relocated the body to the southeast end of Hyde Park before reporting it to the police."

Sinclair stopped pacing, staring at his cousin, dumbfounded. "You're saying that your father arranged for the deliberate alteration of a crime scene? Paul, there may have been clues lost that the police needed to solve those hideous murders!"

"Trust me, Cousin, my father's men combed the grounds for any and all signs, and they delivered each and every detail to Commissioner Henderson. The murderer left no trail. But you can now understand why he was doubly concerned when Trish left Beth here all alone."

"Yes," he said softly. "Where was Connor during all this?"

"India. Father sent a telegram, but a series of peculiar errors delayed its delivery for three days. Of course, once he received it, Connor sought permission for emergency leave, and he took the first ship back to England. Both my father and I remained here until Trish returned. It was during that week that Beth told me about seeing the man in the park. She'd been showing me the horses in the stable. Even then, Beth loved riding, and she had her own pony. I'd started conversing with Frame. He's served here for twenty years, you know. He was introducing me to Pride of Branham. He was sire to King's Dancer, who sired Paladin."

"Paladin will always be a favourite," Charles said fondly.

"He's considered the fastest horse in England, and he has the greatest heart. Though, he cares little for carrying me! Perhaps, it's a blessing I wasn't the one in those tunnels last month."

Both men laughed, and then the earl grew serious. "That day in the stable, Beth had wandered off whilst I spoke with Frame. I'd not even noticed, but my father did. He'd been inside the house talking with the police commissioner, in fact, about the murders. Commissioner Henderson was an old friend and a tangential circle member. Father had been meeting with the London membership in an effort to track down Patricia's whereabouts."

"Your father would have made a formidable detective."

"In a very real way, he served as one. Father joined me inside the stable and asked after Beth. It was only then that I noticed her absence. He and I learnt from a gardener that she'd been seen talking with someone inside the apple grove."

"The man from the park."

"Yes. Father and I immediately headed towards the pond and the plantation nearby, but Beth was already on her way back to the stable, and we met her upon the path. She was very upset, crying in fact, and Father picked her up and asked what had happened. She was only four, Charles, but even then her language skills were remarkable. Despite that, I was shocked when she started speaking to us in Romanian."

"Romanian? Are you certain? Beth told me that the man in the park may have spoken in a language similar to that, but she said she didn't speak it."

"No, she didn't, though she knew some French by then. I recognised it as Romanian, because I'd been studying both that and Russian for two years."

"Did you understand what she said?"

"Yes. She said she didn't want to be queen, and that she was afraid of the wolf."

"She said this. Wolf. In Romanian."

"She did, but after a few minutes, her language changed to English, and when asked about the wolf, later on, she had no recall. She fell asleep in my father's arms, but that night she began having terrible nightmares. She screamed of a wolf attack and blood. She even used the name, Charles. She said the wolf was called Redwing."

"Did she know about them at that time?"

"No. We didn't begin telling Beth of her heritage until after her mother died. Charles, if the shadowy figure you're encountering is the same entity that Beth saw back then—and perhaps the one who murdered my brother—then we must keep him away from our little duchess."

Sinclair stood quietly for a moment, deep in thought. Finally, he returned to his chair, his eyes intense and fixed upon his cousin's face. "Look, from now on, everyone is armed inside this house. You and I keep a weapon handy at all times. And keep Bibles by every beds and scattered about all the rooms. When Trent paid his visit to Beth's bedchamber, he revealed a great dread of that wonderful book. He could go nowhere near it."

"Tomorrow, I'll ask Mac to walk through the house with Martin and anoint all the doors and windows. For tonight, I pray our rest is unbroken," Aubrey said, touching his cousin's forearm.

"As do I. Goodnight, Paul."

Sinclair left the library and climbed the long, winding staircase. As he entered the moonlit bedroom, his eyes fell upon Elizabeth's face. To his relief, her breathing seemed regular, and her expression serene. He moved the long sofa once more, allowing him to recline and still see his beloved. He then locked the windows, taking time to examine the entire park from that vantage point. He could see Frame's men patrolling along the gravel pathways.

"May the Lord protect us all," he whispered.

The brandy's effect had made his eyelids heavy, so the marquess set a cushion at one end of the sofa and pulled two quilts over top of himself. In a few moments, Charles Sinclair had fallen fast asleep.

CHAPTER TWENTY-FOUR
Friday Morning

Thursday passed without event. Based on Aubrey's tale of the body discovered in his gardens in 1872, Sinclair asked Edmund Reid to meet him that morning, and the two policemen now stood inside the Haimsbury spring house, beyond the north gate to Queen Anne Park.

"Thanks for coming on short notice, Ed. I'd considered speaking with you at Leman Street or even at my office at the Yard, but I prefer this remain unofficial. Besides, that office won't be mine much longer. I offered my resignation to Monro, effective the first of December."

The Whitechapel detective sat beside his friend, sharing tea at a small round table inside the beautiful cottage. "Abberline told me about it, and he's already trying to convince me to apply for promotion. I've no ambitions for the Yard, though. How can I help, Charles?"

The spring house that had once served as the sole source of fresh water for the original estate had been converted to a guest cottage when Sinclair's grandfather rebuilt the mansion fifty years earlier. Containing two bedrooms, a parlour, a small kitchen, and a bath, Charles felt comfortable in the simple surroundings, for it reminded him of how he'd spent the majority of his life. "Nice little house, isn't it? I might see if Beth wants to honeymoon here," he joked.

"I'm sure the duchess would be pleased to live anywhere you wish, Charles. Just be sure to hire a cook. From all accounts, Elizabeth knows far more about horses than she does spices."

The marquess laughed. "Then, it is one of the few things my fiancée cannot do well." After a momentary pause, Sinclair grew serious. "Ed, do you recall anything about 'The Songbird Killings' from '72?"

The inspector's face showed surprise. "I've not heard anyone mention those since I was a constable. Why? Do you connect those to Ripper?"

Sinclair poured a second cup of tea. "No, but perhaps I should. I read about them when I first started with the Met. Morehouse had me research it once I was assigned to CID. I'd thought it busywork to be honest, and now I wonder if it might not be related to Redwing. That is why I wanted this to be a quiet conversation. Away from official sources. And official ears."

"I see. Well, in truth, I know very little about those murders. Weren't there half a dozen or so?"

"Seven, according to the earl, though I remember only six. He mentioned them in conversation a few days ago. Apparently, one of the victims was discovered right here. On my estate."

"I don't think so. I'd remember that, Charles."

"No, Ed, you wouldn't, because that information never made it into any of the official reports," the marquess explained. "The woman's body was found by Queen Anne Park gardeners loyal to the duke and to the late Lord Aubrey. It was the latter who made certain that all references to my home were removed from any documents. The gardeners moved the body to Hyde Park before contacting the police."

Reid looked decidedly uncomfortable. "Be careful with whom you discuss this, Charles. As a loyal circle member, I will always defer to our leadership, but there are those inside the Yard whose loyalty lies elsewhere. And I do not refer to police officials."

"Another reason I wanted to sound you out on it first," his superior admitted. "It cannot be coincidence that this happened at a time when Beth was here all alone. She was only four, Ed. Four years old! It was also the summer that Beth first saw 'the man in the park'."

Edmund frowned. "That dark shadow? She saw him that year?"

"Yes, and with Beth expecting, it worries me, Edmund."

"It is definite, then?" he asked. "She is with child?"

Sinclair nodded. "Yes. Emerson insists she remain calm, for he has some concerns about her state of health. I intend to make sure her every day is secure. That is why I would know more about these crimes in '72. Could you make copies of the Yard records on the murders? I cannot do it myself. It would leave a trail for Redwing to follow."

"Yes, but you should speak with Thomas Galton. He's often obtained records through, shall we say, less than legal means that leave no official trail."

"I'd hoped you'd have a way to manage it, just make sure neither your name nor mine is attached in any way."

"I will. Now, if you've nothing else, I should be getting back to Leman Street. Send for me if you have any other need, Charles."

The two men exited the cottage; the inspector returning to Whitechapel, and Charles to his new home to commence a series of meetings with furniture manufacturers. It was afternoon by the time he concluded the interviews, and he'd just left his study, when a footman arrived to announce a visitor—one he'd not seen in many days. Martin Kepelheim.

"My dear friend!" the tailor gushed as the marquess entered the drawing room to greet his guest. "You look more and more like your father now that your attire is improved. That cutaway coat is a masterpiece. One of my finest creations!"

"I completely agree. Martin, I am delighted to see you, and I wonder if perhaps you read my mind, for I've been thinking of you whilst walking the many rooms of this house with the craftsmen. The paintings of my parents always make me think of you. I've read through all their letters now, and my mother spoke of you often. I hadn't realised you and she were such close friends."

"I adored your sweet mother, Charles. Her strength of heart and depth of spirit are matched only by Elizabeth's. Angela Sinclair lives on in her son. I must say, you've transformed this house in record time! Are you happy with the results of your labours?"

"Not all of it is complete," he replied. "Sit, Martin. Have you eaten?"

"I took a late lunch with the duke, and I'm expected at your fiancée's home within the hour. We've scheduled a practise session, you know. Della is learning how to walk with a train for the wedding."

"I've been banished from Queen Anne for the day. Sunday cannot come soon enough."

"We have journeyed far since October, have we not, my friend? But this is where you were always meant to be. In this house and married to Elizabeth."

"Do you think so?"

"Yes, I do! With all my being. But you worry, my friend. Is it the child?"

"You're a mind reader," the detective said with a slight smile. "Or am I that transparent?"

"Only to me, perhaps. The earl tells me that you've learnt of the miscarriages. Moira Stopes was a monstrous witch, if you ask me. I would not be at all surprised if she is connected to Trent. That man wormed his way into Patricia's life long before he married her, if that letter from Connor is any indication."

"I wonder if Stopes is still in England. Perhaps, I should begin an investigation into her, Martin."

"The duke tried to locate her back then, but you'll find little under the name. Oh, yes, there is an official record of a Moira Stopes who studied nursing and midwifery, but this woman's trail vanishes even before Connor supposedly hired her."

"Supposedly? You doubt he did?"

"It does not conform with what I knew of Beth's father. I may be wrong, but if Connor thought his wife required nursing, he would have asked Price to hire someone. But it's more likely that Connor simply would have left government work and remained at home."

"Martin, do you think Redwing prefers a male child?"

The tailor grew pensive for a moment, his gaze falling on a large oil painting, hanging over the drawing room fireplace. "That's you, Charles. The infant in that portrait. Did you know that?"

"No, I've not yet had time to inventory all the paintings. This one has no plaque beneath it, though some do."

"I should be pleased to walk through the house with you one day and help in that endeavour, but yes, that is you in the painting. The woman is not your mother, however, nor the man your father. They are the late Lord Aubrey and his wife, Abigail."

Charles turned to gaze at the portrait. "I cannot believe I failed to notice that! I met Lord Aubrey in '79, of course, and I had the honour to get to know him a little—prior to his death. Paul favours his mother."

"Yes, he does, and strangely enough you look even more like Robert Stuart than Paul does. The late earl's sister was your grandmother, you know."

"I remember hearing that. It makes me a possible heir to the Stuart dynasty."

"It does indeed. Katherine Stuart had black hair and light eyes, and your father inherited the hair; though his eyes were brown like his father's. The painting was commissioned when Robert and Abigail were named your godparents."

Charles rose and walked to the fireplace, touching the canvas as if trying to connect with his past. "I wish I could remember that. My childhood, I mean."

"No more hints or dreams?"

"Some strange dreams," Sinclair admitted. "Ephemeral at best, for they're with me upon waking and then fade. Paul suggested I start writing down all my strange experiences and dreams. In truth, they're beginning to add up to a disturbing picture."

"Ah, yes, I can see how they might," Kepelheim agreed. "Charles, don't try to solve all these mysteries in one day. Allow yourself time to adjust. I worry about your mind, my friend. If you push to remember too much too quickly, it could do damage, I fear."

"Seven years, Martin. Seven years of my life have been stolen from me! How can you ask me to slow down?"

Kepelheim crossed the room to stand beside his friend. "I understand your passion, Charles, but we need you. Beth needs you, and if your mind regresses because of dredging up these ancient memories, then..."

"Then I may prove useless to her cause. I suppose you have a point, but it is frustrating."

"Yes, I imagine it is, for you are a man of action, much like your cousin. However, you are also a remarkable thinker. Use your mental skills and deductive reasoning to ascertain our enemy's plans."

Sinclair sighed, touching the portrait once again. "I'll do my best, Martin. I'd like to think that Uncle Robert and Aunt Abigail look down upon us now and cheer us on in this task. One day, I shall get to meet them both."

"And before that day, you will recall more of your childhood. For now, continue to prepare for your new bride—and your child. Have you looked at the old nursery yet?"

"No, not yet. I've had little time, and in truth, I'm still adjusting to the idea of being a father again. But it is a happy adjustment, I assure you. Beth will make a wonderful mother, and I can picture a little girl with her eyes."

"Or a boy," the tailor suggested. "Well, I must be off. I stopped in only to say hello. Now, spend the afternoon relaxing, for the hours twixt now and Sunday morning will fly past!"

Once the tailor, left, Sinclair decided to take his friend's advice and spend the afternoon reading. He entered the newly furnished and soundproofed library, glancing through the volumes left upon the shelves by his father.

"So many books," he said aloud, unaware that Matthew Laurence had entered the room.

"Your father's collection rivals even the duke's, sir."

Charles spun 'round, his face breaking into a smile. "Laurence, you startled me. Does that gift come naturally, or was it honed in the Drummond household?"

"I'm not sure, sir. My father insisted I keep a soft step, so perhaps it is both."

"You are a man of understatement. I hear from our housekeeper, Mrs. Partridge, that we are now fully staffed, and I know that you are to thank for it, despite the difficulty with Miss Trumper."

"I'm very sorry to have misjudged the girl, sir, but am pleased that you find the staff satisfactory."

"Laurence, I know it's considered bad form for me to ask you to chat with me, but would you? I've hundreds of questions, and truly I know of no one else I might ask. Would you sit?"

The young man thought for a moment and then perched upon the edge of a rather severe chair. "Certainly, sir. Thank you."

"Come now, I've no problem with your sitting comfortably. But look, if I make you self-aware in my manner, then tell me to get stuffed."

"Sir?"

"Ignore me, Laurence. It's just that in two days, I shall be wed to the most beautiful woman in all England."

"And Scotland, sir," the young man added. "Let us not forget that."

"Aye, she is that!" Charles said, slipping into a Scottish accent. "Funny. I'm told I once spoke with a northern brogue. I'm banned from the other house today, you see," he said, his mind returning to the present. "Beth's having her final fitting, and Adele is there so she can practise walking as Kepelheim provides accompaniment. Can you tell I'm a happy man, Mr. Laurence?"

"May I say, sir, that you deserve it? And since you have taken notice of the books, I would suggest you examine a certain leather-bound box, up high on that shelf," he said, pointing to a tall, Chinese cabinet in the corner of the room. "The duke asked me to make sure you saw it. He says it is part of his gift to you—though only a small part. Shall I pour you a claret or anything else before leaving you to it?"

Charles was taller than Laurence by over three inches, but even he had to stand on a stool to reach the mysterious box. "No, nothing at present. I'm filled to the brim with Mrs. Paget's delicious luncheon. Where did you find her? And did I hear that we have two cooks?"

"We do, sir. The ladies are sisters and served together at their last house, that of the Earl of Granddach, an old friend to the duke and your great uncle, I believe. They asked if they might join your staff together, and the duke thought it a good idea. I hope that meets with your approval."

Charles laughed. "Two cooks! I shall get fat eating here every day. Oh, Laurence, has Mrs. Wilsham's apartment been completed?"

"It has, sir, and I believe she will find it very comfortable. It is across the hall from the nursery. I hope that is all right, sir."

"That is perfect, Laurence. Well done."

The young man left, closing the door, and Sinclair settled into a leather chair to see what the duke had sent. He opened the box, and inside was an envelope marked with his name. Beneath were numerous other letters and two small books.

Opening the letter from James, he read:

My Very Dear Nephew,

I hope Laurence remembers to show this box to you before your wedding day, because I believe it will help give you insight into the incredible woman you're about to marry. Since losing Connor twelve years ago, Elizabeth has been more like a daughter to me, and her happiness and safety are uppermost in my mind and heart. I know that you have gone through seasons of doubt regarding whether or not your love for Beth is best *for her*, but my beloved nephew, once you read these letters and the diaries inside the box, I know you will realise it was always meant to be.

Much love and prayers for your happiness,
Uncle James

Sinclair read the letter twice, still finding it remarkable that he had found his true family once again. Setting the duke's letter to one side, he glanced at the others, sorted neatly into stacks by year and tied with white ribbon. Every envelope was addressed to the duke, but as the years passed, the hand that wrote them grew evermore firm and refined.

They're all from Elizabeth! he realised, his heart filled with joy at finding a chance to look into her mind as a growing girl. He untied the first stack of letters, written during '76 and '77. Some came before her father's death, whilst two came after. The first was filled with the joy of a bright child looking forward to seeing her grandfather again.

4th September, 1876

Dearest Grandpapa,

My new tutor says I must call you Grandpapa, because Grandfather is not correct. Is that true? Father (I am to call him 'Papa', isn't that silly?) bought me a new pony for my birthday this year, but he is too fat, so Mother (Mama, I suppose) says I must let him be for now. Father has left for Turkey, and I am all alone once more. Mother suffers great headaches, but Mr. Baxter keeps me company and listens to me practise my piano.

My music lessons are rather boring, but I want to play for you at Christmas, so I practise. Father is coming home in a few months, and we shall visit you then. It's quite dull here, especially since Mother is so often away. When she's not down with her migraines (I hope I spelt that right – it is a new word), she spends time in Hampton, despite the cool weather.

Do you ever see shadows that talk? I hope not, for they are truly terrifying (another new word). There is one that speaks to me each night. He is tall and often stands near Duke Henry's statue. He is much like the man from the park. I shall tell Father about it when he comes home, but until then, I mustn't mention it to Mother. She says it is all in my imagination, and I'm never to speak of it again.

Love,
Beth

My, her command of language was certainly mature for an eight-year-old, he thought as he re-read the letter. *The Shadow Man had already begun to torment her, and she equated him with the man from the park. Perhaps, they are the same entity. How could Patricia refuse to believe her own daughter?*

Charles found it impossible to understand such willful blindness, particularly as it caused Elizabeth more danger.

A second letter arrived the following week.

15ᵗʰ September, 1876

Dearest Grandfather,

Mother is very sad now, and I do not know why. My new tutor has left also. I tried my best to be a good pupil, but I suppose I failed somehow. Mother left yesterday, but she promised to return in a fortnight. Baxter keeps me company, and he is teaching me all about the brewery. His father worked there, you know. May I come to visit you soon? I miss you, and though I've written many times to Cousin Paul, he has not replied. I know he is busy with government work in Paris, but I hoped to talk to him.

You asked me if I dream. The answer is yes. The dreams frighten me, Grandfather. So many faces, like heads within dozens of shadowy mirrors. What could they mean?

Forget what I said about being lonely, Grandfather. There are many here who love me, so I should not complain.

Yours with great affection,
Beth

She sounds so very sad in this letter. So lonely. How could Patricia abandon her only child for weeks at a time? he wondered, growing quite irritated. *Is this ordinary for the aristocracy, or is it more likely that she was already seeing Trent?*

Charles read the letter's date again, calculating backwards from Della's birthday of June, '77. *September of '76. Nine months before—Paul must have been working in disguise at the time, under the name David Saunders—when he met Cozette. That must be why he never wrote. I wonder if he knows how desperately Beth tried to reach him.*

Elizabeth had written again in April—after her father's death.

9th April, 1877

Dearest Grandfather,

Mother is sad all the time, but not because of me. She cries every night, and she sleeps much of the day. I am better and am now able to walk again, but I'm not allowed to ride yet. Mr. Baxter often reads to me. He is a lovely man, is he not? Mrs. Halpern visited yesterday and brought a cake for my birthday. You remember her from last year's fete. She and her very kind husband entered the sheep that won the contest.

Please, please, come to see me soon. There is a man I hate who wants to visit us all the time. I don't like the way he looks at me. He reminds me of the Shadow Man, and he frightens me, Grandfather. When he thinks me not looking, he stares at me—like he could gobble me up! And he has friends who remind me of—of animals. One is exceedingly tall with long arms like a spider. His eyes glow red when no one else is looking. Sometimes, he stands outside my bedchamber. I can hear him breathing, whispering my name over and over. No, it is not my feverish mind imagining this. It is true. All true, though Mother says I make it all up.

I must go now. Mother is calling me, but I shall write again when I am no longer ill. If you hear from Paul, please, tell him that I love him. He is my Scottish knight, and I'm very sorry that Mother was unkind to him. If he will come visit me, I promise to be good.

Love,
Beth

Her final words nearly broke Sinclair's heart. *She's alone again and thinks Paul's absence is because of something she did!* Unconsciously, he began to pace the room, irritation taking hold and banishing his former good mood. *This would have been in the months following Connor's murder by the wolf, when Elizabeth's leg was injured. The Shadow Man—and a clear reference to Trent, but also to this spider creature!*

"My poor darling," he said, tears staining his cheeks. "How terrified you must have been, but how courageous! I wish I could have known you back then, little one—helped you."

The next letter was written in 1879, the very year he'd met her—when she was nearly eleven.

3rd January, 1879

Dearest Grandfather,

Happy New Year to my great love and surrogate father! How I miss my dear, true father, but in your eyes I see his, and that keeps me from becoming too frightened. I often look at your picture and my father's, whenever I am worried and alone—for I keep both upon my night stand, and I pretend you are nearby. I pray you come to visit me soon, even if Sir William does not wish it.

That horrible man continues to fight with Mother daily. Why does he do that? It seems that he despises her; but if so, why would he marry her? The hall rings with their raised voices nearly hour of the day, yet she eventually yields to his every demand like an obedient, docile sheep. Truly, Grandfather, if this is marriage, then I do not look forward to it at all.

Paul would never behave like that, would he? After all, he will be my husband one day, or so I'm told. I do love him, but it's strange to think of being his wife. Still, he is quite wonderful and very handsome. My friend Loretta Briarhurst, Lord Parsington's daughter, told me that she will marry Paul, if I do not. She called him 'rather dreamy'. I suppose he is. Even though he's quite busy, my dreamy cousin visited here all of this past week, and he kept me company, playing games and riding through the woods. He even took me on a picnic.

William despises Paul, I think, and I fear—now that Paul is gone—that Trent will be all the more horrible to my mother, and to me. I care nothing for myself, you understand, but I would dry my mother's tears, if I could. My dear cousin left yesterday, bound for Paris once again. I miss him already.

Mrs. Holloway has taken ill, and our assistant cook, Mrs. Stephens is filling in. I like her dishes very much. Mr. Baxter says I must speak kindly, even if I do not like the food, but I do like it. Mother sleeps most of the time now, and my nanny insists that I not spy upon Sir William. He spends nearly every evening, wandering through the tunnels beneath the hall. Remember, how I discovered them as a girl? I wonder how it is Trent learnt of their existence. Mother may have told him, I suppose. How I wish she would show some backbone with the man!

Oh, there is also this very distressing news. Paul and Mother had words, Grandfather. A terrible argument, and I fear Paul may not come back—ever!—because he was dreadfully angry when he left. He stormed out of the house without even a word of goodbye to me. Please, tell him that I hope he forgives us and will return on my birthday. I would do anything for my darling Paul. Anything.

Much love,
Beth

"Oh, my darling," Charles said aloud. "I shall rid this world of Trent. For your sake and your mother's."

Turning to the next letter, Charles discovered a reference to himself!

23rd July,1879

Dearest Grandfather,

As you know, the fete this year was held three weeks late, and was not the same without Mother. Though, she seldom participated in recent years, her absence was keenly felt by all. The farmers spoke with me, again and again, offering their condolences. They are such gentle souls! I nearly cancelled it, but Paul told me that the villagers look forward to it all year long, so it would be thoughtless of me to do so. My darling cousin remained with me here until a few days ago. With his busy schedule, I thought it quite generous. He is now gone once more. Paul is a kind man, but it is hard to imagine marrying him. Is that wrong of me?

Now that I am eleven, I begin to think ahead to my wedding day, when I shall become Paul's wife. Do most women marry for love, Grandfather? Mrs. Bellringer, my strict governess, says it is never too soon for a duchess to consider a suitable partner. She does not know that I have been promised to Paul, but may I not choose? Are not partners all about business? I've no wish to be part of a business. I wish to be loved, Grandfather. Paul loves me, I know this, but is it silly of me to imagine that someone else might love me, also?

Perhaps a gallant 'Captain' with sea-blue eyes and a ready smile? Of course, I do not refer to anyone we know personally—for that gentleman, handsome and kind and wonderful though he is—well, he is already married. In fact, you must forget I mentioned it.

Much love and many kisses,
Elizabeth

8th April, 1881

Dearest Grandfather,

Today, I am thirteen years old, and I find myself getting taller if you can believe it! Baxter still towers over me, of course, but Mrs. Bellringer marked my height a full inch higher than last year. I hope to grow very tall one day, so that my future husband will not need to bend down just to kiss me. I'm sure you're laughing at this just now—and I can certainly picture you—but I am completely serious.

My kind and brilliant friend, the Captain (Mr. St. Clair, of course) who is now a Chief Inspector in charge of many policemen, stopped by Aubrey House today to visit Paul. I arrived here last week to celebrate my birthday, and Mr. St. Clair was thoughtful enough to wish me a happy one and even brought a gift. Is that not wonderful? Do you think him handsome, Grandfather? I find him so, but I must never tell him. He is married and beyond... Well, beyond all hoping. I understand that I am to marry Paul, whom I adore, but is it wrong of me to wish upon a star sometimes? Oh, if only it were so easy as merely making a wish! If only fears and wishes might be dispelled or granted as easily as thought!

Do you recall the shadows I used to tell you about? I mentioned them to Paul, and he became very angry with me. Why is that? "You've probably imagined it all", he tells me. I suppose I am but a silly girl to my remarkable cousin. Grandfather, am I only that? A silly girl with fanciful dreams? I read and learn, but sometimes I fear that all such effort is in vain. Paul will always be my dearest friend, though. Without him—and you—I should be all alone in this world.

Paul brought Adele with him this time! She is such a lovely child. I find that if I squeeze her with great hugs, she laughs and laughs. Was I the same at that age? I hope one day to have such a darling child. Perhaps one with sea-blue eyes.

Very well, I shall stop. I remember your warning that such vain imaginings will only lead to disappointment. I shall continue to pray that he is well and happy, though. May I at least do that?

Love,
Beth

She'd written the next letter shortly before leaving for Paris.

5th June, 1884

Dearest Grandfather,

I have seen Superintendent St. Clair this day at Aubrey House, and he is as gallant and kind as ever. He is so handsome—or perhaps, that is too forward of me to write, but this letter is to you, my confident and best friend in all the world, and I am free to say what is in my heart, am I not? Do you recall our private talk last Christmas? Am I being too wistful? Yes, I know. I remember your stern reminder that I am promised to Paul, but is it set in stone? Does the circle require that I do so? It seems to me that my cousin's attention is often diverted towards other women; after all, I am only sixteen, and Paul is nearly thirty!

Please, do not ever allow my dear cousin to see this letter, for it would break his heart, I think. He grows ever more protective and quite secretive of late—even more than usual, if you can imagine it. Where did my childhood companion go? He refuses even to allow me to walk my own park without him! Why must my cousin and the circle members always hover about me, as if I am a child and unable to make my own decisions? It drives me mad at times!

Forgive my temper. Yes, I love Paul, truly, but may I not write what is in my heart and mind to you—only for your eyes?

If my mother still lived, I suppose I would confide all these schoolgirl thoughts to her, but you have been both father and mother to me all these years, my loving Grandfather, and I truly do need your counsel. Forget all that nonsense about a duchess not marrying a commoner, because I will simply not hear it! Love knows no social class, my dear. I read Jane Austen's *Pride and Prejudice* last year, and all I could think of is how reversed my own situation is. At least Elizabeth in that lovely story was able to encourage Mr. D'arcy to speak his heart, but how may a peeress speak bold words to the love of her life?

Oh, please, tell me I am not a foolish young woman! Paul says I am at an age where I should spend a few years with Aunt Victoria; therefore, I suppose that will be my fate. The Captain—*my Captain*—is all I can think of these days. What a fool I am, for he is still legally married, is he not? Though his Amelia now resides in Ireland with another man, the law would tell me that my Captain is still hers. Oh, how it tears at my soul, Grandfather! How could she treat him thusly? It breaks my heart to think of him all alone. Were it within my power, I would bring only sunshine to his life. Sunshine and bright smiles. Were I anything other than a duchess, who must live according to an ancient set of laws, I would have kissed him that day at Paul's home! Yes! I would!

Though, he might not wish to return that kiss, I would have told him all that stands inside my soul and risked rejection.

I beg you! Please, do not force me to go to Paris! But if you insist, I shall submit, for I love and respect you. It is only my poor heart you break. Only my future that you determine, but promise me that, should you ever see the Chief Inspector, you will not reveal my pitiful confessions to him. I doubt that Mr. St. Clair returns my affections, and I would not embarrass him for all the world! Surely, if he felt as earnestly in love as I, then he would have told me, would he not?

I must let it go. Leave this burden here in England and give myself to the circle's plans. It drags at my heart, Grandfather, but I shall try to do all you ask of me, for I love you, and I would die rather than hurt or disappoint you.

One last thing, Grandfather mine: A certain someone has been lurking about again. You made me promise to tell you anytime I saw the Shadows, and they have returned. Whilst walking in my garden last night, I saw him—I am certain of it, only this time he did not speak. Perhaps, I imagined it—Paul says I am imaginative, but I think not.

He puzzled me when I was a little girl, but now he truly terrifies me, Grandfather. Why is a mere shadow so very menacing?

All my love,
Elizabeth

The Shadow Man has been following Elizabeth for most of her life, he thought. *She called it 'him' in this letter. Is it possible a part of her dreaming mind knows more than her waking self can recall?*

And finally, there was a letter that, curiously enough, was addressed to him.

12th June, 1884

My Dearest Captain,

I write this letter as a last resort, and it is quite possible that you will never see it. I have instructed my wonderful grandfather (whom you know well, I think, after the many years all of you spent on my mother's murder case) to post it to you once I am gone. I do this, because I love and respect the duke. I leave it to his discretion whether or not to forward this. Grandfather is the best parent in all the world, and if he believes our match to be right, then he will send it. If not, then… Oh, I dare not think of it!

Tomorrow, my darling Captain, I leave for Paris, where I shall spend the next four years, if not longer, learning to be a proper lady and duchess. Since my mother's death, there have been very few female influences in my life, except for Mrs. Alcorn at Branham and my somewhat eccentric aunt, Victoria Stuart. It is to my aunt's château that I go, to linger there until my family approves my return to London. Tory's Paris address is below my signature, should you ever wish to write. I shall understand completely if you prefer not to do so—oh, but I hope you will!

I shall miss you very much, Captain. I know that, to you, I am probably a very tragic young lady whom you met as a little girl, and if that is how you see me, then I thank you for never showing it. You have always made me feel as though you respect me—and perhaps even like me a little. I am sixteen now, and my life is no longer that of a child. Nor are my thoughts—nor my heart.

I doubt that it made much of an impression you, but when I saw you recently at Paul's home in London, I longed to tell you all of this. When you walked into his library that day, I thought my heart had stopped—or perhaps that it had started to beat for the first time in my life. I wanted so much to embrace you; prayed you felt the same and perhaps would reach out for my hand, or even more, that you might wish to kiss me. I dared not do any of those things, though, but how I longed to! Paul said it would be inappropriate to 'throw myself' at a married gentleman, but you've no idea how close I came to doing so.

Yes, I am being foolish, but I can only think of your sea-blue eyes and dashing smile. Oh, how miserable I shall be in Paris, but one word from you would bring me back to England on the first ship! Were it possible, I would fly back, my darling Charles!

I hesitate now to write this, but truly, I—I have come to love you so very, very much.

There I've said it! Now, you may put this letter into your desk or burn it, and then return to your very interesting life whilst I retire to the Parisian countryside to improve my French and perfect my watercolouring.

Honestly, though, I do love you with all my heart, Charles. I truly do, and no matter what your feelings towards me, I shall continue to love you for all the days of my life. I pray that I see you again one day, but if that is not meant to be, then I want you to know that you will always have someone out there who prays for you daily and admires you for who you truly are.

I love you, Captain. I am yours today, tomorrow, and always.

Your Beth
Now and Forever

Why was this letter never been posted? he wondered. *Did she think better of it—perhaps regret it once she arrived in Paris, or had the duke decided to let time pass in the hope she might outgrow her emotions?*

Suddenly, he wanted only to see her, to hold her, to explain why he'd never written or visited—for surely, had he received this letter when written, he would have been on his way to Paris at once, regardless of what English law said at the time!

Shutting the box and ringing the bell for Laurence, the marquess, who had once been a commoner who dreamt of a beautiful peeress, put on his jacket, and with the box under his arm, set out to return to his duchess.

CHAPTER TWENTY-FIVE

It was just after five when Charles Sinclair stepped into the foyer of Queen Anne House, and the entire place was thrown into an uproar, all because of him.

Miss Jenkins, who had begun work as Beth's secretary the previous morning, was clacking away on her portable typewriter, struggling to finish up a stack of letters for Lady Victoria, but hearing the ruckus in the foyer, the bashful young woman rushed out to help. Charles had barely caught a glimpse of his fiancée and Adele, and he could hear Beth laughing and Della squealing in surprise as an arm reached out for him.

"Sir! Oh, Lord Haimsbury, you are early!" Jenkins exclaimed, tugging at the marquess's forearm and pulling him into the front drawing room. "Forgive my impertinence, sir," she continued once Charles stood safely inside the large room, "but we didn't think you would return until much later."

Sinclair grinned. "Is that so?" He winked at the secretary and tried to sneak another peek into the expansive foyer. "I shan't look, really, but if I might just..."

"No, Charles!" his fiancée called out as his face appeared around the door. "You're not to see us!"

Returning to his hiding place, Charles could hear Adele giggling once again and the pitter-patter of her small feet behind Elizabeth's as both ladies fled the foyer, where they had been practising their entrance for the wedding ceremony—to the piano accompaniment of Martin Kepelheim.

The drawing room door opened again, and Lady Victoria appeared, her stern black eyes boring into Sinclair's. "Why are you here?" she bellowed.

Sinclair could not help laughing, his heart was so joyful, but Aunt Victoria's stern reprimand quickly sobered his mood—though only a little—as she removed him from Jenkins forthwith.

"Charles, you should have warned us! Beth thought you intended to be away until six. Well, no matter, keep your eyes shut, Nephew, and follow me."

The happy marquess obeyed, peeking just once, as he followed his domineering but loveable aunt into the yellow morning room where she often spent the day napping. Once he entered, she closed the doors. "There now. Sit down, Charles. I've a few words to speak, so you might as well make yourself comfortable."

"I am all attention, Aunt."

"Good. Well, then, before I say anything else, I just want to mention how pleased I am that you smile more now. When I first arrived, you and Paul both seemed to wear fixed and permanent scowls, and neither of you was the better for it. With the peace of the past days, Aubrey has actually begun to look like his old self again, and you, my dear sister-son, begin to resemble your handsome father all the more."

"Thank you, Tory. I've seen numerous portraits of both my parents now, and being compared to my father always makes me feel closer to him."

"I am glad to hear it." She cleared her throat and continued. "Yes, well, you must think me an odd duck at times, Charles, but I have found my own way in a world of men—not an easy task for a woman with a brain, which is precisely what Elizabeth is, so I want you to assure me that you will not curtail her natural curiosity and courage. I love you dearly, Nephew, but I have noticed in you an unfortunate tendency to overprotect Beth. She is not a hothouse flower. That girl—that *woman*—has lived through horrors many in your old stomping grounds might consider unbearable. Yes, yes, I know the majority of your citizenry have very little, and probably not a bean sometimes, but I tell you that money is not always the blessing it appears. You follow, I hope?"

He nodded, half his mind listening as Beth and Adele returned to the foyer. He could hear Elizabeth instructing Della on how to turn whilst wearing a very long train, amidst the persistent barking of three dogs.

"You are listening, aren't you, Charles?"

"Yes, Aunt, I am. Do forgive me."

"Good, then you must promise me that you will allow Elizabeth to blossom. She has many ideas, some philosophical, some political, but most lie within the realm of how best to use the wealth she's been given to help others. She's told me of her plan to build a teaching hospital, and I applaud it, but she wants to build it in Whitechapel—wait, perhaps it's Spitalfields. Are they the same?"

"Spitalfields and Whitechapel are both in Tower Hamlets borough, yes, so nearly the same, Tory, but Spitalfields is much poorer by far. I'm all in favour of Beth endowing a hospital there. It is much needed, and it will provide education for men and women who've no means to pursue such on their own. I think it's a marvellous idea."

Tory removed a cigarette from her handbag, pursing her lips as she thought best how to respond. Charles automatically lit the smoke for her. "Thank you," she said, returning the silver case to the bag. "So, you have no problem with your wife spending many hours there?"

His brows pinched together. "Has Elizabeth told you she wants to spend time in Spitalfields? Why would she even need to be there?"

Victoria exhaled a thin plume of smoke, sighing. "For a police detective, you're rather thick at times, Nephew. Has it never occurred to you that she might wish to be personally involved? Have you not yet realised just who she is? Elizabeth has never been one to let others do things for her. No, no, let me finish. I see your eyes— my sister's eyes—and I know already what you plan to say. When Elizabeth was a little girl, we taught her to consider how other people in the world must live and work, especially those in service. The year she became duchess, Beth spent the entire summer learning every area of estate life. She learnt to milk a cow, how to make a bed and build a fire, she learnt about plants and how to amend soil. She learnt to saddle her own horse, how to drive a carriage, how to perform basic cooking methods—well, mostly. In truth, Beth baked a cake that could have been used as footing for construction, but in all areas, she tried her best. Why did we ask her to do this? To teach her the toil and sacrifices her servants make for her each and every day. That is why I know, that when she commences this building project, Elizabeth will very likely become personally involved, though I pray she does not try to bake any of them cakes."

Charles smiled as he pictured the little girl he'd met ten years earlier milking a cow or saddling a horse. But then, she had been brave and clever enough to learn the layout of the old tunnel system and even attempt to rescue her mother, all on her own. "I've witnessed Elizabeth's self-reliance many times, Tory, and in most circumstances I think it wonderful. I applaud her courage and dedication to helping others, but when her choices border on foolhardiness, I must and will step in."

Tory laughed as she tapped ash into the silver dish. "Well, my dear, you will find yourself in a constant state of worry if you feel you must follow her every move for fear she might venture into foolish territory. I tell you that she will! When Beth lived with me, she had many admirers; dozens of young men who flocked to my home, day after day, often with no prior notice or courtesy, just to sit and gaze at her."

"She is beautiful, Tory. I often find myself sitting and gazing at her."

"Beth *wants you* to do so, my dear, but not these fellows. Often, when these gawping gentlemen would show up at my door, Beth would speak a few polite words and then hasten to her room, dress as a stable boy, and then dash down the servants' stairs to go riding all by herself." She thought for a moment, and then making up her mind, continued. "Do you know why she did that?"

"Shy?" Sinclair suggested, but deep in his heart he suspected he knew the answer.

"Elizabeth shy? Oh, really, Charles, do be serious. No, my dear, she did it because she had no interest in their admiration. She'd already fallen in love—with you! You cannot know this, but when Elizabeth first arrived at my home in '84, she was in a highly charged, emotional state; and to be frank, it worried me. She was only sixteen at the time, but desperately in love with you, and she feared you would never—could never return her affections. She'd written you a letter, you see, and she waited for a reply each and every day. She hounded our poor postman mercilessly, to see if a letter from Whitechapel or perhaps Scotland Yard had arrived. After three months of this, I told her that either her letter to you had never been received, or that you had chosen not to reply. It was either one or the other. She asked if she should write again, and I told her no; she should not. I know how much she agonised over you, Charles, for

I heard her crying, night after night, praying that your letter would arrive the next day. Elizabeth is loyal and true, and once she gives her heart, she never takes it back. So, I hope you will take good care of that sweet child, Charles. Her love is the rarest of gifts."

Sinclair moved to the sofa and took his aunt's hands in his own. "Tory, I would die for that sweet child. Right now, if it would protect her, I would. I have loved Elizabeth from the first time I saw her as a young girl—only then it was a protective love. But when I saw her at Aubrey House in '84, shortly before she came to live with you, she stole my heart, Tory. That day is forever etched upon my mind. I'd gone there to deliver the last of the Yard's archived documents regarding Patricia's murder. Paul and I'd been secretly removing them to protect Beth from ever learning the extent of her mother's injuries. I'd not seen her in three years, but she was often in my thoughts—again, protectively. I arrived in the afternoon. It had been raining, and the sun had just begun to shine. Paul's butler told me the earl was in the library, and I found my own way there since I'd been to Aubrey House many times over the years. As I entered, Beth was just leaving—and I now know that she'd been arguing with Paul, though I had no idea at that time. All I knew then was this: that time stopped, when I saw her."

His eyes grew misty as he recalled the moment. "She wore a green silk dress with long sleeves that fell softly towards her wrists. It had pink rose petals embroidered upon the skirt, and she'd tied a black velvet sash about her waist, the streamers of the bow following the line of her dress all the way to the floor. Her shoes were black with pearl buttons. Her hair was arranged in long waves down her back, but part of it was braided and accented with pearls. In her beautiful earlobes, hung delicate ear bobs shaped like silver hearts with green bows. I never received that letter, Tory, for if I had, do you think I would have waited for even one second to go to her? I have loved Elizabeth *the woman* since that day. Every cell in my body—every fibre of my being is in love with that woman."

Tory smiled. "That is all I wanted to know, Charles. That she is loved for who she is, for all that she longs to do. Thank you for indulging me, Nephew. I understand Elizabeth's strong attachment. I've grown quite fond of you myself in these short weeks."

He kissed her cheek. "And I love you, too, Tory," he said. "Since I have no memories of my mother, I make new ones with you—her loving sister. I don't think of you as an aunt, but as a surrogate for her. I hope that isn't too strong."

She took his hand, her firm mouth curving into a rare smile. "That is the nicest thing you've ever said to me, and I take it to heart, Charles. Your parents would have been very proud of you. Your mind, your kindness, your gentle heart, but also your unfailing strength of character. I should like to be a mother to you, for her sake, and it pleases me more than I can say," she said with great affection, her eyes growing soft and tearing. She sniffed and straightened her shoulders. "All right, well, that is enough I suppose. Now, Charles, you do realise that you may not sleep here tomorrow night. Bad luck."

He nodded, smiling. "Yes, you've mentioned it a few times. I've already moved my things to Haimsbury House."

"Good. Well, then, we are in our final phase, aren't we? Two days. I must check with our Miss Jenkins now. She's been typewriting some letters for me. All our distant cousins and international friends must receive notice of the wedding and Elizabeth's new London address. She's suggested I remain here at Queen Anne House, but I'm not sure if I wish to live alone."

"Then move in with us," he said and meant it.

"That is a consideration, Nephew. Perhaps I shall. Oh, one more thing. You do know about the ball tomorrow evening?"

"Yes, Prince Anatole reminded me only yesterday, in fact."

"Did he? When?"

"He dropped by Whitehall. Must we go, Tory? I'd prefer a quiet evening, actually."

Victoria stared at her nephew for a moment, considering the strange revelation. "The prince just dropped by? That is quite unlike Romanov. Well, never mind. Yes, we must attend. I know this ball comes when we at our busiest, but we really cannot decline. It is given by the Russian Embassy in concert with the Duke of Edinburgh."

"Why is Edinburgh hosting? Is he a family friend?"

"He is a friend, yes, but he is also married to the Grand Duchess Maria Alexandrovna of Russia, Tsar Alexander's sister. Does it now begin to make sense to you?"

"I suppose so, yes. Is Uncle James attending?"

"We are all going," Stuart answered. "Now, on another topic, I've not spoken with you directly on this, but it's time I do. Has Beth's pregnancy been confirmed?"

"Three doctors have made that diagnosis, so I take it as confirmation," Sinclair replied. "Tory, I hope you don't think I took advantage of Beth," he began, but she held up her hand to stop him.

"You've nothing to explain, my dear. Nothing. I know all about Scotland's troubles, and it's apparent that the goal of that dangerous night has been achieved. But rather than worry about Redwing's motives—which are obvious—let us consider this a blessing, shall we?"

He relaxed and took her hand. "It's a blessing to me. I'd not thought to start a family so soon, but God has kept us safe throughout, so I look to Him to protect Beth and our child. Do you think Anatole was involved in the Scotland attacks?"

"That's hard to say. The prince's behaviour is often inscrutable, which makes it difficult to determine his loyalties. Regardless, he has made a considered effort to befriend you."

"I'm not sure I'd call his actions friendly; though, as you say his motives aren't yet clear."

"No, they are not, which means we must learn more about him and his plans. The simplest path to achieving that aim, is to spend time with him."

"I suppose that's true, but I have no wish to endanger Elizabeth."

"Nor do I. So, have your valet teach you how to dress for this occasion, Charles, for we must attend," she declared.

"Teach me to dress? I have a formal evening suit thanks to Kepelheim, is that not enough? Tails, white waistcoat, and all that?"

"Yes, that would be customary at such an occasion, but this ball has a theme. Everyone is to come costumed in what their ancestors would have worn a century ago. These themed balls are all the rage in Paris, so it's in fashion. You may wish to consult with Laurence about it—or Martin. I should imagine it will involve military dress of some type. Sashes, medals and all that."

Charles laughed. "I'll check my father's trunks and see what I can devise before tomorrow. If nothing else, I'll just wear Connor's kilt," he added, smiling. "Tory, will this be a regular occurrence? Last minute invitations to parties and costume balls. If so, it will take some getting used to. We seldom had call for fancy dress in Whitechapel."

"Don't worry, Charles, most of these invitations will arrive weeks before the event, sometimes months; but yes, you will probably attend many parties. After a year or two, you might even enjoy them."

"Ask me in a year," he said. "Now, is it possible for me to speak to my intended today, or am I permanently banned from the house?"

Victoria took a puff on her cigarette, her head tilting to one side as she considered. "Perhaps, but she's with Adele at present. Speaking of which, we should speak of her as well. And of other things. No, I am not acting as distraction for my niece. Well, in truth, I suppose I am, but you and I haven't had many opportunities to speak alone since my arrival, and I've a few other things to say."

Charles could still hear Elizabeth and Della laughing as Kepelheim played their music, and he longed to join them if only for a moment. "What about Adele?"

Lady Victoria blew several smoke rings, pondering how best to approach the topic. "You don't smoke?" she asked.

He shook his head. "No. I tried it for a few days at Cambridge, but never found it enjoyable."

Stuart tapped the slender cigarette against the dish. "Good. You look surprised. I may smoke, but Elizabeth has never cared for it, though she is kind enough to indulge me. I'd never even considered lighting a cigarette until twenty years ago. That was a hellish year in many ways. I took up the habit to calm my nerves."

Charles thought for a moment. "Twenty years. That would have been '68. The year Beth was born."

The music stopped. "Wait," Victoria told him, motioning for her nephew to remain seated. She walked to the morning room doors, listening intently, her ear pressed against the wood. After a moment, she turned the lock. "It sounds as though Beth and Della have gone upstairs at last, which makes this easier. I've no desire for Elizabeth to hear any of this." She returned to her seat and leaned in close to Sinclair, whispering. "Did Dr. Emerson mention Patricia's miscarriages to you?"

"Yes, which is why I want her to follow his advice to the letter."

She leaned back, her dark eyes rounding. "Now, that is a challenge. Should you find a way to ensure her obedience, then you will have to share it with me, Charles, for Beth is headstrong. However, knowing another life depends upon her compliance might curtail her energies, but do not rely upon that, my dear."

"I do my best," he answered, suddenly worried that 'his best' may not be enough.

"It's a pity about that maid," she continued, blowing smoke towards the ceiling. "How are your injuries?"

"My head still aches, and my entire right side is bruised, but I'll survive. These aren't not my first injuries, Tory, nor will they be the last. I'm just grateful that the girl's plans failed. I pray she is with the Lord now. Poor Gertie was a victim, and I wish I'd been kinder in my actions towards her."

"Hindsight is always perfect, is it not? You aided her in her final moments, Charles. It's quite likely that she is with our Lord now. Life ends when we least expect it."

"Yes. So it does. Tory, did you know about Moira Stopes?" he asked, his voice a whisper.

"No. Not until afterward. Charles, we have tried to keep watch on all children born in the twins' lines. Drummond and Branham. I fear our best efforts are seldom sufficient. But lest you misunderstand, let me assure you that Connor did *not* hire that woman."

"Price seemed to think he did—as did Baxter."

"No," she replied, crushing the spent cigarette and lighting a third, "he did not. The woman brought a letter with her, ostensibly penned by Beth's father, but she only attended the duchess whenever Connor was absent. Patricia later confessed that *she* had hired the nurse. Connor isn't to be blamed, for he travelled a great deal. His talents were much like my brother's, and like Paul's. Despite his great height, Connor Stuart could disappear into any crowd, any city. He also was a consummate athlete: an expert with a sword, a knife, pistol, rifle—any weapon, even a longbow. He was tall and muscular and quite intelligent, and he worried Redwing."

"How so?"

"Connor had uncovered a great deal of information about their plans, and I believe he was on the track of discovering the truth about the Shadow Man's identity."

"He knew about that vile creature? Then how could he leave his daughter to that thing's mercy?" Charles asked, his voice rising. "Tory, I do not understand it! I know Connor loved her, but how could he go away so often if…"

"If he thought her in danger?" she finished for him. "Charles, you are now in Connor Stuart's position. Have there been times when duty calls you from Beth's side?"

Reluctantly, he nodded. "Yes." He then thought of his own son, and how his selfish choices had led to Albert's death. "Forgive me, Tory. I rushed to judgement without thinking. This Shadow Man has plagued Elizabeth since childhood. Did Connor leave any hint to its identity?"

"Sadly, no. He said something to my brother that weekend—the one when he died. I was there, too, and Connor was not himself. I don't know if you're aware of this, but Patricia had remained behind at Branham, which surprised us all, for she usually enjoyed Scotland. In fact, if you want to know the truth, I think Connor was ready to leave her."

"Yes, I know."

The elder Stuart's wide lips parted in shock. "You know? How is that possible? We only surmised it based a few hints."

"I found a letter Connor had written to the duchess, dated the day he died. He told Patricia that he planned to speak to a lawyer the very next day, and that he would seek full custody of Elizabeth. He also accused her of having an affair with William Trent."

Tory's face turned to ash. "No!" she cried out, and Charles instantly regretted blurting out such a distressing truth. He poured his aunt a glass of water and handed it to her.

"Drink this, Tory. I should have broken that dark news with a gentler tone. Forgive me."

She gulped down the water, her eyes tearing. "Poor Connor. Oh that poor darling man. I'd no idea that his marriage had deteriorated to that extent, but I suppose I shouldn't be surprised. But you say, she'd already begun seeing Trent? Did he actually *name* the man in this letter?"

"He did. I showed the letter to Uncle James and to Paul. Both recognised the earl's handwriting, but they, too, were shocked."

"Trent," she whispered bitterly. "How I detest that man! I wonder how far back his influence reaches. Patricia was always impressionable and easily led. She never got over her wild infatuation for Ian Stuart. In truth, she was a very unhappy woman."

Charles moved closer to his aunt, placing an arm 'round her shoulders. "Money and position do not guarantee happiness."

"No, they do not," she agreed, sighing. "Patricia and Connor seldom saw eye to eye, but those miscarriages drove them further apart. Charles, you must never tell Elizabeth what I'm about to say, for she likes to think of her parents as loving one another, but I once had an argument with Trish Stuart that may shock you."

"Yes?"

She took a deep breath and stubbed out the newly lit cigarette. "I should quit these dreadful things," she said. "It was after the second miscarriage. I'd gone to stay with Patricia until she recovered, for the loss had taken a great toll on her physically. In fact, Price despaired of her ever conceiving again."

"How awful," Sinclair said softly.

"Yes, it was. Connor remained at Branham for most of my visit. After a month, he spent the days in London, taking the train each morning but returning at night, and it seemed to me that he and Trish began to grow closer. I couldn't have been more wrong. One evening, I found Trish packing her bags."

"To travel?"

"I assumed as much. I thought the two of them had decided to spend time abroad and rekindle their marriage, but instead she was leaving him. Charles, I did my best to dissuade her, but nothing would alter her plans. Nothing. When Connor returned, the two of them had a terrible argument that resounded throughout the house. He left the next morning for India, and Trish unpacked her bags. It had all been a ploy to force him into leaving, you see. She knew his temperament well enough to predict his reaction. Oh, she could be devious when she wanted to be."

"But they reconciled; they must have," he countered. "If she hated Connor so much, why would she agree to take him back?"

"I've always wondered about that as well; but take him back she did, and only a few months later. Connor consulted with his father before agreeing to reconcile, for he'd begun to contemplate divorce even then. Only a short while after, we learnt about the third miscarriage. Connor nearly lost his mind. I had never seen him weep so, Charles. Not ever. Not once. He blamed himself, you see. After that, he remained at Branham and tended to Trish personally, bringing her meals, feeding her, making sure she grew stronger—for she'd nearly died. That Stopes woman had left her in a deplorable state!"

"Tory, if it takes a lifetime, I shall find that woman and make her account for all her misdeeds."

"Good," his aunt said simply. "I'm glad to hear it."

"Do you think Patricia loved Elizabeth?" he asked.

She snapped the cigarette case shut, and Sinclair noticed that her hands shook. "I think Trish loved Beth as much as she could manage. Duke George was a flinty man, and Trish was much like her father. After Elizabeth's birth, Connor remained at home as long as possible, but Redwing emerged, full force, in India during that time, and our circle ranks were thin. When offered the position in the governor's office there, he chose to take it, but that became the death knell of his marriage."

"And the trip to Drummond Castle that November? When he wrote the letter I found?"

"He'd been transferred from India to Austria; a much better posting. Before commencing his new duties in Vienna, Connor was given a few weeks to spend with family, and they planned a holiday in Glasgow. However, when he arrived at Branham, he and Trish had a terrible row, and Connor stormed out of there, taking Beth with him. That night, after Beth went to bed, he told me about the argument, but said nothing regarding plans for divorce."

"Does Elizabeth know about her parents' embattled marriage?" he asked.

"No, she does not; though she may have suspected. Beth is very good at uncovering secrets, so it is possible. When she and Connor arrived that November, Beth clung to her father nearly every minute. It was as if she knew something was going to happen."

"She did, Tory. Elizabeth told me—told us, Paul and me—about the Shadow Man appearing at her window just before that fateful trip. In September of that year, this creature showed Beth a vision of her father's death and even told her when it would occur."

Victoria's face paled. "No! Oh, Charles, I had no idea! No wonder she stuck to his side. Charles, you must keep watch on her. Redwing has been playing a very long and complex game, and it's still unclear just what their final goal is. I suspect this Shadow Man is but one manifestation of a dark and very powerful entity."

His aunt left the sofa and began to pace the room.

"Victoria, is there something you're not saying?"

"Charles, I have a letter that you should read. It was written to me by your father a few months before he died. I haven't got it here with me. It's in Paris, but I shall send for it. My butler can find it and forward it to Haimsbury House."

"I take it the letter is about Redwing."

"It is—but it's also about you. As you may have guessed, Robby Sinclair also chased after Redwing, but once you were born he remained at home. He was convinced that Redwing had set its sights on you, but most in the circle failed to heed his warnings. It was always assumed by the majority of our members that the Stuart blood—Paul's line—had some major part in the final phases of Redwing's plans. In a way, I suppose it does, since Paul is your cousin thrice over."

He shook his head. "Do you mean my grandmother? I'm still sorting through the many branches of our family tree."

"Your grandmother was Robert Stuart's twin sister. Also, the late earl's great-grandmother was a Sinclair by birth. Our three families have intermarried quite often through the years, but occasionally one of us marries outside these circles. The MacAllens are another linked family. Did you know that your father and Connor Stuart were very close friends? They agreed that your part in all this is quite important. It's imperative that you read through all your father's correspondence and diaries, Charles."

He was about to reply when the butler knocked on their door. Sinclair rose to answer, since Tory had turned the lock.

"Yes, Miles?"

"Sir, forgive me for interrupting, but you've a message from Inspector Reid."

Charles took the telegram, reading the few lines with dismay. "Is there a runner awaiting reply, Miles?"

The butler nodded. "There is, sir. Shall I send him in?"

"No need. Please, tell the duchess that I'll see her later this evening. Victoria, I must be going."

"But Charles, won't you at least stay for supper?"

"I fear I may be away for the remainder of the night, Aunt. There's been another murder in Whitechapel."

CHAPTER TWENTY-SIX

The dead room at 76 Leman Street held three separate cots in addition to the primary autopsy table. Sinclair entered, finding Thomas Sunders explaining his findings to Edmund Reid.

"This one's in four pieces," Reid explained. "As you ordered, I've had France enquiring about any bodies washing up along the embankment. This poor woman was found on the south side of the river, in three different locations. I pulled a dozen strings to obtain all four sections of the body. Lambeth and Southwark both laid claim to her."

Charles joined them at the table. "She's been in the water for days from the looks of it. You can see predation marks on her face. I'd feared this might be Ida Ross, but the hair colour's all wrong. Sunders, can river water darken hair?"

"Not in my experience," the surgeon replied. "We've only just started the autopsy. I'll know more when I examine the hair beneath my lens."

"I assume Abberline's already taken a look at this," Sinclair noted. "Does he think her Ripper?"

"No. Even Fred admits this isn't typical of Jack's work. The arms show signs of torture, meaning someone had access to the woman for hours, perhaps longer."

"Any identifying scars or tattoos?"

Sunders directed the superintendent towards the other tables. "The lower limbs lie here, sir, and the arms next to that." The surgeon lifted the waxed cotton sheets. "I believe a hatchet was used to disarticulate the limbs. Oh, and the torso shows an old tattoo upon the lower spine, but there is also a burn mark, just above it. I'd say the latter was done no more than a day or so before she died."

"More signs of torture," Sinclair said bitterly. Sunders turned the torso over to show the two detectives the marks. "That tattoo is Redwing's sign, Edmund. But this burn looks like a branding iron was used. Multiple times. Again, the same winged dove. Is this woman a Redwing traitor?" Charles paled, even as the words left his lips. "Oh, Edmund, I may know who this woman is, and if I'm right, the earl will be very upset."

"Upset by the death of a Redwing operative?"

"Upset by the death of a woman he tried to help. I think this is Susanna Morgan."

Elizabeth entered the drawing room shortly after six, having finished with her rehearsals and taken off her gown. She'd hoped to find Sinclair, and her countenance fell when she saw he had already gone.

"I thought Charles might still be here," she said, sitting in a chair opposite her aunt. "Has he already returned to Haimsbury House?"

"Yes," Victoria lied. "He had business to finish with his contractors. Something about the lift. I take it your rehearsals went well?"

"Della turns beautifully," the duchess answered. "She's a lovely girl. She asked if she could live with us after the wedding. Are you going to live here? We'd love for you to join our new household, Tory."

Charles had been gone for over an hour, but as it was likely he would be away most of the evening, Victoria looked for means to distract her niece. "I'm not yet sure. Even a large house can feel crowded to a newlywed couple. Did Dr. Emerson call on you today?"

"Briefly. He's quite nice, though I shall miss dear Dr. Price." A shadow passed against the lights of the portico, and the duchess crossed to the large window; looking out. "There's a strange coach in the drive."

"Probably someone delivering another gift," Victoria answered, searching through her handbag. "I've misplaced my spectacles."

"Ring for Miles, Tory. I'm sure he'd be happy to send a maid to fetch them. Are they in your apartment?"

"I've no idea. I won't be long," she said, leaving the room. "Shall I send Della down?"

"Yes, please. I think she'd spend the entire night wearing that new dress, but remind her that is has to remain clean for the wedding. Ask her to come down and play for me, would you?"

"I shan't be long," Tory promised as she headed into the foyer. She passed the butler near the foot of the stairs and mentioned the coach. "Do you mind sending a footman out to see who it might be? No one's bothered to knock yet."

"Of course, Lady Victoria," Miles answered. As he started towards the front door, he noticed it closing. "It looks as though someone has already done so, my lady. Perhaps, Stephens answered."

"No, I think Stephens said he would be at the other house this evening," she said, a dreadful thought suddenly crossing her mind. "Oh, no! I do hope my niece hasn't gone out there!"

The butler still wore a sling upon his left arm whilst his shoulder healed, but he moved quickly towards the door. "I'll see to it, Lady Victoria."

Victoria Stuart followed quickly behind, praying the caller was a friend. "It might be Maisie Churchill. She said something about dropping by with a box of letters."

The butler had reached the door, opened it, and stood within its frame, looking out onto the portico. The lights of the south entry silhouetted his tall form, and beyond, Stuart could see a large black coach, parked upon the gravel drive. A double-headed eagle was painted upon the door. It was the Russian Empire's crest.

"Good heavens!" she gasped, rushing towards the butler. "Tell the duchess to come inside at once, Miles!"

"My lady!" the butler called. "Your aunt asks you to return."

Beth started to reply, but Prince Anatole had already emerged from the coach, and he took her hand, bowing gracefully.

"Good evening, my dear friend. Forgive any presumption, but I wonder if you might join me for supper?"

Victoria stepped onto the portico and called out, doing her best to sound calm. "Your Highness, what a lovely surprise! Won't you come in?" she said, her hand on Elizabeth's forearm. "My nephew will return any moment, and I'm sure he'd be pleased to see you again."

Romanov smiled, his ice blue eyes sparkling in the light of the porch lamps. "Which nephew would that be, Lady Victoria?"

"Why, you may take your pick, Your Highness. Both are staying here as we prepare for the wedding. Won't you come in?"

"I'd hoped to entice your niece into sharing supper with me, as my opportunities to woo her soon end. Do you mind?"

"That depends on Elizabeth," Tory answered with a dry throat. "Beth, surely, you'd prefer to wait for Charles to return."

The duchess appeared confused. "What?"

"Do forgive us, Your Highness. My niece has been ill of late, and the night air might cause a chill."

"Then, she may find warmth inside my coach. Here, my dear, take my hand."

Beth stared at the carriage, turning to the prince with a puzzled expression. "I—supper?" she asked. "No, I think Charles will be back soon."

"Elizabeth, I would cherish a few moments with you," Romanov whispered into her ear as he stroked her hand. "Will you allow it?"

As though sleepwalking, she obediently followed him into the brougham.

Victoria stamped her foot and ran back into the house. "Miles! Send word to my brother at once!"

Inside the coach, Elizabeth listened as the prince spoke in soft tones. "Elizaveta, my darling, I could not risk a telegram, nor would I dare force my way into your home through magical means. My darling, you are in danger."

"I am in danger? Why?" she asked mechanically.

"Oh, my beautiful Elizaveta!" he whispered in the sweetest of tones. "I would remove all hurt, all dangers from your life, but I cannot see the future with perfect eyes. All the rivers of possibility flow towards rapids that indicate falling, but no matter how I try, your future remains in mist. I want only your safety—your happiness. You do know that, do you not?"

"Yes," she whispered as if in a waking dream.

"And I would spare you all that will soon happen, but no matter how I try, no matter what variables I employ, a great danger still finds you. Do you trust me?" She said nothing, and he noticed she had begun to shiver. The prince kissed her forehead. "I love you, Elizaveta."

Nothing. No response.

"Veta, when you were but a child, I vowed to protect you. Always. In doing so—that night on the road to London—I appeared in my true form, and I know that it frightened you. I am sorry for that, but it was the only way I could stop Trent and the Shadow from harming you that night."

"I'm cold," she whispered.

"Soon, you will be warm. You must tell Charles that Trent intends to harm you again. Can you remember that for me?"

She nodded, but her eyes widened in terror. "Trent? No, please! Not Trent!"

He placed his arms 'round her shoulders and kissed her cheek. "I will not permit him to harm you, Veta. Now, look at me." He took her chin into his hand and pulled her face up, towards his. "I know that you are afraid, but I will keep watch over you. Trust me. And, my dear, you must take care. Another life depends upon you."

Elizabeth stared. "Captain," she whispered, trying to break free of the spell.

"Your Captain is coming home to you. Be good for him, Veta. Now, I shall take you back inside. When you awaken, you will remember what I showed you near the stables. The red snow. Say it."

"I will remember the red snow," she whispered.

"Tell Victoria that you have a headache and must lie down. And remember to tell Charles that Trent plans to harm you. Will you do this?"

She nodded as if dreaming. "Tell Charles. He is my Captain. My great love." She blinked, the powerful image of Sinclair tearing at the dense veil. "Charles," she repeated.

"Yes, Charles is your great love. Now, you must lie down." He helped her out of the coach and up the portico steps. Elizabeth felt the wind in her ears and hair. *Have I even been inside a carriage?* she wondered.

Victoria was just coming out again, to meet one of the Branham coaches, intent on going to Whitechapel herself to find Sinclair, but found Elizabeth waiting instead, leaning heavily upon the prince's arm.

"The duchess is ill. She mentioned a headache coming on," he said, carrying her into the drawing room. "Here, allow me to leave you on this comfortable looking sofa. Your aunt will tend to you. Lady Victoria, shall I fetch a doctor?" he asked, genuine concern written across his handsome features.

Tory shook her head. "No, Your Highness, that isn't necessary. Thank you for taking care of Elizabeth. This wedding and all the plans have proven stressful. You are kind to offer, but we'll take care of her now. Charles is due back any moment."

He bowed. "It is nothing. I hope the duchess is well enough to attend tomorrow evening. The Duke of Edinburgh is most anxious to meet Lord Haimsbury. If there is anything I might do, please let me know. Forgive my intrusion."

He bowed again and left, anguish filling his heart. Perhaps, he should not have come, but the visions he'd seen of fire and snow caused Samael to dread Sunday's arrival. No matter what rivers of time he examined, the future always led to the same dark conclusion.

As the coach pulled away, a second spirit being, clad in human flesh, materialised on the seat opposite.

"Your interference begins to annoy me, Brother," Raziel Grigor told him. "Why is she so important to you? If you love her, take her!"

"I do not use human women in such a way."

"Pity. I'm sure she'd be worth it. Have you no desires, Sama? Do Eve's daughters not entice? What visions did you mean, when you spoke to the duchess? Why do you mention snow?"

"Your many sins have corrupted your ability to foresee, haven't they, Raza?" Romanov asked. "You are blind as well as toothless."

The Watcher began to laugh. "Do the fools on Redwing's round table realise that you sit amongst them as a spy? I suspect not. No, no, do not fear, Brother. I've no plans to turn informer on one of my own, despite your treachery."

"Would you have preferred that I kill you, Raza?" Anatole asked the other. "Surely, five thousand years imprisonment is preferable to death."

"Five millennia all alone, unable see my brethren? My children died whilst I slept, Sama! Your regrets do nothing to assuage my anger! Perhaps, I should do to you what you did unto me! Force you to watch those you love suffer and die!"

The Watcher known as Anatole Romanov lifted his cane, causing the sigils carved upon it to glow red. "Try it, Raza, and you will hear me speak these names. Is that what you want? To die at last?"

Raziel Grigor shouted curses in ancient Sumerian, causing the coach's interior to brighten as if fire consumed it. In seconds, he'd vanished, leaving Romanov alone. Brushing sparks from his coat, Samael gazed out the window into the night. He closed his eyes, communing with others of his kind.

A voice spoke inside his mind. A summons.

"I hear and obey," he said, and the entire coach and team vanished from the material world.

It was after nine before Charles returned to Queen Anne House, and Elizabeth still slept on the drawing room sofa where the prince had laid her three hours earlier. The earl arrived with his cousin, having receiving a telegram from Reid. Aubrey appeared distraught and unsettled as the two men entered the mansion, but his aunt failed to notice.

Victoria met them in the foyer, her manner uncharacteristically scattered. Without explanation, she immediately pulled her two nephews into the library, shutting the door behind her.

"Elizabeth is sleeping, but there is much to tell you. The prince was here. Anatole. I've no idea what he said to her, but it struck her hard. She's been asleep ever since."

"Tory, what do you mean?" the detective asked.

"He claimed he'd come to invite her to sup with him this evening, but I insisted she remain home," Victoria answered, pacing about the room.

"I'm sure that went over well," Aubrey said, opening the library doors and motioning to the butler. "Miles, would you bring us a decanter of our uncle's Scotch? Tory, will you join us?"

"No, none for me. I need to keep my head."

"Bring three glasses, Miles, just in case our aunt changes her mind," Aubrey finished. The butler left to follow orders, and Charles looked in quickly on Beth. She slept peacefully, and he had no wish to waken her, so he returned to the library, where his aunt and cousin sat near the fire. "I'll carry her up in a little while. It's been a very long day. I'm afraid the murder Reid called me to investigate is connected to Redwing."

"Is it this Ripper fiend again?" Tory asked as she fiddled with her cigarette case.

"Not directly, no. She's a woman who recently defected from the enemy's ranks. Susanna Morgan."

"I should have taken her to my home," Paul muttered, wiping at his face wearily. "Instead, I left her at a public place."

"You did your best to help her," Sinclair argued. "It isn't your fault that Morgan chose to leave the shelter of the Carlton. Your own operative told you as much. He tried to stop her, but she refused to listen. At least, now, she's out of their reach."

"I just pray she sought the Lord's forgiveness before they tortured her," he whispered. "Why would they do that, Charles? Do you think they sought information, or was it mere spite?"

"We'll never know."

The butler entered, carrying the whisky decanter and glasses.

"A large for me," the earl said dismally. "What a hellish day."

Charles held up his hand. "Nothing for me, Miles. Thank you. Why would Anatole stop by here on the pretense of taking Beth to supper?"

Victoria's hands shook as she tried to light the smoke. Sinclair did it for her. "Thank you, Charles. Perhaps, I will have a small whisky," she said, her voice cracking. "Anatole Romanov is a mystery to me. I consider myself a fine judge of character, but his manner is inscrutable! I cannot tell if he is genuine or merely a consummate actor. It's why I tried to stop her from entering the carriage, but she simply refused to listen!"

"She sat with him inside his coach? For how long? Do you think he may have harmed her? What did he say to her?" Charles asked, taking to his feet.

"Calm down, Charles," Aubrey cautioned. "She's fine. You said so yourself."

Tory took a long drink of the whisky. "I've no idea what he said, but when he carried her inside, she looked ill. In fact, she'd fainted."

Without another word, Sinclair bolted for the door, fearful now regarding his love's condition, but Aubrey held him back. "Listen to the rest of our aunt's story before you run back in there, Charles. Go on, Tory."

Their aunt tried to put the cigarette into her mouth, but her hands refused to work. "Dash it all! I have not felt so helpless in a long, long time! Truly, I have not!" She threw the cigarette into the fire. "I sent word to your uncle, and he's assigned one his agents to keep watch on the Langham, where the prince often stays, but is it enough? Charles, did I hear you say that you've hired someone to act as her bodyguard? Do tell me I am not mistaken in that."

"I've hired an excellent man, Tory. An inspector friend of mine. Arthur France. He and his family are moving into Haimsbury House tomorrow, in fact. He's probably packing up as we speak. Tory, you did all you could."

"Did I? If so, then why do I feel like such a failure? He might have driven off with her, and then what? It's all my fault for trusting him in the first place!"

Charles walked over to her, taking the whisky glass and placing it on a small table. "Come here," he said, drawing her into his strong arms. To the shock of both men, Victoria Stuart began to weep, burying her head in Charles's shoulder.

"Charles, I am so sorry! I should have been more careful. More clever! You place your trust in me, and I simply fall apart. What a stupid woman I am!"

Sinclair held her close, looking at his cousin overtop Victoria's left shoulder. Aubrey had never seen his aunt cry, and he had no idea what to do.

"Paul, would you mind checking on Elizabeth for me?" the detective asked.

Feeling utterly useless, the earl nodded and left the room.

Charles wiped his aunt's tears and kissed her cheek. "Beth is independent and headstrong, and she sometimes makes choices that are counterproductive if not dangerous, but she is unharmed."

The elder Stuart lowered her eyes, her posture stiff as she continued to weep.

"Look at me now, Aunt," he said, lifting her chin. "Remember, you promised to be a mother to me? Well, as your son, I tell you that you are an incredible parent. You are bright, energetic, and wise; but most of all, you selflessly serve those whom you love. Since the moment she was born, you've been more of a mother to Elizabeth than the woman who bore her. And you have shared that same selfless devotion with me. I've come to love you dearly, Aunt. I hope you know that. And I trust you with my darling Beth and with our unborn child. Victoria Stuart, you are the most remarkable woman I know outside of Elizabeth, but most of her personality was formed by you. Believe me when I tell you, that *no one* could have done more."

After taking a deep breath, she wiped her eyes and kissed his hand. "Thank you, Charles. Thank you! You are so like your father. He would have done that. Forgive me for being so very useless, but when I saw Romanov carry her in, all I could think of was that he'd done something to her. Then, when I realised she was all right, I began to think of all the things that could have happened. Charles, my dear, you carry a heavy burden, but you do so with great compassion and quiet strength. During the four years that I kept watch over Beth in Paris, she seldom met with danger. I think Redwing was waiting—for you perhaps. For this year. Oh, don't listen to me! I'm prattling on and on as if I've lost all reason. But thank you, Nephew. Thank you very much."

The earl returned, quietly shutting the doors. "She asked for you, Charles. Oh, and Mrs. Smith's prepared us a late supper."

"I'm sorry your friend was killed," Victoria told her nephew. "Women are pawns to Redwing. I suppose her usefulness was at an end."

Charles stood. "I'll take Beth up, and then I plan to enjoy my last night here as a single man. Paul, are you up for a game of chess after we eat?"

"If you're prepared to lose."

"You do know that I was Cambridge champion three years' running?" Sinclair asked as he left the library.

Victoria opened the cigarette case, but quickly snapped it shut again. "I shall quit these wretched things. Are you all right, Paul?"

"Yes, I suppose so. I only wish I'd done more to protect Morgan. That's all."

"You look quite tired, my dear," she said, reaching for his hand.

"I'm weary to the bone, Aunt. Since Elizabeth returned in late September, the enemy has been relentless. They nip at our heels, and send us running like frightened sheep. If I did not trust in Jesus Christ for comfort and strength—if I did not believe that He is still in control of this world—all of this would surely drive me mad. Look, it's up to us to keep Charles and Elizabeth well and unharmed. He is as much a target as Beth."

"Yes, I know it. Your cousin seldom thinks of himself, I've noticed. Another way that he is like you. I've a strong sense that we've not seen the worst." She sighed. "But let's leave off worrying for tonight. Shall we go to the dining hall?"

Aubrey kissed her cheek. "I dearly love you, Victoria."

She kissed him in return. "Yes, and I love you as well."

"Even if I lose a game to my cousin?"

"Even then," she answered, smiling.

Supper finished at ten, and Charles sat with the earl, enjoying a brandy before a cheerful blaze. "It's beginning to look like snow," he said. "I've installed two boilers at Haimsbury House and radiators in the main apartments. It makes for a more even heat, I'm told. Beth's room here is always cold, even with the windows shut."

"I've noticed that, as well, but Connor's old room remains warm, I wonder why that is," the earl remarked. "Despite the fire's being always lit, I can sometimes see my breath in Beth's chamber. Charles, it occurs to me that this may be more than air temperature."

"What do you mean?" Sinclair asked, pouring himself a cup of strong coffee from the tray of provisions left by Miles.

"Spiritual visitations often leave strange cold spots. As if the apparitions steal all heat from a room."

Charles felt a strange tickle inside his mind at hearing this—a sliver of memory trying to emerge like a harmful splinter from an old wound. "Cold," he muttered. "My nursery was often cold. Freezing cold. Even in summer."

Aubrey sat forward, his face filled with curiosity. "What do you mean? Are you regaining your memory?"

"Perhaps. I'm not sure."

Paul rose and tugged at the bellrope. In a moment, Lester arrived at the door. "Is Mr. Kepelheim about?" asked the earl.

The first footman nodded. "He is, sir. I believe he speaks with Lady Victoria, in her apartment. Shall I fetch him, sir?"

"Yes, if you don't mind—oh, and ask my aunt to join us also. We've something important to discuss."

"Very good, sir."

Paul returned to the fireside. "Charles, I know of no other man better suited to aid you in recovering these memories. Martin has vast experience with the supernatural forces, but he also knew you quite well before your disappearance."

"So, he's said, but Paul I'm not sure these fleeting visions of mine are genuine memory. I really think we should wait, especially with all that's going on right now."

"But that's precisely why we should pursue it! My father once told me that the best way to retrieve information you thought lost is to occupy your mind with something else. Perhaps, that is why you're recovering bits of your old memories now—because of your fears for Beth and the baby. Trust me. Martin will know how to tease these elusive childhood events from your mind. He once helped me to recall incidents I experienced in Austria, when I was held captive there. Oh, I hear him. Never mind. I'll share that adventure with you another time."

The tailor's distinctive voice could be heard speaking softly with Victoria Stuart, and before two ticks of the clock passed, the pair of them stepped through the doorway.

"I hear the chess match went to our marquess," the tailor began in his easy manner. "Here, Tory, sit near the earl. He looks rather glum to me. Lester tells me that we've been summoned. Is the board set for a rematch? If so, Lady Della will wish she'd not gone to bed."

"No rematch. Not tonight, anyway," Aubrey answered, grinning. "Actually, I'd hoped that you might demonstrate your skills, my friend. Charles has begun to remember."

Kepelheim's light eyes rounded. "Is this true? Do you summon up the past?"

"If you're going to begin a session, I'll say goodnight, Martin," Tory told them. "These often stretch on for hours, and I've a great deal to do tomorrow. I'll see you all at breakfast."

"No, dear lady. Stay, won't you?" Kepelheim implored. "I'm sure you're quite weary, but our young marquess requires all his family near him tonight. Would you remain? Please?"

"Very well," she said, returning to her chair. "I'll take one of those brandies, if you're pouring, Paul."

Charles set down the coffee cup, his brows arched high. "Session? Just how long will this take?"

Kepelheim drew his chair close. "It's hard to say. It isn't a formal session, no, and shouldn't be too stressful—at least I pray it is not. I merely want to ask you some questions. There is a new philosophy employed by certain alienists called twilight sleep therapy. Others call it hypnosis after the Greek god *Hypnos*. Now, I shan't be using this precise method, for in truth, I'm not well versed in it, but I shall endeavour to help you relax. And once there, I shall talk. Just talk. Are you willing to try?"

"Yes, I suppose so. Will it hurt?"

"No, not at all, though some memories may bring painful associations. If it looks as if our session might bring too many of those, then we can discontinue it. All right?"

"Yes, all right. So, what do I do?" he asked.

"You need only close your eyes," Kepelheim said. "Paul, could you pour Charles a glass of brandy? Make it a large one." Aubrey poured a full glass of the liquor and handed it to his cousin. Charles started to sip, but the tailor shook his head. "No, my friend, you must gulp it all down at once. A pity with such a lovely vintage, but necessary. It is meant to shock your system."

Sinclair shrugged and tipped back the glass, drinking ten ounces in one large swallow. He wiped his mouth and set down the empty snifter. "Now what?"

"Well, I am impressed," Kepelheim laughed. "You've come a long way since the castle. Your Stuart blood remembers its natural capacity for strong drink, I believe. Now, let's see what your Stuart mind can recover. Lie on this sofa and close your eyes. Breathe normally and listen to my voice, trying to concentrate only on that."

The detective did as instructed, letting his head rest against a plump cushion, eyes shut. He could hear the crackle of the wood fire and the regular ticking of the mantel clock.

"Now, Charles, I am going to begin by telling you a story. I want you to listen, allowing yourself to enter the tale, but if this story gives rise to a memory, then you must interrupt me. Is that clear?"

He nodded. "Yes. It's clear."

"Good. Now, this tale begins in 1859 at Christmas. I was much younger in those days, as you might guess. A slimmer and relatively handsome fellow of twenty-eight. I'd just spent six months in Vienna on behalf of the circle and had come to Carlisle to recuperate from an injury. I'd fallen down a ravine and disturbed the alignment of my spine, and the doctors insisted I do nothing but relax for three months. The Haimsbury family seat, Rose House, is nestled in the quiet of the Eden River Valley, on the bluff of a broad hill overlooking the Vale of Mallerstang, not far from Pendragon Castle. Uther himself is said to have built that old refuge, and it is also said that he and a hundred of his men died there. Locals claim Uther haunts the stones and the well nearby, for Saxons had poisoned that well, and it was this which killed the king. It is a history often told to you by your father, and you even had books on it. That Christmas, it had snowed, leaving a thick blanket of white all along the valley, and as I arrived at your home, your father's men had just installed a magnificent spruce in the main drawing room for the family to decorate."

Sinclair's thoughts drifted into the past, and it was as if he travelled backwards in time on iridescent snowflakes, for as he relaxed, he could hear voices all around, slowly becoming louder and louder, chattering like welcome ghosts, and he fell into a waking dream...

CHAPTER TWENTY-SEVEN

24th December, 1859 – Rose House

"Uncle Marty! Uncle Marty!" the boy shouted, rushing forward to meet the party of winter travellers in the massive foyer. Martin Kepelheim grinned from ear to ear, kneeling as the boy slammed into his arms for a bear hug.

"Charles, my boy, how good it is to see you again! Why, you have grown even taller since I saw you in May. You shall surpass your father soon, I imagine."

The boy's light blue eyes sparkled in the glow of the chandeliers that hung from the lofty ceiling. He was indeed long of limb and far taller than any of his friends, but he smiled readily and had a gentleness of heart seldom seen in one so young. "I shall be very tall," he said in a northern brogue. "So says Auntie Tory."

"And you are very well spoken, also, for a lad of only four years," his friend said as several footmen unloaded luggage from the coach.

"Four-and-a-*half* years," the lad corrected. "Mother will be glad to see you. Are you going to stay for a long time, Uncle Marty?"

"I shall stay until you are quite sick of me," he said with a laugh. Kepelheim took the boy's hand, and the pair of them walked towards a large drawing room, where several footmen had erected a twenty-foot tree. "I see Christmas preparations have begun. Is your father home?"

"He's in the city, but Mother's home. She's going to have a baby. Did you know that, Uncle Marty?"

"Is she?" he teased. "Well, then, it's probably a good thing that I've brought gifts for a newborn Sinclair, isn't it? And I think I've even remembered to bring a few books and toys for a certain young man who likes to look at stars and learn about nature."

Charles Sinclair beamed as he led his friend to a curved leather sofa near the roaring fire. "Father promised me a telescope this year. One he found in Paris when he was there."

"Did he?" Kepelheim asked with a wink. "Well, then, you and I shall be able to examine the stars close up, won't we?"

Victoria Stuart entered, wearing a pair of woolen trousers topped by a crimson riding coat, her dark hair plaited into a thick braid that followed the curve of her back. "Martin, how good to see you!" she greeted the guest, her hands out.

Kepelheim took Stuart's hands, kissing her right. "And a delight to see you again, my dear friend. Is your brother joining us this year?"

"He is. In fact, he should be arriving this evening, if the ice storm holds off. Those forecasts in *The Times* are often wrong, though, aren't they? Robert and Abigail arrived this morning, and Paul's upstairs. He's come down with a cold or something akin to it, though it does little to slow his enthusiasm. It'll be a challenge to keep him in bed. How was Vienna?"

"Long and trying, but I have much to report," Kepelheim answered, casting a quick glance at Charles. "I cannot speak more here, but later, I'll explain. For now, let's enjoy the beauty of this incredible landscape, shall we? How is Angela?"

Tory walked towards a trio of floor to ceiling, arched windows that overlooked the snow-covered valley below. Charles had remained near the tree on the opposite side of the great room; selecting ornaments and candles and handing them to men on ladders, but Victoria kept her voice soft regardless.

"She has suffered from a few odd spells, though Dr. Hendricks thinks it nothing to worry us. Robby seldom leaves the house now, and he's told Palmerston not to expect him in London until well after the start of the year, if then. Angela's due date is only a week away, you know. We're all praying she'll deliver for Christmas."

"But these spells you mention. Are they related to health or to something else?" he whispered.

"Something else, I fear. We'll explain this evening at the meeting. Reggie Whitmore's coming up from London, as is Sir William Galton. Oh, and Duke George sends his regrets. He's dealing with health issues of his own just now. Trish will be here, however, I think. Or at least Connor hopes she'll attend."

"He still keeps faith that she will agree to wed, I take it?"

Tory sighed. "He does, but I wonder if she isn't already looking elsewhere. No, forget I said that, Martin. It is only rumour."

A footman quietly stepped up to the pair, bowing as Victoria turned. "My lady, I'm to tell you and Mr. Kepelheim that Lord Aubrey awaits in the library."

"Ah, well, perhaps Robert has decided to convene a small meeting in advance of this evening's discourse," Martin said. "Please, my good fellow, tell Lord Aubrey that we shall join him in a moment." The circle agent then walked back towards the massive evergreen and tapped the boy on the shoulder. "We're off to speak with your Uncle Robert, Charles. Shan't take long. I hear that your Cousin Paul is ill. Perhaps, he would appreciate a visit."

The boy stood and wiped dust from his hands. "Yes, he's sneezing quite a lot, but Dr. Hendricks says he's not really sick. I'll go see if he's better."

The sensitive child then signalled to his aunt, who bent down, and Charles kissed her cheek. "Love you, Auntie Vic," he said with a great grin.

She kissed his small hand. "Love you, too, Charlie Bob," she replied with a wink. "Tell Paul not to overdo."

The adults left the room, and the youngster watched them leave, whilst his own, much older self wandered the halls of his childhood home, trying to sort through a wealth of mysteries and clues.

In the year 1888, the adult Sinclair's eyes popped open, and he reached out for Martin Kepelheim, his breathing quick.

"I remember!" he gasped. "It was Christmas, and there was a huge spruce tree in the Pendragon room. You gave me a box of Austrian chocolates and two books on astronomy. And father—my father gave me..." he paused, tears running down his cheeks. "Father gave me a hand-crafted German telescope. Uncle Robert was there with Aunt Abigail. I remember them, Martin! I remember how the earl would lift me up and swing me over his head, and my father kept laughing and telling him not to drop me. Mother—oh, Martin. Mother was about to give birth, wasn't she?"

Kepelheim stared, speechless for a moment. He looked to the earl and Victoria. "Perhaps, we should stop for now."

"Why, Martin?" Sinclair asked, anxious to recover more of his memories. "There are so many questions in my mind now that seek answers. Please, don't stop."

The tailor took the detective's hand, his aging eyes filled with worry. "Charles, if you are strong enough to recall these memories, then I encourage doing so, but let us wait until your mind processes these memories first."

Charles shook his head. His mind was alive with a thousand images, and he had no patience to wait. "No, Martin. Whatever method you're using, it's working. Please. My memories have been obscured for a reason, don't you agree?"

"Perhaps," the tailor answered patiently, pouring a glass of water. "Drink this."

Sinclair obeyed. "Then, the memories must contain information Redwing wants buried."

Kepelheim looked at Tory and Aubrey. "Yes, that is likely. Very well, but will you agree to ending the session, if we think you in danger?"

"Danger? What danger lies in memory, Martin?"

"More than you can ever imagine," he muttered.

"What do you mean?" the detective persisted.

Martin sat again, his hands tense. "Consider the implications, my friend. You said that your mother expected a child. Yet, you have no siblings."

Sinclair's mouth opened to speak, but the simple statement suddenly crystallised as his first words emerged. "But... She died," he whispered sadly, as that dark memory returned. "My sister died. Her name was Charlotte Victoria. She died the night she was born. New Year's Eve."

"Yes, Charles. She did. I am so sorry. Do you still wish to continue?"

He wiped at his eyes, dread pulling at his heart. "But my sister was born healthy, Martin. I remember hearing her cries, and the doctor said she was well and strong. But how can that be, if she died? What happened?"

"We never knew. It is a tragic tale, and I confess that it is why I chose to tell you this story, Charles. Not to bring you pain, but to use a time that was both joyful and painful to rouse those indolent memories from their long slumber. Forgive me, my friend. I have worried that you would recall these under circumstances outside our control."

"That's what you meant. In Scotland at my first meeting," Charles whispered. "You said I would begin to remember one day, and that the circle should be ready for it."

"Yes. These memories were stolen from you by design. Redwing must be behind it, but let us use that stratagem against the enemy."

He slumped into the sofa, his breathing coming in anxious pants. "You were there, Tory," he whispered, looking at his aunt with a wan smile. "You called me Charlie Bob."

Victoria's dark eyes filled with tears. "Yes! I did call you that. It seems so long ago now. You were a delightful boy, Charles."

"Then continue with the story, Martin. Help me to recall it all. Please. When I marry Elizabeth, I want to do so as a fully functioning member of this family, and I would know just what truly happened to my mother and father—and perhaps, also, my sister."

Kepelheim took a deep breath, and then returned to the tale...

Rose House – 24ᵗʰ December, 1859

The meeting of the inner circle commenced at eight o'clock that evening, inside the private library. The room had been designed and built by Robby Sinclair's father, Charles Robert Arthur Sinclair I, 9ᵗʰ Marquess of Haimsbury. In the absence of Duke George's attendance, James Stuart, Duke of Drummond, led the meeting. After submitting their praise and petitions to the Lord, he opened the floor to reports. The men and women who gathered 'round the oval table had known one other for many years. Sir William Galton had inherited his position from his father, and his grandfather before him. Galton served in the Palmerston administration, but also in the Foreign Office for ten years, previous to Lord Palmerston's election that June. He was an expert in geopolitics, ancient iconography, Egyptian mythology, Celtic pagan practises, and ciphers.

Beside Galton, sat Lady Victoria Stuart, who'd joined the circle as a twenty-one year old, using her brain but also her beauty to tease information from foreign diplomats. Tory had a knack for insightful examination of a set of seemingly unrelated facts, making her indispensable when trying to interpret the enemy's movements.

Robert Stuart, 11th Earl of Aubrey, sat next to Victoria. The earl's contacts within governments of the world rivalled that of any king or queen, and the circle often jibed that if Redwing truly wanted to install a great ruler upon England's throne, they would have chosen this remarkable descendent of the Stuart monarchy. At forty-six, his black hair had already begun to silver at the temples, but his clear blue eyes were bright, and his mind sharper than any in Redwing's mad membership.

The earl stood, looking at the others at the table: Connor Stuart, able-bodied, quick-witted son to Duke James; Reginald Whitmore, physician to Her Majesty, chemist, and an expert in ancient languages; Edward MacPherson, clergyman, educator, soldier, and expert in spiritual entities and pagan rituals; and the inimitable Martin Kepelheim, musician, astronomer, chemist, linguist and code-breaker; painter, philosopher, poet, and one of the most accomplished field agents the circle had ever trained.

Kepelheim glanced up as Aubrey spoke, his hand raised. "Lord Aubrey, if I may? It will take but a moment, and I believe it relates to what you are about to discuss."

Aubrey smiled. "Forgive me, Martin. I'd forgotten James promised to allow you to open. Your information relates to the American problem?"

"American politics? Is that what you intend to discuss? Well, in truth, this does not connect *directly*, however it will no doubt become an issue if war erupts there."

"I can assure you, Martin, war is inevitable; probably, within the coming year."

Kepelheim sighed. "Ah, well, the group to which I was attached in Vienna will no doubt play a hand in mounting that war, financially at least. They are a fiercely loyal Redwing nest called *Die Herren vom Schwarzen Stein* or Lords of the Black Stone. These serve as the 'hidden hand' behind a more public fellowship of gentlemen philosophers known as The Arcadians. These Arcadians have a London affiliate, but the inner ring of that group calls itself 'The Round Table'."

"The Round Table is already known to us," Aubrey replied bitterly. "If you'll recall, Duke George's traitorous father, Henry, was a member."

"Robert, that is mere speculation," Victoria argued. "We've no proof that Henry attended their meetings, nor that he was Redwing."

"Henry is dead, and debating his loyalties will only divide us," Drummond interrupted. "Martin, this first group in Austria. These so-called 'Lords of the Black Stone'. Did you infiltrate it?"

"Yes, sir, I did. Briefly. Their core doctrine is based partly on Teutonic mythology and partly on Templar mysteries, derived from texts discovered in Damascus during the Crusades."

Victoria glanced at Kepelheim. "This Black Stone they appear to worship. Is it a star?"

"Not exactly," he answered. "It is a stone that fell to earth eons ago and lies, yet undiscovered, somewhere in ancient Assyria. There are numerous theories regarding this stone. Some say it once formed half of the gateway to Eden. Others that it is the stone upon which Jacob's head rested. Still others, that a fallen angel was imprisoned within it before the flood, and that he will emerge and destroy the world of men in the final years before Christ's return. If freed, they say, this creature will summon thirteen brethren, and these will then join together and break the locks of Time, releasing Abaddon and his demonic hoard."

"How can Time be unlocked?" Whitmore asked.

"I cannot say, but the scrolls contain mathematical formulae and symbols that defy interpretation or decipher. I've seen them for myself. They are genuine."

"Martin, if you cannot read them, then how can anyone?" Galton asked.

Drummond put up his hand as a call for calm, for many at the table began to whisper to one another, each questioning the information. "It matters not if we believe in such a possibility. What matters, my friends, is that Redwing believes it. Go on, Martin."

"Thank you, sir," Kepelheim said softly, handing a thick folder to the duke. "This contains detailed information of what I uncovered. The Arcadians have amassed a large and faithful following. These men think themselves nothing more than a fellowship of philosophers and scientists. They've no idea that their leaders meet in secret and employ necromancy and blood rites to summon up spirit guides. Some within their ranks are more than human, by all accounts; altered through ritual magic. But others are devils in disguise.

"These men believe that we are moving into a new, golden age, which will commence within the next one hundred years. I managed to decipher two of their sacred texts, and I've included copies in this report. Their complex calculations predict a great upheaval of the world systems through war and economic collapse. These shakings are viewed as a chaos engine that will drive us out of an 'age of sin', which they call the *Kali Yuga*, and into an age of enlightenment and prosperity. War is ever on their minds and upon their lips. Many have already begun to invest in America, for most see that nation's current, political division as an opportunity to stoke the fires of this chaos machine."

The duke looked at the young Marquess of Haimsbury. Both he and Connor Stuart now scribbled notes on sheets of paper, whispering to each other. "Robby? Is there something you and my son would like to contribute?"

Robert Sinclair stood, bowing slightly to his elder respectfully. "Forgive me, sir, but yes. Connor and I've been working on a project for some months, and Martin's information regarding the timing of this new age fits with what we've surmised."

"And that is?" asked Lord Aubrey.

"It is simply this: Our Lord told us to expect a series of wars in the final years before his return. Europe has certainly had her share, beginning with Napoleon, whom many in the circle thought to be a type of AntiChrist, if not that devil himself. Russia emerges as a challenger to the Ottoman Empire, but Germany and Austria show no sign of relinquishing their chokehold on the economies of Europe. It seems to me—to us," he added, looking to Lord Kesson, "that civil war in America is inevitable, but that this will only strengthen that nation as they move into the next century. We have examined all the geopolitical possibilities that follow a civil war there, and we believe it a domino whose fall will lead to a war for Turkey's empire. This will culminate in a world at war, beginning as early as 1900, but certainly in the first two decades of the next century. If Redwing wishes to place a male of the right age upon the English throne and inhabit him as part of this chaos engine Martin mentioned, then that son *must* be born before the turn of the century."

Aubrey's face paled as the implications of the theory hit home. "If England is to accept this son as king, then he'll have to become wildly popular, else the citizens would never allow it. And he would need to be old enough. At least ten or twelve, I'd say. That means he must born in the 1880s or early '90s. Is that your opinion?"

"That is exactly what we believe, Uncle Robert. And Connor and I also believe that Redwing intends to use Charles to father that child."

"Charles? Why Charles?" the duke asked.

"Because he descends from the Stuarts and the elder twin. But, sir, our research proves that Redwing and all its associated groups such as The Arcadians and the Lords of the Black Stone, have conducted rituals for centuries to produce a purified blood for their endgame. It is the Sinclair blood, sir. As you know, my father was convinced of this, and everything I find confirms it. If Connor and I are right, then Redwing requires a daughter born of the younger twin's line—in fact, a daughter born from both lines would be preferable, as it would strengthen the blood tie."

"And my son?" Aubrey asked. "How does Paul feature in your calculations?"

"We're not sure, but perhaps your great-grandmother's bloodline provides a clue."

"My great-grandmother was adopted, Robby. You know that. How can we know what her bloodline was?"

Martin stood once more. "As Keeper of the Lines, I believe I can provide a provisional answer to that question, my lord. Henrietta Stuart was indeed adopted by the MacAllen family before marrying your great-grandfather, but my investigations last year led me to the Sinclairs as her true forebears; in fact, to a very important Sinclair. Your great-great-grandfather, Lord Haimsbury," he told the young marquess. "And you already know his loyalties."

Robby Sinclair nodded slowly, and his friend Connor Stuart touched his friend's forearm compassionately. "Robby, lad," the earl spoke softly, "we canno' choose our parentage, but we can rise above it. You're a man ta' make your honourable forebears proud. One twist in the tree does not mean that all branches bend."

"I know," Sinclair whispered.

"How is Henrietta related?" Aubrey asked.

"She is listed in an old church record as the seventh marquess's daughter, through a liaison with a young woman named Louise Spaulding. The girl worked at Rose House in the kitchens. When the already married marquess learnt of her pregnancy, he sent her to

371

a convent, which he regularly endowed. The Sinclairs have a long Catholic history, and a few continued to practise the rituals, right up through the 1780s, when the family cut all ties with the Catholics. Poor Louise died giving birth amongst this Carmelite Sisterhood. The prioress, Mother Marie Therese duBois named the baby Henrietta Charlotte Marie Sinclair, and placed her with the MacAllens. I made copies of the documents I uncovered at the convent, which included several letters to Louise from Sinclair."

The earl walked to the young marquess and placed a comforting hand on Haimsbury's shoulder. "Some might claim that your ancestor acted with compassion, for he made certain of the child's welfare, but it stings, regardless. I know. We always want to think the best of our kin. But this means your family and mine are tied even closer together, Robby, which makes me very happy. In addition to our many other blood ties, we also both descend from the seventh marquess, making your son and mine cousins many times over."

Sinclair glanced up, smiling. "You're right. I must choose to see the positives in this."

The earl returned to his seat. "Martin, this group in Austria. Do they also foresee a need for a world king soon?"

"They do. I'm convinced that Lord Kesson and Lord Haimsbury are right, and their conclusions have terrifying implications. Lord Haimsbury, you must begin safeguarding your son at once. I believe Charles is the key to all of Redwing's dark plans. They have been controlling the bloodlines of your families for centuries; in an effort to produce one perfect human child. He is called the King to Come, the Flesh of Fire, but most often, this perfected child is known as Arthur Reborn, the King amongst the Dead."

As the meeting continued, the members argued over Kepelheim's report, discussing possible directions and plans they must now follow.

Unbeknownst to the circle members, their speeches, plans, and arguments were overheard; for hiding behind a tall shelf in the corner of the library, a small boy listened, his sea-blue eyes growing wider with each startling revelation, wondering just who this Redwing group was and why they wanted *his blood*.

Twenty-nine years later, Charles Sinclair opened his eyes, and it all made sense. "I heard it all, Martin," he told the tailor. "Your meeting that night at Rose House. I overheard it."

Kepelheim's mouth opened in shock. "What did you overhear? And how? That room was soundproofed. Nothing reached beyond its doors."

"Yes, but I'd gone to the library to find a book I might read to Paul. Father had arranged a shelf I could reach and filled it with simpler books on science and mathematics. But also poetry and fiction. There was a book in German—a fairy tale—that I planned to read to him. He'd been consigned to bed because of a fever, so I thought I might cheer him up."

The tailor smiled proudly. "Is that so? You always had such a remarkable mind! At four-and-a-half, you not only comprehended English at the level of a ten-year-old, but you also spoke and even read a little French, German, and Italian. Your mother and Victoria used to work with you, as did your governess."

Martin reached for the brandy decanter and poured two glasses, handing one to Sinclair. "Continue. You were hiding in the library as we discussed these matters. Charles, didn't that terrify you? We as much as said that Redwing intended to make you its pawn!"

He nodded, his face remarkably calm. "I overheard all of it. I remember, Martin. And I'm beginning to remember other things, as well. My father was convinced that I formed the heart of Redwing's plans, and he told me so. He and Connor took me aside at Branham the following spring whilst we visited. They warned me that I must report to them at once, if I noticed anything strange, or believed myself followed or watched. Connor kept close to me during that visit. I hadn't realised it at the time, but he was acting as my bodyguard."

Kepelheim sighed. "Yes, he was. Connor Stuart feared for you—as did your father. In fact, Connor later asked the circle to hide you away somewhere, but before we could agree as to how to accomplish that, your father was killed, and you were taken. It was a hellish time, but the Lord worked it all together for His purposes, didn't he? He brought you back to us. And now, you're engaged to the daughter of both twins."

"And we have a child on the way," Sinclair added, sitting up. "Is this the son Redwing has been looking for? Planning for?"

Victoria had been uncharacteristically quiet during the entire session, but she now stood and drew a shawl about her shoulders. "It is an unborn child who knows nothing about his or her blood and only wants to be loved. Let us leave off all this talk of bloodlines and Redwing for now, shall we? It's late. Charles, you should get some rest. Tomorrow will be a long day. If Beth is awake, let her know that we all love her. Did she say anything more about Romanov's visit?"

"Only that he asked her to supper. Her memory of it is unclear, and I had no wish to push her on it. She'd fallen asleep by the time I came back down."

"Good. I like the idea that all this is the Lord's work, Martin. Too often, we dwell on Redwing's plans, but our Saviour also has plans, so it is in those I place my trust. Goodnight, Charles. I'm very glad you now stay with Beth inside her bedroom. At first, I'd thought it highly irregular, but it occurs to me that you're probably already joined as husband and wife in the Lord's eyes, so hang convention. Just don't tell my brother that I said that. He thinks me a prude, you know."

Sinclair smiled and kissed her cheek. "Thank you, Tory. Goodnight, Paul. Martin, thank you for helping me recover my past."

He left them both and climbed the staircase to Beth's apartment, passing through the parlour and into the bedchamber, where he found all three dogs, Samson, Bella, and Briar, lying upon the broad bed, as if the trio had signed a pact to protect the duchess whilst she slept. This canine fellowship formed a ring around the duchess, who breathed rhythmically, softly, peacefully; a Bible in her hands. The three dogs glanced up briefly as Sinclair approached, deeming him 'friend' and quickly returning to their dreams. Smiling, Charles checked the window locks, then sat beside her, gently touching the velvet quilt where it curved over her abdomen.

"Goodnight," he whispered to his unborn child. "May our Lord bring you rest as you grow. I love you—both of you."

"Charles?" she whispered, turning slightly towards him.

"I'm here, little one," he told her, kissing Beth's soft cheek as he held her hand. "And I shall never leave your side. Not ever again."

CHAPTER TWENTY-EIGHT

Saturday, 17ᵗʰ November

Charles arose at eight and ate a leisurely breakfast with Elizabeth, who then left for her grandfather's house, along with Victoria and Paul. The three of them had plans to make, Beth told her fiancé, and last minute shopping to accomplish before that night's costume ball.

Realising he had the day to himself, the marquess dressed and decided to look in at Scotland Yard, where he intended to finalise the last of his unfiled paperwork before meeting with Laurence regarding his costume. However, an unexpected visit from Commissioner Monro and a subsequent celebration delayed him by nearly an hour.

"Tomorrow's the big day," the amiable police commissioner said as he shook Sinclair's hand. "I'd not expected you in today, Charles. Last day as a free man, and all that."

"I prefer to think of it as my last day as a lonely man, sir. Is there something you wished to discuss? Commissioners don't generally stop by this floor without a purpose."

Monro laughed, his full cheeks rounding into fleshy apples. "Sit, Charles, sit. I confess to ulterior motives. I'd asked your commissionaire, Mr. Barton, to bring word to my office should he see you in the building. I'd like to speak to you about this resignation. In fact, I believe I can change your mind."

Sinclair returned to his desk chair, sitting opposite his superior. "Not a chance of it, sir. I prefer this new opportunity with the duke and my cousin."

"The ICI, you mean," Monro answered. "Word of it's spreading throughout Whitehall like wildfire. Lots of whispers and conjecture. Inner Circle Intelligence. Has a nice ring to it."

"You're familiar with the circle, sir?"

"Quite," the commissioner answered. "The duke can tell you of our adventures in India, years ago. Long tale, really." He glanced about the room, as if measuring it. "This office is rather small, don't you think?"

"Perhaps. I rarely spend time here, sir," Sinclair answered, trying to discern the man's true purpose.

"So I gather. You prefer acting, rather than observing. Pencil-pushing must be a chore for a man like you."

"It isn't my favourite part of the job."

"Look, I don't want to lose you, Charles, and neither does the Home Secretary. We've spoken at length with the Prime Minister, and the three of us have come up with an idea that might just entice you to remain with the force. In a new position, of course."

"Forgive the impertinence, but I can think of no promotion that could accomplish that."

"But this is no ordinary promotion," Monro argued. "Sir Robert Morehouse served as liaison 'twixt the Met and government, but we'd like to expand that position. Give it a cabinet seat."

Charles stared, wondering if he'd heard correctly. "Did you just say cabinet seat, Commissioner? How is that possible?"

"It would be an adjunct position, of course. If truth be told, Salisbury intends to offer you a role with the cabinet regardless. You'll be head of this ICI, I take it?"

"I'll be Director-General, yes."

"DG of the ICI. Another nice ring, and the sort of thing these civil servant types like. But being in that position will allow you to observe crime throughout the kingdom."

"That's the idea. Of course, the inner circle has always kept watch on criminal elements in England, so our core activities will not alter," Sinclair explained.

"Lord Aubrey and his many agents have delivered a wealth of intelligence over the years," Monro replied. "He's kept Salisbury out of many a foreign pickle. That's what you can do for *us*, Charles. Warn the police whenever Redwing—or other criminal elements—might engage in crimes like Ripper."

Sinclair stared. "Are you naming Redwing as Ripper, sir?"

"Perhaps. I met with Duke James yesterday, and he implied that very thing. Your uncle and I go back a long way, Charles. I spoke with him about this offer, and he thought you might be interested. You may speak plainly. Are you interested?"

Charles had no idea just how to respond. He'd promised Elizabeth that he'd work from home after the wedding. How would this new position affect that promise?

"I'd like to speak with my family first, Commissioner. This explains the telegram from Lord Salisbury that arrived yesterday. He asked to speak to me after the wedding."

Monro stood. "I hope you'll think long and hard on this, son. I understand that the ICI is warranted as an independent organisation, but your counsel will enable government to make informed decisions. Besides, it would have made your father proud. He always said you'd be important in England's highest tiers one day."

"I promise to give it full and proper consideration, sir."

Shaking his officer's hand, the commissioner smiled. "Do that, but make sure the answer is yes. See you at the wedding tomorrow."

Monro left, and Sinclair sat once more, bowing his head to pray. "Lord, if this is a temptation from Redwing—some part of their master plan—please, help me to discern it. But if it's from you, then help me to see it as your door, opening. I've no wish to be anything more than Elizabeth's husband, but I am willing to do whatever you ask of me."

A hand knocked, and the detective's head lifted. "Yes?" he asked, wiping his eyes.

"A few of us were hoping to visit with you, Superintendent," Haskell said, grinning. "If you can spare the time, that is. Come with me. Third floor lounge."

Moments later, Sinclair entered a parlour filled with men in blue uniforms, laughing amongst others in street dress. The fellowship of policemen and detectives pulled their comrade into the room, and soon every hand reached out to shake his; each man offering to buy Sinclair a drink. By the time he left Whitehall, he could hear the tower chimes ringing out half past two. Charles hailed a hansom and headed for Queen Anne House.

Arriving inside the grand home, he handed his hat to Miles and asked after Elizabeth.

"The duchess and Lady Victoria have not yet returned, sir," the butler answered. "They sent a message about an hour ago, stating their intent to have luncheon at a tea room on Regent Street. Shall I ask Mrs. Smith to prepare something for you, sir?"

"No, I'll eat later, if that suits our cook. Nothing fancy. I imagine we'll have sandwiches and all that at the ball tonight. What time are we to leave, Miles? Do you know?"

"The prince is sending a coach for you and the duchess, which arrives at half past eight, sir. You've plenty of time before then. Mr. Laurence asked if you might stop by Haimsbury House today, if you've a moment. I believe there are questions regarding the lift."

"Yes, I imagine that will work. In fact, I'm to stay there tonight. My aunt insists that anything else would be bad luck. Very well, Miles. It's a sunny day. I'll walk."

"The sun does shine, my lord, but signs point to snow. I'll fetch your warm overcoat, sir."

Bundled into the woolen Chesterfield, Charles crossed through the stately gardens of Queen Anne Park, heading for the stone gate that marked the entrance to his own estate. As he reached the gazebo on the other side, a voice called out from within.

"It looks like snow."

Charles stopped, surprised to find a tall man with dark hair sitting at an ash table. No one had been there a moment before. "So I hear," he said politely, walking up the steps to the gazebo's interior. "I don't believe we've met. May I ask your name?"

The man smiled broadly. "You don't recognise me? How sad. But I'm sure you'll remember eventually, Charles. Remembering is something at which you've grown quite proficient, is it not?"

Ignoring the man's reference to what had happened the previous night, Sinclair persisted. "Your name?"

"You are a typical policeman. All questions, few answers. I'd tell you my name, but they can be misleading. I suppose, it depends on which language one speaks. English. German. Romanian. Russian. French. Hebrew. Akkadian, Sumerian. Of course, all language descends from the original tongue, does it not? That ancient, primordial gloss, which is no longer heard—not here on Earth, at least. Sit, Charles. I would speak to you."

Sinclair remained standing, his blue eyes narrow. "Despite your word games, I've yet to hear your name. English will suffice. I shall be forced to call for security, if you cannot comply with such a simple request."

"Will you lock me up inside your cells? Your police tactics fail with my kind. I suppose that's partly my fault, but look how well it's worked out for you. You've certainly grown into a grand man, Charles. No wonder she finds you so attractive."

Charles thought about drawing his service weapon, but he doubted the creature would succumb to bullets. "You speak in riddles. I presume you are a Watcher?"

The man smiled again, his eyes glittering like a snake's. "Very good. You have come a long way in a short space of time. The inner circle rats told you about our kind, I imagine. Yes, I am one who keeps watch. There are many of us, keeping track of human events of all types. Marriages in this place and that one. Deaths. Births. This man, this woman. This *child*."

"Child?" he pressed, still standing. "Which child might that be?"

"Boy or girl, lad or lassie. It is not yet known. Our vision into the future is limited—a consequence of humanity's free will choices, I fear. The Almighty One cheats, if you ask me. Surely, if we engaged in a fair fight, then he would not intentionally limit us. But then our limitations are minor compared to your own."

The man stood, and Charles saw that he was nearly seven feet in height. "Keep her in your sight at all times, Charles Sinclair. Do not trust my brother. He pretends to do good, to side with the Almighty, but he lies. In fact, most of us do. However, Anatole is to be pitied. He doesn't realise that his tongue is forked. He believes himself on a path to good—to redemption, but he is a fool. Trust in me, Charles. I can fulfill all your dreams. I can return all your memories to you and help you recover all you have lost."

"Vain promises from a nameless creature," Sinclair dared proclaim. "It's clear that your mind is warped beyond all hope."

The creature laughed, and the eyes flamed into crimson orbs. "Foolish man."

"A daring claim, coming from a nameless angel."

A shudder passed through the Watcher's body, and Charles perceived a set of leathery wings emerging—though they seemed hesitant to fully form. The shape of them blurred, as if ready to take flight.

"Afraid?" Charles asked boldly, though his heart felt anything but bold. "Name! Now!"

The semi-emergent wings folded and faded; the eyes softened to a light blue, and he leaned down, grasping the marquess's shoulder.

"I am Saraqael, one of the seven great princes of old," he whispered angrily, his mouth to Sinclair's ear—the breath smelling of death. "And I killed that horse, just as I killed your father. I tried to kill you, but my fool of a brother rescued you and imprisoned me. It was but a reprieve, foolish man. Once the gate is open, and our brethren emerge, then your usefulness is at an end! We've no need for a puny king of clay. King amongst the dead, indeed!" he laughed. "Dead amongst the kings, is more like it! See you soon, *human!*"

The being vanished, leaving only a tall shadow that lingered for a moment, and then twisted aloft into a howling whirlwind. Dropping to his knees, the marquess, buried his head in his hands and began to pray, beseeching God for protection and wisdom. The former for his great love and unborn child—and the latter for himself. He remained there for many minutes, and in the distance, he could hear Westminster's tower bells chime the hour of four o'clock.

"Fear not," he heard a voice whisper, and he opened his eyes to find the same gardener he'd encountered twice before.

"It's you!" he gasped.

The man's face appeared human, but his ageless eyes had a light that warmed the detective's heart as no earthly blaze could.

"I represent the One. I serve within his council, not the infernal realm. I have been tasked to keep watch upon you and the duchess. I am not permitted to interfere, for your free will choices must never be compromised. However, I may aid in the battle against dark spirits. Many of us stand beside you, Charles. Though unseen, we always accompany you on this battlefield."

"Battlefield? What do you mean? What is your name?"

"I am sometimes called Shelumiel. It means 'peace of God', and I am a son of the Most High. My office is as a ministering spirit to those who must engage the adversary directly. You ask which field, I mean. I speak of the world. This earth. Every human is born upon this field of battle, Charles, but most do not recognise it. Some live out their lives in relative ease, as though sitting at a desk. Others rush into the fray, taking constant fire from the enemy. You stand in this latter group; on the front line of a tactic planned by the infernal council in ages past, long before mankind was even born. The Adversary has asked permission to test you and your duchess, but you will never stand alone. Call upon the King, and my regiment and I shall fight on your behalf. Raziel, Saraqael, and all their fallen brethren are no match for us. And there are other spirits who serve you, though their fates are not yet known. Spirits who once walked in darkness and seek the light. These will confound you, but fear not! Choose well, son of the Highest. Trust only in the true King; in Christ, the risen Lord and his redemptive blood. The enemy may seem powerful to human eyes, but they are limited, and nothing is permitted to touch you without our King's permission, so take heart!"

Sinclair felt little comfort in this. "But it is the enemy's dark power which causes so much heartache and injury. Redwing has murdered thousands over the years, and they now set their sights upon people I love!"

"Yes, the men and women who call themselves Redwing have participated in horrendous crimes and rituals that reach back to the dawn of human time. They've called themselves by many names and served myriads of fallen angels. The crimes of these *elohim* reach back further yet, but they and those who serve them will receive judgement soon. All you need do is make the best choice you can today."

"And what choice is that?" he asked. "What of my child? Elizabeth?"

The visitor began to fade. "Do not yield to fear. Trust in Christ, Charles. Trust only in Him."

Moments passed, and the marquess opened his eyes.

"How long have I been kneeling here?" he asked aloud as he stood, his body aching. *Did I just speak with angels from both sides of this battle? One fallen, and one not? Is this really a battlefield upon which I stand? Are there unseen spiritual entities, even now, gathered all around me?*

The sky was darkening, the clouds swirling into twists of midnight black, driven by a cold, easterly wind. "It's going to snow," he said aloud. *Why does Beth fear snow?*

He left the gazebo and entered the mansion, the velvet collar of the overcoat pulled tightly about his ears. One night more, and he'd bring her here—to their new home. Beginning tomorrow, he would never more sleep alone.

Raziel Grigor entered the third floor parlour of 33 Wormwood Street, his sudden appearance punctuated by lightning flashes.

Sir William Trent did not move, not even an inch, though his friends nearly leapt out of their skins at the miraculous display. "Rather showy, don't you think?" the baronet casually asked the Watcher. "What do you want? Can't you see we're having a meeting?"

Dusting sparks from his sleeves, Grigor laughed and took a chair next to Clive Urquhart. "Nice place," the fallen angel told the men. "Lewis Merriweather certainly knows how to construct a sound building. I do like the address. Wormwood evokes so many lovely thoughts."

"Knew," Urquhart corrected, regaining composure. "Poor Lewis knew. Our estate agent is no more, Lord Raziel. Sadly, he succumbed to his weaknesses."

"Ah, yes, those," the angel laughed. "A weak heart and a weak mind—but I suspect the cause of death connected more to his weak friends. I wonder if Inspector Reid and his bumbling policemen noticed the fingermarks on Merriweather's throat?"

"Does it matter? He's buried now and this fine building serves as our new headquarters," Trent stated. "Have you managed to curtail your brother's interference?"

"Which one?" the Watcher asked, waving to one three prostitutes who served as maids for the meeting. "I see that Mrs. Hansen has sent us a delightful collection of playthings. Blonde, brunette, and fiery red. I'll take them all."

"Feel free to enjoy each and every one, old friend, so long as you answer my question. Saraqael is proving tiresome. He's roused the ire of the inner circle by slaying the horse, and his rampage continues. Have you not seen the papers?" Trent shouted, throwing half a dozen broadsheets towards the visitor. "Dead sheep and dead horses in six English counties and two in France! He has only been released a few days. Can you imagine what he'll do in the coming year? We must return him to his prison!"

"Now, why would I do that?" Raziel answered, taking the redhead onto his lap. "Sara is annoying, yes, but he is necessary. Once this wedding is past, we'll have ample time to deal with his compulsions. Let us concentrate on the task at hand. Have you placed the item in his house?"

"Days ago, but your fool of a maid has failed, Raziel. Your so-called son's temptations pushed her into madness and she tried to murder the duchess! Now, the girl is dead, and though no real loss, we have no one inside that house to place the other gateway."

"Do we not?" Raziel asked readily. "Are there not other women who may be used?"

"One may have worked, but she chose to betray us," Trent observed.

Sir Clive sighed heavily, gazing into his wine glass. "Poor Susanna. I shall miss her."

"Miss a traitor?" Trent snapped.

"No, my dear Sir William, no. Of course, not. Only I shall miss her warmth and inventive nature in bed. That is all. The good Lady Margaret is not so much good as she is cold. Can we not summon the doctor from her hiding place?"

"Dr. MacKey wavers in her devotion," Raziel told them. "My traitorous brother would lure her to his side; whatever side that is."

"His own," Trent answered angrily.

"Which brother? Saraqael or Samael? I grow confused, Lord Raziel. You all look alike to my eyes, and your names—they tie themselves into knots in my mind."

"Not surprising," the Watcher replied drily. "Discernment requires a certain amount of wit, after all. We look similar for we are of the same class of elohim. The Ancient Princes of Old—the Seven Wonders of the primordial world. Each of us commanded hundreds of thousands. Such glorious days, they were! Then came the first war, and multitudes were slaughtered. The world split in two."

"First war? What war is that?" Urquhart asked as he poured himself another glass of cognac.

"The war for the throne. So many died. But now we have a chance to avenge their blood, if we reclaim what was lost. This world is ours by right!"

Trent took to his feet, suddenly quite bored. "Yes, so you've said many times. Will Rasha be ready?"

"He is prepared to assume his place in the world. You know this MacKey woman, Trent," said Raziel. "Can she be trusted to place the doorway?"

"Lorena would do anything to achieve great power. Yes, she can be persuaded, but we'll have to offer her a place at the table."

"As a member, or as a meal?" Raziel quipped.

"Perhaps, as both," Trent answered. "Perhaps, she serves us as both."

Lorena MacKey had never felt so afraid in all her life. Though, Anatole had promised to protect her, she'd begun to wonder if even his abilities could overcome Redwing's long reach. The morning papers lay before her, containing stories of politics and peers, with the Haimsbury-Branham wedding featured on every front page. However, tucked amongst these happy reports was one slender column detailing the discovery of a woman, her body dissected into four parts, and washed up along the Thames shoreline. Though no name was given, Lorena knew who it must be. Susanna Morgan. The reporter's frank mention of torture marks and a cruel brand upon the upper back confirmed it. These were the hallmarks of Redwing when dealing with traitors. Death often took days, and women weren't exempt from the procedure—rather they served as sport for the sadistic men who inflicted the injuries.

"If only I'd stayed in Scotland," she told herself. "The duke treated me kindly, and I repaid that kindness with deception. Why? Why do I do this? What have I gained?"

Startled by a soft 'whooshing' sound, she turned towards the door to the luxurious apartment. A white envelope had been slipped beneath it. Taking it from the floor, she opened the message—fearing the worst. Just before their apprehension, Redwing traitors always received a summons from those in charge, listing their crimes.

Unfolding the note, she exhaled in relief. It was a telegram from Anatole Romanov:

Lorena: In two minutes, Trent will knock upon your door. Do all that he asks without fear. I keep watch. You are never out of my sight. I have seen your future. It is bright. - Anatole.

A bright future? she thought. *How can it be bright, when I've chosen darkness?*

As if in answer, she heard a sharp knock on the painted door. Lorena swallowed hard, whispering a prayer inside her mind. *Please, God. If you are there, I beg you! Please, protect me!*

The physician opened the door and found Sir William Trent holding his cane in one hand and a wrapped package in the other.

"I've brought your costume, my dear. It's time to show the earl just how dazzling a temptress you can be."

CHAPTER TWENTY-NINE

The Russian embassy ball began at eight o'clock precisely, and nearly everyone in London high society had been invited. Government officials, bankers, barristers, builders, and peers of all ranks queued up to the majordomo's platform, attired in eighteenth century dress to celebrate the upcoming union of the great houses of Branham and Haimsbury. Victoria had warned Charles that he and Elizabeth shouldn't arrive before nine, for even though they were the guests of honour, protocol demanded they should be announced only after everyone else had arrived and begun to mingle in the ballroom.

Charles sat opposite Elizabeth in the opulent carriage, sent by the prince. The golden coach was an exact replica of Empress Catherine's very own, emblazoned with the Romanov crest and drawn by six white horses in glittering harness. Her gown was one Victoria had found in an old trunk at Queen Anne House; a voluminous dress made in Venice for her great-grandmother, Duchess Antoinette Mérovée de Moiré Linnhe. The elaborate ensemble featured a tiered skirt of pink and gold taffeta overlaid in silk lace, embroidered with scarlet roses. Above the wide skirt, a tight-fitting, boned bodice accented Elizabeth's small waist. Alicia had arranged Elizabeth's raven hair in a high coif, and a waterfall of loose ringlets cascaded down her shoulders. Upon her head, she wore her great-grandmother's coronet, featuring a dozen, ten-carat diamonds set into a gold circlet of strawberry leaves, encrusted in smaller diamonds, and around her throat shone the bejewelled, matching necklace.

"I feel like a princess from a fairy story," Beth said as the carriage pulled through the stone gateway that formed the entrance to Kensington Palace. "Although, I wonder how those princesses endured their clothing. The whalebone in this bodice might serve as a medieval torture device! You, however, are truly Prince Charming. I mean it, Charles. I find myself falling in love with you all over again."

"Then, let's pay the driver to turn 'round and take us home," he teased. "I prefer private dances to a grand ball."

She laughed. "You'll turn my head, Lord Haimsbury! Now, behave. We'll share that private dance tomorrow. Where did you find your costume? Is it your father's?"

"In part," he told her. "Laurence and I found very little at my home, but Booth discovered an absolute treasure trove in the attics at Drummond House. This cavalry uniform was worn by the 8th Duke of Drummond, but the medals belonged to my grandfather. I found them in my father's study. Not bad for a day's hunting. I feel rather out of place, though. Laurence tried to get me to wear the Haimsbury coronet, but that is simply beyond all imagining. A Whitechapel detective in a crown! Good heavens! Beth, I sometimes wonder if I live in a dream, for this life is a far cry from my old policing days. I'm not sure how well I fit into peerage life, but so long as you stand beside me, I shall always feel at home."

"Charles, you need no crown to prove you're my prince. I so look forward to calling you husband. Tomorrow cannot come soon enough."

The carriage pulled to a stop, and a tall footman in satin livery and powdered wig opened the door for the couple. Three additional footmen appeared: one to lower the steps, another to help Elizabeth and Charles descend, and the third walked ahead to open the door to the palace entrance.

Inside the magnificent foyer, James and Paul Stuart met the couple, each peer in full regalia once worn by former dukes and earls. Drummond's broad chest was covered in ribbons and medals. Both the Scottish lords wore a sash and sabre.

"Welcome to the costume club," Aubrey said with a wink at Charles, and then turning to Elizabeth his gaze softened, but to his credit, the earl kept his demeanor appropriate for a cousin.

"Elizabeth, you are the picture of royalty," he said, kissing her hand. "A true princess. Where is Aunt Victoria?" he then asked, his eyes watching every man who walked past.

Charles recognised the look. What did Paul know he did not?

"She arrived here earlier," the marquess answered, "collected by Maisie Churchill. They are still finalising plans for the wedding reception, I think. Honestly, I'd no idea there were so many details involved in getting married."

Elizabeth had stopped to adjust her train, but a small boy in satin livery and powdered wig appeared, as if from nowhere, to do it for her. "Thank you, young sir," she said to the handsome youth. "What's your name?"

The boy smiled, his hazel eyes round with excitement. "Toby, my lady. Toby Ellingham."

"Well, Master Toby, you are quite gallant," she said with a bright smile.

The page bowed and stepped to the side, allowing the footmen to lead whilst he kept watch on the train. As they followed the footmen and youth, Charles marvelled at the gold-leafed interior of the palace. Neither Queen Anne nor Haimsbury House, as grand as both were, came close to rivalling this regal home. The closest would have been Branham, and Charles liked picturing his very own princess as mistress of her Kent county palace, digging in the gardens and baking inedible cakes.

Climbing up two sets of wide, curving steps, the party was approached by the majordomo, an extraordinary looking gentleman with an enormous head, aquiline nose, and arched black brows. He carried a long staff of carved ivory, trimmed in gold leaf, and his livery was of iced blue satin, overlaid in gold stars.

"Your Grace. Lord Haimsbury," he said, bowing low to Elizabeth and Charles. "The Duke and Duchess of Edinburgh and Prince Anatole welcome you to Kensington Palace and are honoured by your presence."

He announced James first and then Paul. Charles noticed that a dozen or more peerage daughters suddenly turned to face the Italian marble and gold-trimmed balcony that led onto the ballroom floor. Clearly, word had travelled throughout the country that the handsome Earl of Aubrey was now available. One of these ingénues was all too familiar to both cousins: Cordelia Wychwright, dressed in a gown of white organza, and standing by her cousins, Lord and Lady Cartringham. For some reason, neither parent stood nearby, but Charles suspected the ambitious Baron and Baroness would never have missed attending.

"Your Royal Highnesses, Most Honourable Dukes and Duchesses, Lords and Ladies, allow me now to present the guests of honour: Her Grace, the Most Honourable Elizabeth Stuart, Duchess of Branham and His Lordship, the Most Honourable Superintendent Charles Sinclair, Marquess of Haimsbury."

The entire room, a dense crowd of four hundred peers, influential bankers, and politicians, began to applaud. Charles bowed, as the duke had instructed, and Elizabeth nodded her head. The majordomo tapped his enormous staff upon the marble, and the couple moved into the room, where they were greeted by the Contessa di Specchio, Russian Ambassador Baron de Staal, and Prince Anatole. The prince's attitude towards the contessa appeared cool, if not icy.

De Staal had chosen a curious combination of Russian and German attire, for his mixed ancestry reached back to both countries. The countess wore a glittering, black silk ensemble that fit tightly 'round every curve, and her throat bore a string of carved rubies.

Anatole wore riding boots and a military style coat over black velvet breeches paired with a red cape, draped casually across his right shoulder. Beneath the coat, a white silk shirt with ruffled lace ascot softened the fierce ensemble, closed with a pin that bore the double-headed eagle of the Romanov crest. Even Charles had to admit that the prince outshone every other male present.

Romanov offered a deep, formal bow and kissed Elizabeth's gloved hand. "My beautiful friend," he whispered as he gazed into her eyes. "You glow, Duchess. Clearly, romance agrees with you."

Beth smiled, gazing first at Charles and then back to Romanov. "You are most kind, Your Highness. Thank you for hosting this ball in our honour. It's quite unexpected, but very much appreciated."

Anatole turned to Charles. "Lord Haimsbury, I concede defeat to the man who has captured the heart of Elizabeth, most beautiful of women. Had I seen her first, I should have given you a contest, but alas, her dark eyes see no other, whenever you are near."

Charles bowed to the prince, noticing Paul's sharp glances at the Russian, but Sinclair smiled. Though the prince's spiritual loyalties remained a mystery, his intervention on behalf of the marquess had proven most helpful. "We are honoured by your friendship, Your Highness. I am delighted that I had the great blessing to meet my duchess first."

Anatole laughed. "Well said, sir. Now, Duke, Lord Aubrey, since you are unaccompanied, I direct your attentions to the bevy of beauty around our ballroom. Most of these you may already know, but a few come from my own country. They are cousins and friends and have noticed the two handsome, Scottish lords in their presence. Enjoy."

The duke grinned mischievously. His moustache curled at the edges, and his dark eyes twinkled. Charles had grown deeply fond of this remarkable man, and he knew that he still had much to learn from both his uncle and cousin. James Stuart had an ease about him even when facing a dangerous foe that Charles hoped one day to achieve.

"Your Highness, you've put together a grand group, and your theme is impressive, particularly for a hastily arranged affair. You must tell me how you pulled it off. We've been working non-stop for a month arranging Beth's wedding, and my sister tells me there are details yet to finish. Perhaps your wife helped?"

The prince stared at the duke for a moment with an odd expression. "I have never married, Duke. It is the one great regret of my life, but I am ever in search of the perfect lady to make my princess. Alas, she will be wed tomorrow at ten."

Paul stood near the contessa, who leaned against his left arm with just enough force to make the earl wince. "Do forgive me, Lord Aubrey! I had forgotten about your poor shoulder. Does it still pain you?"

He managed a smile. "It is nearly healed, Contessa. If you'll excuse me, I believe I see a friend." Aubrey bowed and passed by Charles, whispering, "She is here."

Sinclair assumed he meant Wychwright, but turning, the marquess saw his cousin stride towards a grand marble fountain surrounded by several young women whose generous assets bubbled over tight-bodiced gowns, each fully aware that the dashing earl was now very much available. However, Aubrey continued on, beyond the perfumed throats of this willing gaggle, bowing occasionally to be polite. At last, he stopped before a tall woman in an emerald green gown with an empire waist.

"Good heavens!" Charles gasped, recognising her at last. "James, do you see who's caught my cousin's eye once more?"

The duke accepted a glass of champagne from a passing footman and took Charles by the elbow. "So the spider emerges from her web at last," he said. "One wonders just what mischief the minx intends this time."

"I'll find out," he replied, starting towards her.

"No, son. Leave MacKey to your cousin," Drummond cautioned. "Your only charge now is my granddaughter. If you are not careful, there is a prince ready to steal her."

Charles turned 'round in time to see Elizabeth being led to the dance floor by Anatole. "Is that proper form? May our host claim the first dance?"

"He may, but pay heed to her, Charles. Usually, Elizabeth is more than capable of fending off unwanted advances, but this prince's intent is yet unknown. Speaking of the unknown, who is that?" he added, pointing towards a tall man dressed entirely in scarlet. "Another Romanov?"

"No. At least I don't think so, but I'm sure he's related somehow. He has that same look all these creatures have," Sinclair answered, anger crossing his features. "Keep an eye on Elizabeth for me, will you, James? I believe I'll introduce myself to that gentleman."

The stranger offered a theatrical bow as Charles drew near. "Good evening, Lord Haimsbury. A fitting room for a duel, is it not?"

"How did you manage to secure an invitation?" he asked the Watcher. "Do they even receive letters in Hell's dungeon?"

"You say that, as if you think it derisive, Superintendent. I'll have you know that the nether realm is more real, more powerful— more alive than this puny kingdom. Although, I do enjoy gatherings like these," the being added with a flourish of his satin cape. "Rather dashing, don't you think? I've always loved wearing human trappings, particularly the swords, though you'd never have managed metallurgy without our instruction. You owe much to me and my brethren, Charles. Warfare made England great, after all."

"Prince Alexei," a woman's voice called. Sinclair turned about to find the contessa standing behind him. "I see you are engaged," she continued. "Have you been introduced?"

"Alexei?" Charles asked. "Would that be Alexei Romanov, by any chance?"

"Hardly!" he blustered. "Prince Alexei Nicholai Anghelscu Grigor, at your service. I understand you've met my son, Lord

Haimsbury. Razarit Grigor. A fine lad. He's adopted, of course, but still flesh of my flesh, you might say. You can appreciate such a bond, no? You were also raised by adoptive parents. Edna and Elijah Burke; am I right? Such an honest, loving couple. Pity how they died. Pinned beneath the wheel of a milk wagon is a hideous, painful way to go; and heart failure, though swift, allows the victim to linger for many minutes before crossing beyond the final curtain of life. Such a tragedy!"

Charles felt as if he'd been slapped, and his hand unconsciously rose to do the same to the grinning Romanian.

The contessa grasped his arm, her fingers pressing into his skin. "Lord Haimsbury, join me for a waltz, won't you?"

"This isn't over," Sinclair warned Grigor, forcing himself to go with the Italian.

The countess drew him onto the polished marble dance floor, whispering as she did so. "He will kill you without a thought, Charles. You must let it go."

"What you ask is difficult," he told her, keeping Grigor in sight as they danced. "How can he know anything about my aunt and uncle?"

"He knows many things, and yes, I'm sure it is difficult to control your temper, but Alexei *wanted* you to strike him. Would you please him, my friend? Now, concentrate upon the music and the movement of your feet. It will take your mind off anger. Rash thoughts lead to rash deeds."

"Who is Grigor; and for that matter just who are you?"

"Do we drop all the masks, then?" she asked him seductively. "A pity. I do love mystery, but as I value your friendship, I shall answer your questions. My history might surprise you."

"Very little surprises me these days," he told her as the orchestra began the opening measures of a waltz.

"I grew up in a villa near Milan. My father served Francesco, the first ruler of the powerful Sforza family. I became Francesco's mistress."

"Sforza? I'm not familiar with that name."

"No? Do you know the Borgias, then?"

"As in Lucrezia? Yes. Why?"

"She married Giovanni Sforza. Of course, her father had the marriage annulled. He also had my father killed, claiming he was *upyr*. What some might call a vampire."

"Wait a minute," he said, ignoring the last remark. "Lucrezia's father was said to be Pope Alexander the Sixth. Both lived in the 16th century. How can you possibly be..." He stopped, staring at her. "I see. You are also a vampire. I presume your lifeline extended by such an inheritance."

"I told you that my story would surprise you," she whispered, pulling at his hands. "Dance, Lord Haimsbury. Surely, your recent experiences with my kind open new possibilities in your mind. The world is much more complex than mere humans can imagine."

"So it would seem," he replied, beginning the dance once more. "Tell me about William Trent. Is he also a vampire?"

"The baronet causes an itch beneath your skin, does he not? Shall I scratch that itch for you?"

Rather than answer, Charles turned his eyes towards Beth and Anatole, wondering if he should cut in.

"The duchess enjoys herself," di Specchio whispered. "Are you? Enjoying yourself, I mean?"

In truth, Sinclair considered the countess to be both beautiful and deadly. If he must dance with her, then he intended to make the most of it, by extracting as much information as possible. "Why shouldn't I enjoy myself? You're the second most beautiful woman in the room."

She grew silent for a moment, and he could see a spectrum of emotions playing upon her ageless features. "Beneath your beauty beats a cold heart, my king," she said, revealing a vulnerability he'd not expected.

"Surely you cannot expect me to call you the most beautiful, Serena. After all, I marry the duchess tomorrow. And why do you call me king?"

"I call you by your true title."

"What do you mean?" he pressed, noticing that Beth looked weary.

"You are a king, though you have forgotten it. Soon, those old memories will stir. Old plans and old husbandry begin to yield fruit. Old Saturn's reign returns."

"What?" he asked. "What has Saturn to do with this?"

"Everything. Why do your eyes never leave the duchess? Do my charms not entice?" she asked, her lips full and blood-red in the soft gaslight.

For a moment, for a blink of time, Sinclair experienced a rush of memory, as if reliving primordial scenes from ages past: images of ancient gods upon massive thrones; warriors in battle dress bearing flashing swords that sparked light and fire; worshipping throngs willing to sacrifice children to deities from the heavens; and finally a ring of stone surrounding an uncrowned king.

The king amongst the dead.

All colour drained from his face, and he pushed her back, nearly stumbling as he did so. The contessa drew him down with both hands and kissed him fully on the mouth. "Keep watch on snow, my king," she whispered in his left ear. "That is all I tell you, now leave me before Grigor notices."

The Italian stormed off, pretending she'd been spurned, pushing her way through dozens of dancing couples like an angry salmon.

"What did you say to the Italian?" his cousin's voice asked near Sinclair's elbow.

Turning about, Charles forced a smile, struggling to regain his anchor to the present. "I'm losing my touch. Did you speak with MacKey?"

"Yes, but only for a moment. Lorena claims that she wishes to leave Redwing's shelter, but she's terrified, Charles."

"Has she heard of Morgan's death?"

"She has," the earl answered softly.

"Paul, there was nothing you could do. Morgan chose to leave your protection."

"I know, but does that mean we ignore further cries for help? Lorena's will be the next torso fished from the cold waters of the Thames, if we fail to act." He paused for a moment. "That's why I promised to meet her. After the ball."

The detective gasped. "You did what? Paul, is there a law that says you must fall for the charms of every red-headed physician who flutters her pretty eyelashes?"

"No, but it's difficult to put such a theory to the test, since Lorena is the only red-headed doctor to do so. Let's not forget, that she fluttered those same lashes at you as well, Cousin. Oh, do hide me. Delia's headed this way."

"Shall I call on MacKey to dissuade the Lady Cordelia from pursuing you?" the detective teased. "Do forgive me for deserting you, Lord Aubrey. I need to make sure Elizabeth is all right."

Laughing as he left, Sinclair abandoned the earl to the ingénue's advances and crossed onto the busy dance floor. The third waltz had just ended, and Elizabeth fanned her face. She brightened as her fiancé approached.

"Charles, there you are! I'd feared you'd gone missing."

He placed his right arm around her waist, insinuating himself betwixt her and the prince. "Not a chance of it. Prince Anatole, when you've a moment, I'd love to discuss Russian politics."

Romanov showed surprise. "How very refreshing. So few Englishmen care how our empire advances. Duchess, I hope you will save another dance for me. Your steps are as light as air, and your conversation as bright any star."

"Come, Beth, let's rescue our cousin from Cordelia Wychwright. Anatole, I shan't be long. I'll meet you near the copper fountain."

He led the duchess away from the dancers, towards a secluded dais, where many of the older peers exchanged war stories and stock tips. They sat at a table that had been reserved only for their use, and a livered footman brought champagne, cheese, and glacé fruit.

"I can't remember attending any police dances with so much fancy food," he joked.

"How many dances do policemen attend each year?" she asked, using a silk fan to cool her face.

"Just one, actually. A boring affair at Chiswick Hotel. How are you doing, darling? You're flushed."

"The room grows hot," she answered. "If it weren't so very cold outside, I'd ask you to take me for a walk as we often did during the parties in Kent. How I loved showing you off to everyone, Charles. Did I see you dancing with the countess?"

"Yes, but only to be polite. I met a man who could be Anatole's twin. Have you seen him? A Romanian named Grigor."

"Alexei Grigor?" she asked. "That's Razarit's uncle, I think. I met him once at Dolly Patterson-Smythe's home outside of Paris. Their family name isn't actually Grigor, though. It's Draculesti."

"Then why use the other?"

"The Draculesti family is hunted by Russian soldiers. Paul could explain it better than I. It's to do with the takeover of the Carpathian countries in the early years of the century. Their family once ruled Wallachia. Why do you ask?"

"No reason. I wonder, though, why this Alexei refers to Rasha as his son."

She sighed, still fighting the heat which flushed her cheeks. "When his brother Mikhail died, Alexei adopted Rasha and changed his name. At least, I think that's how it goes. I'm sorry, I'm a bit muddled just now."

Sinclair wondered if her state of health and mind had anything to do with the dance with Romanov. He stood as Victoria arrived, carrying two glasses of champagne.

"They're not both for me," she explained. "My brother is joining us, if he can ever pull himself away from Marlborough. Beth, you look ghastly. Your cheeks have gone all blotchy. Are you ill?"

"No," she whispered. "Just dealing with other issues. Charles, would you mind fetching me some water?"

"I'll have your cousin bring you a cool glass, darling. He needs rescue. Do you mind if I leave you a moment and have that chat with Anatole?"

"No, but don't be gone long."

Raising his arm to signal to the earl, Sinclair waited a beat until Aubrey stepped his way. Sadly, Wychwright followed behind like a faithful duckling.

"I've never been to Kensington Palace before," Delia jabbered as she sat next to Elizabeth. "Why, everyone is here! My father says it's the best chance he's had in six months to speak with the back-benchers. I'm not really sure what that means, but apparently, it's quite important. And there must be half a dozen princes here! Can you believe it? Oh, thank you, Lord Aubrey," she said as Paul handed her a glass of wine in the hope it might slow her constant stream of chatter; which it didn't. "Mother is speaking to the duke about Christmas. Are you returning to Branham for the holidays, Elizabeth, or do you plan to stay in London?"

Beth looked up, the fan in her hand. "What? Oh, Christmas. Well, I'm not sure. That will be up to my husband."

"Husband?" Wychwright asked. "Oh, wait, I see what you mean. Yes, I suppose Lord Haimsbury will be your husband by then."

"He'll be her husband tomorrow, Delia," the earl said. "Have a bite of the brioche," he suggested as a footman set a plate of crustless sandwiches, water crackers, and canapes on their table. "I had one earlier. It's spiced with peppercorns."

Wychwright had been warned by her aunt and mother to refrain from indulging her appetite whilst at the ball, and she shook her head. "I mustn't. Waltzes and a full stomach do not mix; so says my aunt. Is that what happened to you, Duchess? Your colour is very strange. I do hope you're not getting ill again."

"No, merely overheated. Here's Grandfather," she said as the duke approached with Maisie Churchill.

Drummond held the chair for Victoria's friend, sitting beside her. "Now, this is a lovely gathering of beauties! Paul, we're blessed to be the only men to share in their conversation. Princess, what ails you? You're pale and flushed all at once."

"Too much waltzing," she said. "I think I'll take a short walk along the gallery. It isn't far, and I'm sure it's much cooler there. Paul, will you give me your arm?"

"Of course," he said, rising. "We shan't be long, Uncle. Let Charles know where we are, when he returns."

He put his arm out for Beth, and she leaned upon him as they left the main ballroom area, strolled past two fountains, through an indoor garden, and into a quiet hallway lined with forty or more portraits.

"I need to sit again," she told him as they neared a line of chairs. "Thank you, Paul."

"It's you I should thank, Princess. You plucked me from a very tight grip. Delia's a lovely girl, but she pushes much too hard."

"It's her parents who're to blame. The baroness especially. Don't you find Cordelia attractive?"

"Not as a prospective wife, no. Besides, she's far too young for me."

Beth began to laugh, and Paul stared at her. "Am I so funny?"

"In a way. Paul, Cordelia is only a few years younger than I. She'll be eighteen in a few weeks. I'm not even twenty-one yet."

"Well," he muttered, not the least bit happy with her observation, "you're more mature. I don't generally think of you as that young, to be honest."

"My dear Lord Aubrey, you are hardly being honest! I think you admire the Lady Cordelia and don't wish to admit it. Darling, I say this as your dearest friend. You could do much worse, you know. She comes from a good family, and she is very pretty."

"May we change the subject, please?"

"Have I struck a nerve?"

"You have struck no such thing," he insisted as a footman neared. "Lord Aubrey?"

"Yes, I'm Aubrey."

"Lord Salisbury asks to speak with you, sir. His note explains." The servant passed a folded sheet of paper to the earl, who opened it, sighing as he read the contents.

"Beth, I'm very sorry. It's nothing earth-shattering, but Robert insists on meeting with me for five minutes. Do you mind?"

"Not at all. I'm content to sit and wait. It's much cooler here."

"I shan't be long." He turned to the footman. "Have you a pencil and paper?" The young man nodded, and Aubrey scratched a note of his own. "Take this to Lord Haimsbury at once. He probably won't know where the gallery is located, so offer to lead him, won't you?"

The earl kissed Beth and headed towards an upper level meeting room, as the note from the prime minister had instructed. No sooner had he departed, than Alexei Grigor approached, as if he'd been waiting to find her alone.

"How lovely to see you once again, Duchess. It has been how long? Six months?"

Elizabeth startled, for she'd not heard his footsteps. "Your Highness, do forgive me. I'm a little winded from dancing. Six months? Surely not. It was at Dolly's, I think. You were visiting your nephew."

"May I?" he asked, sitting before she could answer. "Rasha had become besotted with you, no?"

She lowered her eyes, somewhat embarrassed. "Razarit did ask permission to court me, but as my aunt explained, I was promised to another."

"Yet, you have broken that promise. It is not the earl standing as your husband tomorrow but this other. Haimsbury. Rasha is understandably disappointed, which is why he is not here this evening. Though invited, he felt unable to attend."

Beth's ordinarily gentle manner bristled at the implication. "Do you think I misled your nephew, Prince? On the contrary, I gave him my friendship, and I thought that it was enough! However, he demonstrated his affections with far too much ardour, if you must know. Your family's importance is the only reason Rasha walks freely today, for he forced himself on me, and when I did not respond in kind, he struck me!"

Grigor feigned surprise. "Your Grace, that is indeed, quite shocking! Had I known, I assure you that I'd have insisted he pay for such insolence. I have no delusions where my adopted son is concerned. He is dear to me, but his behaviour often borders on cruel. I have always taught him to respect ladies. Why did you not write to me?"

His eyes focused upon hers like a pair of dark lamps, lit from within by a cold fire. She hardly noticed when he took her hands.

"I am sorry. Perhaps, I should have," she answered as if in a dream.

"It is easily forgiven," the Watcher told her. "If you would but allow me one dance." She stood, and he led her from the gallery towards a winding staircase. In a moment, they'd disappeared into the upper regions of the palace.

CHAPTER THIRTY

"Why have you arranged this ball?" Sinclair asked Romanov. They sat in a conservatory garden, on a pair of marble benches, beneath the branches of an orange tree. Above them, the moon shone through leaded panes of clear glass, formed into a high dome, and silver played upon the tree's leaves, casting dappled shadows along the floor tiles.

"I find this space soothing, don't you?" the Russian asked.

"Hardly. I find direct replies informative, however. Have you any?"

The handsome elohim smiled as a pair of lovers walked past. The duo showed disappointment at being discovered. The man bowed to Sinclair and the prince, then hastened the young woman away to a more solitary part of the garden.

"He came here to propose," Romanov said as the couple disappeared 'round the corner, seeking privacy. "Her father will say no. The young man's lands and titles include no money, you see. Pity."

"Is this all you can offer? A lesson in peerage romance?"

"No, but rather a lesson in timing. Had you kissed Elizabeth in the Aubrey House library four years ago, her grandfather would have been forced to refuse you. Despite your heritage and despite her love for you."

"I was still married, Anatole. I would never have kissed her."

"So you say, but you were sorely tempted, were you not? I tell you that your friendship with the earl would have soured, and the duchess would now be marrying him, instead. Your child would be his child. Timing, you see. It is everything."

"What is your point?"

"Merely that all opportunities in life, all choices, have consequences. One road taken, leaves another unexplored; and whilst some roads lead to delights, others lead to agony and regret. The birth of one child, may mean the death of another."

"Free will determines our lot in life. I'm aware of all this, you know. I've studied the Bible since I was a boy."

"But have you studied the truths that lie within the original language of that sacred book? Do you truly understand the encrypted plans inscribed within its pages?"

Sinclair checked his timepiece, the words Beth had engraved within its case reminding him of her love—and his dependence upon that steadfast anchor. "Are you saying that both sides in the spiritual war have unknown plans that might yet be discerned?"

"Yes! Yes, I am saying precisely that, Charles. You cannot yet remember it, but I spent two years teaching you. Two years of language lessons. Two years of explanations and revelations, and I did this to arm you for the battle ahead. I warned you, then, that a day would come when your family's enemies would seek to use you through trickery, and that day is here. Timing. And time. They intertwine about you, like twin snakes. These insideous serpents coil about you and your duchess, my friend. They will threaten and cajole, and use any means to gain your obedience to their cause."

"And what cause is that? World domination?"

The angel shook his head. "No. World destruction. Controlling humanity is but a means to an end. The fallen realm seeks to return the world to what it once was: devoid of all God-created humans; a realm of wood and stone and spirit and demon-filled hybrids. A realm of utter darkness."

A chill ran down Sinclair's spine. "How do I fit into this realm of night?"

"The blood—your blood. It contains powers they require to propel a spirit engine. It..."

Victoria Stuart interrupted the prince, appearing in company with Drummond, both flushed with fright. "It's Elizabeth!" Tory shouted as she neared them, her pace quick. "She's been taken!"

Charles jumped to his feet, all colour draining from his face. "What do you mean? Taken by whom? Where?"

"We're not sure, but a footman saw him lead her up the western staircase."

"Saw whom?" the marquess shouted.

Both Stuarts replied at the same time, shock and confusion written upon their faces. "Anatole Romanov!"

Lorena MacKey sipped champagne, watching the two cousins as they pushed through the dense crowd towards the gallery. "How they rush to protect that foolish woman!" she said to her unseen companion. "I cannot understand the allure of that miserable duchess."

Trent laughed. "Don't tell me you're jealous."

"Of her? Not in the least. She is but a small impediment. The prince needs her; that is all."

"He needs her in more ways than one, my dear Lorena. When once he had eyes only for you. Such a shame!"

"And I once had eyes for him, but no longer. The earl, however, his form pleases me."

"I think such a distraction for the oh-so-faithful cousin would be quite helpful, but wait until tomorrow night. We must allow the prince to have his way—only for the present. Once Raziel and his brethren complete their rituals, I shall take my true place in the dark realm! For now, we must keep him on our side. We must be faithful to his plans. Do you understand the concept of fidelity, Doctor?"

Her heart hammering from fear, Lorena slowly lowered her champagne and turned towards the shadow. "Yes. Of course. My life belongs to the fallen realm. Command me and see just how faithful I can be."

"Good. Remember this, my dear. Prince Raziel grew weak during his imprisonment. Others offer greater powers. A civil war brews below, and Redwing will soon have a new, earthly ruler."

She forced a smile, though her hands trembled. "You walk a dangerous path, Sir William. What you suggest requires an army. Have you one?"

"My legions grow," he whispered into her ear, his shadowy hand gripping her arm. "Soon, my armies will cover the city. Loyalty demands sacrifice. Do you wish to join me, Lorena? Are you willing to sacrifice yourself to eternity?"

Two gentlemen in military dress walked past, and MacKey nodded as though completely alone. Both men clearly admired her considerable assets, accentuated by the dress's low neckline.

"What must I do?" she whispered, struggling to hide her terror.

"There is a small task you must perform to prove yourself. Free will, my dear. It is a concept that will soon die, along with the world of men."

"Do you like this room?" Alexei asked Elizabeth. They stood in the centre of an elegant salon, decorated on all sides by mirrors. "I call it my observatory."

The duchess replied slowly, as though half asleep. "You watch the stars? I see no opening to the sky."

Grigor had veiled himself so that he looked identical to Romanov. It was a trick he'd employed many times since emerging from his stone prison in 1871. He'd grown to despise Samael during those five thousand years, and such guises deflected blame from one elohim to another; absolving the true perpetrator but also confusing humans and twisting truth. And who better to blame than the elohim who'd imprisoned him?

"Do you know me?" he asked her, removing the gloves from her small hands. "Can you say my name?"

"Anatole," she whispered.

"Yes," he hissed. "I have brought you to this room because I would show you something quite remarkable. Do you wish to see it?"

"Yes," she answered in a monotone.

Whilst talking with her in the gallery, Grigor had waited until no one observed and then clothed himself in the form of Romanov. When a footman neared the area, Grigor/Romanov deliberately took her by the hand and led the duchess through a connecting archway and up the western staircase. He knew the footman would report his actions to the Stuart clan—and that the real Romanov would be charged with the act.

What Grigor did not know was that the Russian prince had been sitting with Charles Sinclair at that very moment, absolving Anatole of blame.

Turning his captive towards the northeast corner of the hidden chamber, Grigor pointed to one of thirteen mirrors. It stood nine feet high with a breadth of three; its face black as any night.

"Touch it," he commanded.

Obediently, Beth placed her hand upon the surface.

"It's warm," she whispered.

The highly reflective, volcanic glass shimmered with midnight blue lights, but strangely, the chamber's chandelier and candles could not be seen. It was as if she looked into a doorway to another world; a realm of eternal night.

Still pretending to be Romanov, he enticed her with sweet words. "The perfection of this mirror is unsurpassed. It is made from the finest obsidian and anointed with many incantations and spells."

This caused a shudder to overtake her delicate frame, and he held her more tightly as if to bring comfort. "Fear not, little Veta," he cooed in imitation of the Russian. "This mirror does not reflect the material but shows the spiritual. It is a doorway into my realm—a hidden kingdom that will soon reveal itself to all the world of men. Look into the glass, Elizaveta. Look deeply."

"But, I…"

"This is the kingdom to come," he told her. "And you shall be my queen. I'd planned to give you to my son, but Rasha's actions reveal imperfections to his nature, which make him unsuitable for such a lofty position. We shall choose a new king. Do you love your Captain? Would you have him rule this realm of shadow? Rule amongst the dead? If so, then you must do as I command."

He moved her closer to the mirror and whispered into her left ear, as he stroked her hair. The darkling mirror rippled like water, and she began to perceive her own face; her head crowned in spiralling branches of willow. The ball gown changed into diaphanous robes, and her eyes turned from dark brown to icy blue.

"The mirror transforms you, my queen. This is your true self. Do you remember my voice in your mind when you were but a child? I spoke with you in the copse, inside the hidden cottage, and as you grew, it was my voice whispering into your dreams."

"No," she said, her voice trembling. "I must not listen, I must not." She closed her eyes, shutting out the tempting vision; her mind screaming for her to wake up, but his voice was like the softest velvet. *Charles, think of Charles! Do not listen to The Shadow!*

"Gaze deeply into the mirror, and see how much I love you— have always loved you. My desire for you reaches beyond the light of all stars! How can you not know it?"

Her mind resisted, images of her Captain replacing the implanted falsehoods and revealing the true face behind the mask.

She gasped. "Liar! You are Alexei!" she cried, squirming out of his clutches and racing towards the door. As quick as thought, he appeared before her, preventing her from reaching the exit.

"Sinclair's bond with you is strong," he laughed. "Another proof of his blood's power. But my will is stronger yet. Look at me, little mouse! Look at me—now!"

Charles and the Stuarts reached the long gallery within less than two minutes, but there was no sign of Grigor or the duchess.

"Which way did you say they went?" he asked the footman.

"Through the archway, sir. As I told His Grace, Lord Aubrey had asked me to look in on the duchess whilst she remained in the gallery, and I arrived in time to see Prince Anatole take her up the western staircase."

"The prince couldn't have taken her, young man," Drummond answered in as calm a voice as he could muster. "He's right here with us." The duke turned to point towards Romanov, but the Russian was nowhere to be found. "He was just here. I don't understand. Didn't he come with us?"

Charles felt panic overtaking reason, and he pushed towards the terrified servant. "Where do those stairs lead?"

"To the state rooms, sir. I called out, my lord, but neither the prince nor the duchess turned. It seemed to me that she accompanied him willingly. I saw no indication of reluctance."

"What on earth do you mean by that?" Haimsbury shouted.

The footman seemed to shrink, bowing his head as he replied. "Only that beyond the state rooms, is a private staircase, sir."

"And where does that lead?" Aubrey asked, anxiously.

"To the upper level apartments."

Charles began to run.

"Please, let me go," Elizabeth begged her captor. "I'll say nothing, Alexei."

He stepped closer, touching her face. "Of course, you won't," he hissed. "Do you know why I brought you here, my beautiful one? For the same reason that my brother declared himself to Eve. Free will. I could coerce you, yes, but the One's rules require your consent. Of course, there are loopholes within that contract, through which one might slither. I must tell you the truth, but there is no law against a minor twisting of that truth. At least, not as I interpret those laws."

"It's so warm," she said, as his arms drew her into a serpentine embrace. "So...warm…"

He kissed her mouth, all the while his voice echoing inside her head, speaking in hideous whispers that evoked childhood terrors painted in blood. *Captain! Captain!* she thought again and again, silently mouthing the word to keep from falling under the tempter's spell.

"You may have your Captain," he promised. "Your king is our king. Your captain our own—though, he doesn't yet realise it. Our very imprint grows within him, waiting to arise. Do you think it an accident that you fell in love with him?"

You lie! she screamed inside her mind, for her entire body had gone rigid, and her lips would not move. *Charles fights against you, Grigor! He serves God not the Devil!*

"Untrue," he lied. "We control him—have always done. Always will. Your Captain is our creation."

He is God's creation! she shouted inwardly. *Lord Almighty, help me, please! Free from this torment! Help me! Help me to speak—to open my mouth, please!* "Lord Jesus, help me!" she cried out at last, the words springing from her unfrozen lips.

Instantly, the lying creature retreated, as if pulled backwards by a force greater than any earthly mechanism might muster. The chamber brightened with flashes of lightning, and a wail pierced the air, echoing off every one of the thirteen mirrors.

"Begone!" she heard a thunderous voice shout. The room grew quiet, and then a soft hand touched her face.

Elizabeth felt herself falling into nothingness.

And then all went dark.

Charles and the others found Elizabeth sitting beneath a large, indoor fig tree, Prince Anatole fanning her face.

"She's fainted," he told them, his voice filled with deep concern.

"Where did you find her?" Sinclair asked, taking her from the prince's arms.

"In an upper level chamber. She is unharmed."

"She's so pale. What did he do to her?" Aubrey asked, kneeling beside the bench.

"He frightened her; that is all, but leave Grigor to me," the Russian said, standing. "Take her home, Lord Haimsbury. There is a side exit not far from here. Follow me. I shall take you."

Charles lifted her into his arms, and the movement caused her coronet to fall, but the prince caught it before it struck the tiles, and handed it to James. "She is more regal than any queen, Duke. Take care of her, and please let me know if you require anything—anything at all."

Though no one in the family fully trusted the Russian, it was clear that Anatole cared deeply for the duchess. "Just ahead, we turn to the left, and this hallway leads to a side entrance. If you will walk in that direction, I shall alert my driver to meet you there."

James shook the Russian's hand. "Thank you, Your Highness. You've been a great help. I'll go with them. I think my sister took a different turn from us. She may be with her friend, Maisie Churchill. Would you be good enough to find her and then send her in a separate carriage?"

"Of course," Anatole replied, bowing. "I regret the way this evening ended, Duke. I'd hoped to bring you a night of relaxation and enjoyment, but it has ended the opposite. Forgive me."

Sinclair felt confused, and he suspected Romanov could provide further answers—though not tonight. He mustered up a polite smile. "Thank you, Your Highness."

Paul Stuart helped his cousin place Elizabeth into the carriage, relieved to see her eyes beginning to open. "Princess, are you all right?"

She gripped his hand. "The redhead," she muttered, nearly asleep. "Don't trust her..."

Sinclair and the duke entered the carriage, but the earl remained. "Take her home, Charles. There are other guests here tonight that deserve my attention—if not my wroth. I shall meet you at Haimsbury House later and explain."

The earl shut the carriage door, and the horses led them away from the magnificent palace towards Queen Anne House. Charles had promised he would not sleep there this night, but even though France had arrived to keep watch over the premises, the marquess made up his mind to disobey Victoria, if the earl were delayed.

"Beth?" he whispered as he held her close. She opened her eyes, and they appeared glassy, the pupils large. "James, I fear she may have suffered more than a faint. Perhaps, I should send for Emerson."

"Something is not right," Drummond said. "How does a footman see one prince, when another is involved?"

"The two are similar. One might easily mistake them."

"No, I think this more than similarity. It reminds me of tales my father once told the circle of spirits who could appear in any guise. We must investigate this Romanian."

"Beth says he's Rasha Grigor's uncle. Are they both spirits then?"

"Both are evil, that much we know!" the duke exclaimed angrily.

"It's all my fault," Charles moaned. "I should never have left her. In fact, coming at all was a mistake. I wish we'd just run away and gotten married in Scotland."

Stuart's face softened. "If it's anyone's fault, it's mine, son. You begged me to let you wed before coming back, and I insisted on a show. I pray my foolishness hasn't caused her harm."

She opened her eyes again, her lips parting slightly. "Snow," she said suddenly. "Red snow. And fire. Cold. So cold," she whispered, shivering.

"James, would you hand me that blanket?" Charles draped the thick wool across her shoulders and pulled it down to cover her small feet. "Is that better?"

Elizabeth nodded, but she still shivered. "The monster. In the glass. Red snow."

The duke and Charles exchanged worried glances. "What monster, darling?"

"Snow and fire," she repeated.

"What can she mean by snow and fire?" Drummond asked.

Charles kissed her head. "She's asked me about snow before, but when I pursue the thread, it's as if the reason behind her question vanishes. As though her memory were tampered with, if you get my meaning. What if someone intentionally removes them—or rather obscures them?"

"Who?" his uncle asked as the coach turned down Queen Anne Walk.

"When I first met Elizabeth, she had no recollection of the tragedy that brought her to Commercial Street. No memory of her own name."

"Yes, but that was caused by the blow to her head," Drummond argued.

"Was it? We all assumed it was, but what if one of these spirits interferes with her natural ability to recall? What puzzles me most is why they continually assault her mind." Stroking her hair, he continued. "I should have listened. She told both Paul and me of a nightmare that took place in a ballroom, and we dismissed it. Why didn't I listen?"

The coach stopped near the entrance to the mansion, and the duke placed a comforting hand on his nephew's arm. "Come, now, no more self-doubt, son. That's what the enemy wants. Hand her to me. I'll carry her in. It'll be my last time to do so before she becomes yours alone."

The duke cradled Elizabeth in his strong arms and kissed her face as he carried her into the house. Miles met the trio at the door, opening it wide to allow them ingress.

"Is my lady unwell, sir?" he asked, his face filled with concern.

"Just weary," Drummond answered. The duke settled Elizabeth upon a long sofa inside the front drawing room and kissed her face. "Sleep, Princess. Your Captain is here with you."

Charles saw the duke's tears, and he clutched at the older man's shoulder. "Sir, I am so very proud to call you uncle."

Drummond laughed it off, in typical fashion. "A blood nephew, yes, Charles, but you're more like a son," he whispered.

Just then, the men overheard Miles speaking with another—the voice deep and delightfully familiar. In seconds, the massive presence of Cornelius Baxter strode into the drawing room, worry creasing his brow, and those magnificent brows pinching together as if shaking hands.

"Good heavens! Is the little duchess ill, sirs?" he asked, bending to feel her forehead.

Drummond began to laugh. "She'll be right as rain now, Mr. Baxter. Now that you're here. Does my sister have you down as guests, or are you to serve? It had best be the former, for our duchess will much complain if she discovers you're expected to work whilst here."

"Mrs. Alcorn and I are honoured to be included as guests, sir," the gentle giant explained. "Mr. Miles has been kind enough to show us to our guest quarters. I've quite missed this old house, but Branham will always be my home, Your Grace."

Charles shook the large man's hand warmly. "Baxter, my dear friend, I'm so pleased to see you! Tory didn't mention anything about sending you an invitation, and I'm ashamed to say I didn't think of it, but I'm sure it was Beth. She loves you like a second father."

Baxter's animated brows rose to new heights. "That is well said, sir, and I am most grateful. I've brought further information regarding that, uh, skirmish at the hall," he whispered. "Shall I wait until the duchess is out of earshot, sir?"

"Yes, I think it's best," the marquess replied, grinning. "Let me see Beth to bed, and then I shall return to talk for an hour before I leave. Now that I know she is safely in your hands, old friend, I must spend my final night as a bachelor elsewhere. Aunt Victoria says it must be so."

"Ah, yes, that inestimable lady must be obeyed at all cost," the Branham butler replied with a gleam in his eye. "Very good, sir. You will find me in the library. Mr. Kepelheim and I had begun a game of chess, to which I promised to return."

Charles lifted Elizabeth into his arms, heading towards the staircase. James kissed her once more and Charles carried Beth up the steps, realising the next time he carried her would be as her husband—after their wedding.

Alicia Mallory, who'd fallen asleep on the parlour sofa whilst waiting, nearly leapt out of her skin when the marquess entered.

"Oh, Lord Haimsbury! I am sorry, sir! I was told you would sleep at your own home tonight." She shut the door that led to the bath and dressing rooms to prevent him from accidentally viewing the duchess's gown, which hung upon a closet door. "Was the ball a success, sir?"

"It was...interesting, you might say. Quite crowded. The duchess is worn through from dancing. Could you turn down her bed? I'll leave her to sleep, but it would be best for her to change into something more comfortable right away. This gown looks most uncomfortable to me."

"It's a good thing men don't wear corsets," she said with an impish grin. "Begging your pardon, sir."

"Oh, I agree wholeheartedly, Alicia. You are coming to live with us at Haimsbury House, I hope?"

She began removing Elizabeth's gloves and shoes. "Yes, sir, most of my things are already there, as are my lady's. Mr. France arrived tonight also, my lord, and awaits downstairs. Also, Mr. Baxter and Mrs. Alcorn came just after supper. Mrs. Wilsham sent word that there are several wedding gifts at your home, sir. One is from the queen!"

"Ah, but this dear lady is my queen, Alicia," he said, kissing Beth's hand.

"Charles?" she asked, opening her eyes at his touch.

"I'm here, little one. Alicia, do you mind giving us a moment?"

"Not at all, sir. I'll be next door, turning down Lord Aubrey's bed. Goodnight, sir."

"Goodnight, Alicia. What is it, darling?" he asked, sitting beside the duchess.

"What time is it?"

"Past midnight, so I can tell you that as of today, you will be my wife. Isn't that marvellous?"

She nodded, and he noticed that her eyes still seemed unfocused.

"Sleep now, little one. Rest well, for I make no guarantee regarding the sleep you'll have tomorrow night," he teased, hoping to make her smile.

"Snow," she muttered, closing her eyes once more. "Red snow... and fire."

Reluctantly, Charles left her and walked down the steps, thinking how this would be his final journey down the staircase as a single man. The thought pleased him very much. He was still smiling when he entered the library to find Kepelheim, France, and Baxter deep in conversation.

"Hail to the new laird!" Baxter cried happily as he took to his feet, a raised glass in one hand and a half-filled decanter in the other. "We have taken the liberty, sir, of pouring ourselves glasses of the little duchess's best claret. She was kind enough to write both Mrs. Alcorn and myself personal letters of invitation, in which my lady insisted we consider ourselves guests rather than servants. The duchess even added her written permission that we should raid both kitchen and wine cellar, which I have done, my lord." The men all raised their glasses. "To you, Lord Haimsbury. To the gentleman who's won the greatest heart in all the realm!"

"Hear, hear!" the other men shouted in unison.

Baxter filled another glass and handed it to Charles, who sat down after accepting it, happy to be with men he considered his closest friends. "Thank you all," the marquess said. "Truly, I am a wealthy man. As a man who's lived much of life alone, I've not formed many strong attachments, but you three are much more than friends. You are also fellow warriors, and with that in mind, I now ask our esteemed Mr. Baxter to tell us how Branham fares these days. Have there been any other incursions from the spirit realm since I left?"

The butler refilled all their glasses and then sat into a leather upholstered wingback chair. "Branham lives on, Lord Haimsbury. And may I say before this company just how very glad it makes me that you have returned to your family? I recall your father and mother well, and, as I've already told you, I met you a few times when you were a boy. Your parents often visited Branham, and before Mr. Miles took over, I served them here as well. The Duchess Patricia dearly loved your mother as friend, sir."

"Thank you, Baxter. Perhaps, when we've the time, you can share tales of my parents."

"It would be my honour, sir. Now, as to the affairs at Branham, you may have received Mr. Marsden's report regarding Ambrose Aurelius. Twas a curious diagnosis, or so thought Mr. Clark and our own vet Mr. Stillwell. I cannot speak to the liver damage, but the marks upon the animal's neck were peculiar. Mr. Marsden thought them caused by a rat."

"And you, Baxter? And Clark? What are your conclusions?"

Taking a deep breath, the butler's brows spoke before his mouth. "Ghosts, sir. Or what we of the material world might call spirits. Can it be coincidence that the stallion died the very night that you were attacked? Perhaps, but a logical man would never deny a possible connexion."

Kepelheim nodded, his back against an embroidered cushion. "Nor would a logical man neglect the implication of cause and effect. The cause is Redwing; the effect a dead horse. But, Baxter, you must tell our marquess of the events of last night!"

After taking a long sip of the wine, he continued, eyes wide. "Yes, last night left us in quite a state, my lord. I can tell you that. In fact, Mrs. Alcorn and I very nearly sent out regrets and remained at the hall, but as we feared it would only cause the duchess needless worry, we decided against it."

"Whatever happened?" Sinclair asked, sitting forward. "More ghosts?"

"More dead sheep, which is distressing enough, but then there are the bells, sir."

"Bells?"

"The abbot's bells, my lord. Those still mounted in the steeple over the old abbey. They had not rung in over sixty years. Not once. Not until last night."

"What caused them to ring, sir?" asked France, his lean face open in anticipation.

"That old abbey, Inspector France, was burnt long ago because of the devilish practises of those who lived within its walls. Claiming to be men of God, these were spawns of Satan, and before he was burnt for witchcraft, the abbot, Simeon Lemures, was parted from his hands by a very sharp broadax, courtesy of King James the Sixth—as the Scots number it, of course," he added with a glance towards Sinclair.

"I grow more Scottish with each passing day," the marquess said, smiling. "Go on, Baxter."

"Well, gentlemen, it is said that on certain nights of the year, the old abbot's severed hands reach up, out of the aether, and pull the ropes, causing the bells to sound. A superstition, yes, but until last night, I had never heard those bells. Yet, at midnight precisely, all three clanged together, not stopping until an hour later."

"Did you send men to inspect the abbey?" Sinclair asked, convinced that one of Trent's altered hybrids, rather than the disembodied hands of a long-dead abbot, lay behind it.

"Mr. Powers, Mr. Clark, and I attended, along with half a dozen of our younger men. Despite our best efforts, my lord, no answer was forthcoming, for though the clanging continued, the bells themselves were silent."

The tailor waved his hands in irritation. "Wait, wait! How is this possible? Either the bells chimed, or they did not!"

"There were no bells, Mr. Kepelheim. When Clark's son mounted the steeple—a very dangerous feat in such weather, and at night, I might add—his lantern revealed an empty belfry. Tis a mystery, I know, but it was witnessed by many men."

"Might the ringing have originated elsewhere?" asked the tailor. "Hampton-on-Sea, perhaps?"

Baxter shook his large head. "No, sir. It did not. Young Master Clark still has minor hearing loss, for having climbed that tower. He said it was as if phantom bells sounded within the belfry. A ghostly presence indeed!"

"Is Clark's son going to be all right?" Sinclair asked, concerned.

"Dr. Price's young assistant, Mr. Emory—who is quite competent, I might add—does not think the loss permanent, which is a blessing." The butler sipped the last of his claret, gazing momentarily at the empty glass. "Ah, but the next morning, we discovered three dead ewes in one of the folds and a pony too ill to eat. Poor thing died that afternoon. I dread telling the duchess, my lord. She loves all her animals, but particularly the horses."

"I'll find a way to break it, Mr. Baxter, but not until next week. Allow her to enjoy her special day first."

"It is a special day for you both, my friend!" Kepelheim insisted, as he refilled their glasses. "Mr. Baxter, have your men reported further incursions of those wolf creatures since last month? Trent's men might still be behind those mysterious bells, but also the deaths of the animals. These hybrids have a powerful hunger."

"So I've come to understand, Mr. Kepelheim, and I am very glad that the little duchess did not have to witness their ferocity! I must say, the sight of Mr. Reid's magnificent balloon rising into the clouds above was something most gratifying."

Charles reached over and grasped the butler's forearm. "Baxter, it was the sight of you, Kepelheim, and so many other brave men that I shall cherish until my last days. You safeguarded our passage to those heights. I never heard how you dealt with their bodies. Did you bury them?"

Kepelheim answered. "Burnt them, of course. A hideous smell, I can tell you! We counted forty in all, and we searched every pocket before adding each to the pit. Very few had any papers, only one or two, which I brought to you at the castle. One wonders at their science, for the aberrations were startling!"

"Foul creatures!" Baxter huffed angrily. "Misfits—all of them! Monsters with one driving instinct: to kill."

The tailor nodded. "Well said, Mr. Baxter. There is a guiding hand behind these animal mixtures. These were monstrous beings, Charles. Tall, stout, hairy like a wolf, and massively muscled. They demonstrated little knack for strategy, however, which was to our benefit. We had a good long look at their—oh I suppose one might call them malformations—for each had claws, not fingernails, and their canine teeth were long, strong, and sharp. The wounds you've described on the horses does not sound like the work of these creatures, however. If Marsden thought it the work of a rat, then the culprit possesses finer, sharper fangs than Trent's hybrids."

"But where do these creatures originate?" Charles asked, sitting forward. "If they're a devilish army fashioned by Redwing, then where is this army's birthplace?"

"A sensible question," Kepelheim said, turning towards Arthur. "Poor Mr. France must wonder what we speak of—such hideous criminal elements are not part of Metropolitan Police training, are they, Inspector France?"

Arthur shook his head. "No, sir, they are not, but I've seen creatures such as you describe—and only recently. In Whitechapel, in fact."

"Really?" Kepelheim asked, his face filled with interest. "Where? When?"

"Only last night, sir."

Sinclair set aside his wine. "You saw them?"

France nodded. "I did, sir. My wife Brenda had just finished packing up all our belongings, and I was loading the crates and furnishings into a large wagon that your staff provided for our use. Thank you, by the way, sir."

Charles's face widened into a bright smile. "On the contrary, Arthur, it's I should thank you. By accepting a position as Beth's bodyguard, you've removed a heavy weight from my mind. Besides, you were born for this, lad. I've known few men with keener investigative skills. And your aim's almost a match for mine."

France smiled, a bit embarrassed. "Thank you, sir. I'd not wish to challenge you to a shooting match, but you're kind to say it, Superintendent."

"Not for long," Charles replied.

"Sir?"

"The rank. I've tendered my resignation to Monro. Superintendent becomes my former title soon."

"Oh?" France replied, clearly surprised at the news. "Well, as I said, I'd packed up the wagon and was walking back towards our house when I saw something flash past me—like in my side vision, you follow? I turned to see what it might be, and what do I see but a very large man, completely naked, sirs, his body covered in blood, and his mouth—or maw—or whatever, open as if panting. Like a dog or a wolf does. This thing had thick hair over most of its body, like a wolf, but it was clearly a man. It stood on two legs, its arms upraised, and then it howled! Such a pitiful sound, sir. It sent chills down my spine!"

"I can imagine," the tailor whispered. "Do go on, Mr. France. What then? Did it see you?"

"Yes, sir, it did. My first instinct was to protect my family, of course, and I reached into my coat to draw my weapon. Then I remembered it was still inside the house, so I rushed back in to fetch it. Armed with the revolver, I ran out to meet the thing, but the man—or I suppose I should say more rightly that *monster*—was gone."

The others grew pensive. Finally, Baxter broke the silence. "You're very brave, sir, for one so young. Lord Haimsbury, is it possible these creatures are behind the horrible crimes in your quarter?"

"Possibly, but I can assure you that no one investigating, save France and Reid, would believe that a hell-hound committed the crimes. Arthur, this man most definitely looked like he was part wolf? That is your assessment?"

"It is, sir. Only partly, though, for it mostly resembled a very tall, muscular man. He seemed in pain, though, sir. I cannot explain why I say it, but that was my impression."

Baxter cleared his throat and sat back against the chair, causing the leather to creak. "There is a story, sirs, that Lord Aubrey asked me never to repeat, but I think he would now approve of my recalling it for your ears. Twas the time Lord Kesson and our Duchess Elizabeth—when she was very young—encountered a great wolf at Branham."

"What?" Charles asked. "I've not heard either the duchess or the earl speak of this. Where did this happen? When?"

France looked puzzled. "Who is Lord Kesson?"

The butler took a long drink and then refilled his glass once more. "To fortify myself," he explained. "To answer your question, Mr. France, the Duke of Drummond is also the Earl of Kesson amongst many other distinguished titles, and so his late son Connor Stuart—the little duchess's father—took that as his courtesy title at birth. It was the fall of '74. The little duchess—then holding a great courtesy title herself for one so small, that of Marchioness of Anjou—well, she would have been six. Her father had come home for a short stay following a six-month posting to India. I tell you, gentlemen, that wonderful man adored his daughter. Twas a shame his sons never survived."

"Baxter, I've only just learnt about those sons," the marquess answered. "Does the duchess know?"

The butler's eyes grew moist. "No, sir, she does not. Her father made us all swear never to tell her, and even the graves were moved to a different part of the cemetery after she was born. And they are unmarked. Look for three small crosses in the northwest corner when you are there. Those tiny graves tell a woeful tale. Indeed, those were tragic days, my lord. Tragic. There were two sons that we know of, but it is likely there was also a third who passed to our heavenly Father. That third, small grave holds no body, only a letter written by the earl to the child he never knew existed. It was by far the saddest of three funerals, I can tell you that. And Lord Kesson, I think because of those losses, threw all his love into his daughter. He would have remained beside her every moment, were he not required to serve our country abroad. You may know this already, Lord Haimsbury, but His Lordship also travelled the world hunting down Redwing scum. Perhaps, you wondered how our estate rounded up a small army so quickly, sir, but that is due to Lord Kesson. He formed us into a military camp each summer, and every servant had to learn to use a variety of weapons. I bless that man for keeping us in trim! Last month was not the first time we were so rallied. The first was that summer in '74. When the wolf appeared."

The butler sipped once again, his greying brows climbing up his forehead as he did so. "It was the autumn of the year, and the marchioness—our little duchess now—as I said, was six. His Lordship challenged her to a race into the centre of the maze; something they often did together. Sirs, the little marchioness knew that formation with all its twists and turns better than anyone, and she easily beat him, though his legs were long and quick. His Lordship stood taller than even you, Lord Haimsbury. Six feet and five inches tall he was! A great, manly gentleman! I was standing on the lawn when the race began, for we'd served luncheon in the rose garden. Duchess Patricia had retired with a headache, something which afflicted many of her days, I am sorry to say. I was setting the lemonade glasses onto a tray, when I heard the little marchioness scream."

Suddenly, the door to the library opened, and all four men jumped at once. Baxter nearly dropped his wine, but being quick with his hands, managed to keep hold of the stem.

It was Aubrey, and he shut the door behind him. "Sorry to startle you, gentlemen. Charles, is Beth all right?"

"She's sleeping," he said as Baxter poured the earl a glass of claret, emptying the second decanter.

"It seems I shall have to make another trip to that fine cellar," the butler said, gazing wistfully at his own empty glass, for he had gulped down the last. "Lord Aubrey, I was just telling the wolf story from when the little duchess was six. Shall I go on, sir?"

Paul sat next to Charles and nodded. "I think it's a tale now best told to our friends. And when you've done, Baxter, I'll share my evening, which oddly enough follows that theme. But go on, I've not heard your version before. Only Cousin Conner's."

The butler took a moment to collect his thoughts. "Where was I then—oh yes! As I was saying, the race began. I was stacking glasses, and then I heard the scream. I've mentioned our military precision, gentlemen, and it was those months of drilling that ignited into a rush of men brandishing weapons of all sorts—hedge clippers, rakes, pitchforks, and several with drawn pistols, for His Lordship kept four to six men armed and on duty at all times. Even Mrs. Alcorn, who was then acting as our housekeeper's assistant, came flying into the north garden, a fire poker in her hands. The earl was already inside the maze, and we all rushed in, but the marchioness's screams continued, growing ever more shrill with each repeat.

"I tell you now, sirs, that I was absolutely terrified. Never before in all her life had that child screamed. Not once. Not even once—not even when a snake crept into the dining hall one evening—no, not the snake Lord Aubrey left in my pantry, no, not that one—but I tell you this: that darling girl was stalwart and unflappable; unlike her mother who screamed at the sight of a button falling off one's coat.

Well, I loved Duchess Patricia, so I say it with affection, but she was imminently flappable. No, sirs, I had never heard that child scream before, and it was that which so terrified me! I'd barely made it past the first few turnings in the maze, when she darted past me, legs all a-blur. Then, to my astonishment, that brave child wrenched the fire poker from Mrs. Alcorn's hands and ran back towards the centre of the maze, shouting something about her father and how dare that wolf hurt him!"

"She ran *back* into the maze?" Kepelheim asked. "That dear lady has the heart of a lion!"

Charles thought of her actions the night the wolf attacked in Scotland, and how Beth had stood up to that hideous, supernatural beast, putting her own life on the line, to save Adele. "She does at that," he said proudly. "But then what happened?"

Paul continued the story. "I think I can help with this, Baxter, for my cousin told me what he saw. Connor had raced Beth into the centre of the maze, and as usual she won. It was when she reached the centre, that she saw an enormous grey wolf. Connor later told me that he'd once seen that same wolf in Scotland as a boy, and he recognised it the moment he saw it. A massive silver grey with immense legs and head and eyes of crimson fire. When he heard Elizabeth scream, he ran towards the middle—for in truth he knew the maze as well as Beth, but he always let her win. He told me that she stood as if frozen; the wolf not more than three feet from her. Terrified, Connor ran to Beth, ordering her to run back to the house. Then, he blocked the exit so the wolf could not follow.

"Now, here is where it becomes even more chilling, my friends. Connor told me that the wolf actually *spoke* to him—but not with its mouth. He heard the words inside his head, and it told him that he would die very soon, but that Elizabeth was his and only his. Connor said he found that he couldn't move, as if his limbs were pinned to the ground somehow. But all he could think of was Beth and her safety. After that day, he took to carrying his pistol with him at all times, but we now know it would have done no good had he been armed that day. Connor learnt that lesson too late, two years later in Scotland. But that day, as he faced this thing inside the maze—unable to move—suddenly Beth came flying back into the centre, darted past him, and she stabbed at the wolf with the fire poker. Connor said the creature gave a great cry and vanished into a pillar of fire and smoke. It was at that same moment that Mr. Baxter and the others arrived. Connor had collapsed, and Beth was kissing his face."

Baxter had begun to weep. "So she was, sir. That precious child had indeed rushed back into the fray, and *she'd won*. I did not see the wolf, myself, but I saw the pillar of fire and smoke, and it was like a door to another world had opened and shut. Most strange, sirs." He turned to the earl. "Lord Aubrey, I beg your indulgence for telling the tale, for I know I promised never to repeat it, but…"

Paul smiled at the butler. "But Charles and our company have need to hear this tale, Baxter. I only asked you to keep it to yourself to reduce any risk that Beth might hear of it. She had no recollection of the encounter, and I hoped to keep it that way. But despite our attempts to shield her, she must have recalled something. After the attack in Scotland, the duchess told us she'd seen such a wolf before. But why do we talk of wolves, Charles? What did I miss?"

The marquess glanced at his pocket watch: half past midnight. "Paul, we talk of wolves because France saw a hybrid in Whitechapel. I'll leave you to hear the tale from him, for I must now bid you all goodnight. I'd love to stay and talk until dawn, for this company cheers me much, but I'm weary to the bone. Goodnight, all. I'll see you at the church."

Paul walked Charles to the door. "Is Beth really all right?"

"She is," he assured the earl. "She sleeps now, and tomorrow we wed. I hope you've put off your trip to Egypt for now."

"In fact, I convinced Salisbury of it at the ball tonight, but it is only a postponement. I'll keep watch tonight along with Inspector France. And I'll tell you my tale about Dr. MacKey tomorrow. For now, go home! And enjoy your last night of freedom!"

CHAPTER THIRTY-ONE

18th November

Elizabeth slept until quarter past eight, rising only when Alicia Mallory insisted the duchess must ready herself for the wedding. Worried that her cousin hadn't joined the family for breakfast, Della crept into Beth's room, peering 'round the door. Seeing Elizabeth already awake, Adele rushed in to kiss her.

"Do hurry, Cousin Beth!" she sang, bouncing onto the edge of the bed. "Today is your wedding day! Are you thrilled to be getting married?"

"How could I not be?" the duchess replied as she kissed her little cousin. "Have I missed breakfast?"

"Mrs. Smith served it early," the girl answered. "But it wasn't much at all. Toast and oatmeal with fruit. Aunt Victoria says we mustn't fill up before going, because we'll have so much to eat afterward. I had three slices of toast as a precaution, though. Mrs. Smith promised to send up a tray for you. Do hurry, Cousin Beth. We'll be late, and I want to see Winston before the service begins."

"I'm afraid you won't be able to do that, Della. We arrive after everyone's seated. Alicia, could you run me a quick bath? I'll start brushing out my hair."

"Yes, my lady," the maid answered, turning the taps to the porcelain tub. "Shall I arrange it the same way? Like we practised?"

"The curls or the fishbone braid? Which looks better?"

"Either, my lady. We can try both, if you wish. They cannot begin the ceremony without you, after all."

Laughing, Elizabeth unbraided her hair and used a boar's hair brush to smooth the persistent waves. The waist-length locks shone in the morning sunlight.

"Shall I?" Della asked, taking the brush and stroking the raven strands. "Your dress is so very pretty. I like it much better than the one you wore last night."

"As do I, darling. Has it warmed up?" Beth asked.

"A little. Mr. Miles said it might snow," the girl answered happily.

"Snow?" Elizabeth whispered, a slight headache starting in her right temple. "I pray not."

"I love snow," Della said. "There. All ready for the new style."

Beth gazed at herself in the dressing table mirror, a strange memory teasing at her thoughts. *A mirror. Why does that bother me?* As she stood, the room spun a bit and Beth gripped the table, fighting an intense wave of nausea.

"Cousin Beth?" Della asked her, reaching to steady the duchess. "You stood too quickly. Paul says the blood can fly out of your head, when you do that. Sit down again until it returns."

Beth obeyed, sitting upon the upholstered bench.

The door stood ajar, and Mary Wilsham entered, carrying a silver tray, laden with a pot of weak tea, one slice of dry toast, and a bowl of oatmeal. After Gertrude Trumper's vociferous announcement regarding the pregnancy, Mrs. Meyer had spoken with the household servants and explained the full truth of the matter. Everyone understood and now went out of their way to make certain that the duchess never traversed stairs or walked alone. The cook prepared special meals, and Wilsham took great pains to make sure Elizabeth ate a little something at each meal.

"Here, my lady. I've brought a bit of breakfast. Try to manage a few bites of the oatmeal. It'll fortify ya for the day an' help that little one ta grow."

Beth smiled. "I'll see what I can do, Mary. Thank you. What time is it?"

"Already half eight," Wilsham answered as she helped the duchess to a soft chair, where she might eat the meal. "Did ya hear the finches singin' this mornin'? I used ta set out seeds for 'em back at the old house. They'd sing fer hours sometimes."

"Is it warmer, then?" Beth asked as Alicia began to lay out the clothing on the bed.

"It's cold but sunny," Wilsham answered. "Here now, Lady Della, let me help you with your hair whilst your cousin eats."

Mary Wilsham had never raised a daughter, but always wished for one. She and Adele had grown quite close. "Very well, Aunt Mary," the girl answered sweetly. "Could you arrange my hair just like Elizabeth's? And with my little coronet, too, please!"

Alicia looked up from her work. "I think yours is called a tiara, Lady Della. The Branham coronet is what my lady wears, but yours is ever so pretty."

"Isn't it, though?" the girl said dreamily. "And I may meet my handsome prince today at the wedding, so I must look my very best. Oh, Cousin Beth, I'm so happy!"

Elizabeth sipped the weak tea, praying the nausea wouldn't overwhelm her on this day—of all days. "I'm glad, Della, but if I do not dress, then there will be no wedding, and that would break my poor Captain's heart, would it not?"

Della grew serious. "Oh, we mustn't do that. Poor Cousin Charles would be forever sad. You must finish quickly, and I'll see you downstairs."

The child bounced out of the room, and Mary Wilsham shut the door.

"I'm sure Aggie MacGowan can tend to Lady Della. She's turned into a real good lady's maid," she told Beth. "Is there aught I can fetch for ya?"

"No, thank you, Mary. If I can keep this down, then I'll be fine. Thank you for thinking of me. Oh, I do hope I can fit into that gown without a corset! Either Madam du Monde's measuring tape is faulty, or else my waistline expands almost daily. Is this rate of growth normal?"

"Some ladies grow quick, others do not," Wilsham replied as she sat in the other chair. "I hardly showed at all wiv my first boy, bu' the second pushed me out somethin' fierce."

Hoping to help, Alicia made a suggestion. "We can try the dress without it first, if it makes it more comfortable. I'm not inclined to wear them either, but most gentlemen seem to prefer the way they make me look. Not that I've had that any young men court me, of course."

"Your day'll come, Alicia," Mary said, helping Beth to her feet. "Here now, let's do the bath, and then consider our options for the dress."

Downstairs, Victoria had already breakfasted and dressed for the day. She'd promised to meet her friend Maisie Churchill at the chapel by nine. The morning papers were filled with news about the nuptials, listing all the peers who would be attending, most notably the queen. The service was to begin at ten, and afterward, the duke was hosting a reception for five hundred in the ballroom of his home. Had the wedding been in the warmer months, the celebration would have been outdoors, but colder air and the promise of snow made indoors a requirement.

"Paul, I shall leave without you, if you do not hurry!" Victoria called as Miles helped her into a coat. "Nephew! Are you coming or not?"

Aubrey bounded down the steps, still fastening the left cufflink. Even when at home, the earl seldom used a valet, but today he'd employed Baxter's expert assistance. However, one of the collar buttons had popped off, requiring repair, and then, the right cufflink refused to remain latched. "Sorry, Tory. We ran into a few snags, but I'm all yours."

The elder Stuart frowned. "I thought you'd promised to cut your hair."

Aubrey laughed, his chestnut locks bouncing. "Beth said she prefers it this length."

"Yes, so she's said many times. I thought she also liked the beard, yet you've shaved. Does this mean your Egypt adventure is off?"

"For the present."

"I see," Tory answered flatly. "Then, you're still going?"

"Eventually, I must, but let's not speak of it today, all right? This is Elizabeth's day, and I'll not spoil it. Shall we away to Drummond Chapel?"

"Yes, I think so. Is Elizabeth on time, do you think? She slept in far too late, in my opinion. She should have risen at six."

"She had a difficult night," the earl said, stifling a yawn. "And when all this is over, I shall spend at least a week sleeping myself. Is it snowing yet?"

Miles walked the pair to the main doors, where the duke's carriage awaited to take them to the church. "Not yet, sir, but there are suspicious clouds overhead," the butler said, handing the earl his top hat. "I've taken the liberty of placing a warm blanket and two umbrellas inside the coach, just in case."

"Good thinking, Miles," Aubrey said happily, offering his arm to his aunt. "Lady Victoria?"

She put her arm through Paul's, and the two made their way to the black brougham. "Maisie will be cross. Ah well, it cannot be helped."

She stepped into the coach with the footman's assistance, and Paul followed. As they drove the short distance to the duke's estate, Aubrey gazed out the window.

"I hope you're not moping, Nephew," Victoria said, her eyes sharp. "This was to be your wedding once."

Paul sighed, brushing the hair back behind his left ear. "I've decided to let it go, Tory. And I'm beginning to succeed, though I'd be lying if I said my heart is fully healed. I doubt that wound will ever mend completely. No man could love her more than Charles does. He deserves her, Tory. He really does."

"I'm glad to hear you say it. Now, just what were you doing with that auburn-haired woman last night? Oh, yes, I saw you, my dear. Who is she?"

"One of Redwing's softer ranks," he explained. "Only this one is subtler than most. Dr. MacKey isn't the first female operative I've encountered, nor will she be the last I imagine, but she is persistent," he said, smiling. "Despite her rushed departure from Drummond castle on a stolen horse, she's found a way to explain her behaviour to me. Can you believe it? I think she is friend to this Romanian prince, too, for I saw him speaking with her last night in the garden after Uncle James and Charles left with Beth. Alexei is a deceiver, if ever I've seen one. It was all I could manage not to throttle the man!"

Victoria buttoned her gloves. "You know, this battle is about far more than an earthly realm. It is about heavenly rewards, too. Siding with God's enemy leaves one damned for all eternity. Do you think this woman is worth our prayers?"

"I've already begun petitioning the Lord on her behalf, Tory," he said, and she could see deep emotion in his face. "It's why I plan to meet her tonight. If there is any chance at all that she might jump from that hellish ship, then I'd like to help."

"Be careful, Paul. A drowning woman might just as easily pull you under with her. Well, I see we're here. I must find Maisie. Beware of feminine traps. Keep on the whole armour of God at all times."

"I do, and I will, Victoria. Now, I'm off to find our groom. I'll see you inside."

Charles Sinclair had been waiting in the chapel's vestry for half an hour, kept company by Martin Kepelheim. The groom wore a beautifully tailored formal suit, specially made for him by Martin's loving and talented hands. The trousers were of black-dyed Merino wool that broke at just the right spot upon the gleaming, black leather boots. He wore a white silk shirt and a white, double-breasted waistcoat made of the finest silk, embroidered in gold thread forming the inner circle's trademark symbol: a P crossed by an S, enclosed within a gold ring.

"Subtle, but it makes a statement, does it not?" Kepelheim said as Charles noticed the needlework.

"It's beautiful, Martin. I don't think anyone ever explained what our symbol actually represents. I presume the P stands for Plantagenet, but what of the S?"

Kepelheim laughed. "You are most likely correct as regards the P, although some have joked that the initials actually refer to Paul Stuart, since he's been our leader in the field for so long. Yes, it goes back to the Plantagenet twins, of course. The two sons of Henry the Fifth and Catherine."

"Wait, you just said 'most likely correct' about what the P stands for. I cannot let that pass, Martin. If not Plantagenet, then what?"

"Allow me to defer that conversation until after your wedding, my friend. I stand amongst a minority within the circle who've begun to consider another possibility, but it is based on scant—though mounting—evidence, so allow me to pass for now."

"Very well, but only if you give me a hint."

"No, for if I do, it would be impossible for you to let it drop, Charles. If you will set it aside in your remarkable mind for the present, I shall tell you all I know tonight."

"You do realise that I shan't forget."

Kepelheim grinned, deep dimples creasing his fleshy face. "Yes, Superintendent, I'm aware of your dogged nature and that you'll pursue questions on this topic without mercy, therefore I promise not to leave the city."

Both men laughed, and Sinclair looked once more at the exquisite workmanship on both the tie and waistcoat. "And the S?"

"Well, the S does stand for Stuart, according to current thought, but some—even as lately as a hundred years ago—believed it stood for Sinclair."

"Do you refer to the meeting at Rose House? The one I overheard?" Charles asked.

The tailor nodded, making sure his protégé's shoulders fit correctly. "Yes, but Stuart and Sinclair may both be correct, for our duchess will soon possess both those names, and you very nearly did. When your grandfather married into the Stuart clan, your great-grandfather—I think he would have been the 9th Lord Aubrey—insisted that as part of the marriage contract, any issue would take the name Stuart-Sinclair, but the Sinclairs refused, hence your unhyphenated surname. So perhaps both theories have merit. Elizabeth embodies both twins, the Branham and Drummond lines, and she is a Stuart. However, she is about to marry the other 'S', becoming Elizabeth Stuart Sinclair. Here, let me tie this cravat. The knot is all wrong. You are nothing but thumbs today, my friend."

Kepelheim expertly knotted the bespoke tie—gold silk with narrow white and black stripes—and he brushed at the cutaway coat to make sure the groom looked perfect.

"You are every inch a marquess," the tailor said proudly. "Our duchess will swoon, when she sees her Captain in his new attire; will she not, Lord Aubrey?"

Paul had entered the room, dressed in a matching suit, but with a black striped cravat and gold waistcoat. "Martin's right, Cousin. You look quite handsome. No looking in the mirror now. You'll have plenty of time to admire yourself later. It's nearly ten, and I've a few things to tell you before the ceremony."

"About Lorena?" he asked his cousin.

"Yes, how did you…oh, your detective skills, I suppose. I managed to corner her for half an hour after you and James left with Beth. As I was leaving, I noticed her talking with the Romanian."

"Alexei?"

"Yes, though it's hard to tell from a distance. He and Romanov bear a striking resemblance to one another."

"What excuse did Lorena give for fleeing the castle?" Sinclair asked.

Aubrey laughed. "A feeble one. She claimed that she left the castle because she feared the wolf!"

Charles's brows rose high. "Oh, really?"

Paul nodded, smiling. "Yes, I know. She is brazen, is she not? Lorena claimed she'd seen it approach the house whilst she was out walking—though walking at that hour sounds suspicious in itself—and that she panicked and ran to the mews, where the wolf then followed her. She told me that the horses were startled by the animal, so she hastened towards the first horse she found and quickly saddled it—again, so she claims—and that she'd ridden halfway to Glasgow before the wolf left off chase."

Charles could hardly believe his ears. "Did she honestly expect you to believe any part of that?"

"Of course, she did. I smiled and nodded during the entire performance, but all the while, I perceived a kind of sadness in her voice. Charles, I think Lorena regrets leaving us."

"You think her a possible traitor to Redwing? If so, Paul, then we must find a way to help. I'd not want any woman to suffer the way Morgan did."

"Nor would I, which is why I'm meeting her tonight at ten."

"Paul, I wish you wouldn't. Postpone until I can go with you, will you? Beth is still worried that you're in danger."

"Cousin, I've lived most of my life in danger of one kind or another. I'll be perfectly safe. Your only worry today is making sure you don't trip on Beth's skirts, when you walk beside her."

Sinclair smiled, placing his hand on the earl's arm. "You are a truly good man, Paul Stuart. Another man would search for ways to ruin this day for me, but instead you find ways to ease it. Thank you, Cousin. Thank you, but promise to be careful. The thrill of danger can be a harsh and addictive mistress. I say it as someone who's experienced that lady's charms. Besides, we need you in our lives. Beth and I."

Aubrey's eyes—so similar to Haimsbury's—began to tear up as well. "Charles, you're as dear to me as any brother. I will never allow harm to befall you or your bride."

"Well, well," a strong male voice called from the entrance to the vestry. "Are my nephews going to spend the entire morning talking, or shall we have a wedding?"

Charles put his arms around his uncle, giving him a great hug. "James, you are making me the happiest man on this earth! I cannot tell you all that's in my heart; it's so full. I'm actually overwhelmed with joy!"

James touched Charles's face. "I know, son. I do know it, and all I ask is that you make Beth happy and keep her safe. Well, Nephews, shall we drink to this union? I know it's early, but I've had Booth mix champagne into a bit of apple juice, so we can share a private toast." The sober-eyed butler entered the cramped room, carrying a silver pitcher, from which he poured a sparkling concoction into four crystal flûtes.

Drummond raised his glass high. "To my remarkable nephews, Charles and Paul. May the love you feel for one another today never falter. May your minds be ever sharp, and may you always look to Christ for His divine guidance."

"Amen," both young men said in response as all four clinked glasses. Charles wiped his eyes and looked up just as Edward MacPherson entered.

"Champagne so early in the day? Ah, well, it is a special occasion, after all. The archbishop has arrived, so it looks as though we're ready. Benson's invariably longwinded, but I've asked him to keep it brief. We'll see how well he complies."

"Yes, my uncle told me as much. If it pleases Her Majesty, then I'm happy to oblige," Sinclair replied with a wide smile.

"Gentlemen, if I may offer a prayer before we leave?"

The duke, Sinclair, Stuart, and Kepelheim bowed their heads along with MacPherson, whose soft voice rose up into the vestry's high ceiling. "Saviour of all who claim your precious blood, you and you alone have created the worlds, both seen and unseen. You raise up and you tear down. Your elevate some to positions of great authority, and others you reduce to the lowest of the low. How you choose to use Charles Sinclair is up to you, but I pray that no matter where you might lead him and his new bride following this service, that you will strengthen them both for the task. Equip them and guide them for each phase of their journey. Whether that journey be filled with joys, triumphs, tears, or sorrow, it all begins today. Thank you, Lord, for the honour you have bestowed upon me to pronounce them as one. Thank you for the lives they will now share with all of us. In your name, we ask it; even the name of Christ Almighty. Amen."

"Well, son," MacPherson said to Charles, "put on your best smile and get ready to greet your bride."

Lorena MacKey watched from a position across the street from Drummond chapel. Trent stood beside her, dressed in his finest clothes, tapping a rosewood cane against the palm of his gloved hand. "Do you know what to do?" he asked.

"Yes, of course. It's as simple as a maiden's thoughts," she said. "And my reward?"

"You will learn all the wonderful tricks of form and function which you so desire, my dear. So long as you obey only my commands. Remember that traitors meet very dark ends."

"Why would I betray you, when you promise such gifts?"

"That is wise, my dear," he said, touching her hair. "You're very pretty, Lorena. 'twould be a shame to ruin such a face."

Fearing that any reply to the threat might reveal her true feelings, MacKey forced a smile. "I'll leave now to make sure the mirror is ready. Arrive no earlier than nine, for these parties go on far into the evening."

"Excellent, my dear," he answered, still playing with her hair. "Do not fail me. I offer no second chances."

Lorena prayed inwardly to God, wondering if he cared—if he even noticed her predicament, for fear raked at her heart with clawed hands. She bowed her head to Trent and forced a smile, and then departed for Queen Anne House.

CHAPTER THIRTY-TWO

The chimes of Westminster proclaimed the hour of ten, and the main door to Drummond Chapel opened. Charles waited near the altar with Paul to his left, and he anxiously watched the doorway for the first sign of Adele and Beth. The chapel was packed to overflowing, forcing those who arrived late to remain in their coaches or stand outside in the morning chill, in order to witness this rare, peerage event. News reporters and photographers from all of Europe's major papers waited near their carriages, though a few lucky ones sat inside the chapel, near the back.

The chamber orchestra, which had played a selection of hymns as prelude, now commenced the first processional arrangement, '*And the mountains shall depart*' from Mendelssohn's oratorio *Elijah.* Lady Adele entered, and Paul's eyes began to grow moist as he watched his beloved daughter walk slowly and carefully towards the altar; arrayed all in white organza and embroidered satin, a gown to match Elizabeth's. Della's chestnut hair curled into a ladylike coif of tight spirals, and upon her head sat a dazzling white gold tiara encrusted with tiny diamonds that Paul had borrowed from his mother's jewellery box. Seeing her thus, he suddenly realised just how quickly his child was growing up. Della was nearly eleven, and in only a few more years, she might walk this same aisle as a bride.

"Isn't she beautiful?" Paul said to his cousin proudly. "That's my lassie."

As Della reached the front, she took a step to the side opposite her father, the man she knew as her brother (though Paul was beginning to wonder if he shouldn't tell her the truth soon). He winked at her, and she very carefully took her place, keeping the six-foot train out of Elizabeth's way, just as she had practised. The orchestra concluded the first selection and began to play '*I Know that My Redeemer Liveth*' from Handel's *Messiah*, one of Elizabeth's favourite sacred works. Everyone stood and turned to look at James Stuart, the Duke of Drummond, proudly holding his granddaughter's delicate arm.

Charles gasped, as did everyone in the pews. The handsome Scottish duke wore full formal attire that matched the style and fabrics of his nephews, but it was Beth whose dazzling beauty demanded all their attention. She wore white satin, overlaid with fine gold embroidery, wrought in a double ring pattern, that covered the entire skirt and high-necked bodice. Although she'd wanted to leave the corset behind, the pearl buttons at the dress's waist had refused to fasten without one, so Beth walked carefully, keeping her back straight and trying not to become dizzy with all the excitement; for, just as Charles could see her, she could see him, and her heart beat wildly as she neared her Captain.

Atop the wedding veil, shone the dazzling pink diamonds of the Branham ducal coronet. The veil had once been worn by her maternal great-great grandmother, Antoinette Mérovée de Moiré Linnhe, and was finely woven in white silk tulle, trimmed in beautifully stitched tambour lace, shaped like roses of purest white that reached out as long as the gown's magnificent train. The veil covered her face, but its delicate lacework permitted Elizabeth's dark eyes to see and be seen; and above it, the crown's diamonds shone like a rosy dawn as she walked beneath the lights of the chandeliers.

Her wide train stretched behind for thirty feet, sweeping majestically across the red carpet as she passed the rows of pews; each filled with dignitaries and peers, amongst them the Duke and Duchess of Edinburgh, Duke and Duchess of Marlborough, and, in the very front, the heir presumptive Prince Albert Victor the Duke of Clarence and his father Edward, Prince of Wales. On the aisle, next to the prince, sat Her Majesty Queen Victoria, alongside her daughter-in-law Princess Alexandra.

Just behind the queen, sat two more rows of royal dignitaries, including Prince Anatole Romanov, who sat beside Prince Nicholai Aleksandrovich Romanov, the *tesarevich,* or crown prince, of the Russian Empire, who had once shown a keen interest in Elizabeth. The twenty-year-old Russian heir offered the little duchess a wide grin as she passed, and Anatole nodded his head politely.

Just before reaching the altar, Elizabeth paused to curtsy to the queen, who leaned over to kiss her upon the forehead. As she straightened, Beth nearly lost her balance, but no one noticed, save Charles, for she appeared to move flawlessly to her position next to Adele.

Years later, when speaking of the ceremony, neither Elizabeth nor Charles would remember much. Beth would recall how his hand trembled a little, and that she'd yawned during the impromptu homily given by the Archbishop of Canterbury, followed by his ten minute prayer of supplication and blessing. The one moment that would remain fixed in both their memories was when Ed MacPherson said the words that forever changed their relationship: "Before God and in the presence of this congregation, Elizabeth and Charles have made their solemn vows to each other. They have confirmed their promises by the joining of hands and by the giving and receiving of rings. Therefore, I proclaim to all here present that they are now husband and wife. Lord Haimsbury, you may now kiss your bride."

And so he did. Charles Robert Arthur Sinclair III gently lifted the veil of his beloved bride and sweetly kissed her.

"I love you, Captain. Always and forever," she said as their lips parted.

"And I love you, little one. You make me the happiest man in all the earth today."

The orchestra commenced a final hymn of praise, and Charles and Elizabeth turned towards the congregation, the couple's joyful smiles more radiant than any sunrise. After a final blessing, a recessional hymn commenced, and Charles took Beth's arm, leading her through the main doors and into the morning air.

Just before reaching the end of the long, carpeted sidewalk, the elated marquess pulled her close and kissed her once again. As a result, the long lines of well-wishers and newspapermen broke into applause, and church bells began to peal across Westminster. Adele and the earl followed, along with the Duke of Drummond, who escorted Queen Victoria. The aged sovereign moved slowly, limping slightly on her left foot, but stopped to speak with the newlyweds before returning to her carriage.

"My beautiful girl," she said to Elizabeth. "I admit to disappointment that you and my grandson couldn't make a go of it, but it seems as though you've found someone who suits you very well. Charles, you must keep her always in your care and make her happy, as my beloved Albert did for me. And may you have many, many children, my dears! Now, if you will forgive an old woman, I must retire to my coach. Gout, you know," she added, whispering the confession to Beth. "I pray it never comes to your family, but if it does, a bit of baking soda in water each morning offers relief—but one must remember to make it a daily ritual. Sadly, with all that's occupied me of late, I've not been as faithful as needs require."

"I take all your advice to heart, Your Majesty. Thank you," Beth said as the queen held her hand.

Victoria then looked to Sinclair. "Charles, you must come see us next time we are in Edinburgh. I have many marvellous tales about your father. Oh what a man he was!"

"You're very kind to say so, Your Majesty. Beth and I shall be honoured."

"Goodbye, my dears," she said and kissed Elizabeth once more on the forehead. The queen then turned to Drummond, whispering something which caused the duke to laugh. Prince Edward had been speaking in the narthex with the Duke of Marlborough, but seeing his mother departing, quickly ended his conversation and helped her to the royal coach, where three footmen in full livery assisted her up the folding steps.

Returning to his granddaughter, Drummond kissed her cheek, and Beth noticed tears glistening on his face. "Did you see the queen's face when you kissed? It made her cry. I saw it! She had such hopes for you and Eddy, but she's all right. Now that the legalities are ended, it's time for the party! Charles, we'll see you both at Drummond House as quickly as you can finish here, and then I fear it's a long, formal line of congratulations and best wishes from all the muckety-mucks in London. But after that folderol's finished, we'll adjourn to Queen Anne for the real celebration. Princess, are you up for a full day?"

She nodded, her hand tightly held by her new husband. "I am, Grandfather. A full day and more, even if it goes past midnight. Can you believe it? I have a new title, and it is the best of all. Missus! I shall always want to have that as my primary title, Captain. Mrs. Charles Sinclair."

Charles kissed her once more, his eyes filled with admiration and affection. "Mrs. Sinclair, I love you madly. Are you aware of that?"

She nodded, and the duke laughed, happier than he'd been in years. "All right. I'm off," he told them. "Charles, have her there as soon as possible, though I expect you're going to find it a challenge, working your way through this crowd. Granger stands ready with your carriage, whenever you wish to go. Now is better than later."

Elizabeth kissed the duke, and Charles saw the great man weep openly, tears glistening upon his moustache. "Thank you for making this possible, Grandpa. And for saying yes when Charles asked for my hand. You'll never know how happy you've made me!"

Drummond kissed her hand and headed towards the first carriage in a long line, parked on the gravel circle. Aunt Victoria came next, but she stopped only for a moment.

"Well done, both of you," she said simply. "Don't be late to the house. Paul and Adele have already left, and I strongly suggest you follow their example. There will be ample time for chitchat and visiting at my brother's home. Don't dawdle now!"

She kissed Beth's cheek and winked at her nephew, who winked in return.

"Well, Mrs. Sinclair?" he asked his bride. "Shall we? Our carriage awaits, and we dare not dawdle."

Charles signalled to Granger, and the decorated coach pulled forward. Two footmen assisted Charles and Elizabeth into the ornate carriage's interior, taking great care with the wedding gown's train so that it did not wrinkle.

As the horses began trotting, Charles kissed her once more. "Mrs. Sinclair! I never knew two words could be so wonderful or have such meaning to me. Beth, you've made me the happiest man alive! With you by my side, I can even face hours of droning well-wishers and endless toasts."

"There is no joy greater than this, my Captain: to call you husband," she said, sitting as straight as she could, for the corset was already biting into her flesh.

He laughed. "Husband. It almost sounds like a foreign word after being alone for so many years. You may need to repeat it a thousand times or so, until I grow used to it."

"Husband, husband, husband," she whispered, leaning close. "I'll say it again and again, my darling, if it makes you smile." She winced, twisting slightly in the seat. "It will be a long day, I fear, and

I shall be glad to exchange this dress for something less elegant. Truly, it seems the fancier the gown, the more impossible the torture!"

He put his hand to her waist and felt the whalebone ribs that formed the corset. "I hope you didn't wear this to impress me," he said honestly. "I like your natural waistline—prefer it actually."

She took a careful breath. "As do I, husband. It was not out of vanity that I put on this medieval device, but out of necessity. It seems, I have expanded since Friday. I fear that without the corset, the dress was an inch too small. My waistline widens to make room for your son."

He touched her waist, lovingly. "How our lives have changed," he whispered. "If this causes you discomfort, do you prefer changing now? I can ask Granger to take us home first."

"No, that would take an hour or more, and we've guests waiting. I'll manage, but I doubt I'll be able to eat much. I shall change as soon as we get back to Queen Anne."

"And after, we go to our home, Beth. Our home. How I love saying that! Beth, I hope you will always be happy. I want only to see you smile."

"Captain, I can think of no time when I would not smile in your company—not if you, too, are smiling."

"In plenty and want, joy and sorrow, sickness and health," he said, a moment's worry crossing his thoughts.

"Do I hear darkness in your voice? Charles, no matter what our future holds, the bond betwixt us will never weaken, but only grow stronger. I've no fear when you hold me. None at all."

"Then I promise to hold you always. If not in my arms, then know that you are eternally in my heart."

As they came to a stop, Charles could see two footmen unrolling a red carpet, leading from the duke's front door and ending at the coach. "It's rather like being royalty," he joked as Granger opened the carriage door, and a footman lowered the steps into place. He and Granger then helped the couple exit the carriage, and Charles took his bride's arm as they followed the carpeted path up the steps. The entire portico had been festooned with boughs, ribbons, and swags of dried orange blossoms, adding a festive touch to the mansion.

The doors opened, and Booth greeted them, wearing a rare smile. "Congratulations, my lady, my lord. Your Grace, your aunt awaits you in the green room. Lord Haimsbury, may I escort you to the blue room?"

Charles sighed as he watched Beth follow a footman towards the green room, and then disappear behind a set of panelled doors. "Very well, Booth, let's begin the party, shall we?"

"Very good, sir. You'll find this room is reserved for family and close friends only. We've set out a cold luncheon, available anytime you require nourishment. The formal reception commences in the ballroom in half an hour's time. Please, take a few moments to relax until then, sir."

Charles entered and realised at once that it was the very same room where he and Amelia had first met the duke nearly ten years earlier. Standing here now, he thought of his first marriage—and of his son—and prayed Amelia had found peace before her death. *I've forgiven her,* he thought. *Finally, I've let it all go.* It was a free-ing moment.

As he took a seat upon the same couch where eleven-year-old Beth had told her grandfather that Charles was to be called 'Captain', he found himself weeping. *Thank you, Lord! Thank you for converting all these years of pain and sorry into joy and happiness!*

His internal reverie was abruptly interrupted by the abrasive call of an all too familiar voice.

"Well done, old man! She's a looker and loaded."

Sinclair cringed, but determined not to permit even this lout to disturb the peace of the day, he managed a smile. "Albert Wendaway," he said, deliberately avoiding the insolent baronet's title. "I'm surprised to see you here."

Wendaway, attired in a charcoal cutaway and garish waist-coat of red silk, offered his hand. "Where else would I be today, old man? Got the invite and all, you know. My cousin is around here, somewhere. You remember him, Charles. John Pike. Second son of Sir Winston Pike. A knight, not a baronet, but still he's kin. I say! You've done rather well for yourself. Who'd have thought that beneath that mundane exterior you were actually a marquess—and an important one at that. I'd imagine your properties provide a very pretty income."

"They suffice," Sinclair replied vaguely.

Wendaway laughed, his upturned nose crinkling above a ginger moustache. "Droll, old man. Very droll. My banker friend says your portfolio can match any in England, and when you include the Branham properties, why, you're rich as Croesus! You've entered the world of financial power, Cousin. Well done!"

"I've no intention of lending you money, Albert. Nor of paying your gambling debts."

Wendaway laughed, his thick skin impervious to insult. "My debts are paid, old man," he lied. "And I've no need for a loan. However, my friend at Barings has word of a sure-thing, which only a fool would refuse."

"I've my own investment banker," the marquess began, but the persistent baronet forged ahead nonetheless.

"Yes, yes, I'm sure you do, but this man just returned from six months in the Argentine, and he knows of a yet unregistered silver mine that is scratching for investors. He guarantees tripling your money in less than a month. A thousand pounds could net you three thousand; ten, thirty; a hundred could buy the entire mine at this point and leave you in a very pretty position."

"If your friend is so certain of his facts, have him contact my man at National Provencial. His name is Sir Percival Wilders."

"Oh, yes, I suppose I could do that, but then Wilders would take his cut of the profits. Or he might neglect to report all your returns, old man."

Charles wanted to kick the annoying baronet's backside, but he counted to ten as all the reasons why he detested the shiftless gambler flooded his memory. Then, it occurred to him that if Wendaway were here, then Amelia's parents could not be far behind. Only seconds after this thought flickered through his mind, Margaret Winstone's unmistakable, high-pitched laughter rose up and echoed off the panelled walls in the duke's foyer. Sinclair flinched, fearing his temper, and continued to count well past ten to twenty, thirty, and higher. Before reaching triple digits, a much more welcome voice modified the strident laughter, blending Margaret's guffaws into a tolerable duet of gentility.

The Earl of Aubrey entered with Adele on his arm.

"Charles, is this not the loveliest of all ladies today—our Beth notwithstanding, of course?"

Albert Wendaway finally stopped talking, turned, and bowed to Adele. His lips curled into a sugary smile. "What a vision you are! Your beauty rivals that of Helen. A face to launch ten thousand ships! I'm Charles's cousin, Sir Albert Wendaway, at your service. You were marvellous today, Lady Adele. Absolutely smashing."

Della's cheeks pinked at the overt praise, but Paul interrupted before she could answer. "You say you're my cousin's cousin? Now that is interesting. I don't recall any Wendaways in the family tree. I'm Lord Aubrey, and Adele is my much beloved sister."

Wendaway's right eyelid began to twitch in an odd fashion—something both Charles and Paul noticed—and he offered the earl a tense bow. "Lord Aubrey, your reputation precedes you, sir. You are Lady Adele's brother? Then, I'm all the more pleased to make your acquaintance, for she cuts a fine figure."

What little smile remained on Paul's face vanished completely, and he took a step towards the baronet. "I keep careful watch on my sister, sir. A wise man would do well to remember that."

Wendaway audibly gulped and moved backwards. "Wisdom is finer than any gold, so they say. Tis a pleasure to meet you—at last."

Della watched as the young man left to mingle in the foyer. "He's very handsome," she said, her face aglow.

"So are tigers, darling. Let's spend some time with our cousin, shall we? He looks lonely." Paul led his sister towards the punch bowl, where a footman poured two cups of the citrus and cranberry beverage. "Charles, where's your bride?" he asked as he and Della took seats near the fireplace.

"Closeted with our aunt."

The duke entered, chatting with Frederick and Margaret Winstone. "We're all in here," he was saying, "but we'll be moving on to the ballroom shortly. Mrs. Winstone, have you met the Russian royal family? The tsar couldn't make it, but he sent his son and several cousins, including Prince Anatole Romanov. The prince is very powerful in St. Petersburg, you know. And I hear that many others begin to arrive. The Dukes of Marlborough and Edinburgh, the Prime Minister—but also Cartringham, Boughton, and a whole roster of high-ranking dignitaries from all across Europe. I believe they're gathering in the ballroom, or perhaps it's the gallery. Booth would know. Booth!" he called.

The butler appeared as if by magic. "Your Grace?"

"Booth, old man, Mr. and Mrs. Winstone are to be escorted to the special room upstairs. Has the Russian party arrived yet? No?

Well, I'm sure there are lots of highbrows there already—no doubt enjoying the refreshments."

Margaret was practically drooling, and Sir Albert had already gone ahead of the butler towards the 'special' receiving area in the upper level gallery. The duke joined his nephews.

"You'll need to keep an eye on that baronet," he told the earl. "I doubt the Winstones have any idea of the true extent of his debts, but I'm told gambling is his more charming side. The rest of his vices might even make him eligible for a set of bracelets in Her Majesty's cells at Newgate."

Charles sighed, casting his eyes on Della, who sat alone near the window. "I'd dearly love to throttle that man, but it may not be wise to speak of him here. Young hearts break easily. And speaking of hearts, have you seen any sign of my wife?" he asked, breaking into a wide smile. "Oh, I do love calling her that."

The duke took a cup of punch from the footman. "Thank you, Wilson. Beth should join us directly, son. I think my sister had some motherly advice to pass along. She'd planned on giving that speech this morning, but Beth slept in—or so Tory tells it. Is our girl all right? She looks a bit pale to me."

Charles and Paul sat in matching armchairs, the smooth motion so similar that the duke began to laugh. "You two are certainly alike at times!"

The cousins exchanged glances and each crossed his left leg over the right, as if on cue. "I don't know what you mean," Aubrey said with a grin. "So," he continued turning to his cousin, "*is* Beth all right?"

"She is—at least I think she is. Her dress has tightened slightly since Friday. Apparently, our son or daughter has decided to commence a growing spurt. That aside, Beth's feeling better than she has in some time."

"Good," both Stuarts said in unison, and this time it was Charles who laughed.

"We truly are a family, that much is certain!" he said happily. "Oh, before I forget, James, I want to thank you for the wedding gift. The box of Beth's letters is a treasure trove. I've not yet read the diaries, but I shall once I've the time. Thank you, sir."

The duke drained the punch cup in two gulps, swiping at moustache. "Needs whisky. You're welcome, Charles, but that box is but a part of the gift. You'll find in your stables, four matched Friesian horses, and your carriage house contains a new Frey landau with five windows. I've had a new crest painted on it, as well and all the other coaches you and Beth will use. The design represents the combined Branham and Haimsbury Houses. The House of Lords heraldic committee approved, and Her Majesty used the new design on the dinnerware she gave you. That old woman surely loves Beth. She also had a soft spot for your father once."

Charles smiled as he touched his uncle's forearm. "Thank you, James. A new crest? I can think of nothing that symbolises my love for Beth better—except for children, of course."

Drummond's black eyes began to dance. "Now you're talking! And I canno' wait ta teach that new great-grandson how ta fish and ride a horse."

"And what if that great-grandson turns out to be a great-grand-daughter?" Paul asked, laughing.

James Stuart shrugged. "Then, I'll teach her to do all those things. Did I not teach our Beth to do them? Charles, your wife is the finest horsewoman in the entire kingdom. She even beat your cousin in a race when she was only twelve. There's a photograph of her with the trophy to prove it."

"I'm sorry to admit it's all true, Charles," Aubrey confessed. "Elizabeth can make horses do anything she wishes, and because she's light as a feather, she takes jumps as if flying!"

"I'll look for that photograph when we go to Branham next month, but seeing Beth ride again will have to wait until the end of next summer."

The duke nodded. "Aye, it will, but isn't it worth it?" he asked with a grin. "Children are the best of blessings, son. Ah, here comes the champion horsewoman now."

The three men stood, for Elizabeth had returned, her train re-moved, and the long veil replaced with just the coronet. The new wedding ring sparkled alongside the pink diamond upon her hand, and she gazed at Charles with adoring eyes. The marquess walked towards her, recalling how the little duchess had stood in that very spot ten years before—mourning the loss of her mother, dressed in somber clothes. How things had changed!

He took her into his arms. "I love you, Mrs. Sinclair," he said, kissing her lips.

She blushed slightly, her face glowing. "And I love you, too, my darling husband. And I love my new name! Mrs. Sinclair. You may call me that again and again, Captain," she continued as he walked her through the foyer towards the staircase. "Ah, but we have many people to greet, and the queue has already begun to form. Once we've shaken all their hands and listened to all their good wishes and reminiscences, I'm told we'll have a break for a light meal. Afterward, we'll endure many hours of dancing and lots more handshaking, and probably an endless stream of stories about our parents, but that all ends when we depart for Queen Anne at eight. Grandfather has deviously told his staff to keep the party going until long after you and I depart. Then following the family celebration, you and I shall leave for our new home."

"I like that last part the best," he whispered as he bent to kiss her once more. "All right, Mrs. Sinclair, the sooner we begin, the sooner we leave, correct?"

"Correct," she laughed, and the duke accompanied his grand-daughter and nephew up the broad staircase that led to the mansion's grand ballroom.

The newlyweds arrived to a room packed with peers, princes, ministers, bankers, and all the *nouveau riche* merchants and businessmen of the kingdom. Charles kept close to his new bride, shaking hundreds of hands as a long queue formed near the orchestra stand.

At the head of the line stood a balding man with a grizzled beard and regal bearing. He smiled as he approached Elizabeth, bowing slightly. "My dear Duchess," he said fondly. "May I offer my sincerest congratulations and best wishes to you and your new husband?"

Beth smiled as the portly man kissed her hand. "Thank you, Prime Minister. Allow me to introduce that husband to you, though it is quite possible you've already met, seeing that he is with Scotland Yard, for the moment, at least. Lord Salisbury, this is my husband, Superintendent Charles Sinclair, Lord Haimsbury."

The prime minister shook Charles's hand. "A pleasure to see you again, Superintendent. Duchess, your husband may not recall it, but I have met with him several times previously. Congratulations on finding your heritage. I assume your resignation is because of this this new ICI venture you and Aubrey have begun with Drummond. If you'll meet with me soon, I hope to convince you to take an official position with government. If you must give up your rank as superintendent, allow me to replace with something that makes use of your police experience but allows you to serve a higher cause."

"Commissioner Monro mentioned something to that effect, Prime Minister. I'd be pleased to discuss it, but only if it doesn't require travel outside England. I prefer to stay close to London, in fact."

"It will permit you to live in London, if you wish," Salisbury said.

"Then, I'm interested. And I do recall those first meetings with you, sir, though I was rather young at the time, and I believe brashly outspoken."

The prime minister laughed, his beard shaking along with his chin. "So you were! Duchess, your new husband had the audacity to barge into my office when I was Secretary of State for India—oh, I suppose it was back in '77 or so—and he insisted I address a problem with a crime involving Indian immigrants in Whitechapel. He was quite indignant about the whole thing as I recall, but he made a positive impression on me, nonetheless. Your husband is like a dog with a bone, when he's passionate about a thing."

Charles laughed. "Yes, well, I was rather full of myself in those days. Beth, I received a painful dressing down from the police commissioner for my effort, but Lord Salisbury was kind enough to lend a hand, and we arrested the men involved. One suspect had very high connexions to Indian royalty, you see, and the Foreign Office couldn't help meddling. If I never thanked you for your aid, sir, I do so now."

Salisbury bowed. "My pleasure. Do you intend to serve in the House of Lords, Charles?"

Beth took her husband's arm and shook her head. "Allow me to answer, Charles. Robert, do you recall what I once told you about that august membership?" she asked, calling the prime minister by his Christian name. "You told me that as a female, I could not serve in the House of Lords, but that my husband might do so, and…"

"And you said that if you could not serve, then neither would he. Charles, your wife was thirteen at the time and quite passionate about politics. I regret not allowing her to serve. I imagine Elizabeth's input would have aided our country and perhaps kept us from many errors of judgement."

"Well said," she replied with a bright smile.

The prime minister moved along, and a tall young man stepped forward to take his place. His features were strong and classically handsome with large eyes and a thin moustache. He wore striped trousers and a morning coat. He took Beth's hand, holding it firmly.

"Elizabeth, you make a smashing bride. It's a shame this wasn't a royal wedding."

"Thank you for coming, Eddy," she said. "Charles, allow me to introduce His Royal Highness, Prince Albert Victor, Duke of Clarence."

Sinclair bowed slightly, and the young man shook the marquess's hand. "Good to meet you at last, Haimsbury."

"It's an honour, Your Highness," Charles said, bowing.

The prince laughed. "No need for that, old man! I concede defeat to you. My grandmother has always loved your wife dearly, as have I. May your lives together be blessed and filled with joy. I hope to see you at my club."

"Thank you, Your Highness. That means a great deal to both of us."

The prince leaned in to whisper something to Beth, which caused her to smile, and she kissed his cheek. "I hope the same for you, Eddy," she said, and the prince moved on.

"What did he say?" Charles asked.

She squeezed his hand. "He said he's glad I found true happiness, even though it isn't with him. Eddy's a soft-hearted man and very sweet. The press often makes great fun of him, but the reporters have no idea the struggles he's had to endure."

"Such as?"

"Eddy's father is quite demanding. I cannot say more than that."

He let it go, continuing to greet dukes, earls, bankers, and the like, noting that the number of those awaiting never seemed to lessen. The long queue continued for over two hours as each person offered congratulations and best wishes along with endless anecdotes. Finally, at half past one, the couple escaped for a short meal in the dining hall with family and a few special guests.

Charles noticed Beth's colour had paled, and she had little to eat. "If nothing appeals, darling, I'm sure the duke's cook will be happy to make you something else."

Elizabeth sipped a cup of weak tea and took a few bites of bread and cheese. "Sorry, husband, I'm simply unable to eat any more," she whispered. "It is all I can do to keep down what little break-fast I ate."

He squeezed her hand. Amelia had never suffered from morning sickness as he remembered, at least not that he noticed. Charles now wondered if he'd ever truly loved his first wife. Had he merely married her because it seemed the right thing to do? Certainly, back then, his heart held nothing close to the deep emotion it did now.

"I'll take you home, if you wish it, darling. You've only to speak the word."

She shook her head, smiling at Adele who waved as she entered the room from the crowded hallway. "No, I can make it. I just need to be careful." Her cheeks whitened, and she stood suddenly. "You must excuse me for a moment. I need air."

She left by the side door, and Charles rushed after, taking her hand. "I'm not to let you out of my sight, Beth."

"I'm so hot, Charles. A moment in the day's chill is all I need," she said, and he led her out the rear doors and into a large garden, where their passage was impeded by a dozen well-wishers and glad-handers taking a shortcut from the solarium to the main dining hall.

One was Edmund Reid.

"Congratulations to you both!" he called as he pumped his col-league's hand. "Your Grace, are you all right? You're very pale. Too much excitement, perhaps."

"Yes, I'm all right, Inspector Reid. Just a trifle warm. Too many people. Do you think it will snow?" she asked.

Her question caught him by surprise. "I'm told it will likely hold off through Tuesday, but shipping forecasts are often inaccurate. I think we're safe until tomorrow, though."

She appeared relieved. "Thank goodness! Is Mrs. Reid with you?"

"She is. Emily's chatting with your aunt, in fact. I know it's none of my business, but you appear a trifle off balance, Duchess. May I help?"

"No, I'm...I'm really just overly warm," she insisted, but her gait was unsteady.

Charles kept watch on her eyes, which had taken on a listless appearance. "Beth, I insist you sit down. Edmund, would you mind going with us? I believe there's a side entrance to the conservatory just over here, beyond the fountain."

Reid took a position in front and parted the crowd as the married couple followed the cobbled pathway to a large white door, opened by Mr. Harold, the duke's underbutler. "Come in, my lady, my lord. Is the duchess unwell? Shall I fetch Mrs. Dalborough?"

"My wife grows weary, Harold. Would you mind standing outside to ensure our privacy?"

"Not at all, sir," the stout young man replied, disappearing through the exterior door.

"This way, darling. Sit here," her husband said.

Elizabeth dropped onto a wicker sofa, padded by sumptuous pillows and fabrics. A centrally placed fireplace had been lit, and the cheerful blaze warmed the floor tiles, but the afternoon sun had begun to disappear behind a bank of thick clouds, leaving the conservatory somewhat chilly.

"Rest here for a moment. Is the room too cold?"

"Not at all. It feels wonderful, actually," she answered, fanning herself with her hand. "Charles, can you help me with this coronet? It's quite heavy, and my poor neck is about to break."

He removed the combs that held the magnificent crown in place and handed all to Reid. "Better?"

Edmund set the combs and coronet on a nearby table. "Though the air's chilly, she looks flushed," he told Sinclair. "Emily had troubles like this with both our children in the early weeks. Perhaps, a glass of punch or tonic water would help."

Beth shook her head. "That will only make it worse, I fear. Peppermint tea sounds better, if Mrs. Carson has any."

"I'll have a footman bring it right away," Reid said, casting a worried look at Charles.

The inspector left to find a servant, and Charles turned towards his wife. "Beth, let me take you home. I'm sure everyone would understand."

"No, Charles, I'd rather stay, but would you mind if I rest my head on your shoulder, only for a few minutes?"

"You may rest it there for a lifetime," he whispered. "Put your feet up, darling. Those shoes look uncomfortable."

"I'd love to, but if I remove them, I shan't want to put them on again. They fit fine this morning, but grow tighter just as my clothing now does. Getting off my feet helps, though."

He smiled. "We've come a long way, haven't we? I'd never pictured Prince Albert Victor as being so nice, but he is. Do you regret not marrying him?"

"Eddy's a lovely man, but I prefer being Mrs. Sinclair, thank you very much. Charles, you do know that you've made me the happiest woman alive?"

"I hope you'll always feel that way, little one. Did you sleep well last night? The ball seemed to take a lot out of you."

"Not especially well, but I'll sleep tonight."

"Will you?" he teased, and she looked up at him, her cheeks pinking. "I see that you know what I mean," he said, stroking her soft face.

"I imagine I do," she replied. "How many children shall we have, Captain? Two? Four? The queen has nine children. Shall we try to outdo her?"

Charles laughed. "My darling, I'm content with just the one for now. Let's see him or her safely born, and then if you wish for more, we'll do our best to achieve it."

"How wonderful to imagine this child, Charles. Do you think he or she will be tall? I hope so. Nearly everyone in both our families is tall, so it's likely."

"What about a petite daughter with dark eyes and raven hair like her mother? Beth, there is no woman more beautiful, none more wonderful and kind. I'm glad to see the colour returning to your cheeks. You had me worried."

She sat up, taking as deep a breath as the corset permitted. "Being with you always brings me strength, Captain. I wonder what position Salisbury has in mind for you."

"Monro mentioned something to do with the cabinet."

"The cabinet? It must be an entirely new office. Did he offer any hints as to what it might entail?"

"Not much, to be honest. I want to get the ICI operating first, though. Here's Edmund with your tea."

The policeman entered with a footman, who carried a pot of tea and two cups. Beth took a few minutes to sip half a cup of the warm beverage. Charles helped to reposition her coronet, and the trio returned to the interior of the house, arriving at the dining hall just as Paul Stuart was leaving it.

"I'd wondered where the two of you went," he said, taking Beth's hand. "Are you all right, Princess?"

"Much better now. I'd grown overly warm; that's all."

"The orchestra has set up in the ballroom. Are you up to dancing?" he asked, looking into her eyes with great concern. "Beth, you still seemed flushed to me. Why not let Charles take you home?"

"It's very bad form for a bride to leave her own wedding," Elizabeth insisted. "It's only a few hours more. I can endure that, surely. Besides, who'll protect you from Delia Wychwright, if we leave? I saw her glancing in your direction during luncheon with a very intense look upon her face."

"I think she was looking at Uncle James, actually. Delia's given up on me and set her eyes on a much higher title," he jibed.

"Did I see Señor Puccini earlier?" asked Charles.

"You did," Aubrey answered. "Victoria had three pianos delivered to provide a variety of music and musicians. I overheard Martin say that Puccini is playing at four o'clock in the Argyle Salon."

"Tory knows how much I love music," Beth answered. "We'll have to look in on all the salons and say hello."

The couple and Aubrey passed through long corridors, stopping several times to receive handshakes and fondest wishes from guests. Finally, after quarter of an hour, they entered the larger of two picture galleries, where the eyes of four centuries of Drummonds watched them pass.

"Soon, your portrait will join those," Aubrey told his cousin. "James couldn't be happier, Charles. Not only that you've married Beth, but that you've agreed to be his heir."

"You're sure you don't mind?" asked Sinclair.

"Not at all! It takes a great weight off my shoulders, to be honest. The Drummond properties are vast and require regular attention, which would have meant forsaking travel in favour of sitting behind a desk once a week. The very thought makes me shudder! Plus, James attends Parliament several times a year and sits on the privy council. It's all rather dull, if you ask me."

"Desks have never appealed to me either, but I suspect we'll have plenty to engage our minds here in London. Besides, it's a moot point. Our uncle will outlive us all," Sinclair laughed as they reached an enormous portrait of two young men in 15th century dress. "Who are these? More Drummond ancestors?"

"You've never seen this?" asked the earl. "That's the royal princes, Henry Charles and Henry Edward. The twin sons who started it all. Charles is the taller one, there on the left, and Edward, who was three minutes younger, stands on the right. The men surrounding the twins are the original inner circle. Just to Charles's right is Lord Aubrey, and to Edward's left is Lord Anjou. They shared leadership in that first fellowship. Twelve members in all. Many of their descendants sit on the circle today."

Beth took a seat in a plush chair opposite the painting, resting her aching feet whilst her cousins explored the gallery. The long, rectangular space was panelled in mahogany, and many of the portraits hung within specially designed mouldings, stained in a rich red hue. Behind her chair, a mullioned window overlooked a courtyard garden, and the duchess turned to watch a gaggle of youngsters, apparently searching for distraction from the somewhat staid and lackluster activities their parents enjoyed.

The air temperatures had dropped precipitously since they'd left the chapel, and the iron grey clouds overhead threatened cold rain or snow within the hour.

"I fear Mr. Reid is mistaken. It looks like snow could fall at any moment," she sighed.

Charles turned, worried at her continued questions regarding snow. "Edmund's rarely wrong about these things. I suppose as an aeronaut, he's learnt to read clouds. Don't worry about it, darling." He gazed once more at the painting. "Paul, is it my imagination, or do these two men look familiar?"

"Which men?" he asked as Cordelia Wychwright entered the gallery on Albert Wendaway's arm.

"You said there were twelve men on the first circle, but I count fourteen standing with the twins. Those in the very back are nearly hidden by the curtains, but they—no, it can't be!" he gasped. "Paul? Paul, are you listening?"

The earl had left the painting and now stood near the archway, staring at Wychwright. "Cordelia, do you know this man?"

The ingénue giggled. "Of course, I do! He's Sir Albert. He's quite nice, too. Bertie tells me that he's Lord Haimsbury's cousin, so he's your family as well, I should think."

Aubrey took her hand. "Let me escort you to the ballroom, Delia."

She appeared puzzled and pulled away. "But Bertie asked for the first three dances, and I've promised."

"Promises can be broken," the earl said firmly. "And dances should be shared only with those deemed trustworthy."

Wendaway laughed, removing a cigar from his pocket. "Meaning that I am not?"

Charles started to intervene, but Elizabeth appeared at Cordelia's side and reached for the girl's hand. "Come help me with my coronet, Delia. It's starting to slip. There's a little powder room just up here."

The duchess left, her arm through Wychwright's, leaving Wendaway to face both Sinclair and Stuart—alone.

"Allow me, Paul," the marquess told his cousin. "See that Beth and Cordelia arrive safely at the ballroom, will you? I'll catch you up."

"You're sure?"

"Yes. Very sure. Now go."

Reluctantly, the earl left, following the ladies' path through the archway to the rooms beyond the lower gallery.

Charles snatched the baronet's unlit cigar and crushed it beneath his boot. "I suggest you leave now, Albert. I've learnt to tolerate, perhaps even like Amelia's parents, but that does not imply that I tolerate you. Cordelia Wychwright is a friend, and I will not have you insinuate yourself into her life."

"Or what?"

Sinclair leaned in to whisper, careful to avoid prying ears beyond the doors. "Or I shall revisit the file I've kept on you since meeting you, old chum."

Foolishly, Albert merely grinned, as if he believed himself invulnerable. "Former Scotland Yard detectives have no power to arrest, Cousin. Or aren't you aware of that?"

"How do you know I'm leaving the Yard?"

"Word travels. I have eyes all over the city, Charles. Important eyes. Men who keep watch."

A horrible thought shot into Sinclair's mind, and its implications caused a hundred suspicions to crystallize into a single word.

"Watchers," he said, angrily denting the baronet's red waistcoat with his forefinger. "Watchers! I should have known you'd be part of that hellish group! Should have guessed that a man like you would seek fellowship with a murderous mob like Redwing. Wendaway, if I so much as hear your name spoken in the same sentence as a crime, I'll come after you. I may be leaving the Yard, but my influence and my reach increase."

"You refer to your little circle?" he dared ask. "Their influence wanes, old man."

"Get out. Leave now whilst your legs still function."

Wendaway removed a second cigar from his coat pocket and clipped the end. "Very well, I'll leave, but don't expect me to be gone for long, Cousin." The insolent gambler offered a shallow, mocking bow and turned about, heading into the salons.

"He isn't worth it," a soft voice said.

Sinclair spun on his heel, finding a beautiful woman with auburn hair and green eyes. "Lorena?" he asked in shock. "How did you get in? What are you doing here?"

"A barrage of questions. Ever the policeman," MacKey said, taking his arm and pulling Sinclair to a quiet spot near the window. "If you don't mind, I prefer to remain in the shadows."

"Yes, I'd imagine you would. Shadows fit well with your agenda, I should think. Paul told me that you'd dyed your hair blonde. Why change it back, if you're trying to hide?"

"Hiding won't help me. Not now. Charles, I know that you and the earl think me wicked, but there are aspects to my actions I cannot reveal yet. I only came to warn you."

"Warn me about what?"

She reached for his left hand, touching the shining, gold wedding band. "Elizabeth is so lucky," she whispered to herself. Then, glancing up, her words came quickly, urgently. "She's in danger, Charles. I cannot stop what's about to happen. Those behind it are far too powerful, and I'm but a little cog in their machine. Just remember that I tried to stop it. If the prince is right, then she'll be safe; if not, then we're all lost."

"What do you mean?" he insisted. "Lorena, if you're trying to make amends, then do it. Tell me what is about to happen!"

Tears filled her green eyes, and he could see great anguish upon her face. "Don't leave her side. Not even for a minute. That's all I can say. Goodbye, Charles. I hope one day, you can forgive me."

She reached up and kissed his cheek, and before he could react, she'd rushed out the side door and into the courtyard. MacKey passed by the gaggle of playing children, dashed around the statue of Duke Henry Charles, and re-entered the house on the far side of the garden.

Shocked, the newlywed marquess rubbed his cheek as he walked through the gallery towards the ballroom stairs, pausing again at the portrait, his gaze falling once more on the two, mysterious figures. The brushstrokes that formed the men's faces seemed strong and purposeful, and the figures' positions, behind and slightly above the main grouping, made it appear as if the two secretly watched the twins.

All colour drained from Sinclair's face as frank realisation replaced idle curiosity. The long dark hair and muscularly tall form of the one was unmistakable. It was Anatole Romanov, wearing a crown and dressed in a crimson, 15th century Russian tunic and a black robe trimmed in sable. Romanov, whose name had most likely differed at the time of painting, stood several inches taller than the second observer, who wore a cap crown that obscured his hair colour. Might this second man be Grigor? Perhaps, not, if Warren's theory were correct, regarding the release of a Watcher in 1871.

Do three of these devils now roam loose in London? He thought of Susanna Morgan's claim that Redwing had freed a Watcher from within a long-buried obsidian mirror. Suddenly, Charles Sinclair actually *wanted* to speak to Anatole Romanov. And soon, he'd have the chance.

CHAPTER THIRTY-THREE

"Mrs. Sinclair, may I have this dance?" Charles asked as the orchestra began the first waltz.

As music for her first public dance as a married woman, Elizabeth had chosen Chopin's *Valse,* Opus 64, No. 2. Long one of the duchess's favourite pieces, the lead instrument of this special, orchestral arrangement featured the gifted hands of famed pianist Arabella Goddard, who'd come out of retirement as a favour to the duke.

Everyone applauded as Charles led his bride onto the expansive, marble-tiled ballroom floor. Chopin's lilting music allowed him to gently lead her through the steps and twirls with ease, and during the *piu mosso*, the fluid eighth note passage propelled their feet into a cascade of turnings that showcased Elizabeth's effortless ability to dance, but also permitted Sinclair to draw his bride ever closer to him.

"You make my heart race," he told her as the music took them 'round the floor. "Yet, every eye is upon us, my darling, making this dance quite public. Shall we dance more privately later?"

She blushed and squeezed his hands. "I look forward to it, husband. I hope I do not disappoint. I've led a rather sheltered life, despite my...condition."

"A condition which pleases me more than you could ever imagine, Beth. You and I are made for each other. I believe that with all my heart. I've been in love with you ever since '84, when I saw you at Paul's house. I never saw the letter you wrote before going to Paris. If I had, I'd have come to you immediately, no matter what the law might have said. I loved you then, just as I love you now."

"I realised that when you visited Queen Anne in October, Charles. Your eyes spoke everything my heart had longed to hear you say."

Slowly, other couples began to populate the dance floor, and Charles kept watch on Prince Anatole, who danced with a Russian woman a few yards away. "Does the prince distress you, Beth?"

Elizabeth had been looking towards the tall Russian royal, and she turned back to gaze at Charles. "Sometimes, though I cannot say why. He reminds me of someone, I think."

"Alexei Grigor?" Her hands tensed, and he instantly wished he'd said nothing. "Forgive me, Beth. This is our wedding day, and I've caused you to worry. Let's speak of brighter things. Oh, the music has stopped."

She said little as he led her back towards the chairs. "I think we'll sit this next one out, dear wife. You look pale again, and it's probably my fault."

"I say, Duchess!" a man's voice called in an obnoxiously loud voice.

Elizabeth offered a cool but polite response. "Hello, Sir Albert." Taking the perfunctory greeting as an open invitation, Wendaway boldly sat down beside her.

"Smashing party. Did I see old 'collars and cuffs' talking with you at the reception line?"

"Collars and cuffs?" she asked. "I'm afraid I don't know who you mean."

"Eddy, of course. The prince. Just a nickname amongst his nearest and dearest. He's a bit of a dandy, if you ask me. Charles, I've been speaking to Kip Mycroft-Jones. He's a clerk in the House of Lords, you know, and he mentioned that Salisbury's creating a special advisor position for you on his cabinet. Well, well! Your influence is indeed rising."

Sinclair put his arm around Elizabeth protectively, casting a warning glance at the baronet. "I thought you intended to leave, Albert. Pressing business elsewhere, you said."

"No, not at the moment." Wendaway started to light a cigarette. "Oh, forgive me," he said to the duchess. "Do you mind?"

Charles answered for her. "Yes, she does. The duke has a drawing room for that, Wendaway. My wife is sensitive to smoke."

"Oh, righto," he said, winking. "Delicate condition and all that."

"What did you say?" Sinclair shot back angrily.

"I mean Cousin Elizabeth's lungs, of course. I'm sure she's unaccustomed to a gentleman's habits. Charles, didn't you used to smoke?"

"No. You're remembering Katherine's husband."

"Oh, right. Joshua Calendar. Kate's my cousin, you know, Duchess. Charles's first wife's sister. Such a shame about Amelia. Awful way to go."

Charles jumped to his feet, ready to bite the man's head off, but Elizabeth spoke, cutting off her husband's words before they even formed. "Yes, it was a dreadful business. I met her many times before she left for Ireland. Your cousin was a kind woman. She often mentioned you, Sir Albert."

Wendaway looked at her strangely. "Yes, that's right. I'd quite forgotten all that. You met Amelia when you met Charles. What's it been now, ten years? Tragic. Just tragic. Happened in Whitechapel of all places. I say, wasn't your mother completely torn apart, in the manner of old Jack?"

Beth's face drained of all colour, and she gripped her husband's hand tightly. Charles was ready to call the man out, but despite her distress, Beth spoke first.

"Charles, would you fetch me a glass of water, please?"

Sinclair stared at her in disbelief. "Beth, I should remain here."

"Darling, I'm parched and quite warm. I know it's an imposition, but a glass of water would really help. Would you mind terribly?" she persisted sweetly.

Reluctantly, the marquess left, glaring back at Wendaway. "Albert, I shan't forget this," he seethed before leaving.

The baronet grinned as if he'd won a round of poker with an ace up his sleeve and a jack in his boot. "Poor old Charles. Ever the policeman. I imagine he'll miss all that authority."

Beth turned towards the unwelcome guest, her voice low and serious. "My husband may have resigned from Scotland Yard, but his arm and reach have only lengthened. Do you really want to find out just how important Charles has become? Or do you imagine him somehow malleable and acquiescent because of your connexion to his first wife. If so, then you are as great a fool as you are a liar."

"Well, I, uh..." the baronet blustered, finding her frank language disquieting.

Her voice softened to a mere whisper as Beth continued, her dark eyes points of jet black. "You labour under the mistaken impression that you have some sort of leverage with my family, Sir Albert, but I assure you, my husband will not permit *anyone* to harm or distress me. Nor will the Stuarts allow it. My grandfather wields a mighty stick in government, and when he speaks, all ears open. But lest you think you might find a way to reach or cajole me in their absence, understand this: I may be young, but I am one of the wealthiest women in Europe; making me as influential as any sovereign—perhaps more so. Her Majesty loves me like a granddaughter, and bankers cater to me with shouts of sycophantic euphoria. One snap of my delicate fingers, and you will find yourself stripped of that title you so proudly wear and berthed within a transport ship, bound for Australia before that day's sun sets. Is that clear? If you value your title and your freedom, then I suggest you *do not test me*."

"Duchess, I assure you that..." he entreated, but she cut him off.

"Do *not* presume to call me Duchess. Your rank is far too low to make such a blunder, Sir Albert. You will address me as *Your Grace*, and I am not your cousin!"

"Ah, yes, uh, of course, Your Grace," he stammered, but once more, she interrupted, her dark eyes sparking fire.

"I know much more about you than you might surmise, Albert Wendaway. More than my husband may even know. Do not look surprised. Shall we discuss what really happened in Dublin? The illegal activities twixt you and your cousin Amelia's paramour, Harold Lowry? I suspect those are secrets you prefer to remain buried. I can think of several police detectives who would find your penchant for non-existent silver mines of interest. Shall I mention those to my husband?"

"What? I say, how did you...?"

"I may be petite, but my arm is long and my intelligence high. And if you are wise, you will steer clear of my Cousin Paul," she continued. "His manner is gracious and kind, but the earl's aim is true and deadly."

As if on cue, Aubrey joined them, his face serious. "Princess, may I have this dance?" he asked. "Or shall I teach this upstart baronet a few steps first?"

Wendaway immediately stood and adjusted his garish waist-coat. "As I said, Your Grace. Congratulations." The baronet was walking away just as Charles returned with the water.

"You'd have been proud of your wife, Charles," Stuart told his cousin. "She sent Wendaway off with a rather painful flea in his ear."

Sinclair handed Beth the glass and sat down once again. "Yes, I noticed him scratching a bit. Well done, darling."

She drank half the water, her face flushed with anger. "We've not seen the last of Wendaway. His kind have no good sense, only ambition."

Paul reached for her hand and kissed it. "You were wonderful," he told her proudly. "I considered stepping in, but honestly, I was having far too much fun watching you dress him down. Wendaway has much to learn about the Stuart clan. Especially you, Princess."

Still angry, Charles kept watch on the baronet, who wove in and out of the crowd, pausing here and there. He stopped to speak with a middle-aged man with a receding hairline, stooped shoulders, and a slight paunch. "Well, now, that is a depressing picture. Look who just sidled up to my shiftless former cousin." Sinclair declared.

"Sir Clive Urquhart," Aubrey said with a sigh. "Apparently, like attracts like. Charles, if you could find a crime with which to prosecute that man at last, you would only please your wife. And your cousin. Otherwise, I may just have to find a less legal way to deal with the man."

Sinclair took Elizabeth's hand, and found it trembling. "Darling, is it the company, the conversation, or something else?"

"If you mean present company, of course not. I love and adore you both, but the mixture of Sir Clive Urquhart and Albert Wendaway is worrisome. Clive has taken control of the Royal Estate Agency in the city. Did you know that? My lawyer told me on Friday. Urquhart's reopening it as a financial institution called Blackstone Investments."

"Blackstone?" Sinclair asked. "What is it about that name sounds familiar?"

"I can think of no businessman in Clive's orbit named Blackstone," Aubrey mused. "Beth, do you know of any?"

"None—no wait. There's a Jacob Blackstone who used to sit on the Branham Charity's board of governors. He died last year, though. Oh, no," she spoke quickly, "here comes Prince Anatole. Please, both of you, keep your manner civil."

The enigmatic Russian bowed politely. "Congratulations, Duchess—or perhaps, it is more apt to the occasion to call you Mrs. Sinclair. I watched you and your husband on the dance floor. A most handsome couple, if I may say so."

Elizabeth glanced up, doing her best to manage a sincere smile. "Thank you, Your Highness. You've been very kind to us."

"Paul, would you mind keeping Beth company for a few minutes, whilst the prince and I speak?"

The earl's brows pinched together in dismay. "I'm sure Beth prefers your company to mine."

"Nonsense, Elizabeth cherishes any time she might share with you. Isn't that right, darling?"

"Yes, of course," the duchess answered, assuming her husband had a very good reason for leaving. "Take all the time you need."

"Your Highness, might we find a quiet spot? I'd love to learn more about Russian politics."

The marquess disappeared through a side door that led into a smoking parlour, and the earl turned towards the duchess. "Are you happy?"

"Yes. Very happy, but also quite tired. Why do you think Charles wanted to speak with the prince?"

Rather than worry her, Aubrey offered innocuous speculation. "Most likely, he wants to talk to Romanov about Russian spies in London. I'm sure our new investigative venture will run afoul of countless government factions in the years to come, but the Okhrana make a second home in England, requiring the establishment of firm rules at the start."

"The Okhrana? The Russian secret police, you mean."

"Yes, they've infiltrated all aspects of society, even the Met Police, I'm told. Their stated aim is to root out anarchists, but in truth, they're spying on England."

"Is that what Salisbury wants Charles to do? To uncover spy rings?"

"Possibly. As an independent intelligence service, the ICI will provide information to government without accountability. It's a politician's dream come true. Oh, but speaking of spying," he said, hoping to make her smile, "it looks as though I'll be giving Egypt a miss this year. That's why the prime minister asked to meet with me last night. Robert said it was his wedding gift to you and Charles. The trip is cancelled for the present. I shan't be leaving England for a good long while."

Elizabeth's face brightened into a wide smile, and she jumped to her feet to embrace him. "Oh, Paul! That is the best news I've had in such a long time! And it explains your smooth face, I imagine. Tory told me you'd shaved the beard to impress Cordelia Wychwright. I've no idea how Lady Delia feels, but I much prefer you this way. Your cheeks are far more kissable."

She leaned in to offer said kiss to his smooth cheek but caught the toe of her shoe on his, causing her to tumble into his lap. "Oh!" Beth cried out, instantly trying to regain her feet.

The earl helped the duchess back to her chair, his face red. "Careful, Mrs. Sinclair," he exclaimed just as Cordelia Wychwright's mother walked past.

The baroness glared at Aubrey, her disgruntled breaths sounding rather like a steam engine as she turned towards a long table filled with refreshments. Suddenly, however, the angry engine spun about and she addressed the earl directly.

"Where is Lord Haimsbury?" the baroness asked pointedly.

"Charles has gone to have a chat with Prince Anatole," Elizabeth answered, her face flushed. "Baroness, I'm so glad you and the baron were able to attend the wedding. I saw your daughter earlier. She's looks quite lovely—as always. When again is her debutante ball?"

"Next March," the woman answered sternly. "We'd hoped to introduce Delia to a few *suitable* gentlemen in advance of the party, but it's so difficult to find men who are trustworthy."

"Yes, I imagine it is," Elizabeth answered, intentionally taking her cousin's hand. "I've the honour to know two such men, however. My husband, of course, but also my beloved cousin, Lord Aubrey. Did you know that Paul became my protector when I was but a child? He faithfully kept watch on me all those years, never once complaining. I suppose it's one reason we've grown to love one another so much. The young woman who finally wins his heart will indeed be blessed, and I shall be delighted to call her cousin."

The speech seemed to cool the steam engine's boiler to a more moderate heat, and the puffing slowed to a lighter rhythm. "I'd not heard that story before, Duchess. Since childhood? Lord Aubrey, you must have been quite young yourself."

The earl exhaled, for he'd been holding his breath, dreading the woman's assault. "Relatively young. Beth is twelve and half years younger than I, and Charles four months my elder. Though, he's still struggling to regain his early memories, mine are intact. He and I were like brothers as children. I'm grateful to the Lord each day that he's returned my cousin to us."

A smile crept across the stern woman's wrinkled face. "Well, it all begins to make sense. Delia is our only child, you know. It's very important that we make the best choices for her life. I'm sure you agree, Duchess?"

"Yes, of course. Forgive me, won't you, Baroness? We're to have photographs taken in the gallery. Paul, may I have your arm? I'm not sure I trust these shoes. The left heel's beginning to wobble."

Paul helped her to stand. "It's always a pleasure, Baroness. Please, tell your husband that, if he's still in London, I hope to see him at my club next week."

"Of course, Lord Aubrey," she answered, nearly giddy as his final words and their possible meaning stirred in her brain.

The earl offered Wychwright a bow before escorting Elizabeth out the side door, where a footman handed the earl a note. After reading it, Paul began to laugh. "Well, your excuse regarding photographs appears to be prescient. It's from Tory, and she calls the entire family to the lower gallery. I imagine Mr. Blackwood and his camera await. Come, dear, let's make these portraits as memorable as the day."

CHAPTER THIRTY-FOUR

After closing the door to the duke's library, Charles turned to face the prince. "I'd rather not leave my wife alone for too long, so let's get right to it, shall we?"

Romanov appeared relaxed, even confident. Calmly, he took a seat near the fire, spreading his hands as if to offer complete transparency. "What would you ask of me?"

"No limits this time. No games."

"I assure you, Lord Haimsbury, I never play games."

"So you keep saying, yet your deliberate obfuscation leaves an entirely opposite impression!" He paused a moment to regain his sense of calm, for the prince invariably caused the marquess's blood pressure to soar.

Romanov's expression remained serene. "I shall answer plainly. Ask your questions."

"No limit to the number?"

"Not to the number, no, but your time is limited, Charles. As you say."

"Do you deliberately bait me?"

A slight smile crossed the Russian's face. "No, not deliberately. You want to know about last night."

"Yes," Sinclair replied, stepping towards the prince. "Who is Grigor, and why did he pretend to be you?"

"Please, sit, Charles. A satisfying answer will take a little time, but a thorough one requires far more time than you can spare at the moment. To begin, as you've long suspected, I am not human."

Taking a chair next to the mysterious Russian, the all too human detective exhaled, releasing tension along with carbon dioxide. "You're a hybrid."

"No. Much more. I am elohim."

"Elohim? I don't understand. What is that? Some new breed of altered human?"

"It is a generalised class, referring to those whose realm lies beyond your ability to perceive. Some call it the heavenly realm."

Sinclair laughed. "You're claiming to be an angel?"

"An imprecise word, but according to your understanding, yes. That is what I am. The term 'angel' implies a mission. My presence upon the earth does include a mission, but one that has altered from its original purpose. As I told you before, we've no time for complete answers. The person you know as Prince Alexei Grigor is also elohim. Once, he and I were as close as brothers, but our paths diverged many thousands of years ago. It is why I imprisoned him within the stone Warren found on Mt. Hermon."

"*You* imprisoned him?" Sinclair asked. "Is your mission as a kind of jailer, then?"

"No. Forgive me for being vague—I promise to tell you everything one day—but my history requires many hours to explain. For now, let us keep to a single issue: Grigor. He is sometimes called Raziel in our realm. Names have purpose and power, and each of us possess dozens, sometimes hundreds of names."

"Yours are carved upon your cane," Sinclair recalled, pointing to the prince's walking stick.

He smiled. "Yes, some are. I have far more names than this slender stick can display. Raziel and I had similar positions in the council once. We served at his side. The One, I mean. The Creator whom you call God."

"Until you were cast out," Charles dared to say.

The prince sighed. "Not entirely. Raziel chose to leave, and I was dispatched to apprehend him. Raziel is a special kind of scribe, a member of the Seven. He recorded every word spoken by the One. Every word heard, that is. None of us knows what our Lord spoke before Creation commenced. But each of his words contains power. Raziel compiled a book, which he brought with him to this realm— to Earth. His intent was to reveal these sacred and most powerful words to Adam's sons and daughters."

"Did he succeed?"

"Yes. Before the great flood, Raziel's secrets allowed the proliferation of great evil within this world; though only a very small portion had been revealed. Mankind had to decipher the words, you see. They are written in a very convoluted and difficult language. That was Raziel's plan. He gave the kings of old the book, but would only translate it in exchange for reward and worship."

"He sold the secrets."

Romanov nodded. "Yes. Such avarice and treachery revealed a rebellious heart within Raziel. He was summoned to the council, but refused to attend. He was, therefore, tried *in absentia* and found guilty." The angel paused, intense regret upon his face. "The sentence was death."

"How can that be? The creature still lives!"

"Yes, he does. I'd known Raziel for millennia, and I believed he might yet be redeemed and returned to the host. We of the divine realm have free will, you understand, but the One sets rules and boundaries. I entreated with him for Raziel's life, and our Lord repented of his anger, saying that he could live and be given one more chance, but that he must be removed from the Earth until the time of the end."

"And you did so by imprisoning him in that rock?"

He nodded. "Yes. I laid the stone within the Grotto of Pan at the foot of Hermon, placing hundreds of wards upon it so that it might go unnoticed. After the great flood's waters subsided, the stone's location filled with silt and debris, and it remained undiscovered until Alexander the Great conquered the region. Alexander believed himself descended from the great gods of antiquity, so when his men uncovered the stone, he felt compelled to use it as a marker. He forced his soldiers to convey the great slab up the sides of Hermon, finding a temple."

"And he left the stone there?"

"Yes. First, he had it inscribed with the words of the Watchers. Those who descended to Hermon before the flood. Alexander thought this all his idea, but the inspiration, you might say, came to him from spiritual guides. The spirits who haunt that region are very old and very angry, and devious beyond human imagination."

Sinclair understood. "They used Alexander to advance their own aims."

"Precisely. When I discovered that the stone had been moved, I renewed the wards, making it less visible to human eyes. Those wards had worn away by the time Warren's team arrived at the mount."

"Thus, the stone came to London."

"And Raziel with it. He hates the One, and he hates me for my obedience to Him."

Charles thought for a moment, running through possibilities in his mind. "That's why he posed as you last night. He wanted me to blame you for harming Beth."

"Yes. Since emerging in 1871, Raziel has committed great evil in this world, and his plans are vast and convoluted. My ability to see and foresee is limited. I can only be in one place at a time. However, based on all I know of his activities, I think Raziel intends to kill you and use Elizabeth for his own ends."

Fear took hold of Sinclair's heart, turning it to ice. Not for himself—for his wife. "Use her? How?"

"To engender a new race of kings. Elizabeth's blood is unique, as is yours, but Raziel has foreseen your future, and it causes him great concern. Your actions will impact the entire world and lead to the end of all things, but they are ordained by the One as part of his plan. Raziel hopes to stop that plan by slaying you—but failing that, he will seek to turn you to his cause."

Romanov stood. "Your family is gathering for photographs. You must go, Charles. Keep watch on the duchess. Do not let her out of your sight."

"What do you mean? What is Raziel planning? Is she in danger? What about Rasha?" the marquess asked.

"Rasha is a fool. Do not concern yourself with him. He is a failed and unmanageable experiment. Raziel knows this and will soon terminate the test."

"The Romanian prince is a test? What do you mean?"

"Razarit Grigor's human form has been altered through blood magic, but he has become hard to control. Raziel will end him and begin again. Now, I must go."

"No, wait, there are other questions I would ask!" Sinclair cried out, but the prince had vanished. Reluctantly, the marquess left the room and headed out to join his family.

At Queen Anne House, a package arrived in a tall, wooden crate. Mr. Miles, who had remained behind to oversee last minute details for the family celebration, signed for the package and read the card which stated the gift was to be installed immediately in the duchess's bedchamber, on orders from the sender. Two strong footmen carried the heavy box up the steps. Inside, they discovered a beautifully polished mirror, set in a carved Indian rosewood frame. Instructions included within the box insisted the gift be placed opposite the door, at the foot of the duchess's bed.

Nothing about the strange present sounded alarm bells, for hundreds of gifts had arrived over the past ten days, many with puzzling if not outlandish instructions from givers, who wished to ensure their presents received immediate attention. Even the envelope tied to the frame failed to raise concern. Its handwritten greeting was to 'Supt. Sinclair, Lord Haimsbury', and the footmen reasoned that the master suite now belonged to the marquess, and that the main bedchamber would be used by both husband and wife.

Having satisfied all the instructions, the busy footmen returned to their duties, giving no thought to the true purpose behind the enigmatic mirror.

On the main floor, with the foyer empty, no one noticed a woman enter through the unlocked door and tiptoe up the staircase to the bedchamber, where she hid within the interior of the bathroom closet, a vial of laudanum stashed inside her purse.

CHAPTER THIRTY-FIVE
8:55 pm – Queen Anne House

The wedding reception and associated activities lasted until after eight, and by the time the Sinclairs and their entourage left Drummond House, all were exhausted. Now, they stood in the elegant and roomy foyer of Queen Anne House, celebrating as a family.

The duke, his sister Victoria, Paul Stuart, Adele, Martin Kepelheim, Arthur France and his wife and two children, Mr. Baxter, Mrs. Alcorn, Mrs. Wilsham, Miss Jenkins (Beth's new secretary, who had spent most of the night crying and telling all she was amazed to have received an invitation), Edmund Reid and his wife Emily, Michael Emerson (who'd spent much of his time speaking to Miss Jenkins), and all the Queen Anne servants gathered together beneath the glass rotunda, gazing not at the stars above, but at the newly wedded couple now facing them as they prepared for one last, farewell toast.

Charles stood next to the duke, and already many toasts had been offered, stories told, and songs sung. The marquess turned to his uncle, his glass raised high: "To Uncle James, my friends. He is our patriarch, our leader, and our best friend in all this world. May he live to see many more such weddings!"

Everyone heartily agreed, lifting their glasses and drinking, and the duke patted his nephew on the shoulder proudly.

"Charles, my dear boy, you bring a light to my granddaughter's eyes that is akin to nothing I've ever seen there before. She's loved you for years, and today is only the beginning of your lives together. May our Saviour bring you his blessings and his protection. I only wish that your parents could have been here today to see the two of you wed. Elizabeth, my dearest Princess, may you never have an unhappy day and may you walk always in the light of our Lord's lamp. To Charles and Elizabeth Sinclair, everyone!"

All drank to the toast, and applause erupted amidst a round of 'hear, hears' and 'jolly goods'. Baxter and Alcorn wiped tears from their eyes, for both felt a special kinship to the duchess, and they clinked their glasses together, feeling as proud as if they were parents of the bride.

Mr. Kepelheim then called for all the eligible ladies in the room—including the maids and kitchen staff—to gather at the base of the staircase to catch Elizabeth's bouquet. She had carried a cascade of orange blossoms and white roses, accented by a spray of ivy, and she took her husband's hand and climbed to the third, broad step on the winding case.

"Are you all ready?" she asked, after making sure Adele had joined the group. "All right, here goes," she said, turning her back and tossing the bouquet over her shoulder.

Adele rushed forward and nearly caught the arrangement, but it was Miss Jenkins who found herself in possession of the flowers, much to her surprise. "Oh, I mean—well, I didn't think—I'd. Well!" she sputtered, looking at Michael Emerson with a sense of profound embarrassment.

Adele offered the secretary a wide, conciliatory smile. "Miss Jenkins, does this mean you will be next?"

"It may," Beth answered for her secretary. "Well, dear friends. Now that I've completed all my duties for the day, I must leave you."

Alicia Mallory pushed through the dense pack of females and climbed the other staircase towards the master apartment. "Shall I meet you upstairs, my lady?"

Beth nodded. "Charles, I shan't be long. I'll change into my travelling clothes, and then, we'll leave for our new home."

He pulled her close and kissed her. "I love you, wife."

"And I you, husband, my dashing Captain. Give me fifteen minutes, at least. There are nearly fifty pearl buttons and many hooks to manage, but I'll be as quick as possible." She turned to walk up the steps, and Charles watched her disappear into the upper hallway, his heart full.

"Now, let's have another round of songs," the duke called out merrily. "Della, play that highland tune you learned last week. The quick one. I think it's time we danced like true Scots!"

Adele skipped off with France's children close behind, and she began a lively reel. Hamish Granger took up his bagpipes and

Frame his fiddle, and soon the entire main level echoed with the sounds of the Hebrides. Brenda France sat close by, turning pages as Adele's quick fingers played the complicated tune. Kepelheim and Reid joined Sinclair, who'd left the staircase in favour of one of fifty chairs, scattered around the perimeter of the cavernous foyer.

Kepelheim sighed loudly as he sat. "Ah! It's always sad to see the end of such an enjoyable evening. Of course, my friend, yours has only begun," he added with a wink. "Mr. France now lives with you, I take it? Good. He seems an able man and quick with his wits. This doctor, Michael Emerson; I like him, Charles. He, too, may be a candidate. What do you think?"

Charles tried to keep his eyes open, but the champagne had begun to go to his head. "I think... I think that I could sleep for a week. Emerson? Yes, he's interesting. He has a detective's instincts and a medical man's knowledge, and he is an ardent follower of Christ. He mentioned that his father knows MacPherson and has even consulted with the inner circle."

"Really? The Emersons. I know no family by that name other than…wait, is his father an earl?"

"Yes. Lord Braxton. Michael's the second son. He lost his first wife, you know—and their child."

"How sad. As he is now Beth's doctor, we might want to bring him into our confidence soon. Keep your eyes on her always, Charles—something which you are happy to do, yes, I know—but our enemy lurks ever in the shadows. Trent in particular. I'm disturbed by Paul's report about MacKey. If she's in London, then it's likely she's allied with Trent."

Charles turned, his mind growing more alert. "I saw MacKey at Drummond House."

Kepelheim stared. "When?"

"Late afternoon. She spoke to me in the lower gallery, and then ran off into the garden. I considered going after her, but it seemed a fool's errand. I wish I understood that woman."

"Redwing's females are past comprehension. Put it out of your mind. Do you plan to remand Trent for questioning? Is that stickpin sufficient to bring him in?"

"Yes, but Reid will have to handle it. Tonight, I've other things on my mind."

The tailor laughed. "Oh, but of course! It is your wedding night, my friend. Let us put all these dangers out of our heads!"

Charles looked at his pocket watch. Beth had been upstairs now for ten minutes. "I'd love to, but isn't that precisely when the enemy might choose to strike? When we relax our resolve? Oh, I know, I'm beginning to see danger everywhere. Look, I hope you'll join us for a little gathering next month. Beth plans a small dinner party on the twenty-fourth of December at Branham. Assuming she still wants to have Christmas there. Otherwise, we'll host it at my home. I mean our home, of course," he added smiling.

"So she told me. Did I hear correctly? The queen sent you a set of magnificent bone china?"

"She did. It arrived yesterday, and it had a card instructing Laurence to open it at once. It was a huge set, four dozen engraved plates with all the bits and pieces that go with them I guess, each with an entwined H and B on them—for Haimsbury and Branham, along with today's date. James had the queen's own heraldry artist design the new crest, and it's on all our coaches now. That queen. She's a kind old lady, Martin. She kissed Beth twice! Yet, surely she recalls the Plantagenet bloodline and the pact she signed on becoming sovereign?"

Martin nodded. "She knows all. It's the reason she tried so hard to make a match with the Duke of Clarence. It's been fifteen minutes."

Charles rose and straightened his jacket and waistcoat. "Well, then I shall go upstairs and see what is keeping my wife. Oh, I do love saying that, Martin."

The tailor watched happily as his friend passed through the jovial crowd, pausing here and there to say a word or shake a hand, and then he stopped near the staircase to speak with the duke.

"May I now knock upon your granddaughter's door, sir?"

James laughed, his cheeks rosy. "Aye, but beware when women are shut up in their rooms. A man might walk in on anything! But she's your wife now, son. Go fetch her!"

Grinning with joy, Charles dashed up the long staircase and followed the hallway until he reached Elizabeth's apartment, passing through the parlour and knocking on the bedchamber door. No one answered. He listened, and hearing no voices, knocked again before turning the knob.

A faint and plaintive voice responded.

"Help!"

A knot formed in Sinclair's stomach. "Alicia?" he called, praying he'd misheard.

"Help, please!" she called again. "Help me!"

"Paul! Something's wrong! Hurry!" he shouted down the stairwell to Aubrey. The earl had been standing near the front entry, saying goodnight to Adele, preparing to leave for his appointment with Lorena MacKey. At the sound of his cousin's cries, the earl ran through the crowd and took the steps three at a time, his uncle and France close behind.

"Alicia!" Charles called, pounding on the door. "Beth! What's going on? The door is locked. Let me in!"

"Sir!" the maid called again, her voice barely audible. "Help me, please!"

The two cousins put their shoulders to the door, but it wouldn't budge. Miles, Frame, and Granger arrived, followed by Baxter.

"On three, sirs," the hulking Chief of the Mews said as he joined the cousins in the effort. All three men threw their weight at the door, and it gave way, splintering the frame. Charles rushed into the apartment and found the maid lying on the dark blue carpet, her face flushed, hair in disarray.

"Oh, sir!" she wept. "He took her! He just came and took her!"

"Who, Alicia? Who?"

"The man—I don't know his name. I'd never seen him before, sir. A tall man with a cane. He came out of the mirror, and he took her!"

Paul knelt beside the maid. "Say that again, Alicia. Tell us everything that happened. Leave nothing out."

The earl helped her to a chair, and the slender maid's entire body trembled. By now Emerson had joined them, and he began to examine her eyes. "She's been drugged," he said plainly.

"I had one glass o' wine, sir. Downstairs, but I felt fine until I got up here, and then I was so sleepy. It made me stumble, and when the duchess came into the room, she ran to me, asking what was wrong. My lady started for the door to call for aid, but then the man just—well, he was there—all of a sudden. He came out of that new mirror. He put a cloth over her mouth, and she fell into his arms. And then—like a flash—they were both gone! Back into that mirror!"

Charles nearly collapsed, his mind numb, but his cousin caught him. "Paul, we have to find her. It's Trent, I know it. He always carries that cane. But, how can he travel through a mirror? It's impossible!"

Aubrey helped Charles to a chair and then examined the looking glass. "Charles, there is a card here. Addressed to you."

Charles took the card from his cousin, his eyes blurring with tears. He wiped his face and opened the envelope. "It's from Trent. It says only this: 'Follow the map, Detective. You have one hour before she dies.' Paul, what can he mean? Map? What map?"

Reid stood near the back of the group of men, and he raised his hand, pushing forward. "The map of Whitechapel, Charles. It must be that. The one we found with Redwing's marks upon it."

"Where is it?" Aubrey asked.

"It's in the library downstairs," the duke answered. "Kepelheim put it there along with the other items we've been discussing this week. Martin?"

Kepelheim nodded. "Yes, yes! It is there! Come, let us see what this fiend means when he refers to the map."

In a few minutes, all but Emerson had joined up in the library, the doctor remaining with Alicia for the present. Kepelheim unlocked a small safe tucked behind a portrait of Beth as a child, and he removed a white box. "Here it is."

"Let me see it," Charles said as he entered the room.

The tailor brought the marquess the creased and stained map, marked in thirty-three places with the shape of a dove.

"Edmund, you told the circle that there are thirty-three marks upon this map. Miller's Court murder was the last. Number thirty-three, correct?"

"Yes, but another murder was reported last night, at a pub on Gascoigne. Why?"

"Gascoigne?" Sinclair asked. He nearly fell again, his face white.

Aubrey caught him and helped him to sit. "Charles, this is too much for you."

"That pub," the marquess insisted. "Find it on the map. Is there a mark beside it?"

Reid pored over the extensive sheet. "It might be a faint mark. No dove, though. It looks like an upper case 'I'."

Paul took the map and held it up to the light. "An 'I'? Why would Trent use... Wait, Edmund. Not an 'I'. It's a Roman numeral. This is the number one. Good heavens, is this starting all over? I remember seeing nothing marked on this part of the map. When did these get here? Who's had access to this?"

"Find the next Roman numeral," Kepelheim told the men.

Charles had no need to even look. Suddenly, it all made a dreadful sort of sense. "It's on Columbia Road."

Reid placed a lamp beside the stained map. "Columbia Road? Not far from Gascoigne, I take it. Yes, there might be a small mark there, although it could also be just a smudge. The map is so stained it's difficult to make it out clearly. Does anyone have a hand lens?"

Kepelheim reached into his pocket and withdrew a small brass lens. "Will this suffice?" he asked.

Running the lens along the length of the map, the inspector paused at a street on the northwest end of Whitechapel. "It's there. Two small marks, like the letters 'II'. The Roman numeral for two. But what does it mean?"

Sinclair felt bile rise to the back of his throat, and he glanced up at his cousin. "It's my old house. He's taken her there, Paul. Trent has taken Beth to my home!"

Aubrey spurred into action. "Then, we find her! Everyone to the coaches. We've six of them in the Queen Anne mews, and there are several from Drummond House parked in the front. We'll need a few men to remain here. Baxter, you and Miles are both handy with a shotgun. I've a collection of weapons in the west wing. The key to the gun cabinet is in my top bureau drawer. Martin, you ride with the duke. Charles and I shall leave now. Reid can give you the address!"

In a flash, the cousins had armed themselves and flown out the front door, bound for a two-storey house on Columbia Road. "How far is it from here?" Aubrey asked, checking his weapon and making sure he had additional cartridges.

Charles looked grim. "More than half an hour at this pace," he said as he watched Westminster disappear behind them. "Paul, I bless the fact that Beth chose to go up when she did. If she'd waited until you'd already left, then I would be alone in this."

"That was the plan, Charles," Aubrey answered. "Lorena was supposed to keep me from going with you. This is a trap. You do know that?"

"Of course, it's a trap," the detective answered. "But I don't care. All that matters is Elizabeth. If I die tonight, I intend to save her."

CHAPTER THIRTY-SIX

Elizabeth awoke to find herself lying on the floor. Her head ached, her beautiful wedding dress had been torn at the shoulder, and she could barely breathe. Sitting up, the strange room spun as a wave of nausea took hold, causing her to fall back against the bare wood.

"Poor Elizabeth," a man's voice said softly from the corner of the room. "Too much champagne?"

Beth fought against the sickness, blinking to clear her vision. Her mind felt numb, but she knew she was not where she belonged.

"I thought this place infinitely appropriate, my dear. Although, your meddlesome knight errant will never make it here in time. I've positioned a band of my soldiers to delay him, you see. And if my friend Lorena has succeeded, then that interfering cousin of yours is also occupied. Expect no help there either."

The room was dark, lit only by the moon, and Beth tried to determine where she now lay. "I know your voice, monster," she said, pushing against a wall to stabilise her position. "What did you do to me? To my maid?"

"Just a little laudanum for the sweet Alicia. The fair Lorena was good enough to add it to her champagne. But you—well, I could not risk your screaming, so I had to use chloroform on you. I expect your rescuers are on their way, but it's unlikely they'll make it past my hybrids. Such a shame. Those fine wedding suits the noisome Mr. Kepelheim created will be torn and bloody soon."

Beth's ribs ached, and her nose and throat felt raw from the chloroform. "Where am I?"

"Here, there, and everywhere. Actually, it's an old and familiar place to you. Historical in some respects. It struck me a few months ago that this would be the perfect place to begin the next phase of the rituals. The place that brought you such joy will now cause you much pain."

The room was freezing cold, for the fireplace hadn't been lit since Mary Wilsham's departure. Elizabeth kicked as Trent's approach, but he proved too strong. "You are a heartless fiend! I hate you!"

"Yes, I know you do. And as much as I would love to have first turn at your beautiful body, my dear, another claims that privilege. I've brought you a groom, Elizabeth. Every bride needs a groom. Shall I introduce you?"

A second shadow flickered into the cold room, and its form resolved into that of Rasha Grigor. "I always said you'd be my wife," he whispered huskily. "And now you will be. My eternal bride and mother to all my children."

"No!" she shouted, pressing against the wall. "Leave me alone!"

"Eventually, I will, but first I intend to take what is mine."

Grigor removed his jacket and waistcoat, and Elizabeth began to scream.

"How much farther?" Paul asked as they passed Bishopsgate Station.

"Five minutes, perhaps. My old home is several blocks to the north from here. Wait! What is that?" Sinclair shouted.

The carriage had stopped abruptly, and now began to sway back and forth upon its springs. Both men could hear the horses neighing as if panicked, and in another second they understood why. A team of hybrids had attacked, their unnatural claws raking through the horses' flesh and eyes. Screams split the night air as a pair of wolfmen mounted the driver's seat and were now tearing the poor man apart.

Paul and Charles began firing into the melee, hitting purchase every time, but each creature required many bullets to take down.

"Charles, look out!" Aubrey shouted as a gigantic hybrid leapt towards the window. Another pulled at the earl's door, and both men soon exhausted their supply of ammunition, but mercifully the wave of hybrids had finally halted, apparently beaten.

The two cousins stepped out of the coach onto a cobbled street streaked in blood, and flesh, and gore. Locals were screaming and shouting for police, and Charles could hear a chorus of constables' whistles summoning comrades to their cause.

Behind them, the other coaches halted, and the duke and the rest of the circle rushed to the overturned brougham. "Are you all right?" he asked his nephews, his face flushed.

"Yes, for the moment," Sinclair called in return. "We're out of ammunition, though."

"Take these," Drummond told them, handing each a new weapon and plenty of cartridges—and just in time, for a second wave of hybrids had emerged from the south side of the train tracks. The three Stuart men began firing as teeth, claws, and fire-red eyes descended upon them.

"You may take my body, but that is all. I loathe you both!"

Rasha Grigor unbuttoned his shirt, smiling as he tormented the duchess. "I'm sure you do, but it makes no difference."

Trent watched, his lips twisted into a sneering smile. "Such a pity."

Grigor nodded, reaching for the pearl buttons on Beth's gown. "That our comrades aren't here to see this, or that she's so very pitiable? Which?"

"I meant you, Rasha. I pity you."

The hybrid prince turned to stare at the baronet. "Why would you pity me? I have all I've ever wanted."

"Yes, but your father is displeased with you, Rasha. Aren't you, my lord?"

A shadow moved in the next room, blotting out the faint moonlight. "I warned you, Razarit. Your impetuous actions reveal too many flaws in your character. I fear that your time is up."

Beth said nothing, praying inwardly that all this was but a nightmare.

"I may hate my brother," the Shadow continued, "but he is right about you. You are a failed experiment. I considered allowing Samael remove you, but as you are my creation, that duty falls to me."

"But Father!" the wayward prince cried out. "Why?"

A bright flash illuminated the upper storey. Rasha Grigor's body jerked with a thousand spasms, his skin cracking and splintering—the flesh burning. His final, plaintive words echoed within the now empty space. Razarit Grigor had disappeared, leaving nothing but glittering dust and sparks.

Trent clapped his hands together, as if wiping the residual particles of the now-dead Romanian from his palms. "Well done, Lord Raziel! Rasha had become overly proud and irritating, if you must know. And with him gone, you'll require another human to take his position within the round table."

Grigor's head tilted to one side. "You imagine that replacement should be you, I presume?" he asked. "Why? What actions qualify you for such an honour, Trent?"

Sir William answered proudly. "I've served as a vanguard, my lord. Hoping for your release—all these many years. I've prepared this girl for your use!"

"And I hate you for it!" Beth shouted. "I hate you both!"

The baronet grinned. "Yes, your mother hated me as well, did you know that? Oh, Patricia never loved me, not for a moment," he bragged. "Not even during our mad affair. Oh, perhaps you were unaware of that."

She stared at him, her mind processing this tease of information. *Is he trying to keep me off balance? Is this a trick?* "What do you mean?"

He laughed as he bent down, deciding to continue what Rasha had begun. "Surely, even as a child, you noticed your parents had grown apart. Not that your mother ever really cared for Connor Stuart. Not really. I met her in Paris. Long before your father's death."

Raziel stepped towards them. "I've never heard this tale. Do continue."

"And then I may take her?" Trent asked.

"Prove your worth, and I shall consider it."

William sat upon the floor as he continued the confession, his breath clouding the air of the unheated bedroom. "It took me a very long time to plan it all out. Trish was such a willing dupe. Luring her into bed was far too easy."

"You lie!" Elizabeth shouted.

"Do I? Yes, I suppose I do, but not about this. There is no need. Patricia and I began a torrid affair six years before the beast took your father's life."

"*You* are the beast!" she shouted, kicking her feet as he grasped her legs.

"Am I? Perhaps, but not as you imagine it, my dear. Another had the privilege of devouring Lord Kesson's flesh. I was not even there that night, though it benefited me. I was entertaining your mother in my bed whilst your father breathed his last upon Drummond's heath. Isn't that true, Lord Raziel?"

She'd gone quiet, her mind shutting down, and she tried to summon up her husband's image in hopes it might calm her. *Captain, where are you?*

Trent leered at her, lifting the hem of the gown and running a hand along her right calf. "There. That's the spot," he said, touching the long scar that ran along the back of her leg. "That's where the wolf bit you, isn't it? Did your flesh taste warm, I wonder? Was your blood sweet? You would know, wouldn't you, Lord Raziel?" he said, looking at the shadow. "Did you intentionally mangle her leg, or was your animal nature too strong that night?"

The other offered no reply, so Trent continued. "How your mother began to loathe me after a time," he told Elizabeth. "She never truly loved me, of course. Not of her own free will. I'd hypnotized her, and I tried to do the same to you, but your mind would never yield to mine for some reason. However, controlling your mother allowed me to control you, for when under my spell she would do whatever I commanded. Well, except for one thing. I demanded she give you to me, and she refused. Patricia simply would not see it my way. Such a shame. She had her charms, but not enough to keep her alive. It's been a very long game, this one, but so worth it. And no one will come to your rescue. If, however, that wretched detective does make it past my creatures, then he will die. And you, my dear, will get to watch me tear him apart."

"Charles *will* be here, and so will Paul!" she shouted.

This last surprised Trent, and he froze, his face less certain, and he glanced at Raziel for assurance. "Is she right?"

The Shadow said nothing.

"No, I don't think so," Trent whispered, almost to himself. "The meddlesome earl is lying in the seductive arms of my friend, Lorena MacKey, this night. Your faithful Scottish guardian has deserted you for another, Elizabeth. You are all alone in this world."

"He is coming!" she shouted as bile stung the back of her throat. "He'd not left, William. Paul was still at Queen Anne when you took me!"

Trent began to laugh. "Then that interfering Scotsman has died on the streets of Whitechapel, alongside your husband!"

In the distance, Elizabeth could hear wolves howling, and shouts; hundreds of gunshots echoing in the nearby streets. "Spare them, William, and I'll go with you! I'll do whatever you say! Please, Prince Raziel—I'll not fight you. I beg you to spare them! Please, call off your pack!"

"You would bargain for their lives?" Trent sneered. "What a pretty mouth to speak such lies. You would save your knights, but you'd never give yourself to us willingly, not whilst your husband lives. No, that will not do. Charles must die, Elizabeth. He must. Now, to our pleasures," he said.

Trent's large hands ripped at the dress, popping the pearl buttons and satin thread. It came apart, and he tugged it free of her body, tossing the gown into the cold fireplace.

"All mine," he said, Trent's eyes turning yellow like a wolf's; the sharp teeth clicking as hot breath fell upon her face.

Reid had emptied his shotgun and revolver, but the duke continued firing. Every man's pistol smoked, and now all of Leman Street had arrived—brave men in blue, most armed only with billy clubs, smashing at the wolfmen, breaking teeth, skulls, and legs.

"Get to the house!" the duke shouted to his nephews. "We'll manage here!"

Charles needed no more encouragement. Tapping Paul on the arm, the two cousins ran northward into the darkness, praying they'd reach Columbia Street in time.

Elizabeth kicked her feet as hard as she could, doing all within her strength to fight Trent's powerful weight. His hands had moved to her underskirt, and she screamed.

Raziel's image then did a very strange thing. It began to shimmer, altering form, as though he could no longer maintain his human guise. All ambient light instantly snuffed out, and the room went completely black.

Trent paused. "What are you doing, my lord prince? Raziel?"

Slowly, a faint light pierced the pitch darkness, and a pair of red pinpoints appeared, floating within something large, dense, and blacker than any night.

"You think me Raziel?" a familiar voice whispered. "Who is the fool now, Trent?"

"Samael!" the baronet shouted in terror. "But how?"

"Do you imagine that I do not keep watch on your round table, Sir William? That the deeds of my brethren go unnoticed? You thought me weak, only because it is what I wanted you to think. I told you that if you *ever* touched her again, I would kill you. Do you think me so limited in my vision that I did not foresee this? You thought to make devious plans with my brother? Never, little human. *Never!*"

Romanov's voice boomed like thunder, and Elizabeth trembled, pushing against the cold wall, trying to put as much distance betwixt herself and the horrifying apparition as she could manage.

"Let me go!" Trent's voice cried out, blustering. "Raziel will hear of your treachery! He will tell Lucifer!"

The angel's grip tightened on William Trent's throat, long fingers of smoke and fire squeezing muscle and sinews. "Raziel is not my master, and neither is Lucifer! Now, as your kind is so fond of saying, Sir William: *Go to Hell!*"

The fiery elohim shook the human as if he were nothing but a dry leaf caught in a maelstrom, dashing the bloodied body about the room—crashing it into corners, closet doors, and walls—breaking every bone. Then he threw the splintered remains out the bedroom window. Trent's mortality smashed through the thick mullions and panes of glass, and then crashed into the small courtyard below.

Gently, Samael bent beside the cowering duchess. "Elizabeth, my sweet one, forgive me for not interceding before—for allowing him to hurt you. But he will hurt you no longer. Not ever again. Here, let me take you from this place."

Beth felt herself lifted, carried, and cold wind chilled her entire body as they passed *through* the ceiling, into the night air. As they sailed aloft, snowflakes began to fall, quickly accumulating upon the grass and cobbles below.

"Snow," she whispered, tears filling her eyes.

"Yes, my dear friend. Snow."

Beth clutched at his long arms. "Charles?" she asked him as he landed upon the roof of a nearby building. "Where is he?"

"Are you all right? Are you undamaged?"

Elizabeth looked into the eyes, no longer composed of fire and smoke, but now icy blue.

"Anatole?" she asked, her mind shutting down from shock.

"Fear not, my beautiful friend. I shall take you to a place where you may rest and recover." He waved his hands, and a woolen cloak appeared out of nothing. He wrapped it around her, pulling her close to further warm her. "I cannot remain, Elizabeth. Close your eyes now. You will be warm soon."

Below, the falling snow had already blanketed the ground in white, and Beth obediently closed her eyes.

Without warning, the real Raziel Grigor materialised upon the roofline of Sinclair's old house. Two gargoyles emerged alongside their master, clenching their sharp teeth angrily. The elohim's face contorted with anger. "Deceiver!" he shouted. "I shall see you dead for this, Samael!"

Anatole didn't dare put her down, for fear that Raziel's powerful minions might try to take her. Instead, he ascended into the air, calling out a single word: "Flames!"

The home ignited into a raging fire, and Raziel and his followers screamed as the rapidly spreading blaze forced them to retreat.

Anatole Romanov flew high into the night sky, the high-born prince, known in ancient times as Samael, poison of God, angel of death, primordial elohim, one of the Seven. He gently carried the duchess to a secret place, far from the reach of his fallen brethren.

Charles and Paul turned the corner and found the house completely engulfed in flames.

"No!" Sinclair cried out as he reached the courtyard.

Trent's torn and bloodied body, the eyes open and empty, lay several yards from the door, and Sinclair looked up to see the smashed window to his bedroom.

"Beth's up there!" he cried, rushing at the door, but the entire house was ablaze, and the intense heat threw him back against the earl. "I have to try!" Charles shouted above the roar of the inferno, rushing again towards the door.

He kicked it in, but a massive explosion threw him backward several feet, and his head struck a metal hitching post. He lay there motionless, and a deep wound at the back of his head slowly beginning to bleed, the thin stream of red staining the white snow.

Bells clanged as the local fire brigade arrived along with dozens of policemen. The duke and Kepelheim ran to Charles.

"Is she out?" the duke shouted, finding the earl kneeling beside his cousin.

"We cannot get up there," Paul said, tears streaming down his face. "Trent is dead. We have no idea about Beth, but…"

Another explosion hurled glass and shattered wood into the street, and the firemen pulled everyone back.

Though they saw her not, the explosion caused Beth to open her eyes, and she helplessly watched from the angel's arms.

"Snow," she said as he carried her higher. "Red snow."

TO BE CONTINUED IN BOOK 4:

REALMS
OF
STONE

PLANNED RELEASE DATE: APRIL, 2018

ABOUT THE AUTHOR

 Science, writing, opera, and geopolitics are just a few of the many 'hats' worn by Sharon K. Gilbert. She has been married to SkyWatchTV host and fellow writer Derek P. Gilbert for nearly twenty years, and during that time, helped to raise a brilliant and beautiful stepdaughter, Nicole Gilbert.

The Gilberts have shared their talents and insights for over a decade with the pioneering Christian podcasts, *PID Radio, Gilbert House Fellowship,* and *View from the Bunker*. In addition to co-hosting SkyWatchTV's flagship interview program and *SciFriday* each week, Sharon also hosts *SkyWatch Women* and *SkyWatch Women One-on-One*. She and Derek speak several times each year at conferences, where they love to discuss news and prophecy with viewers, listeners, and readers.

Sharon's been following and studying Bible prophecy for over fifty years, and she often says that she's only scratched the surface. When not immersed in study, a writing project, or scouring the Internet for the latest science news, you can usually find her relaxing in the garden with their faithful hound, Sam T. Dachshund.

Learn more about Sharon and *The Redwing Saga* at her websites: www.sharonkgilbert.com and www.theredwingsaga.com

OTHER BOOKS BY SHARON K. GILBERT

Ebola and the Fourth Horseman of the Apocalypse (non-fiction)

Blood Lies: Book One of The Redwing Saga (fiction)

Blood Rites: Book Two of The Redwing Saga (fiction)

Winds of Evil (fiction)

Signs and Wonders (fiction)

The Armageddon Strain (fiction)

Contributing Author:

God's Ghostbusters (non-fiction)

Blood on the Altar (non-fiction)

Pandemonium's Engine (non-fiction)

I Predict (non-fiction)

When Once We Were a Nation (non-fiction)